F1992 ANTASY BASKETBALL DIGEST

1992 FANTASY BASKETBALL DIGEST

by
Troy Boeldt, Jim Ulrich, Chris Crawley, and Alex Ferrari

Lerner Publications Company • Minneapolis

The authors and the publisher believe all information regarding NBA player transactions to be accurate up to June 24, 1992, when this book was set to go to press. For subsequent information, please consult the authors' Fantasy Basketball Updates. An order form is at the back of this book.

DISCLAIMER: This book's references to newspapers, on-line computer services, and other media are presented for informational purposes only. The authors and the publisher intend no endorsement of any medium or product and are not liable for any consequences of the use of such media or products.

Cover photo by John Leyba.

Composed in Times Roman and Helvie Light
by Dahl & Curry, Minneapolis, Minnesota.

International Standard Book Number: 0-8225-9851-5
1 2 3 4 5 6 7 8 9 10 01 00 99 98 97 96 95 94 93 92

DEDICATION

To our families, who have supported us through this endeavor.

To Russell Alm, for his wit and sarcasm, and for being our fourth team.

To our leaguemates, who put up with us play-testing ideas.

Because it should have been here last year, but wasn't, Thanks, Mom.

"Dedico questo libro ai miai familiari in Italia."

CONTENTS

INTRODUCTION

Fantasy Basketball gets you into the NBA-basketball action. You are the owner, general manager, and coach of your own squad. As owner, you decide the salaries of your players within the constraints of a salary cap, just as in the NBA. As general manager, you trade real NBA players with other franchises, just as in the NBA. Finally, as coach, you choose a starting lineup for your team on a daily basis, just as in the NBA.

Your most important duties as an owner will come on draft day. You have only so many player-purchase units to spend in putting together a whole team, so you have to decide what each player deserves to be paid. When you only have 250 units to spend on 18 players, you must make wise decisions. If the average player costs 14 units, who is worth more than that? Who is worth buying only for much less? How can you know a bargain when you see one? Hot Rod Williams is worth almost five million dollars a year to the Cleveland Cavaliers; is he worth 25 units to you?

Once the season begins, your roles as general manager and coach come into play. As general manager you make all the necessary roster transactions. When your team needs help, you may have to trade with other franchises in the league. The Blazers probably would not trade Clyde the Glide for the entire Sacramento team, but if your franchise lacks depth (as would any Fantasy Franchise that paid Drexler's price in the league's auction draft), you might do well to give him up for L-Train, Causwell, and Spud Webb. Your team that lacked depth before, and was forced to play Cartwright and Mario Elie along with Mr. Drexler, would now be stronger in every statistical category. Is this a wise move? Is Clyde Drexler worth more than that? That may not be apparent until the end of the season, but these judgment calls keep the game interesting.

As coach, your main function is to decide who your 12 best players are for any given week. You will need to assess your team's strengths and weaknesses and decide on a strategy. You probably won't have to worry about K.J. riding the pines. However, when a Bill Laimbeer starts "buying the farm," you may want to bench him in favor of a hot Ed Pinckney, who saw some productive minutes when Bird and McHale were out with injuries. You may shift your lineup to get balanced production in all the statistical categories your league uses, or you may decide to give away one category in order to excel in the others. Most likely you will have to use both strategies at various points in your season. You don't just draft a team and sit back. You must stay involved and active throughout the entire season. That is the fun of Fantasy Basketball.

The most important thing to remember is just that: Have fun. It is okay to be competitive; in fact a competitive streak will help you give the other franchises in your league an interesting season. However, you should be able to enjoy yourself even if your team is in last place. (If nothing else, you can amuse yourself by just watching your players on TV and trying to be a spoiler.) Obviously, the league championship—and the bragging rights that go along with it—can go to only one franchise. We hope that our advice is helpful in making sure that the top franchise is yours. Good Luck!

CHAPTER 1

ORGANIZING A LEAGUE

GETTING STARTED

Creating a league is a four-step process: Owners must be recruited, a league commissioner must be chosen, the owners must meet, and your league must follow up on the decisions made at that meeting—especially by having a smooth and timely draft. If you get all four of these steps right, your Fantasy League will be off to a good start. You may still wind up crying in your beer at the end of the season, but at least it won't be because your league crashed and burned on takeoff.

RECRUITING OWNERS

You may already be involved in other fantasy sports, so recruiting owners may be easy. If you don't have this ready pool of eager fantasy owners, you might have to put some effort into recruitment. Look for owners with three very important qualities: a hard-core enthusiasm for basketball, a good disposition, and a strong sense of fair play. Recruiting your friends first will probably create the most fun for you. A league of friends might not be the most competitive at the beginning, but after a couple of years of languishing in the cellar, even your most noncompetitive leaguemates will be too embarrassed to continue producing a Sacramento-like team.

Getting friends of friends is also okay, but this may cause problems. Someone who knows only one person in the league may not have that sense of obligation that inspires owners to play within the spirit of the rules. While having people you get along with in your league is important, don't bring in your little brother, your grandma, or your better half just to fill the league—unless that person knows more about basketball than you do. (On second thought, don't bring them in even if they do know more than you. Just think about the embarrassment of finishing fourth behind Little Timmy, Grandma, and your significant other.)

CHOOSING A LEAGUE COMMISSIONER

Being a league commissioner is not easy. The hours are bad. The pay stinks. People are always griping, and generally the commissioner is treated with about as much respect as Rodney Dangerfield. However, a commissioner does enjoy a position of almost dictatorial power. If that's your thing, go for it. Alternatively, you could do it just because you know that your league needs a reasonable, fair commissioner (and none of your leaguemates fit that description).

If possible the commissioner should be a nonowner, but someone from outside the league will probably lose interest very quickly. If you can't have a nonplaying commissioner, we suggest a three-owner committee to perform the commissioner's duties. Each of the three has a vote in making decisions, and the majority rules. This should prevent most conflicts of interest. (NOTE: From this point forward we will talk about the commissioner as if he were male and as if he were one person, even if he, or she, or some combination thereof, has three heads and six arms.)

Whoever the commissioner is, he should have an analytical mind. He will be bombarded with questions and arguments whenever a conflict arises. He will have to dissect the problem effectively, consider the implications of any decision, and lay down the law. Also, he must be extremely well organized; nothing infuriates an owner more than statistics that arrive two days after they are needed. When *USA Today* prints the NBA stats on Tuesday, your league's stats should be compiled and mailed on Wednesday to give an owner four days to analyze his team's performance and make any necessary changes to his roster. The commissioner must also be patient; even well-run and well-organized leagues include owners who feel they're not getting a fair shake. The commissioner must be able to handle such dissatisfied whiners and still remain fair to ALL the owners.

THE OWNERS MEETING

An owners meeting is very important, especially in your first year. At the meeting, the owners gather to squabble about what the rules should be and what variations they want to play: "Let's try head-to-head scoring." "We had a problem with this rule last year, so let's make sure it won't happen again." "That trade smacked of collusion." It is up to the commissioner to listen to everyone's ideas and decide what is best for the league. Here is a list of the major issues to be decided at the meeting:

1) Amount of NBA talent to use
2) Drafting method
3) Trades
4) Pickups
5) Franchise fees
6) Draft date
7) Scoring method (Weekly or Head-to-Head)
   a) Intra-Squad transactions
   b) Playoffs and payoffs
   c) Transaction fees

As a rule, the league meeting—where all this is discussed—is at a tavern that happens to serve food. This makes the meeting fun, and sometimes it becomes much easier by the end of the evening to convince someone that you are right. The commissioner may want each owner to self-address and stamp enough envelopes to receive an entire season's stats in the mail. Or he may choose to set up a time and place for the owners to pick up a copy of the stats each week. While the official reason for the owners meeting is to iron out the rules, the real reason is to pass on as much false information as humanly possible: "I read that Hakeem is unhappy in Houston and thinking about playing overseas." "I saw on Sportcenter that Dominique's knee operation went badly." "I'm ready for the auction right now." "The Spurs think that Rod Strickland has an attitude problem." Well, sometimes you have to tell the truth just to get someone to believe your lies. Remember, just because you need a sense of fair play does not mean you have to play fair.

THE TALENT POOL

When deciding how much NBA talent should be available in your Fantasy League, strive for a competitive atmosphere. If only six owners are in your league, for example, it would be unwise to use all 27 NBA teams. This would result in six teams composed purely of superstars, and the winner would be the owner whose team had the fewest injuries. It would also deprive some lucky owner the pleasure of having Les Jepsen grace his roster. The ideal setup is to have a talent pool larger, but not much larger, than your league needs to fill its rosters. Try to maintain about a two-to-one ratio of NBA teams in your talent pool to fantasy teams in your league. Only a league with 14 owners should use the entire NBA slate of 27 teams in its talent pool. If you have fewer owners, use fewer teams. Trust us. We know what we're doing. A 14-team Fantasy League can have a talent pool of all 27 NBA teams and will have to use 9 to 10 players from each NBA team. Since even the World Champion Chicago Bulls don't have more than three competent players, some very marginal selections will be made. This is a good thing. It rewards the owners who do their homework. While you may be grimacing over the prospect of having Ron Anderson as your best reserve forward, you can laugh at the guy who is starting Kenny Anderson. This is how the fate of your team will be determined. Everyone will have some superstars, but the quality of your fringe players can make you a winner.

Selecting which NBA teams to use can be done in one of three ways. You can pick them out of a hat. You can, provided you have only six or seven owners, choose only the East or only the West Conference. Or you can use the method our league has used in the past: Each owner nominates two NBA teams for the talent pool, and any slots left open because of duplicate NBA nominations are filled by NBA teams chosen out of a hat.

PLAYER ACQUISITION

Only two acquisition options make sense—an auction or an ordered draft. What do we suggest? GO WITH AN AUCTION. An auction—in which every owner starts with a total of 250 player-purchase units to spend in building a team—allows every owner a chance at every player and most closely resembles the NBA's salary cap. It also allows owners to judge how much their favorite players are worth and how many of these players they can accumulate. Many owners in a league will shy away from hometown players because they believe those players will cost more than they're worth—simply because everyone knows who they are and what they can do. It is an interesting, and often successful, draft strategy. But the owners who acquire the hometown players do get to root for their boys at the arena 41 times a year.

AUCTION

Finally the moment of truth has arrived. The draft will take about eight hours, so get an early start in a big, comfortable room. We suggest making lunch arrangements well in advance to maximize the quantity discount. The commissioner should be the auctioneer and the bookkeeper. As the auctioneer, he must announce the player being auctioned and the current price. ("Mark Aguirre—we have 60, do I hear 61?") And no auction would be complete without that famous call "Going once. Going twice. Last call Mark Aguirre for 60. Sold American!" (By the way, if Mark Aguirre goes for 60 in your league, call us. We want to join.)

As a bookkeeper, the commissioner must record which franchise bought which players and must keep a running total of the player-purchase units remaining for each franchise. Because running the auction can be very time-consuming, any commissioner with a team of his own will have trouble executing his duties and drafting his own team at the same time. If you have a playing commissioner, we suggest finding a very good nonplaying friend to do the busy work.

Choose some random order in which owners will nominate NBA players. We like going clockwise around the room, but you could be bold, new, and innovative by going counterclockwise. The first owner calls out the name of an NBA player, thereby nominating that player. Nominating a player is an automatic bid of 1 unit. Bidding continues to escalate, in increments of no less than 1 unit, until none of the other owners wants to increase the bid. The highest bidder buys the nominated player.

EXAMPLE: I nominate Shaquille O'Neal, someone bids 55, I bid 59, he bids 60, I bid 61, and no one cares to bid 62. I would then own Shaq's contract for 61 units.

Each owner's budget of 250 units acts as a salary cap—the maximum he can spend in compiling a team of 18 players. Only a portion of these players will ever be active at any one time; the others will be either on the taxi squad or on injured reserve. An owner can use these units any way he chooses, and on any player he chooses. If an owner wants 18 guards, he can have them. If an owner wishes to spend 233 units on Michael (He Who Leaps and Never Lands) Jordan and 1 unit on each of his 17 other players, he can do that too. (A piece of advice: Michael may be able to stay suspended in midair forever, but he's still not worth 233 units.) An owner may bid on any player he wants as long as all of the following are true:

    1) The owner does not already have 18 players.
    2) The player is a member of the talent pool.
    3) The owner can afford whatever bid he is proposing.
    4) The owner can fill the rest of his team with a bid of at least 1.

EXAMPLE: An owner has four players left to acquire and 12 units to spend on them. If someone calls a player he wants, his maximum bid for that player is 9 units, leaving him with 1 unit for each of his last three players. Any owner caught illegally bidding should be drawn and quartered—or at least fined a substantial amount, whichever is easier. After an owner has acquired his 18 players, he becomes a spectator, and any leftover units are wasted.

ORDERED DRAFT

If for some reason your league does not want to use an auction, your other option is an ordered draft. The NBA uses an ordered draft to acquire its college talent. Each franchise, when its turn comes around, picks a player, and that player's rights belong to that team. In Fantasy Basketball this kind of draft can also be used. The order in which the franchises pick should be randomly determined for every odd round, and the order should be flipped for the even rounds. On draft day, each franchise, in the predetermined order, selects one NBA player per round. Since each team needs 18 players, the draft will be 18 rounds long. As an example, the first two rounds of an eight-team league might look something like this:

First Round	Franchise	Second Round	Franchise
1st pick	Team #1	1st pick	Team #8
2nd pick	Team #2	2nd pick	Team #7
3rd pick	Team #3	3rd pick	Team #6
4th pick	Team #4	4th pick	Team #5
5th pick	Team #5	5th pick	Team #4
6th pick	Team #6	6th pick	Team #3
7th pick	Team #7	7th pick	Team #2
8th pick	Team #8	8th pick	Team #1

Every successive odd round would then have a different order, selected randomly, with the corresponding even round being the reverse. In the third round, maybe Team #6 would get the first pick, so in the fourth round Team #6 would pick last.

Regardless of whether you use an auction or an ordered draft, one or more owners may not be able to participate, in person, at the draft site. If the absent owners cannot send servants to represent them, turn to technology. The league can arrange a conference call or a party call, although either way there will be someone with a cauliflower ear the day after the draft. If an owner has to leave the draft before choosing a complete team, allow him to fill his team with whatever hack players remain unclaimed at the end of the draft. If your league has more than one owner who is not able to stay for the duration, the delinquents can fill their rosters on a first-come, first-served basis.

TRADES

In Fantasy Basketball, totally unregulated trading would lead to chaos. Certain rules have to be observed, both by the owners in their trading and by the commissioner in his regulation of their trading. First off, both teams in a trade must give up an equal number of players; a trade must be a one-player-for-one-player deal (or two-for-two, or three-for-three, etc.). This does not mean that you cannot trade three good players for one great player. You will just have to take two pine riders to accompany the superstar in order to close the deal. For example, an owner in our league gave away Hersey Hawkins, Sam Mitchell, Robert Parish, and Moses Malone to obtain the services of David Robinson—and the bench-warming abilities of Tony Smith, Jim Les, and Orlando Woolridge. This was a good trade because the owner who obtained Robinson did not have to use the other three hacks in his starting lineup. Meanwhile, the other owner, who had been starting Les and Woolridge, was able to improve his lineup from top to bottom.

Trades must be turned in to the commissioner for consideration before Friday night of any given week. This gives the commissioner the entire weekend to consider the trade before it can go into effect on the following Monday.

No matter which scoring method your league uses, you'll need an additional rule—a provision to prevent the suicidal trading that Fantasy Basketball owners call "dumping." In the interest of fairness, complete league-wide trading should be allowed only up to the All-Star break. Any deadline later than that is likely to generate bad trades, since many cellar-dwelling owners who are approaching elimination will fail to keep track of their players and will not make intelligent trades.

This does not mean, however, that no trading at all is allowed late in the season. Trading can occur, but with some restrictions. During each week after the All-Star break, the teams of your league are divided into three groups according to each week's standings. In a 14-team league, for example, the first group would contain the top 4 teams, the second group would contain teams 5 though 10, and the third group would contain the last 4 teams. An owner may trade only with the other owners in his group, who (because their standings are similar) are striving for the same goal. The owners in the first group want first place, those in the middle group want to finish in the money, and those in the last group want to avoid the stigma of being called the Minnesota Timberwolves of the league. It is unlikely that an owner would throw his team away to another owner who is competing for the same goal. More than any other aspect of the game, trades need to be closely scrutinized by the commissioner. The commissioner should have the power to approve or block all trades, so that a multitude of bad trades does not unbalance the league. An owner desperate to improve his team and possibly move up in the standings will try to get the best deal he can—even if it concentrates far too much talent in too few teams.

A trade that works out especially well for one of the teams involved usually leaves the other with nothing but regrets. And, as sorry as we feel for the ill-informed owner who has been ripped off, we have to pity the league even more. All the other owners in the league get ripped off—through no fault of their own—when some unscrupulous franchise owner sweet-talks some other owner into making a couple of Cleveland Cavalier–style deals that vault Mr. Unscrupulous to the top of the league standings. The other owners have very little chance to catch him in such a case, without resorting to similar shady tactics. Without some kind of system to check this kind of trading, your league will probably degenerate into wide-scale nonsense by the All-Star break.

We hope that we have not completely turned you and your league against trades; trading is a lot of fun for owners and can help a team shore up its weak areas. While bad trades hurt everyone, fair trades between well-informed owners benefit all parties involved and make the league more competitive. A good trade should position both of the trading teams to rise in the standings. An owner wishing to trade should identify his team's statistical shortages and abundances. Where can he make a move and, more importantly, what can his team afford to give up? He can then seek potential trading partners— other teams in the league that have what he needs and need what he wants to trade away.

So let's say you've found this match made in heaven. Now the haggling can begin. While you may want to give up only Mookie Blaylock for Detlef Schrempf, your esteemed colleague may want you to part with Karl Malone. Although you would probably decline that deal, the haggling is far from over. It is this give-and-take that makes trades such an interesting and challenging method of improving your team.

Teams that have improved through wise trades may become the envy of other franchises. Some disgruntled owner who thinks he can win with the team he drafted may start to whine as he finds his own franchise outpaced by two teams that have just completed a trade. He may even consider the trade unfair, but that's up to the commissioner to decide. Maybe the grumbling owner simply needs to start making a few deals of his own.

PICKUPS

Since its inception, our league has tried and rejected several systems for handling pickups. At first, the teams in our league could pick up an unlimited number of players from a pool of free agents. (Free agents are players who were included in the talent pool on draft day but are not currently on any fantasy team's roster.) Owners were using this rule, however, to replace their bad personnel with better players. Shrewd and intelligent as this maneuver was, it led to a lot of collusion among teams, which made it unfair. Never mind how this was done; we don't recommend it. The arguments over such shady tactics almost ripped our league apart while it was still in its infancy. We then imposed rules specifically to curtail such collusion, but franchise owners learned how to bend the rules. Finally, we just froze the teams after the draft, not allowing any pickups at all.

This method worked quite well, and the owners were happy until some of them lost high-priced talent to injuries. They screamed, and the rest of us told them that they should have drafted for depth so they could withstand the loss of their injured players. This was a valid point, but so was their counterargument—that they were already being penalized enough by losing a starting player with no compensation. In the end, we devised an alternate method for pickups, and it has worked very well. For those leagues that decide not to freeze team rosters after the draft, we recommend our system. It's a no-nonsense way of dealing with pickups.

Allow a free agent to be picked up only if a Fantasy League player is PLACED ON INJURED RESERVE OR SUSPENDED. The owner has only one week after the player is placed on IR to make this pickup; after that, the fantasy team has to live with the injury and no pickups are allowed. The owner may pick up only a free agent who plays the same position as his injured player. The owner at this point retains the rights to the player on IR. When the original team member is removed from IR, the fantasy owner must place the original player back on his roster and drop the replacement player he picked up. There is no grace period for this change, and the owner has no choice as to which one of the players he can keep on the roster. The replacement player becomes a free agent, and he may be claimed by another fantasy team with a player on IR. Once an owner has picked up a free agent for an injured player, the replacement may never be traded to another team. If the owner decides to trade the injured player, he must immediately drop the replacement. The fantasy team that trades for an injured player does not have the option to call up a free agent for that injured player. After all, the owner knew full well that the player was injured when he made the trade. If a franchise owner decides to acquire the services of a player who has been placed on IR before the league's draft day, that owner is not allowed to pick up a free agent for that player.

If your league decides not to allow any pickups, only those NBA players who are bid upon on draft day are relevant to your league's season. All other players are off-limits. There are no free agents. Except for players you acquire or discard in trades, the team you draft is the team you have. Hopefully, you'll have some depth in case of injury. If not, it may be a long way down to the bottom of the standings, but you'll get there eventually.

FRANCHISE FEES

While the purpose of a Fantasy Basketball league is to have fun, we suggest you play for something. This need not be money, but do not just play for pride. It is demoralizing to realize how little pride you have when you are wallowing in the cellar with no chance of ever seeing the light of day. By putting something on the line—pizza, beer, dinner, basketball cards, boyfriend/girlfriend, husband/wife, anything—you can encourage franchise owners to take their moves seriously.

Before the season starts, each franchise owner should pay the franchise fee, in the form of money or whatever. These payments go into the prize pool, to be divided later among the top teams in your league. If you do play for money (this is much easier to collect than blood), make the franchise fee small so you don't financially burden the owners.

THE DRAFT DATE

No matter which scoring method you choose, the best time to have your Fantasy League draft is the second weekend of the NBA season. The NBA always has its first game on a Friday, so the draft should not be on the next day, but rather the following Saturday or Sunday. Some leagues hold their draft before the season begins, but we think this is a dangerous practice. Especially if your league does not allow pickups, a preseason draft exposes you to an inordinate risk of drafting—and being stuck with—injured, benched, or cut players. That risk can't be totally eliminated, but it can be reduced if you draft on the second weekend. That way, all the owners at least get a chance to see who is starting, who is getting the minutes, who is riding the pines, and who is gone.

It is important to note that *USA Today* does not publish team-by-team statistics until the second Tuesday of the NBA season, so only the owners who dissect the daily box scores will have this extremely valuable information before the draft—a just and ample reward for 10 minutes of work every morning. If the draft is held any later, early-season developments will paint a very clear picture of the upcoming season, thereby penalizing the franchise owners who were well prepared.

SCORING METHODS

At the owners meeting, choosing a scoring method will be your most important decision. Your choice of either the Weekly Scoring Method or the Head-to-Head Scoring Method will profoundly affect the way you set up your league—especially how you handle intra-squad transactions, transaction fees, and playoffs and payoffs. Let's look briefly at the basics of the two scoring methods.

If your league chooses the Weekly Scoring Method, you, as an owner, will draft a team. Weekly, you will submit a roster of active players. These players will compete in seven categories—rebounds, assists, steals, blocks, turnovers, three-pointers made, and total points scored. At the end of each NBA week, your team's total statistics will be calculated and added to the previous week's statistics in those seven categories. Then the totals will be compared to those earned by the other teams in your league. Points will be assigned each week depending on how your team compares to the others. The team with the most points after the last week of the regular NBA season wins.

In the Head-to-Head Scoring Method, your team has a schedule of opponents it faces. When game day arrives, you will select your best players to go head-to-head against your opponent's best players. They will compete in seven categories—rebounds, assists, steals, blocks, total points scored, three-pointers made, and turnovers. The team that outperforms the other team in four of the seven categories wins the game. At the end of the season, the teams with the most wins advance to the playoffs and through a process of elimination, a single champion will prevail.

The beauty of the Weekly Scoring Method lies in its simplicity. Because player transactions are few, the commissioner is not harried by thousands of telephone calls a day. The league stats need only be dealt with on a weekly basis, and all the stats are already compiled into a nice table. Simple as it is, however, the Weekly Scoring Method still promotes a very competitive atmosphere. Even teams in the lower half of the standings affect the league by besting the upper-echelon teams in one or two categories. (This spoiler role may even console some humble franchises through the long summer of their discontent.) Standings in the league are highly volatile. The loss of David Robinson at the end of last season probably cost hundreds of teams a shot at their leagues' championships.

We found that leagues using the weekly method have a much better success rate than those using head-to-head. Because it does not entail as much work for the owners or the commissioner, even the busiest—or laziest—franchise owners stick with it.

The Head-to-Head Scoring Method is quite a bit more complicated and time-consuming, but it has several advantages. Head-to-head creates a more exciting style of play because teams compile wins and losses and compete for a berth in the playoffs, just as teams do in the NBA. Head-to-head creates a more intense, competitive atmosphere because teams will play actual games in which there is a winner and a loser. Any two owners in your league will be in direct competition about every four weeks. This fuels rivalries—and may even strain some great friendships. Your season will not be a total loss, even when you finish in last place, if just once during the year you beat the champion.

However, head-to-head has an inherent problem—keeping the owners interested throughout the long NBA season. Each owner will need to do more homework, and the commissioner will have his hands (and ears) full handling calls. Also, the information you need to play head-to-head can be hard to get. If no one in your league has a computer, you may be forced to play only two games each week instead of three. *USA Today,* the bible of fantasy sports addicts, is inconsiderate enough not to publish a paper on weekends. By Monday, the box scores from late Thursday, Friday, and Saturday are old news, so *USA Today* doesn't print them. What? No box scores from almost three days of NBA action? This audacity is matched only by that of the average local paper, which gives you only a skeleton box score. The rebounds, assists, steals, or blocked shots will not be found for a Friday or Saturday game. This is not a good thing.

The technological way around this dilemma is for someone in your league (preferably one of the commissioners) to equip his computer with a modem and subscribe to the *USA Today Sports Line* or *Computer Sports World* to get weekend box scores. CSW (702-294-0191) charges $29.95 as a one-time fee and then 53 cents per minute at discount times. The *USA Today Sports Line* (1-800-826-9688) costs $19.95, and the on-line charge is 10 cents per minute with a minimum charge of $9.95 per month. After painstaking research (meaning: after receiving a phone call from someone who gave us this information), we have also discovered another method. There are at least two newspapers on the West Coast with the foresight and intelligence to print complete box scores of all the NBA weekend games. You could subscribe to the *Los Angeles Times* or the *Sacramento Bee* and get all the needed stats, although they would be a little late.

WEEKLY SCORING METHOD

The mechanics of the Weekly Scoring Method are quite simple. Each team's roster consists of 18 players: 12 starters (who accumulate statistics) and 6 members of the taxi squad. The first step in scoring is to buy a Tuesday *USA Today* for the weekly NBA team-by-team stats. The commissioner should then make a list of each fantasy team's 12 active players, write down the players' number of rebounds, and add these numbers to get a team total for rebounds. Once the commissioner has done this for all the teams in your league, he compares the team totals and makes a list ranking the league's teams from the one with the highest rebound total to the one with the lowest. Points are assigned to each team depending on where it ranks. For example, if you have 14 teams in your league, the highest-ranking team will receive 14 points, the second-highest will receive 13 points, and so on down to the lowest team, which will receive 1 point.

It is possible that, when the total rebounds are added for each of the league's teams, two teams will be tied. If two teams do have the same amount of rebounds, they will obviously be adjacent in the ranking; add the points allocated to these two positions, divide by two, and give each of the tied teams half. For example, Team #1 and Team #2 (in a 14-team league) have 120 rebounds each after the first week, which ties them for first place. One team would be placed in first and one team in second. That would give them 14 points and 13 points respectively. The commissioner would then add 13 and 14 together to get 27, divide by two, and give each team 13.5 points. If there is a three-way tie, the same process is used except that the three positional ranking points are used and then divided by three.

This process is repeated for each of the categories that your league uses— blocks, assists, points scored, and so forth. The points received from your ranking in each category are then totaled for each team to get the weekly score for each team. The team with the most ranking points is the current week's leader. Each week, the ranking points are redone and the team with the most ranking points for the final week is the winner.

To help you understand this system, we have reproduced an example of our weekly score sheet from early in a season. (See pages 26–28.) It lists the starting lineup for each team along with each player's appropriate stats for that week. It also lists the inactive players or taxi squad for each team. You will notice that some players have numbers in parentheses on their stat lines. This indicates that an intra-team transaction was made, or that the player was acquired through a trade at some time in the past. The numbers inside the parentheses represent the stats that the player accumulated while not in the fantasy team's starting lineup. The numbers that are used are found in the *USA Today* that is published the Tuesday after the move is made. These numbers would be all the stats accumulated by these players up until the last day of the stat period before the move was made. These numbers in parentheses must be subtracted from their respective fantasy teams' totals. The numbers in parentheses are kept on the stat line for bookkeeping purposes, just in case an owner should complain about his starting lineup. You can show him when he moved whom; and in case you are wrong, you can easily make the correction.

Now to explain the mysterious "Others" line in the statistics. This is where the stats of the players who are replaced in the starting lineup during an intrasquad transaction, or a trade, are kept. The stat line here can be kept as a running total because the bookkeeping is done through the subtractions. If we look at our example, Team 1 switched Gerald Wilkins for Kenny Norman (Kenny was hurt). So Kenny's stats went down to the "Others" line and the stats that Gerald had already accumulated were put in parentheses on his stat line to be subtracted when the team's totals are done. The unparenthesized numbers on Wilkins's stat line represent his total stats as shown in *USA Today* for that week, minus the number in parentheses.

When looking at each category's weekly standings, you will notice that the teams are listed from best to worst for that statistic and that the points awarded are listed next to the teams. You will also notice in the "steals" category that Team 4 and Team 1 both have 206 steals. That leaves them tied in third and fourth place, for which they would normally receive 2 and 1 standing points respectively. Since they are tied, however, these points are added together and divided by 2; each team thus receives the resulting 1.5 points.

COMPUTING WEEKLY STANDINGS: A SAMPLE

TEAM #1

PLAYER	TEAM	REBs	ASTs	STLs	BLKs	TOs	3-PTs	PTs
Willis, K.	ATL	145	30	12	9	38	0	203
Johnson, A.	DEN	14	60	7	2	22	0	51
Person, C.	IND	93	46	6	4	46	18	304
Grant, Ga.	LAC	57	167	27	4	62	2	164
Campbell, T.	MIN	75	42	33	10	49	4	326
Corbin, T.	MIN	126	58	29	16	51	0	294
Coleman, D.	NJ	174	23	15	29	59	3	263
Theus, R.	NJ	31	61	15	1	62	12	281
Dudley, C.	NJ	105	14	9	33	26	0	103
Wilkins, G.	NY	(31)8	(49)12	(11)4	(8)6	(38)9	(2)1	(171)46
Jackson, M.	NY	45	133	17	3	38	4	179
King, B.	WAS	68	71	11	6	80	2	435
Webb, S.	ATL							
King, S.	CHI							
Ehlo, C.	CLV		**T A X I**					
Johnson, V.	DET		**S Q U A D**					
Norman, K.	LAC							
Reynolds, J.	ORL							
OTHERS		81	31	21	15	49	3	218
TOTAL		1022	748	206	138	591	48	2867

TEAM #2

PLAYER	TEAM	REBs	ASTs	STLs	BLKs	TOs	3-PTs	PTs
Gattison, K.	CHA	105	14	14	22	28	0	158
Donaldson, J.	DAL	95	9	5	25	36	0	123
Mullin, C.	GS	90	73	36	23	60	10	462
Hardaway, T.	GS	78	174	50	1	66	24	362
Lister, A.	GS	120	31	5	18	28	0	112
Tolbert, T.	GS	(59)48	(13)6	(5)5	(6)5	(15)13	(1)0	(108)83
Burton, W.	MIA	(15)33	(4)12	(4)11	(2)2	(9)29	(0)0	(42)114
Douglas, S.	MIA	24	112	29	2	74	1	192
Rice, G.	MIA	79	41	10	11	43	18	200
Ewing, P.	NY	170	34	18	58	72	0	403
Majerle, D.	PHX	74	44	34	8	30	7	149
Jones, C.	WAS	91	16	16	30	15	0	56
Brown, C.	CLV							
Vaught, L.	LAC							
Davis, T.	MIA		**T A X I**					
Breuer, R.	MIN		**S Q U A D**					
Spenser, F.	MIN							
Perry, T.	PHI							
OTHERS		89	5	8	18	31	0	100
TOTAL		1096	571	241	223	523	60	2514

TEAM #3

PLAYER	TEAM	REBs	ASTs	STLs	BLKs	TOs	3-PTs	PTs
Bogues, M.	CHA	48	175	38	1	30	1	130
Jordan, M.	CHI	93	98	43	10	49	7	460
Levingston, C.	CHI	65	16	7	11	13	0	70
Price, M.	CLV	45	166	42	2	56	18	271
Laimbeer, B.	DET	158	38	14	13	24	9	202
Olajuwon, H.	HOS	199	46	37	53	62	0	372
Johnson, B.	HOS	(16)16	(6)7	(7)4	(1)1	(16)16	1	(50)42
Brickowski, F.	MIL	90	21	15	11	43	0	151
Grayer, J.	MIL	(14)31	(10)21	(2)8	(2)5	(14)7	0	(36)48
Cummings, T.	SA	111	44	12	5	39	2	284
Mays, T.	SAC	(26)13	(39)14	(12)8	(1)1	(34)16	(9)7	(116)63
Eaton, M.	UT	107	3	9	43	25	0	60
Tarpley, R.	DAL							
Cook, A.	DEN							
Kessler, G.	MIA		**T A X I**					
Schayes, D.	MIL		**S Q U A D**					
Anderson, G.	DEN							
McMillan, N.	SEA							
OTHERS		145	25	18	22	28	0	264
TOTAL		1121	674	255	178	408	44	2417

TEAM #4

PLAYER	TEAM	REBs	ASTs	STLs	BLKs	TOs	3-PTs	PTs
Malone, M.	ATL	127	26	4	13	33	0	175
Rodman, D.	DET	152	21	14	10	23	1	80
Maxwell, V.	HOS	48	64	27	2	42	43	237
Fleming, V.	IND	60	122	20	6	40	1	219
Murphy, T.	MIN	52	11	5	4	12	0	79
Richardson, P.	MIN	55	152	25	1	42	10	242
Blaylock, M.	NJ	29	84	40	5	58	4	208
Gilliam, A.	PHI	119	19	20	12	46	0	249
Williams, B.	POR	146	23	11	8	34	0	201
Duckworth, K.	POR	93	15	7	4	46	0	242
Tisdale, W.	SAC	130	37	11	9	50	0	322
Robinson, D.	SA	145	34	22	46	66	0	363
Scheffler, S.	CHA							
Roberts, F.	MIL							
Petrovic, D.	NJ		**T A X I**					
Scott, D.	ORL		**S Q U A D**					
Green, R.	PHI							
Schintzius, D.	SA							
OTHERS								
TOTAL		1156	608	206	120	492	59	2617

TEAM	RANKING REBOUNDS	POINTS		TEAM	RANKING BLOCKS	POINTS
Team 4	1156	4		Team 2	223	4
Team 3	1121	3		Team3	178	3
Team 2	1096	2		Team 1	138	2
Team 1	1022	1		Team 4	120	1

TEAM	RANKING ASSISTS	POINTS		TEAM	RANKING TURNOVERS	POINTS
Team 1	748	4		Team 3	408	4
Team 3	674	3		Team 4	492	3
Team 4	608	2		Team 2	523	2
Team 2	571	1		Team 1	591	1

TEAM	RANKING STEALS	POINTS		TEAM	RANKING 3-POINTERS	POINTS
Team3	255	4		Team 2	60	4
Team 2	241	3		Team 4	59	3
Team 4	206	1.5		Team 1	48	2
Team 1	206	1.5		Team 3	44	1

TEAM	RANKING POINTS	POINTS
Team 1	2867	4
Team 4	2617	3
Team 2	2514	2
Team 3	2417	1

FINAL STANDINGS FOR THIS WEEK

TEAM	STANDING	POINTS
Team 3	1	19.0
Team 2	2	18.0
Team 4	3	17.5
Team 1	4	15.5

This stat period was very early in the season and, as we said, things can change in a hurry. Team 1, which was in even worse shape in our 14-team league, ended the season in third. Team 2 ended its season in fifth. Team 4 ended its season in sixth. Team 3 ended up second to last. Our advice to you is: Never feel comfortable with your team until the season is over and you have won.

INTRA-TEAM TRANSACTIONS

We have already explained the two roster moves—trades, and, if your league allows them, pickups for injuries—that can be made in both the Weekly and the Head-to-Head scoring methods. The only other type of roster move is the intra-team transaction, and it is used only if your league uses the Weekly Scoring Method. Head-to-head does not need this feature because a lineup is called in for every game. The key element in an intra-team transaction is the taxi squad—a squad of six inactive players kept in reserve to give you some staffing flexibility. The taxi squad in Fantasy Basketball is the equivalent of the bench in the NBA. Whether your team allows pickups or freezes fantasy teams after the draft, the proper use of your taxi squad is a key element in your team's success. These reserves are especially significant in a frozen-roster league, because they are then your only recourse should your team be crippled by injury.

Ideally your taxi squad should serve two purposes (three if you count the comic relief derived from owning John "Hot Plate" Williams and Bobby Hansen). It should provide you with enough depth to replace an injured or a suddenly unproductive starter. It should also allow you the luxury of making an occasional, but highly advantageous, short-term roster move. For example, let's say that you take a look at your weekly stats and notice that you could pass three other franchises and gain three points in the weekly standings—if only your fantasy team had 10 more steals. So, you decide to replace Johnny Dawkins with Mookie Blaylock. You sacrifice some points and assists in exchange for the necessary steals to vault your team past those other franchises. In a couple of weeks you will have surpassed those three teams in steals and gained the accompanying three standings points. If you also manage to hold your position in assists, you will have made a fine short-term roster move.

Intra-squad transactions are subject to some restrictions. First of all, there's a weekly transaction deadline. To move a player from your starting lineup to your taxi squad, and vice versa, you must call the league commissioner before any games are played on Monday, the first day of each new stat period. This deadline prevents an owner from seeing that a player has had a great game on Monday and then trying to use that player in the same week. Also, a position freeze applies. When an owner pulls the trigger and calls a player up from his taxi squad (and, consequently, sends another one down), both players are frozen in their new positions. These players must, barring any injuries, remain frozen in their new positions for at least three weeks. Only if a starting player is PLACED ON INJURED RESERVE (not just injured), can the three-week minimum restriction be waived. In such a case, the injured starter can be replaced by any player on the taxi squad.

This three-week minimum makes keeping stats easier and offers an element of risk. A fantasy team owner might call up a taxi-squad player who has been piling up numbers, only to find that his supposed phenom is a mere flash in the pan. Should a different starter get banged up (but not go on IR) later on, the team's best reserve will already have been called up. In addition, the team's worst starter, now probably the best taxi-squad player, is inactive for three weeks. This leaves the risk-taking owner an unenviable choice: (1)

playing his banged-up starter or (2) calling up some hack and freezing another two players for three more weeks. It can be a vicious circle.

EXAMPLE: One of our teams was deep enough to have Grant Long, the Miami Heat's forward, on its taxi squad. About mid-season, Grant started to have some statistically successful games while Terry Cummings, a starter for this same Fantasy Franchise, found himself in a slump. The fantasy owner decided to replace Terry with Grant, at the time a seemingly good move. Unfortunately for this owner, an injury to David Robinson forced Cummings to elevate his game a notch. Terry was playing much better than Grant, but the owner could only sit and watch, because they both had to stay where they were. The owner lost some very valuable stats in this exchange. Now, to complicate matters, Rik Smits started to have knee problems. He sat for a couple of games, and when he came back, his playing time was reduced. But for how long? The owner now had to decide: Would Rik's stats be better than a replacement's? Well, if the owner hadn't made the original switch of Grant Long for Terry Cummings, he could have placed all of his best performers in his starting lineup by substituting Grant Long for Rik Smits. But because the original move was made, the owner was stuck with a slumping Long and an ailing Smits (or his best bench player, who was now Tim McCormick) in his starting lineup. Meanwhile, Terry Cummings rampaged his way along the West Coast. Again, the owner lost valuable stats—not many, but little things like these add up and can make quite a difference by the end of the season. Now if Rik Smits, who was still in the starting lineup, had ever been put on IR, the owner could have exchanged Terry Cummings for Rik because the three-week minimum would have been waived.

Here's where your coaching prowess must shine. While the best-coached teams may not always win, we can almost guarantee that a team with Danny Ferry in its starting lineup and John Starks riding the pines will plummet to astonishing new lows by season's end. Likewise, a team that keeps its production at a maximum—that gets hot players into the lineup and slumping players out at the right times—will be competing for the money when spring comes.

TRANSACTION FEES

Your league should assess transaction fees for intra-team transactions and for trades. The following numbers can be used as guidelines for the amounts that should be charged. For an intra-team transaction, charge 5 percent of the franchise fee for any moves made before the All-Star break; charge 10 percent for any moves made after that. Waive the fee only for a move that replaces a player placed on injured reserve. For trades, charge 20 percent of the franchise fee. The responsibility for paying this fee is negotiable as part of the trade. These fees are assessed to minimize transactions made on a whim, and to make bookkeeping easier. All transaction fees go into the prize pool to be divided up by the winners at the end of the season.

PAYOFFS

The payoff for your league should be determined before your season begins. In a 14-team league, for example, the five top owners would receive part of the bounty. The fifth-place prize should equal the franchise fee (that is, the owner recovers his franchise fee—but not any transaction fees). The remainder of the money in the prize pool should be given out in the following percentages:

        4th place   —   10
        3rd place   —   20
        2nd place   —   30
        1st place   —   40

SUMMARY OF RULES: WEEKLY SCORING METHOD

Draft:
1. Owner drafts 18 players.
2. Owner has 250 units to spend.
3. Team can draft a player if:
   a. The owner does not already have 18 players.
   b. The player is a member of the talent pool.
   c. The owner can afford whatever bid he is proposing.
   d. The owner can fill the rest of his team with a bid of at least 1 unit.

Play:
1. Choose 12 starters.
2. Compete in seven categories.
   a. Rebounds
   b. Assists
   c. Steals
   d. Blocks
   e. Turnovers
   f. Three-point field goals made
   g. Points

Pickups (Option 1):
1. Replaced player must be on injured reserve.
2. New player must be a free agent.
3. New player must play the same position as player replaced.
4. Owner retains right to injured player.
5. New player must be dropped when injured player is taken off IR.
6. New player may never be traded.
7. If the injured player is traded the new player is immediately dropped.
8. No pickup is allowed to a team that has traded for an injured player.

Frozen Roster (Option 2):
No pickups are allowed.

Trades:
1. Both teams involved must trade same number of players.
2. Trades must be submitted by Friday.
3. Trades must be approved by commissioner.
4. Teams are charged 20 percent of franchise fee (responsibility of payment is negotiable as part of trade).
5. Before All-Star break, league-wide trading is allowed.
6. After All-Star break:
   a. League is divided into three groups.
   b. Owners may only trade within their own group.

Intra-Team Transactions:
1. Call-up must be called in to commissioner before first Monday game.
2. Players are frozen in new position for three weeks.
3. Fee is 5 percent of franchise fee before All-Star break.
4. Fee is 10 percent of franchise fee after All-Star break.
5. Rules 2, 3, and 4 are void if a starter goes on IR.

Payoff (14-team league):
1. Fifth-place team receives franchise fee back.
2. Fourth—10 percent of pot.
3. Third—20 percent of pot.
4. Second—30 percent of pot.
5. First—40 percent of pot.

HEAD-TO-HEAD SCORING METHOD

If you choose to play head-to-head, the steps you will use to organize a league will remain the same. The rules, with a few exceptions will change. In recruiting owners, you are still looking for the same qualities, but the owners have much more responsibility and therefore must be much more dedicated. For instance, owners have to phone in their lineups every week. The commissioner's job description is longer than that of the weekly-method commissioner. Every week he will get many more phone calls with three games worth of lineups and last-minute lineup changes. He may also have to meet an additional requirement: having an answering machine and/or a computer. In addition, there are a few specific aspects of the head-to-head method that need to be discussed during the owners meeting, although this will certainly provoke more fights. The number of games played per week must be discussed, as well as the positions allowed for some players. Some things, however, are not very different from what they would be in the weekly method— how to choose the talent pool, the rules for trading, and most draft procedures (except that player-position requirements have to be met). And, of course, the head-to-head commissioner must be just as wise, fair, trustworthy, etcetera as the weekly-method commissioner.

Since no fees are assessed for intra-team transactions, you may wish to make the original franchise fee larger if your league wants more money in the pot at the end of the season. Trade fees are the same.

So much for the similarities. Now let's discuss the differences between the head-to-head and weekly versions of play.

Head-to-head play is much more realistic than the Weekly Scoring Method, but it is much more complicated. There are 27 weeks in the NBA's regular season, and during each week your teams will play either two or three games, depending on where you get your stats. If you use *USA Today*, only two games a week can be played, because the box scores from late Thursday, Friday, and Saturday are not printed in the paper. If someone in your league has a computer with a modem—and if you decide to subscribe to some online sports service like the *USA Today Sports Line* or *Computer Sports*

World—you can play three games a week, because the weekend box scores can be downloaded to enable you to calculate the results of your league's games. (The cost will be roughly $10 to $15 a month, but it is worth the extra dollar per person for the realism of three games a week. The number to call for information on joining the *USA Today Sports Line* is 1-800-826-9688. The number for *Computer Sports World* is 1-702-294-0191.)

In head-to-head competition with two games per week, calculate the results of your first game by using NBA games played on Sunday and Monday. Calculate the results of your second game by using NBA games played on Wednesday and Thursday. A word to the wise: Watch out for Thursday games on the West Coast, the box scores of which may not make Friday's paper. Games played on Tuesdays are swing games; players' statistics from Tuesday's games can be used to fill a lineup spot in either the first or second game of your league each week. However, you can never use the same player's game twice. For example, if Chris Mullin plays on Tuesday, you can only use his stats from that game for either the Sunday/Monday game or the Wednesday/Thursday game, not both. (For an illustration of how this works, see our sample matchups in this chapter.)

If you can play three games a week, do it. It is more realistic. With a 3-game-per-week setup, you can play 61 games in your season, plus the playoffs—very close to the 82 games plus playoffs that each NBA team plays. In a three-game-per-week system, your first game uses the stats from Sunday and Monday NBA games, the second game uses stats from Wednesday and Thursday games, and the third game uses stats from Friday and Saturday games. Tuesday is again a swing day; players' stats from Tuesday can be used for either of the first two games of each week. Again, the stats for a player from Tuesday's game can be used for either the Sunday/Monday matchup or the Wednesday/Thursday matchup, but not both. Remember that someone is going to have to access some kind of score-reporting service like the *USA Today Sports Line* to get the weekend box scores and determine the results of the Friday/Saturday games. *USA Today* leaves the box scores in its computer for quite a long time, so accessing them can be put off for a couple of days. Still, the sooner the better. People want to know the results as soon as possible to find out how they did over the weekend and where they are in the standings.

Now that you know how many games you are going to play each week, let's consider how you are going to try to win them. While your draft in head-to-head is conducted in the same fashion as in the weekly method, you only play 8 of your 18 players in each game. For each game, you match your starting eight (three guards, three forwards, and two centers) against the starting eight of one other team in your league, according to a predetermined schedule. (For a sample schedule, see the appendix to this book.) Your players compete with your opponent's players in seven different categories: points, rebounds, blocked shots, assists, steals, turnovers, and three-point field goals. (In the turnover category, the team with the fewest wins.) To win a game, your team must win four of the seven categories. To win a category, your starting eight must outperform your opponent's starting eight in that category. (For an illustration of this system, see our sample matchups later in this chapter.)

Head-to-head puts an emphasis on team management, not just on drafting the best team. As a coach, you must analyze the comparative strengths of your team and your opponent's. You might conclude, "Well, I can't win rebounds, blocks, or steals, but I have him in assists, turnovers, and three-point field goals. Can I sub a player who won't hurt me in the three categories I'm winning, but will get me more points?" If you're lucky, one of your players in this case will be playing in Oakland against those running Warriors and you'll win.

We settled on a starting team of eight players because almost no owner will have the luxury of having eight superstars available for every game. Also, few (if any) NBA teams go more than eight deep on their bench, and we are trying to get as close to the real thing as possible, aren't we? The position restrictions—requiring each team to play three forwards, three guards, and two centers—prevent an owner from just teaming six big men with Stockton and Hardaway. These lineup restrictions make the games a better reflection of who has the better team, or more likely, which team has the hottest eight players in a particular time frame.

INTRA-TEAM TRANSACTIONS

The calling in and recording of lineups for each game is a time-consuming task for all of the team owners—and much more so for the commissioner. Who needs a million phone calls a day? It's far better to limit team owners to a single phone call, with the lineups for all two or three league games, in a given week. This call should be on the Friday or Saturday prior to the next week's games. A helpful hint to the commissioner: give the phone calls a format: "The players for my first game are: _____. The players for my second game are: _____. The players for my third game are: _____." Have the owners list the two centers first, the three forwards second, and the three guards last. If someone forgets to make a call, use the last lineup that was called in.

If a player is injured, allow the team owner to replace the injured player in the lineup, but this does not mean that if Ewing gets hurt in Sunday's game a team owner could replace him with a different player who is playing on Monday (which, in head-to-head, is considered as the same game). The owner could, however, exchange Ewing for Brad Daugherty in the league's second game of the week. To minimize the bookkeeping involved, we suggest allowing owners only one substitution per league game. (This does not include injury substitutions.) No player substitution is allowed if either party in the proposed move—the player to be substituted or the player to be replaced—has already played or if an NBA game involving either party has already started. Establish a clear line of communication so the owners are confident that their lineups and lineup changes are received.

SCHEDULES AND PLAYOFFS

This is the true benefit of playing head-to-head: You can hope to make the playoffs with your team peaking at the right time. When playoffs roll around for your league, we hope that they resemble the NBA Championships of the '70s, and not the dull stuff they called playoffs in the '80s. Boy, don't you just love that Celtic-Laker rivalry? Gag me with Kareem's goggles.

Three Games a Week

A playoff round can be a three-, five-, or seven-game series. Whoever takes two of three, three of five, or four of seven games is the series winner. If a game ends in a tie, the sudden-death tie breaker is the number of free throws made (draft the Mailman for this). The number of regular-season games you play depends on the number of teams in your league and how many teams make the playoffs. If your league has 10–14 teams in it, you can play 61 games in the regular season and save the last 9 for the playoffs. If your league has eight or fewer teams, you can play as many as 64 games and set aside the last 6 for the playoffs, or you can play as few as 58 games and set aside the last 12 for the playoffs. (Please refer to Appendix C: League Schedules for a wider variety of playoff options for leagues of different sizes.) The number of teams that make the playoffs are as follows:

> 14-Team League — 8 teams (no first-round byes)
> 12-Team League — 6 teams (2 get byes)
> 10-Team League — 6 teams (2 get byes)
> 8-Team League — 4 teams (no byes)

We recommend not using any divisions in your league. Let the seedings for the playoffs go straight down the standings. That is, the team with the best record is the top seed in the playoffs, and the team with the eighth-best record is the number eight seed in the playoffs.

NOTE: In case of a tie for a playoff spot or for a seed in the playoffs, the team with the best record in the regular-season meetings between the two teams gets the playoff spot or the better seed.

The pairings for the playoffs are as follows:

FOURTEEN-TEAM LEAGUE

TEN- OR TWELVE-TEAM LEAGUE

For a 10- or 12-team league, teams 7 and 8 do not make the playoffs. Teams 1 and 2 receive byes in the first round as a reward for their excellent play in the regular season.

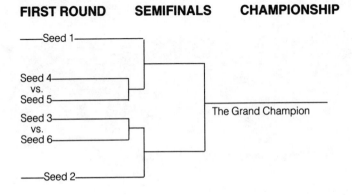

EIGHT-TEAM LEAGUE

In a league with eight or fewer teams, the first round is lost to the regular season. The top four teams make the playoffs and start their playoffs at the semifinal stage.

SEMIFINALS   **CHAMPIONSHIP**

Seed 1
vs.
Seed 4

The Grand Champion

Seed 3
vs.
Seed 2

Two Games a Week

If your league plays two games a week, your playoffs are limited to two-game, total-stat playoff rounds. Both owners submit lineups for each of the two games. The lineups for both games must be submitted by the first game on Sunday—with no last-minute substitutions allowed, except in the case of injury. The stats for both games are totaled for each team. The team that wins the most categories moves on to the next round. Any ties are broken by a sudden-death tally of the free throws made by each team over the course of both games; more free throws, you win.

If you have 10, 12, or 14 teams in your league, your league will play 48 games in the regular season, and play 6 in the playoffs. If you have eight or fewer teams in your league, you play 50 games and save 4 for the playoffs. The seedings and pairings are the same as for the three-game-a-week playoffs.

PAYOFFS

In a league with 14, 12, or 10 teams, give the losers of the first round one-half of their franchise fee back. During the championship game, also have a consolation game to determine third and fourth places. Third place receives 20 percent, and fourth place 10 percent of the remaining pot. The winner receives 40 percent, while the runner-up receives 30 percent. In an eight-team league, there is no first round, so fourth place simply receives 10 percent of the total pot, third place gets 20 percent, second place gets 30 percent, and the champion gets 40 percent.

SAMPLE MATCHUPS AND ANALYSIS

To show how these rules apply to actual Fantasy Basketball play, let's take a look at how our league's matchups went during one week of actual NBA games (from January 5, 1992, through January 11, 1992). For some (very biased) analysis of these matchups, we'll ask each of the four franchise owners to dish out a few lame excuses and outrageous boasts about their fortunes during that week.

For the league's first game (Sunday and Monday):

Detroit at San Antonio	Sacramento at Boston
Miami at L.A. Lakers	Houston at Atlanta
Philadelphia at Portland	Indiana at Utah
Phoenix at New York	L.A. Clippers at New Jersey

Tuesday (the swing day):

Atlanta at New York	Washington at Chicago
Cleveland at Minnesota	L.A. Lakers at Dallas
Seattle at Denver	Orlando at Portland

For the league's second game (Wednesday and Thursday):

New York at Boston	Chicago at Miami
Houston at Philadelphia	L.A. Clippers at Indiana
Sacramento at Detroit	L.A. Lakers at San Antonio
Utah at Milwaukee	Orlando at Seattle
Denver at Phoenix	Cleveland at Washington
Minnesota at New Jersey	Sacramento at Charlotte

Dallas at Atlanta

For the third and final game of the week (Friday and Saturday)

Minnesota at Boston	Miami at Chicago
L.A. Clippers at Philadelphia	Portland at Charlotte
Portland at Detroit	New Jersey at Detroit
Seattle at Dallas	Utah at Minnesota
Denver at L.A. Lakers	San Antonio at Denver
Milwaukee at New Jersey	L.A. Clippers at Washington
Houston at Miami	Philadelphia at Cleveland
Utah at Chicago	Atlanta at Indiana
Orlando at Phoenix	Sacramento at Milwaukee
San Antonio at Golden State	Seattle at Houston
Boston at New York	Golden State at Phoenix

Team #1

Edwards, J.	LAC
Longley, L.	MIN
Salley, J.	DET
Lohaus, B.	MIL
Kessler, A.	MIA
Pippen, S.	CHI
Elliott, S.	SA
Schrempf, D.	IND
Catledge, T.	ORL
Volkov, A.	ATL
Smith, D.	DAL
Murphy, T.	MIN
Anderson, R.	PHI
Price, M.	CLE
Strickland, R.	SA
Richardson, P.	MIN
Dawkins, J.	PHI
Anderson, K.	NJ

Team #2

Mutombo, D.	DEN
Dudley, C.	NJ
Alexander, V.	GS
Jones, C.	WAS
Bird, L.	BOS
Anderson, G.	DEN
Majerle, D.	PHX
Perry, T.	PHX
Williams, Jo.	ORL
Gamble, K.	BOS
Reynolds, J.	ORL
Newman, J.	CHA
Starks, J.	NY
Adams, M.	WAS
Skiles, S.	ORL
Brandon, T.	CLE
Smith, S.	MIA
Marciulionis, S.	GS

Team #3

Smits, R.	IND
Seikaly, R.	MIA
Smith, L.	HOU
McCormick, T.	NY
Green, S.	SA
Manning, D.	LAC
Grant, H.	CHI
Hill, T.	GS
McCray, R.	DAL
Williams, Ja.	PHI
Anderson, W.	SA
Johnson, K	PHX
Maxwell, V.	HOU
Robinson, R.	ATL
Oliver, B.	PHI
Vincent, S.	ORL
Hansen, B.	CHI
Coles, B.	MIA

Team #4

Robinson, D.	SA
Benjamin, B.	SEA
Thompson, L.	IND
Robinson, C.	POR
McKey, D.	SEA
Long, G.	MIA
Bailey, T.	MIN
Williams, B.	POR
Woolridge, O.	DET
Edwards, T.	UT
Fox, R.	BOS
Stockton, J.	UT
Hornacek, J.	PHX
Bogues, M.	CHA
Shaw, B.	MIA
Smith, T.	LAL
Les, J.	SAC
Ceballos, C.	PHX

The fantasy league schedule sets the following matchups:

In Game 1: Team #1 vs. Team #2
Team #3 vs. Team #4

In Game 2: Team #1 vs. Team #3
Team #2 vs. Team #4

In Game 3: Team #1 vs. Team #4
Team #2 vs. Team #3

Word from the Owner: Team 1

THE DRAFT

I know what you're saying: "How can a guy expect to win any games without a center?" Well, you should have seen my team before I traded Greg Kite for John Salley. The problem was that, after performing a certain predraft ritual with the owner of Team 3, I spent most of draft day lying on the floor with a towel over my eyes, trying to kick start my brain. Needless to say, the old brain failed me. After paying 50 for Scottie Pippen as my third player, I decided that I could play this game without a center. Worse, I kept this strategy throughout the entire draft, even though I could have gotten capable centers such as Moses Malone and Rik Smits for prices in the low 20s. Also, I was told that I drafted Rod Strickland for 21. To this day, I deny ever mentioning the number 21.

My team paid severely for my errors in judgment. After an abysmal 3–17 start, I decided it was time for action. Interestingly enough, I contacted the other team in the league with a 3–17 record. As we examined our teams, it became clear that each should be built around its major superstar—Scottie Pippen in my case, and Hakeem Olajuwon in his. We then tried to find four categories we each could win and tried to make a trade that would boost both teams in these respective categories (this may be the only strategy available to you if your team ends up as bad as ours were).

After much discussion, I gave him Dominique Wilkins (and later apologized when Wilkins got injured), Kendall Gill, and Greg Kite. In return I got Mark Price, Sean Elliott, and John Salley. I gave him a good rebounding and scoring guard (Gill), a dominant scorer (Dominique), and a decent center (Kite) to help him try to improve on points, rebounds, blocks, and maybe turnovers or steals as his four winnable categories. I got a reasonably capable center (Salley), a third point guard (Price), and an all-around forward (Elliott). A bit of good fortune came my way when Rod Strickland signed with the Spurs and gave me three very effective point guards available for every game, plus Johnny Dawkins if one of them had a day off. With the three point guards and Scottie Pippen, who led all forwards in assists, I didn't lose assists in any game the rest of the season. The other categories I was favoring were steals and three-pointers, and after that I hoped to get lucky in one other category—turnovers (my point guards were good here); points (if Pippen and Elliott had big games); or blocks (if Salley had a monster game).

The trade had some tremendous results (one of them being that I get to mention Hank and Jim's names in the book—I told them I'd make them famous if they traded with me). Although both of our teams missed the playoffs, we had the two best records in the league from the time of the trade to the end of the regular season. My team even swept all seven categories in a few games, believe it or not. Since the chances are slim that such an astoundingly successful trade will occur again in the foreseeable future, you can expect to read about this one for years. (My coauthors will be hearing about it for the rest of their lives.)

Even after this great trade, my team still had precious little depth. (Luckily, I had almost no injuries.) My starting eight rarely changed until Alexander Volkov and Luc Longley started playing more because of injuries to others. The only changes I made were to sub occasionally for a starter who wasn't available during a particular time frame.

GAME ONE

So, without further ado, here is my starting lineup for Game 1:

C—John Salley   F—Scottie Pippen
C—James Edwards   G—Mark Price
F—Detlef Schrempf   G—Rod Strickland
F—Sean Elliott   G—Pooh Richardson

This is my normal starting eight. Against Team 2, a team with Adams, Skiles, and Bird, I am in danger of losing my precious assist category if I don't throw my best passing lineup at them. Unfortunately, my team always has matchup problems against Alex. He does well in threes, turnovers, and steals—categories in which I can usually compete—and he always wins rebounds, blocks, and points.

GAME TWO

Against Team 3, which only has one respectable assist man (I refuse to consider Rumeal Robinson an assist man), I would like to make a substitution that would strengthen my rebounding. I figure I might be able to sneak by in this category since I shouldn't have to worry about assists. Unfortunately, at this point, I have no shooting guards at all on my roster (later I will trade Brad Lohaus for Blue Edwards in order to add some depth to my guard and forward positions), and the only rebounding forward I have is Terry Catledge. There's no reason Sean Elliott can't get more rebounds than Catledge, so, grudgingly, I play my normal starting eight and hope that Detlef comes up with a freakishly big rebounding game. My lineup is again:

C—John Salley   F—Scottie Pippen
C—James Edwards   G—Mark Price
F—Detlef Schrempf   G—Rod Strickland
F—Sean Elliott   G—Pooh Richardson

This one shocked me. I beat a very strong team in rebounds, 55–49. Granted, his team had an off-game in rebounds, but Detlef must have been inspired by my pep talk. He pulled down 17 boards, and Pooh must have had a career high with his 9. (These are the kinds of statistics, by the way, that are lost when the Weekly Scoring Method is used.) Finally, I would like to gloat briefly over my five-to-one assist-to-turnover ratio. Thank you.

GAME THREE

Again I'm in the unenviable position of not being able to change lineups according to my opponent's strengths and weaknesses. So, instead of talking about my unchanged lineup, I'll pass along a handy bit of information I learned this season: The better teams, or, more accurately, the teams with the highest attendance figures, will tend to play more games on weekends than during the week. When they play on both Friday and Saturday, as, for instance, the Bulls and Blazers do this week, any players you own from these teams will miss some fantasy games over the course of the season. Before your draft next year, you might want to examine the NBA schedule closely to check out who loses the most fantasy games that season. Oh yes, by the way, here's my lineup for Game 3:

C—John Salley	F—Scottie Pippen
C—James Edwards	G—Mark Price
F—Detlef Schrempf	G—Rod Strickland
F—Sean Elliott	G—Pooh Richardson

Jim's team is another that I can rarely compete with, for the same reasons that I can't beat Alex's team. In fact, I beat him only once during the regular season, and even then I win three of my four categories by a margin of only one. I'm not so fortunate this time.

Word from the Owner: Team 2

THE DRAFT

My draft strategy was simple. I made a mock roster just before the draft, filling it with players I thought would do well this year (what I call bargain players). Then I checked what superstars I needed to give me a good balanced performance in all seven categories (with an emphasis on rebounds, blocks, and three-pointers). All my hard work and planning went to hell, though, when Mutombo was the first player called in our auction draft. I had imagined teams both with and without Mutombo, and had decided that my units would be better spent on other players who didn't have the big rookie's price tag. Unfortunately, as I was bidding him up, I said "50," and everyone else shut up. Still, he was a bargain at 50. You've got to be flexible on draft day.

Next (still early in the draft) I took Adams from Washington, who'd had a good preseason and was an excellent three-point shooter. Another 50 units were gone. Bird was my next selection, costing me 42 units. Was he worth the risk of injury? With hindsight my answer would be, "NO!" But when Bird was healthy I was a tough team to beat. My next pick was a mascot, of sorts. John "Hot Plate" Williams was suspended for being grossly overweight, and I figured anyone with a physique like that belonged on my team. Plus I only had to pay 2 units for him.

At this point in the draft, there were still some players left whom I liked and would be willing to bid on. But mostly I was looking for bargain players who would cost me less than 10 units each. My spending reserve looked meager compared to those of other franchises (not the best position to be in). Thunder Dan came home at 25. Greg "Beemer" Anderson cost 15. Skiles and Dudley went for 27 and 9 respectively. Jerry "Ice Ice Baby" Reynolds went for 2, and Gamble and Brandon for 4. Marciulionis cost me 7 units and Starks cost me 4. I picked up these players sporadically throughout the draft, waiting a long time for other franchises either to fill their rosters or to be left with fewer units than the 10 I had to spend. This gave me plenty of time to examine my team and figure out which of the players left in the draft might produce the numbers I needed. Steve Smith (4), Tim Perry (1), and Johnny Newman (2) seemed like good choices. Finally, I needed centers since I only had Mutombo and Dudley. I took C. Jones from Washington and Victor "The House" Alexander from Golden State to complete my team.

I had a good mix of talent and depth, and would end up being especially thankful I had drafted for depth. My team was riddled with injuries during the season. And to make matters worse, I eventually traded Dudley and some of my depth for Rik Smits, who wound up with tendonitis in both knees. When we were deciding on a week to use for this example, I tried to find one in which my team had been completely healthy and discovered that there had been no such week.

Still, I thrived, getting off to a fast start and managing to squeak into the playoffs with a battered and bruised team. Of course, during the playoffs, I was without the services of Mutombo and Smits and lost in the first round. I did manage to force a third game in a best of three series by a stroke of good coaching. Since my team could no longer compete in rebounds or blocks (two strong categories for my opponent), I played a combination of Smith, Skiles, Adams, Majerle, Bird, Starks (a guard/forward), Alexander, and C. Jones. I tried to win assists, steals, threes, and turnovers. When I didn't win steals in my third and deciding playoff game, my season came to an end.

GAME ONE

This week I lose Larry Bird, Golden State doesn't play until the weekend, Ice is hurt, Scott Skiles is out, and Steve Smith is on IR. Left with few options, I play Gamble in a guard position and hope he picks up the slack for Bird (and McHale who is also out). Luckily I'm playing Troy, whose team I match up well against. I would normally coach Troy into a loss, but even without a choice of which players to start this week, I think I can beat him. Here are my starters:

C—Dikembe Mutombo	F—Dan Majerle
C—Chris Dudley	G—Michael Adams
F—"Cadillac" Anderson	G—John Starks
F—Tim Perry	G—Kevin Gamble

As expected I stuff Troy into a sack. To be fair, however, I should mention that I had two players DNP (Did Not Play) for this game and substituted active players for them for the purposes of this book. Without the substitutions, Troy would have crushed me 6–1. Hey, call it what you like. I'm not above a little cheating if I can make it look respectable.

GAME TWO

This is not a game to be banged–up for. Once Jim traded away his depth for David Robinson, he became very hard to beat. I can normally beat Jim's team in rebounding and three-pointers. I'm competitive in points, but I need to beat him in steals to have a chance of winning. Unfortunately I do not have the services of Ice Reynolds, so winning steals is not going to be easy. Oh well, I'll try.

C—Dikembe Mutombo	F—Dan Majerle
C—Chris Dudley	G—Michael Adams
F—"Cadillac" Anderson	G—John Starks
F—Tim Perry	G—Kevin Gamble

After this game, I just want to take my ball and go home.

GAME THREE

To end this week with a win would be a big morale builder for my belea-guered troops. I'm playing Russ, whose well-balanced team matches up nicely with mine. The team that wins blocked shots normally wins our matchups. If my team were healthy in this case, I would make Majerle a guard and play Bird, Perry, and "Cadillac" Anderson at the forward positions. But, alas, I have little choice again in the players I can start. Marciulionis is now available, but since I can't imagine him helping me, I let him ride the pines.

C—Dikembe Mutombo	F—Dan Majerle
C—Chris Dudley	G—Michael Adams
F—"Cadillac" Anderson	G—Kevin Gamble
F—Tim Perry	G—John Starks

Yet another demoralizing defeat, added to another demoralizing week, which will eventually build to a kind of crescendo of demoralization by sea-son's end. It's a good thing I don't take this stuff seriously or I might run away to hide somewhere in the hills of Peru.

Word from the Owner: Team 3

THE DRAFT

Hi. I'm Russ, and this is a story about how to draft a team with no depth. Unfortunately, I spent draft day suffering from the same affliction as the owner of Team 1, and was therefore unable to keep my mind (what there was of it) on the quality of my choices all the way down the line.

I determined early in the draft that I could win with nine players, so I drafted Rony Seikaly, Rik Smits, Danny Manning, Horace Grant, Willie Anderson, Kevin Johnson, Vernon Maxwell, Rumeal Robinson, and Rodney McCray. (I'm convinced it is possible for a team to win a championship with nonnative-born centers. I just didn't have a chance to prove it this year.) For-tunately, when McCray was injured, I was able to sub Bimbo Coles, whom I picked up for Travis Mays. The fatal mistake I made was to assume that Vernon could make me competitive in three-pointers all by his lonesome. He was so inconsistent from the launching stripe that I had to settle for an occa-sional game of four three-pointers sandwiched between weeks of shutouts.

On the upside, Grant and Manning made an excellent one-two forward combination, getting plenty of points, rebounds, blocks, and steals, with a minimum of turnovers. When K.J. got hot, my team became a force to be reckoned with. My team lived under a good sign, remaining remarkably injury-free for the entire season (Rik Smits was traded for Chris Dudley and some desperately needed depth before Rik's tendonitis sidelined him). In case you are wondering, I finished one game shy of the last playoff spot, after winning seven of my last nine games. Final record: 29–26. Too bad this wasn't the actual NBA.

GAME ONE

Here I play Jim's Bruising Berthas, home of the beloved Mr. Robinson. I can kiss blocks and steals good-bye. Robinson and Stockton should easily outdistance my crew, barring some major rear-end kicking on the part of Ho Grant and Danny Manning. You might as well memorize this lineup, because it's not going to change much this week or, alas, for the rest of the season. A team full of almosts. Maybe I can almost win.

C—Rony Seikaly	F—Willie Anderson
C—Rik Smits	G—Kevin Johnson
F—Danny Manning	G—Vernon Maxwell
F—Horace Grant	G—Rumeal Robinson

Ah, a loss. . . . Gentlemen, you have a choice. Either the level of play improves, or you find yourselves in LaCrosse Catbirds uniforms. Do I make myself clear?

GAME TWO

In this case, I play Troy's Assist Monsters. I suppose I could concede assists and bench K.J., but I cannot in good conscience bench the star guard of my team (and Phoenix's, with apologies to Mr. Hornacek). After finding out that Rumeal has missed the previous game, I consider substituting McCray or Bimbo Coles, but I find out that whatever kept Rumeal out will not keep him out again. So my lineup is set. Assists are lost, rebounds and blocks won easily, and turnovers probably won. I need one of the remaining three categories. Shoot it, Vernon! Now shoot it again! And again!

C—Rony Seikaly	F—Willie Anderson
C—Rik Smits	G—Kevin Johnson
F—Danny Manning	G—Vernon Maxwell
F—Horace Grant	G—Rumeal Robinson

Losing to this bunch is about as pleasant as having teeth pulled. It's going to be a long offseason. Gentlemen, I think it may be time for some owner-friendly R-E-N-E-G-O-T-I-A-T-I-O-N. How does that sound, knaves?

GAME THREE

Alex's team provides the most interesting matchup. Even when he's battered and bruised, he can put in a lineup that can take almost any category. My best move in this situation? You guessed it. Send the same guys out there again and hope that a healthy starting eight will overcome the Backfiring Ferraris.

C—Rony Seikaly	F—Willie Anderson
C—Rik Smits	G—Kevin Johnson
F—Danny Manning	G—Vernon Maxwell
F—Horace Grant	G—Rumeal Robinson

There is some joy in Sudsville. This game proves, if nothing else, that you can't lose them all. The worst part about this season is that I don't even get a lottery pick after my gross misfortune/mismanagement. Then again, none of these guys has any kind of long-term deal with me, so I can start fresh next year.

Word from the Owner: Team 4

THE DRAFT

My team consisted of one superstar (John Stockton), one player I was forced to take because of his skills and position in the draft (Hersey Hawkins), and 14 guys who were just too good to pass up. Let me explain this in further detail. During the first week of the season, Stockton was having some "monster" games. By the day of the draft, he was averaging five steals and 15 assists per game. I just had to have him, no matter what the price (57 units as it turned out, but well worth it). Once I had Stockton (the first player I drafted), I proceeded to bid on anyone who seemed to be a bargain. I picked up Benoit Benjamin for 28 units using this method. But then Hersey Hawkins came up on the auction block, and I was faced with a big dilemma. All the great steal artists in the league had been taken, and after Hawkins the best guy left was Mugsy Bogues. Settling for Mugsy would have meant giving up over half a steal per game, so I decided I had to pay the 40 for Hersey and wait for some more bargains to come my way.

As it turned out, I had nothing to worry about. The players I thought would do well seemed to get ignored (I got Grant Long for 3 and Derrick McKey for 11, for example). And even when I did reach a little bit, it didn't do any harm (Jeff Hornacek for 20, Moses Malone for 19, and Robert Parish for 27). I even ended up getting Mugsy Bogues after all, for 4 units. By the time the draft was over, I was content with my team. I had three good centers, three good guards, and a lot of guys with potential at the forward spot.

The first week of the season, I went 1–2. Then, the second week of the season, I went . . . 1–2. I said to myself, "Something is wrong here. I have more talent than this." Then I realized what the problem was—too much depth at center. It's great to have three good forwards and three good guards, but three good centers, unless injury strikes, are a waste. I looked over the rosters of my fellow owners, looking for a potential trade. I thought about trading one of the centers for an established forward, but nothing came of that. I thought about trading two of them for a great forward, but nothing came of that. I finally realized what I had to do. I decided I could package Robert Parish, Moses Malone, Hersey Hawkins, and Sam Mitchell for DAVID ROBINSON and anyone else. By trading my depth for superior talent, I was able to fashion the best team in the league for the majority of the season. This move would cost me when playoff time rolled around, because both

Robinson and Benjamin were hurt, and I was forced to play Brad Lohaus and LaSalle Thompson at center. If I had to do it over again, however, I would do exactly the same thing. After all, he is DAVID ROBINSON, our MVP.

GAME ONE

Now I know what Pat Riley felt like when he coached the Lakers. At this point in the season, my players were so dominant that all I had to do was throw the ball out on the floor and watch them play. Nobody had better centers, nobody had better guards, and my forwards (the supposed weakness of my team) were holding their own with anybody.

C—David Robinson	F—Buck Williams
C—Benoit Benjamin	G—John Stockton
F—Grant Long	G—Brian Shaw
F—Derrick McKey	G—Jeff Hornacek

This turned out to be my only close game all week. But my horses still prevailed, winning three-pointers, points, steals, and assists. How did we ever lose blocks? If this keeps up, heads will roll.

GAME TWO

Next I play Alex. Who cares? My team will continue on its path of cold, calculated devastation. Nobody can stop us, not even a coauthor. I have it all. Dave and Benoit are blocking the shots and getting the rebounds. Stockton and Mugsy are dishing and swiping. Hornacek is throwing down the threes. Life is good.

C—David Robinson	F—Derrick McKey
C—Benoit Benjamin	G—John Stockton
F—Buck Williams	G—Mugsy Bogues
G—Grant Long	G—Jeff Hornacek

This is more like it—a convincing victory instead of a squeaker like last time. We should have won steals too; our season average was somewhere around 14. Boy would we be awesome if we were firing on all cylinders.

GAME THREE

Troy is next on the hit list, and boy will he fall hard. His team is so pathetic that we considered suspending him as a coauthor at one point. Oh well, one more in the win column for me. Better enjoy it while it lasts.

C—David Robinson	F—Derrick McKey
C—Benoit Benjamin	G—John Stockton
F—Buck Williams	G—Mugsy Bogues
F—Grant Long	G—Jeff Hornacek

Troy's was the only team in the league that beat us in assists on a regular basis. Thank goodness we hammered him in five other categories, on our way to our third easy victory this week.

RESULTS

Now that you've heard from the owners, let's get back to reality. Here are the results of the week's play—just the facts:

Fantasy Results: Game One

Category	Team #1	Team #2	Winner
Rebounds	39	59	Team 2
Assists	35	22	Team 1
Steals	12	14	Team 2
Turnovers	10	18	Team 1
Points	111	141	Team 2
Blocks	1	9	Team 2
3-Pointers	1	1	tie

Final Score	
Team 1	2.5
Team 2	4.5

Category	Team 3	Team 4	Winner
Rebounds	49	44	Team 3
Assists	29	45	Team 4
Steals	7	22	Team 4
Turnovers	12	23	Team 3
Points	124	130	Team 4
Blocks	13	9	Team 3
3-Pointers	3	6	Team 4

Final Score	
Team 3	3
Team 4	4

Fantasy Results: Game Two

Category	Team 1	Team 3	Winner
Rebounds	53	49	Team 1
Assists	55	35	Team 1
Steals	10	10	tie
Turnovers	11	19	Team 1
Points	130	132	Team 3
Blocks	2	2	tie
3-Pointers	6	1	Team 1

Final Score	
Team 1	5
Team 3	2

Category	Team 2	Team 4	Winner
Rebounds	50	52	Team 4
Assists	25	45	Team 4
Steals	11	8	Team 2
Turnovers	20	15	Team 4
Points	114	134	Team 4
Blocks	7	15	Team 4
3-Pointers	2	2	tie

Final Score	
Team 2	1.5
Team 4	5.5

Fantasy Results: Game Three

Category	Team 1	Team 4	Winner
Rebounds	44	50	Team 4
Assists	35	31	Team 1
Steals	10	12	Team 4
Turnovers	22	20	Team 4
Points	99	125	Team 4
Blocks	3	5	Team 4
3-Pointers	2	2	tie

Final Score	
Team 1	1.5
Team 4	5.5

Category	Team 2	Team 3	Winner
Rebounds	41	61	Team 3
Assists	31	31	tie
Steals	12	6	Team 2
Turnovers	17	14	Team 3
Points	101	130	Team 3
Blocks	8	10	Team 3
3-Pointers	4	2	Team 2

Final Score	
Team 3	4.5
Team 2	2.5

WEEKLY STANDINGS

TEAM	WINS	LOSSES
Team 4	3	0
Team 3	1	2
Team 2	1	2
Team 1	1	2

SUMMARY OF RULES: HEAD-TO-HEAD SCORING METHOD

Draft:

1. Owner drafts 18 players.
2. Owner has 250 units to spend.
3. Team can draft a player if:
   a. The owner does not already have 18 players.
   b. The player is a member of the talent pool.
   c. The owner can afford whatever bid he is proposing.
   d. The owner can fill the rest of his team with a bid of at least 1 unit.

Play:

1. Eight starters are chosen.
   a. Three guards
   b. Three forwards
   c. Two centers
2. Fantasy games are broken up according to NBA games played during the week.
   a. NBA players playing on Sunday and Monday can be used for Fantasy Game 1.
   b. NBA players playing on Tuesday can be used in either Fantasy Game 1 or Fantasy Game 2.
   c. NBA players playing on Wednesday and Thursday can be used for Fantasy Game 2.
   d. NBA players playing on Friday and Saturday can be used for Fantasy Game 3.
3. Teams compete in seven categories.
   a. Rebounds
   b. Assists
   c. Steals
   d. Blocks
   e. Points
   f. Three-point shots made
   g. Turnovers (the team with the fewest turnovers wins)
4. To win, a team must beat its opponent in four of seven categories.
5. Ties are broken by free throws made.

Pickups (Option 1):

1. Replaced player must be on injured reserve or suspended list.
2. New player must be a free agent.
3. New player must be of the same position as player replaced.
4. Owner retains right to injured player.
5. New player must be dropped when injured player is off IR.
6. New player may never be traded.
7. If the injured player is traded the new player is immediately dropped.
8. No pickup is allowed to a team that has traded for an injured player.

Frozen Roster (Option 2):
> No pickups arc allowed.

Trades:
1. Both teams involved must trade same number of players.
2. Trades must be submitted by Friday.
3. Trades must be approved by commissioner.
4. The fee per trade is 20 percent of franchise fee.
   (Responsibility of payment is negotiable as part of trade).
5. Before All-Star break, league-wide trading is allowed.
6. After All-Star break:
   a. League is divided into three parts.
   b. Owners may only trade within their own group.

Intra-team transactions:
1. Starters for all three games must be called in by Saturday night.
2. If no lineup is phoned in, use the last lineup given.
3. Owner may have as many injury substitutions as he or she has injured starters.
   a. Injured players may not have played already in the present fantasy game.
   b. Replacement players may not have played already in the present fantasy game.

Playoffs:
1. Three games a week: The team that wins two out of three is the winner.
2. Two games a week: Cumulative stats over two games determine winner.
3. Setup:
   a. 14-Team League—8 teams (no first-round byes)
   b. 12-Team League—6 teams (2 get byes)
   c. 10-Team League—6 teams (2 get byes)
   d. 8-Team League—4 teams (no byes)
   e. Teams are seeded according to record:
      i. Best record vs. worst (of playoff teams)
      ii. Second best vs. second worst
      iii. Etc.
      iv. Don't forget that some teams get byes.
4. Sudden Death: Winner determined by total free throws made.

Payoff (14-team league):
1. Losers of first round receive half of original franchise fee.
2. Fourth place receives 10 percent of pot.
3. Third place receives 20 percent of pot.
4. Second place receives 30 percent of pot.
5. First place receives 40 percent of pot.

VARIATIONS

Two of the variations that appeared in this section last year have been incorporated directly into the rules section of the Weekly Scoring Method. We play-tested these variations—turnovers and three-point field goals—and found them to work extremely well. They were both already used in the Head-to-Head Method, but this year we have added them to the Weekly Scoring Method, as well.

So now all that remains of our once plentiful "Variations" are two additional statistical categories and one section about keeping teams from year to year. For those of you who live for statistics like free-throw percentage and field-goal percentage, we still list them in this section as possibilities, and we still list the stats themselves in the "Statistical Results" section.

ADDITIONAL CATEGORIES
FOR WEEKLY-METHOD LEAGUES

Remember that in Fantasy Basketball, unlike in other fantasy sports, each player contributes in every statistical category (with the exceptions of Mugsy Bogues and Spud Webb, who don't block any shots except each other's). This makes evaluating NBA players in preparation for the draft a difficult task. An owner who must not only evaluate each player's potential in the seven basic categories, but then decide how he'll do in one or more additional categories, will have difficulty achieving the proper balance needed to win.

If the owners in your league decide to use additional categories, make sure that the new categories do not upset the balance provided by the seven basic ones. Don't pick a category that might further enhance the value of centers and point guards, for instance, since these positions already enjoy a slight edge in the seven basic categories. The average center contributes heavily in scoring, rebounding, and blocked shots, while the average point guard contributes heavily in scoring, assists, and steals. For additional categories, choose some in which shooting guards and small forwards—the positions slighted by the seven basic categories—excel.

After numerous hours spent in consultation with various owners and commissioners, we've determined that the only other categories of any consequence are: field-goal percentage and free-throw percentage. We do not ourselves use, recommend, or even like these categories, but we still respect others' interest in using them. For that reason, they deserve to be included in this book.

We still welcome suggestions for any new categories our readers may have tried and found to work well. If you have a suggestion, please send it (along with the category's pros and cons) to:

Fantastic Sports
P.O. Box 93425
Milwaukee, WI 53203

FREE-THROW PERCENTAGE

If you feel the need to add an extra category, free-throw percentage is not a bad choice. In the NBA, a team's free-throw percentage can often mean the difference between a winning and losing record. In Fantasy Basketball, if this category is added, you will have to plan your draft strategies to include a mix of productive players who are good free-throw shooters, along with those who have the proverbial "touch of the blacksmith." You will have to decide what an acceptable percentage will be for your team, and draft accordingly. If you have Messrs. Jordan and Dudley, you have to live with what Dudley does to Michael's numbers. Will Michael shoot enough free throws to compensate for Dudley's 0-for-14 binges?

In scoring free-throw percentage, all you have to do is add up the total free throws that your active players make and divide that number by the number of free throws that they attempted. The higher the percentage, the better.

FIELD-GOAL PERCENTAGE

We will mention field-goal percentage only because we feel obligated to state all possible additional categories. We think this could very well be the dumbest statistical category on the face of the earth. When designing Fantasy Basketball we tried to select a mix of categories that would make all five positions as equal as possible. To include a category in which the last guard ever to lead the league was Dave Twardzik really, really irks us. (Dave, however, did get his number retired for his efforts.) Big men will crush little men in this category every time. Go out to a hoop, shoot 20 layups and 20 shots from the top of the key, and see how many you make from each spot. Anyone is going to have a better percentage as they get closer to the basket; this is just common sense. We beg you not to use this category unless you are held at gunpoint. And even then you should carefully weigh all your options.

KEEPING PLAYERS FROM YEAR TO YEAR

One of the first things you will discover after your league's initial draft is that a fantasy draft is easily the most fun you can have for six hours in a room full of sweat-soaked, smelly people. This alone should convince your league to redraft every year.

However, if your league intends to continue for several years with the same owners, you may want the added commitment of keeping players from year to year. This does make the game a little too much like marriage. (And isn't marriage half the reason why some people seek the sanctuary of fantasy leagues?)

The biggest problem with keeping players from year to year is that the upper-echelon teams are usually those that managed to draft the best bargains. Should your league decide to keep players from year to year, this disparity will remain for years to come. Also the possibility of "dumping" becomes stronger. Owners at the bottom of the standings may opt to trade better talent to the leaders for cheaper talent and the chance to build for next year. This may in turn destroy the competitive spirit of the league. We feel that it is much easier for each team to start over next year and let the owners who finished at the bottom "prove" that the leaders just "got lucky."

Keeping players from year to year causes other problems too. For one, it provides only one fantasy owner the services of David Robinson. Let's try to spread the wealth, okay? Who wouldn't enjoy yelling "That's my guy!" after David slams over Mutombo (or any other feeble hack who tries to get in his way)? Also, people move, people marry, and people finish last three or four years in a row. If you do commit your league to a year-to-year format, one owner's leaving poses numerous problems. Replacing an owner is always difficult, but imagine trying to get someone to join your league if he knows he will inherit a team that finished near the bottom. If you do find such a weirdo, do you really want him in your league? One final problem occurs with drafting injured players. An owner whose draft is going poorly may decide to draft Dominique Wilkins and Bernard King for a cheap price so that he can save them, and their cheap price, for next year.

Still, despite all our advice, you may decide to keep players from year to year. The following are some rules to follow if you go that route. We try to account for as many potential problems as humanly possible. Some wise guy will always try to skirt the rules, and he will be even tougher to get rid of if you are playing head-to-head, so beware.

Your league should decide, before its initial draft, the maximum number of seasons that a fantasy team can keep a player at his original price. We recommend two seasons (the one in which he was drafted and the next) as a maximum. This rewards the owner for his discovery of talent for a little while but does not allow him to monopolize these players forever and build a Laker-like dynasty. After two seasons, the owner will either have to release the player or sign him for five more years at double his price. After signing him to this five-year deal, he cannot release him until the deal has expired. He may, however, trade the player if someone is willing to take the hack off his hands. An owner may keep up to eight players for the next year. He may not, however, keep any player who was injured when he was drafted. The price of the players who are kept is subtracted from the 250 units the owner is allowed for the next year's draft.

CHAPTER 2

PLAYER ANALYSIS

PLAYER REVIEWS

Forget Miller Lite, this is it and that's that. It's time for our player reviews. This is where we prove our true worth and you get what you need to know to win. But first, our disclaimer: Yes, it takes true talent even to make a CBA roster. And all the players we are about to review have done even better than that (well, almost all of them). We know they're all really good basketball players, but if that's all we tell you, you get no useful draft information. And giving you useful information (as opposed to pampering the egos of professional athletes) is what we're here for. Also keep in mind, as you read these player appraisals, that this isn't a review of the NBA; this is a review of Fantasy Basketball. If we destroy your favorite player, it doesn't mean he isn't a good basketball player; it means he isn't a good Fantasy Basketball player.

These reviews have taken a whole season to compile—a season of listening to complaints from owners in our league; of talking to new friends who called us from other leagues; of getting all the stats we could lay our hands on; and of generally digesting as much basketball as humanly possible. While we don't review all players, if there is a player who should be drafted, you'll get the straight story on him from us. We also list a few players who absolutely should not be drafted. We do this because—we admit it—we can't resist the cheap shots. (Please see the disclaimer above.) These reviews are written before the NBA draft, so if a particular draft pick will have an effect on one of these players, we mention that in our Rookie Review section.

Included in each review are the player's team at the time of publication, the position(s) the player may play for head-to-head scoring, and a few carefully crafted words about the player in question. To help you at draft time, we list, for each player, the price he should be worth in a 14-team league. This price should be the same for both head-to-head and weekly scoring. The only difference might be that in head-to-head, good centers could go a little higher because there aren't enough good centers to fill out every head-to-head roster.

What you do with our reviews is up to you. Whether or not you agree with our review, or our price, never let the price limit you. We are only suggesting what we think a player is worth at the beginning of the draft, when everyone has units left to bid with. If you need a good assist man and you have the money, you might pay more than our price for John Stockton, the best assist man in the business. Also, if one of our high-priced players gets called late in the draft, when money's tight, it's very unlikely that he'll go for the price we quote. Just remember that nothing is concrete.

Another thing to keep in mind is that in the offseason there will probably be more than a few player moves (probably several by each team). To help you cope with these changes, we offer our Fantasy Basketball Update, which lists, by team, all the player moves that have occurred in the offseason, as well as how these moves will affect the teams' plans. We also include training camp reports for every team and estimates of whose fantasy stock is rising and whose is plummeting. (To order the update, please use the order form in the back of the book, or call toll-free, 1-800-944-7665.)

Finally, we hope you enjoy our reviews. Just remember, we're professionals. We know what we're doing.

GUARDS

Guards used to be a very easy group to draft. You just picked up a couple of point guards for assists and steals and then loaded up on centers and forwards. Or else you drafted a few shooting guards, who were cheaper than the point guards, and sacrificed assists and steals for added scoring. Or, finally, you paid the price and got Michael Jordan or Clyde Drexler, who could do everything for you. Now things are completely different. Several shooting guards have improved their games so that they can almost compete with Jordan and Drexler as multi-category players. Kendall Gill, Willie Anderson, and Jeff Hornacek are just a few examples. There are also a few shooting guards who have emerged as such tremendous players in a particular category (Billy Owens in rebounds and Vern Maxwell in threes, for example) that they have to be considered in any drafting strategy. Finally, the importance of the assist category has diminished. Only three point guards had double-digit assists per game. With all these changes in the fantasy game, careful consideration is now required as you plan which guards to draft.

Michael Adams   Wash   (G)   Price: 37
Although Michael Adams put together some great point-guard numbers last season, every category was down from his season in the "Paul Westhead–Denver Nuggets Experiment." Gosh, now wasn't that a surprising development. Moral of the story: Expect "human" numbers, plus a lot of three-pointers, from Michael next year. And don't draft Reggie Williams.

Rafael Addison   NJ   (G)   Price: 1
What can be said about Rafael Addison that hasn't already been said? Wait a minute, nothing has been said about Rafael, ever. Precisely.

Danny Ainge   Port   (G)   Price: 4
Danny put up some spectacular numbers in the playoffs last year and hit a stellar 78 three-pointers in the regular season. There are less desirable reserves to have on a fantasy team, that's for sure.

Kenny Anderson   NJ   (G)   Price: 15
Eventually someone will give Kenny Anderson some playing time. This will likely be good for whoever drafts Kenny, but it most certainly will hurt the Nets.

Nick Anderson   Orl   (G,F)   Price: 32
Orlando was probably planning on building its team around Nick Anderson until it won the rights to draft a guy named O'Neal. Anderson's still a worthy player to build your fantasy team around. Let's see, 20 points and over six boards a game from a shooting guard/small forward. Yes, he could find a place on most teams. Also note the steal-and-a-half and the half-block per game, and then try not to salivate too much on draft day.

Willie Anderson   SA   (G)   Price: 30
How much is a swingman worth who can post fives in rebounds and assists? Well, do a little math and pay 5/7 of what you are thinking of paying for Scottie Pippen. (Round down. Willie did only score 13 a game last season.)

Greg Anthony   NY   (G)   **Price: 5 (As insurance only)**
Greg Anthony had flashes of mediocrity last season and looks to be the best backup point guard the Knicks have had in two years.

B.J. Armstrong   Chi   (G)   **Price: 6 (3 if he doesn't start)**
How many playoff games did B.J. pull out for the Bulls last season? Certainly more than enough to win him a starting job over John Paxson. But be careful, assists don't come easily when you have Michael and Scottie handling the ball all the time.

Vincent Askew   GS   (G)   **Price: 2**
Another of the great Golden State role players. This doesn't mean that he does one thing very well. In Golden State, a role player is someone who can come in and do anything, depending on the situation. Isn't Don Nelson a fabulous coach?

Stacey Augmon   Atl   (G,F)   **Price: 16**
Stacey had a pretty good rookie season, especially considering that Atlanta lost its entire team concept after Dominique's injury. Stacey should turn into a fine Fantasy Basketball player, mostly because of his versatility (he can play guard or forward) and his rebounding (over five per game).

John Bagley   Bos   (G)   **Price: 5 (Who, truly, can know?)**
Who could ever have imagined that the ''Baglady'' would find a season like this in his shopping cart? But let's look at the season closely: He only averaged 6.6 assists per game, he got less than one steal per game and more than two turnovers, and he shot only 10 three-pointers all year. And this was Bagley's career year?

Dana Barros   Sea   (G)   **Price: 5 (For taxi-squad threes)**
Imagine this concept: A basketball player comes off of Seattle's bench, with Eddie Johnson, and his job is to shoot when Eddie doesn't. This is Dana Barros. Dana does fire up a huge number of threes, but his lack of balanced production makes him exclusively taxi-squad material.

John Battle   Clev   (G)   **Price: 3**
John Battle was expected to come to Cleveland and help shore up the Cavs' guard problems. Well, the guard problems are gone, but unfortunately for John, it was Terrell Brandon and Mark Price who did the shoring.

Rolando Blackman   Dal   (G)   **Price: 8**
It's a shame that Rolando couldn't, like Mark Aguirre, get out of Dallas while the getting was good. Rolando put up his usual good shooting-guard numbers last year, and he still makes a fine reserve to look to in a pinch. But he's lost in that whirlpool called the Mavericks, and it doesn't appear he'll be able to keep his head above water.

Mookie Blaylock   NJ   (G)   **Price: 20 (30 if he's not a Net)**
Mookie Blaylock is as good a point guard now as he was last year. He still gets a ton of steals, a good number of assists, and a tremendous number of blocks for a point guard. Unfortunately for Mookie, there's this Kenny Anderson guy sitting on the bench making an awful lot of money, and there

aren't many coaches who will make player changes that might cost them their jobs. Hope that someone else sees his worth and rescues Mookie from the Meadowlands.

Mugsy Bogues   Char   (G)   Price: 24
You know, eventually the Hornets are going to draft a point guard, and Mugsy's fine NBA career will go the way of the Dodo bird. Luckily for Mugsy, the Hornets have the second pick in the draft and (sigh) will have to live another season with nine-plus assists and two-plus steals from their point guard. Those poor Hornets.

Anthony Bowie   Orl   (G,F)   Price: 15 (But he won't go that high)
Anthony came on when Nick Anderson got injured, and played well enough to get Nick moved to small forward. With a healthy Anderson and a healthy Dennis Scott, Anthony won't get all the playing time he got last season, but he has the sixth-man spot wrapped up in Orlando. We can almost guarantee that Anthony will be a steal in your draft. And since you own this book, we even suspect he'll be a steal for you.

Terrell Brandon   Clev   (G)   Price: 9
Terrell was a fine pick for Cleveland and should be a good backup for Mark Price. Eventually he'll become a good starting point guard in his own right. But remember, for Fantasy Basketball purposes this season, he's only a nice insurance policy for Mark Price.

Scott Brooks   Minn   (G)   Price: 1 (Double that if he starts)
With every trade rumor in the league somehow involving Pooh Richardson, you wonder if the T-Wolves are actually planning on starting Scott Brooks at point guard. No, not even the Wolves are that lost.

Dee Brown   Bos   (G)   Price: 15
With Brian Shaw gone, with John Bagley turning older than dirt, and with Sherman Douglas becoming nothing more than a future throw-in, Dee Brown appears to have the point-guard position in hand for the Celts if he can stay healthy. And think about this: If Bird retires, or is injured, or whatever, a point guard in Boston might be able to get a reasonable number of assists.

Rex Chapman   Wash   (G)   Price: Why ask?
Washington, huh? You know, Rex could do really well in Washington. Isn't there a CBA team in Spokane?

Maurice Cheeks   Atl   (G)   Price: Less than 0
The Knicks gave away Maurice Cheeks for a backup center who played 108 minutes this year. You're probably asking yourself, "Who got the better deal?"

Bimbo Coles   Mia   (G)   Price: 12
Bimbo probably won't start for the Heat this season, but he should be the team's only true point guard. This makes him a good final starter or high taxi-squad player. And his price is right.

Del Curry   Char   (G)   Price: 10
Del seemed to like the Hornets' new, quicker pace, and he certainly loved
their Rex Chapman solution. Now all he has to do is play the same number of
minutes and shoot 49% again. Bets, anyone?

Walter Davis   Den   (G)   Price: Easily 1
Walter went out last season and put up the type of numbers that Denver needed—the type of numbers that sent coach Paul Westhead back to the unem-
ployment line.

Johnny Dawkins   Phil   (G)   Price: 18
Johnny Dawkins could be the least respected point guard in the league. He
certainly got no respect from Sir Charles while Sir Charles was still a resi-
dent of Philadelphia. Despite this, however, Johnny dished out seven assists
a game, scored 12 points a game, and played all 82 games of the season. And
this was a season in which he was supposed to take it easy on his knees. The
only other thing in Philly that was consistent for 82 games was Barkley's
mouth.

Sherman Douglas   Bos   (G)   Price: 5 (How the mighty have fallen)
If only the Heat would have let Sherm go to the Lakers. . . . But seriously, if
he couldn't even live up to being the next John Bagley, how was he planning
on being the next Magic Johnson? Don't expect Sherm to be playing in Boston, even if he's still on the roster.

Clyde Drexler   Port   (G)   Price: 47
So Clyde was finally put on the Olympic team. Gee, only 11 months late.
But then again, how can those poor Olympic selection committee members
be expected to notice a guy who gets over 6.5 rebounds and assists a game,
scores 25 points, and keeps his team in every game they play? Who has time
to scour the NBA for mediocrity like that?

Joe Dumars   Det   (G)   Price: 22
Joe Dumars made the NBA All-Defensive team while collecting 71 steals in
82 games. Is it just us, or have most NBA awards become like Gold Gloves
in baseball? If you made the team last year, and had a pulse this year, you're
in. But hey, Joe did raise his assist average to 4.5 per game. That, added to
30% fewer blocks and 100 fewer steals than Mookie Blaylock, in 10 more
games, certainly makes Joe a defensive force to be reckoned with.

Kevin Edwards   Mia   (G)   Price: 4
Kevin found time to score 10 a game last season. Unfortunately for him,
however, the Heat find themselves in a drafting position that usually only
offers good backup guards or forwards. Sorry, Kevin, your team got good
without you.

Craig Ehlo   Clev   (G,F)   Price: 26
Craig put together some great numbers last season and should easily do it
again, since the Cavs have stopped asking him to play point guard even when
Price is resting. Hey, wait a minute, when did the Cavs figure out what they
were doing? Keep Craig in the back of your mind during your draft, and hope
you have the most money when he's called.

Mario Elie   **GS**   **(G,F)**   **Price: 3**

Mario was given an expanded role last season and put together the kind of all-around, but thoroughly mediocre, performance that Don Nelson likes out of his reserves. Personally, we like better production even out of our taxi-squad players.

A.J. English   **Wash**   **(G)**   **Price: 2**

A.J. put up the kinds of numbers last season that should land him behind LaBradford Smith on the depth chart this season. If LaBradford still isn't healthy, well, A.J. should still end up behind him.

Vern Fleming   **Ind**   **(G)**   **Price: 4**

While it seemed to take ol' Vern a little while to adjust to his new role, he finally made the adjustment and became a competent backup. Still, this offers very little in the way of fantasy value.

Eric "Sleepy" Floyd   **Hou**   **(G)**   **Price: 4**

Floyd keeps living up to his nickname. But if he continues to fade this fast, the Rockets will have to put Sleepy to sleep.

Rick Fox   **Bos**   **(G,F)**   **Price: 7**

Another great, late-first-round pick by the Boston Celtics. The problem for Rick is that the Celtics now have four players—all late picks—who can all play both guard and forward. So when is Rick going to get enough playing time to prove he can play? The answer is: When Larry Bird finally hangs it up. Rick could be a steal if Larry calls it quits.

Kevin Gamble   **Bos**   **(F)**   **Price:13**

Last year we told you that Gamble would get better. He didn't. We also told you that his numbers were pretty solid. They still are. If you can get him for around 10, he might be worth it.

Winston Garland   **Den**   **(G)**   **Price: 8**

Believe it or not, this was Denver's best point guard last season. Sure, Paul Westhead didn't really deserve a chance, but you look at the personnel he had to work with, and you wonder if the deck wasn't stacked against him.

Tate George   **NJ**   **(G)**   **Price: 5**

Tate was easily the second best point guard for the Nets, behind Mookie, and the second best shooting guard, behind Drazen. Bill Fitch complained that he didn't need Kenny Anderson, and would you believe that he was right? (Mental note: Imagine the future of the Nets had they taken Billy O.) But back to reality, pick up George for next to nothing at the end of the draft and hope New Jersey trades Mookie or benches Kenny.

Kendall Gill   **Char**   **(G)**   **Price: 34**

Let's take a look at Gill's numbers per game: 20 points, five boards, four assists, two steals, and only 2.3 turnovers. Not bad for an off guard. These kinds of numbers put Mr. Gill in some very exclusive company, behind only Jordan and Drexler. With a nucleus of Kendall and Larry Johnson, had the Hornets gotten the first pick in this year's draft, it would not have been too early at all to start measuring fingers in Charlotte for championship rings.

Gerald Glass   Minn   (G)   Price: 6
After watching Gerald hang around with the Timberwolves for a couple of years, we wondered what he could do with some minutes. Having seen that, we now hope that he can improve and actually become a decent fantasy player.

Paul Graham   Atl   (G)   Price: 3
Paul Graham got a lot of playing time that he won't ever get again if Travis Mays or Dominique Wilkins is healthy. So forget it. Whatever you were thinking, he hasn't got a chance.

Gary Grant   LAC   (G)   Price: 15 (25 if he's elsewhere)
Gary Grant still got a lot of assists and steals even after the Clippers traded for another point guard. It seems obvious that the only way the Clippers are going to keep Gary from producing for them is to trade him. This should happen soon, and Gary should become an even better fantasy player when it does. The team he's traded to probably won't like him either, though.

Greg Grant   Phil   (G)   Price: 2
Doesn't this guy look exactly like all the other backup point guards in Philadelphia over the last couple of seasons? Ricky Green. Andre Turner. It's amazing we can even remember these guys at all.

Jeff Grayer   Mil   (G,F)   Price: 3
Jeff Grayer does just enough to keep himself on an NBA roster. For some reason, the Bucks have never learned when to cut their losses on a first-round pick.

Bobby Hansen   Chi   (G)   Price: Almost 1
As much as we make fun of Dennis Hopson, we think he's worth more than Bobby Hansen.

Tim Hardaway   GS   (G)   Price: 48
As you examine Tim's numbers this year, don't overlook perhaps the most amazing one—nearly four rebounds per game. Isn't this guy smaller than Mugsy Bogues? We're kidding. Expect to pay a ton for Timmy and his incredible stats; but if he continues to keep firing all those threes, expect to be more than pleased with your purchase.

Derek Harper   Dal   (G)   Price: 18
Remember when Derek Harper was the best Illinois guard in the NBA? Now he wouldn't even start on an all-Illinois team. (But in an Illinois guard drafting strategy, he's still worth taking if you get Nick Anderson and Kendall Gill.)

Ron Harper   LAC   (G)   Price: 33
Ron is another member of the five-rebound/five-assist club at shooting guard. Also, don't forget his supplementary numbers of almost two steals a game and almost a block a game—both of which are higher than Drexler's production.

Hersey Hawkins   Phil   (G)   Price: 25
While Hersey's production dropped off a lot last season, he's now the focal point in Philly. With Charles out west, Hersey will be free to shoot when he

wants without worrying what his Royal Roundness thinks of his shot selection. Expect a big turnaround for Hersey this season, especially with Doug Moe running a wild show in Philly.

Craig Hodges   Chi   (G)   Price: 2 (Only 36 threes)
The Chicago Bulls have such a good second string that Phil Jackson didn't have both Pippen and Jordan out of a game at the same time all season. Not once in 3936 minutes did he trust his second unit to be out there by themselves! And Craig Hodges is the shooter of this group. Wow!

Dennis Hopson   Sac   (G)   Price: 6
You could knock us over with a feather, but Dennis Hopson put up some respectable numbers in Sacramento. Unfortunately, Sacramento is now trying to trade Mitch Richmond so that Dennis can get more playing time. Won't the Kings ever learn?

Jeff Hornacek   Phil   (G)   Price: 36
Last season, Jeff Hornacek (along with Tim Perry and Dan Majerle) kept the Suns near the top in the West. He and Perry were rewarded with tickets to Philly. How unfortunate for them. But luckily for Jeff, his role in Philly should be similar to the one he had in Phoenix. He may come off the bench, but he'll still get a lot of minutes; he'll probably run the team when Dawkins is resting; and he should get to shoot a lot when Hawkins is resting. All in all, Jeff should have an opportunity to repeat last year's career season.

Jay Humphries   Mil   (G)   Price: 20
The Bucks had Rockets' disease this year. The guards who were great two years ago were mediocre last year. OK, maybe Jay wasn't mediocre, but the steady improvement he'd been showing definitely dropped off. Luckily for Jay, Mike Dunleavy probably won't be subbing Lester Conner in for him too often. Jay is our bet to be this year's Mark Jackson. Take the risk.

Mike Iuzzolino   Dal   (G)   Price: 2
If Dallas gets rid of all their guards in the offseason, which they said they might do, Iuzzolino could be a steal. Then again, he could be a complete waste; he is a Maverick, after all.

Chris Jackson   Den   (G)   Price: 3
Forget the new name. Forget the new coach. What Chris really needs is a new jump shot. But he is still very young and has plenty of time to continue to prove that he's a bust.

Mark Jackson   NYK   (G)   Price: 27
Pat Riley's star pupil. Mark's reemergence almost makes the Knicks wish they hadn't taken Greg Anthony last year. Oh well, now if Mark slips up, they can have another point-guard controversy. Don't bet on that, though.

Kevin Johnson   Phx   (G)   Price: 39
K.J. is one of the best point guards in the business. He does the things a point guard should do. He dishes, he steals, and he scores. If you like these things, be ready to pay dearly for his services. You won't be disappointed, unless you notice that he tied John Stockton for the league lead in turnovers among point guards.

Vinnie Johnson   SA   (G)   Price: 1
Vinnie made a living being able to shoot. Now in San Antonio he scores eight points a game while playing 22 minutes. I can't see what use Vinnie would be on any fantasy team, unless he was some kind of injury insurance for Willie Anderson. And even then. . . .

Michael Jordan   Chi   (G)   Price: 50
What can we say about Jordan on a basketball court except that he is a force? As a fantasy player, he'll contribute in all categories. If only he didn't cost so much. If you take Mike, be sure you have a good plan for how—and on whom—you will spend the rest of your units.

Steve Kerr   Clev   (G)   Price: 1
Steve's days in Cleveland are numbered. His playing time in Cleveland is nonexistent.

Bo Kimble   LAC   (G,F)   Price: 0
Maybe he should start shooting left-handed from the field too.

Negele Knight   Phx   (G)   Price: 10
Phoenix missed Negele's services late in the season and in the playoffs. The Suns really like him and so do a lot of other teams. If you want to take a gamble that he'll be traded, or that K.J. will get hurt, Negele could be a steal.

Jim Les   Sac   (G)   Price: 2 (For the threes)
Part of the Sacramento combination of Les and Les (Jepson and Jim). And believe us, there's never been a Les-ser combination in NBA history.

Lafayette "Fat" Lever   Dal   (G)   Price: 15
Can Fat stay healthy next year? If he's healthy, will Dallas use him? Fat put up some very good numbers over 31 games last season, but there are too many questions surrounding him to make him a good pick.

Reggie Lewis   Bos   (G)   Price: 28
Without Reggie Lewis, the Celts would probably go from winning their division to cheering their NBA lottery balls. Reggie's numbers were very good last year—including a steal and a half and over a block a game. If Larry finally calls it quits, pay large sums for Reggie's services next year. If not, draft Reggie anyway. Bird can't stay healthy all season even if he doesn't retire.

Mark Macon   Den   (G)   Price: 5
If you look at Greg Anderson's numbers from last season and wonder how he got all those rebounds, remember: Anderson had Mark Macon taking outside shots on his team. Yes, Mark does get some steals (two per game), but he's a huge liability if you use shooting percentage (37.5%).

Jeff Malone   Ut   (G)   Price: 9
Jeff puts up your typical shooting-guard numbers and is mostly useless except for his 51% from the field (if you play with field-goal percentage).

Sarunas Marciulionis GS   (G)   Price: 11
Sarunas puts up your typical shooting guard numbers (if this sounds familiar, see Jeff Malone), only more so. The big exceptions are his 54% from the field and 2.68 turnovers/game. It's amazing that the man can shoot but can't

pass. Oh well, be that as it may, Sarunas gained a starting job when the Warriors traded Richmond, then lost that starting job when Billy Owens started playing well. All in all, his minutes should stay about the same as last year's, and so should his numbers.

Vernon Maxwell　　Hou　　(G)　　Price: 22
Vern was the only Houston guard not to disappear last season, but he had to start firing like a disgruntled post office employee in order to get his three-point totals up where they belong. Vern had a good many turnovers last year, but then, he did have to carry the Rockets from the guard position.

Travis Mays　　Atl　　(G)　　Price: 10
What is going to happen in Atlanta if Travis and Dominique come back healthy? Well, our best guess is that Travis will play in more than the two games he played in last season.

George McCloud　　Ind　　(G)　　Price: 2
George finally got off the Pacer bench a few times last season. Not bad for a guy who was once a lottery pick.

Nate McMillan　　Sea　　(G,F)　　Price: 6
Those of you who took our advice and payed 2 for Nate on the chance he would play must have been very happy late last year, when Nate was "tearing up the league." (Well, as much as Nate McMillan can be expected to tear up the league.) Still, most of his minutes were at small forward, and it may be a risk to pay too much for Nate if the 'Sonics don't give him those minutes again next year.

Reggie Miller　　Ind　　(G)　　Price: 26
Reggie dropped last season to the second best shooting-guard-named-Reggie in the league, although Mr. Lewis had to play out of his mind to pass Mr. Miller up. Every one of Reggie's numbers is good (save his 0.32 block per game), and if the Pacers would finally confirm a starting lineup, or trade Chuck Person, Reggie's numbers could be great.

Rodney Monroe　　Atl　　(G)　　Price: 1
Last year in our draft review, we couldn't understand why everyone passed up on Rodney. Now we know. While he didn't actually get enough playing time to prove himself, with a .368 shooting percentage, he didn't deserve the chance.

Eric Murdock　　Ut　　(G)　　Price: 4 (Enough insurance jokes)
Eric got a vote of confidence when, immediately after the playoffs, the Jazz cut longtime backup Delaney Rudd. Gosh, this means that Eric gets to play behind John Stockton. That should add up to some productive minutes. We won't bother to put the "Not!" after this statement.

Brian Oliver　　Phil　　(G)　　Price: 2
Bold Prediction of the Year: "Brian Oliver will benefit most from the hiring of Doug Moe." OK, Hersey Hawkins may benefit more than Brian does, but Brian should get a lot more playing time and the chance to shoot an awful lot more. Pick up Brian at the end of the draft on the "off-chance" that we're right.

Billy Owens   **GS**   **(G,F)**   **Price: 25**
Billy Owens is the type of player Don Nelson has been dreaming about for his entire life. Billy can play point guard when Hardaway needs a rest. Billy can run the break. Billy can drive on just about anybody. Billy can even match up with some of the smaller centers in the league. Oh yeah, and Billy is the rebounder that Nellie's needed since he got to Golden State. And Billy doesn't sacrifice the Golden State style of play to do all this.

Gerald Pack   **Port**   **(G)**   **Price: 1**
There was a noteworthy event in Gerald Pack's season last year. During a regular-season game, he called for play #3. Portland doesn't have a play #3. But Rick Adelman is thinking of inventing one just for Gerald, and our guess is that it will somehow involve Drexler's shooting the ball.

John Paxson   **Chi**   **(G)**   **Price: 3 (2 if he doesn't start)**
Not only will John Paxson not play as well as he did in the playoffs, but he probably won't start next season. B.J. should take his starting spot, as well as some more of his minutes, and John should slip even further down the ranks of unused taxi-squaders.

Gary Payton   **Sea**   **(G)**   **Price: 19**
Gary just might turn himself into a quality point guard. He raised his assist total to over six per game while keeping his turnovers down to just over two per game. Not too shabby for a guy from a team that can't ever decide on a regular lineup. Sure, Gary only scored nine points a game, but what do you want from a guy who has to play with Ricky Pierce and Eddie Johnson? Expect Gary and the 'Sonics to ride their playoff momentum to an even better showing next season.

Drazen Petrovic   **NJ**   **(G,F)**   **Price: 20**
Drazen became a fine shooting guard last season, and don't worry about next season, the Nets have nobody else. Our only concern with Drazen is his high turnover rate (2.6 a game). On the other hand, his 123 three-pointers more than make up for our concern.

Ricky Pierce   **Sea**   **(G,F)**   **Price: 8**
Ricky Pierce was given more minutes in Seattle and his scoring improved slightly. But his turnovers were high, 2.4 a game, and his three-point total dropped to 33. With improved play by Gary Payton, Ricky's role should be reduced to scoring, and nothing but scoring.

Terry Porter   **Port**   **(G)**   **Price: 23**
Always remember, the NBA playoffs don't count in your Fantasy Basketball league. Don't get trapped into paying for a reputation that was earned in the playoffs and not in the regular season. Terry couldn't possibly keep up the pace he set in the first three rounds of the playoffs, and, on the other hand, he almost certainly won't continue to play as badly as he did in the finals. Beyond that, Terry still didn't get up to six assists per game last year. He has a reputation for thinking like a shooting guard at the point-guard position, so beat the odds and draft him as a shooting guard who gets a lot of assists. Unless he's overpriced.

Paul Pressey   SA   (G,F)   Price: 1
Here's a little trivia for the youngsters reading our book: Paul Pressey was
the first player to be referred to as a "point forward." You will notice that
we talk about Paul Pressey in the past tense.

Mark Price   Clev   (G)   Price: 32
If you didn't have Mark on your team last year, it will probably shock you to
learn that he played in 72 games. His minutes were down early in the season,
but by the end he was getting a lot of playing time. Mark was exactly what
the Cavs needed to live up to their potential. Almost. With the arrival of
Terrell Brandon, Mark will spend a lot more time at shooting guard, but don't
worry, the only stats that should change are points and three-pointers (and
those should go up). Pay the "Price" for Mark because few realize his true
worth.

Jerry "Ice" Reynolds Orl   (G,F)   Price: 4
Only in Orlando would Ice get enough playing time to score 12 points a
game.

Pooh Richardson   Minn   (G)   Price: 31
Pooh's numbers are surprisingly good for a guy mentioned in every trade
rumor in the NBA. Hopefully, for Minnesota fans, the T-Wolves will wise
up and realize that Pooh is a point guard to build a team around—and a darn
good fantasy team too.

Mitch Richmond   Sac   (G)   Price: 28
Too good a player to be stuck in Sacramento. But they'll probably trade him
for Steve Scheffler and a second-round pick. Mitch had the same kinds of
numbers in Sacramento as in Golden State, except for the 103 three-pointers
he shot. He's even becoming a leader, but in Sacramento, being a leader
means resembling General Custer.

Glenn "Doc" Rivers LAC   (G)   Price: 13
The Clippers finally got their precious point guard, and Doc went out there
and proved that he's not the point guard he used to be. He finished more than
2.5 assists per game behind Gary Grant.

Alvin Robertson   Mil   (G)   Price: 26
An "off-year" for the other Robertson from Milwaukee. (You youngsters
out there can ask your dads about the Big O.) Alvin is one of the few players
in the NBA who can completely take over a game. (When he wants to, that
is.) If Alvin ever decides he "wants to" for an entire season, and you happen
to draft him that year, you'll win your league. Even if that never happens,
however, his four rebounds and four assists per game, plus over 2.5 steals
per game, are pretty nice. Especially for an "off-year."

Rumeal Robinson   Atl   (G)   Price: 16
As much as we disliked Atlanta's decision to trade Doc Rivers and start
Rumeal at point guard, Rumeal had a better season than Doc did. That would
make Rumeal the 26th best starting point guard in the league last year. OK,
25th—John Paxson isn't really a point guard.

Byron Scott   LAL   (G)   **Price: 10**
There used to be a fine line separating Byron from your typical, dull shooting guard. But these days he's on the other side of the line, and from this side it doesn't look so fine anymore—it looks like a wall.

Brian Shaw   Mia   (G)   **Price: 15**
Larry Bird must have demanded that Brian Shaw be traded after Shaw averaged more assists than Larry. It's probably Boston's loss. Expect Brian to fit in well with the Heat, in a lineup that won't feature a "true point guard" unless Bimbo Coles is in. This will hurt Brian's assists but help all his other numbers.

Scott Skiles   Orl   (G)   **Price: 27**
Scott spent most of the 91–92 season banged-up, if not outright injured. His steals, less than one per game, were awful for a point guard, and his turn-overs, over three per game, were high considering his limited minutes. On the other hand, his 91 three-pointers and 7.3 assists per game are respectable for a healthy point guard. His numbers should go up next season, especially if he masters a nice little inlet pass to Shaq.

Kenny Smith   Hou   (G)   **Price: 21**
Kenny Smith was a letdown last season. Remember this line. Repeat it incessantly to your co-owners. Mention that everyone in Houston was tremendously let down by Kenny's play last year. Even throw in that he might get benched in favor of Sleepy Floyd. (If you can keep a straight face during this line, you should consider a career in politics.) Then, at the draft, steal Kenny for a song and get numbers that no one could argue with.

Otis Smith   Orl   (G)   **Price: 1**
It's a shame that Orlando had the first pick in the draft; now they won't have a low enough pick to replace Otis. Wait a minute, they still have a second round pick, don't they?

Steve Smith   Mia   (G)   **Price: 24**
Steve made the Heat more than pleased with their decision to draft him and trade Sherman Douglas. While his numbers may not look that great on the surface, remember that this was his rookie year and he was hurt for much of the season. In 1992–93, with Steve and Brian Shaw learning to play together, Smith should move right up the fantasy ranks.

Tony Smith   LAL   (G)   **Price: 2**
After the '91 finals, everyone in L.A. was beaming about Tony. After last season, no one could remember his name.

Rory Sparrow   LAL   (G)   **Price: 0**
Did you know that Rory Sparrow finished the season with the Lakers? Now you know why you bought our book. Where else can you find crucial info like this?

John Starks   NY   (G)   **Price: 11**
John leaped into a key sixth-man position for the Knicks and showed more than a little bit of potential. And remember, if you're going to draft one of the "lesser" shooting guards, make sure he does something besides score. Like nail 94 three-pointers, for example.

John Stockton   Ut   (G)   Price: 49
OK, so you know how good John Stockton really is. You may even realize that some aspects of his game (his ability to run the break, for example) are actually slightly underrated. Does this make him worth more than Michael Jordan? Well, who is better—a dominant two-category player (Stockton led the league in both assists and steals last year), or a heavy contributor in all categories? The answer depends on your needs and on the talents of the other players on your team. Stockton and Jordan usually go for about the same price, so make your choice and bid away.

Rod Strickland   SA   (G)   Price: 30 (If he's anywhere)
Rod may not have made any friends in San Antonio with his holdout last season, but with his 4.7 rebounds, the most for a point guard last season, and his 8.6 assists per game, Rod made some friends among fantasy owners. Now if he can stay out of trouble (unlikely, if not impossible), we'll see how many friends he makes this season.

Terry Teagle   LAL   (G,F)   Price: 3
Terry's a "scorer" who scored 10 points in 30 minutes a game. That's hot.

Isiah Thomas   Det   (G)   Price: 23
Last season marked what is most likely the beginning of the end for Isiah. His assists dropped to just over seven a game, and his turnovers were over three a game. If you're lucky, someone in your league is a Pistons fan (a dying breed to say the least) and still thinks Isiah can return to his past glory. We suspect he will, but only for the All-Star game.

Sedale Threatt   LAL   (G)   Price: 20
Who would have thought that Sedale Threatt would be the savior of the Lakers? But then, when the Lakers were eliminated in the first round, did you think to yourself that they might have made a better pick? Oh well. You shouldn't expect Sedale to continue to put up last year's numbers, but it is tempting to check out how low his turnovers were and how high his steals were.

Sam Vincent   Orl   (G)   Price: 5
Sam put together some tremendous numbers backing up the oft-injured Scott Skiles last season. Almost makes you wish you could see what he'd do starting a whole season. Almost makes you ashamed, some of the things you think about when you become a Fantasy Basketball owner.

Darrell Walker   Det   (G)   Price: 4
Darrell's rebounds were down an awful lot last season, and it probably dragged his whole game down. Darrell could get a few more minutes this season, but it won't be enough to make him productive. Just remember those great numbers from Darrell's Washington past, and be glad you had him back then. You did have him back then, didn't you?

Anthony "Spud" Webb   Sac   (G)   Price: 29
If you bothered to notice last season, both Spud and Mugsy had some pretty good seasons starting at point guard. In fact, for the second half of the season, Spud was probably one of the top five point guards in the league. If you're smart, you'll lose that "Height Envy" and pick up two pretty good point guards for practically nothing.

Doug West   Minn   (G)   Price: 7
Go back and read our review of Byron Scott. Now notice that Doug West's numbers were very comparable to Byron's last season.

Gerald Wilkins   NYK   (G)   Price: 4
Gerald lost his starting job, and most of his minutes, to John Starks last season. Don't expect this trend to be reversed—Pat Riley is a pretty smart guy.

Michael Williams   Ind   (G)   Price: 27
Michael sprang into the lineup and stunned a lot of people with his speed and quickness. It reminds you of the quickness with which he was let go by more than a few NBA teams. Michael put up some tremendous numbers in his first full season starting at point guard. And while he may not be ranked with the best point guards in the league, over eight assists and almost three steals a game are certainly nice. Especially when you find out his price.

David Wingate   Wash   (G)   Price: 3
David's back in Washington and could get a few minutes at shooting guard next season. Whom that helps, we have no idea.

Danny Young   LAC   (G)   Price: 2
The former Blazer deep-bencher is now a Clipper deep-bencher. The more things change, the more they stay the same. At least he's better than Bo Kimble.

FORWARDS

As NBA players become more versatile, so does the category of forwards in Fantasy Basketball. Forwards are not just the rebounders and shooters they were in the old days. Guys like Scottie Pippen, Chris Mullin, and Danny Manning run the floor for their teams at times (Pippen most of the time). There are more than a few forwards who will make a legitimate impact on your fantasy team's assist, steal, and three-point totals—categories previously dominated only by guards. As the NBA looks for more complete players, you should also look to these players to fulfill a wider range of functions for your fantasy teams. Still, as you develop a draft strategy for forwards, it's important to get the scoring and rebounding that forwards are known for. On the whole, they still shine the brightest in these categories.

Mark Aguirre   Det   (F)   Price: 3
Mark says that he wants to play for the Mexican Olympic team in Barcelona. It should be fun watching him score 40 against everyone else and 10 against the USA. Back in the NBA, Mark's numbers dropped again last year to 11.3 points and 3.2 rebounds a game. No reason to think they will be any better this year.

Greg Anderson   Den   (F)   Price: 22
Cadillac raised his game (it would have been hard to lower it) after he was given the starting power-forward job in training camp (we mentioned this in our update). He responded by averaging 11.5 points and 11.5 rebounds per game. The Nuggets, however, now have a new coach and probably a new system, so there is no telling if Greg will retain his starting job. But if the signs look good early in the season, a Cadillac might very well be worth leasing this year.

Ron Anderson   Phil   (F)   Price: 3
Remember last year, when we told you that any team whose #1 forward off the bench averaged 4.5 rebounds was in trouble? Well Ron's rebounds dropped to 3.4, and the 'Sixers became a lottery team. He did average 13.7 points and over a steal a game, however. If the end of the draft rolls around and Ron is cheap, grab him. If you ever have to start him, you'd better have some aspirin.

Thurl Bailey   Minn   (F)   Price: 9
Thurl's game started to show some age last year. Getting traded to Minnesota couldn't have helped his numbers any either. He still has a pretty adequate all-around game though, and is quite useful as a situational player.

Charles Barkley   Phx   (F)   Price: 35
Sir Charles got his wish; he's on a winning team and, more importantly, he's still the star. Charles should produce even more with a real team around him; but that's only because he's in the West now, and Phoenix likes to run. Look for Charles to have another great year, but he probably won't win his championship and will start whining again next season.

William Bedford   Det   (F,C)   Price: 2
Bedford managed to get some playing time early, but was not very productive. New coach, new ideas, but don't count on anything new from William.

David Benoit   Ut   (F)   **Price: 4**
David missed the last two games of the Utah-Portland series. In that series, the Jazz collapsed. Therefore. . . . We'll let you find the flawed logic in that particular syllogism. But seriously, don't forget about Benoit (that's Ben-whaaa not Benjamin) at the end of your draft; if the situation in Utah is just right, he could put together some tremendously mediocre numbers.

Larry Bird   Bos   (F)   **Price: 35 (50 with a back)**
Once again Larry provided the Boston fans (and more importantly his fantasy owners) with a bittersweet mixture of spectacular games and time spent on IR last year. When he played, he was brilliant: 20 points, over nine rebounds, and almost seven assists a game. When he didn't play, the Celtics (and a lot of fantasy teams) were in trouble. He missed 37 games this year after missing 20 the year before. Maybe it is time for Mr. Legend to hang it up; he has openly considered retirement in the not-too-distant future. If Larry comes back, he's worth the money as long as he's healthy for the last three weeks of the regular season (fantasy playoff time).

Anthony Bonner   Sac   (F)   **Price: 10**
Bonner averaged 9.4 points and 6.1 rebounds in under 29 minutes a game last year. He is one of the bright spots in the Sacramento organization. Try to get him cheap at the end of the draft. We think you will be pleasantly surprised at the results.

Frank Brickowski   Mil   (F)   **Price: 9**
Brickowski's stats are a lot like Bonner's—5.3 rebounds and 11.4 points in 24 minutes a game. However, since Brick Man is quite a bit older, and probably won't see increased playing time, we recommend that you stay away from him unless he's super cheap.

Willie Burton   Mia   (F,G)   **Price: 4**
The Miami Heat is well on its way to becoming a very good franchise and Willie Burton can take none of the credit for it. As the guard situation in Miami shapes up to include Steve Smith, Brian Shaw, and Bimbo Coles, with Kevin Edwards seeing tiny minutes, all that's left for Willie is to back up Glenn Rice. We can all see those big numbers rolling in next season, can't we?

Michael Cage   Sea   (F)   **Price: 13**
Seattle seems to have forgotten about Michael, but with about nine boards, nine points, and more than a steal a game, he shouldn't be forgotten at your draft.

Tony Campbell   Minn   (F)   **Price: 14**
The Wolves decided in their infinite wisdom to move Tony to small forward, cut his minutes, and win 17 games. Maybe they are planning to start Scott Brooks at point guard if (sorry, when) they trade Pooh.

Antoine Carr   Sac   (F)   **Price: 7**
Carr got traded to San Antonio, where he fought Cummings and Elliott for playing time. He lost that fight more often than not, which explains the dramatic drop in his productivity. There is good news: His numbers shouldn't get much worse. There is also bad news: His numbers *can't* get much worse.

Terry Catledge   Orl   (F)   **Price: 13**
Terry got 14 points and seven rebounds a game last year—exactly what he got the year before (and exactly what we predicted he would get). Looking on the bright side, however, those are not bad numbers, and you always know exactly what you're paying for—to the decimal.

Cedric Ceballos   Phx   (F)   **Price: 8**
7.2 points and 2.4 rebounds in just over 11 minutes a game. This guy could be as good as Terry Cummings if he ever got playing time. With Chambers's role in the offense being reduced, and with Tim Perry traded, Ceballos should get the playing time he needs to prove himself.

Tom Chambers   Phx   (F)   **Price: 12**
Phoenix finally wised up and realized that this guy is a chump. He no longer plays the fourth quarter of most games, and his playing time varies from night to night depending on the accuracy of his shooting. The Suns have given up trying to get him to play defense, and are even considering trading him if they can. If he stays in Phoenix, he is worth little. If he goes to a team that can tolerate his numerous defensive lapses, and if he can shoot better than the 43% he shot last year, he may be able to put up the kind of offensive numbers that will make him worth 20 again.

Derrick Coleman   NJ   (F)   **Price: 29**
When Derrick won Rookie of the Year, we said that we preferred Lionel Simmons because of his better all-around game. We still do, but it's like choosing between a 15-pound northern and a 15-pound muskie. Chances are you're not going to throw either one back. Derrick has arrived as a very good player. He might turn the ball over a lot (he was the undisputed turnover champion last year), but live with it because his other stats (19.8 points and 9.5 rebounds) will win you some games.

Tyrone Corbin   Ut   (F)   **Price: 12**
One small gust of the trade winds blew Ty from his position as one of the best bargains in Fantasy Basketball to his new position as just another sixth man. When he was in a Timberwolves' uniform, he was expected to do almost everything, and he usually did. In Utah, however, all he has to do is play 27 minutes a game, score 10, and rebound six—a far cry from the awesome numbers he was putting up in Minnesota.

Terry Cummings   SA   (F)   **Price: 23**
Terry had another consistent year—17 points and nine rebounds night after night. When Robinson got hurt, he raised his game a notch and really put up some numbers. Look for him to do the same thing this year; unfortunately he will be priced a little higher because of his great finish.

Dale Davis   Ind   (F)   **Price: 12**
Dale showed promise in his injury-plagued rookie year—enough to assure him of a starting job this season. While his numbers probably won't reach awe-inspiring levels, he could be the steal of your draft for the price you'll pay.

Terry Davis   Dal   (F,C)   Price: 16
We may rip on a few players sometimes, but Terry Davis proves how good you have to be just to make an NBA roster. Terry spent two years wallowing on the Miami bench before the Mavs brought him in and gave him an opportunity to play. Terry made the most of his chance with almost 10 boards and over 10 points a game. Not bad for a guy who couldn't catch on with an expansion team.

Ledell Eackles   Wash   (F)   Price: 4
Ledell found his way off the fat farm and managed to play 65 games last year. But have you noticed that you never see Eackles and "Hot Plate" Williams in the same place at the same time? Food for thought (pun intended).

Theodore "Blue" Edwards Ut (F,G) Price: 6
What kind of slime is Jerry Sloan anyway? First, he finally benches Thurl Bailey so that Blue can get his rightful starting assignment, and then turns around and benches Blue in the playoffs for David Benoit! If he hasn't noticed, we have—Blue is exactly what Utah needs from a starting small forward.

Sean Elliott   SA   (F)   Price: 18
Let us start by saying that Sean Elliott has a tremendous amount of talent. Let us go on to say that we also have a tremendous amount of respect for the man, because he sacrifices his individual talent to do what the club needs him to do. Let us conclude by saying that although he puts up good numbers, he will be overpriced because someone is always going to pay for his talent instead of his numbers.

Dale Ellis   Mil   (F,G)   Price: 12 (Just for the threes)
At times last season, the Milwaukee Bucks finally appeared to understand what type of player Dale Ellis is. They would play him 35 minutes and feed him the ball when he got hot. And, lo and behold, Dale would score 28 or 30 points. But then, in the next game, they would play him 20 minutes and refuse to show him the ball if he was alone under the basket. Is it any wonder the Bucks have a new GM and head coach this season? Does Mike Dunleavy know what to do with Dale Ellis? What do you think?

Dwayne Ferrell   Atl   (F)   Price: 4
Dwayne was the early benefactor of the Human Highlight Film's injury, but he was not impressive and lost his minutes by the end of the season to Alexander Volkov. This makes him a gamble for a gambling fool.

Danny Ferry   Clev   (F)   Price: 2
Danny may have come close to justifying Cleveland's trade for him when he sucker-punched Jordan in the playoffs. If he had gotten Michael to retaliate and get ejected, he would have been worth the trade right there. No matter how well Danny ever plays, though, he will never be worth Ron Harper and two first-rounders. Unfortunately for the Cavs, he is not even playing well enough to make people think about it.

Greg Foster   **Wash**   **(F)**   **Price: 2**
Greg got some minutes when everybody, and we mean everybody, on Washington's front line got hurt. Many more lives would have to be wasted for Greg to turn into something good.

Armon Gilliam   **Phil**   **(F)**   **Price: 20**
Gilliam pulls down over eight rebounds a game. Not bad when your small forward pulls down over 11. "The Hammer" also throws down about 17 points a game. Include a block, and half a steal per game, and you've got a pretty good player. And with Chuckles now off to Phoenix, who knows? Gilliam could become an All-Star.

Harvey Grant   **Wash**   **(F)**   **Price: 15**
Harvey kept his game right where it was, despite myriad injuries that limited him to 64 games. The only noticeable decline was in blocked shots. Look for him to return to normal as soon as his health does.

Horace Grant   **Chi**   **(F)**   **Price: 26**
While he still doesn't score as much as Harvey, he is definitely the better all-around player. 10 rebounds, 1.23 steals, 1.62 blocks, and a mere 1.21 turnovers are darn fine numbers. A lot of people who talk about basketball for a living think that Horace will make the step to superstardom next year. We talk about basketball for a living, and we agree. Pay up to 30 for him and watch the stats roll in.

A.C. Green   **LAL**   **(F,C)**   **Price: 20**
A.C. was one of the bright spots in an otherwise dismal season for the Lakers. He raised his entire game back to a level of respectability. However, with a healthy Divac and an emerging Campbell around, Green probably won't be able to match those numbers this year. We will wait for the preseason, however, before we hand down our final judgment.

Sidney Green   **SA**   **(F)**   **Price: 4**
If you're looking for a backup power forward who gets about four rebounds and four points a game, then here's your man. Why you're looking for him is your problem. (What we're trying to tell you here is pass on Mr. Green.)

Tom Hammonds   **Wash**   **(F)**   **Price: 4**
Hammonds started to play well toward the end of the season. His 12 points and five rebounds per game almost doubled his stats from the previous year. Look for even more improvement from Tom this year as his playing time increases.

Rod Higgins   **GS**   **(F)**   **Price: 5**
Double-digit points and some three-pointers—not bad—but still not worth more than 5.

Tyrone Hill   **GS**   **(F)**   **Price: 11**
Given the opportunity to start most of the year, Hill responded by ripping down 7.2 rebounds and swiping almost one ball a game. He is rumored to be on the trading block, however, and if he lands with the right team, he could really produce. If he remains with Golden State, expect roughly the same numbers.

Henry James   Clev   (F)   Price: 1
Showed he had something in the playoffs, but we're not sure what. Still, he's a third-string forward in Cleveland and that's not worth anything.

Buck Johnson   Hou   (F)   Price: 4
Here's a name you can throw out during your auction and try to get someone else to pay some money for him. Buck had some really good games, but in the end he only managed to average 3.9 rebounds and 8.6 points per game. Don't let the fact that he is a starter on the Rockets sucker you into paying anything for him, because he is just not worth it.

Eddie Johnson   Sea   (F)   Price: 6
Eddie managed to raise all his stats with the exception of three-point field goals. Unfortunately, that was his best stat. He still threw down 29 of them, which is a fairly respectable number. He is probably worth more than last year, but not much more.

Larry Johnson   Char   (F)   Price: 24
Larry Johnson is looking like the second, albeit shorter, coming of Karl Malone. He already has the Mailman beat with his 83% from the free-throw line. While Larry will probably become a great spokesperson for several shoe companies, he still needs to work on his all-around game.

Shawn Kemp   Sea   (F,C)   Price: 25
Do the words rising superstar mean anything to you? About the only thing Kemp can't do is pass. His 10.4 rebounds and 15.5 points per game are impressive enough. Throw in over a steal and almost two blocks per game, and you can see why we are so high on him. The best part is that he will most likely be cheap because not a lot of people know how good he is.

Jerome Kersey   Port   (F)   Price: 22
Jerome put up some really nice numbers last year. What we don't understand is how a guy can average almost 1.5 steals and less than two turnovers a game, and still have hands of stone. There wasn't a pass that went into or out of his hands cleanly in the finals. Oh well, don't try to figure it out; just pay the money to get him because he is worth it.

Bernard King   Wash   (F)   Price: Only the Dr. knows
Not one of Bernard's best seasons, but on the bright side he didn't have a single turnover all year.

Stacey King   Chi   (F,C)   Price: 3
Stacey is the guy you see on the highway with the left turn indicator flashing continuously. He can only go around the world to the left. He did raise his scoring by 1.5 points, all the way up to 7 a game. This doesn't make him worth the lottery pick the Bulls spent on him; nor does it make him worth drafting in your league. But at least his mom can say that her son is starting to play better.

Larry Krystkowiak   Mil   (F)   Price: 8
Before Larry's knee injury, he was a fine garbage-man player. When he came back from the injury, he was a power forward with a shot selection reminiscent of World B. Free. There was an article in the newspaper that described Larry as an impact player. Now, we have two questions. First,

how does a player go from being a hardworking, pick-up-the-loose-ball, garbage-baskets type, to being an impact player by blowing out a knee? And second, how much of an impact is nine points and 5.4 rebounds?

Marcus Liberty   **Den**   **(F)**   **Price: 4**
9.3 points and 4.1 rebounds per game. These numbers are hideous for a man with this kind of talent. If he had any kind of desire and work ethic he could be a superstar. Unfortunately, they don't sell those things at the corner store.

Grant Long   **Mia**   **(F)**   **Price: 17**
Why Grant Long is such a well-kept secret in the NBA is a question that seemingly will plague mankind for years to come. All this guy does is score 15 points, tear down over eight boards, and get 1.7 steals per game. And for this one of our authors paid the princely sum of 3 units last year. Look to steal him cheap at the end of the draft, and you won't be disappointed.

Dan Majerle   **Phx**   **(F,G)**   **Price: 30**
Thunder Dan went from appearing on highlight films to appearing in the All-Star game. It's a progression we documented in our update last season. Dan's numbers should continue to improve with the deterioration of Tom Chambers. Note also the tremendous amount of threes Dan threw down last year.

Karl Malone   **Ut**   **(F)**   **Price: 38**
Last year we told you that you would be better off saving 15–20 units by drafting Tyrone Corbin instead of the Mailman. Now that Corbin is Malone's backup, and Karl had another year just like the last one, we are going to tell you to save 8–10 units and draft Dan Majerle.

Danny Manning   **LAC**   **(F)**   **Price: 33**
With the knee finally healthy, Manning put up some incredible numbers for a small forward. These numbers are even more impressive when you consider the amount of talent that the Clippers have fighting for the ball. In fact Danny is even starting to look like he may have been worth the first pick in the draft. Now that he is reunited with Larry Brown, his numbers should be even better.

Anthony Mason   **NY**   **(F)**   **Price: 10**
It's funny that a guy named Mason is built like a brick wall. He even puts up brick-wall numbers—seven rebounds and seven points. As the forwards in New York continue to age, Mason looks to be standing on a solid foundation.

Rodney McCray   **Dal**   **(F)**   **Price: 11**
Rodney's numbers dropped a bit, but then again, the Mavericks' dropped a whole bunch. With 6.2 rebounds and three assists per game, he is still a draftable player, but don't pay too much for him.

Xavier McDaniel   **NY**   **(F)**   **Price: 13**
X-Man got himself traded to New York, where he proceeded to blend very nicely into Pat Riley's offense. Unfortunately, his 13.7 points and 5.6 rebounds represent quite a dropoff from last year, and there is no reason to imagine those numbers will get any better.

Kevin McHale   Bos   (F,C)   Price: 14
McHale only managed to show up for 56 of Boston's games last year. Although that was 11 more than Bird showed up for, McHale was not nearly as productive. His blocks, rebounds, and points all went down significantly. He is also not getting any younger. Unless the price is really cheap, we think you should pass on Kevin.

Derrick McKey   Sea   (F)   Price: 19
Derrick's numbers dropped slightly due to the 29 games he missed last year. With a return to good health, his numbers should be better than ever. He is also one of those players who always seem to be a bargain. Look to steal him late in the draft at much less than he is worth.

Terry Mills   NJ   (F)   Price: 8
His points and rebounds went up slightly. Not enough to make him worth any more than any other backup power forward though.

Sam Mitchell   Minn   (F)   Price: 10
Sam was another victim of the turmoil in Minnesota (see also Pooh Richardson, Tony Campbell, and Tyrone Corbin). His points and rebounds dropped, as did his playing time. With the Wolves looking at forwards in the draft, Sam's odds for a good season are reaching longshot proportions.

Chris Morris   NJ   (F)   Price: 20 (For steals and blocks)
When Chris wasn't throwing a childlike tantrum and finding himself in Bill Fitch's doghouse (and on the bench), he was still putting up some pretty good numbers. With Chuck Daly as his new coach, he should be all right. Daly has a habit of straightening out malcontents. Look for Chris to rebound (and steal and block) to a big year.

Chris Mullin   GS   (F,G)   Price: 33
With Mitch Richmond gone, Mullin was asked to generate the same offense as usual while being double-teamed even more. He responded by increasing his rebounds and three-pointers, while maintaining the rest of his game. He was rewarded with a gold medal and a free trip to Barcelona. Now all he wants is a championship ring. Despite having the best coach in the league, he will need a good center to do it. Until then, look for Chris to keep doing what he is doing, and to do it well.

Jerrod Mustaf   Phx   (F)   Price: 5
Everybody in New York liked Jerrod, but he didn't get any playing time. The Suns liked Jerrod enough to give up Xavier McDaniel for him. Still he didn't get any playing time. Now that the Suns have traded Andrew Lang and Tim Perry, Jerrod will have to get playing time. Let's hope he still has some of the things that everybody liked.

Larry Nance   Clev   (F)   Price: 29
On the surface, it would appear that Larry had an off-year. His points and rebounds dropped slightly. However, his blocks and steals (far more valuable categories) went up significantly. Larry may actually have had a better year than the year before. Now that the Cavs are a quality team again, you can expect Nance to have another quality year.

Johnny Newman   **Char**   **(F,G)**   **Price: 8**
Every year you think Johnny Newman can't possibly be a starter again, and every year he averages 16 points and three rebounds. This year, again, we're assuming Charlotte will draft someone who can send this clown to the bench. But if not, you know what he's going to do.

Ken Norman   **LAC**   **(F)**   **Price: 9 (20 on another team)**
What happened to Ken Norman? He has gone from being one of the really good forwards in the league to being a 12-point, six-rebound player off the bench. Maybe Larry Brown just couldn't live with his attitude. If he gets traded somewhere he can be happy, look for great numbers. If he stays with the Clippers, he will be average.

Charles Oakley   **NYK**   **(F)**   **Price: 12**
A few of Charles's rebounding buddies, Dennis Rodman and Kevin Willis, had breakout seasons. Charles couldn't keep up, dropping his rebounds to 8.5 per game and his scoring to 6.2 per game. Look for him to bounce back slightly in the rebounds and not so much in the scoring.

Sam Perkins   **LAL**   **(F,C)**   **Price: 24**
With another year in L.A. under his belt (and Magic and Vlade MIA), Perkins was able to raise his game to the level he had attained when he was a Maverick. This makes him a pretty good all-around player. Whatever his role with the team is this year, he should continue to put up some impressive stats.

Tim Perry   **Phil**   **(F)**   **Price: 18**
While Tim Perry had a great season (especially for someone who had barely played in his first three years), he would probably never have matched it if he had remained in Phoenix. Now that he's in Philadelphia, however, he may have a chance to expand on those numbers. But how much more do you think this guy can pull out of his bag of tricks? Don't expect Tim to improve as much as he did last season. If he continued that way, he'd probably end up our Fantasy MVP.

Chuck Person   **Ind**   **(F)**   **Price: 28**
While everybody is busy picking on Chuckie for almost everything he does, no one seems to notice his numbers. Let's talk about those numbers for a minute. First of all, Chuckie threw down 116 three-pointers last year. The rest of his stats are roughly equivalent to two-thirds of Scottie Pippen's; which makes him pretty darn great. The best part of the whole deal is that you can get Person for about half of Pippen's price, not two-thirds..

Ed Pinckney   **Bos**   **(F)**   **Price: 12**
"Easy Ed" did stuff last season. He did lots of stuff last season. He probably did enough stuff to warrant his graduating from the taxi-squad to the big leagues. We don't want to say that Pinckney will start and be more productive next season, but he is the only Celtic big man who is too young to run for President.

Scottie Pippen   **Chi**   **(F)**   **Price: 48**
Scottie improved his scoring and assists, and asserted himself as one of the top five players in the game. He does, however, have a sort of Jeckyll and

Hyde problem. He tends to disappear in some games, but he tends to dominate others. He complains that he doesn't get enough offensive opportunities in some games, but then he goes out and creates a triple-double in others. If Pippen can find the mythical fountain of consistency that Larry Bird once bathed in daily, he can probably wind up as good as Larry Legend himself.

Kurt Rambis   Phx   (F)   Price: 1
The best thing we can say about Kurt Rambis is that he has more championship rings than Bernard King—once again proving that the only Justice in the world plays right field for Atlanta.

J.R. Reid   Char   (F,C)   Price: 11
Having been given another year (and another chance) to fit into the Charlotte lineup, Reid put up the exact same numbers as the year before. This year Charlotte has the second pick in the draft, and if J.R. wants more playing time, he will have to learn to be a backup point guard.

Glenn Rice   Mia   (F)   Price: 28
Glenn fired up 155 three-pointers last year. That was how many he made, not how many he attempted. Surprisingly enough, his scoring was up by six points a game. He also managed to maintain the rest of his stats at a pretty respectable level. Pay the money for Glenn, and you will be quite happy.

Fred Roberts   Mil   (F)   Price: 3
Rumor in Milwaukee has it that if the Bucks don't ax Fredly, the Bucks' fans will.

Cliff Robinson   Port   (F)   Price: 14
Let's start by saying that Cliff is becoming a respectable all-around player. Let's continue by saying that there is no way he should be taking the most shots per minute on this team after Drexler. When it was crunch time, Cliff usually came up 2-for-14. Meanwhile on the sidelines, Rick Adelman just stood there nodding his head, looking like he "picked the wrong week to stop sniffing glue." Seriously, though, draft Cliff for his stats, just don't watch the games.

Dennis Rodman   Det   (F)   Price: 30
Rodman started to rebound with a vengeance, and it must have gone to his head. Every stat that we track went up also, including an astounding 32 three-pointers. Dennis was playing like he wanted to make up for not earning those Defensive Player of the Year awards. We don't know what to tell you about this year. Are 20 rebounds a game out of his reach? Nothing else seems to be.

Tree Rollins   Hou   (F,C)   Price: 2
He's older than dirt, he only saw 12 minutes a game, and he still averaged over a block a game. You can't make an old dog forget his one trick.

Mike Sanders   Clev   (F)   Price: 4
7.1 points and 3.1 rebounds a game. But enough about Mike Sanders; let's move on to Detlef Schrempf.

Detlef Schrempf   Ind   (F)   Price: 26
Detlef may not look like the typical power forward, but he puts up power-forward numbers—17.2 points and 9.6 rebounds a game, despite coming off

the bench. He was deservedly named Sixth Man of the Year last year, and there is no reason to think that he won't win it again. Oh yeah, learn to spell his name correctly; it makes a great bar bet.

Dennis Scott　　　　**Orl**　　**(F)**　　**Price: 23**
Dennis Scott may have had the longest day-to-day injury in the history of sports. He played the first 18 games of the season, hurt his leg, and was never seen again. Oh, they kept telling us he was coming back, but they were just pulling our chains. When he did play, he was mighty impressive; throwing down 20 points a game, including 29 three-pointers, in those 18 games. Assuming he has finally recovered from that injury, look for him to put up some really good numbers this year.

Lionel Simmons　　　**Sac**　　**(F)**　　**Price: 29**
Simmons followed up a fine rookie year with a fine sophomore year. His scoring and rebounding dropped off slightly, but he more than made up for that by increasing his blocks and steals. No reason to think he will be any worse this year, and (who knows?) he could get better.

Charles Smith　　　**LAC**　　**(F,C)**　　**Price: 19**
Just when we were saying how lucky the Clippers were that their leading scorer didn't get hurt, just when we were touting Charles Smith as a premier power forward, Charles Smith gets hurt and has a subpar year. We are not really sure if there was some cause-and-effect here, but we are willing to give him the benefit of the doubt. Anyway, the Clippers are looking to trade him, so stay tuned for an update on his productivity.

Doug Smith　　　　**Dal**　　**(F)**　　**Price: 8**
Yeah, we know he's a Maverick, but he still could get good. It probably won't be this season, however, so we suggest you pass.

Larry Smith　　　　**Hou**　　**(F,C)**　　**Price: 5**
Larry Smith would have to play 48 minutes a game somewhere if he wanted to challenge Dennis Rodman for the rebound title. Since Larry probably won't even start anywhere (and certainly not in Houston), his chances look pretty grim at this point.

Larry Stewart　　　**Wash**　　**(F)**　　**Price: 10**
Larry Stewart came in as a non-drafted free agent and put up some great numbers for about a month and a half. He finished the season with six boards and 10 points a game, and probably guaranteed himself the backup job behind Harvey Grant. We've seen worse reserves.

LaSalle Thompson　　**Ind**　　**(F,C)**　　**Price: 2**
LaSalle proved last season that he will easily fit into his new role as the backup to Greg Dreiling.

Otis Thorpe　　　　**Hou**　　**(F,C)**　　**Price: 21**
Another in an amazingly long line of great players to find their way out of Sacramento. The year before last, Otis needed Hakeem to get injured before he could prove what kinds of numbers he could put together. With the trade winds gusting in Houston, Otis may have to become the Rockets' impact player. And we bet he can do it.

Waymon Tisdale   Sac   (F)   Price: 16
Waymon had been appealing his death-row sentence in Sacramento for a long time. Now Sacramento may have enough talent to keep him around and keep him happy. In fact, Waymon is not even the best player on the team anymore. He still put up some good numbers last year (6.5 rebounds and 16.6 points), but as the talent in town gets better and younger, Waymon's numbers can only get worse.

Jeff Turner   Orl   (F)   Price: 3
Turner was lost in the shuffle before Shaq came to town. Now he looks more like a busted flush.

Kiki Vandeweghe   NYK   (F)   Price: 3
Kiki is still hoping that Rick Patino will come back to the Knicks, so Kiki can again set up camp behind the three-point line.

Loy Vaught   LAC   (F)   Price: 7
Loy could be good (no, really, we're serious) if only he didn't have to fight so many Clippers for playing time. With the Clippers looking to trade for better talent, don't expect Loy's fight to get any easier.

Alexander Volkov   Atl   (F)   Price: 10
Don't let Alex's final numbers fool you. At the end of the season, he was putting up some great numbers. He is going to be a steal, even when Dominique returns to town.

Randy White   Dal   (F)   Price: 3
Didn't Randy have a short career as a kick-boxer? Wait, that was Too Tall Jones. We always get those old Dallas players confused. Expect Randy to get a couple of sacks and about 100 solo tackles.

Dominique Wilkins   Atl   (F)   Price: 18 (For the good half-season)
Dominique's injury reduced what would have been a very good fantasy season to just 42 games. It was a shame. With seven boards, 3.8 assists, 1.24 steals, less than three turnovers, and 28.1 points a game, 'Nique was again proving himself to be a Fantasy Basketball force. His injury is serious, so don't look for a Mark Price–like return. But we do wish him well. It would be a shame for all those sportscasters to lose all those minutes of highlight film.

Buck Williams   Port   (F)   Price: 15
Buck is a very good player to have on your team if FG% and FT% are used. He is a perennial leader in FG% and doesn't shoot enough free throws to hurt you at 75%. If you play in a league that doesn't use percentages, just be careful not to pay for a reputation. His numbers are only average: 8.8 boards, 0.78 steals, 0.51 blocks, 11.3 points.

Brian Williams   Orl   (F)   Price: 11
Last season at draft time, we felt very sad that the Magic only managed to land Brian Williams in the first round. Maybe we were wrong, since Williams, when healthy, put up some decent numbers. In fact, his numbers were comparable to Bonner's, who we already told you is a bright, young talent. The only question mark now is how O'Neal will affect the team. If he can coexist with Shaq, Brian may be a good player.

Herb Williams   Dal   (F)   Price: 12
Herb was looking for one last chance, and luckily he found himself in Dallas where everyone gets another chance. Everyone except Roy Tarpley.

John "Hot Rod" Williams Clev (F,C)   Price: 20
Don't think about how much the Cavs pay "Hot Rod." Just think about how good he'll look on your team. Over two blocks a game, to go with seven-plus rebounds and 12 points. Those numbers will go a long way in Fantasy Basketball.

John "Hot Plate" Williams Wash (F,C) Price: 0 (Plus 15% for the tip)
They finally got fed up with "Hot Plate" (after plate, after plate, after plate), and sat him for the whole year. Those of you who had access to *USA Today*'s computer sports line will know that he was suspended for being "grossly overweight." He was Alex's mascot last year. Alex was hoping that John would show up on his doorstep and they could tour all the restaurants in the area for a month.

Reggie Williams   Den   (F)   Price: 15
Reggie gets the generic Denver review. He had a great statistical season last year, but unfortunately Dan Issel is the new coach in Denver, and Dan probably cares more about wins than about Reggie's stats.

Scott Williams   Chi   (F)   Price: 5
For the second straight year, Scott's performance in the playoffs should earn him more time and maybe better numbers. But then again, Will Perdue played all season and saw no time in the playoffs.

Kevin Willis   Atl   (F,C)   Price: 28
Kevin had a monster rebounding season. When he and Dennis Rodman played each other, the game looked like King Kong vs. Godzilla. But beyond the rebounds, all Kevin really did for fantasy owners was score 18 points a game. While this was still a steal for those who got him last year, this year everybody knows, and no one will let a theft take place.

Orlando Woolridge Det   (F)   Price: 7
Orlando went from a phenomenal season in Denver to being just one of the boys in Detroit. Maybe the Pistons will ship him off to Doug Moe in Philadelphia, and we'll see shades of 1990–91.

James Worthy   LAL   (F)   Price: 22
Early last season, James came out and became the productive all-around player that we never thought he could be. Despite his later injury, James increased his worth enough that the Lakers will probably pull the trigger and trade him. If they don't, there's almost no reason to believe he'll repeat last year's performance. Almost.

CENTERS

There is almost no way to win at Fantasy Basketball without at least one good center to shore up the middle of your team, and if you play head-to-head, it's virtually impossible to win without two decent centers. Centers are about the only players who accumulate large numbers of blocked shots. They also average more rebounds than guards and forwards. When comparing centers, look at these two categories first. What separates a good center from a great center can be determined when assists, steals, and scoring are compared.

Right now the ranks of centers in the NBA are changing. Hakeem Olajuwon, David Robinson, and Patrick Ewing used to be the only dominant big men in Fantasy Basketball, but there are now several players snapping at their heels, fighting to enter the "Elite" category. The emergence of Pervis Ellison, Rony Seikaly, and Dikembe Mutombo—in addition to the already-emerged Brad Daugherty—has created a second tier of centers to build a team around. What will the arrivals of Shaquille O'Neal and Alonzo Mourning do to this grouping? Whatever happens, it will be fun to watch. Despite all these changes, however, David Robinson was our Fantasy MVP last year, for the second year in a row. Can he be caught?

Finally, a word of advice: Near the end of a fantasy draft, don't get desperate and draft just any center; sometimes a good power forward will do more for you than a mediocre center. In head-to-head, however, you can't afford to get caught without at least two decent centers at the end of the draft. Plan your center strategy early and try to avoid last-minute, desperation moves.

Here are our impressions of this year's crop of big men:

Alaa Abdelnaby   Port   (C,F)   Price: 1
Alaa made a fairly important contribution to the Blazers during the regular season—he kept them from having to bring in Wayne Cooper very often. But during the playoffs, and especially the finals, he was lost in the shuffle. Just remember, Cliff Robinson didn't get much playing time two years ago either.

Victor Alexander   GS   (C)   Price: 8
If Victor ever got into Don Nelson's doghouse, there wouldn't be any room left for Nellie's dog. Victor had a tremendously mediocre rookie season, but at least he saw some playing time. Given an opportunity, "The House" could turn himself into the next Kevin Duckworth. Wouldn't that be awesome.

Benoit Benjamin   Sea   (C)   Price: 26
Benoit finally started to play well although he disappeared at times last season. Still his numbers looked good—8.1 rebounds, 1.87 blocks, and 14 points per game. Not up to his potential, but, all things considered, we'd rather have him working for us than against us.

Manute Bol   Phil   (C)   Price: 8
Manute may get enough blocks (2.89 per game) to warrant consideration as a fantasy player, but he won't get you anything else, including self-respect.

Sam Bowie   NJ   (C)   Price: 27 (And maybe an extra knee)
The oft-injured Bowie managed a relatively healthy season (71 games) and
had some relatively healthy numbers (8.1 boards, 2.6 assists, 1.69 blocks,
and 15 points per game). You could look at these numbers as an indication of
good things to come. Or you could say to yourself that since he's normally
good for only half a season, he'll make up for last season's 71 games by only
playing 11 next year. "Feel lucky, punk?"

Randy Breuer   Minn   (C)   Price: 2
We think it's a darn good thing that Randy stands at 7'4", because if he were
2" shorter, he'd be just another gleepy white guy who couldn't play basketball. For a working definition of "gleepy," just think of every other white,
ex–Big Ten center.

Mike Brown   Ut   (C)   Price: 6
When Mike Brown and Karl Malone both box out for a rebound, only Mugsy
Bogues is small enough to fit between them. Mike is a "wide body" in every
sense of the term, but that also means he'll pull down a few boards. And
being in Utah, he should score 10 points a game on dazzling passes from
John Stockton alone.

Michael Cage   Sea   (C)   Price: 10
Can you say, "A good backup?" Sure! I thought you could.

Elden Campbell   LAL   (C)   Price: 8
Elden got his shot at stardom and proved that he's a fine backup center.
Campbell won't win a game for you but he probably won't lose a game for
you either.

Bill Cartwright   Chi   (C)   Price: 4
There are an awful lot of backup centers who can help your team more than
Bill can. Let the obnoxious Bulls' fan in your league take Cartwright. Then
watch that obnoxious Bulls' fan suffer as all Bulls' fans should.

Dwayne Causwell   Sac   (C)   Price: 18
Dwayne did all right as a sophomore—7.3 boards, 2.69 blocks, but only
eight points per game. With Dwayne Schintzius as his backup, Causwell
should get increased playing time, and should continue to improve his numbers (although the blocks probably won't improve much since they're already phenomenal).

Brad Daugherty   Clev   (C)   Price: 37
Brad has been undervalued in our league for years. We don't expect this trend
to continue. He is a quality center who hasn't commanded as high a price as
the "big" centers, but whose time has come. After averaging 10.4 rebounds,
21 points, and more than a block a game last season, he will not come cheap.
Oh, yes, and let's not forget what the playoff announcers managed to state
about 400 times per telecast: "Brad's the best passing center in basketball."

Vlade Divac   LAL   (C)   Price: 20
Vlade had an injury-riddled season, coupled with trouble in his homeland,
but he still managed to have a few good games at center for the Lakers. His
rebounding was down (6.9 from 8.1) as were his blocked shots (0.97 from

1.55), but he should be back in form next season. When you check his stats, note also that he steals the ball well for a center (1.53 steals per game). Maybe it was Vlade's disappointing season that caused all the strife in Yugoslavia. If only the world's problems could be solved by a good NBA season. This concludes our social commentary for this year.

James Donaldson   NY   (C)   Price: 2
Derek Harper called James a seven-foot punk, but we just can't picture James with a mohawk.

Greg Dreiling   Ind   (C)   Price: 1
Greg started for a while when Smits was sidelined with tendonitis in both knees. Let's hope, for Indiana's sake, that Rik will be healthy next year.

Kevin Duckworth   Port   (C)   Price: 10
"What's a Duck worth?" As much as you're willing to pay for 6.1 boards and 10 points a game.

Chris Dudley   NJ   (C)   Price: 15 (Much less if you use FT%)
Chris's stats are skewed because of injuries to Bowie. Wait, injuries to Bowie? Hmmm. Dudley might not get any points (especially from the free-throw line), but most teams could use nine boards and over two blocks a game. (And almost twice that if Bowie gets hurt.) It's seems a pretty safe bet.

Mark Eaton   Ut   (C)   Price: 8
Mark Eaton, or "Sasquatch" as a friend of ours calls him, is moving up in years and doesn't pull down the boards he used to (6.1 per game last season). But he does still take up enough room in the lane to block over 2.5 shots a game.

James Edwards   LAC   (C)   Price:2
James Edwards was brought to the Clippers for his leadership and experience. He certainly wasn't brought in for his production at center.

Pervis Ellison   Wash   (C,F)   Price: 42
"Out of service" Pervis has finally been given a clean bill of health and has taken his place among the second-tier centers in the league (joining such notables as Brad Daugherty and Rony Seikaly). He is still prone to injury, but his production/price ratio should be very good.

Patrick Ewing   NYK   (C)   Price: 50
The New York Ewings (or is it the Rileys now?) played better than anyone thought they would, amazing the Bulls by pushing them to a seventh game. Ewing is still the weakest of the "Big Three" centers, but he might still be a bargain. His assists and scoring could even increase next year, should the Knicks acquire the outside shooter they are so desperately seeking. And with Pervis, Dikembe, and possibly Shaq threatening to make it the "Big Six," look for Ewing to respond with a possible career year.

Chris Gatling   GS   (C)   Price: 2
He almost gives the Warriors depth at center. He certainly gives them weight at center.

Kenny Gattison   Char   (C,F)   Price: 12
Kenny put up some fine numbers this year and will be rewarded with a powerful backup role next year, behind Alonzo Mourning. Still, if everyone else thinks like that, he might be a steal in a backup role.

Michael Gminski   Char   (C)   **Price: A Wooden Nickel**
WHY ?!?

Donald Hodge   Dal   (C)   **Price: 8**
Donald Hodge put up the kind of numbers last season that show clearly why he is a mediocre taxi-squad center. But he'll probably go for less than half of what Kevin Duckworth goes for in your league. Think about it.

Les Jepsen   Sac   (C)   **Price: "Les" than 0**
Les was the key man in the Billy Owens trade as you can tell by reading the Kings' press guide. There the team philosophy is stated as, "Less is more, so we want more Les." When you add Jim Les to Les Jepsen, Sacramento has got less (and Les).

Charles Jones   Wash   (C,F)   **Price: 2**
A competent backup with an incompetent shot.

Alec Kessler   Mia   (C,F)   **Price: 3**
Alec is passing up a profitable career as the CEO of a Fortune 500 company to play in the NBA. Some lucky company will be happy when Alec gives up basketball. So will we.

Greg Kite   Orl   (C)   **Price: Not quite 1**
A team would have to be desperate to have Greg Kite on its roster. In such a case, however, Kite might be worth up to 70 units to the desperate owner. While the rest of us avoid such thoughts, Jim (one of our fellow authors) still wakes up in the middle of the night in a cold sweat after just such a nightmare.

Joe Kleine   Bos   (C)   **Price: 2**
Let's just say, "DeKleine."

John Koncak   Atl   (C)   **Price: 2**
John Koncak was one of the best centers in basketball last year. He far outpaced the best of the league's big men on his way to a Hall of Fame season. NOT! Fish! (Apologies to Wayne and Garth.)

Bill Laimbeer   Det   (C)   **Price: 7**
Bill thinks that if Detroit will use him in a backup role, he can play a couple more years. Oh, thank you, Bill! Thank you! We're all so grateful. A couple more years of whining and even less production. What a treat. (But always remember, Bill should have been given an opportunity to make the Olympic team.)

Andrew Lang   Phil   (C)   **Price: 15**
Andrew Lang was finally given a starting job by the Suns; unfortunately the job is in Philadelphia. In Philly, Lang will be asked to rebound more than 6.7 times a game, and his blocks may rise even higher than last year's impressive 2.48 a game. He may even average more than seven points a game for a whole season.

Alton Lister   **GS**   **(C)**   **Price: 3**
Lister the listless. Granted he was injured most of the year, but, still—3.5 rebounds and 3.9 points a game? Brrrr! Sends a chill down our collective spine. Actually, so does the thought of Nellie with a real center.

Brad Lohaus   **Mil**   **(C,F)**   **Price: 3**
B.L. was not worth the $1.7 million Milwaukee paid him last year, and he's not worth much as a fantasy player either. If he goes somewhere besides Milwaukee, to some team that will give him playing time, he might be worth, say, 4.

Luc Longley   **Minn**   **(C)**   **Price: 5**
Use the force Luc! Worth 5 units because just having potential at center is better than half the centers in the league.

Moses Malone   **Atl**   **(C)**   **Price: 21**
He's Mo. He's still Mo after all these years. 9.1 boards, almost one steal, and 15.6 points per game. Respectable numbers for the last holdover from the ABA. Remember, "Only Moses knows what Moses is capable of!"

Dikembe Mutombo   **Den**   **(C)**   **Price: 45**
With the emergence of Dikembe and Pervis Ellison, and considering the bright future of Shaquille O'Neal, there are actually more than a couple of good centers to draft in Fantasy Basketball. Isn't that amazing? Dikembe was our Fantasy Rookie of the Year last season. He had more rebounds and blocks than Larry Johnson, and only scored three fewer points per game. And we all know how vitally important three points a game can be, don't we? The author who drafted Dikembe would like it mentioned that he had more than a few turnovers last season, but even Robinson and Olajuwon get a lot of turnovers. With Dan Issel, a former center, as Denver's new head coach, the Nuggets should go to Dikembe even more this season. Isn't it great to have more than three good centers to choose from?

Hakeem Olajuwon   **Hou**   **(C)**   **Price: 57**
Hakeem was as impressive as ever, even though everyone in Houston thought he had an awful season. 12.1 rebounds, 2.2 assists, 1.81 steals, 4.34 blocks, and 21.6 points a game—not bad for a guy on the trading block. If you had him last year, you couldn't complain about his production, unless you were looking for three-pointers. He's worth what you pay for him as long as you can give him a supporting cast. By the way, if he starts to play badly, don't suspend him; he hates that.

Robert Parish   **Bos**   **(C)**   **Price: 16 (Plus two knees)**
Tick. Tick. Tick. We've been hearing that noise for years as Parish has gotten older. And older. And older. Bob managed to sidestep Father Time for another year and put up some good numbers. Can you roll the bones and get a natural seven again, or are you going to crap out with snake eyes?

Will Perdue   **Chi**   **(C)**   **Price: 2**
If dishing out punishment were a category, Will might be worth something. It was amazing how little we saw Will in the playoffs last season. Kind of nice, actually.

Oldin Polynice   **LAC**   **(C)**   **Price: 12**
The fact that Oldin can come down with seven boards a game, despite sharing the floor with all those rebounders on the Clippers, must mean he screens out his own teammates as well as the opposition. Unfortunately, he does so little else. As long as he's not your #1 center, we don't foresee too much trouble in your future.

Blair Rasmussen   **Den**   **(C)**   **Price: 7**
Blair's rebounding suffered in Atlanta (4.9) because he'd grown accustomed to all those missed shots in Denver. Of course, it didn't help that Willis ripped down every board in sight. Still, when he got some playing time, Blair didn't perform too badly—just well enough to make you dig a little deeper into your pocketbook for his services.

Stanley Roberts   **Orl**   **(C)**   **Price: 15 (Double without Shaq)**
Stanley's numbers last year were skewed by a lack of minutes early in the season. But for a stretch of about 20 games before he was injured, Stanley was becoming the second "Center of the Future" from last year's draft, along with Dikembe Mutombo. With his ol' buddy Shaq arriving in Orlando, Stanley might have to become the second "Power Forward of the Future" from last year's draft, along with that Johnson fellow. We don't know how Shaq's presence will affect Stanley. Heck, we don't know what a full season will do to Stanley. The one thing we do know: Stanley is worth a risk.

David Robinson   **SA**   **(C)**   **Price: 60**
Well, we were "forced" to pick David as our Fantasy Player of the Year for the second straight year. (Look at these numbers: 12.2 rebounds, 2.7 assists, 2.32 steals, 2.63 turnovers, 4.49 blocks, and 23.2 points a game. If only he had made more than one three-pointer. . . .) We only say that we were "forced," because we had to make our selection before he got injured. But with those kinds of numbers, we'll be more than happy to admit, a year or two from now, that David was our Player of the Year for several seasons before the NBA figured out what was what and gave him its MVP award.

John Salley   **Det**   **(C,F)**   **Price: 8**
Why would you want to draft a center from a team that gets all of its rebounding from one forward? Spider's numbers slipped this year (4.1 boards, 1.53 blocks, 9.5 points), but there is room for improvement if he gets continued help from Bill Laimbeer. The help would be Laimbeer's spending more time on the bench.

Dan Schayes   **Mil**   **(C)**   **Price: 1 (2 if he's on a team)**
Dan was injured during the latter part of the year (and his numbers actually got better). Even for a backup, 3.9 boards and 5.6 points are atrocious.

Dwayne Schintzius   **Sac**   **(C)**   **Price: 1**
Dwayne finally found a place where he fits in—Sacramento.

Rony Seikaly   **Mia**   **(C)**   **Price: 34**
Last season, after a lot of good play, Rony moved into the second-tier center group. Don't be afraid to pay for Rony; remember, his backup is only Alec Kessler.

Charles Shackleford   Phil   (C)   Price: 5
You gotta "Love Shack, baby," except "his tin roof's rusted." Eat your heart out, Chris Berman.

Rik Smits   Ind   (C)   Price: 18
Rik had tendonitis in both knees, so his numbers were down (but still not bad). Keep an eye on his progress; he hasn't been healthy for two years. But if he is going to be healthy this year, you might be able to get him for a song.

Felton Spencer   Minn   (C)   Price: 14
Felton improved his numbers last year: He averaged 7.8 fouls per 48 minutes. Two years ago, he was only averaging 7.7 fouls per 48 minutes. Mr. Spencer grabbed 7.1 boards and got 1.30 blocks a game, but scored only 6.6 points. Keep your eye on him this year; with a better supporting cast, he may improve. (Of course, he may not.)

Roy Tarpley   Dal   (C,F)   Price: We're Kidding
We decided to review Roy one more time just for the sheer excessiveness of it. No, really, we did have to mention Roy because he was our CBA Fantasy Player of the Year.

Mark West   Phx   (C)   Price: 13
Mark West should be the major beneficiary of the Barkley deal. First of all, he now has a low-post companion, something he's never had in Phoenix. And second, his backups are now Jerrod Mustaf and Ed Nealy. While West will never be a great center, he may recapture some of his late-80s form based on extra playing time alone.

ROOKIE REVIEWS

The 1992 NBA draft looks to be the deepest in many years. In addition to its one guaranteed superstar (Shaquille O'Neal), it has a lot of depth at the top, with players who can step into starting lineups and make major contributions. There is talent all the way through the first round and even into the second round, and there are sleepers everywhere. In no other recent draft, for instance, could the Bulls have dreamed of getting a talent like Byron Houston with the last pick of the first round. This is a draft that could send a smart owner to the top of his fantasy league. If you want to take some taxi-squad gambles this year, look for their names in this chapter. Many of these rookies are good bets. Keep an eye on preseason reports for almost every team, and when the need for more information becomes too great, order our Fantasy Basketball Update. The update lists all transactions for each team, how all these moves will affect the teams involved, and what news is coming out of summer and preseason camps. To order the update, please check out the flyer in the back of the book.

This year we take the plunge and list prices that we'd pay for each rookie. The price listed is what you should pay for the rookie if he is going to start or get significant minutes (25-plus per game). We list in each review what we feel has to happen for each player to get those minutes. If these requirements aren't fulfilled, our suggested prices must be adjusted accordingly. Again, our update will list revised prices depending on the word we get out of the camps.

As happened last year, our two college scouts, Jim and Troy, don't often seen eye-to-eye on the merits of each player. When they do agree, it's often a case of agreeing that the player is utterly unworthy of praise, if not unworthy even of a review. So to alleviate the strain on the typewriter, Jim and Troy will give separate reviews of rookies over whom there is some disagreement. Alex's complete lack of interest in the college game (as well as some religious beliefs that are better left unspoken of) make him less than useful in these reviews. He won't be heard from.

What follow are our impressions (collective or individual) of each player taken in the first round of the draft. We will not rate any second-round selections, although we will provide a list of the players taken in the second round at the end of this section. If a player taken in the second round appears likely to break through and make a contribution in his rookie season, we'll bring this to light in our update.

TOP ROOKIE DRAFT PICKS

Shaquille O'Neal   **(C)**   **Orlando**   **LSU**

TROY'S REVIEW: Here's the easiest question I'll ever get asked: What does Shaquille O'Neal have to do to break into the starting lineup? Answer: He has to sign a contract. Shaq will be twice as good as any other rookie this year and should break his way into the Fantasy Top Five. Does this mean that Rookie of the Year is assured? Hah! As if sportswriters cared about blocked shots, or even rebounds. (Dikembe Mutombo beat Larry Johnson by an awful lot of blocks and by more than one rebound a game.) If you've noticed, what sportswriters care about is scoring. And what else? Scoring. Scoring in the clutch to win games. Scoring in every way humanly possible. And then scoring just a little bit more. Shaquille should get his eight dunks every game, but with a scoring average of 16 points, he will be edged out for Rookie of the Year. For the winning selection, read on.
PRICE: 48 if Fort Knox relocates to Orlando.

JIM'S REVIEW: There you go again, Troy. We can't seem to agree on anything. That's what I get for coauthoring a book with someone from the Land of Lincoln. Shaq will be so totally dominant that Rookie of the Year will not even be a contest. First of all, he will score more like 22 a game rather than 16. Second of all, rebounds and blocks will matter when he pulls down 13 a game and swats away almost four. And third of all (third of all?), you'd better have saved a couple of paychecks to afford the dinner at the Hyatt you will once again owe me this year. Well, enough picking on Troy; what I am trying to tell you people out there is that Shaq is a superstar from Day 1, and well worth the price.
PRICE: 56

Alonzo Mourning   **(C,F)**   **Charlotte**   **Georgetown**

TROY: Alonzo will start, likely at center, for the Hornets. With Larry Johnson at power forward, this makes Charlotte too small a team to be a contender for many years (it will seem like an eternity to their talented players). What will Alonzo do? I've asked myself this question since his awful junior year at Georgetown. Yes, I did predict that he'd have a great senior year after Dikembe left. So, I'm still left with the ultimate question, and it's time for an answer. And the answer is . . . I'm going to defer. Let the Georgetown fan in your draft (and if you don't have a Georgetown fan in your league I envy you) pay more than Alonzo could possibly be worth and check out his numbers for next year.
PRICE: 45 if you're a Georgetown fan. 16 if you have a brain.

JIM: With thinking like that, it's no wonder that your team was so horrid last year. "I'm going to defer." Is this a man of conviction or what? Take a stand, Troy. Be someone. Even if you were wrong (and you usually are), at least I'd have some respect for you. As for Mourning, he has more talent than Mutombo. Unfortunately, Charlotte has tons more talent than Denver, so Mourning won't have to do as much. He will probably average around 12 points, eight rebounds, and two blocks a game. Respectable numbers that will only get better.
PRICE: 21

Christian Laettner   (F,C)   Minnesota   Duke

JIM: I honestly don't know what to tell you about Laettner. My gut feeling is that he is going to bomb big-time. On the other hand, a lot of people are saying that this guy has major amounts of talent and that he can't miss. I do know this much: He has a terrific outside shot and he was one hell of a college player. The same, however, can also be said of many a Duke player, including Mike Gminski, Mark Alarie, Alaa Abdelnaby, and the original Duke washout, Jim Spanarkle. Basically, I think that the jury is still out on Christian. He will probably score about 11, rebound about five, and throw down about 60 three-pointers. This makes him three times as good as Brad Lohaus. Let some fool in your league, someone who thinks Laettner will win Rookie of the Year, someone like Troy in other words, pay the really big bucks for him.
PRICE: 9

TROY: Man of conviction, huh? "Take a stand," he says. "Be someone," he says. 'Atta boy, Jim. (By the way, deferring on Mourning was the only smart move.) Anyway, now it's time to go out on that limb. Christian Laettner will win Rookie of the Year. I don't recant my statement that Shaquille will be twice as good as any other rookie, I just think that the nation's sportswriters, in their infinite wisdom, will overlook Shaquille's tremendous all-around stats in favor of Christian's clutch scoring. Hey, Jim, why don't you skip those other useless names and just say you think Laettner will be the next Danny Ferry? The thing is, Christian has a distinct advantage over those other dorks you mention. Christian played inside on both offense and defense, something Danny never did. Christian also has a fighting spirit that no one seems to remember when they ask if he can take the NBA's pounding. Doesn't anyone remember Laettner stepping on that guy in the NCAA tourney? Besides, every one of Christian's Olympic Dream-Teammates, with the exception of Sir Charles, thinks Christian will be great. (Charles, of course, thinks he'll make a great bellhop.) Anyway, here are Christian's numbers for his "Rookie of the Year" season: 20 points, nine rebounds, 3.5 assists, 1.25 steals, and one block a game.
PRICE: 28 (OK, maybe I'm reaching.)

Jim Jackson   (G)   Dallas   Ohio State

Jim is probably the best all-around player in the draft. He will step right into the starting lineup at shooting guard, especially considering the Rolando Blackman trade. He should score upwards of 20 points and haul down at least five boards a game. He's capable of playing point guard, but until Dallas surrounds him with players who can score, he probably won't get more than four assists a game. People worry about his range, but they said that about Scottie Pippen when he was a rookie too.
PRICE: 21

LaPhonso Ellis   (F)   Denver   Notre Dame

JIM: This pick seems to indicate that Cadillac Anderson is no longer a part of Denver's plans, but you never really know what Denver is up to. At 6'8" Ellis is a little too small to play power forward, but he lacks the passing ability to play small forward. He's an intense rebounder and runs the court well. He should be a solid starter, but will probably never be a superstar.
PRICE: 11

TROY: How soon they forget. Jim, how can you say LaPhonso is too small to play power forward, when we project Alonzo Mourning at center, and Ellis manhandled Mourning as a freshman in the NCAA tourney? OK, LaPhonso did have problems in college, but that was only because he was at Notre Dame, and they actually have academic standards there. Also, Jim, don't worry about Cadillac; he was a Band-Aid solution anyway. LaPhonso is such a tremendous leaper that he should easily put up the rebounding numbers that Cadillac got last year. He could even score 15 a game if Denver still lacks an offensive strategy.
PRICE: 23

Tom Gugliotta   **(F)**   **Washington**   **N.C. State**
Nobody could understand why the Bullets wanted this guy over hometown hero Walt Williams. Nobody in our elite circle of basketball aficionados, anyway. We also couldn't understand why Washington, the only team really interested in Gugliotta, didn't trade down. Tom should leap into the starting lineup, especially if the Knicks steal Harvey Grant from the Bullets. Tom should be able to get a few defensive rebounds, since he was the ACC's leading rebounder, and he'll probably score a few points. Tom reminds Jim an awful lot of Danny Ferry. Troy thinks Jim should come up with another comparison sometime during these reviews.
PRICE: 11 if you think the Bullets were right.

Walt Williams   **(G)**   **Sacramento**   **Maryland**
Even though the Kings told everybody they wouldn't take Walt, even if he was available, they couldn't pass up his talent. With Mitch Richmond at shooting guard, Walt probably isn't looking at a starting job, but he should be the third guard and get plenty of minutes. This was guaranteed by the release of Dennis Hopson. While Walt can play the point, don't look for the Kings to play him too much there; he turned the ball over a lot in college. Walt can score a ton and should put up some good, possibly very good, numbers. Walt could be the best gamble in this draft.
PRICE: 15, but he won't go that high in your draft.

Todd Day   **(G,F)**   **Milwaukee**   **Arkansas**
Todd Day should be the key beneficiary of the Milwaukee Bucks' fire sale. As the Bucks build for the future, Todd will probably be given every opportunity to step in quickly and be the Bucks' future star. Todd's a great all-around player who might have slipped to the eighth pick because of an attitude problem. He could easily start at small forward or shooting guard for the Bucks, depending on how many more moves they decide to make. But even if he doesn't start, he should get plenty of playing time. The Bucks also drafted his Arkansas teammate, Lee Mayberry, to be their future point guard, which should help Todd leap into the offense even more quickly than might have been expected. Todd should be a solid contributor, and will most likely achieve stardom two or three years down the road.
PRICE: 15, but, like Walt Williams, he shouldn't go that high.

Clarence Weatherspoon (F)   **Philadelphia**   **Southern Mississippi**
TROY: Immediately after the 76ers took Clarence, the comparisons to Charles Barkley began. While Clarence is a wide body like Charles, and is known for his rebounds like Charles, there are precious few people in bas-

ketball like Charles Barkley. Actually, there's only one. Clarence could be good this year and he might become a great rebounder, but the odds of his becoming Charles Barkley are much slimmer than he is.
PRICE: 8

JIM: Weatherspoon will step in and start at small forward now that Barkley is a Phoenix Sun. Clarence dislikes being compared to Sir Charles, and with good reason; he will never be as good. However, he should contribute some decent numbers right away—14 points and nine rebounds, for starters. This makes him as good as Grant Long, who is a perennial steal in fantasy drafts.
PRICE: 21

Adam Keefe   (F,C)   **Atlanta**   **Stanford**
Adam is a big, physical bruiser who should find minutes tough to come by in Atlanta. With the emergence of Kevin Willis as a All-Star rebounder, Adam will have to supplant Jon Koncak or Blair Rasmussen if he wants to play a significant number of minutes. Adam could turn into a good player, but it could take a while.
PRICE: 4

Robert Horry   (F)   **Houston**   **Alabama**
Robert really helped himself in the draft with his play in the predraft camps. Barring a trade for another small forward, Robert should move right into a starting small-forward spot (especially since Houston's release of Buck Johnson). Robert is another one of those all-around players who were so popular in this draft. He should put up some decent rookie numbers and should be a nice gamble for some interested fantasy owner.
PRICE: 14, but he'll be on sale for at least 50% off.

Harold Miner   (G)   **Miami**   **USC**
There are two major problems we see with Harold Miner. First, barring an Olajuwon trade, the Heat are so stocked at guard, with Brian Shaw, Steve Smith, Kevin Edwards, Willie Burton, and even occasionally Glenn Rice, that Harold will have to fight very hard for any playing time. Harold's second problem is his glaring lack of defensive ability. The CBA is full of explosive offensive players who can't play defense. Defense wins games in the NBA, and if you can't play it, a team won't play you. This doesn't have to happen to Harold, but it's probably a good prognosis for his rookie season.
PRICE: 12 if two of those other guards are gone.

Bryant Stith   (G,F)   **Denver**   **Virginia**
Could Denver actually be thinking? They get a great rebounder with their first pick, and then a solid (and, more importantly, smart) swingman with their second pick. While Denver did need a point guard, getting the best available player was more important for a team of their caliber. Bryant is another of those all-around players, and after Mark Macon's poor rookie performance, he could move right into the starting lineup. Even if he doesn't start, his minutes should be significant enough to help him put up some solid numbers in several categories.
PRICE: 10

Malik Sealy   **(F)**   **Indiana**   **St. John's**
Malik would have been a great pick here, if the Pacers were a rebuilding team that could offer him the minutes to grow, literally, into the NBA. Unfortunately for Malik, Indiana is too full of talent to give him the minutes he needs. The future for Malik will probably consist of two or three years on the Pacer bench, followed by a trade that might give him a chance to be an NBA player. But that can only happen if he bulks up from his 185 pounds.
PRICE: Not this year

Anthony Peeler   **(G)**   **LA Lakers**   **Missouri**
Anthony was probably the steal of the draft. He was always considered one of the top five talents in college ball, but run-ins with the law dropped him down the list—to the Lakers' delight. The Lakers were in desperate need of a player with this kind of talent who could also generate some excitement in the Great Western Forum. Look for Anthony to explode into the starting lineup; the Lakers are too smart to keep Byron in the starting lineup out of respect for his past. L.A. should be quite happy with Peeler's production, and so should his fantasy owners.
PRICE: 16, and he might go that high.

Randy Woods   **(G)**   **LA Clippers**   **LaSalle**
Randy was the fifth-leading scorer in the NCAA last season and was still rated the top point guard in the draft. Doesn't it seem as if everyone in the NBA wants a point guard who will pass before he'll shoot? We guess the Clippers don't. Randy reminds some people of Tim Hardaway because of his quickness, defense, and outstanding range. His major problem this season should be finding playing time behind veterans Doc Rivers and Gary Grant. Don't look for enough moves out of the Clips to get him into the starting lineup. His future problems should be finding enough time to shoot while still distributing the ball to all that talent in L.A.
PRICE: 5

Doug Christie   **(G)**   **Seattle**   **Pepperdine**
At 6'6", Christie is a very big point guard. He also shoots well enough to play shooting guard and rebounds well enough to play small forward. He should be able to back up Gary Payton (or possibly beat him out) as well as Derrick McKey. The only concern about Doug was his knee problem, which cost him several places in the draft. If his knees hold up, look for Doug to produce some very reasonable numbers.
PRICE: 10

Tracy Murray   **(G,F)**   **Portland**   **UCLA**
Tracy had been in the NBA less than a week when he became the property of his third team. He should be happy in Portland, especially with the Blazers talking about using him the way they used Danny Ainge. At 6'8", Tracy could be a great shooting guard. He has outstanding range on his jump shot and should be able to shoot over most other shooting guards. At small forward, his inability to create his own offense will be a liability. But standing on the perimeter and firing up three-pointers is a role Tracy is well suited for, and that seems to be Portland's plan for him.
PRICE: 9

Don MacLean   (F)   LA Clippers   UCLA
Don was drafted by the Pistons and then traded to the Clippers before the first round was over. He has two major obstacles in his path to NBA stardom, or even NBA mediocrity. First, he isn't going to get much playing time at forward for the Clippers. Second, he isn't tough enough to handle NBA power forwards, and he isn't quick enough to handle NBA small forwards. There is a positive; he can do anything on offense. But that isn't enough to earn him the kind of minutes he needs to produce decent numbers.
PRICE: 2

Hubert Davis   (G)   New York   North Carolina
After the Knicks traded for Rolando Blackman, their interest in Hubert Davis (as the shooter they needed) should have faded, right? Well, the Knicks must really dislike the shooters they have to go out and get two new ones on the same day. Before the trade, Hubert might be have been a good pick, but now he's a 1-unit insurance policy for Rolando.
PRICE: 1

Jon Barry   (G)   Boston   Georgia Tech
JIM: Jon could be what the Celtics are looking for at point guard. It sounds scary, but it could be true. Sherman Douglas is on the trading block, leaving only John Bagley to beat out. Barry is probably good enough to beat out Bagley and should make a decent point guard. He has NBA range on his three-point shot, and at 6'5" he can rebound well for a point guard.
PRICE: 18 if he starts.
TROY: OK, Jim, I have only one argument with your review: What happened to Dee Brown? Yes, I think that Sherm will be traded, and yes, I think that Jon is probably better than Bagley; but the Celtics' starting point-guard spot is already guaranteed to Dee Brown. Jon could be a good backup, but so what? I do agree with your price, though . . . I mean to say, with the disclaimer.
PRICE: 2 if he's the first backup.

Oliver Miller   (C,F)   Phoenix   Arkansas
Oliver is an immense talent, with the emphasis on "immense." Oliver could be the next Benoit Benjamin—all the talent, none of the work ethic. With Andrew Lang and Tim Perry sent east, Oliver is the likely choice to step into the backup center spot for the Suns. He might even be able to beat out Mark West as the starter. All of this is contingent on Oliver's working hard in camp and taking the weight off before camp.
PRICE: 10

Lee Mayberry   (G)   Milwaukee   Arkansas
Lee is the kind of point guard the Bucks like. He's great on defense, a good perimeter shooter, and a decent penetrator. He also averaged an incredible 1.6 turnovers a game his senior season. If he can do that for the Bucks, he'll easily beat out Eric Murdock (acquired in a draft-day trade from Utah) for the starting spot. Lee should make Milwaukee forget about Jay Humphries in a season or two.
PRICE: 13

Latrell Sprewell   (G)   Golden State   Alabama
Latrell has NBA three-point range and can create on offense, which already
makes him one of Nellie's Warriors. He has speed and quickness but will
have to improve his ballhandling to command major minutes on a team as
good as Golden State. We trust Nellie as a judge of talent, but we just can't
see where Latrell will find the playing time to prove Nellie right.
PRICE: 4 because of his coach

Elmore Spencer   (C)   LA Clippers   UNLV
After the trade of Oldin Polynice, Elmore was brought in to be the backup
center (backing up either Charles Smith or someone else if there's another
trade). Elmore will need plenty of time to develop both his offensive and
defensive skills, but he is already a good shot blocker. Look for him to be a
decent backup, especially in years to come.
PRICE: 6

Dave Johnson   (G,F)   Portland   Syracuse
Dave played very well in a predraft camp and was the leading scorer. However, with all the talent Portland already had before they acquired Tracy
Murray and Rod Strickland, this pick struck us as odd. With their front line
aging much more quickly than their guards, shouldn't the Trailblazers have
taken a big man , if only as a project for the future? Oh well, none of this
bodes well for Dave, who shouldn't even get enough playing time to work up
a sweat this season.
PRICE: Don't waste the effort.

Byron Houston   (G,F)   Chicago   Oklahoma State
Byron was the second biggest steal of the draft. At the beginning of the year,
Byron was touted as one of the top ten players in the draft. One bad game in
the NCAA tourney, and a lack of height (6'4"), left Byron for the fortunate
Chicago Bulls. Two things should come to mind concerning Mr. Houston.
First, Charles Barkley is only 6'4" and look what he does. (Not that Byron is
the next Barkley; that's Clarence Weatherspoon's job.) And second, so what
if he's only 6'4"—that just makes the numbers he put up at Oklahoma State
even more impressive. Look for Byron to be a decent backup for both Jordan
and Pippen, and look for him to contribute right away.
PRICE: 13

1992 NBA DRAFT
SECOND-ROUND SELECTIONS

No.	Team	Player	Pos	College
28.	Minnesota	Marlon Maxey	(F)	Texas-El Paso
29.	New Jersey	P.J. Brown	(C)	Louisiana Tech
30.	Dallas	Sean Rooks	(F)	Arizona
31.	Portland	Reggie Smith	(F)	Texas Christian
32.	Washington	Brent Price	(G)	Oklahoma
33.	Chicago	Corey Williams	(G)	Oklahoma State
34.	Minnesota	Chris Smith	(G)	Connecticut
35.	Charlotte	Tony Bennett	(G)	Wisconsin-Green Bay
36.	L.A. Lakers	Duane Cooper	(G)	Southern Cal.
37.	Miami	Isaiah Morris	(F)	Arkansas
38.	Atlanta	Elmer Bennett	(G)	Notre Dame
39.	Chicago	Litterial Green	(G)	Georgia
40.	New Jersey	Steve Rogers	(G)	Alabama State
41.	Houston	Popeye Jones	(F)	Murray State
42.	Miami	Matt Geiger	(C)	Georgia Tech
43.	Golden State	Pedrag Danilovic	(F)	Belgrade
44.	San Antonio	Henry Williams	(G)	N.C.-Charlotte
45.	Seattle	Chris King	(F)	Wake Forest
46.	Denver	Robert Werdann	(C)	St. John's
47.	Boston	Darren Morningstar	(C)	Pittsburgh
48.	Phoenix	Brian Davis	(F)	Duke
49.	Phoenix	Ron Ellis	(F)	Louisiana Tech
50.	Golden State	Matt Fish	(C)	N.C.-Wilmington
51.	Minnesota	Tim Burroughs	(F)	Jacksonville
52.	Chicago	Matt Steigenga	(F)	Michigan State
53.	Houston	Curtis Blair	(G)	Richmond
54.	Sacramento	Brett Roberts	(F)	Morehead State

THE TWENTY-FIVE BEST PLAYERS FOR FANTASY BASKETBALL

This top-25 list was compiled based on how useful (using 1991–92 statistics) each player would have been to a team using the basic seven categories. We did not take previous performances into consideration, and we did not penalize players for missing games because of injury. Finally, we favored the all-around player over the devastating two-category player.

The task of naming the top 25 Fantasy Basketball players may be the most difficult thing we authors must do each year. "Oh sure," you say, "that's easy; there's Dave, Hakeem, Jordan, Pippen, Drexler. . . ." Yes, but where do you place the players on the lower half of the list? Do Coleman and Grant belong on the list, or should Daugherty and Gill be there instead? Or is some combination of the four the most accurate rating? Should we have fun and put Shaquille O'Neal somewhere a year early? We tried turning to technology for the answers, but we didn't like the results our computer gave us. So, when all was said and done, we really just made it up.

1. David Robinson (C) San Antonio
Dave continues his Fantasy MVP reign.

2. Hakeem Olajuwon (C) Houston
Why wasn't Hakeem leading Nigeria to an Olympic Silver Medal?

3. Clyde Drexler (G) Portland
Could this be the year "The Glide" gets his ring?

4. Michael Jordan (G) Chicago
Can Michael deny Clyde his title and Dave his MVP award again this year?

5. Scottie Pippen (F) Chicago
When will Scottie be granted his wish to become a point guard?

6. Larry Bird (F) Boston
Even with limited time, Larry Legend can still produce.

7. Patrick Ewing (C) New York
Giving Patrick a team cost him several places on our list.

8. Pervis Ellison (C) Washington
"Never Nervous" is starting to look like a #1 draft choice.

9. Chris Mullin (F) Golden State
An "off-year" for Mullin and he drops all the way to #9.

10. Charles Barkley (F) Phoenix
Is the land of the Sun the promised land for Sir Charles?

11. Tim Hardaway (G) Golden State
His "SKILLS" keep him moving up our list.

12. Ron Harper (G) LA Clippers
Rated higher than any Cavalier, especially Danny Ferry.

13. Jeff Hornacek (G) **Philadelphia**
Poor Jeff takes his show to Philly.

14. John Stockton (G) **Utah**
Repeat this phrase: "Assists and steals. Assists and steals."

15. Dikembe Mutombo (C) **Denver**
Our Fantasy Rookie of the Year and the only rookie addition to this list.

16. Karl Malone (F) **Utah**
The best truck driver in the NBA.

17. Lionel Simmons (F) **Sacramento**
A consistent sophomore season is rare in sports these days.

18. Dominique Wilkins (F) **Atlanta**
Another good half-season, but can they rebuild him?

19. Kevin Willis (F) **Atlanta**
One of the new rebounding forces in the NBA.

20. Larry Nance (F) **Cleveland**
Will Larry ever slow down?

21. Mitch Richmond (G) **Sacramento**
Eventually Sacramento has to win with all their talent.

22. Chuck Person (F) **Indiana**
Why are the statistical greats always on the trading block?

23. Dan Majerle (F) **Phoenix**
Thunder Dan breaks into the NBA elite.

24. Derrick Coleman (F) **New Jersey**
Can Chuck Daly reform this spoiled brat?

25. Horace Grant (F) **Chicago**
The big difference in the Bulls' "repeat" season.

CHAPTER 3

1991–92 STATISTICAL RESULTS

1991–92 REGULAR-SEASON STATISTICAL RESULTS
NBA PLAYERS ORDERED BY ASSISTS PER GAME

NAME	POS	TEAM	GMs	MINs	MINs per GM	ASTs	ASTs per MIN	ASTs per GM	FG PCT
◄1. STOCKTON, J.	g	UT	82	3002	36.6	1126	0.375	13.7	0.482
◄2. JOHNSON, K.	g	PHX	78	2899	37.2	836	0.288	10.7	0.479
◄3. HARDAWAY, T.	g	GS	81	3332	41.1	807	0.242	10.0	0.461
4. BOGUES, M.	g	CHA	82	2790	34.0	743	0.266	9.1	0.472
5. STRICKLAND, R.	g	SA	57	2053	36.0	491	0.239	8.6	0.455
6. JACKSON, M.	g	NY	81	2461	30.4	694	0.282	8.6	0.491
• 7. RICHARDSON, P.	g	MIN	82	2922	35.6	685	0.234	8.4	0.466
8. WILLIAMS, M.	g	IND	79	2750	34.8	647	0.235	8.2	0.490
• 9. ADAMS, M.	g	WAS	78	2795	35.8	594	0.213	7.6	0.393
◄10. PRICE, M.	g	CLE	72	2138	29.7	535	0.250	7.4	0.488
►11. SKILES, S.	g	ORL	75	2377	31.7	544	0.229	7.3	0.414
•12. THREATT, S.	g	LAL	82	3070	37.4	593	0.193	7.2	0.489
►13. THOMAS, I.	g	DET	78	2918	37.4	560	0.192	7.2	0.446
◄14. WEBB, S.	g	SAC	77	2724	35.4	547	0.201	7.1	0.445
►15. PIPPEN, S.	f	CHI	82	3164	38.6	572	0.181	7.0	0.506
16. SMITH, K.	g	HOU	81	2735	33.8	562	0.206	6.9	0.475
17. DAWKINS, J.	g	PHI	82	2815	34.3	567	0.201	6.9	0.437
18. GRANT, Ga.	g	LAC	78	2049	26.3	538	0.263	6.9	0.462
19. BLAYLOCK, M.	g	NJ	72	2548	35.4	492	0.193	6.8	0.432
• 20. BIRD, L.	f	BOS	45	1662	36.9	306	0.184	6.8	0.466
ι 21. DREXLER, C.	g	POR	76	2751	36.2	512	0.186	6.7	0.470
22. BAGLEY, J.	g	BOS	73	1742	23.9	480	0.276	6.6	0.441
23. HUMPHRIES, J.	g	MIL	71	2261	31.8	466	0.206	6.6	0.470
• 24. PAYTON, G.	g	SEA	81	2549	31.5	506	0.199	6.3	0.451
ι 25. JORDAN, M.	g	CHI	80	3102	38.8	489	0.158	6.1	0.519
ι 26. PORTER, T.	g	POR	82	2784	34.0	477	0.171	5.8	0.462
ι 27. HARPER, D.	g	DAL	65	2252	34.6	373	0.166	5.7	0.443
28. ROBINSON, R.	g	ATL	81	2220	27.4	446	0.201	5.5	0.456
29. ANDERSON, W.	g/f	SA	57	1889	33.1	302	0.160	5.3	0.456
30. BROWN, D.	g	BOS	31	883	28.5	164	0.186	5.3	0.426
31. GARLAND, W.	g	DEN	78	2209	28.3	411	0.186	5.3	0.444
✓ 32. RICHMOND, M.	g	SAC	80	3095	38.7	411	0.133	5.1	0.468
‾ 33. HARPER, R.	g	LAC	82	3144	38.3	417	0.133	5.1	0.440
✓34. HORNACEK, J.	g	PHX	81	3078	38.0	411	0.134	5.1	0.512
35. McMILLAN, N.	g/f	SEA	72	1652	22.9	359	0.217	5.0	0.437
36. PERSON, C.	f	IND	81	2923	36.1	382	0.131	4.7	0.480
37. WORTHY, J.	f	LAL	54	2108	39.0	252	0.120	4.7	0.447
38. DUMARS, J.	g	DET	82	3192	38.9	375	0.118	4.6	0.448
39. SMITH, S.	g	MIA	61	1806	29.6	278	0.154	4.6	0.454
40. COLES, B.	g	MIA	81	1976	24.4	366	0.185	4.5	0.455
41. ROBERTSON, A.	g	MIL	82	2463	30.0	360	0.146	4.4	0.430
42. SIMMONS, L.	f	SAC	78	2895	37.1	337	0.116	4.3	0.454
43. GILL, K.	g/f	CHA	79	2906	36.8	329	0.113	4.2	0.467
44. BARKLEY, C.	f	PHI	75	2881	38.4	308	0.107	4.1	0.552
45. DOUGLAS, S.	g	BOS	42	752	17.9	172	0.229	4.1	0.463
46. MAXWELL, V.	g	HOU	80	2700	33.7	326	0.121	4.1	0.413
47. CHAPMAN, R.	g	WAS	22	567	25.8	89	0.157	4.1	0.448
48. SHAW, B.	g	MIA	63	1423	22.6	250	0.176	4.0	0.407
49. RIVERS, Do.	g	LAC	59	1657	28.1	233	0.141	4.0	0.424
50. SCHREMPF, D.	f	IND	80	2605	32.6	312	0.120	3.9	0.536
51. JOHNSON, A.	g	HOU	69	1235	17.9	266	0.215	3.9	0.479
52. BRANDON, T.	g	CLE	82	1605	19.6	316	0.197	3.9	0.419
53. ANTHONY, G.	g	NY	82	1510	18.4	314	0.208	3.8	0.370
54. MILLER, R.	g	IND	82	3120	38.0	314	0.101	3.8	0.501
55. VINCENT, S.	g	ORL	39	885	22.7	148	0.167	3.8	0.430
56. EHLO, C.	g/f	CLE	63	2016	32.0	238	0.118	3.8	0.453

(NAME)	FT PCT	3-PT SHOTS MADE	3-PT SHOTS TRIED	REBs	STLs	TURN-OVERS	BLKs	PTs
(STOCKTON, J.)	0.842	83	204	270	244	286	22	1297
(JOHNSON, K.)	0.807	10	46	292	116	272	23	1536
(HARDAWAY, T.)	0.766	127	376	310	164	267	13	1893
(BOGUES, M.)	0.783	2	27	235	170	156	6	730
(STRICKLAND, R.)	0.687	5	15	265	118	160	17	787
(JACKSON, M.)	0.770	11	43	305	112	211	13	916
(RICHARDSON, P.)	0.691	53	155	301	119	204	25	1350
(WILLIAMS, M.)	0.871	8	33	282	233	240	22	1188
(ADAMS, M.)	0.869	125	386	310	145	212	9	1408
(PRICE, M.)	0.947	101	261	173	94	159	12	1247
(SKILES, S.)	0.895	91	250	202	74	233	5	1057
(THREATT, S.)	0.831	20	62	253	168	182	16	1240
(THOMAS, I.)	0.773	25	86	247	118	252	15	1445
(WEBB, S.)	0.859	73	199	223	125	229	24	1231
(PIPPEN, S.)	0.760	16	80	630	155	253	93	1720
(SMITH, K.)	0.866	54	137	177	104	227	7	1137
(DAWKINS, J.)	0.882	36	101	227	89	183	5	988
(GRANT, Ga.)	0.815	15	51	184	138	187	14	609
(BLAYLOCK, M.)	0.712	12	54	269	170	152	40	996
(BIRD, L.)	0.926	52	128	434	42	125	33	908
(DREXLER, C.)	0.794	114	338	500	138	240	70	1903
(BAGLEY, J.)	0.716	10	42	161	57	148	4	524
(HUMPHRIES, J.)	0.783	42	144	184	119	148	13	991
(PAYTON, G.)	0.669	3	23	295	147	174	21	764
(JORDAN, M.)	0.832	27	100	511	182	200	75	2404
(PORTER, T.)	0.856	128	324	255	127	188	12	1485
(HARPER, D.)	0.759	58	186	170	101	154	17	1152
(ROBINSON, R.)	0.636	34	104	219	105	206	24	1055
(ANDERSON, W.)	0.775	13	56	300	54	140	51	744
(BROWN, D.)	0.769	5	22	79	33	59	7	363
(GARLAND, W.)	0.859	9	28	190	98	175	22	846
(RICHMOND, M.)	0.813	103	268	319	92	247	34	1803
(HARPER, R.)	0.736	64	211	447	152	252	72	1495
(HORNACEK, J.)	0.886	83	189	407	158	170	31	1632
(McMILLAN, N.)	0.643	27	98	252	129	112	29	435
(PERSON, C.)	0.675	132	354	426	68	216	18	1497
(WORTHY, J.)	0.814	9	43	305	76	127	23	1075
(DUMARS, J.)	0.867	49	120	188	71	193	12	1635
(SMITH, S.)	0.748	40	125	188	59	152	19	729
(COLES, B.)	0.824	10	52	189	73	167	13	816
(ROBERTSON, A.)	0.763	67	210	350	210	223	32	1010
(SIMMONS, L.)	0.770	1	5	634	135	218	132	1336
(GILL, K.)	0.745	6	25	402	154	180	46	1622
(BARKLEY, C.)	0.695	32	137	830	136	235	44	1730
(DOUGLAS, S.)	0.682	1	10	63	25	68	9	308
(MAXWELL, V.)	0.772	162	473	243	104	178	28	1372
(CHAPMAN, R.)	0.679	8	29	58	15	45	8	270
(SHAW, B.)	0.791	5	23	204	57	99	22	495
(RIVERS, Do.)	0.832	26	92	147	111	92	19	641
(SCHREMPF, D.)	0.828	23	71	770	62	191	37	1380
(JOHNSON, A.)	0.654	4	15	80	61	110	9	386
(BRANDON, T.)	0.807	1	23	162	81	136	22	605
(ANTHONY, G.)	0.741	8	55	136	59	98	9	447
(MILLER, R.)	0.858	129	341	318	105	157	26	1695
(VINCENT, S.)	0.846	1	13	101	35	72	4	411
(EHLO, C.)	0.707	69	167	307	78	104	22	776

1991–92 REGULAR-SEASON STATISTICAL RESULTS
NBA PLAYERS ORDERED BY ASSISTS PER GAME

	NAME	POS	TEAM	GMs	MINs	MINs per GM	ASTs	ASTs per MIN	ASTs per GM	FG PCT
57.	WILKINS, D.	f	ATL	42	1601	38.1	158	0.099	3.8	0.464
58.	IUZZOLINO, M.	g	DAL	52	1280	24.6	194	0.152	3.7	0.451
59.	CONNER, L.	g	MIL	81	1420	17.5	294	0.207	3.6	0.431
60.	DAUGHERTY, B.	c	CLE	73	2643	36.2	262	0.099	3.6	0.570
61.	JOHNSON, L.	f	CHA	82	3047	37.2	292	0.096	3.6	0.490
62.	MULLIN, C.	f	GS	81	3346	41.3	286	0.086	3.5	0.524
63.	WEST, D.	g	MIN	80	2540	31.7	281	0.111	3.5	0.518
64.	MANNING, D.	f	LAC	82	2904	35.4	285	0.098	3.5	0.542
65.	LEVER, F.	g	DAL	31	884	28.5	107	0.121	3.5	0.387
66.	WILEY, M.	g	ATL	53	870	16.4	180	0.207	3.4	0.430
67.	MARCIULIONIS, S.	g	GS	72	2117	29.4	243	0.115	3.4	0.538
68.	STARKS, J.	g	NY	82	2118	25.8	276	0.130	3.4	0.449
69.	MAJERLE, D.	g/f	PHX	82	2853	34.8	274	0.096	3.3	0.478
70.	CHEEKS, M.	g	ATL	56	1086	19.4	185	0.170	3.3	0.462
71.	REYNOLDS, J.	g/f	ORL	46	1159	25.2	151	0.130	3.3	0.380
72.	VOLKOV, A.	f	ATL	77	1516	19.7	250	0.165	3.3	0.441
73.	ARMSTRONG, B.J.	g	CHI	82	1875	22.9	266	0.142	3.2	0.481
74.	FLEMING, V.	g	IND	82	1737	21.2	266	0.153	3.2	0.482
75.	GRANT, Gr.	g	PHI	68	891	13.1	217	0.244	3.2	0.440
76.	ANDERSON, K.	g	NJ	64	1086	17.0	203	0.187	3.2	0.390
77.	KERSEY, J.	f	POR	77	2553	33.2	243	0.095	3.2	0.467
78.	COLEMAN, D.	f	NJ	65	2207	34.0	205	0.093	3.2	0.504
79.	BOWIE, D.	g/f	ORL	52	1721	33.1	163	0.095	3.1	0.493
80.	PIERCE, R.	g	SEA	78	2658	34.1	241	0.091	3.1	0.475
81.	PETROVIC, D.	g	NJ	82	3027	36.9	252	0.083	3.1	0.508
82.	HAWKINS, H.	g	PHI	81	3013	37.2	248	0.082	3.1	0.462
83.	PAXSON, J.	g	CHI	79	1946	24.6	241	0.124	3.1	0.528
84.	WINGATE, D.	g	WAS	81	2127	26.3	247	0.116	3.1	0.465
85.	THORPE, O.	f	HOU	82	3056	37.3	250	0.082	3.1	0.592
86.	MALONE, K.	f	UT	81	3054	37.7	241	0.079	3.0	0.526
87.	CAMPBELL, T.	f/g	MIN	78	2441	31.3	229	0.094	2.9	0.464
88.	McCRAY, R.	f	DAL	75	2106	28.1	219	0.104	2.9	0.436
89.	FLOYD, S.	g	HOU	82	1662	20.3	239	0.144	2.9	0.406
90.	WILLIAMS, R.	f	DEN	81	2623	32.4	235	0.090	2.9	0.471
91.	ELLISON, P.	c	WAS	66	2511	38.0	190	0.076	2.9	0.539
92.	NANCE, L.	f	CLE	81	2880	35.6	232	0.081	2.9	0.539
93.	YOUNG, D.	g	LAC	62	1023	16.5	172	0.168	2.8	0.392
94.	WALKER, D.	g	DET	74	1541	20.8	205	0.133	2.8	0.423
95.	CORCHIANI, C.	g	ORL	51	741	14.5	141	0.190	2.8	0.399
96.	SCOTT, B.	g	LAL	82	2679	32.7	226	0.084	2.8	0.458
97.	LONG, G.	f	MIA	82	3063	37.4	225	0.074	2.7	0.494
98.	PRITCHARD, K.	g	BOS	11	136	12.4	30	0.221	2.7	0.471
99.	BLACKMAN, R.	g	DAL	75	2527	33.7	204	0.081	2.7	0.461
100.	ANDERSON, N.	g/f	ORL	60	2203	36.7	163	0.074	2.7	0.463
101.	GRANT, Ho.	f	CHI	81	2859	35.3	217	0.076	2.7	0.579
102.	GAMBLE, K.	g/f	BOS	82	2496	30.4	219	0.088	2.7	0.529
103.	WILKINS, G.	g	NY	82	2344	28.6	219	0.093	2.7	0.447
104.	KNIGHT, N.	g	PHX	42	631	15.0	112	0.178	2.7	0.475
105.	ROBINSON, D.	c	SA	68	2564	37.7	181	0.071	2.7	0.551
106.	GRANT, Ha.	f	WAS	64	2388	37.3	170	0.071	2.7	0.479
107.	NEWMAN, J.	f/g	CHA	55	1651	30.0	146	0.088	2.7	0.477
108.	BOWIE, S.	c	NJ	71	2179	30.7	186	0.085	2.6	0.445
109.	GREEN, R.	g	BOS	26	367	14.1	68	0.185	2.6	0.447
110.	ELLIOTT, S.	f	SA	82	3120	38.0	214	0.069	2.6	0.494
111.	MORRIS, C.	f	NJ	77	2394	31.1	197	0.082	2.6	0.477
112.	PRESSEY, P.	g	SA	56	759	13.6	142	0.187	2.5	0.373

(NAME)	FT PCT	3-PT SHOTS MADE	3-PT SHOTS TRIED	REBs	STLs	TURN-OVERS	BLKs	PTs
(WILKINS, D.)	0.835	37	128	295	52	122	24	1179
(IUZZOLINO, M.)	0.836	59	136	98	33	92	1	486
(CONNER, L.)	0.704	0	7	184	97	79	10	287
(DAUGHERTY, B.)	0.777	0	2	760	65	185	78	1566
(JOHNSON, L.)	0.829	5	22	899	81	160	51	1576
(MULLIN, C.)	0.833	64	175	450	173	202	62	2074
(WEST, D.)	0.805	4	23	257	66	120	26	1116
(MANNING, D.)	0.725	0	5	564	135	210	122	1579
(LEVER, F.)	0.750	17	52	161	46	36	12	347
(WILEY, M.)	0.686	14	42	81	47	60	3	204
(MARCIULIONIS, S.)	0.788	3	10	208	116	193	10	1361
(STARKS, J.)	0.778	94	270	191	103	150	18	1139
(MAJERLE, D.)	0.756	87	228	483	131	101	43	1418
(CHEEKS, M.)	0.605	3	6	95	83	36	0	259
(REYNOLDS, J.)	0.836	3	24	149	63	96	17	555
(VOLKOV, A.)	0.631	35	110	265	66	102	30	662
(ARMSTRONG, B.J.)	0.806	35	87	145	46	94	5	809
(FLEMING, V.)	0.737	6	27	209	56	140	7	726
(GRANT, Gr.)	0.833	7	18	69	45	46	2	225
(ANDERSON, K.)	0.745	3	13	127	67	97	9	450
(KERSEY, J.)	0.664	1	8	633	114	151	71	971
(COLEMAN, D.)	0.763	23	76	618	54	248	98	1289
(BOWIE, D.)	0.860	17	44	245	55	107	38	758
(PIERCE, R.)	0.917	33	123	233	86	189	20	1690
(PETROVIC, D.)	0.808	123	277	258	105	215	11	1691
(HAWKINS, H.)	0.874	91	229	271	157	189	43	1536
(PAXSON, J.)	0.784	12	44	96	49	44	9	555
(WINGATE, D.)	0.719	1	18	269	123	124	21	638
(THORPE, O.)	0.657	0	7	862	52	237	37	1420
(MALONE, K.)	0.778	3	17	909	108	248	51	2272
(CAMPBELL, T.)	0.803	13	37	286	84	165	31	1307
(McCRAY, R.)	0.719	25	85	468	48	115	30	677
(FLOYD, S.)	0.794	37	123	150	57	128	21	744
(WILLIAMS, R.)	0.803	56	156	405	148	173	68	1474
(ELLISON, P.)	0.728	1	3	740	62	196	177	1322
(NANCE, L.)	0.822	0	6	670	80	87	243	1375
(YOUNG, D.)	0.851	23	70	75	46	47	4	280
(WALKER, D.)	0.619	0	10	238	63	79	18	387
(CORCHIANI, C.)	0.875	10	37	78	45	74	2	255
(SCOTT, B.)	0.839	54	157	310	105	119	28	1218
(LONG, G.)	0.807	6	22	691	139	185	40	1212
(PRITCHARD, K.)	0.778	0	3	11	3	11	4	46
(BLACKMAN, R.)	0.899	65	169	239	50	153	22	1374
(ANDERSON, N.)	0.667	30	85	384	97	125	33	1196
(GRANT, Ho.)	0.741	0	2	807	100	98	131	1149
(GAMBLE, K.)	0.885	9	31	286	75	97	37	1108
(WILKINS, G.)	0.730	38	108	206	76	113	17	1016
(KNIGHT, N.)	0.688	4	13	46	24	58	3	243
(ROBINSON, D.)	0.701	1	8	829	158	182	305	1578
(GRANT, Ha.)	0.800	1	8	432	74	109	27	1155
(NEWMAN, J.)	0.766	13	46	179	70	129	14	839
(BOWIE, S.)	0.757	8	25	578	41	150	120	1062
(GREEN, R.)	0.722	1	4	24	17	18	1	106
(ELLIOTT, S.)	0.861	25	82	439	84	152	29	1338
(MORRIS, C.)	0.714	22	110	494	129	171	81	879
(PRESSEY, P.)	0.683	3	21	95	29	64	19	151

1991–92 REGULAR-SEASON STATISTICAL RESULTS
NBA PLAYERS ORDERED BY ASSISTS PER GAME

	NAME	POS	TEAM	GMs	MINs	MINs per GM	ASTs	ASTs per MIN	ASTs per GM	FG PCT
113.	TURNER, A.	g	WAS	70	871	12.4	177	0.203	2.5	0.425
114.	BROOKS, S.	g	MIN	82	1082	13.2	205	0.190	2.5	0.447
115.	AINGE, D.	g	POR	81	1595	19.7	202	0.127	2.5	0.442
116.	AUGMON, S.	g/f	ATL	82	2505	30.5	201	0.080	2.5	0.489
117.	GARRICK, T.	g	DAL	40	549	13.7	98	0.179	2.5	0.413
118.	WILLIAMS, J.	f/c	CLE	80	2432	30.4	196	0.081	2.5	0.503
119.	JOHNSON, V.	g	SA	60	1350	22.5	145	0.107	2.4	0.405
120.	JACKSON, C.	g	DEN	81	1538	19.0	192	0.125	2.4	0.421
121.	ASKEW, V.	g	GS	80	1496	18.7	188	0.126	2.4	0.509
122.	OWENS, B.	g/f	GS	80	2510	31.4	188	0.075	2.4	0.525
123.	GLASS, G.	g	MIN	75	1822	24.3	175	0.096	2.3	0.440
124.	RODMAN, D.	f	DET	82	3301	40.3	191	0.058	2.3	0.539
125.	RICE, G.	f	MIA	79	3007	38.1	184	0.061	2.3	0.469
126.	GEORGE, T.	g	NJ	70	1037	14.8	162	0.156	2.3	0.428
127.	McKEY, D.	f	SEA	52	1757	33.8	120	0.068	2.3	0.472
128.	LES, J.	g	SAC	62	712	11.5	143	0.201	2.3	0.385
129.	CURRY, D.	g	CHA	77	2020	26.2	177	0.088	2.3	0.486
130.	KERR, S.	g	CLE	48	847	17.6	110	0.130	2.3	0.511
131.	McCLOUD, G.	g	IND	51	892	17.5	116	0.130	2.3	0.409
132.	LEWIS, Re.	g	BOS	82	3070	37.4	185	0.060	2.3	0.503
133.	GRAHAM, P.	g	ATL	78	1718	22.0	175	0.102	2.2	0.447
134.	OLAJUWON, H.	c	HOU	70	2636	37.7	157	0.060	2.2	0.502
135.	PERKINS, S.	f/c	LAL	63	2332	37.0	141	0.061	2.2	0.450
136.	MALONE, J.	g	UT	81	2922	36.1	180	0.062	2.2	0.511
137.	MACON, M.	g	DEN	76	2304	30.3	168	0.073	2.2	0.375
138.	ELIE, M.	g/f	GS	79	1677	21.2	174	0.104	2.2	0.521
139.	MUTOMBO, D.	c	DEN	71	2716	38.3	156	0.057	2.2	0.493
140.	WILLIS, K.	f/c	ATL	81	2962	36.6	173	0.058	2.1	0.483
141.	EDWARDS, K.	g	MIA	81	1840	22.7	170	0.092	2.1	0.454
142.	BATTLE, J.	g	CLE	76	1637	21.5	159	0.097	2.1	0.480
143.	SMITH, La.	g	WAS	48	708	14.7	99	0.140	2.1	0.407
144.	CHAMBERS, T.	f	PHX	69	1948	28.2	142	0.073	2.1	0.431
145.	DAVIS, B.	f	DAL	33	429	13.0	66	0.154	2.0	0.442
146.	JOHNSON, E.	f	SEA	81	2366	29.2	161	0.068	2.0	0.459
147.	LAIMBEER, B.	c	DET	81	2234	27.6	160	0.072	2.0	0.470
148.	JOHNSON, B.	f	HOU	80	2202	27.5	158	0.072	2.0	0.458
149.	PACK, R.	g	POR	72	894	12.4	140	0.157	1.9	0.423
150.	SCOTT, D.	f	ORL	18	608	33.8	35	0.058	1.9	0.402
151.	EACKLES, L.	f	WAS	65	1463	22.5	125	0.085	1.9	0.468
152.	BURTT, S.	g	PHX	31	356	11.5	59	0.166	1.9	0.463
153.	EWING, P.	c	NY	82	3150	38.4	156	0.050	1.9	0.522
154.	BRICKOWSKI, F.	f	MIL	65	1556	23.9	122	0.078	1.9	0.524
155.	MURDOCK, E.	g	UT	50	478	9.6	92	0.193	1.8	0.415
156.	GRAYER, J.	g	MIL	82	1659	20.2	150	0.090	1.8	0.449
157.	McDANIEL, X.	f	NY	82	2344	28.6	149	0.064	1.8	0.478
158.	BURTON, W.	g/f	MIA	68	1585	23.3	123	0.078	1.8	0.450
159.	SPARROW, R.	g	LAL	46	489	10.6	83	0.170	1.8	0.384
160.	ENGLISH, A.J.	g	WAS	81	1665	20.6	143	0.086	1.8	0.433
161.	CORBIN, T.	f	UT	80	2207	27.6	140	0.063	1.8	0.481
162.	SMITH, To.	g	LAL	63	820	13.0	109	0.133	1.7	0.399
163.	KONCAK, J.	c	ATL	77	1489	19.3	132	0.089	1.7	0.391
164.	SANDERS, M.	f	CLE	31	633	20.4	53	0.084	1.7	0.571
165.	SMITH, Do.	f	DAL	76	1707	22.5	129	0.076	1.7	0.415
166.	EDWARDS, T.	g/f	UT	81	2283	28.2	137	0.060	1.7	0.522
167.	AGUIRRE, M.	f	DET	75	1582	21.1	126	0.080	1.7	0.431
168.	RUDD, D.	g	UT	65	538	8.3	109	0.203	1.7	0.399

(NAME)	FT PCT	3-PT SHOTS MADE	3-PT SHOTS TRIED	REBs	STLs	TURN-OVERS	BLKs	PTs
(TURNER, A.)	0.792	1	16	90	57	84	2	284
(BROOKS, S.)	0.810	32	90	99	66	51	7	417
(AINGE, D.)	0.824	78	230	148	73	70	13	784
(AUGMON, S.)	0.666	1	6	420	124	181	27	1094
(GARRICK, T.)	0.692	1	4	56	36	44	4	137
(WILLIAMS, J.)	0.752	0	4	607	60	83	182	952
(JOHNSON, V.)	0.647	19	60	182	41	74	14	478
(JACKSON, C.)	0.870	31	94	114	44	117	4	837
(ASKEW, V.)	0.694	1	10	233	47	84	23	498
(OWENS, B.)	0.654	1	9	639	90	179	65	1141
(GLASS, G.)	0.616	16	54	260	66	103	30	859
(RODMAN, D.)	0.600	32	101	1530	68	140	70	800
(RICE, G.)	0.837	155	396	394	90	145	35	1765
(GEORGE, T.)	0.821	1	6	105	41	82	3	418
(McKEY, D.)	0.847	19	50	268	61	114	47	777
(LES, J.)	0.809	45	131	63	31	42	3	231
(CURRY, D.)	0.836	74	183	259	93	134	20	1209
(KERR, S.)	0.833	32	74	78	27	31	10	319
(McCLOUD, G.)	0.781	32	94	132	26	62	11	338
(LEWIS, Re.)	0.851	5	21	394	125	136	105	1703
(GRAHAM, P.)	0.741	55	141	231	96	91	21	791
(OLAJUWON, H.)	0.766	0	1	845	127	187	304	1510
(PERKINS, S.)	0.817	15	69	556	64	83	62	1041
(MALONE, J.)	0.898	1	12	233	56	140	5	1639
(MACON, M.)	0.730	4	30	220	154	155	14	805
(ELIE, M.)	0.852	23	70	227	68	83	15	620
(MUTOMBO, D.)	0.642	0	0	870	43	252	210	1177
(WILLIS, K.)	0.804	6	37	1258	72	197	54	1480
(EDWARDS, K.)	0.848	7	32	211	99	120	20	819
(BATTLE, J.)	0.848	2	17	112	36	91	5	779
(SMITH, La.)	0.804	2	21	81	44	63	1	247
(CHAMBERS, T.)	0.830	18	49	401	57	103	37	1128
(DAVIS, B.)	0.733	5	18	33	11	27	3	92
(JOHNSON, E.)	0.861	27	107	292	55	130	11	1386
(LAIMBEER, B.)	0.893	32	85	451	51	102	54	783
(JOHNSON, B.)	0.727	1	9	312	72	104	49	685
(PACK, R.)	0.803	0	10	97	40	92	4	332
(SCOTT, D.)	0.901	29	89	66	20	31	9	359
(EACKLES, L.)	0.743	7	35	178	47	75	7	856
(BURTT, S.)	0.704	1	6	34	16	33	4	187
(EWING, P.)	0.738	1	6	921	88	209	245	1970
(BRICKOWSKI, F.)	0.767	3	6	344	60	112	23	740
(MURDOCK, E.)	0.754	5	26	54	30	50	7	203
(GRAYER, J.)	0.667	19	66	257	64	105	13	739
(McDANIEL, X.)	0.714	12	39	460	57	147	24	1125
(BURTON, W.)	0.800	6	15	244	46	119	37	762
(SPARROW, R.)	0.615	3	15	28	12	33	5	127
(ENGLISH, A.J.)	0.841	6	34	168	32	89	9	886
(CORBIN, T.)	0.866	0	4	472	82	97	20	780
(SMITH, To.)	0.653	0	11	76	39	50	8	275
(KONCAK, J.)	0.655	0	12	261	50	54	67	241
(SANDERS, M.)	0.766	1	3	96	24	22	10	221
(SMITH, Do.)	0.736	0	11	391	62	97	34	671
(EDWARDS, T.)	0.774	39	103	298	81	122	46	1018
(AGUIRRE, M.)	0.687	15	71	236	51	105	11	851
(RUDD, D.)	0.762	11	47	54	15	49	1	193

1991–92 REGULAR-SEASON STATISTICAL RESULTS
NBA PLAYERS ORDERED BY ASSISTS PER GAME

	NAME	POS	TEAM	GMs	MINs	MINs per GM	ASTs	ASTs per MIN	ASTs per GM	FG PCT
169.	PERRY, T.	f	PHX	80	2483	31.0	134	0.054	1.7	0.523
170.	ROBINSON, C.	f	POR	82	2124	25.9	137	0.065	1.7	0.466
171.	BARROS, D.	g	SEA	75	1331	17.7	125	0.094	1.7	0.483
172.	DIVAC, V.	c	LAL	36	979	27.2	60	0.061	1.7	0.495
173.	ANDERSON, Ro.	f	PHI	82	2432	29.7	135	0.056	1.7	0.465
174.	HENSON, S.	g	MIL	50	386	7.7	82	0.212	1.6	0.361
175.	NORMAN, K.	f	LAC	77	2009	26.1	125	0.062	1.6	0.490
176.	OAKLEY, C.	f	NY	82	2309	28.2	133	0.058	1.6	0.522
177.	SALLEY, J.	f/c	DET	72	1774	24.6	116	0.065	1.6	0.512
178.	GATTISON, K.	f/c	CHA	82	2223	27.1	131	0.059	1.6	0.529
179.	REID, J.R.	c/f	CHA	51	1257	24.6	81	0.064	1.6	0.490
180.	BONNER, A.	f	SAC	79	2287	28.9	125	0.055	1.6	0.447
181.	STEWART, L.	f	WAS	76	2229	29.3	120	0.054	1.6	0.514
182.	SMITS, R.	c	IND	74	1772	23.9	116	0.066	1.6	0.510
183.	PERRY, E.	g	CHA	50	437	8.7	78	0.179	1.6	0.380
184.	FOX, R.	g/f	BOS	81	1535	19.0	126	0.082	1.6	0.459
185.	ROBERTS, F.	f	MIL	80	1746	21.8	122	0.070	1.5	0.482
186.	LYNCH, K.	g	CHA	55	819	14.9	83	0.101	1.5	0.417
187.	DAVIS, W.	g	DEN	46	741	16.1	68	0.092	1.5	0.459
188.	WHATLEY, E.	g	POR	23	209	9.1	34	0.163	1.5	0.412
189.	TISDALE, W.	f	SAC	72	2521	35.0	106	0.042	1.5	0.501
190.	McHALE, K.	f/c	BOS	56	1398	25.0	82	0.059	1.5	0.510
191.	MAYES, Th.	g	LAC	24	255	10.6	35	0.137	1.5	0.303
192.	CUMMINGS, T.	f	SA	70	2149	30.7	102	0.048	1.5	0.488
193.	GILLIAM, A.	f/c	PHI	81	2771	34.2	118	0.043	1.5	0.512
194.	KRYSTKOWIAK, L.	f	MIL	79	1848	23.4	114	0.062	1.4	0.444
195.	HOPSON, D.	g/f	SAC	71	1314	18.5	102	0.078	1.4	0.465
196.	GREEN, A.C.	f	LAL	82	2902	35.4	117	0.040	1.4	0.476
197.	RIVERS, Da.	g	LAC	15	122	8.1	21	0.172	1.4	0.333
198.	CATLEDGE, T.	f	ORL	78	2430	31.2	109	0.045	1.4	0.496
199.	FERRELL, D.	f	ATL	66	1598	24.2	92	0.058	1.4	0.524
200.	SEIKALY, R.	c	MIA	79	2800	35.4	109	0.039	1.4	0.489
201.	TEAGLE, T.	f	LAL	82	1602	19.5	113	0.071	1.4	0.452
202.	CARTWRIGHT, B.	c	CHI	64	1471	23.0	87	0.059	1.4	0.467
203.	SUTTON, S.	g	SA	67	601	9.0	91	0.151	1.4	0.388
204.	WILLIAMS, Bu.	f	POR	80	2519	31.5	108	0.043	1.4	0.604
205.	KEMP, S.	f/c	SEA	64	1808	28.2	86	0.048	1.3	0.504
206.	BREUER, R.	c	MIN	67	1176	17.6	89	0.076	1.3	0.468
207.	RAMBIS, K.	f	PHX	28	381	13.6	37	0.097	1.3	0.463
208.	RASMUSSEN, B.	c	ATL	81	1968	24.3	107	0.054	1.3	0.478
209.	MASON, A.	f	NY	82	2198	26.8	106	0.048	1.3	0.509
210.	ELLIS, D.	f	MIL	81	2191	27.0	104	0.048	1.3	0.469
211.	MORTON, J.	g	MIA	25	270	10.8	32	0.119	1.3	0.387
212.	THOMPSON, L.	f/c	IND	80	1299	16.2	102	0.079	1.3	0.468
213.	WILLIAMS, H.	f/c	DAL	75	2040	27.2	94	0.046	1.3	0.431
214.	TURNER, J.	f	ORL	75	1591	21.2	92	0.058	1.2	0.451
215.	LANE, J.	f	MIL	14	177	12.6	17	0.096	1.2	0.304
216.	DUCKWORTH, K.	c	POR	82	2222	27.1	99	0.045	1.2	0.461
217.	BENJAMIN, B.	c	SEA	63	1941	30.8	76	0.039	1.2	0.478
218.	KOFOED, B.	g	SEA	44	239	5.4	51	0.213	1.2	0.472
219.	MITCHELL, S.	f	MIN	82	2151	26.2	94	0.044	1.2	0.423
220.	MOORE, T.	f	DAL	42	782	18.6	48	0.061	1.1	0.400
221.	SMITH, C.	f/c	LAC	49	1310	26.7	56	0.043	1.1	0.466
222.	MALONE, M.	c	MIL	82	2511	30.6	93	0.037	1.1	0.474
223.	TUCKER, T.	g	SA	24	415	17.3	27	0.065	1.1	0.465
224.	CAGE, M.	f	SEA	82	2461	30.0	92	0.037	1.1	0.566

(NAME)	FT PCT	3-PT SHOTS MADE	3-PT SHOTS TRIED	REBs	STLs	TURN-OVERS	BLKs	PTs
(PERRY, T.)	0.712	3	8	551	44	141	116	982
(ROBINSON, C.)	0.664	1	11	416	85	154	107	1016
(BARROS, D.)	0.760	83	186	81	51	56	4	619
(DIVAC, V.)	0.768	5	19	247	55	88	35	405
(ANDERSON, Ro.)	0.877	42	127	278	86	109	11	1123
(HENSON, S.)	0.793	23	48	41	15	40	1	150
(NORMAN, K.)	0.535	4	28	448	53	100	66	929
(OAKLEY, C.)	0.735	0	3	700	67	123	15	506
(SALLEY, J.)	0.715	0	3	296	49	102	110	684
(GATTISON, K.)	0.688	0	2	580	59	140	69	1042
(REID, J.R.)	0.705	0	3	317	49	84	23	560
(BONNER, A.)	0.627	1	4	485	94	133	26	740
(STEWART, L.)	0.807	0	3	449	51	112	44	794
(SMITS, R.)	0.788	0	2	417	29	130	100	1024
(PERRY, E.)	0.659	1	7	39	34	50	3	126
(FOX, R.)	0.755	23	70	220	78	123	30	644
(ROBERTS, F.)	0.749	19	37	257	52	122	40	769
(LYNCH, K.)	0.761	3	8	85	37	44	9	224
(DAVIS, W.)	0.872	5	16	70	29	45	1	457
(WHATLEY, E.)	0.871	0	4	21	14	14	3	69
(TISDALE, W.)	0.763	0	2	469	55	124	79	1195
(McHALE, K.)	0.822	0	13	330	11	82	59	780
(MAYES, Th.)	0.667	15	41	16	16	31	2	99
(CUMMINGS, T.)	0.711	5	13	631	58	115	34	1210
(GILLIAM, A.)	0.807	0	2	660	51	166	85	1367
(KRYSTKOWIAK, L.)	0.757	0	5	429	54	115	12	714
(HOPSON, D.)	0.708	12	47	206	67	100	39	743
(GREEN, A.C.)	0.744	12	56	762	91	111	36	1116
(RIVERS, Da.)	0.909	0	1	19	7	17	1	30
(CATLEDGE, T.)	0.694	0	4	549	58	138	16	1154
(FERRELL, D.)	0.762	11	33	210	49	99	17	839
(SEIKALY, R.)	0.733	0	3	934	40	216	121	1296
(TEAGLE, T.)	0.767	1	4	183	66	114	9	880
(CARTWRIGHT, B.)	0.604	0	0	324	22	75	14	512
(SUTTON, S.)	0.756	26	89	47	26	70	9	246
(WILLIAMS, Bu.)	0.754	0	1	704	62	130	41	901
(KEMP, S.)	0.748	0	3	665	70	156	124	994
(BREUER, R.)	0.533	0	1	281	27	41	99	363
(RAMBIS, K.)	0.778	0	0	106	12	25	14	90
(RASMUSSEN, B.)	0.750	5	23	393	35	51	48	729
(MASON, A.)	0.642	0	0	573	46	101	20	573
(ELLIS, D.)	0.774	138	329	253	57	119	18	1272
(MORTON, J.)	0.842	2	16	26	13	28	1	106
(THOMPSON, L.)	0.817	0	2	381	52	98	34	394
(WILLIAMS, H.)	0.725	1	6	454	35	114	98	859
(TURNER, J.)	0.693	1	8	246	24	106	16	530
(LANE, J.)	0.333	0	0	66	2	14	1	37
(DUCKWORTH, K.)	0.690	0	3	497	38	143	37	880
(BENJAMIN, B.)	0.687	0	2	513	39	175	118	879
(KOFOED, B.)	0.577	1	7	26	2	20	2	66
(MITCHELL, S.)	0.786	2	11	473	53	97	39	825
(MOORE, T.)	0.833	30	84	82	32	44	4	355
(SMITH, C.)	0.785	0	6	301	41	69	98	714
(MALONE, M.)	0.786	3	8	744	74	150	64	1279
(TUCKER, T.)	0.800	19	48	37	21	14	3	155
(CAGE, M.)	0.620	0	5	728	99	78	55	720

	NAME	POS	TEAM	GMs	MINs	MINs per GM	ASTs	ASTs per MIN	ASTs per GM	FG PCT
225.	FERRY, D.	f	CLE	68	937	13.8	75	0.080	1.1	0.409
226.	LICHTI, T.	g	DEN	68	1176	17.3	74	0.063	1.1	0.460
227.	HIGGINS, S.	f	ORL	38	616	16.2	41	0.067	1.1	0.459
228.	FREDERICK, A.	f	CHA	66	852	12.9	71	0.083	1.1	0.435
229.	WOOLRIDGE, O.	f	DET	82	2113	25.8	88	0.042	1.1	0.498
230.	LOHAUS, B.	f/c	MIL	70	1081	15.4	74	0.069	1.1	0.450
231.	BROWN, R.	g	SAC	56	535	9.6	59	0.110	1.1	0.456
232.	PERDUE, W.	c	CHI	77	1007	13.1	80	0.079	1.0	0.547
233.	SMITH, O.	g	ORL	55	877	15.9	57	0.065	1.0	0.365
234.	MILLS, T.	f	NJ	82	1714	20.9	84	0.049	1.0	0.463
235.	HANSEN, B.	g	CHI	68	809	11.9	69	0.085	1.0	0.444
236.	BROWN, M.	c/f	UT	82	1783	21.7	81	0.045	1.0	0.453
237.	KING, S.	f/c	CHI	79	1268	16.1	77	0.061	1.0	0.506
238.	HAMMONDS, T.	f	CHA	37	984	26.6	36	0.037	1.0	0.488
239.	HODGES, C.	g	CHI	56	555	9.9	54	0.097	1.0	0.384
240.	ANDERSON, G.	f	DEN	82	2793	34.1	78	0.028	1.0	0.456
241.	BULLARD, M.	f	HOU	80	1278	16.0	75	0.059	0.9	0.459
242.	BAILEY, T.	f	MIN	84	2104	25.0	78	0.037	0.9	0.440
243.	WOLF, J.	f	DEN	67	1160	17.3	61	0.053	0.9	0.361
244.	VAUGHT, L.	f	LAC	79	1687	21.4	71	0.042	0.9	0.492
245.	ADDISON, R.	g	NJ	76	1175	15.5	68	0.058	0.9	0.433
246.	PARISH, R.	c	BOS	79	2285	28.9	70	0.031	0.9	0.536
247.	GMINSKI, M.	c	CHA	35	499	14.3	31	0.062	0.9	0.452
248.	HIGGINS, R.	f	GS	25	535	21.4	22	0.041	0.9	0.412
249.	SPENCER, F.	c	MIN	61	1481	24.3	53	0.036	0.9	0.426
250.	MUSTAF, J.	f	PHX	52	545	10.5	45	0.083	0.9	0.477
251.	VANDEWEGHE, K.	f	NY	67	956	14.3	57	0.060	0.9	0.491
252.	BROWN, T.	f	SEA	57	655	11.5	48	0.073	0.8	0.410
253.	DAVIS, T.	f/c	DAL	68	2149	31.6	57	0.027	0.8	0.482
254.	LEVINGSTON, C.	f	CHI	79	1020	12.9	66	0.065	0.8	0.498
255.	JONES, Ch.	c/f	WAS	75	1365	18.2	62	0.045	0.8	0.367
256.	BUECHLER, J.	f	GS	28	290	10.4	23	0.079	0.8	0.409
257.	LONGLEY, L.	c	MIN	66	991	15.0	53	0.054	0.8	0.458
258.	FRANK, T.	f	MIN	10	140	14.0	8	0.057	0.8	0.546
259.	WILLIAMS, S.	f	CHI	63	690	11.0	50	0.073	0.8	0.483
260.	SCHAYES, D.	c	MIL	43	726	16.9	34	0.047	0.8	0.417
261.	CEBALLOS, C.	f	PHX	64	725	11.3	50	0.069	0.8	0.482
262.	CARR, A.	f/c	SA	81	1867	23.0	63	0.034	0.8	0.490
263.	LIBERTY, M.	f/g	DEN	75	1527	20.4	58	0.038	0.8	0.443
264.	PINCKNEY, E.	f	BOS	81	1917	23.7	62	0.032	0.8	0.537
265.	HODGE, D.	c/f	DAL	51	1058	20.7	39	0.037	0.8	0.497
266.	SANDERS, J.	f	ATL	12	117	9.8	9	0.077	0.8	0.444
267.	OLIVER, J.	g/f	CLE	27	252	9.3	20	0.079	0.7	0.398
268.	CAUSWELL, D.	c	SAC	80	2291	28.6	59	0.026	0.7	0.550
269.	EDWARDS, Ja.	c	LAC	72	1437	20.0	53	0.037	0.7	0.465
270.	SMITH, L.	f/c	HOU	45	800	17.8	33	0.041	0.7	0.544
271.	BRYANT, M.	c	POR	56	800	14.3	41	0.051	0.7	0.480
272.	CAMPBELL, E.	c	LAL	81	1876	23.2	59	0.032	0.7	0.448
273.	FOSTER, G.	f	WAS	49	548	11.2	35	0.064	0.7	0.461
274.	NEALY, E.	f	PHX	52	505	9.7	37	0.073	0.7	0.512
275.	MONROE, R.	g	ATL	38	313	8.2	27	0.086	0.7	0.368
276.	ROBERTS, S.	c	ORL	55	1118	20.3	39	0.035	0.7	0.529
277.	DUDLEY, C.	c	NJ	82	1902	23.2	58	0.031	0.7	0.403
278.	BENNETT, W.	f	MIA	54	833	15.4	38	0.046	0.7	0.379
279.	JAMERSON, D.	f	HOU	48	378	7.9	33	0.087	0.7	0.414
280.	WILLIAMS, Br.	f	ORL	48	905	18.9	33	0.037	0.7	0.528

(NAME)	FT PCT	3-PT SHOTS MADE	3-PT SHOTS TRIED	REBs	STLs	TURN-OVERS	BLKs	PTs
(FERRY, D.)	0.836	17	48	213	22	46	15	346
(LICHTI, T.)	0.839	1	9	118	43	72	12	446
(HIGGINS, S.)	0.861	6	25	102	16	41	6	291
(FREDERICK, A.)	0.685	4	17	144	40	58	26	389
(WOOLRIDGE, O.)	0.683	1	9	260	41	133	33	1146
(LOHAUS, B.)	0.659	57	144	249	40	46	71	408
(BROWN, R.)	0.655	0	6	69	35	42	12	192
(PERDUE, W.)	0.495	1	2	312	16	72	43	350
(SMITH, O.)	0.769	8	21	116	36	62	13	310
(MILLS, T.)	0.750	8	23	453	48	82	41	742
(HANSEN, B.)	0.364	7	27	77	27	28	3	173
(BROWN, M.)	0.667	0	1	476	42	105	34	632
(KING, S.)	0.753	2	5	205	21	76	25	551
(HAMMONDS, T.)	0.610	0	1	185	22	58	13	440
(HODGES, C.)	0.941	36	96	24	14	22	1	238
(ANDERSON, G.)	0.623	0	4	941	88	201	65	945
(BULLARD, M.)	0.760	64	166	223	26	56	21	512
(BAILEY, T.)	0.796	0	2	485	35	108	117	951
(WOLF, J.)	0.803	1	11	240	32	60	14	254
(VAUGHT, L.)	0.797	4	5	512	37	66	31	601
(ADDISON, R.)	0.737	14	49	165	28	46	28	444
(PARISH, R.)	0.772	0	0	705	68	131	97	1115
(GMINSKI, M.)	0.750	1	3	118	11	20	16	202
(HIGGINS, R.)	0.814	33	95	85	15	15	13	255
(SPENCER, F.)	0.691	0	0	435	27	70	79	405
(MUSTAF, J.)	0.690	0	0	145	21	51	16	233
(VANDEWEGHE, K.)	0.803	26	66	88	15	27	8	467
(BROWN, T.)	0.727	19	63	84	30	35	5	271
(DAVIS, T.)	0.635	0	5	672	26	117	29	693
(LEVINGSTON, C.)	0.625	1	6	227	27	42	45	311
(JONES, Ch.)	0.500	0	0	317	43	39	92	86
(BUECHLER, J.)	0.571	0	1	52	19	13	7	70
(LONGLEY, L.)	0.663	0	0	257	35	83	64	281
(FRANK, T.)	0.667	0	0	26	5	5	4	46
(WILLIAMS, S.)	0.649	0	3	247	13	35	36	214
(SCHAYES, D.)	0.771	0	0	168	19	41	19	240
(CEBALLOS, C.)	0.737	1	6	152	16	71	11	462
(CARR, A.)	0.764	1	5	346	32	114	96	881
(LIBERTY, M.)	0.728	17	50	308	66	90	29	698
(PINCKNEY, E.)	0.812	0	1	564	70	73	56	613
(HODGE, D.)	0.667	0	0	275	25	75	23	426
(SANDERS, J.)	0.778	0	0	26	5	5	3	47
(OLIVER, J.)	0.773	1	9	27	9	9	2	96
(CAUSWELL, D.)	0.613	0	1	580	47	124	215	636
(EDWARDS, Ja.)	0.731	0	1	202	24	72	33	698
(SMITH, L.)	0.364	0	1	256	21	44	7	104
(BRYANT, M.)	0.667	0	3	201	26	30	8	230
(CAMPBELL, E.)	0.619	0	2	423	53	73	159	578
(FOSTER, G.)	0.714	0	1	145	6	36	12	213
(NEALY, E.)	0.667	20	50	111	16	17	2	160
(MONROE, R.)	0.826	6	27	33	12	23	2	131
(ROBERTS, S.)	0.515	0	1	336	22	78	83	573
(DUDLEY, C.)	0.468	0	0	739	38	79	179	460
(BENNETT, W.)	0.700	0	1	162	19	33	9	195
(JAMERSON, D.)	0.926	8	28	43	17	24	0	191
(WILLIAMS, Br.)	0.669	0	0	272	41	86	53	437

	NAME	POS	TEAM	GMs	MINs	MINs per GM	ASTs	ASTs per MIN	ASTs per GM	FG PCT
281.	WILLIAMS, K	f	IND	60	565	9.4	40	0.071	0.7	0.518
282.	HASTINGS, S.	f	DEN	40	421	10.5	26	0.062	0.7	0.340
283.	ASKINS, K	g/f	MIA	59	843	14.3	38	0.045	0.6	0.410
284.	SHACKLEFORD, C.	c	PHI	72	1399	19.4	46	0.033	0.6	0.486
285.	GREEN, Se.	g	IND	35	256	7.3	22	0.086	0.6	0.392
286.	HERRERA, C.	f	HOU	43	566	13.2	27	0.048	0.6	0.516
287.	HENDERSON, G.	g	DET	16	96	6.0	10	0.104	0.6	0.375
288.	BROWN, C.	f	LAL	42	431	10.3	26	0.060	0.6	0.469
289.	KITE, G.	c	ORL	72	1479	20.5	44	0.030	0.6	0.437
290.	RANDALL, M.	f	MIN	54	441	8.2	33	0.075	0.6	0.456
291.	SCHINTZIUS, D.	c	SAC	33	400	12.1	20	0.050	0.6	0.427
292.	POLYNICE, O.	c	LAC	76	1834	24.1	46	0.025	0.6	0.519
293.	COOPER, W.	f	POR	35	344	9.8	21	0.061	0.6	0.427
294.	TOLBERT, T.	f	GS	35	310	8.9	21	0.068	0.6	0.384
295.	THOMAS, C.	g	DET	37	156	4.2	22	0.141	0.6	0.353
296.	OLIVER, B.	g	PHI	34	279	8.2	20	0.072	0.6	0.330
297.	HILL, T.	c/f	GS	82	1886	23.0	47	0.025	0.6	0.522
298.	DONALDSON, J.	c	NY	58	1075	18.5	33	0.031	0.6	0.457
299.	ROYAL, D.	f	SA	60	718	12.0	34	0.047	0.6	0.449
300.	CHILCUTT, P.	f/c	SAC	69	817	11.8	38	0.047	0.6	0.452
301.	LISTER, A.	c	GS	26	293	11.3	14	0.048	0.5	0.557
302.	LANG, A.	c	PHX	81	1965	24.3	43	0.022	0.5	0.522
303.	LECKNER, E.	c	CHA	59	716	12.1	31	0.043	0.5	0.513
304.	HOWARD, B.	f	DAL	27	318	11.8	14	0.044	0.5	0.519
305.	KIMBLE, B.	f	LAC	34	277	8.2	17	0.061	0.5	0.396
306.	MAYS, T.	g	ATL	2	32	16.0	1	0.031	0.5	0.429
307.	EATON, M.	c	UT	81	2023	25.0	40	0.020	0.5	0.446
308.	LEE, D.	g	NJ	46	307	6.7	22	0.072	0.5	0.431
309.	WHITE, R.	f	DAL	65	1021	15.7	31	0.030	0.5	0.380
310.	DAVIS, D.	f	IND	64	1301	20.3	30	0.023	0.5	0.552
311.	WITTMAN, R.	g	IND	24	115	4.8	11	0.096	0.5	0.421
312.	KLEINE, J.	c	BOS	70	991	14.2	32	0.032	0.5	0.492
313.	GREEN, S.	f	SA	80	1127	14.1	36	0.032	0.5	0.427
314.	WIGGINS, M.	g	PHI	49	569	11.6	22	0.039	0.5	0.384
315.	BLANKS, L.	g	DET	43	189	4.4	19	0.101	0.4	0.455
316.	BENOIT, D.	f	UT	77	1161	15.1	34	0.029	0.4	0.467
317.	KESSLER, A.	c	MIA	77	1197	15.5	34	0.028	0.4	0.413
318.	ABDELNABY, A.	f/c	POR	71	934	13.2	30	0.032	0.4	0.493
319.	THOMPSON, S.	g	SAC	19	91	4.8	8	0.088	0.4	0.378
320.	WINCHESTER, K.	f	NY	19	81	4.3	8	0.099	0.4	0.433
321.	DREILING, G.	c	IND	60	509	8.5	25	0.049	0.4	0.494
322.	McCORMICK, T.	c	NY	22	108	4.9	9	0.083	0.4	0.424
323.	ALEXANDER, V.	c	GS	80	1350	16.9	32	0.024	0.4	0.529
324.	PHILLS, B.	g	CLE	10	65	6.5	4	0.062	0.4	0.429
325.	SAMPSON, R.	c	WAS	10	108	10.8	4	0.037	0.4	0.310
326.	JAMES, H.	f	CLE	65	866	13.3	25	0.029	0.4	0.407
327.	RULAND, J.	c	PHI	13	209	16.1	5	0.024	0.4	0.526
328.	BEDFORD, W.	f/c	DET	32	363	11.3	12	0.033	0.4	0.413
329.	DAILEY, Q.	f	SEA	11	98	8.9	4	0.041	0.4	0.243
330.	PAYNE, K	f	PHI	49	353	7.2	17	0.048	0.4	0.448
331.	CROWDER, C.	g/f	UT	51	328	6.4	17	0.052	0.3	0.384
332.	PETERSEN, J.	c	GS	27	169	6.3	9	0.053	0.3	0.450
333.	SELLERS, B.	f/c	DET	43	226	5.3	14	0.062	0.3	0.466
334.	ACRES, M.	c	ORL	68	926	13.6	22	0.024	0.3	0.517
335.	BOL, M.	c	PHI	71	1267	17.8	22	0.017	0.3	0.383
336.	QUINNETT, B.	f	DAL	39	326	8.4	12	0.037	0.3	0.347

(NAME)	FT PCT	3-PT SHOTS MADE	3-PT SHOTS TRIED	REBs	STLs	TURN-OVERS	BLKs	PTs
(WILLIAMS, K)	0.605	0	4	129	20	22	41	252
(HASTINGS, S.)	0.857	0	9	98	10	22	15	58
(ASKINS, K)	0.703	25	73	142	40	47	15	219
(SHACKLEFORD, C.)	0.663	0	1	415	38	62	51	473
(GREEN, Se.)	0.536	2	10	42	13	27	6	141
(HERRERA, C.)	0.568	0	1	99	16	37	25	191
(HENDERSON, G.)	0.818	3	8	8	3	8	0	36
(BROWN, C.)	0.612	0	3	82	12	29	7	150
(KITE, G.)	0.588	0	1	402	30	61	57	228
(RANDALL, M.)	0.744	3	16	71	12	25	3	171
(SCHINTZIUS, D.)	0.833	0	4	118	6	19	28	110
(POLYNICE, O.)	0.622	0	1	536	45	83	20	613
(COOPER, W.)	0.636	0	0	101	4	15	27	77
(TOLBERT, T.)	0.550	2	8	55	10	20	6	90
(THOMAS, C.)	0.667	2	17	22	4	17	1	48
(OLIVER, B.)	0.682	0	4	30	10	24	2	81
(HILL, T.)	0.694	0	1	593	73	106	43	671
(DONALDSON, J.)	0.709	0	0	289	8	48	49	285
(ROYAL, D.)	0.692	0	0	124	25	39	7	252
(CHILCUTT, P.)	0.821	2	2	187	32	41	17	251
(LISTER, A.)	0.424	0	0	92	5	20	16	102
(LANG, A.)	0.768	0	1	546	48	87	201	622
(LECKNER, E.)	0.745	0	1	206	9	39	18	196
(HOWARD, B.)	0.710	1	2	51	11	15	8	131
(KIMBLE, B.)	0.645	4	13	32	10	15	6	112
(MAYS, T.)	1.000	3	6	2	0	3	0	17
(EATON, M.)	0.598	0	0	491	36	60	205	266
(LEE, D.)	0.526	10	37	35	11	12	1	120
(WHITE, R.)	0.765	4	27	236	31	68	22	418
(DAVIS, D.)	0.572	0	1	410	27	49	74	395
(WITTMAN, R.)	0.500	0	0	9	2	3	0	17
(KLEINE, J.)	0.708	4	8	296	23	27	14	326
(GREEN, S.)	0.820	0	0	342	29	62	11	367
(WIGGINS, M.)	0.686	0	1	94	20	25	1	211
(BLANKS, L.)	0.727	6	16	22	14	14	1	64
(BENOIT, D.)	0.810	3	14	296	19	71	44	434
(KESSLER, A.)	0.817	0	0	314	17	58	32	410
(ABDELNABY, A.)	0.753	0	0	260	25	66	16	432
(THOMPSON, S.)	0.375	0	1	19	6	5	3	31
(WINCHESTER, K.)	0.800	1	2	15	2	2	2	35
(DREILING, G.)	0.750	1	1	96	10	31	16	117
(McCORMICK, T.)	0.667	0	0	34	2	8	0	42
(ALEXANDER, V.)	0.691	0	1	336	45	91	62	589
(PHILLS, B.)	0.636	0	2	8	3	8	1	31
(SAMPSON, R.)	0.667	0	2	30	3	10	8	22
(JAMES, H.)	0.803	29	90	112	16	43	11	418
(RULAND, J.)	0.688	0	0	47	7	20	4	51
(BEDFORD, W.)	0.636	0	1	63	6	15	18	114
(DAILEY, Q.)	0.813	0	1	12	5	10	1	31
(PAYNE, K)	0.692	5	12	54	16	19	8	144
(CROWDER, C.)	0.833	13	30	41	7	13	2	114
(PETERSEN, J.)	0.700	0	2	45	5	5	6	43
(SELLERS, B.)	0.769	0	1	42	1	15	10	102
(ACRES, M.)	0.761	1	3	252	25	33	15	208
(BOL, M.)	0.462	0	9	222	11	41	205	110
(QUINNETT, B.)	0.615	13	41	51	16	16	8	115

1991–92 REGULAR-SEASON STATISTICAL RESULTS
NBA PLAYERS ORDERED BY ASSISTS PER GAME

	NAME	POS	TEAM	GMs	MINs	MINs per GM	ASTs	ASTs per MIN	ASTs per GM	FG PCT
337.	KING, R.	c	SEA	40	213	5.3	12	0.056	0.3	0.380
338.	BROOKS, K.	f	DEN	37	270	7.3	11	0.041	0.3	0.443
339.	GATLING, C.	c	GS	54	612	11.3	16	0.026	0.3	0.568
340.	TURNER, Jo.	f	HOU	42	345	8.2	12	0.035	0.3	0.439
341.	WEST, M.	c	PHX	82	1436	17.5	22	0.015	0.3	0.632
342.	CONLON, M.	c	SEA	45	381	8.5	12	0.032	0.3	0.475
343.	VRANKOVIC, S.	c	BOS	19	110	5.8	5	0.046	0.3	0.469
344.	ROLLINS, T.	f/c	HOU	59	697	11.8	15	0.022	0.3	0.535
345.	BATTLE, K.	f	GS	16	92	5.8	4	0.044	0.3	0.647
346.	WILLIAMS, Ja.	f/c	PHI	50	646	12.9	12	0.019	0.2	0.364
347.	MURPHY, T.	f	MIN	47	429	9.1	11	0.026	0.2	0.488
348.	McCANN, B.	f	DET	26	129	5.0	6	0.047	0.2	0.394
349.	ANSLEY, M.	f	CHA	10	45	4.5	2	0.044	0.2	0.444
350.	FEITL, D.	c	NJ	34	175	5.2	6	0.034	0.2	0.429
351.	OGG, A.	c	MIA	43	367	8.5	7	0.019	0.2	0.548
352.	AUSTIN, I.	c	UT	31	112	3.6	5	0.045	0.2	0.457
353.	OWENS, K.	f	LAL	20	80	4.0	3	0.038	0.2	0.281
354.	HALEY, J.	f/c	LAL	49	394	8.0	7	0.018	0.1	0.369
355.	COOK, A.	f	DEN	22	115	5.2	2	0.017	0.1	0.600
356.	COPA, T.	f/c	SA	33	132	4.0	3	0.023	0.1	0.550
357.	ELLIS, L.	f	LAC	29	103	3.6	1	0.010	0.0	0.340
358.	JEPSEN, L.	c	SAC	31	87	2.8	1	0.012	0.0	0.375

(NAME)	FT PCT	3-PT SHOTS MADE	3-PT SHOTS TRIED	REBs	STLs	TURN-OVERS	BLKs	PTs
(KING, R.)	0.756	0	1	49	4	18	5	88
(BROOKS, K.)	0.810	2	11	39	8	18	2	105
(GATLING, C.)	0.661	0	4	182	31	44	36	306
(TURNER, Jo.)	0.525	0	0	78	6	32	4	117
(WEST, M.)	0.637	0	0	372	14	82	81	501
(CONLON, M.)	0.750	0	0	69	9	27	7	120
(VRANKOVIC, S.)	0.583	0	0	28	0	10	17	37
(ROLLINS, T.)	0.867	0	0	171	14	18	62	118
(BATTLE, K.)	0.833	0	1	16	2	4	2	32
(WILLIAMS, Ja.)	0.636	0	0	145	20	44	20	206
(MURPHY, T.)	0.559	1	2	110	9	18	8	98
(McCANN, B.)	0.308	0	1	30	6	7	4	30
(ANSLEY, M.)	0.833	0	0	6	0	3	0	21
(FEITL, D.)	0.842	0	0	61	2	19	3	82
(OGG, A.)	0.533	0	0	74	5	19	28	108
(AUSTIN, I.)	0.633	0	0	35	2	8	2	61
(OWENS, K.)	0.800	0	0	15	5	2	4	26
(HALEY, J.)	0.483	0	0	95	7	25	8	76
(COOK, A.)	0.667	0	0	34	5	3	4	34
(COPA, T.)	0.308	0	0	36	2	8	6	48
(ELLIS, L.)	0.474	0	0	24	6	11	9	43
(JEPSEN, L.)	0.636	0	1	30	1	3	5	25

1991–92 REGULAR-SEASON STATISTICAL RESULTS
NBA PLAYERS ORDERED BY BLOCKS PER GAME

	NAME	POS	TEAM	GMs	MINs	MINs per GM	BLKs	BLKs per MIN	BLKs per GM	FG PCT
. 1.	ROBINSON, D.	c	SA	68	2564	37.7	305	0.119	4.49	0.551
. 2.	OLAJUWON, A.	c	HOU	70	2636	37.7	304	0.115	4.34	0.502
. 3.	NANCE, L.	f	CLE	81	2880	35.6	243	0.084	3.00	0.539
. 4.	EWING, P.	c	NY	82	3150	38.4	245	0.078	2.99	0.522
.5.	MUTOMBO, D.	c	DEN	71	2716	38.3	210	0.077	2.96	0.493
6.	BOL, M.	c	PHI	71	1267	17.8	205	0.162	2.89	0.383
7.	CAUSWELL, D.	c	SAC	80	2291	28.6	215	0.094	2.69	0.550
. 8.	ELLISON, P.	c	WAS	66	2511	38.0	177	0.071	2.68	0.539
9.	EATON, M.	c	UT	81	2023	25.0	205	0.101	2.53	0.446
10.	LANG, A.	c	PHX	81	1965	24.3	201	0.102	2.48	0.522
11.	WILLIAMS, Jo.	f/c	CLE	80	2432	30.4	182	0.075	2.28	0.503
12.	DUDLEY, C.	c	NJ	82	1902	23.2	179	0.094	2.18	0.403
13.	SMITH, C.	f/c	LAC	49	1310	26.7	98	0.075	2.00	0.466
14.	CAMPBELL, E.	c	LAL	81	1876	23.2	159	0.085	1.96	0.448
.15.	KEMP, S.	f/c	SEA	64	1808	28.2	124	0.069	1.94	0.504
.16.	BENJAMIN, B.	c	SEA	63	1941	30.8	118	0.061	1.87	0.478
.17.	BOWIE, S.	c	NJ	71	2179	30.7	120	0.055	1.69	0.445
18.	SIMMONS, L.	f	SAC	78	2895	37.1	132	0.046	1.69	0.454
.19.	GRANT, Ho.	f	CHI	81	2859	35.3	131	0.046	1.62	0.579
20.	SALLEY, J.	f/c	DET	72	1774	24.6	110	0.062	1.53	0.512
.21.	SEIKALY, R.	c	MIA	79	2800	35.4	121	0.043	1.53	0.489
.22.	COLEMAN, D.	f	NJ	65	2207	34.0	98	0.044	1.51	0.504
23.	ROBERTS, S.	c	ORL	55	1118	20.3	83	0.074	1.51	0.529
.24.	MANNING, D.	f	LAC	82	2904	35.4	122	0.042	1.49	0.542
25.	BREUER, R.	c	MIN	67	1176	17.6	99	0.084	1.48	0.468
26.	PERRY, T.	f	PHX	80	2483	31.0	116	0.047	1.45	0.523
27.	BAILEY, T.	f	MIN	84	2104	25.0	117	0.056	1.39	0.440
28.	SMITS, R.	c	IND	74	1772	23.9	100	0.056	1.35	0.510
29.	WILLIAMS, H.	f/c	DAL	75	2040	27.2	98	0.048	1.31	0.431
30.	ROBINSON, C.	f	POR	82	2124	25.9	107	0.050	1.30	0.466
31.	SPENCER, F.	c	MIN	61	1481	24.3	79	0.053	1.30	0.426
32.	LEWIS, Re.	g	BOS	82	3070	37.4	105	0.034	1.28	0.503
33.	JONES, Ch.	c/f	WAS	75	1365	18.2	92	0.067	1.23	0.367
34.	PARISH, R.	c	BOS	79	2285	28.9	97	0.043	1.23	0.536
35.	CARR, A.	f/c	SA	81	1867	23.0	96	0.051	1.19	0.490
36.	DAVIS, D.	f	IND	64	1301	20.3	74	0.057	1.16	0.552
37.	PIPPEN, S.	f	CHI	82	3164	38.6	93	0.029	1.13	0.506
38.	TISDALE, W.	f	SAC	72	2521	35.0	79	0.031	1.10	0.501
39.	WILLIAMS, Br.	f	ORL	48	905	18.9	53	0.059	1.10	0.528
40.	DAUGHERTY, B.	c	CLE	73	2643	36.2	78	0.030	1.07	0.570
41.	GILLIAM, A.	f/c	PHI	81	2771	34.2	85	0.031	1.05	0.512
42.	McHALE, K,	f/c	BOS	56	1398	25.0	59	0.042	1.05	0.510
43.	MORRIS, C.	f	NJ	77	2394	31.1	81	0.034	1.05	0.477
44.	ROLLINS, T.	f/c	HOU	59	697	11.8	62	0.089	1.05	0.535
45.	LOHAUS, B.	f/c	MIL	70	1081	15.4	71	0.066	1.01	0.450
46.	WEST, M.	c	PHX	82	1436	17.5	81	0.056	0.99	0.632
47.	PERKINS, S.	f/c	LAL	63	2332	37.0	62	0.027	0.98	0.450
48.	DIVAC, V.	c	LAL	36	979	27.2	35	0.036	0.97	0.495
49.	LONGLEY, L.	c	MIN	66	991	15.0	64	0.065	0.97	0.458
50.	JORDAN, M.	g	CHI	80	3102	38.8	75	0.024	0.94	0.519
51.	DREXLER, C.	g	POR	76	2751	36.2	70	0.026	0.92	0.470
52.	KERSEY, J.	f	POR	77	2553	33.2	71	0.028	0.92	0.467
53.	McKEY, D.	f	SEA	52	1757	33.8	47	0.027	0.90	0.472
54.	ANDERSON, W.	g/f	SA	57	1889	33.1	51	0.027	0.89	0.456
55.	VRANKOVIC, S.	c	BOS	19	110	5.8	17	0.155	0.89	0.469
56.	HARPER, R.	g	LAC	82	3144	38.3	72	0.023	0.88	0.440

(NAME)	FT PCT	3-PT SHOTS MADE	3-PT SHOTS TRIED	REBs	ASTs	STLs	TURN-OVERS	PTs
(ROBINSON, D.)	0.701	1	8	829	181	158	182	1578
(OLAJUWON, A.)	0.766	0	1	845	157	127	187	1510
(NANCE, L.)	0.822	0	6	670	232	80	87	1375
(EWING, P.)	0.738	1	6	921	156	88	209	1970
(MUTOMBO, D.)	0.642	0	0	870	156	43	252	1177
(BOL, M.)	0.462	0	9	222	22	11	41	110
(CAUSWELL, D.)	0.613	0	1	580	59	47	124	636
(ELLISON, P.)	0.728	1	3	740	190	62	196	1322
(EATON, M.)	0.598	0	0	491	40	36	60	266
(LANG, A.)	0.768	0	1	546	43	48	87	622
(WILLIAMS, Jo.)	0.752	0	4	607	196	60	83	952
(DUDLEY, C.)	0.468	0	0	739	58	38	79	460
(SMITH, C.)	0.785	0	6	301	56	41	69	714
(CAMPBELL, E.)	0.619	0	2	423	59	53	73	578
(KEMP, S.)	0.748	0	3	665	86	70	156	994
(BENJAMIN, B.)	0.687	0	2	513	76	39	175	879
(BOWIE, S.)	0.757	8	25	578	186	41	150	1062
(SIMMONS, L.)	0.770	1	5	634	337	135	218	1336
(GRANT, Ho.)	0.741	0	2	807	217	100	98	1149
(SALLEY, J.)	0.715	0	3	296	116	49	102	684
(SEIKALY, R.)	0.733	0	3	934	109	40	216	1296
(COLEMAN, D.)	0.763	23	76	618	205	54	248	1289
(ROBERTS, S.)	0.515	0	1	336	39	22	78	573
(MANNING, D.)	0.725	0	5	564	285	135	210	1579
(BREUER, R.)	0.533	0	1	281	89	27	41	363
(PERRY, T.)	0.712	3	8	551	134	44	141	982
(BAILEY, T.)	0.796	0	2	485	78	35	108	951
(SMITS, R.)	0.788	0	2	417	116	29	130	1024
(WILLIAMS, H.)	0.725	1	6	454	94	35	114	859
(ROBINSON, C.)	0.664	1	11	416	137	85	154	1016
(SPENCER, F.)	0.691	0	0	435	53	27	70	405
(LEWIS, Re.)	0.851	5	21	394	185	125	136	1703
(JONES, Ch.)	0.500	0	0	317	62	43	39	86
(PARISH, R.)	0.772	0	0	705	70	68	131	1115
(CARR, A.)	0.764	1	5	346	63	32	114	881
(DAVIS, D.)	0.572	0	1	410	30	27	49	395
(PIPPEN, S.)	0.760	16	80	630	572	155	253	1720
(TISDALE, W.)	0.763	0	2	469	106	55	124	1195
(WILLIAMS, Br.)	0.669	0	0	272	33	41	86	437
(DAUGHERTY, B.)	0.777	0	2	760	262	65	185	1566
(GILLIAM, A.)	0.807	0	2	660	118	51	166	1367
(McHALE, K,)	0.822	0	13	330	82	11	82	780
(MORRIS, C.)	0.714	22	110	494	197	129	171	879
(ROLLINS, T.)	0.867	0	0	171	15	14	18	118
(LOHAUS, B.)	0.659	57	144	249	74	40	46	408
(WEST, M.)	0.637	0	0	372	22	14	82	501
(PERKINS, S.)	0.817	15	69	556	141	64	83	1041
(DIVAC, V.)	0.768	5	19	247	60	55	88	405
(LONGLEY, L.)	0.663	0	0	257	53	35	83	281
(JORDAN, M.)	0.832	27	100	511	489	182	200	2404
(DREXLER, C.)	0.794	114	338	500	512	138	240	1903
(KERSEY, J.)	0.664	1	8	633	243	114	151	971
(McKEY, D.)	0.847	019	50	268	120	61	114	777
(ANDERSON, W.)	0.775	13	56	300	302	54	140	744
(VRANKOVIC, S.)	0.583	0	0	28	5	0	10	37
(HARPER, R.)	0.736	64	211	447	417	152	252	1495

1991–92 REGULAR-SEASON STATISTICAL RESULTS
NBA PLAYERS ORDERED BY BLOCKS PER GAME

NAME	POS	TEAM	GMs	MINs	MINs per GM	BLKs	BLKs per MIN	BLKs per GM	FG PCT
57. KONCAK, J.	c	ATL	77	1489	19.3	67	0.045	0.87	0.391
58. NORMAN, K.	f	LAC	77	2009	26.1	66	0.033	0.86	0.490
59. RODMAN, D.	f	DET	82	3301	40.3	70	0.021	0.85	0.539
60. SCHINTZIUS, D.	c	SAC	33	400	12.1	28	0.070	0.85	0.427
61. DONALDSON, J.	c	NY	58	1075	18.5	49	0.046	0.84	0.457
62. GATTISON, K.	f/c	CHA	82	2223	27.1	69	0.031	0.84	0.529
63. WILLIAMS, R.	f	DEN	81	2623	32.4	68	0.026	0.84	0.471
64. OWENS, B.	g/f	GS	80	2510	31.4	65	0.026	0.81	0.525
65. SAMPSON, R.	c	WAS	10	108	10.8	8	0.074	0.80	0.310
66. ANDERSON, G.	f	DEN	82	2793	34.1	65	0.023	0.79	0.456
67. KITE, G.	c	ORL	72	1479	20.5	57	0.039	0.79	0.437
68. ALEXANDER, V.	c	GS	80	1350	16.9	62	0.046	0.78	0.529
69. MALONE, M.	c	MIL	82	2511	30.6	64	0.026	0.78	0.474
70. COOPER, W.	f	POR	35	344	9.8	27	0.079	0.77	0.427
71. MULLIN, C.	f	GS	81	3346	41.3	62	0.019	0.77	0.524
72. BIRD, L	f	BOS	45	1662	36.9	33	0.020	0.73	0.466
73. BOWIE, A.	g/f	ORL	52	1721	33.1	38	0.022	0.73	0.493
74. SHACKLEFORD, C.	c	PHI	72	1399	19.4	51	0.037	0.71	0.486
75. PINCKNEY, E.	f	BOS	81	1917	23.7	56	0.029	0.69	0.537
76. WILLIAMS, K.	f	IND	60	565	9.4	41	0.073	0.68	0.518
77. CAGE, M.	f	SEA	82	2461	30.0	55	0.022	0.67	0.566
78. GATLING, C.	c	GS	54	612	11.3	36	0.059	0.67	0.568
79. LAIMBEER, B.	c	DET	81	2234	27.6	54	0.024	0.67	0.470
80. WILLIS, K.	f/c	ATL	81	2962	36.6	54	0.018	0.67	0.483
81. OGG, A.	c	MIA	43	367	8.5	28	0.076	0.65	0.548
82. MALONE, K.	f	UT	81	3054	37.7	51	0.017	0.63	0.526
83. JOHNSON, L.	f	CHA	82	3047	37.2	51	0.017	0.62	0.490
84. LISTER, A.	c	GS	26	293	11.3	16	0.055	0.62	0.557
85. JOHNSON, B.	f	HOU	80	2202	27.5	49	0.022	0.61	0.458
86. BARKLEY, C.	f	PHI	75	2881	38.4	44	0.015	0.59	0.552
87. RASMUSSEN, B.	c	ATL	81	1968	24.3	48	0.024	0.59	0.478
88. GILL, K.	g/f	CHA	79	2906	36.8	46	0.016	0.58	0.467
89. HERRERA, C.	f	HOU	43	566	13.2	25	0.044	0.58	0.516
90. STEWART, L.	f	WAS	76	2229	29.3	44	0.020	0.58	0.514
91. BENOIT, D.	f	UT	77	1161	15.1	44	0.038	0.57	0.467
92. EDWARDS, T.	g/f	UT	81	2283	28.2	46	0.020	0.57	0.522
93. LEVINGSTON, C.	f	CHI	79	1020	12.9	45	0.044	0.57	0.498
94. WILKINS, D.	f	ATL	42	1601	38.1	24	0.015	0.57	0.464
95. WILLIAMS, S.	f	CHI	63	690	11.0	36	0.052	0.57	0.483
96. BEDFORD, W.	f/c	DET	32	363	11.3	18	0.050	0.56	0.413
97. BLAYLOCK, M.	g	NJ	72	2548	35.4	40	0.016	0.56	0.432
98. PERDUE, W.	c	CHI	77	1007	13.1	43	0.043	0.56	0.547
99. ANDERSON, N.	g/f	ORL	60	2203	36.7	33	0.015	0.55	0.463
100. HOPSON, D.	g/f	SAC	71	1314	18.5	39	0.030	0.55	0.465
101. BURTON, W.	g/f	MIA	68	1585	23.3	37	0.023	0.54	0.450
102. CHAMBERS, T.	f	PHX	69	1948	28.2	37	0.019	0.54	0.431
103. HAWKINS, H.	g	PHI	81	3013	37.2	43	0.014	0.53	0.462
104. HIGGINS, R.	f	GS	25	535	21.4	13	0.024	0.52	0.412
105. HILL, T.	c/f	GS	82	1886	23.0	43	0.023	0.52	0.522
106. MAJERLE, D.	g/f	PHX	82	2853	34.8	43	0.015	0.52	0.478
107. WILLIAMS, Bu.	f	POR	80	2519	31.5	41	0.016	0.51	0.604
108. MILLS, T.	f	NJ	82	1714	20.9	41	0.024	0.50	0.463
109. RAMBIS, K.	f	PHX	28	381	13.6	14	0.037	0.50	0.463
110. ROBERTS, G.	f	MIL	80	1746	21.8	40	0.023	0.50	0.482
111. SCOTT, D.	f	ORL	18	608	33.8	9	0.015	0.50	0.402
112. CUMMINGS, T.	f	SA	70	2149	30.7	34	0.016	0.49	0.488

(NAME)	FT PCT	3-PT SHOTS MADE	3-PT SHOTS TRIED	REBs	ASTs	STLs	TURN-OVERS	PTs
(KONCAK, J.)	0.655	0	12	261	132	50	54	241
(NORMAN, K.)	0.535	4	28	448	125	53	100	929
(RODMAN, D.)	0.600	32	101	1530	191	68	140	800
(SCHINTZIUS, D.)	0.833	0	4	118	20	6	19	110
(DONALDSON, J.)	0.709	0	0	289	33	8	48	285
(GATTISON, K.)	0.688	0	2	580	131	59	140	1042
(WILLIAMS, R.)	0.803	56	156	405	235	148	173	1474
(OWENS, B.)	0.654	1	9	639	188	90	179	1141
(SAMPSON, R.)	0.667	0	2	30	4	3	10	22
(ANDERSON, G.)	0.623	0	4	941	78	88	201	945
(KITE, G.)	0.588	0	1	402	44	30	61	228
(ALEXANDER, V.)	0.691	0	1	336	32	45	91	589
(MALONE, M.)	0.786	3	8	744	93	74	150	1279
(COOPER, W.)	0.636	0	0	101	21	4	15	77
(MULLIN, C.)	0.833	64	175	450	286	173	202	2074
(BIRD, L)	0.926	52	128	434	306	42	125	908
(BOWIE, A.)	0.860	17	44	245	163	55	107	758
(SHACKLEFORD, C.)	0.663	0	1	415	46	38	62	473
(PINCKNEY, E.)	0.812	0	1	564	62	70	73	613
(WILLIAMS, K.)	0.605	0	4	129	40	20	22	252
(CAGE, M.)	0.620	0	5	728	92	99	78	720
(GATLING, C.)	0.661	0	4	182	16	31	44	306
(LAIMBEER, B.)	0.893	32	85	451	160	51	102	783
(WILLIS, K.)	0.804	6	37	1258	173	72	197	1480
(OGG, A.)	0.533	0	0	74	7	5	19	108
(MALONE, K.)	0.778	3	17	909	241	108	248	2272
(JOHNSON, L.)	0.829	5	22	899	292	81	160	1576
(LISTER, A.)	0.424	0	0	92	14	5	20	102
(JOHNSON, B.)	0.727	1	9	312	158	72	104	685
(BARKLEY, C.)	0.695	32	137	830	308	136	235	1730
(RASMUSSEN, B.)	0.750	5	23	393	107	35	51	729
(GILL, K.)	0.745	6	25	402	329	154	180	1622
(HERRERA, C.)	0.568	0	1	99	27	16	37	191
(STEWART, L.)	0.807	0	3	449	120	51	112	794
(BENOIT, D.)	0.810	3	14	296	34	19	71	434
(EDWARDS, T.)	0.774	39	103	298	137	81	122	1018
(LEVINGSTON, C.)	0.625	1	6	227	66	27	42	311
(WILKINS, D.)	0.835	037	128	295	158	52	122	1179
(WILLIAMS, S.)	0.649	0	3	247	50	13	35	214
(BEDFORD, W.)	0.636	0	1	63	12	6	15	114
(BLAYLOCK, M.)	0.712	12	54	269	492	170	152	996
(PERDUE, W.)	0.495	1	2	312	80	16	72	350
(ANDERSON, N.)	0.667	30	85	384	163	97	125	1196
(HOPSON, D.)	0.708	12	47	206	102	67	100	743
(BURTON, W.)	0.800	6	15	244	123	46	119	762
(CHAMBERS, T.)	0.830	18	49	401	142	57	103	1128
(HAWKINS, H.)	0.874	91	229	271	248	157	189	1536
(HIGGINS, R.)	0.814	33	95	85	22	15	15	255
(HILL, T.)	0.694	0	1	593	47	73	106	671
(MAJERLE, D.)	0.756	87	228	483	274	131	101	1418
(WILLIAMS, Bu.)	0.754	0	1	704	108	62	130	901
(MILLS, T.)	0.750	8	23	453	84	48	82	742
(RAMBIS, K.)	0.778	0	0	106	37	12	25	90
(ROBERTS, G.)	0.749	19	37	257	122	52	122	769
(SCOTT, D.)	0.901	29	89	66	35	20	31	359
(CUMMINGS, T.)	0.711	5	13	631	102	58	115	1210

1991–92 REGULAR-SEASON STATISTICAL RESULTS
NBA PLAYERS ORDERED BY BLOCKS PER GAME

	NAME	POS	TEAM	GMs	MINs	MINs per GM	BLKs	BLKs per MIN	BLKs per GM	FG PCT
113.	LONG, G.	f	MIA	82	3063	37.4	40	0.013	0.49	0.494
114.	MITCHELL, S.	f	MIN	82	2151	26.2	39	0.018	0.48	0.423
115.	EDWARDS, Ja.	c	LAC	72	1437	20.0	33	0.023	0.46	0.465
116.	GMINSKI, M.	c	CHA	35	499	14.3	16	0.032	0.46	0.452
117.	SCHREMPF, D.	f	IND	80	2605	32.6	37	0.014	0.46	0.536
118.	DUCKWORTH, K.	c	POR	82	2222	27.1	37	0.017	0.45	0.461
119.	GAMBLE, K.	g/f	BOS	82	2496	30.4	37	0.015	0.45	0.529
120.	HODGE, D.	c/f	DAL	51	1058	20.7	23	0.022	0.45	0.497
121.	REID, J.R.	c/f	CHA	51	1257	24.6	23	0.018	0.45	0.490
122.	SMITH, Do.	f	DAL	76	1707	22.5	34	0.020	0.45	0.415
123.	THORPE, O.	f	HOU	82	3056	37.3	37	0.012	0.45	0.592
124.	GREEN, A.C.	f	LAL	82	2902	35.4	36	0.012	0.44	0.476
125.	RICE, G.	f	MIA	79	3007	38.1	35	0.012	0.44	0.469
126.	SCHAYES, D.	c	MIL	43	726	16.9	19	0.026	0.44	0.417
127.	DAVIS, T.	f/c	DAL	68	2149	31.6	29	0.014	0.43	0.482
128.	RICHMOND, M.	g	SAC	80	3095	38.7	34	0.011	0.43	0.468
129.	THOMPSON, L.	f/c	IND	80	1299	16.2	34	0.026	0.43	0.468
130.	WORTHY, J.	f	LAL	54	2108	39.0	23	0.011	0.43	0.447
131.	GRANT, Ha.	f	WAS	64	2388	37.3	27	0.011	0.42	0.479
132.	KESSLER, A.	c	MIA	77	1197	15.5	32	0.027	0.42	0.413
133.	BROWN, M.	c/f	UT	82	1783	21.7	34	0.019	0.41	0.453
134.	CAMPBELL, T.	f/g	MIN	78	2441	31.3	31	0.013	0.40	0.464
135.	FRANK, T.	f	MIN	10	140	14.0	4	0.029	0.40	0.546
136.	GLASS, G.	g	MIN	75	1822	24.3	30	0.017	0.40	0.440
137.	McCRAY, R.	f	DAL	75	2106	28.1	30	0.014	0.40	0.436
138.	McMILLAN, N.	g/f	SEA	72	1652	22.9	29	0.018	0.40	0.437
139.	WILLIAMS, Ja.	f/c	PHI	50	646	12.9	20	0.031	0.40	0.364
140.	WOOLRIDGE, O.	f	DET	82	2113	25.8	33	0.016	0.40	0.498
141.	FREDERICK, A.	f	CHA	66	852	12.9	26	0.031	0.39	0.435
142.	LEVER, F.	g	DAL	31	884	28.5	12	0.014	0.39	0.387
143.	LIBERTY, M.	f/g	DEN	75	1527	20.4	29	0.019	0.39	0.443
144.	ROBERTSON, A.	g	MIL	82	2463	30.0	32	0.013	0.39	0.430
145.	VAUGHT, L.	f	LAC	79	1687	21.4	31	0.018	0.39	0.492
146.	VOLKOV, A.	f	ATL	77	1516	19.7	30	0.020	0.39	0.441
147.	HASTINGS, S.	f	DEN	40	421	10.5	15	0.036	0.38	0.340
148.	HORNACEK, J.	g	PHX	81	3078	38.0	31	0.010	0.38	0.512
149.	ADDISON, R.	g	NJ	76	1175	15.5	28	0.024	0.37	0.433
150.	FOX, R.	g/f	BOS	81	1535	19.0	30	0.020	0.37	0.459
151.	REYNOLDS, J.	g/f	ORL	46	1159	25.2	17	0.015	0.37	0.380
152.	CHAPMAN, R.	g	WAS	22	567	25.8	8	0.014	0.36	0.448
153.	PRITCHARD, K.	g	BOS	11	136	12.4	4	0.029	0.36	0.471
154.	BRICKOWSKI, F.	f	MIL	65	1556	23.9	23	0.015	0.35	0.524
155.	EHLO, C.	g/f	CLE	63	2016	32.0	22	0.011	0.35	0.453
156.	ELLIOTT, S.	f	SA	82	3120	38.0	29	0.009	0.35	0.494
157.	HAMMONDS, T.	f	CHA	37	984	26.6	13	0.013	0.35	0.488
158.	MAXWELL, V.	g	HOU	80	2700	33.7	28	0.010	0.35	0.413
159.	SHAW, B.	g	MIA	63	1423	22.6	22	0.016	0.35	0.407
160.	PRESSEY, P.	g	SA	56	759	13.6	19	0.025	0.34	0.373
161.	SCOTT, B.	g	LAL	82	2679	32.7	28	0.011	0.34	0.458
162.	WHITE, R.	f	DAL	65	1021	15.7	22	0.022	0.34	0.380
163.	AUGMON, S.	g/f	ATL	82	2505	30.5	27	0.011	0.33	0.489
164.	BONNER, A.	f	SAC	79	2287	28.9	26	0.011	0.33	0.447
165.	WEST, D.	g	MIN	80	2540	31.7	26	0.010	0.33	0.518
166.	KING, S.	f/c	CHI	79	1268	16.1	25	0.020	0.32	0.506
167.	MILLER, R.	g	IND	82	3120	38.0	26	0.008	0.32	0.501
168.	RIVERS, Do.	g	LAC	59	1657	28.1	19	0.012	0.32	0.424

(NAME)	FT PCT	3-PT SHOTS MADE	3-PT SHOTS TRIED	REBs	ASTs	STLs	TURN-OVERS	PTs
(LONG, G.)	0.807	6	22	691	225	139	185	1212
(MITCHELL, S.)	0.786	2	11	473	94	53	97	825
(EDWARDS, Ja.)	0.731	0	1	202	53	24	72	698
(GMINSKI, M.)	0.750	1	3	118	31	11	20	202
(SCHREMPF, D.)	0.828	23	71	770	312	62	191	1380
(DUCKWORTH, K.)	0.690	0	3	497	99	38	143	880
(GAMBLE, K.)	0.885	9	31	286	219	75	97	1108
(HODGE, D.)	0.667	0	0	275	39	25	75	426
(REID, J.R.)	0.705	0	3	317	81	49	84	560
(SMITH, Do.)	0.736	0	11	391	129	62	97	671
(THORPE, O.)	0.657	0	7	862	250	52	237	1420
(GREEN, A.C.)	0.744	12	56	762	117	91	111	1116
(RICE, G.)	0.837	155	396	394	184	90	145	1765
(SCHAYES, D.)	0.771	0	0	168	34	19	41	240
(DAVIS, T.)	0.635	0	5	672	57	26	117	693
(RICHMOND, M.)	0.813	103	268	319	411	92	247	1803
(THOMPSON, L.)	0.817	0	2	381	102	52	98	394
(WORTHY, J.)	0.814	9	43	305	252	76	127	1075
(GRANT, Ha.)	0.800	1	8	432	170	74	109	1155
(KESSLER, A.)	0.817	0	0	314	34	17	58	410
(BROWN, M.)	0.667	0	1	476	81	42	105	632
(CAMPBELL, T.)	0.803	13	37	286	229	84	165	1307
(FRANK, T.)	0.667	0	0	26	8	5	5	46
(GLASS, G.)	0.616	16	54	260	175	66	103	859
(McCRAY, R.)	0.719	25	85	468	219	48	115	677
(McMILLAN, N.)	0.643	27	98	252	359	129	112	435
(WILLIAMS, Ja.)	0.636	0	0	145	12	20	44	206
(WOOLRIDGE, O.)	0.683	1	9	260	88	41	133	1146
(FREDERICK, A.)	0.685	4	17	144	71	40	58	389
(LEVER, F.)	0.750	17	52	161	107	46	36	347
(LIBERTY, M.)	0.728	17	50	308	58	66	90	698
(ROBERTSON, A.)	0.763	67	210	350	360	210	223	1010
(VAUGHT, L.)	0.797	4	5	512	71	37	66	601
(VOLKOV, A.)	0.631	35	110	265	250	66	102	662
(HASTINGS, S.)	0.857	0	9	98	26	10	22	58
(HORNACEK, J.)	0.886	83	189	407	411	158	170	1632
(ADDISON, R.)	0.737	14	49	165	68	28	46	444
(FOX, R.)	0.755	23	70	220	126	78	123	644
(REYNOLDS, J.)	0.836	3	24	149	151	63	96	555
(CHAPMAN, R.)	0.679	8	29	58	89	15	45	270
(PRITCHARD, K.)	0.778	0	3	11	30	3	11	46
(BRICKOWSKI, F.)	0.767	3	6	344	122	60	112	740
(EHLO, C.)	0.707	69	167	307	238	78	104	776
(ELLIOTT, S.)	0.861	25	82	439	214	84	152	1338
(HAMMONDS, T.)	0.610	0	1	185	36	22	58	440
(MAXWELL, V.)	0.772	162	473	243	326	104	178	1372
(SHAW, B.)	0.791	5	23	204	250	57	99	495
(PRESSEY, P.)	0.683	3	21	95	142	29	64	151
(SCOTT, B.)	0.839	54	157	310	226	105	119	1218
(WHITE, R.)	0.765	4	27	236	31	31	68	418
(AUGMON, S.)	0.666	1	6	420	201	124	181	1094
(BONNER, A.)	0.627	1	4	485	125	94	133	740
(WEST, D.)	0.805	4	23	257	281	66	120	1111
(KING, S.)	0.753	2	5	205	77	21	76	551
(MILLER, R.)	0.858	129	341	318	314	105	157	1695
(RIVERS, Do.)	0.832	26	92	147	233	111	92	641

1991–92 REGULAR-SEASON STATISTICAL RESULTS
NBA PLAYERS ORDERED BY BLOCKS PER GAME

	NAME	POS	TEAM	GMs	MINs	MINs per GM	BLKs	BLKs per MIN	BLKs per GM	FG PCT
169.	SANDERS, M.	f	CLE	31	633	20.4	10	0.016	0.32	0.571
170.	ELLIS, L.	f	LAC	29	103	3.6	9	0.087	0.31	0.340
171.	LECKNER, E.	c	CHA	59	716	12.1	18	0.025	0.31	0.513
172.	MUSTAF, J.	f	PHX	52	545	10.5	16	0.029	0.31	0.477
173.	RULAND, J.	c	PHI	13	209	16.1	4	0.019	0.31	0.526
174.	SMITH, S.	g	MIA	61	1806	29.6	19	0.011	0.31	0.454
175.	WEBB, S.	g	SAC	77	2724	35.4	24	0.009	0.31	0.445
176.	HOWARD, B.	f	DAL	27	318	11.8	8	0.025	0.30	0.519
177.	RICHARDSON, P.	g	MIN	82	2922	35.6	25	0.009	0.30	0.466
178.	ROBINSON, R.	g	ATL	81	2220	27.4	24	0.011	0.30	0.456
179.	STRICKLAND, R.	g	SA	57	2053	36.0	17	0.008	0.30	0.455
180.	ASKEW, V.	g	GS	80	1496	18.7	23	0.015	0.29	0.509
181.	BLACKMAN, R.	g	DAL	75	2527	33.7	22	0.009	0.29	0.461
182.	JOHNSON, K.	g	PHX	78	2899	37.2	23	0.008	0.29	0.479
183.	McDANIEL, X.	f	NY	82	2344	28.6	24	0.010	0.29	0.478
184.	GARLAND, W.	g	DEN	78	2209	28.3	22	0.010	0.28	0.444
185.	WILLIAMS, M.	g	IND	79	2750	34.8	22	0.008	0.28	0.490
186.	BRANDON, T.	g	CLE	82	1605	19.6	22	0.014	0.27	0.419
187.	DREILING, G.	c	IND	60	509	8.5	16	0.031	0.27	0.494
188.	GRAHAM, P.	g	ATL	78	1718	22.0	21	0.012	0.27	0.447
189.	STOCKTON, J.	g	UT	82	3002	36.6	22	0.007	0.27	0.482
190.	BULLARD, M.	f	HOU	80	1278	16.0	21	0.016	0.26	0.459
191.	CURRY, D.	g	CHA	77	2020	26.2	20	0.010	0.26	0.486
192.	FERRELL, D.	f	ATL	66	1598	24.2	17	0.011	0.26	0.524
193.	FLOYD, S.	g	HOU	82	1662	20.3	21	0.013	0.26	0.406
194.	HARPER, D.	g	DAL	65	2252	34.6	17	0.008	0.26	0.443
195.	PAYTON, G.	g	SEA	81	2549	31.5	21	0.008	0.26	0.451
196.	PIERCE, R.	g	SEA	78	2658	34.1	20	0.008	0.26	0.475
197.	POLYNICE, O.	c	LAC	76	1834	24.1	20	0.011	0.26	0.519
198.	WINGATE, D.	g	WAS	81	2127	26.3	21	0.010	0.26	0.465
199.	ASKINS, K.	g/f	MIA	59	843	14.3	15	0.018	0.25	0.410
200.	BUECHLER, J.	f	GS	28	290	10.4	7	0.024	0.25	0.409
201.	CHILCUTT, P.	f/c	SAC	69	817	11.8	17	0.021	0.25	0.452
202.	CORBIN, T.	f	UT	80	2207	27.6	20	0.009	0.25	0.481
203.	EDWARDS, K.	g	MIA	81	1840	22.7	20	0.011	0.25	0.454
204.	NEWMAN, J.	f/g	CHA	55	1651	30.0	14	0.009	0.25	0.477
205.	SANDERS, J.	f	ATL	12	117	9.8	3	0.026	0.25	0.444
206.	FOSTER, G.	f	WAS	49	548	11.2	12	0.022	0.24	0.461
207.	MASON, A.	f	NY	82	2198	26.8	20	0.009	0.24	0.509
208.	SMITH, O.	g	ORL	55	877	15.9	13	0.015	0.24	0.365
209.	WALKER, D.	g	DET	74	1541	20.8	18	0.012	0.24	0.423
210.	ABDELNABY, A.	f/c	POR	71	934	13.2	16	0.017	0.23	0.493
211.	BROWN, D.	g	BOS	31	883	28.5	7	0.008	0.23	0.426
212.	JOHNSON, V.	g	SA	60	1350	22.5	14	0.010	0.23	0.405
213.	SELLERS, B.	f/c	DET	43	226	5.3	10	0.044	0.23	0.466
214.	ACRES, M.	c	ORL	68	926	13.6	15	0.016	0.22	0.517
215.	CARTWRIGHT, B.	c	CHI	64	1471	23.0	14	0.010	0.22	0.467
216.	ELLIS, D.	f	MIL	81	2191	27.0	18	0.008	0.22	0.469
217.	FERRY, D.	f	CLE	68	937	13.8	15	0.016	0.22	0.409
218.	McCLOUD, G.	g	IND	51	892	17.5	11	0.012	0.22	0.409
219.	PERSON, C.	f	IND	81	2923	36.1	18	0.006	0.22	0.480
220.	PETERSEN, J.	c	GS	27	169	6.3	6	0.036	0.22	0.450
221.	STARKS, J.	g	NY	82	2118	25.8	18	0.009	0.22	0.449
222.	BROWN, R.	g	SAC	56	535	9.6	12	0.022	0.21	0.456
223.	CATLEDGE, T.	f	ORL	78	2430	31.2	16	0.007	0.21	0.496
224.	DOUGLAS, S.	g	BOS	42	752	17.9	9	0.012	0.21	0.463

(NAME)	FT PCT	3-PT SHOTS MADE	3-PT SHOTS TRIED	REBs	ASTs	STLs	TURN-OVERS	PTs
(SANDERS, M.)	0.766	1	3	96	53	24	22	221
(ELLIS, L.)	0.474	0	0	24	1	6	11	43
(LECKNER, E.)	0.745	0	1	206	31	9	39	196
(MUSTAF, J.)	0.690	0	0	145	45	21	51	233
(RULAND, J.)	0.688	0	0	47	5	7	20	51
(SMITH, S.)	0.748	40	125	188	278	59	152	729
(WEBB, S.)	0.859	73	199	223	547	125	229	1231
(HOWARD, B.)	0.710	1	2	51	14	11	15	131
(RICHARDSON, P.)	0.691	53	155	301	685	119	204	1350
(ROBINSON, R.)	0.636	34	104	219	446	105	206	1055
(STRICKLAND, R.)	0.687	5	15	265	491	118	160	787
(ASKEW, V.)	0.694	1	10	233	188	47	84	498
(BLACKMAN, R.)	0.899	65	169	239	204	50	153	1374
(JOHNSON, K.)	0.807	10	46	292	836	116	272	1536
(McDANIEL, X.)	0.714	12	39	460	149	57	147	1125
(GARLAND, W.)	0.859	9	28	190	411	98	175	846
(WILLIAMS, M.)	0.871	8	33	282	647	233	240	1188
(BRANDON, T.)	0.807	1	23	162	316	81	136	605
(DREILING, G.)	0.750	1	1	96	25	10	31	117
(GRAHAM, P.)	0.741	55	141	231	175	96	91	791
(STOCKTON, J.)	0.842	83	204	270	1126	244	286	1297
(BULLARD, M.)	0.760	64	166	223	75	26	56	512
(CURRY, D.)	0.836	74	183	259	177	93	134	1209
(FERRELL, D.)	0.762	11	33	210	92	49	99	839
(FLOYD, S.)	0.794	37	123	150	239	57	128	744
(HARPER, D.)	0.759	58	186	170	373	101	154	1152
(PAYTON, G.)	0.669	3	23	295	506	147	174	764
(PIERCE, R.)	0.917	33	123	233	241	86	189	1690
(POLYNICE, O.)	0.622	0	1	536	46	45	83	613
(WINGATE, D.)	0.719	1	18	269	247	123	124	638
(ASKINS, K.)	0.703	25	73	142	38	40	47	219
(BUECHLER, J.)	0.571	0	1	52	23	19	13	70
(CHILCUTT, P.)	0.821	2	2	187	38	32	41	251
(CORBIN, T.)	0.866	0	4	472	140	82	97	780
(EDWARDS, K.)	0.848	7	32	211	170	99	120	819
(NEWMAN, J.)	0.766	13	46	179	146	70	129	839
(SANDERS, J.)	0.778	0	0	26	9	5	5	47
(FOSTER, G.)	0.714	0	1	145	35	6	36	213
(MASON, A.)	0.642	0	0	573	106	46	101	573
(SMITH, O.)	0.769	8	21	116	57	36	62	310
(WALKER, D.)	0.619	0	10	238	205	63	79	387
(ABDELNABY, A.)	0.753	0	0	260	30	25	66	432
(BROWN, D.)	0.769	5	22	79	164	33	59	363
(JOHNSON, V.)	0.647	19	60	182	145	41	74	478
(SELLERS, B.)	0.769	0	1	42	14	1	15	102
(ACRES, M.)	0.761	1	3	252	22	25	33	208
(CARTWRIGHT, B.)	0.604	0	0	324	87	22	75	512
(ELLIS, D.)	0.774	138	329	253	104	57	119	1272
(FERRY, D.)	0.836	17	48	213	75	22	46	346
(McCLOUD, G.)	0.781	32	94	132	116	26	62	338
(PERSON, C.)	0.675	132	354	426	382	68	216	1497
(PETERSEN, J.)	0.700	0	2	45	9	5	5	43
(STARKS, J.)	0.778	94	270	191	276	103	150	1139
(BROWN, R.)	0.655	0	6	69	59	35	42	192
(CATLEDGE, T.)	0.694	0	4	549	109	58	138	1154
(DOUGLAS, S.)	0.682	1	10	63	172	25	68	308

1991–92 REGULAR-SEASON STATISTICAL RESULTS
NBA PLAYERS ORDERED BY BLOCKS PER GAME

	NAME	POS	TEAM	GMs	MINs	MINs per GM	BLKs	BLKs per MIN	BLKs per GM	FG PCT
225.	KERR, S.	g	CLE	48	847	17.6	10	0.012	0.21	0.511
226.	QUINNETT, B.	f	DAL	39	326	8.4	8	0.025	0.21	0.347
227.	TURNER, J.	f	ORL	75	1591	21.2	16	0.010	0.21	0.451
228.	WILKINS, G.	g	NY	82	2344	28.6	17	0.007	0.21	0.447
229.	WOLF, J.	f	DEN	67	1160	17.3	14	0.012	0.21	0.361
230.	KLEINE, J.	c	BOS	70	991	14.2	14	0.014	0.20	0.492
231.	OWENS, K.	f	LAL	20	80	4.0	4	0.050	0.20	0.281
232.	THREATT, S.	g	LAL	82	3070	37.4	16	0.005	0.20	0.489
233.	ELIE, M.	g/f	GS	79	1677	21.2	15	0.009	0.19	0.521
234.	THOMAS, I.	g	DET	78	2918	37.4	15	0.005	0.19	0.446
235.	COOK, A.	f	DEN	22	115	5.2	4	0.035	0.18	0.600
236.	COPA, T.	f/c	SA	33	132	4.0	6	0.046	0.18	0.550
237.	GRANT, Ga.	g	LAC	78	2049	26.3	14	0.007	0.18	0.462
238.	HUMPHRIES, J.	g	MIL	71	2261	31.8	13	0.006	0.18	0.470
239.	KIMBLE, B.	f	LAC	34	277	8.2	6	0.022	0.18	0.396
240.	LICHTI, T.	g	DEN	68	1176	17.3	12	0.010	0.18	0.460
241.	MACON, M.	g	DEN	76	2304	30.3	14	0.006	0.18	0.375
242.	OAKLEY, C.	f	NY	82	2309	28.2	15	0.007	0.18	0.522
243.	BENNETT, W.	f	MIA	54	833	15.4	9	0.011	0.17	0.379
244.	BROWN, C.	f	LAL	42	431	10.3	7	0.016	0.17	0.469
245.	CEBALLOS, C.	f	PHX	64	725	11.3	11	0.015	0.17	0.482
246.	GREEN, Se.	g	IND	35	256	7.3	6	0.023	0.17	0.392
247.	JAMES, H.	f	CLE	65	866	13.3	11	0.013	0.17	0.407
248.	MURPHY, T.	f	MIN	47	429	9.1	8	0.019	0.17	0.488
249.	PRICE, M.	g	CLE	72	2138	29.7	12	0.006	0.17	0.488
250.	TOLBERT, T.	f	GS	35	310	8.9	6	0.019	0.17	0.384
251.	AINGE, D.	g	POR	81	1595	19.7	13	0.008	0.16	0.442
252.	COLES, B.	g	MIA	81	1976	24.4	13	0.007	0.16	0.455
253.	CONLON, M.	c	SEA	45	381	8.5	7	0.018	0.16	0.475
254.	GRAYER, J.	g	MIL	82	1659	20.2	13	0.008	0.16	0.449
255.	HALEY, J.	f/c	LAL	49	394	8.0	8	0.020	0.16	0.369
256.	HARDAWAY, T.	g	GS	81	3332	41.1	13	0.004	0.16	0.461
257.	HIGGINS, S.	f	ORL	38	616	16.2	6	0.010	0.16	0.459
258.	JACKSON, M.	g	NY	81	2461	30.4	13	0.005	0.16	0.491
259.	JEPSEN, L.	c	SAC	31	87	2.8	5	0.058	0.16	0.375
260.	LYNCH, K.	g	CHA	55	819	14.9	9	0.011	0.16	0.417
261.	PAYNE, K.	f	PHI	49	353	7.2	8	0.023	0.16	0.448
262.	SMITH, L.	f/c	HOU	45	800	17.8	7	0.009	0.16	0.544
263.	THOMPSON, S.	g	SAC	19	91	4.8	3	0.033	0.16	0.378
264.	AGUIRRE, M.	f	DET	75	1582	21.1	11	0.007	0.15	0.431
265.	DUMARS, J.	g	DET	82	3192	38.9	12	0.004	0.15	0.448
266.	KRYSTKOWIAK, L.	f	MIL	79	1848	23.4	12	0.007	0.15	0.444
267.	McCANN, B	f	DET	26	129	5.0	4	0.031	0.15	0.394
268.	PORTER, T.	g	POR	82	2784	34.0	12	0.004	0.15	0.462
269.	ANDERSON, K.	g	NJ	64	1086	17.0	9	0.008	0.14	0.390
270.	BRYANT, M.	c	POR	56	800	14.3	8	0.010	0.14	0.480
271.	GREEN, S.	f	SA	80	1127	14.1	11	0.010	0.14	0.427
272.	JOHNSON, E.	f	SEA	81	2366	29.2	11	0.005	0.14	0.459
273.	MARCIULIONIS, S.	g	GS	72	2117	29.4	10	0.005	0.14	0.538
274.	MURDOCK, E.	g	UT	50	478	9.6	7	0.015	0.14	0.415
275.	ANDERSON, Ro.	f	PHI	82	2432	29.7	11	0.005	0.13	0.465
276.	BATTLE, K.	f	GS	16	92	5.8	2	0.022	0.13	0.647
277.	BURTT, S.	g	PHX	31	356	11.5	4	0.011	0.13	0.463
278.	JOHNSON, A.	g	HOU	69	1235	17.9	9	0.007	0.13	0.479
279.	KING, R.	c	SEA	40	213	5.3	5	0.024	0.13	0.380
280.	PETROVIC, D.	g	NJ	82	3027	36.9	11	0.004	0.13	0.508

(NAME)	FT PCT	3-PT SHOTS MADE	3-PT SHOTS TRIED	REBs	ASTs	STLs	TURN-OVERS	PTs
(KERR, S.)	0.833	32	74	78	110	27	31	319
(QUINNETT, B.)	0.615	13	41	51	12	16	16	115
(TURNER, J.)	0.693	1	8	246	92	24	106	530
(WILKINS, G.)	0.730	38	108	206	219	76	113	1016
(WOLF, J.)	0.803	1	11	240	61	32	60	254
(KLEINE, J.)	0.708	4	8	296	32	23	27	326
(OWENS, K.)	0.800	0	0	15	3	5	2	26
(THREATT, S.)	0.831	20	62	253	593	168	182	1240
(ELIE, M.)	0.852	23	70	227	174	68	83	620
(THOMAS, I.)	0.773	25	86	247	560	118	252	1445
(COOK, A.)	0.667	0	0	34	2	5	3	34
(COPA, T.)	0.308	0	0	36	3	2	8	48
(GRANT, Ga.)	0.815	15	51	184	538	138	187	609
(HUMPHRIES, J.)	0.783	42	144	184	466	119	148	991
(KIMBLE, B.)	0.645	4	13	32	17	10	15	112
(LICHTI, T.)	0.839	1	9	118	74	43	72	446
(MACON, M.)	0.730	4	30	220	168	154	155	805
(OAKLEY, C.)	0.735	0	3	700	133	67	123	506
(BENNETT, W.)	0.700	0	1	162	38	19	33	195
(BROWN, C.)	0.612	0	3	82	26	12	29	150
(CEBALLOS, C.)	0.737	1	6	152	50	16	71	462
(GREEN, Se.)	0.536	2	10	42	22	13	27	141
(JAMES, H.)	0.803	29	90	112	25	16	43	418
(MURPHY, T.)	0.559	1	2	110	11	9	18	98
(PRICE, M.)	0.947	101	261	173	535	94	159	1247
(TOLBERT, T.)	0.550	2	8	55	21	10	20	90
(AINGE, D.)	0.824	78	230	148	202	73	70	784
(COLES, B.)	0.824	10	52	189	366	73	167	816
(CONLON, M.)	0.750	0	0	69	12	9	27	120
(GRAYER, J.)	0.667	19	66	257	150	64	105	739
(HALEY, J.)	0.483	0	0	95	7	7	25	76
(HARDAWAY, T.)	0.766	127	376	310	807	164	267	1893
(HIGGINS, S.)	0.861	6	25	102	41	16	41	291
(JACKSON, M.)	0.770	11	43	305	694	112	211	916
(JEPSEN, L.)	0.636	0	1	30	1	1	3	25
(LYNCH, K.)	0.761	3	8	85	83	37	44	224
(PAYNE, K.)	0.692	5	12	54	17	16	19	144
(SMITH, L.)	0.364	0	1	256	33	21	44	104
(THOMPSON, S.)	0.375	0	1	19	8	6	5	31
(AGUIRRE, M.)	0.687	15	71	236	126	51	105	851
(DUMARS, J.)	0.867	49	120	188	375	71	193	1635
(KRYSTKOWIAK, L.)	0.757	0	5	429	114	54	115	714
(McCANN, B)	0.308	0	1	30	6	6	7	30
(PORTER, T.)	0.856	128	324	255	477	127	188	1485
(ANDERSON, K.)	0.745	3	13	127	203	67	97	450
(BRYANT, M.)	0.667	0	3	201	41	26	30	230
(GREEN, S.)	0.820	0	0	342	36	29	62	367
(JOHNSON, E.)	0.861	27	107	292	161	55	130	1386
(MARCIULIONIS, S.)	0.788	3	10	208	243	116	193	1361
(MURDOCK, E.)	0.754	5	26	54	92	30	50	203
(ANDERSON, Ro.)	0.877	42	127	278	135	86	109	1123
(BATTLE, K.)	0.833	0	1	16	4	2	4	32
(BURTT, S.)	0.704	1	6	34	59	16	33	187
(JOHNSON, A.)	0.654	4	15	80	266	61	110	386
(KING, R.)	0.756	0	1	49	12	4	18	88
(PETROVIC, D.)	0.808	123	277	258	252	105	215	1691

1991–92 REGULAR-SEASON STATISTICAL RESULTS
NBA PLAYERS ORDERED BY BLOCKS PER GAME

	NAME	POS	TEAM	GMs	MINs	MINs per GM	BLKs	BLKs per MIN	BLKs per GM	FG PCT
281.	SMITH, To.	g	LAL	63	820	13.0	8	0.010	0.13	0.399
282.	SUTTON, G.	g	SA	67	601	9.0	9	0.015	0.13	0.388
283.	TUCKER, T.	g	SA	24	415	17.3	3	0.007	0.13	0.465
284.	WHATLEY, E.	g	POR	23	209	9.1	3	0.014	0.13	0.412
285.	ADAMS, M.	g	WAS	78	2795	35.8	9	0.003	0.12	0.393
286.	CONNER, L.	g	MIL	81	1420	17.5	10	0.007	0.12	0.431
287.	ROYAL, D.	f	SA	60	718	12.0	7	0.010	0.12	0.449
288.	VANDEWEGHE, K.	f	NY	67	956	14.3	8	0.008	0.12	0.491
289.	ANTHONY, G.	g	NY	82	1510	18.4	9	0.006	0.11	0.370
290.	EACKLES, L.	f	WAS	65	1463	22.5	7	0.005	0.11	0.468
291.	ENGLISH, A.J.	g	WAS	81	1665	20.6	9	0.005	0.11	0.433
292.	PAXSON, Jo.	g	CHI	79	1946	24.6	9	0.005	0.11	0.528
293.	SPARROW, R.	g	LAL	46	489	10.6	5	0.010	0.11	0.384
294.	TEAGLE, T.	f	LAL	82	1602	19.5	9	0.006	0.11	0.452
295.	WINCHESTER, K.	f	NY	19	81	4.3	2	0.025	0.11	0.433
296.	GARRICK, T.	g	DAL	40	549	13.7	4	0.007	0.10	0.413
297.	MOORE, T.	f	DAL	42	782	18.6	4	0.005	0.10	0.400
298.	PHILLS, B.	g	CLE	10	65	6.5	1	0.015	0.10	0.429
299.	TURNER, Jo.	f	HOU	42	345	8.2	4	0.012	0.10	0.439
300.	VINCENT, S.	g	ORL	39	885	22.7	4	0.005	0.10	0.430
301.	BROOKS, S.	g	MIN	82	1082	13.2	7	0.007	0.09	0.447
302.	BROWN, T.	f	SEA	57	655	11.5	5	0.008	0.09	0.410
303.	DAILEY, Q.	f	SEA	11	98	8.9	1	0.010	0.09	0.243
304.	DAVIS, B.	f	DAL	33	429	13.0	3	0.007	0.09	0.442
305.	FEITL, D.	c	NJ	34	175	5.2	3	0.017	0.09	0.429
306.	FLEMING, V.	g	IND	82	1737	21.2	7	0.004	0.09	0.482
307.	SCHEFFLER, S.	f	DEN	11	61	5.6	1	0.016	0.09	0.667
308.	SMITH, K.	g	HOU	81	2735	33.8	7	0.003	0.09	0.475
309.	MAYES, Th.	g	LAC	24	255	10.6	2	0.008	0.08	0.303
310.	BATTLE, J.	g	CLE	76	1637	21.5	5	0.003	0.07	0.480
311.	BOGUES, M.	g	CHA	82	2790	34.0	6	0.002	0.07	0.472
312.	KNIGHT, N.	g	PHX	42	631	15.0	3	0.005	0.07	0.475
313.	LANE, J.	f	MIL	14	177	12.6	1	0.006	0.07	0.304
314.	OLIVER, J.	g/f	CLE	27	252	9.3	2	0.008	0.07	0.398
315.	RIVERS, Da.	g	LAC	15	122	8.1	1	0.008	0.07	0.333
316.	SKILES, S.	g	ORL	75	2377	31.7	5	0.002	0.07	0.414
317.	ARMSTRONG, B.J.	g	CHI	82	1875	22.9	5	0.003	0.06	0.481
318.	AUSTIN, I.	c	UT	31	112	3.6	2	0.018	0.06	0.457
319.	DAWKINS, J.	g	PHI	82	2815	34.3	5	0.002	0.06	0.437
320.	MALONE, J.	g	UT	81	2922	36.1	5	0.002	0.06	0.511
321.	OLIVER, B.	g	PHI	34	279	8.2	2	0.007	0.06	0.330
322.	PACK, R.	g	POR	72	894	12.4	4	0.005	0.06	0.423
323.	PERRY, E.	g	CHA	50	437	8.7	3	0.007	0.06	0.380
324.	RANDALL, M.	f	MIN	54	441	8.2	3	0.007	0.06	0.456
325.	WILEY, M.	g	ATL	53	870	16.4	3	0.004	0.06	0.430
326.	YOUNG, D.	g	LAC	62	1023	16.5	4	0.004	0.06	0.392
327.	BAGLEY, J.	g	BOS	73	1742	23.9	4	0.002	0.05	0.441
328.	BARROS, D.	g	SEA	75	1331	17.7	4	0.003	0.05	0.483
329.	BROOKS, K.	f	DEN	37	270	7.3	2	0.007	0.05	0.443
330.	JACKSON, C.	g	DEN	81	1538	19.0	4	0.003	0.05	0.421
331.	KOFOED, B.	g	SEA	44	239	5.4	2	0.008	0.05	0.472
332.	LES, J.	g	SAC	62	712	11.5	3	0.004	0.05	0.385
333.	MONROE, R.	g	ATL	38	313	8.2	2	0.006	0.05	0.368
334.	CORCHIANI, C.	g	ORL	51	741	14.5	2	0.003	0.04	0.399
335.	CROWDER, C.	g/f	UT	51	328	6.4	2	0.006	0.04	0.384
336.	GEORGE, T.	g	NJ	70	1037	14.8	3	0.003	0.04	0.428

(NAME)	FT PCT	3-PT SHOTS MADE	3-PT SHOTS TRIED	REBs	ASTs	STLs	TURN-OVERS	PTs
(SMITH, To.)	0.653	0	11	76	109	39	50	275
(SUTTON, G.)	0.756	26	89	47	91	26	70	246
(TUCKER, T.)	0.800	19	48	37	27	21	14	155
(WHATLEY, E.)	0.871	0	4	21	34	14	14	69
(ADAMS, M.)	0.869	125	386	310	594	145	212	1408
(CONNER, L.)	0.704	0	7	184	294	97	79	287
(ROYAL, D.)	0.692	0	0	124	34	25	39	252
(VANDEWEGHE, K.)	0.803	26	66	88	57	15	27	467
(ANTHONY, G.)	0.741	8	55	136	314	59	98	447
(EACKLES, L.)	0.743	7	35	178	125	47	75	856
(ENGLISH, A.J.)	0.841	6	34	168	143	32	89	886
(PAXSON, Jo.)	0.784	12	44	96	241	49	44	555
(SPARROW, R.)	0.615	3	15	28	83	12	33	127
(TEAGLE, T.)	0.767	1	4	183	113	66	114	880
(WINCHESTER, K.)	0.800	1	2	15	8	2	2	35
(GARRICK, T.)	0.692	1	4	56	98	36	44	137
(MOORE, T.)	0.833	30	84	82	48	32	44	355
(PHILLS, B.)	0.636	0	2	8	4	3	8	31
(TURNER, Jo.)	0.525	0	0	78	12	6	32	117
(VINCENT, S.)	0.846	1	13	101	148	35	72	411
(BROOKS, S.)	0.810	32	90	99	205	66	51	417
(BROWN, T.)	0.727	19	63	84	48	30	35	271
(DAILEY, Q.)	0.813	0	1	12	4	5	10	31
(DAVIS, B.)	0.733	5	18	33	66	11	27	92
(FEITL, D.)	0.842	0	0	61	6	2	19	82
(FLEMING, V.)	0.737	6	27	209	266	56	140	726
(SCHEFFLER, S.)	0.750	0	0	14	0	3	1	21
(SMITH, K.)	0.866	54	137	177	562	104	227	1137
(MAYES, Th.)	0.667	15	41	16	35	16	31	99
(BATTLE, J.)	0.848	2	17	112	159	36	91	779
(BOGUES, M.)	0.783	2	27	235	743	170	156	730
(KNIGHT, N.)	0.688	4	13	46	112	24	58	243
(LANE, J.)	0.333	0	0	66	17	2	14	37
(OLIVER, J.)	0.773	1	9	27	20	9	9	96
(RIVERS, Da.)	0.909	0	1	19	21	7	17	30
(SKILES, S.)	0.895	91	250	202	544	74	233	1057
(ARMSTRONG, B.J.)	0.806	35	87	145	266	46	94	809
(AUSTIN, I.)	0.633	0	0	35	5	2	8	61
(DAWKINS, J.)	0.882	36	101	227	567	89	183	988
(MALONE, J.)	0.898	1	12	233	180	56	140	1639
(OLIVER, B.)	0.682	0	4	30	20	10	24	81
(PACK, R.)	0.803	0	10	97	140	40	92	332
(PERRY, E.)	0.659	1	7	39	78	34	50	126
(RANDALL, M.)	0.744	03	16	71	33	12	25	171
(WILEY, M.)	0.686	14	42	81	180	47	60	204
(YOUNG, D.)	0.851	23	70	75	172	46	47	280
(BAGLEY, J.)	0.716	10	42	161	480	57	148	524
(BARROS, D.)	0.760	83	186	81	125	51	56	619
(BROOKS, K.)	0.810	2	11	39	11	8	18	105
(JACKSON, C.)	0.870	31	94	114	192	44	117	837
(KOFOED, B.)	0.577	1	7	26	51	2	20	66
(LES, J.)	0.809	45	131	63	143	31	42	231
(MONROE, R.)	0.826	6	27	33	27	12	23	131
(CORCHIANI, C.)	0.875	10	37	78	141	45	74	255
(CROWDER, C.)	0.833	13	30	41	17	7	13	114
(GEORGE, T.)	0.821	1	6	105	162	41	82	418

1991–92 REGULAR-SEASON STATISTICAL RESULTS
NBA PLAYERS ORDERED BY BLOCKS PER GAME

	NAME	POS	TEAM	GMs	MINs	MINs per GM	BLKs	BLKs per MIN	BLKs per GM	FG PCT
337.	GREEN, R.	g	BOS	26	367	14.1	1	0.003	0.04	0.447
338.	HANSEN, B.	g	CHI	68	809	11.9	3	0.004	0.04	0.444
339.	MORTON, J.	g	MIA	25	270	10.8	1	0.004	0.04	0.387
340.	NEALY, E.	f	PHX	52	505	9.7	2	0.004	0.04	0.512
341.	GRANT, Gr.	g	PHI	68	891	13.1	2	0.002	0.03	0.440
342.	THOMAS, C.	g	DET	37	156	4.2	1	0.006	0.03	0.353
343.	TURNER, A.	g	WAS	70	871	12.4	2	0.002	0.03	0.425
344.	BLANKS, L.	g	DET	43	189	4.4	1	0.005	0.02	0.455
345.	DAVIS, W.	g	DEN	46	741	16.1	1	0.001	0.02	0.459
346.	HENSON, S.	g	MIL	50	386	7.7	1	0.003	0.02	0.361
347.	HODGES, C.	g	CHI	56	555	9.9	1	0.002	0.02	0.384
348.	IUZZOLINO, M.	g	DAL	52	1280	24.6	1	0.001	0.02	0.451
349.	LEE, D.	g	NJ	46	307	6.7	1	0.003	0.02	0.431
350.	RUDD, D.	g	UT	65	538	8.3	1	0.002	0.02	0.399
351.	SMITH, La.	g	WAS	48	708	14.7	1	0.001	0.02	0.407
352.	WIGGINS, M.	g	PHI	49	569	11.6	1	0.002	0.02	0.384
353.	ANSLEY, M.	f	CHA	10	45	4.5	0	0.000	0.00	0.444
354.	CHEEKS, M.	g	ATL	56	1086	19.4	0	0.000	0.00	0.462
355.	HENDERSON, G.	g	DET	16	96	6.0	0	0.000	0.00	0.375
356.	JAMERSON, D.	f	HOU	48	378	7.9	0	0.000	0.00	0.414
357.	MAYS, T.	g	ATL	2	32	16.0	0	0.000	0.00	0.429
358.	McCORMICK, T.	c	NY	22	108	4.9	0	0.000	0.00	0.424
359.	WITTMAN, R.	g	IND	24	115	4.8	0	0.000	0.00	0.421

(NAME)	FT PCT	3-PT SHOTS MADE	3-PT SHOTS TRIED	REBs	ASTs	STLs	TURN-OVERS	PTs
(GREEN, R.)	0.722	1	4	24	68	17	18	106
(HANSEN, B.)	0.364	7	27	77	69	27	28	173
(MORTON, J.)	0.842	2	16	26	32	13	28	106
(NEALY, E.)	0.667	20	50	111	37	16	17	160
(GRANT, Gr.)	0.833	7	18	69	217	45	46	225
(THOMAS, C.)	0.667	2	17	22	22	4	17	48
(TURNER, A.)	0.792	1	16	90	177	57	84	284
(BLANKS, L.)	0.727	6	16	22	19	14	14	64
(DAVIS, W.)	0.872	5	16	70	68	29	45	457
(HENSON, S.)	0.793	23	48	41	82	15	40	150
(HODGES, C.)	0.941	36	96	24	54	14	22	238
(IUZZOLINO, M.)	0.836	59	136	98	194	33	92	486
(LEE, D.)	0.526	10	37	35	22	11	12	120
(RUDD, D.)	0.762	11	47	54	109	15	49	193
(SMITH, La.)	0.804	2	21	81	99	44	63	247
(WIGGINS, M.)	0.686	0	1	94	22	20	25	211
(ANSLEY, M.)	0.833	0	0	6	2	0	3	21
(CHEEKS, M.)	0.605	3	6	95	185	83	36	259
(HENDERSON, G.)	0.818	3	8	8	10	3	8	36
(JAMERSON, D.)	0.926	8	28	43	33	17	24	191
(MAYS, T.)	1.000	3	6	2	1	0	3	17
(McCORMICK, T.)	0.667	0	0	34	9	2	8	42
(WITTMAN, R.)	0.500	0	0	9	11	2	3	17

1991–92 REGULAR-SEASON STATISTICAL RESULTS
NBA PLAYERS ORDERED BY FIELD-GOAL PERCENTAGE

	NAME	POS	TEAM	GMs	MINs	MINs per GM	FGs MADE	FGs TRIED	FG PCT	FT PCT
1.	SCHEFFLER, S.	f	DEN	11	61	5.6	6	9	0.667	0.750
2.	BATTLE, K.	f	GS	16	92	5.8	11	17	0.647	0.833
• 3.	WEST, M.	c	PHX	82	1436	17.5	196	310	0.632	0.637
4.	WILLIAMS, B.	f	POR	80	2519	31.5	340	563	0.604	0.754
5.	COOK, A.	f	DEN	22	115	5.2	15	25	0.600	0.667
✔ 6.	THORPE, O.	f	HOU	82	3056	37.3	558	943	0.592	0.657
7.	GRANT, Ho.	f	CHI	81	2859	35.3	457	790	0.579	0.741
8.	SANDERS, M.	f	CLE	31	633	20.4	92	161	0.571	0.766
9.	DAUGHERTY, B.	c	CLE	73	2643	36.2	576	1010	0.570	0.777
10.	GATLING, C.	c	GS	54	612	11.3	117	206	0.568	0.661
•11.	CAGE, M.	f	SEA	82	2461	30.0	307	542	0.566	0.620
12.	LISTER, A.	c	GS	26	293	11.3	44	79	0.557	0.424
13.	BARKLEY, C.	f	PHI	75	2881	38.4	622	1126	0.552	0.695
14.	DAVIS, D.	f	IND	64	1301	20.3	154	279	0.552	0.572
15.	ROBINSON, D.	c	SA	68	2564	37.7	592	1074	0.551	0.701
16.	COPA, T.	f/c	SA	33	132	4.0	22	40	0.550	0.308
▪17.	CAUSWELL, D.	c	SAC	80	2291	28.6	250	455	0.550	0.613
18.	OGG, A.	c	MIA	43	367	8.5	46	84	0.548	0.533
~19.	PERDUE, W.	c	CHI	77	1007	13.1	152	278	0.547	0.495
20.	FRANK, T.	f	MIN	10	140	14.0	18	33	0.546	0.667
21.	SMITH, L.	f/c	HOU	45	800	17.8	50	92	0.544	0.364
22.	MANNING, D.	f	LAC	82	2904	35.4	650	1199	0.542	0.725
23.	ELLISON, P.	c	WAS	66	2511	38.0	547	1014	0.539	0.728
24.	NANCE, L.	f	CLE	81	2880	35.6	556	1032	0.539	0.822
25.	RODMAN, D.	f	DET	82	3301	40.3	342	635	0.539	0.600
26.	MARCIULIONIS, S.	g	GS	72	2117	29.4	491	912	0.538	0.788
27.	PINCKNEY, E.	f	BOS	81	1917	23.7	203	378	0.537	0.812
28.	SCHREMPF, D.	f	IND	80	2605	32.6	496	925	0.536	0.828
29.	PARISH, R.	c	BOS	79	2285	28.9	468	874	0.536	0.772
30.	ROLLINS, T.	f/c	HOU	59	697	11.8	46	86	0.535	0.867
31.	ALEXANDER, V.	c	GS	80	1350	16.9	243	459	0.529	0.691
32.	GATTISON, K.	f/c	CHA	82	2223	27.1	423	799	0.529	0.688
33.	ROBERTS, S.	c	ORL	55	1118	20.3	236	446	0.529	0.515
34.	GAMBLE, K.	g/f	BOS	82	2496	30.4	480	908	0.529	0.885
35.	WILLIAMS, Br.	f	ORL	48	905	18.9	171	324	0.528	0.669
36.	PAXSON, J.	g	CHI	79	1946	24.6	257	487	0.528	0.784
37.	MALONE, K.	f	UT	81	3054	37.7	798	1516	0.526	0.778
38.	RULAND, J.	c	PHI	13	209	16.1	20	38	0.526	0.688
39.	OWENS, B.	g/f	GS	80	2510	31.4	468	891	0.525	0.654
40.	MULLIN, C.	f	GS	81	3346	41.3	830	1584	0.524	0.833
41.	BRICKOWSKI, F.	f	MIL	65	1556	23.9	306	584	0.524	0.767
42.	FERRELL, D.	f	ATL	66	1598	24.2	331	632	0.524	0.762
43.	PERRY, T.	f	PHX	80	2483	31.0	413	789	0.523	0.712
44.	OAKLEY, C.	f	NY	82	2309	28.2	210	402	0.522	0.735
45.	LANG, A.	c	PHX	81	1965	24.3	248	475	0.522	0.768
46.	EWING, P.	c	NY	82	3150	38.4	796	1525	0.522	0.738
47.	EDWARDS, T.	g/f	UT	81	2283	28.2	433	830	0.522	0.774
48.	HILL, T.	c/f	GS	82	1886	23.0	254	487	0.522	0.694
49.	ELIE, M.	g/f	GS	79	1677	21.2	221	424	0.521	0.852
50.	HOWARD, B.	f	DAL	27	318	11.8	54	104	0.519	0.710
51.	POLYNICE, O.	c	LAC	76	1834	24.1	244	470	0.519	0.622
52.	JORDAN, M.	g	CHI	80	3102	38.8	943	1818	0.519	0.832
53.	WILLIAMS, K.	f	IND	60	565	9.4	113	218	0.518	0.605
54.	WEST, D.	g	MIN	80	2540	31.7	463	894	0.518	0.805
55.	ACRES, M.	c	ORL	68	926	13.6	78	151	0.517	0.761
56.	HERRERA, C.	f	HOU	43	566	13.2	83	161	0.516	0.568

(NAME)	3-PT SHOTS MADE	3-PT SHOTS TRIED	REBs	ASTs	STLs	TURN-OVERS	BLKs	PTs
(SCHEFFLER, S.)	0	0	14	0	3	1	1	21
(BATTLE, K.)	0	1	16	4	2	4	2	32
(WEST, M.)	0	0	372	22	14	82	81	501
(WILLIAMS, B.)	0	1	704	108	62	130	41	901
(COOK, A.)	0	0	34	2	5	3	4	34
(THORPE, O.)	0	7	862	250	52	237	37	1420
(GRANT, Ho.)	0	2	807	217	100	98	131	1149
(SANDERS, M.)	1	3	96	53	24	22	10	221
(DAUGHERTY, B.)	0	2	760	262	65	185	78	1566
(GATLING, C.)	0	4	182	16	31	44	36	306
(CAGE, M.)	0	5	728	92	99	78	55	720
(LISTER, A.)	0	0	92	14	5	20	16	102
(BARKLEY, C.)	32	137	830	308	136	235	44	1730
(DAVIS, D.)	0	1	410	30	27	49	74	395
(ROBINSON, D.)	1	8	829	181	158	182	305	1578
(COPA, T.)	0	0	36	3	2	8	6	48
(CAUSWELL, D.)	0	1	580	59	47	124	215	636
(OGG, A.)	0	0	74	7	5	19	28	108
(PERDUE, W.)	1	2	312	80	16	72	43	350
(FRANK, T.)	0	0	26	8	5	5	4	46
(SMITH, L.)	0	1	256	33	21	44	7	104
(MANNING, D.)	0	5	564	285	135	210	122	1579
(ELLISON, P.)	1	3	740	190	62	196	177	1322
(NANCE, L.)	0	6	670	232	80	87	243	1375
(RODMAN, D.)	32	101	1530	191	68	140	70	800
(MARCIULIONIS, S.)	3	10	208	243	116	193	10	1361
(PINCKNEY, E.)	0	1	564	62	70	73	56	613
(SCHREMPF, D.)	23	71	770	312	62	191	37	1380
(PARISH, R.)	0	0	705	70	68	131	97	1115
(ROLLINS, T.)	0	0	171	15	14	18	62	118
(ALEXANDER, V.)	0	1	336	32	45	91	62	589
(GATTISON, K.)	0	2	580	131	59	140	69	142
(ROBERTS, S.)	0	1	336	39	22	78	83	573
(GAMBLE, K.)	9	31	286	219	75	97	37	1108
(WILLIAMS, Br.)	0	0	272	33	41	86	53	437
(PAXSON, J.)	12	44	96	241	49	44	9	555
(MALONE, K.)	3	17	909	241	108	248	51	2272
(RULAND, J.)	0	0	47	5	7	20	4	51
(OWENS, B.)	1	9	639	188	90	179	65	1141
(MULLIN, C.)	64	175	450	286	173	202	62	2074
(BRICKOWSKI, F.)	3	6	344	122	60	112	23	740
(FERRELL, D.)	11	33	210	92	49	99	17	839
(PERRY, T.)	3	8	551	134	44	141	116	982
(OAKLEY, C.)	0	3	700	133	67	123	15	506
(LANG, A.)	0	1	546	43	48	87	201	622
(EWING, P.)	1	6	921	156	88	209	245	1970
(EDWARDS, T.)	39	103	298	137	81	122	46	1018
(HILL, T.)	0	1	593	47	73	106	43	671
(ELIE, M.)	23	70	227	174	68	83	15	620
(HOWARD, B.)	1	2	51	14	11	15	8	131
(POLYNICE, O.)	0	1	536	46	45	83	20	613
(JORDAN, M.)	27	100	511	489	182	200	75	2404
(WILLIAMS, K.)	0	4	129	40	20	22	41	252
(WEST, D.)	4	23	257	281	66	120	26	1116
(ACRES, M.)	1	3	252	22	25	33	15	208
(HERRERA, C.)	0	1	99	27	16	37	25	191

1991-92 REGULAR-SEASON STATISTICAL RESULTS
NBA PLAYERS ORDERED BY FIELD-GOAL PERCENTAGE

	NAME	POS	TEAM	GMs	MINs	MINs per GM	FGs MADE	FGs TRIED	FG PCT	FT PCT
57.	STEWART, L.	f	WAS	76	2229	29.3	303	590	0.514	0.807
58.	LECKNER, E.	c	CHA	59	716	12.1	79	154	0.513	0.745
59.	NEALY, E.	f	PHX	52	505	9.7	62	121	0.512	0.667
60.	SALLEY, J.	f/c	DET	72	1774	24.6	249	486	0.512	0.715
61.	HORNACEK, J.	g	PHX	81	3078	38.0	635	1240	0.512	0.886
62.	GILLIAM, A.	f/c	PHI	81	2771	34.2	512	1001	0.512	0.807
63.	MALONE, J.	g	UT	81	2922	36.1	691	1353	0.511	0.898
64.	KERR, S.	g	CLE	48	847	17.6	121	237	0.511	0.833
65.	SMITS, R.	c	IND	74	1772	23.9	436	855	0.510	0.788
66.	McHALE, K.	f/c	BOS	56	1398	25.0	323	634	0.510	0.822
67.	ASKEW, V.	g	GS	80	1496	18.7	193	379	0.509	0.694
68.	MASON, A.	f	NY	82	2198	26.8	203	399	0.509	0.642
69.	PETROVIC, D.	g	NJ	82	3027	36.9	668	1315	0.508	0.808
70.	KING, S.	f/c	CHI	79	1268	16.1	215	425	0.506	0.753
71.	PIPPEN, S.	f	CHI	82	3164	38.6	687	1359	0.506	0.760
72.	KEMP, S.	f/c	SEA	64	1808	28.2	362	718	0.504	0.748
73.	COLEMAN, D.	f	NJ	65	2207	34.0	483	958	0.504	0.763
74.	LEWIS, Re.	g	BOS	82	3070	37.4	703	1397	0.503	0.851
75.	WILLIAMS, J.	f/c	CLE	80	2432	30.4	341	678	0.503	0.752
76.	OLAJUWON, H.	c	HOU	70	2636	37.7	591	1177	0.502	0.766
77.	MILLER, R.	g	IND	82	3120	38.0	562	1121	0.501	0.858
78.	TISDALE, W.	f	SAC	72	2521	35.0	522	1043	0.501	0.763
79.	WOOLRIDGE, O.	f	DET	82	2113	25.8	452	907	0.498	0.683
80.	LEVINGSTON, C.	f	CHI	79	1020	12.9	125	251	0.498	0.625
81.	HODGE, D.	c/f	DAL	51	1058	20.7	163	328	0.497	0.667
82.	CATLEDGE, T.	f	ORL	78	2430	31.2	457	922	0.496	0.694
83.	DIVAC, V.	c	LAL	36	979	27.2	157	317	0.495	0.768
84.	LONG, G.	f	MIA	82	3063	37.4	440	890	0.494	0.807
85.	DREILING, G.	c	IND	60	509	8.5	43	87	0.494	0.750
86.	ELLIOTT, S.	f	SA	82	3120	38.0	514	1040	0.494	0.861
87.	ABDELNABY, A.	f/c	POR	71	934	13.2	178	361	0.493	0.753
88.	BOWIE, A.	g/f	ORL	52	1721	33.1	312	633	0.493	0.860
89.	MUTOMBO, D.	c	DEN	71	2716	38.3	428	869	0.493	0.642
90.	VAUGHT, L.	f	LAC	79	1687	21.4	271	551	0.492	0.797
91.	KLEINE, J.	c	BOS	70	991	14.2	144	293	0.492	0.708
92.	JACKSON, M.	g	NY	81	2461	30.4	367	747	0.491	0.770
93.	VANDEWEGHE, K.	f	NY	67	956	14.3	188	383	0.491	0.803
94.	CARR, A.	f/c	SA	81	1867	23.0	359	732	0.490	0.764
95.	WILLIAMS, M.	g	IND	79	2750	34.8	404	824	0.490	0.871
96.	JOHNSON, L.	f	CHA	82	3047	37.2	616	1258	0.490	0.829
97.	REID, J.R.	c/f	CHA	51	1257	24.6	213	435	0.490	0.705
98.	NORMAN, K.	f	LAC	77	2009	26.1	402	821	0.490	0.535
99.	AUGMON, S.	g/f	ATL	82	2505	30.5	440	899	0.489	0.666
100.	THREATT, S.	g	LAL	82	3070	37.4	509	1041	0.489	0.831
101.	SEIKALY, R.	c	MIA	79	2800	35.4	463	947	0.489	0.733
102.	PRICE, M.	g	CLE	72	2138	29.7	438	897	0.488	0.947
103.	CUMMINGS, T.	f	SA	70	2149	30.7	514	1053	0.488	0.711
104.	HAMMONDS, T.	f	CHA	37	984	26.6	195	400	0.488	0.610
105.	MURPHY, T.	f	MIN	47	429	9.1	39	80	0.488	0.559
106.	SHACKLEFORD, C.	c	PHI	72	1399	19.4	205	422	0.486	0.663
107.	CURRY, D.	g	CHA	77	2020	26.2	504	1038	0.486	0.836
108.	WILLIS, K.	f/c	ATL	81	2962	36.6	591	1224	0.483	0.804
109.	BARROS, D.	g	SEA	75	1331	17.7	238	493	0.483	0.760
110.	WILLIAMS, S.	f	CHI	63	690	11.0	83	172	0.483	0.649
111.	STOCKTON, J.	g	UT	82	3002	36.6	453	939	0.482	0.842
112.	CEBALLOS, C.	f	PHX	64	725	11.3	176	365	0.482	0.737

(NAME)	3-PT SHOTS MADE	3-PT SHOTS TRIED	REBs	ASTs	STLs	TURN-OVERS	BLKs	PTs
(STEWART, L.)	0	3	449	120	51	112	44	794
(LECKNER, E.)	0	1	206	31	9	39	18	196
(NEALY, E.)	20	50	111	37	16	17	2	160
(SALLEY, J.)	0	3	296	116	49	102	110	684
(HORNACEK, J.)	83	189	407	411	158	170	31	1632
(GILLIAM, A.)	0	2	660	118	51	166	85	1367
(MALONE, J.)	1	12	233	180	56	140	5	1639
(KERR, S.)	32	74	78	110	27	31	10	319
(SMITS, R.)	0	2	417	116	29	130	100	1024
(McHALE, K.)	0	13	330	82	11	82	59	780
(ASKEW, V.)	1	10	233	188	47	84	23	498
(MASON, A.)	0	0	573	106	46	101	20	573
(PETROVIC, D.)	123	277	258	252	105	215	11	1691
(KING, S.)	2	5	205	77	21	76	25	551
(PIPPEN, S.)	16	80	630	572	155	253	93	1720
(KEMP, S.)	0	3	665	86	70	156	124	994
(COLEMAN, D.)	23	76	618	205	54	248	98	1289
(LEWIS, Re.)	5	21	394	185	125	136	105	1703
(WILLIAMS, J.)	0	4	607	196	60	83	182	952
(OLAJUWON, H.)	0	1	845	157	127	187	304	1510
(MILLER, R.)	129	341	318	314	105	157	26	1695
(TISDALE, W.)	0	2	469	106	55	124	79	1195
(WOOLRIDGE, O.)	1	9	260	88	41	133	33	1146
(LEVINGSTON, C.)	1	6	227	66	27	42	45	311
(HODGE, D.)	0	0	275	39	25	75	23	426
(CATLEDGE, T.)	0	4	549	109	58	138	16	1154
(DIVAC, V.)	5	19	247	60	55	88	35	405
(LONG, G.)	6	22	691	225	139	185	40	1212
(DREILING, G.)	1	1	96	25	10	31	16	117
(ELLIOTT, S.)	25	82	439	214	84	152	29	1338
(ABDELNABY, A.)	0	0	260	30	25	66	16	432
(BOWIE, A.)	17	44	245	163	55	107	38	758
(MUTOMBO, D.)	0	0	870	156	43	252	210	1177
(VAUGHT, L.)	4	5	512	71	37	66	31	601
(KLEINE, J.)	4	8	296	32	23	27	14	326
(JACKSON, M.)	11	43	305	694	112	211	13	916
(VANDEWEGHE, K.)	26	66	88	57	15	27	8	467
(CARR, A.)	1	5	346	63	32	114	96	881
(WILLIAMS, M.)	8	33	282	647	233	240	22	1188
(JOHNSON, L.)	5	22	899	292	81	160	51	1576
(REID, J.R.)	0	3	317	81	49	84	23	560
(NORMAN, K.)	4	28	448	125	53	100	66	929
(AUGMON, S.)	1	6	420	201	124	181	27	1094
(THREATT, S.)	20	62	253	593	168	182	16	1240
(SEIKALY, R.)	0	3	934	109	40	216	121	1296
(PRICE, M.)	101	261	173	535	94	159	12	1247
(CUMMINGS, T.)	5	13	631	102	58	115	34	1210
(HAMMONDS, T.)	0	1	185	36	22	58	13	440
(MURPHY, T.)	1	2	110	11	9	18	8	98
(SHACKLEFORD, C.)	0	1	415	46	38	62	51	473
(CURRY, D.)	74	183	259	177	93	134	20	1209
(WILLIS, K.)	6	37	1258	173	72	197	54	1480
(BARROS, D.)	83	186	81	125	51	56	4	619
(WILLIAMS, S.)	0	3	247	50	13	35	36	214
(STOCKTON, J.)	83	204	270	1126	244	286	22	1297
(CEBALLOS, C.)	1	6	152	50	16	71	11	462

1991-92 REGULAR-SEASON STATISTICAL RESULTS
NBA PLAYERS ORDERED BY FIELD-GOAL PERCENTAGE

	NAME	POS	TEAM	GMs	MINs	MINs per GM	FGs MADE	FGs TRIED	FG PCT	FT PCT
113.	ROBERTS, F.	f	MIL	80	1746	21.8	311	645	0.482	0.749
114.	DAVIS, T.	f/c	DAL	68	2149	31.6	256	531	0.482	0.635
115.	FLEMING, V.	g	IND	82	1737	21.2	294	610	0.482	0.737
116.	CORBIN, T.	f	UT	80	2207	27.6	303	630	0.481	0.866
117.	ARMSTRONG, B.J.	g	CHI	82	1875	22.9	335	697	0.481	0.806
118.	BRYANT, M.	c	POR	56	800	14.3	95	198	0.480	0.667
119.	PERSON, C.	f	IND	81	2923	36.1	616	1284	0.480	0.675
120.	BATTLE, J.	g	CLE	76	1637	21.5	316	659	0.480	0.848
121.	JOHNSON, K.	g	PHX	78	2899	37.2	539	1125	0.479	0.807
122.	JOHNSON, A.	g	HOU	69	1235	17.9	158	330	0.479	0.654
123.	GRANT, Ha.	f	WAS	64	2388	37.3	489	1022	0.479	0.800
124.	BENJAMIN, B.	c	SEA	63	1941	30.8	354	740	0.478	0.687
125.	McDANIEL, X.	f	NY	82	2344	28.6	488	1021	0.478	0.714
126.	RASMUSSEN, B.	c	ATL	81	1968	24.3	347	726	0.478	0.750
127.	MAJERLE, D.	g/f	PHX	82	2853	34.8	551	1153	0.478	0.756
128.	NEWMAN, J.	f/g	CHA	55	1651	30.0	295	618	0.477	0.766
129.	MUSTAF, J.	f	PHX	52	545	10.5	92	193	0.477	0.690
130.	MORRIS, C.	f	NJ	77	2394	31.1	346	726	0.477	0.714
131.	GREEN, A.C.	f	LAL	82	2902	35.4	382	803	0.476	0.744
132.	CONLON, M.	c	SEA	45	381	8.5	48	101	0.475	0.750
133.	PIERCE, R.	g	SEA	78	2658	34.1	620	1306	0.475	0.917
134.	SMITH, K.	g	HOU	81	2735	33.8	432	910	0.475	0.866
135.	KNIGHT, N.	g	PHX	42	631	15.0	103	217	0.475	0.688
136.	MALONE, M.	c	MIL	82	2511	30.6	440	929	0.474	0.786
137.	BOGUES, M.	g	CHA	82	2790	34.0	317	671	0.472	0.783
138.	McKEY, D.	f	SEA	52	1757	33.8	285	604	0.472	0.847
139.	KOFOED, B.	g	SEA	44	239	5.4	25	53	0.472	0.577
140.	WILLIAMS, R.	f	DEN	81	2623	32.4	601	1277	0.471	0.803
141.	PRITCHARD, K.	g	BOS	11	136	12.4	16	34	0.471	0.778
142.	LAIMBEER, B.	c	DET	81	2234	27.6	342	727	0.470	0.893
143.	DREXLER, C.	g	POR	76	2751	36.2	694	1476	0.470	0.794
144.	HUMPHRIES, J.	g	MIL	71	2261	31.8	377	803	0.470	0.783
145.	RICE, G.	f	MIA	79	3007	38.1	672	1432	0.469	0.837
146.	ELLIS, D.	f	MIL	81	2191	27.0	485	1034	0.469	0.774
147.	BROWN, C.	f	LAL	42	431	10.3	60	128	0.469	0.612
148.	VRANKOVIC, S.	c	BOS	19	110	5.8	15	32	0.469	0.583
149.	BREUER, R.	c	MIN	67	1176	17.6	161	344	0.468	0.533
150.	THOMPSON, L.	f/c	IND	80	1299	16.2	168	359	0.468	0.817
151.	EACKLES, L.	f	WAS	65	1463	22.5	355	759	0.468	0.743
152.	RICHMOND, M.	g	SAC	80	3095	38.7	685	1465	0.468	0.813
153.	CARTWRIGHT, B.	c	CHI	64	1471	23.0	208	445	0.467	0.604
154.	KERSEY, J.	f	POR	77	2553	33.2	398	852	0.467	0.664
155.	GILL, K.	g/f	CHA	79	2906	36.8	666	1427	0.467	0.745
156.	BENOIT, D.	f	UT	77	1161	15.1	175	375	0.467	0.810
157.	ROBINSON, C.	f	POR	82	2124	25.9	398	854	0.466	0.664
158.	SELLERS, B.	f/c	DET	43	226	5.3	41	88	0.466	0.769
159.	BIRD, L.	f	BOS	45	1662	36.9	353	758	0.466	0.926
160.	SMITH, C.	f/c	LAC	49	1310	26.7	251	539	0.466	0.785
161.	RICHARDSON, P.	g	MIN	82	2922	35.6	587	1261	0.466	0.691
162.	HOPSON, D.	g/f	SAC	71	1314	18.5	276	593	0.465	0.708
163.	ANDERSON, Ro.	f	PHI	82	2432	29.7	469	1008	0.465	0.877
164.	TUCKER, T.	g	SA	24	415	17.3	60	129	0.465	0.800
165.	WINGATE, D.	g	WAS	81	2127	26.3	266	572	0.465	0.719
166.	EDWARDS, Ja.	c	LAC	72	1437	20.0	250	538	0.465	0.731
167.	WILKINS, D.	f	ATL	42	1601	38.1	424	914	0.464	0.835
168.	CAMPBELL, T.	f/g	MIN	78	2441	31.3	527	1137	0.464	0.803

(NAME)	3-PT SHOTS MADE	3-PT SHOTS TRIED	REBs	ASTs	STLs	TURN-OVERS	BLKs	PTs
(ROBERTS, F.)	19	37	257	122	52	122	40	769
(DAVIS, T.)	0	5	672	57	26	117	29	693
(FLEMING, V.)	6	27	209	266	56	140	7	726
(CORBIN, T.)	0	4	472	140	82	97	20	780
(ARMSTRONG, B.J.)	35	87	145	266	46	94	5	809
(BRYANT, M.)	0	3	201	41	26	30	8	230
(PERSON, C.)	132	354	426	382	68	216	18	1497
(BATTLE, J.)	2	17	112	159	36	91	5	779
(JOHNSON, K.)	10	46	292	836	116	272	23	1536
(JOHNSON, A.)	4	15	80	266	61	110	9	386
(GRANT, Ha.)	1	8	432	170	74	109	27	1155
(BENJAMIN, B.)	0	2	513	76	39	175	118	879
(McDANIEL, X.)	12	39	460	149	57	147	24	1125
(RASMUSSEN, B.)	5	23	393	107	35	51	48	729
(MAJERLE, D.)	87	228	483	274	131	101	43	1418
(NEWMAN, J.)	13	46	179	146	70	129	14	839
(MUSTAF, J.)	0	0	145	45	21	51	16	233
(MORRIS, C.)	22	110	494	197	129	171	81	879
(GREEN, A.C.)	12	56	762	117	91	111	36	1116
(CONLON, M.)	0	0	69	12	9	27	7	120
(PIERCE, R.)	33	123	233	241	86	189	20	1690
(SMITH, K.)	54	137	177	562	104	227	7	1137
(KNIGHT, N.)	4	13	46	112	24	58	3	243
(MALONE, M.)°	3	8	744	93	74	150	64	1279
(BOGUES, M.)	2	27	235	743	170	156	6	730
(McKEY, D.)	19	50	268	120	61	114	47	777
(KOFOED, B.)	1	7	26	51	2	20	2	66
(WILLIAMS, R.)	56	156	405	235	148	173	68	1474
(PRITCHARD, K.)	0	3	11	30	3	011	4	46
(LAIMBEER, B.)	32	85	451	160	51	102	54	783
(DREXLER, C.)	114	338	500	512	138	240	70	1903
(HUMPHRIES, J.)	42	144	184	466	119	148	13	991
(RICE, G.)	155	396	394	184	90	145	35	1765
(ELLIS, D.)	138	329	253	104	57	119	18	1272
(BROWN, C.)	0	3	82	26	12	29	7	150
(VRANKOVIC, S.)	0	0	28	5	0	10	17	37
(BREUER, R.)	0	1	281	89	27	41	99	363
(THOMPSON, L.)	0	2	381	102	52	98	34	394
(EACKLES, L.)	7	35	178	125	47	75	7	856
(RICHMOND, M.)	103	268	319	411	92	247	34	1803
(CARTWRIGHT, B.)	0	0	324	87	22	75	14	512
(KERSEY, J.)	1	8	633	243	114	151	71	971
(GILL, K.)	6	25	402	329	154	180	46	1622
(BENOIT, D.)	3	14	296	34	19	71	44	434
(ROBINSON, C.)	1	11	416	137	85	154	107	1016
(SELLERS, B.)	0	1	42	14	1	15	10	102
(BIRD, L.)	52	128	434	306	42	125	33	908
(SMITH, C.)	0	6	301	56	41	69	98	714
(RICHARDSON, P.)	53	155	301	685	119	204	25	1350
(HOPSON, D.)	12	47	206	102	67	100	39	743
(ANDERSON, Ro.)	42	127	278	135	86	109	11	1123
(TUCKER, T.)	19	48	37	27	21	14	3	155
(WINGATE, D.)	1	18	269	247	123	124	21	638
(EDWARDS, Ja.)	0	1	202	53	24	72	33	698
(WILKINS, D.)	37	128	295	158	52	122	24	1179
(CAMPBELL, T.)	13	37	286	229	84	165	31	1307

1991–92 REGULAR-SEASON STATISTICAL RESULTS
NBA PLAYERS ORDERED BY FIELD-GOAL PERCENTAGE

	NAME	POS	TEAM	GMs	MINs	MINs per GM	FGs MADE	FGs TRIED	FG PCT	FT PCT
169.	RAMBIS, K.	f	PHX	28	381	13.6	38	82	0.463	0.778
170.	MILLS, T.	f	NJ	82	1714	20.9	310	670	0.463	0.750
171.	ANDERSON, N.	g/f	ORL	60	2203	36.7	482	1042	0.463	0.667
172.	BURTT, S.	g	PHX	31	356	11.5	74	160	0.463	0.704
173.	DOUGLAS, S.	g	BOS	42	752	17.9	117	253	0.463	0.682
174.	HAWKINS, H.	g	PHI	81	3013	37.2	521	1127	0.462	0.874
175.	GRANT, Ga.	g	LAC	78	2049	26.3	275	595	0.462	0.815
176.	CHEEKS, M.	g	ATL	56	1086	19.4	115	249	0.462	0.605
177.	PORTER, T.	g	POR	82	2784	34.0	521	1129	0.462	0.856
178.	FOSTER, G.	f	WAS	49	548	11.2	89	193	0.461	0.714
179.	HARDAWAY, T.	g	GS	81	3332	41.1	734	1592	0.461	0.766
180.	BLACKMAN, R.	g	DAL	75	2527	33.7	535	1161	0.461	0.899
181.	DUCKWORTH, K.	c	POR	82	2222	27.1	362	786	0.461	0.690
182.	LICHTI, T.	g	DEN	68	1176	17.3	173	376	0.460	0.839
183.	DAVIS, W.	g	DEN	46	741	16.1	185	403	0.459	0.872
184.	FOX, R.	g/f	BOS	81	1535	19.0	241	525	0.459	0.755
185.	JOHNSON, E.	f	SEA	81	2366	29.2	534	1164	0.459	0.861
186.	BULLARD, M.	f	HOU	80	1278	16.0	205	447	0.459	0.760
187.	HIGGINS, S.	f	ORL	38	616	16.2	127	277	0.459	0.861
188.	JOHNSON, B.	f	HOU	80	2202	27.5	290	633	0.458	0.727
189.	LONGLEY, L.	c	MIN	66	991	15.0	114	249	0.458	0.663
190.	SCOTT, B.	g	LAL	82	2679	32.7	460	1005	0.458	0.839
191.	DONALDSON, J.	c	NY	58	1075	18.5	112	245	0.457	0.709
192.	AUSTIN, I.	c	UT	31	112	3.6	21	46	0.457	0.633
193.	RANDALL, M.	f	MIN	54	441	8.2	68	149	0.456	0.744
194.	ROBINSON, R.	g	ATL	81	2220	27.4	423	928	0.456	0.636
195.	BROWN, R.	g	SAC	56	535	9.6	77	169	0.456	0.655
196.	ANDERSON, G.	f	DEN	82	2793	34.1	389	854	0.456	0.623
197.	ANDERSON, W.	g/f	SA	57	1889	33.1	312	685	0.456	0.775
198.	STRICKLAND, R.	g	SA	57	2053	36.0	300	659	0.455	0.687
199.	BLANKS, L.	g	DET	43	189	4.4	25	55	0.455	0.727
200.	COLES, B.	g	MIA	81	1976	24.4	295	649	0.455	0.824
201.	SMITH, S.	g	MIA	61	1806	29.6	297	654	0.454	0.748
202.	EDWARDS, K.	g	MIA	81	1840	22.7	325	716	0.454	0.848
203.	SIMMONS, L.	f	SAC	78	2895	37.1	527	1162	0.454	0.770
204.	EHLO, C.	g/f	CLE	63	2016	32.0	310	684	0.453	0.707
205.	BROWN, M.	c/f	UT	82	1783	21.7	221	488	0.453	0.667
206.	GMINSKI, M.	c	CHA	35	499	14.3	90	199	0.452	0.750
207.	TEAGLE, T.	f	LAL	82	1602	19.5	364	805	0.452	0.767
208.	CHILCUTT, P.	f/c	SAC	69	817	11.8	113	250	0.452	0.821
209.	PAYTON, G.	g	SEA	81	2549	31.5	331	734	0.451	0.669
210.	TURNER, J.	f	ORL	75	1591	21.2	225	499	0.451	0.693
211.	IUZZOLINO, M.	g	DAL	52	1280	24.6	160	355	0.451	0.836
212.	BURTON, W.	g/f	MIA	68	1585	23.3	280	622	0.450	0.800
213.	LOHAUS, B.	f/c	MIL	70	1081	15.4	162	360	0.450	0.659
214.	PETERSEN, J.	c	GS	27	169	6.3	18	40	0.450	0.700
215.	PERKINS, S.	f/c	LAL	63	2332	37.0	361	803	0.450	0.817
216.	ROYAL, D.	f	SA	60	718	12.0	80	178	0.449	0.692
217.	STARKS, J.	g	NY	82	2118	25.8	405	902	0.449	0.778
218.	GRAYER, J.	g	MIL	82	1659	20.2	309	689	0.449	0.667
219.	CHAPMAN, R.	g	WAS	22	567	25.8	113	252	0.448	0.679
220.	PAYNE, K.	f	PHI	49	353	7.2	65	145	0.448	0.692
221.	CAMPBELL, E.	c	LAL	81	1876	23.2	220	491	0.448	0.619
222.	DUMARS, J.	g	DET	82	3192	38.9	587	1311	0.448	0.867
223.	GRAHAM, P.	g	ATL	78	1718	22.0	305	682	0.447	0.741
224.	WILKINS, G.	g	NY	82	2344	28.6	431	964	0.447	0.730

(NAME)	3-PT SHOTS MADE	3-PT SHOTS TRIED	REBs	ASTs	STLs	TURN-OVERS	BLKs	PTs
(RAMBIS, K.)	0	0	106	37	12	25	14	90
(MILLS, T.)	8	23	453	84	48	82	41	742
(ANDERSON, N.)	30	85	384	163	97	125	33	1196
(BURTT, S.)	1	6	34	59	16	33	4	187
(DOUGLAS, S.)	1	10	63	172	25	68	9	308
(HAWKINS, H.)	91	229	271	248	157	189	43	1536
(GRANT, Ga.)	15	51	184	538	138	187	14	609
(CHEEKS, M.)	3	6	95	185	83	36	0	259
(PORTER, T.)	128	324	255	477	127	188	12	1485
(FOSTER, G.)	0	1	145	35	6	36	12	213
(HARDAWAY, T.)	127	376	310	807	164	267	13	1893
(BLACKMAN, R.)	65	169	239	204	50	153	22	1374
(DUCKWORTH, K.)	0	3	497	99	38	143	37	880
(LICHTI, T.)	1	9	118	74	43	72	12	446
(DAVIS, W.)	5	16	70	68	29	45	1	457
(FOX, R.)	23	70	220	126	78	123	30	644
(JOHNSON, E.)	27	107	292	161	55	130	11	1386
(BULLARD, M.)	64	166	223	75	26	056	21	512
(HIGGINS, S.)	6	25	102	41	16	41	6	291
(JOHNSON, B.)	1	9	312	158	72	104	49	685
(LONGLEY, L.)	0	0	257	53	35	83	64	281
(SCOTT, B.)	54	157	310	226	105	119	28	1218
(DONALDSON, J.)	0	0	289	33	8	48	49	285
(AUSTIN, I.)	0	0	35	5	2	8	2	61
(RANDALL, M.)	3	16	71	33	12	25	3	171
(ROBINSON, R.)	34	104	219	446	105	206	24	1055
(BROWN, R.)	0	6	69	59	35	42	12	192
(ANDERSON, G.)	0	4	941	78	88	201	65	945
(ANDERSON, W.)	13	56	300	302	54	140	51	744
(STRICKLAND, R.)	5	15	265	491	118	160	17	787
(BLANKS, L.)	6	16	22	19	14	14	1	64
(COLES, B.)	10	52	189	366	73	167	13	816
(SMITH, S.)	40	125	188	278	59	152	19	729
(EDWARDS, K.)	7	32	211	170	99	120	20	819
(SIMMONS, L.)	1	5	634	337	135	218	132	1336
(EHLO, C.)	69	167	307	238	78	104	22	776
(BROWN, M.)	0	1	476	81	42	105	34	632
(GMINSKI, M.)	1	3	118	31	11	20	16	202
(TEAGLE, T.)	1	4	183	113	66	114	9	880
(CHILCUTT, P.)	2	2	187	38	32	41	17	251
(PAYTON, G.)	3	23	295	506	147	174	21	764
(TURNER, J.)	1	8	246	92	24	106	16	530
(IUZZOLINO, M.)	59	136	98	194	33	92	1	486
(BURTON, W.)	6	15	244	123	46	119	37	762
(LOHAUS, B.)	57	144	249	74	40	46	71	408
(PETERSEN, J.)	0	2	45	9	5	5	6	43
(PERKINS, S.)	15	69	556	141	64	83	62	1041
(ROYAL, D.)	0	0	124	34	25	39	7	252
(STARKS, J.)	94	270	191	276	103	150	18	1139
(GRAYER, J.)	19	66	257	150	64	105	13	739
(CHAPMAN, R.)	8	29	58	89	15	45	8	270
(PAYNE, K.)	5	12	54	17	16	19	8	144
(CAMPBELL, E.)	0	2	423	59	53	73	159	578
(DUMARS, J.)	49	120	188	375	71	193	12	1635
(GRAHAM, P.)	55	141	231	175	96	91	21	791
(WILKINS, G.)	38	108	206	219	76	113	17	1016

1991–92 REGULAR-SEASON STATISTICAL RESULTS
NBA PLAYERS ORDERED BY FIELD-GOAL PERCENTAGE

	NAME	POS	TEAM	GMs	MINs	MINs per GM	FGs MADE	FGs TRIED	FG PCT	FT PCT
225.	WORTHY, J.	f	LAL	54	2108	39.0	450	1007	0.447	0.814
226.	BONNER, A.	f	SAC	79	2287	28.9	294	658	0.447	0.627
227.	GREEN, R.	g	BOS	26	367	14.1	46	103	0.447	0.722
228.	BROOKS, S.	g	MIN	82	1082	13.2	167	374	0.447	0.810
229.	THOMAS, I.	g	DET	78	2918	37.4	564	1264	0.446	0.773
230.	EATON, M.	c	UT	81	2023	25.0	107	240	0.446	0.598
231.	WEBB, S.	g	SAC	77	2724	35.4	448	1006	0.445	0.859
232.	BOWIE, S.	c	NJ	71	2179	30.7	421	947	0.445	0.757
233.	ANSLEY, M.	f	CHA	10	45	4.5	8	18	0.444	0.833
234.	SANDERS, J.	f	ATL	12	117	9.8	20	45	0.444	0.778
235.	GARLAND, W.	g	DEN	78	2209	28.3	333	750	0.444	0.859
236.	KRYSTKOWIAK, L.	f	MIL	79	1848	23.4	293	660	0.444	0.757
237.	HANSEN, B.	g	CHI	68	809	11.9	79	178	0.444	0.364
238.	BROOKS, K.	f	DEN	37	270	7.3	43	97	0.443	0.810
239.	HARPER, D.	g	DAL	65	2252	34.6	448	1011	0.443	0.759
240.	LIBERTY, M.	f/g	DEN	75	1527	20.4	275	621	0,443	0.728
241.	AINGE, D.	g	POR	81	1595	19.7	299	676	0.442	0.824
242.	DAVIS, B.	f	DAL	33	429	13.0	38	86	0.442	0.733
243.	VOLKOV, A.	f	ATL	77	1516	19.7	251	569	0.441	0.631
244.	BAGLEY, J.	g	BOS	73	1742	23.9	223	506	0.441	0.716
245.	HARPER, R.	g	LAC	82	3144	38.3	569	1292	0.440	0.736
246.	BAILEY, T.	f	MIN	84	2104	25.0	368	836	0.440	0.796
247.	GRANT, Gr.	g	PHI	68	891	13.1	99	225	0.440	0.833
248.	GLASS, G.	g	MIN	75	1822	24.3	383	871	0.440	0.616
249.	TURNER, Jo.	f	HOU	42	345	8.2	43	98	0.439	0.525
250.	KITE, G.	c	ORL	72	1479	20.5	94	215	0.437	0.588
251.	McMILLAN, N.	g/f	SEA	72	1652	22.9	177	405	0.437	0.643
252.	DAWKINS, J.	g	PHI	82	2815	34.3	394	902	0.437	0.882
253.	McCRAY, R.	f	DAL	75	2106	28.1	271	622	0.436	0.719
254.	FREDERICK, A.	f	CHA	66	852	12.9	161	370	0.435	0.685
255.	WINCHESTER, K.	f	NY	19	81	4.3	13	30	0.433	0.800
256.	ADDISON, R.	g	NJ	76	1175	15.5	187	432	0.433	0.737
257.	ENGLISH, A.J.	g	WAS	81	1665	20.6	366	846	0.433	0.841
258.	BLAYLOCK, M.	g	NJ	72	2548	35.4	429	993	0.432	0.712
259.	WILLIAMS, H.	f/c	DAL	75	2040	27.2	367	851	0.431	0.725
260.	LEE, D.	g	NJ	46	307	6.7	50	116	0.431	0.526
261.	CONNER, L.	g	MIL	81	1420	17.5	103	239	0.431	0.704
262.	AGUIRRE, M.	f	DET	75	1582	21.1	339	787	0.431	0.687
263.	CHAMBERS, T.	f	PHX	69	1948	28.2	426	989	0.431	0.830
264.	WILEY, M.	g	ATL	53	870	16.4	83	193	0.430	0.686
265.	VINCENT, S.	g	ORL	39	885	22.7	150	349	0.430	0.846
266.	ROBERTSON, A.	g	MIL	82	2463	30.0	396	922	0.430	0.763
267.	FEITL, D.	c	NJ	34	175	5.2	33	77	0.429	0.842
268.	MAYS, T.	g	ATL	2	32	16.0	6	14	0.429	1.000
269.	PHILLS, B.	g	CLE	10	65	6.5	12	28	0.429	0.636
270.	GEORGE, T.	g	NJ	70	1037	14.8	165	386	0.428	0.821
271.	SCHINTZIUS, D.	c	SAC	33	400	12.1	50	117	0.427	0.833
272.	GREEN, S.	f	SA	80	1127	14.1	147	344	0.427	0.820
273.	COOPER, W.	f	POR	35	344	9.8	35	82	0.427	0.636
274.	SPENCER, F.	c	MIN	61	1481	24.3	141	331	0.426	0.691
275.	BROWN, D.	g	BOS	31	883	28.5	149	350	0.426	0.769
276.	TURNER, A.	g	WAS	70	871	12.4	111	261	0.425	0.792
277.	McCORMICK, T.	c	NY	22	108	4.9	14	33	0.424	0.667
278.	RIVERS, Do.	g	LAC	59	1657	28.1	226	533	0.424	0.832
279.	MITCHELL, S.	f	MIN	82	2151	26.2	307	725	0.423	0.786
280.	PACK, R.	g	POR	72	894	12.4	115	272	0.423	0.803

(NAME)	3-PT SHOTS MADE	3-PT SHOTS TRIED	REBs	ASTs	STLs	TURN-OVERS	BLKs	PTs
(WORTHY, J.)	9	43	305	252	76	127	23	1075
(BONNER, A.)	1	4	485	125	94	133	26	740
(GREEN, R.)	1	4	24	68	17	18	1	106
(BROOKS, S.)	32	90	99	205	66	51	7	417
(THOMAS, I.)	25	86	247	560	118	252	15	1445
(EATON, M.)	0	0	491	40	36	60	205	266
(WEBB, S.)	73	199	223	547	125	229	24	1231
(BOWIE, S.)	8	25	578	186	41	150	120	1062
(ANSLEY, M.)	0	0	6	2	0	3	0	21
(SANDERS, J.)	0	0	26	9	5	5	3	47
(GARLAND, W.)	9	28	190	411	98	175	22	846
(KRYSTKOWIAK, L.)	0	5	429	114	54	115	12	714
(HANSEN, B.)	7	27	77	69	27	28	3	173
(BROOKS, K.)	2	11	39	11	8	18	2	105
(HARPER, D.)	58	186	170	373	101	154	17	1152
(LIBERTY, M.)	17	50	308	58	66	90	29	698
(AINGE, D.)	78	230	148	202	73	70	13	784
(DAVIS, B.)	5	18	33	66	11	27	3	92
(VOLKOV, A.)	35	110	265	250	66	102	30	662
(BAGLEY, J.)	10	42	161	480	57	148	4	524
(HARPER, R.)	64	211	447	417	152	252	72	1495
(BAILEY, T.)	0	2	485	78	35	108	117	951
(GRANT, Gr.)	7	18	69	217	45	46	2	225
(GLASS, G.)	16	54	260	175	66	103	30	859
(TURNER, Jo.)	0	0	78	12	6	32	4	117
(KITE, G.)	0	1	402	44	30	61	57	228
(McMILLAN, N.)	27	98	252	359	129	112	29	435
(DAWKINS, J.)	36	101	227	567	89	183	5	988
(McCRAY, R.)	25	85	468	219	48	115	30	677
(FREDERICK, A.)	4	17	144	71	40	58	26	389
(WINCHESTER, K.)	1	2	15	8	2	2	2	35
(ADDISON, R.)	14	49	165	68	28	46	28	444
(ENGLISH, A.J.)	6	34	168	143	32	89	9	886
(BLAYLOCK, M.)	12	54	269	492	170	152	40	996
(WILLIAMS, H.)	1	6	454	94	35	114	98	859
(LEE, D.)	10	37	35	22	11	12	1	120
(CONNER, L.)	0	7	184	294	97	79	10	287
(AGUIRRE, M.)	15	71	236	126	51	105	11	851
(CHAMBERS, T.)	18	49	401	142	57	103	37	1128
(WILEY, M.)	14	42	81	180	47	60	3	204
(VINCENT, S.)	1	13	101	148	35	72	4	411
(ROBERTSON, A.)	67	210	350	360	210	223	32	1010
(FEITL, D.)	0	0	61	6	2	19	3	82
(MAYS, T.)	3	6	2	1	0	3	0	17
(PHILLS, B.)	0	2	8	4	3	8	1	31
(GEORGE, T.)	1	6	105	162	41	82	3	418
(SCHINTZIUS, D.)	0	4	118	20	6	19	28	110
(GREEN, S.)	0	0	342	36	29	62	11	367
(COOPER, W.)	0	0	101	21	4	15	27	77
(SPENCER, F.)	0	0	435	53	27	70	79	405
(BROWN, D.)	5	22	79	164	33	59	7	363
(TURNER, A.)	1	16	90	177	57	84	2	284
(McCORMICK, T.)	0	0	34	9	2	8	0	42
(RIVERS, Do.)	26	92	147	233	111	92	19	641
(MITCHELL, S.)	2	11	473	94	53	97	39	825
(PACK, R.)	0	10	97	140	40	92	4	332

1991-92 REGULAR-SEASON STATISTICAL RESULTS
NBA PLAYERS ORDERED BY FIELD-GOAL PERCENTAGE

	NAME	POS	TEAM	GMs	MINs	MINs per GM	FGs MADE	FGs TRIED	FG PCT	FT PCT
281.	WALKER, D.	g	DET	74	1541	20.8	161	381	0.423	0.619
282.	JACKSON, C.	g	DEN	81	1538	19.0	356	845	0.421	0.870
283.	WITTMAN, R.	g	IND	24	115	4.8	8	19	0.421	0.500
284.	BRANDON, T.	g	CLE	82	1605	19.6	252	601	0.419	0.807
285.	SCHAYES, D.	c	MIL	43	726	16.9	83	199	0.417	0.771
286.	LYNCH, K.	g	CHA	55	819	14.9	93	223	0.417	0.761
287.	MURDOCK, E.	g	UT	50	478	9.6	76	183	0.415	0.754
288.	SMITH, Do.	f	DAL	76	1707	22.5	291	702	0.415	0.736
289.	JAMERSON, D.	f	HOU	48	378	7.9	79	191	0.414	0.926
290.	SKILES, S.	g	ORL	75	2377	31.7	359	868	0.414	0.895
291.	BEDFORD, W.	f/c	DET	32	363	11.3	50	121	0.413	0.636
292.	MAXWELL, V.	g	HOU	80	2700	33.7	502	1216	0.413	0.772
293.	GARRICK, T.	g	DAL	40	549	13.7	59	143	0.413	0.692
294.	KESSLER, A.	c	MIA	77	1197	15.5	158	383	0.413	0.817
295.	HIGGINS, R.	f	GS	25	535	21.4	87	211	0.412	0.814
296.	WHATLEY, E.	g	POR	23	209	9.1	21	51	0.412	0.871
297.	ASKINS, K.	g/f	MIA	59	843	14.3	84	205	0.410	0.703
298.	BROWN, T.	f	SEA	57	655	11.5	102	249	0.410	0.727
299.	McCLOUD, G.	g	IND	51	892	17.5	128	313	0.409	0.781
300.	FERRY, D.	f	CLE	68	937	13.8	134	328	0.409	0.836
301.	BUECHLER, J.	f	GS	28	290	10.4	29	71	0.409	0.571
302.	SHAW, B.	g	MIA	63	1423	22.6	209	513	0.407	0.791
303.	JAMES, H.	f	CLE	65	866	13.3	164	403	0.407	0.803
304.	SMITH, La.	g	WAS	48	708	14.7	100	246	0.407	0.804
305.	FLOYD, S.	g	HOU	82	1662	20.3	286	704	0.406	0.794
306.	JOHNSON, V.	g	SA	60	1350	22.5	202	499	0.405	0.647
307.	DUDLEY, C.	c	NJ	82	1902	23.2	190	472	0.403	0.468
308.	SCOTT, D.	f	ORL	18	608	33.8	133	331	0.402	0.901
309.	MOORE, T.	f	DAL	42	782	18.6	130	325	0.400	0.833
310.	SMITH, To.	g	LAL	63	820	13.0	113	283	0.399	0.653
311.	CORCHIANI, C.	g	ORL	51	741	14.5	77	193	0.399	0.875
312.	RUDD, D.	g	UT	65	538	8.3	75	188	0.399	0.762
313.	OLIVER, J.	g/f	CLE	27	252	9.3	39	98	0.398	0.773
314.	KIMBLE, B.	f	LAC	34	277	8.2	44	111	0.396	0.645
315.	McCANN, B.	f	DET	26	129	5.0	13	33	0.394	0.308
316.	ADAMS, M.	g	WAS	78	2795	35.8	485	1233	0.393	0.869
317.	GREEN, Se.	g	IND	35	256	7.3	62	158	0.392	0.536
318.	YOUNG, D.	g	LAC	62	1023	16.5	100	255	0.392	0.851
319.	KONCAK, J.	c	ATL	77	1489	19.3	111	284	0.391	0.655
320.	ANDERSON, K.	g	NJ	64	1086	17.0	187	480	0.390	0.745
321.	SUTTON, G.	g	SA	67	601	9.0	93	240	0.388	0.756
322.	MORTON, J.	g	MIA	25	270	10.8	36	93	0.387	0.842
323.	LEVER, F.	g	DAL	31	884	28.5	135	349	0.387	0.750
324.	LES, J.	g	SAC	62	712	11.5	74	192	0.385	0.809
325.	HODGES, C.	g	CHI	56	555	9.9	93	242	0.384	0.941
326.	WIGGINS, M.	g	PHI	49	569	11.6	88	229	0.384	0.686
327.	SPARROW, R.	g	LAL	46	489	10.6	58	151	0.384	0.615
328.	CROWDER, C.	g/f	UT	51	328	6.4	43	112	0.384	0.833
329.	TOLBERT, T.	f	GS	35	310	8.9	33	86	0.384	0.550
330.	BOL, M.	c	PHI	71	1267	17.8	49	128	0.383	0.462
331.	REYNOLDS, J.	g/f	ORL	46	1159	25.2	197	518	0.380	0.836
332.	KING, R.	c	SEA	40	213	5.3	27	71	0.380	0.756
333.	PERRY, E.	g	CHA	50	437	8.7	49	129	0.380	0.659
334.	WHITE, R.	f	DAL	65	1021	15.7	145	382	0.380	0.765
335.	BENNETT, W.	f	MIA	54	833	15.4	80	211	0.379	0.700
336.	THOMPSON, S.	g	SAC	19	91	4.8	14	37	0.378	0.375

(NAME)	3-PT SHOTS MADE	3-PT SHOTS TRIED	REBs	ASTs	STLs	TURN-OVERS	BLKs	PTs
(WALKER, D.)	0	10	238	205	63	79	18	387
(JACKSON, C.)	31	94	114	192	44	117	4	837
(WITTMAN, R.)	0	0	9	11	2	3	0	17
(BRANDON, T.)	1	23	162	316	81	136	22	605
(SCHAYES, D.)	0	0	168	34	19	41	19	240
(LYNCH, K.)	3	8	85	83	37	44	9	224
(MURDOCK, E.)	5	26	54	92	30	50	7	203
(SMITH, Do.)	0	11	391	129	62	97	34	671
(JAMERSON, D.)	8	28	43	33	17	24	0	191
(SKILES, S.)	91	250	202	544	74	233	5	1057
(BEDFORD, W.)	0	1	63	12	6	15	18	114
(MAXWELL, V.)	162	473	243	326	104	178	28	1372
(GARRICK, T.)	1	4	56	98	36	44	4	137
(KESSLER, A.)	0	0	314	34	17	58	32	410
(HIGGINS, R.)	33	95	85	22	15	15	13	255
(WHATLEY, E.)	0	4	21	34	14	14	3	69
(ASKINS, K.)	25	73	142	38	40	47	15	219
(BROWN, T.)	19	63	84	48	30	35	5	271
(McCLOUD, G.)	32	94	132	116	26	62	11	338
(FERRY, D.)	17	48	213	75	22	46	15	346
(BUECHLER, J.)	0	1	52	23	19	13	7	70
(SHAW, B.)	5	23	204	250	57	99	22	495
(JAMES, H.)	29	90	112	25	16	43	11	418
(SMITH, La.)	2	21	81	99	44	63	1	247
(FLOYD, S.)	37	123	150	239	57	128	21	744
(JOHNSON, V.)	19	60	182	145	41	74	14	478
(DUDLEY, C.)	0	0	739	58	38	79	179	460
(SCOTT, D.)	29	89	66	35	20	31	9	359
(MOORE, T.)	30	84	82	48	32	44	4	355
(SMITH, To.)	0	11	76	109	39	50	8	275
(CORCHIANI, C.)	10	37	78	141	45	74	2	255
(RUDD, D.)	11	47	54	109	15	49	1	193
(OLIVER, J.)	1	9	27	20	9	9	2	96
(KIMBLE, B.)	4	13	32	17	10	15	6	112
(McCANN, B.)	0	1	30	6	6	7	4	30
(ADAMS, M.)	125	386	310	594	145	212	9	1408
(GREEN, Se.)	2	10	42	22	13	27	6	141
(YOUNG, D.)	23	70	75	172	46	47	4	280
(KONCAK, J.)	0	12	261	132	50	54	67	241
(ANDERSON, K.)	3	13	127	203	67	97	9	450
(SUTTON, G.)	26	89	47	91	26	70	9	246
(MORTON, J.)	2	16	26	32	13	28	1	106
(LEVER, F.)	17	52	161	107	46	36	12	347
(LES, J.)	45	131	63	143	31	42	3	231
(HODGES, C.)	36	96	24	54	14	22	1	238
(WIGGINS, M.)	0	1	94	22	20	25	1	211
(SPARROW, R.)	3	15	28	83	12	33	5	127
(CROWDER, C.)	13	30	41	17	7	13	2	114
(TOLBERT, T.)	2	8	55	21	10	20	6	90
(BOL, M.)	0	9	222	22	11	41	205	110
(REYNOLDS, J.)	3	24	149	151	63	96	17	555
(KING, R.)	0	1	49	12	4	18	5	88
(PERRY, E.)	1	7	39	78	34	50	3	126
(WHITE, R.)	4	27	236	31	31	68	22	418
(BENNETT, W.)	0	1	162	38	19	33	9	195
(THOMPSON, S.)	0	1	19	8	6	5	3	31

1991–92 REGULAR-SEASON STATISTICAL RESULTS
NBA PLAYERS ORDERED BY FIELD-GOAL PERCENTAGE

	NAME	POS	TEAM	GMs	MINs	MINs per GM	FGs MADE	FGs TRIED	FG PCT	FT PCT
337.	HENDERSON, G.	g	DET	16	96	6.0	12	32	0.375	0.818
338.	JEPSEN, L.	c	SAC	31	87	2.8	9	24	0.375	0.636
339.	MACON, M.	g	DEN	76	2304	30.3	333	889	0.375	0.730
340.	PRESSEY, P.	g	SA	56	759	13.6	60	161	0.373	0.683
341.	ANTHONY, G.	g	NY	82	1510	18.4	161	435	0.370	0.741
342.	HALEY, J.	f/c	LAL	49	394	8.0	31	84	0.369	0.483
343.	MONROE, R.	g	ATL	38	313	8.2	53	144	0.368	0.826
344.	JONES, Ch.	c/f	WAS	75	1365	18.2	33	90	0.367	0.500
345.	SMITH, O.	g	ORL	55	877	15.9	116	318	0.365	0.769
346.	WILLIAMS, Ja.	f/c	PHI	50	646	12.9	75	206	0.364	0.636
347.	HENSON, S.	g	MIL	50	386	7.7	52	144	0.361	0.793
348.	WOLF, J.	f	DEN	67	1160	17.3	100	277	0.361	0.803
349.	THOMAS, C.	g	DET	37	156	4.2	18	51	0.353	0.667
350.	QUINNETT, B.	f	DAL	39	326	8.4	43	124	0.347	0.615
351.	ELLIS, L.	f	LAC	29	103	3.6	17	50	0.340	0.474
352.	HASTINGS, S.	f	DEN	40	421	10.5	17	50	0.340	0.857
353.	RIVERS, Da.	g	LAC	15	122	8.1	10	30	0.333	0.909
354.	OLIVER, B.	g	PHI	34	279	8.2	33	100	0.330	0.682
355.	SAMPSON, R.	c	WAS	10	108	10.8	9	29	0.310	0.667
356.	LANE, J.	f	MIL	14	177	12.6	14	46	0.304	0.333
357.	MAYES, Th.	g	LAC	24	255	10.6	30	99	0.303	0.667
358.	OWENS, K.	f	LAL	20	80	4.0	9	32	0.281	0.800
359.	DAILEY, Q.	f	SEA	11	98	8.9	9	37	0.243	0.813

(NAME)	3-PT SHOTS MADE	3-PT SHOTS TRIED	REBs	ASTs	STLs	TURN-OVERS	BLKs	PTs
(HENDERSON, G.)	3	8	8	10	3	8	0	36
(JEPSEN, L.)	0	1	30	1	1	3	5	25
(MACON, M.)	4	30	220	168	154	155	14	805
(PRESSEY, P.)	3	21	95	142	29	64	19	151
(ANTHONY, G.)	8	55	136	314	59	98	9	447
(HALEY, J.)	0	0	95	7	7	25	8	76
(MONROE, R.)	6	27	33	27	12	23	2	131
(JONES, Ch.)	0	0	317	62	43	39	92	86
(SMITH, O.)	8	21	116	57	36	62	13	310
(WILLIAMS, Ja.)	0	0	145	12	20	44	20	206
(HENSON, S.)	23	48	41	82	15	40	1	150
(WOLF, J.)	1	11	240	61	32	60	14	254
(THOMAS, C.)	2	17	22	22	4	17	1	48
(QUINNETT, B.)	13	41	51	12	16	16	8	115
(ELLIS, L.)	0	0	24	1	6	11	9	43
(HASTINGS, S.)	0	9	98	26	10	22	15	58
(RIVERS, Da.)	0	1	19	21	7	17	1	30
(OLIVER, B.)	0	4	30	20	10	24	2	81
(SAMPSON, R.)	0	2	30	4	3	10	8	22
(LANE, J.)	0	0	66	17	2	14	1	37
(MAYES, Th.)	15	41	16	35	16	31	2	99
(OWENS, K.)	0	0	15	3	5	2	4	26
(DAILEY, Q.)	0	1	12	4	5	10	1	31

1991–92 REGULAR-SEASON STATISTICAL RESULTS
NBA PLAYERS ORDERED BY FREE-THROW PERCENTAGE

	NAME	POS	TEAM	GMs	MINs	MINs per GM	FTs MADE	FTs TRIED	FT PCT	FG PCT
1.	MAYS, T.	g	ATL	2	32	16.0	2	2	1.000	0.429
2.	PRICE, M.	g	CLE	72	2138	29.7	270	285	0.947	0.488
3.	HODGES, C.	g	CHI	56	555	9.9	16	17	0.941	0.384
4.	BIRD, L.	f	BOS	45	1662	36.9	150	162	0.926	0.466
5.	JAMERSON, D.	f	HOU	48	378	7.9	25	27	0.926	0.414
6.	PIERCE, R.	g	SEA	78	2658	34.1	417	455	0.917	0.475
7.	RIVERS, DA.	g	LAC	15	122	8.1	10	11	0.909	0.333
8.	SCOTT, D.	f	ORL	18	608	33.8	64	71	0.901	0.402
9.	BLACKMAN, R.	g	DAL	75	2527	33.7	239	266	0.899	0.461
10.	MALONE, J.	g	UT	81	2922	36.1	256	285	0.898	0.511
11.	SKILES, S.	g	ORL	75	2377	31.7	248	277	0.895	0.414
12.	LAIMBEER, B.	c	DET	81	2234	27.6	67	75	0.893	0.470
13.	HORNACEK, J.	g	PHX	81	3078	38.0	279	315	0.886	0.512
14.	GAMBLE, K.	g/f	BOS	82	2496	30.4	139	157	0.885	0.529
15.	DAWKINS, J.	g	PHI	82	2815	34.3	164	186	0.882	0.437
16.	ANDERSON, Ro.	f	PHI	82	2432	29.7	143	163	0.877	0.465
17.	CORCHIANI, C.	g	ORL	51	741	14.5	91	104	0.875	0.399
18.	HAWKINS, H.	g	PHI	81	3013	37.2	403	461	0.874	0.462
19.	DAVIS, W.	g	DEN	46	741	16.1	82	94	0.872	0.459
20.	WILLIAMS, M.	g	IND	79	2750	34.8	372	427	0.871	0.490
21.	WHATLEY, E.	g	POR	23	209	9.1	27	31	0.871	0.412
22.	JACKSON, C.	g	DEN	81	1538	19.0	94	108	0.870	0.421
23.	ADAMS, M.	g	WAS	78	2795	35.8	313	360	0.869	0.393
24.	DUMARS, J.	g	DET	82	3192	38.9	412	475	0.867	0.448
25.	ROLLINS, T.	f/c	HOU	59	697	11.8	26	30	0.867	0.535
26.	CORBIN, T.	f	UT	80	2207	27.6	174	201	0.866	0.481
27.	SMITH, K.	g	HOU	81	2735	33.8	ʹ219	253	0.866	0.475
28.	HIGGINS, S.	f	ORL	38	616	16.2	31	36	0.861	0.459
29.	ELLIOTT, S.	f	SA	82	3120	38.0	285	331	0.861	0.494
30.	JOHNSON, E.	f	SEA	81	2366	29.2	291	338	0.861	0.459
31.	BOWIE, A.	g/f	ORL	52	1721	33.1	117	136	0.860	0.493
32.	GARLAND, W.	g	DEN	78	2209	28.3	171	199	0.859	0.444
33.	WEBB, S.	g	SAC	77	2724	35.4	262	305	0.859	0.445
34.	MILLER, R.	g	IND	82	3120	38.0	442	515	0.858	0.501
35.	HASTINGS, S.	f	DEN	40	421	10.5	24	28	0.857	0.340
36.	PORTER, T.	g	POR	82	2784	34.0	315	368	0.856	0.462
37.	ELIE, M.	g/f	GS	79	1677	21.2	155	182	0.852	0.521
38.	LEWIS, Re.	g	BOS	82	3070	37.4	292	343	0.851	0.503
39.	YOUNG, D.	g	LAC	62	1023	16.5	57	67	0.851	0.392
40.	EDWARDS, K.	g	MIA	81	1840	22.7	162	191	0.848	0.454
41.	BATTLE, J.	g	CLE	76	1637	21.5	145	171	0.848	0.480
42.	McKEY, D.	f	SEA	52	1757	33.8	188	222	0.847	0.472
43.	VINCENT, S.	g	ORL	39	885	22.7	110	130	0.846	0.430
44.	FEITL, D.	c	NJ	34	175	5.2	16	19	0.842	0.429
45.	MORTON, J.	g	MIA	25	270	10.8	32	38	0.842	0.387
46.	STOCKTON, J.	g	UT	82	3002	36.6	308	366	0.842	0.482
47.	ENGLISH, A.J.	g	WAS	81	1665	20.6	148	176	0.841	0.433
48.	LICHTI, T.	g	DEN	68	1176	17.3	99	118	0.839	0.460
49.	SCOTT, B.	g	LAL	82	2679	32.7	244	291	0.839	0.458
50.	RICE, G.	f	MIA	79	3007	38.1	266	318	0.837	0.469
51.	REYNOLDS, J.	g/f	ORL	46	1159	25.2	158	189	0.836	0.380
52.	IUZZOLINO, M.	g	DAL	52	1280	24.6	107	128	0.836	0.451
53.	FERRY, D.	f	CLE	68	937	13.8	61	73	0.836	0.409
54.	CURRY, D.	g	CHA	77	2020	26.2	127	152	0.836	0.486
55.	WILKINS, D.	f	ATL	42	1601	38.1	294	352	0.835	0.464
56.	ANSLEY, M.	f	CHA	10	45	4.5	5	6	0.833	0.444

(NAME)	3-PT SHOTS MADE	3-PT SHOTS TRIED	REBs	ASTs	STLs	TURN-OVERS	BLKs	PTs
(MAYS, T.)	3	6	2	1	0	3	0	17
(PRICE, M.)	101	261	173	535	94	159	12	1247
(HODGES, C.)	36	96	24	54	14	22	1	238
(BIRD, L.)	52	128	434	306	42	125	33	908
(JAMERSON, D.)	8	28	43	33	17	24	0	191
(PIERCE, R.)	33	123	233	241	86	189	20	1690
(RIVERS, DA.)	0	1	19	21	7	17	1	30
(SCOTT, D.)	29	89	66	35	20	31	9	359
(BLACKMAN, R.)	65	169	239	204	50	153	22	1374
(MALONE, J.)	1	12	233	180	56	140	5	1639
(SKILES, S.)	91	250	202	544	74	233	5	1057
(LAIMBEER, B.)	32	85	451	160	51	102	54	783
(HORNACEK, J.)	83	189	407	411	158	170	31	1632
(GAMBLE, K.)	9	31	286	219	75	97	37	1108
(DAWKINS, J.)	36	101	227	567	89	183	5	988
(ANDERSON, Ro.)	42	127	278	135	86	109	11	1123
(CORCHIANI, C.)	10	37	78	141	45	74	2	255
(HAWKINS, H.)	91	229	271	248	157	189	43	1536
(DAVIS, W.)	5	16	70	68	29	45	1	457
(WILLIAMS, M.)	8	33	282	647	233	240	22	1188
(WHATLEY, E.)	0	4	21	34	14	14	3	69
(JACKSON, C.)	31	94	114	192	44	117	4	837
(ADAMS, M.)	125	386	310	594	145	212	9	1408
(DUMARS, J.)	49	120	188	375	71	193	12	1635
(ROLLINS, T.)	0	0	171	15	14	18	62	118
(CORBIN, T.)	0	4	472	140	82	97	20	780
(SMITH, K.)	54	137	177	562	104	227	7	1137
(HIGGINS, S.)	6	25	102	41	16	41	6	291
(ELLIOTT, S.)	25	82	439	214	84	152	29	1338
(JOHNSON, E.)	27	107	292	161	55	130	11	1386
(BOWIE, A.)	17	44	245	163	55	107	38	758
(GARLAND, W.)	9	28	190	411	98	175	22	846
(WEBB, S.)	73	199	223	547	125	229	24	1231
(MILLER, R.)	129	341	318	314	105	157	26	1695
(HASTINGS, S.)	0	9	98	26	10	22	15	58
(PORTER, T.)	128	324	255	477	127	188	12	1485
(ELIE, M.)	23	70	227	174	68	83	15	620
(LEWIS, Re.)	5	21	394	185	125	136	105	1703
(YOUNG, D.)	23	70	75	172	46	47	4	280
(EDWARDS, K.)	7	32	211	170	99	120	20	819
(BATTLE, J.)	2	17	112	159	36	91	5	779
(McKEY, D.)	19	50	268	120	61	114	47	777
(VINCENT, S.)	1	13	101	148	35	72	4	411
(FEITL, D.)	0	0	61	6	2	19	3	82
(MORTON, J.)	2	16	26	32	13	28	1	106
(STOCKTON, J.)	83	204	270	1126	244	286	22	1297
(ENGLISH, A.J.)	6	34	168	143	32	89	9	886
(LICHTI, T.)	1	9	118	74	43	72	12	446
(SCOTT, B.)	54	157	310	226	105	119	28	1218
(RICE, G.)	155	396	394	184	90	145	35	1765
(REYNOLDS, J.)	3	24	149	151	63	96	17	555
(IUZZOLINO, M.)	59	136	98	194	33	92	1	486
(FERRY, D.)	17	48	213	75	22	46	15	346
(CURRY, D.)	74	183	259	177	93	134	20	1209
(WILKINS, D.)	37	128	295	158	52	122	24	1179
(ANSLEY, M.)	0	0	6	2	0	3	0	21

	NAME	POS	TEAM	GMs	MINs	MINs per GM	FTs MADE	FTs TRIED	FT PCT	FG PCT
57.	BATTLE, K.	f	GS	16	92	5.8	10	12	0.833	0.647
58.	CROWDER, C.	g/f	UT	51	328	6.4	15	18	0.833	0.384
59.	GRANT, Gr.	g	PHI	68	891	13.1	20	24	0.833	0.440
60.	KERR, S.	g	CLE	48	847	17.6	45	54	0.833	0.511
61.	MOORE, T.	f	DAL	42	782	18.6	65	78	0.833	0.400
62.	MULLIN, C.	f	GS	81	3346	41.3	350	420	0.833	0.524
63.	SCHINTZIUS, D.	c	SAC	33	400	12.1	10	12	0.833	0.427
64.	JORDAN, M.	g	CHI	80	3102	38.8	491	590	0.832	0.519
65.	RIVERS, Do.	g	LAC	59	1657	28.1	163	196	0.832	0.424
66.	THREATT, S.	g	LAL	82	3070	37.4	202	243	0.831	0.489
67.	CHAMBERS, T.	f	PHX	69	1948	28.2	258	311	0.830	0.431
68.	JOHNSON, L.	f	CHA	82	3047	37.2	339	409	0.829	0.490
69.	SCHREMPF, D.	f	IND	80	2605	32.6	365	441	0.828	0.536
70.	MONROE, R.	g	ATL	38	313	8.2	19	23	0.826	0.368
71.	AINGE, D.	g	POR	81	1595	19.7	108	131	0.824	0.442
72.	COLES, B.	g	MIA	81	1976	24.4	216	262	0.824	0.455
73.	McHALE, K.	f/c	BOS	56	1398	25.0	134	163	0.822	0.510
74.	NANCE, L.	f	CLE	81	2880	35.6	263	320	0.822	0.539
75.	CHILCUTT, P.	f/c	SAC	69	817	11.8	23	28	0.821	0.452
76.	GEORGE, T.	g	NJ	70	1037	14.8	87	106	0.821	0.428
77.	GREEN, S.	f	SA	80	1127	14.1	73	89	0.820	0.427
78.	HENDERSON, G.	g	DET	16	96	6.0	9	11	0.818	0.375
79.	KESSLER, A.	c	MIA	77	1197	15.5	94	115	0.817	0.413
80.	PERKINS, S.	f/c	LAL	63	2332	37.0	304	372	0.817	0.450
81.	THOMPSON, L.	f/c	IND	80	1299	16.2	58	71	0.817	0.468
82.	GRANT, Ga.	g	LAC	78	2049	26.3	44	54	0.815	0.462
83.	WORTHY, J.	f	LAL	54	2108	39.0	166	204	0.814	0.447
84.	HIGGINS, R.	f	GS	25	535	21.4	48	59	0.814	0.412
85.	RICHMOND, M.	g	SAC	80	3095	38.7	330	406	0.813	0.468
86.	DAILEY, Q.	f	SEA	11	98	8.9	13	16	0.813	0.243
87.	PINCKNEY, E.	f	BOS	81	1917	23.7	207	255	0.812	0.537
88.	BENOIT, D.	f	UT	77	1161	15.1	81	100	0.810	0.467
89.	BROOKS, K.	f	DEN	37	270	7.3	17	21	0.810	0.443
90.	BROOKS, S.	g	MIN	82	1082	13.2	51	63	0.810	0.447
91.	LES, J.	g	SAC	62	712	11.5	38	47	0.809	0.385
92.	PETROVIC, D.	g	NJ	82	3027	36.9	232	287	0.808	0.508
93.	JOHNSON, K.	g	PHX	78	2899	37.2	448	555	0.807	0.479
94.	GILLIAM, A.	f/c	PHI	81	2771	34.2	343	425	0.807	0.512
95.	LONG, G.	f	MIA	82	3063	37.4	326	404	0.807	0.494
96.	STEWART, L.	f	WAS	76	2229	29.3	188	233	0.807	0.514
97.	BRANDON, T.	g	CLE	82	1605	19.6	100	124	0.807	0.419
98.	ARMSTRONG, B.J.	g	CHI	82	1875	22.9	104	129	0.806	0.481
99.	WEST, D.	g	MIN	80	2540	31.7	186	231	0.805	0.518
100.	WILLIS, K.	f/c	ATL	81	2962	36.6	292	363	0.804	0.483
101.	SMITH, La.	g	WAS	48	708	14.7	45	56	0.804	0.407
102.	PACK, R.	g	POR	72	894	12.4	102	127	0.803	0.423
103.	WOLF, J.	f	DEN	67	1160	17.3	53	66	0.803	0.361
104.	WILLIAMS, R.	f	DEN	81	2623	32.4	216	269	0.803	0.471
105.	CAMPBELL, T.	f/g	MIN	78	2441	31.3	240	299	0.803	0.464
106.	JAMES, H.	f	CLE	65	866	13.3	61	76	0.803	0.407
107.	VANDEWEGHE, K.	f	NY	67	956	14.3	65	81	0.803	0.491
108.	BURTON, W.	g/f	MIA	68	1585	23.3	196	245	0.800	0.450
109.	GRANT, Ha.	f	WAS	64	2388	37.3	176	220	0.800	0.479
110.	OWENS, K.	f	LAL	20	80	4.0	8	10	0.800	0.281
111.	TUCKER, T.	g	SA	24	415	17.3	16	20	0.800	0.465
112.	WINCHESTER, K.	f	NY	19	81	4.3	8	10	0.800	0.433

(NAME)	3-PT SHOTS MADE	3-PT SHOTS TRIED	REBs	ASTs	STLs	TURN-OVERS	BLKs	PTs
(BATTLE, K.)	0	1	16	4	2	4	2	32
(CROWDER, C.)	13	30	41	17	7	13	2	114
(GRANT, Gr.)	7	18	69	217	45	46	2	225
(KERR, S.)	32	74	78	110	27	31	10	319
(MOORE, T.)	30	84	82	48	32	44	4	355
(MULLIN, C.)	64	175	450	286	173	202	62	2074
(SCHINTZIUS, D.)	0	4	118	20	6	19	28	110
(JORDAN, M.)	27	100	511	489	182	200	75	2404
(RIVERS, Do.)	26	92	147	233	111	92	19	641
(THREATT, S.)	20	62	253	593	168	182	16	1240
(CHAMBERS, T.)	18	49	401	142	57	103	37	1128
(JOHNSON, L.)	5	22	899	292	81	160	51	1576
(SCHREMPF, D.)	23	71	770	312	62	191	37	1380
(MONROE, R.)	6	27	33	27	12	23	2	131
(AINGE, D.)	78	230	148	202	73	70	13	784
(COLES, B.)	10	52	189	366	73	167	13	816
(McHALE, K.)	0	13	330	82	11	82	59	780
(NANCE, L.)	0	6	670	232	80	87	243	1375
(CHILCUTT, P.)	2	2	187	38	32	41	17	251
(GEORGE, T.)	1	6	105	162	41	82	3	418
(GREEN, S.)	0	0	342	36	29	62	11	367
(HENDERSON, G.)	3	8	8	10	3	8	0	36
(KESSLER, A.)	0	0	314	34	17	58	32	410
(PERKINS, S.)	15	69	556	141	64	83	62	1041
(THOMPSON, L.)	0	2	381	102	52	98	34	394
(GRANT, Ga.)	15	51	184	538	138	187	14	609
(WORTHY, J.)	9	43	305	252	76	127	23	1075
(HIGGINS, R.)	33	95	85	22	15	15	13	255
(RICHMOND, M.)	103	268	319	411	92	247	34	1803
(DAILEY, Q.)	0	1	12	4	5	10	1	31
(PINCKNEY, E.)	0	1	564	62	70	73	56	613
(BENOIT, D.)	3	14	296	34	19	71	44	434
(BROOKS, K.)	2	11	39	11	8	18	2	105
(BROOKS, S.)	32	90	99	205	66	51	7	417
(LES, J.)	45	131	63	143	31	42	3	231
(PETROVIC, D.)	123	277	258	252	105	215	11	1691
(JOHNSON, K.)	10	46	292	836	116	272	23	1536
(GILLIAM, A.)	0	2	660	118	51	166	85	1367
(LONG, G.)	6	22	691	225	139	185	40	1212
(STEWART, L.)	0	3	449	120	51	112	44	794
(BRANDON, T.)	1	23	162	316	81	136	22	605
(ARMSTRONG, B.J.)	35	87	145	266	46	94	5	809
(WEST, D.)	4	23	257	281	66	120	26	1116
(WILLIS, K.)	6	37	1258	173	72	197	54	1480
(SMITH, La.)	2	21	81	99	44	63	1	247
(PACK, R.)	0	10	97	140	40	92	4	332
(WOLF, J.)	1	11	240	61	32	60	14	254
(WILLIAMS, R.)	56	156	405	235	148	173	68	1474
(CAMPBELL, T.)	13	37	286	229	84	165	31	1307
(JAMES, H.)	29	90	112	25	16	43	11	418
(VANDEWEGHE, K.)	26	66	88	57	15	27	8	467
(BURTON, W.)	6	15	244	123	46	119	37	762
(GRANT, Ha.)	1	8	432	170	74	109	27	1155
(OWENS, K.)	0	0	15	3	5	2	4	26
(TUCKER, T.)	19	48	37	27	21	14	3	155
(WINCHESTER, K.)	1	2	15	8	2	2	2	35

	NAME	POS	TEAM	GMs	MINs	MINs per GM	FTs MADE	FTs TRIED	FT PCT	FG PCT
113.	VAUGHT, L.	f	LAC	79	1687	21.4	55	69	0.797	0.492
114.	BAILEY, T.	f	MIN	84	2104	25.0	215	270	0.796	0.440
115.	FLOYD, S.	g	HOU	82	1662	20.3	135	170	0.794	0.406
116.	DREXLER, C.	g	POR	76	2751	36.2	401	505	0.794	0.470
117.	HENSON, S.	g	MIL	50	386	7.7	23	29	0.793	0.361
118.	TURNER, A.	g	WAS	70	871	12.4	61	77	0.792	0.425
119.	SHAW, B.	g	MIA	63	1423	22.6	72	91	0.791	0.407
120.	MARCIULIONIS, S.	g	GS	72	2117	29.4	376	477	0.788	0.538
121.	SMITS, R.	c	IND	74	1772	23.9	152	193	0.788	0.510
122.	MALONE, M.	c	MIL	82	2511	30.6	396	504	0.786	0.474
123.	MITCHELL, S.	f	MIN	82	2151	26.2	209	266	0.786	0.423
124.	SMITH, C.	f/c	LAC	49	1310	26.7	212	270	0.785	0.466
125.	PAXSON, J.	g	CHI	79	1946	24.6	29	37	0.784	0.528
126.	BOGUES, M.	g	CHA	82	2790	34.0	94	120	0.783	0.472
127.	HUMPHRIES, J.	g	MIL	71	2261	31.8	195	249	0.783	0.470
128.	McCLOUD, G.	g	IND	51	892	17.5	50	64	0.781	0.409
129.	STARKS, J.	g	NY	82	2118	25.8	235	302	0.778	0.449
130.	MALONE, K.	f	UT	81	3054	37.7	673	865	0.778	0.526
131.	PRITCHARD, K.	g	BOS	11	136	12.4	14	18	0.778	0.471
132.	RAMBIS, K.	f	PHX	28	381	13.6	14	18	0.778	0.463
133.	SANDERS, J.	f	ATL	12	117	9.8	7	9	0.778	0.444
134.	DAUGHERTY, B.	c	CLE	73	2643	36.2	414	533	0.777	0.570
135.	ANDERSON, W.	g/f	SA	57	1889	33.1	107	138	0.775	0.456
136.	EDWARDS, T.	g/f	UT	81	2283	28.2	113	146	0.774	0.522
137.	ELLIS, D.	f	MIL	81	2191	27.0	164	212	0.774	0.469
138.	OLIVER, J.	g/f	CLE	27	252	9.3	17	22	0.773	0.398
139.	THOMAS, I.	g	DET	78	2918	37.4	292	378	0.773	0.446
140.	PARISH, R.	c	BOS	79	2285	28.9	179	232	0.772	0.536
141.	MAXWELL, V.	g	HOU	80	2700	33.7	206	267	0.772	0.413
142.	SCHAYES, D.	c	MIL	43	726	16.9	74	96	0.771	0.417
143.	JACKSON, M.	g	NY	81	2461	30.4	171	222	0.770	0.491
144.	SIMMONS, L.	f	SAC	78	2895	37.1	281	365	0.770	0.454
145.	BROWN, D.	g	BOS	31	883	28.5	60	78	0.769	0.426
146.	SELLERS, B.	f/c	DET	43	226	5.3	20	26	0.769	0.466
147.	SMITH, O.	g	ORL	55	877	15.9	70	91	0.769	0.365
148.	LANG, A.	c	PHX	81	1965	24.3	126	164	0.768	0.522
149.	DIVAC, V.	c	LAL	36	979	27.2	86	112	0.768	0.495
150.	BRICKOWSKI, F.	f	MIL	65	1556	23.9	125	163	0.767	0.524
151.	TEAGLE, T.	f	LAL	82	1602	19.5	151	197	0.767	0.452
152.	OLAJUWON, H.	c	HOU	70	2636	37.7	328	428	0.766	0.502
153.	NEWMAN, J.	f/g	CHA	55	1651	30.0	236	308	0.766	0.477
154.	HARDAWAY, T.	g	GS	81	3332	41.1	298	389	0.766	0.461
155.	SANDERS, M.	f	CLE	31	633	20.4	36	47	0.766	0.571
156.	WHITE, R.	f	DAL	65	1021	15.7	124	162	0.765	0.380
157.	CARR, A.	f/c	SA	81	1867	23.0	162	212	0.764	0.490
158.	COLEMAN, D.	f	NJ	65	2207	34.0	300	393	0.763	0.504
159.	ROBERTSON, A.	g	MIL	82	2463	30.0	151	198	0.763	0.430
160.	TISDALE, W.	f	SAC	72	2521	35.0	151	198	0.763	0.501
161.	RUDD, D.	g	UT	65	538	8.3	32	42	0.762	0.399
162.	FERRELL, D.	f	ATL	66	1598	24.2	166	218	0.762	0.524
163.	ACRES, M.	c	ORL	68	926	13.6	51	67	0.761	0.517
164.	LYNCH, K.	g	CHA	55	819	14.9	35	46	0.761	0.417
165.	PIPPEN, S.	f	CHI	82	3164	38.6	330	434	0.760	0.506
166.	BULLARD, M.	f	HOU	80	1278	16.0	38	50	0.760	0.459
167.	BARROS, D.	g	SEA	75	1331	17.7	60	79	0.760	0.483
168.	HARPER, D.	g	DAL	65	2252	34.6	198	261	0.759	0.443

(NAME)	3-PT SHOTS MADE	3-PT SHOTS TRIED	REBs	ASTs	STLs	TURN-OVERS	BLKs	PTs
(VAUGHT, L.)	4	5	512	71	37	66	31	601
(BAILEY, T.)	0	2	485	78	35	108	117	951
(FLOYD, S.)	37	123	150	239	57	128	21	744
(DREXLER, C.)	114	338	500	512	138	240	70	1903
(HENSON, S.)	23	48	41	82	15	40	1	150
(TURNER, A.)	1	16	90	177	57	84	2	284
(SHAW, B.)	5	23	204	250	57	99	22	495
(MARCIULIONIS, S.)	3	10	208	243	116	193	10	1361
(SMITS, R.)	0	2	417	116	29	130	100	1024
(MALONE, M.)	3	8	744	93	74	150	64	1279
(MITCHELL, S.)	2	11	473	94	53	97	39	825
(SMITH, C.)	0	6	301	56	41	69	98	714
(PAXSON, J.)	12	44	96	241	49	44	9	555
(BOGUES, M.)	2	27	235	743	170	156	6	730
(HUMPHRIES, J.)	42	144	184	466	119	148	13	991
(McCLOUD, G.)	32	94	132	116	26	62	11	338
(STARKS, J.)	94	270	191	276	103	150	18	1139
(MALONE, K.)	3	17	909	241	108	248	51	2272
(PRITCHARD, K.)	0	3	11	30	3	11	4	46
(RAMBIS, K.)	0	0	106	37	12	25	14	90
(SANDERS, J.)	0	0	26	9	5	5	3	47
(DAUGHERTY, B.)	0	2	760	262	65	185	78	1566
(ANDERSON, W.)	13	56	300	302	54	140	51	744
(EDWARDS, T.)	39	103	298	137	81	122	46	1018
(ELLIS, D.)	138	329	253	104	57	119	18	1272
(OLIVER, J.)	1	9	27	20	9	9	2	96
(THOMAS, I.)	25	86	247	560	118	252	15	1445
(PARISH, R.)	0	0	705	70	68	131	97	1115
(MAXWELL, V.)	162	473	243	326	104	178	28	1372
(SCHAYES, D.)	0	0	168	34	19	41	19	240
(JACKSON, M.)	11	43	305	694	112	211	13	916
(SIMMONS, L.)	1	5	634	337	135	218	132	1336
(BROWN, D.)	5	22	79	164	33	59	7	363
(SELLERS, B.)	0	1	42	14	1	15	10	102
(SMITH, O.)	8	21	116	57	36	62	13	310
(LANG, A.)	0	1	546	43	48	87	201	622
(DIVAC, V.)	5	19	247	60	55	88	35	405
(BRICKOWSKI, F.)	3	6	344	122	60	112	23	740
(TEAGLE, T.)	1	4	183	113	66	114	9	880
(OLAJUWON, H.)	0	1	845	157	127	187	304	1510
(NEWMAN, J.)	13	46	179	146	70	129	14	839
(HARDAWAY, T.)	127	376	310	807	164	267	13	1893
(SANDERS, M.)	1	3	96	53	24	22	10	221
(WHITE, R.)	4	27	236	31	31	68	22	418
(CARR, A.)	1	5	346	63	32	114	96	881
(COLEMAN, D.)	23	76	618	205	54	248	98	1289
(ROBERTSON, A.)	67	210	350	360	210	223	32	1010
(TISDALE, W.)	0	2	469	106	55	124	79	1195
(RUDD, D.)	11	47	54	109	15	49	1	193
(FERRELL, D.)	11	33	210	92	49	99	17	839
(ACRES, M.)	1	3	252	22	25	33	15	208
(LYNCH, K.)	3	8	85	83	37	44	9	224
(PIPPEN, S.)	16	80	630	572	155	253	93	1720
(BULLARD, M.)	64	166	223	75	26	56	21	512
(BARROS, D.)	83	186	81	125	51	56	4	619
(HARPER, D.)	58	186	170	373	101	154	17	1152

1991–92 REGULAR-SEASON STATISTICAL RESULTS
NBA PLAYERS ORDERED BY FREE-THROW PERCENTAGE

	NAME	POS	TEAM	GMs	MINs	MINs per GM	FTs MADE	FTs TRIED	FT PCT	FG PCT
169.	KRYSTKOWIAK, L.	f	MIL	79	1848	23.4	128	169	0.757	0.444
170.	BOWIE, S.	c	NJ	71	2179	30.7	212	280	0.757	0.445
171.	MAJERLE, D.	g/f	PHX	82	2853	34.8	229	303	0.756	0.478
172.	KING, R.	c	SEA	40	213	5.3	34	45	0.756	0.380
173.	SUTTON, G.	g	SA	67	601	9.0	34	45	0.756	0.388
174.	FOX, R.	g/f	BOS	81	1535	19.0	139	184	0.755	0.459
175.	WILLIAMS, Bu.	f	POR	80	2519	31.5	221	293	0.754	0.604
176.	MURDOCK, E.	g	UT	50	478	9.6	46	61	0.754	0.415
177.	KING, S.	f/c	CHI	79	1268	16.1	119	158	0.753	0.506
178.	ABDELNABY, A.	f/c	POR	71	934	13.2	76	101	0.753	0.493
179.	WILLIAMS, J.	f/c	CLE	80	2432	30.4	270	359	0.752	0.503
180.	CONLON, M.	c	SEA	45	381	8.5	24	32	0.750	0.475
181.	DREILING, G.	c	IND	60	509	8.5	30	40	0.750	0.494
182.	GMINSKI, M.	c	CHA	35	499	14.3	21	28	0.750	0.452
183.	LEVER, F.	g	DAL	31	884	28.5	60	80	0.750	0.387
184.	MILLS, T.	f	NJ	82	1714	20.9	114	152	0.750	0.463
185.	RASMUSSEN, B.	c	ATL	81	1968	24.3	30	40	0.750	0.478
186.	SCHEFFLER, S.	f	DEN	11	61	5.6	9	12	0.750	0.667
187.	ROBERTS, F.	f	MIL	80	1746	21.8	128	171	0.749	0.482
188.	SMITH, S.	g	MIA	61	1806	29.6	95	127	0.748	0.454
189.	KEMP, S.	f/c	SEA	64	1808	28.2	270	361	0.748	0.504
190.	GILL, K.	g/f	CHA	79	2906	36.8	284	381	0.745	0.467
191.	LECKNER, E.	c	CHA	59	716	12.1	38	51	0.745	0.513
192.	ANDERSON, K.	g	NJ	64	1086	17.0	73	98	0.745	0.390
193.	RANDALL, M.	f	MIN	54	441	8.2	32	43	0.744	0.456
194.	GREEN, A.C.	f	LAL	82	2902	35.4	340	457	0.744	0.476
195.	EACKLES, L.	f	WAS	65	1463	22.5	139	187	0.743	0.468
196.	GRANT, Ho.	f	CHI	81	2859	35.3	235	317	0.741	0.579
197.	GRAHAM, P.	g	ATL	78	1718	22.0	126	170	0.741	0.447
198.	ANTHONY, G.	g	NY	82	1510	18.4	117	158	0.741	0.370
199.	EWING, P.	c	NY	82	3150	38.4	377	511	0.738	0.522
200.	FLEMING, V.	g	IND	82	1737	21.2	132	179	0.737	0.482
201.	ADDISON, R.	g	NJ	76	1175	15.5	56	76	0.737	0.433
202.	CEBALLOS, C.	f	PHX	64	725	11.3	109	148	0.737	0.482
203.	HARPER, R.	g	LAC	82	3144	38.3	293	398	0.736	0.440
204.	SMITH, Do.	f	DAL	76	1707	22.5	89	121	0.736	0.415
205.	OAKLEY, C.	f	NY	82	2309	28.2	86	117	0.735	0.522
206.	DAVIS, B.	f	DAL	33	429	13.0	11	15	0.733	0.442
207.	SEIKALY, R.	c	MIA	79	2800	35.4	370	505	0.733	0.489
208.	EDWARDS, Ja.	c	LAC	72	1437	20.0	198	271	0.731	0.465
209.	MACON, M.	g	DEN	76	2304	30.3	135	185	0.730	0.375
210.	WILKINS, G.	g	NY	82	2344	28.6	116	159	0.730	0.447
211.	LIBERTY, M.	f/g	DEN	75	1527	20.4	131	180	0.728	0.443
212.	ELLISON, P.	c	WAS	66	2511	38.0	227	312	0.728	0.539
213.	BLANKS, L.	g	DET	43	189	4.4	8	11	0.727	0.455
214.	BROWN, T.	f	SEA	57	655	11.5	48	66	0.727	0.410
215.	JOHNSON, B.	f	HOU	80	2202	27.5	104	143	0.727	0.458
216.	WILLIAMS, H.	f/c	DAL	75	2040	27.2	124	171	0.725	0.431
217.	MANNING, D.	f	LAC	82	2904	35.4	279	385	0.725	0.542
218.	GREEN, R.	g	BOS	26	367	14.1	13	18	0.722	0.447
219.	WINGATE, D.	g	WAS	81	2127	26.3	105	146	0.719	0.465
220.	McCRAY, R.	f	DAL	75	2106	28.1	110	153	0.719	0.436
221.	BAGLEY, J.	g	BOS	73	1742	23.9	68	95	0.716	0.441
222.	SALLEY, J.	f/c	DET	72	1774	24.6	186	260	0.715	0.512
223.	FOSTER, G.	f	WAS	49	548	11.2	35	49	0.714	0.461
224.	MORRIS, C.	f	NJ	77	2394	31.1	165	231	0.714	0.477

(NAME)	3-PT SHOTS MADE	3-PT SHOTS TRIED	REBs	ASTs	STLs	TURN-OVERS	BLKs	PTs
(KRYSTKOWIAK, L.)	0	5	429	114	54	115	12	714
(BOWIE, S.)	8	25	578	186	41	150	120	1062
(MAJERLE, D.)	87	228	483	274	131	101	43	1418
(KING, R.)	0	1	49	12	4	18	5	88
(SUTTON, G.)	26	89	47	91	26	70	9	246
(FOX, R.)	23	70	220	126	78	123	30	644
(WILLIAMS, Bu.)	0	1	704	108	62	130	41	901
(MURDOCK, E.)	5	26	54	92	30	50	7	203
(KING, S.)	2	5	205	77	21	76	25	551
(ABDELNABY, A.)	0	0	260	30	25	66	16	432
(WILLIAMS, J.)	0	4	607	196	60	83	182	952
(CONLON, M.)	0	0	69	12	9	27	7	120
(DREILING, G.)	1	1	96	25	10	31	16	117
(GMINSKI, M.)	1	3	118	31	11	20	16	202
(LEVER, F.)	17	52	161	107	46	36	12	347
(MILLS, T.)	8	23	453	84	48	82	41	742
(RASMUSSEN, B.)	5	23	393	107	35	51	48	729
(SCHEFFLER, S.)	0	0	14	0	3	1	1	21
(ROBERTS, F.)	19	37	257	122	52	122	40	769
(SMITH, S.)	40	125	188	278	59	152	19	729
(KEMP, S.)	0	3	665	86	70	156	124	994
(GILL, K.)	6	25	402	329	154	180	46	1622
(LECKNER, E.)	0	1	206	31	9	39	18	196
(ANDERSON, K.)	3	13	127	203	67	97	9	450
(RANDALL, M.)	3	16	71	33	12	25	3	171
(GREEN, A.C.)	12	56	762	117	91	111	36	1116
(EACKLES, L.)	7	35	178	125	47	75	7	856
(GRANT, Ho.)	0	2	807	217	100	98	131	1149
(GRAHAM, P.)	55	141	231	175	96	91	21	791
(ANTHONY, G.)	8	55	136	314	59	98	9	447
(EWING, P.)	1	6	921	156	88	209	245	1970
(FLEMING, V.)	6	27	209	266	56	140	7	726
(ADDISON, R.)	14	49	165	68	28	46	28	444
(CEBALLOS, C.)	1	6	152	50	16	71	11	462
(HARPER, R.)	64	211	447	417	152	252	72	1495
(SMITH, Do.)	0	11	391	129	62	97	34	671
(OAKLEY, C.)	0	3	700	133	67	123	15	506
(DAVIS, B.)	5	18	33	66	11	27	3	92
(SEIKALY, R.)	0	3	934	109	40	216	121	1296
(EDWARDS, Ja.)	0	1	202	53	24	72	33	698
(MACON, M.)	4	30	220	168	154	155	14	805
(WILKINS, G.)	38	108	206	219	76	113	17	1016
(LIBERTY, M.)	17	50	308	58	66	90	29	698
(ELLISON, P.)	1	3	740	190	62	196	177	1322
(BLANKS, L.)	6	16	22	19	14	14	1	64
(BROWN, T.)	19	63	84	48	30	35	5	271
(JOHNSON, B.)	1	9	312	158	72	104	49	685
(WILLIAMS, H.)	1	6	454	94	35	114	98	859
(MANNING, D.)	0	5	564	285	135	210	122	1579
(GREEN, R.)	1	4	24	68	17	18	1	106
(WINGATE, D.)	1	18	269	247	123	124	21	638
(McCRAY, R.)	25	85	468	219	48	115	30	677
(BAGLEY, J.)	10	42	161	480	57	148	4	524
(SALLEY, J.)	0	3	296	116	49	102	110	684
(FOSTER, G.)	0	1	145	35	6	36	12	213
(MORRIS, C.)	22	110	494	197	129	171	81	879

1991–92 REGULAR-SEASON STATISTICAL RESULTS
NBA PLAYERS ORDERED BY FREE-THROW PERCENTAGE

	NAME	POS	TEAM	GMs	MINs	MINs per GM	FTs MADE	FTs TRIED	FT PCT	FG PCT
225.	McDANIEL, X.	f	NY	82	2344	28.6	137	192	0.714	0.478
226.	BLAYLOCK, M.	g	NJ	72	2548	35.4	126	177	0.712	0.432
227.	PERRY, T.	f	PHX	80	2483	31.0	153	215	0.712	0.523
228.	CUMMINGS, T.	f	SA	70	2149	30.7	177	249	0.711	0.488
229.	HOWARD, B.	f	DAL	27	318	11.8	22	31	0.710	0.519
230.	DONALDSON, J.	c	NY	58	1075	18.5	61	86	0.709	0.457
231.	KLEINE, J.	c	BOS	70	991	14.2	34	48	0.708	0.492
232.	HOPSON, D.	g/f	SAC	71	1314	18.5	179	253	0.708	0.465
233.	EHLO, C.	g/f	CLE	63	2016	32.0	87	123	0.707	0.453
234.	REID, J.R.	c/f	CHA	51	1257	24.6	134	190	0.705	0.490
235.	CONNER, L.	g	MIL	81	1420	17.5	81	115	0.704	0.431
236.	BURTT, S.	g	PHX	31	356	11.5	38	54	0.704	0.463
237.	ASKINS, K.	g/f	MIA	59	843	14.3	26	37	0.703	0.410
238.	ROBINSON, D.	c	SA	68	2564	37.7	393	561	0.701	0.551
239.	BENNETT, W.	f	MIA	54	833	15.4	35	50	0.700	0.379
240.	PETERSEN, J.	c	GS	27	169	6.3	7	10	0.700	0.450
241.	BARKLEY, C.	f	PHI	75	2881	38.4	454	653	0.695	0.552
242.	ASKEW, V.	g	GS	80	1496	18.7	111	160	0.694	0.509
243.	CATLEDGE, T.	f	ORL	78	2430	31.2	240	346	0.694	0.496
244.	HILL, T.	c/f	GS	82	1886	23.0	163	235	0.694	0.522
245.	TURNER, J.	f	ORL	75	1591	21.2	79	114	0.693	0.451
246.	GARRICK, T.	g	DAL	40	549	13.7	18	26	0.692	0.413
247.	PAYNE, K.	f	PHI	49	353	7.2	9	13	0.692	0.448
248.	ROYAL, D.	f	SA	60	718	12.0	92	133	0.692	0.449
249.	ALEXANDER, V.	c	GS	80	1350	16.9	103	149	0.691	0.529
250.	RICHARDSON, P.	g	MIN	82	2922	35.6	123	178	0.691	0.466
251.	SPENCER, F.	c	MIN	61	1481	24.3	123	178	0.691	0.426
252.	DUCKWORTH, K.	c	POR	82	2222	27.1	156	226	0.690	0.461
253.	MUSTAF, J.	f	PHX	52	545	10.5	49	71	0.690	0.477
254.	GATTISON, K.	f/c	CHA	82	2223	27.1	196	285	0.688	0.529
255.	KNIGHT, N.	g	PHX	42	631	15.0	33	48	0.688	0.475
256.	RULAND, J.	c	PHI	13	209	16.1	11	16	0.688	0.526
257.	AGUIRRE, M.	f	DET	75	1582	21.1	158	230	0.687	0.431
258.	STRICKLAND, R.	g	SA	57	2053	36.0	182	265	0.687	0.455
259.	BENJAMIN, B.	c	SEA	63	1941	30.8	171	249	0.687	0.478
260.	WIGGINS, M.	g	PHI	49	569	11.6	35	51	0.686	0.384
261.	WILEY, M.	g	ATL	53	870	16.4	24	35	0.686	0.430
262.	FREDERICK, A.	f	CHA	66	852	12.9	63	92	0.685	0.435
263.	PRESSEY, P.	g	SA	56	759	13.6	28	41	0.683	0.373
264.	WOOLRIDGE, O.	f	DET	82	2113	25.8	241	353	0.683	0.498
265.	DOUGLAS, S.	g	BOS	42	752	17.9	73	107	0.682	0.463
266.	OLIVER, B.	g	PHI	34	279	8.2	15	22	0.682	0.330
267.	CHAPMAN, R.	g	WAS	22	567	25.8	36	53	0.679	0.448
268.	PERSON, C.	f	IND	81	2923	36.1	133	197	0.675	0.480
269.	WILLIAMS, Br.	f	ORL	48	905	18.9	95	142	0.669	0.528
270.	PAYTON, G.	g	SEA	81	2549	31.5	99	148	0.669	0.451
271.	ANDERSON, N.	g/f	ORL	60	2203	36.7	202	303	0.667	0.463
272.	BROWN, M.	c/f	UT	82	1783	21.7	190	285	0.667	0.453
273.	BRYANT, M.	c	POR	56	800	14.3	40	60	0.667	0.480
274.	COOK, A.	f	DEN	22	115	5.2	4	6	0.667	0.600
275.	FRANK, T.	f	MIN	10	140	14.0	10	15	0.667	0.546
276.	GRAYER, J.	g	MIL	82	1659	20.2	102	153	0.667	0.449
277.	HODGE, D.	c/f	DAL	51	1058	20.7	100	150	0.667	0.497
278.	MAYES, Th.	g	LAC	24	255	10.6	24	36	0.667	0.303
279.	McCORMICK, T.	c	NY	22	108	4.9	14	21	0.667	0.424
280.	NEALY, E.	f	PHX	52	505	9.7	16	24	0.667	0.512

(NAME)	3-PT SHOTS MADE	3-PT SHOTS TRIED	REBs	ASTs	STLs	TURN-OVERS	BLKs	PTs
(McDANIEL, X.)	12	39	460	149	57	147	24	1125
(BLAYLOCK, M.)	12	54	269	492	170	152	40	996
(PERRY, T.)	3	8	551	134	44	141	116	982
(CUMMINGS, T.)	5	13	631	102	58	115	34	1210
(HOWARD, B.)	1	2	51	14	11	15	8	131
(DONALDSON, J.)	0	0	289	33	8	48	49	285
(KLEINE, J.)	4	8	296	32	23	27	14	326
(HOPSON, D.)	12	47	206	102	67	100	39	743
(EHLO, C.)	69	167	307	238	78	104	22	776
(REID, J.R.)	0	3	317	81	49	84	23	560
(CONNER, L.)	0	7	184	294	97	79	10	287
(BURTT, S.)	1	6	34	59	16	33	4	187
(ASKINS, K.)	25	73	142	38	40	47	15	219
(ROBINSON, D.)	1	8	829	181	158	182	305	1578
(BENNETT, W.)	0	1	162	38	19	33	9	195
(PETERSEN, J.)	0	2	45	9	5	5	6	43
(BARKLEY, C.)	32	137	830	308	136	235	44	1730
(ASKEW, V.)	1	10	233	188	47	84	23	498
(CATLEDGE, T.)	0	4	549	109	58	138	16	1154
(HILL, T.)	0	1	593	47	73	106	43	671
(TURNER, J.)	1	8	246	92	24	106	16	530
(GARRICK, T.)	1	4	56	98	36	44	4	137
(PAYNE, K.)	5	12	54	17	16	19	8	144
(ROYAL, D.)	0	00	124	34	25	39	7	252
(ALEXANDER, V.)	0	1	336	32	45	91	62	589
(RICHARDSON, P.)	53	155	301	685	119	204	25	1350
(SPENCER, F.)	0	0	435	53	27	70	79	405
(DUCKWORTH, K.)	0	3	497	99	38	143	37	880
(MUSTAF, J.)	0	0	145	45	21	51	16	233
(GATTISON, K.)	0	2	580	131	59	140	69	1042
(KNIGHT, N.)	4	13	46	112	24	58	3	243
(RULAND, J.)	0	0	47	5	7	20	4	51
(AGUIRRE, M.)	15	71	236	126	51	105	11	851
(STRICKLAND, R.)	5	15	265	491	118	160	17	787
(BENJAMIN, B.)	0	2	513	76	39	175	118	879
(WIGGINS, M.)	0	1	94	22	20	25	1	211
(WILEY, M.)	14	42	81	180	47	60	3	204
(FREDERICK, A.)	4	17	144	71	40	58	26	389
(PRESSEY, P.)	3	21	95	142	29	64	19	151
(WOOLRIDGE, O.)	1	9	260	88	41	133	33	1146
(DOUGLAS, S.)	1	10	63	172	25	68	9	308
(OLIVER, B.)	0	4	30	20	10	24	2	81
(CHAPMAN, R.)	8	29	58	89	15	45	8	270
(PERSON, C.)	132	354	426	382	68	216	18	1497
(WILLIAMS, Br.)	0	0	272	33	41	86	53	437
(PAYTON, G.)	3	23	295	506	147	174	21	764
(ANDERSON, N.)	30	85	384	163	97	125	33	1196
(BROWN, M.)	0	1	476	81	42	105	34	632
(BRYANT, M.)	0	3	201	41	26	30	8	230
(COOK, A.)	0	0	34	2	5	3	4	34
(FRANK, T.)	0	0	26	8	5	5	4	46
(GRAYER, J.)	19	66	257	150	64	105	13	739
(HODGE, D.)	0	0	275	39	25	75	23	426
(MAYES, Th.)	15	41	16	35	16	31	2	99
(McCORMICK, T.)	0	0	34	9	2	8	0	42
(NEALY, E.)	20	50	111	37	16	17	2	160

1991–92 REGULAR-SEASON STATISTICAL RESULTS
NBA PLAYERS ORDERED BY FREE-THROW PERCENTAGE

	NAME	POS	TEAM	GMs	MINs	MINs per GM	FTs MADE	FTs TRIED	FT PCT	FG PCT
281.	SAMPSON, R.	c	WAS	10	108	10.8	4	6	0.667	0.310
282.	THOMAS,. C	g	DET	37	156	4.2	10	15	0.667	0.353
283.	AUGMON, S.	g/f	ATL	82	2505	30.5	213	320	0.666	0.489
284.	KERSEY, J.	f	POR	77	2553	33.2	174	262	0.664	0.467
285.	ROBINSON, C.	f	POR	82	2124	25.9	219	330	0.664	0.466
286.	SHACKLEFORD, C.	c	PHI	72	1399	19.4	63	95	0.663	0.486
287.	LONGLEY, L.	c	MIN	66	991	15.0	53	80	0.663	0.458
288.	GATLING, C.	c	GS	54	612	11.3	72	109	0.661	0.568
289.	LOHAUS, B.	f/c	MIL	70	1081	15.4	27	41	0.659	0.450
290.	PERRY, E.	g	CHA	50	437	8.7	27	41	0.659	0.380
291.	THORPE, O.	f	HOU	82	3056	37.3	304	463	0.657	0.592
292.	BROWN, R.	g	SAC	56	535	9.6	38	58	0.655	0.456
293.	KONCAK, J.	c	ATL	77	1489	19.3	19	29	0.655	0.391
294.	OWENS, B.	g/f	GS	80	2510	31.4	204	312	0.654	0.525
295.	JOHNSON, A.	g	HOU	69	1235	17.9	66	101	0.654	0.479
296.	SMITH, To.	g	LAL	63	820	13.0	49	75	0.653	0.399
297.	WILLIAMS, S.	f	CHI	63	690	11.0	48	74	0.649	0.483
298.	JOHNSON, V.	g	SA	60	1350	22.5	55	85	0.647	0.405
299.	KIMBLE, B.	f	LAC	34	277	8.2	20	31	0.645	0.396
300.	McMILLAN, N.	g/f	SEA	72	1652	22.9	54	84	0.643	0.437
301.	MASON, A.	f	NY	82	2198	26.8	167	260	0.642	0.509
302.	MUTOMBO, D.	c	DEN	71	2716	38.3	321	500	0.642	0.493
303.	WEST, M.	c	PHX	82	1436	17.5	109	171	0.637	0.632
304.	BEDFORD, W.	f/c	DET	32	363	11.3	14	22	0.636	0.413
305.	COOPER, W.	f	POR	35	344	9.8	7	11	0.636	0.427
306.	JEPSEN, L.	c	SAC	31	87	2.8	7	11	0.636	0.375
307.	PHILLS, B.	g	CLE	10	65	6.5	7	11	0.636	0.429
308.	ROBINSON, R.	g	ATL	81	2220	27.4	175	275	0.636	0.456
309.	WILLIAMS, Ja.	f/c	PHI	50	646	12.9	56	88	0.636	0.364
310.	DAVIS, T.	f/c	DAL	68	2149	31.6	181	285	0.635	0.482
311.	AUSTIN, I.	c	UT	31	112	3.6	19	30	0.633	0.457
312.	VOLKOV, A.	f	ATL	77	1516	19.7	125	198	0.631	0.441
313.	BONNER, A.	f	SAC	79	2287	28.9	151	241	0.627	0.447
314.	LEVINGSTON, C.	f	CHI	79	1020	12.9	60	96	0.625	0.498
315.	ANDERSON, G.	f	DEN	82	2793	34.1	167	268	0.623	0.456
316.	POLYNICE, O.	c	LAC	76	1834	24.1	125	201	0.622	0.519
317.	CAGE, M.	f	SEA	82	2461	30.0	106	171	0.620	0.566
318.	WALKER, D.	g	DET	74	1541	20.8	65	105	0.619	0.423
319.	CAMPBELL, E.	c	LAL	81	1876	23.2	138	223	0.619	0.448
320.	GLASS, G.	g	MIN	75	1822	24.3	77	125	0.616	0.440
321.	QUINNETT, B.	f	DAL	39	326	8.4	16	26	0.615	0.347
322.	SPARROW, R.	g	LAL	46	489	10.6	8	13	0.615	0.384
323.	CAUSWELL, D.	c	SAC	80	2291	28.6	136	222	0.613	0.550
324.	BROWN, C.	f	LAL	42	431	10.3	30	49	0.612	0.469
325.	HAMMONDS, T.	f	CHA	37	984	26.6	50	82	0.610	0.488
326.	CHEEKS, M.	g	ATL	56	1086	19.4	26	43	0.605	0.462
327.	WILLIAMS, K.	f	IND	60	565	9.4	26	43	0.605	0.518
328.	CARTWRIGHT, B.	c	CHI	64	1471	23.0	96	159	0.604	0.467
329.	RODMAN, D.	f	DET	82	3301	40.3	84	140	0.600	0.539
330.	EATON, M.	c	UT	81	2023	25.0	52	87	0.598	0.446
331.	KITE, G.	c	ORL	72	1479	20.5	40	68	0.588	0.437
332.	VRANKOVIC, S.	c	BOS	19	110	5.8	7	12	0.583	0.469
333.	KOFOED, B.	g	SEA	44	239	5.4	15	26	0.577	0.472
334.	DAVIS, D.	f	IND	64	1301	20.3	87	152	0.572	0.552
335.	BUECHLER, J.	f	GS	28	290	10.4	12	21	0.571	0.409
336.	HERRERA, C.	f	HOU	43	566	13.2	25	44	0.568	0.516

(NAME)	3-PT SHOTS MADE	3-PT SHOTS TRIED	REBs	ASTs	STLs	TURN-OVERS	BLKs	PTs
(SAMPSON, R.)	0	2	30	4	3	10	8	22
(THOMAS,. C)	2	17	22	22	4	17	1	48
(AUGMON, S.)	1	6	420	201	124	181	27	1094
(KERSEY, J.)	1	8	633	243	114	151	71	971
(ROBINSON, C.)	1	11	416	137	85	154	107	1016
(SHACKLEFORD, C.)	0	1	415	46	38	62	51	473
(LONGLEY, L.)	0	0	257	53	35	83	64	281
(GATLING, C.)	0	4	182	16	31	44	36	306
(LOHAUS, B.)	57	144	249	74	40	46	71	408
(PERRY, E.)	1	7	39	78	34	50	3	126
(THORPE; O.)	0	7	862	250	52	237	37	1420
(BROWN, R.)	0	6	69	59	35	42	12	192
(KONCAK, J.)	0	12	261	132	50	54	67	241
(OWENS, B.)	1	9	639	188	90	179	65	1141
(JOHNSON, A.)	4	15	80	266	61	110	9	386
(SMITH, To.)	0	11	76	109	39	50	8	275
(WILLIAMS, S.)	0	3	247	50	13	35	36	214
(JOHNSON, V.)	19	60	182	145	41	74	14	478
(KIMBLE, B.)	4	13	32	17	10	15	6	112
(McMILLAN, N.)	27	98	252	359	129	112	29	435
(MASON, A.)	0	0	573	106	46	101	20	573
(MUTOMBO, D.)	0	0	870	156	43	252	210	1177
(WEST, M.)	0	0	372	22	14	82	81	501
(BEDFORD, W.)	0	1	63	12	6	15	18	114
(COOPER, W.)	0	0	101	21	4	15	27	77
(JEPSEN, L.)	0	1	30	1	1	3	5	25
(PHILLS, B.)	0	2	8	4	3	8	1	31
(ROBINSON, R.)	34	104	219	446	105	206	24	1055
(WILLIAMS, Ja.)	0	0	145	12	20	44	20	206
(DAVIS, T.)	0	5	672	57	26	117	29	693
(AUSTIN, I.)	0	0	35	5	2	8	2	61
(VOLKOV, A.)	35	110	265	250	66	102	30	662
(BONNER, A.)	1	4	485	125	94	133	26	740
(LEVINGSTON, C.)	1	6	227	66	27	42	45	311
(ANDERSON, G.)	0	4	941	78	88	201	65	945
(POLYNICE, O.)	0	1	536	46	45	83	20	613
(CAGE, M.)	0	5	728	92	99	78	55	720
(WALKER, D.)	0	10	238	205	63	79	18	387
(CAMPBELL, E.)	0	2	423	59	53	73	159	578
(GLASS, G.)	16	54	260	175	66	103	30	859
(QUINNETT, B.)	13	41	51	12	16	16	8	115
(SPARROW, R.)	3	15	28	83	12	33	5	127
(CAUSWELL, D.)	0	1	580	59	47	124	215	636
(BROWN, C.)	0	3	82	26	12	29	7	150
(HAMMONDS, T.)	0	1	185	36	22	58	13	440
(CHEEKS, M.)	3	6	95	185	83	36	0	259
(WILLIAMS, K.)	0	4	129	40	20	22	41	252
(CARTWRIGHT, B.)	0	0	324	87	22	75	14	512
(RODMAN, D.)	32	101	1530	191	68	140	70	800
(EATON, M.)	0	0	491	40	36	60	205	266
(KITE, G.)	0	1	402	44	30	61	57	228
(VRANKOVIC, S.)	0	0	28	5	0	10	17	37
(KOFOED, B.)	1	7	26	51	2	20	2	66
(DAVIS, D.)	0	1	410	30	27	49	74	395
(BUECHLER, J.)	0	1	52	23	19	13	7	70
(HERRERA, C.)	0	1	99	27	16	37	25	191

1991–92 REGULAR-SEASON STATISTICAL RESULTS
NBA PLAYERS ORDERED BY FREE-THROW PERCENTAGE

NAME	POS	TEAM	GMs	MINs	MINs per GM	FTs MADE	FTs TRIED	FT PCT	FG PCT
337. MURPHY, T.	f	MIN	47	429	9.1	19	34	0.559	0.488
338. TOLBERT, T.	f	GS	35	310	8.9	22	40	0.550	0.384
339. GREEN, Se.	g	IND	35	256	7.3	15	28	0.536	0.392
340. NORMAN, K.	f	LAC	77	2009	26.1	121	226	0.535	0.490
341. OGG, A.	c	MIA	43	367	8.5	16	30	0.533	0.548
342. BREUER, R.	c	MIN	67	1176	17.6	41	77	0.533	0.468
343. LEE, D.	g	NJ	46	307	6.7	10	19	0.526	0.431
344. TURNER, Jo.	f	HOU	42	345	8.2	31	59	0.525	0.439
345. ROBERTS, S.	c	ORL	55	1118	20.3	101	196	0.515	0.529
346. JONES, Ch.	c/f	WAS	75	1365	18.2	20	40	0.500	0.367
347. WITTMAN, R.	g	IND	24	115	4.8	1	2	0.500	0.421
348. PERDUE, W.	c	CHI	77	1007	13.1	45	91	0.495	0.547
349. HALEY, J.	f/c	LAL	49	394	8.0	14	29	0.483	0.369
350. ELLIS, L.	f	LAC	29	103	3.6	9	19	0.474	0.340
351. DUDLEY, C.	c	NJ	82	1902	23.2	80	171	0.468	0.403
352. BOL, M.	c	PHI	71	1267	17.8	12	26	0.462	0.383
353. LISTER, A.	c	GS	26	293	11.3	14	33	0.424	0.557
354. THOMPSON, S.	g	SAC	19	91	4.8	3	8	0.375	0.378
355. HANSEN, B.	g	CHI	68	809	11.9	8	22	0.364	0.444
356. SMITH, L.	f/c	HOU	45	800	17.8	4	11	0.364	0.544
357. LANE, J.	f	MIL	14	177	12.6	9	27	0.333	0.304
358. COPA, T.	f/c	SA	33	132	4.0	4	13	0.308	0.550
359. McCANN, B.	f	DET	26	129	5.0	4	13	0.308	0.394

(NAME)	3-PT SHOTS MADE	3-PT SHOTS TRIED	REBs	ASTs	STLs	TURN-OVERS	BLKs	PTs
(MURPHY, T.)	1	2	110	11	9	18	8	98
(TOLBERT, T.)	2	8	55	21	10	20	6	90
(GREEN, Se.)	2	10	42	22	13	27	6	141
(NORMAN, K.)	4	28	448	125	53	100	66	929
(OGG, A.)	0	0	74	7	5	19	28	108
(BREUER, R.)	0	1	281	89	27	41	99	363
(LEE, D.)	10	37	35	22	11	12	1	120
(TURNER, Jo.)	0	0	78	12	6	32	4	117
(ROBERTS, S.)	0	1	336	39	22	78	83	573
(JONES, Ch.)	0	0	317	62	43	39	92	86
(WITTMAN, R.)	0	0	9	11	2	3	0	17
(PERDUE, W.)	1	2	312	80	16	72	43	350
(HALEY, J.)	0	0	95	7	7	25	8	76
(ELLIS, L.)	0	0	24	1	6	11	9	43
(DUDLEY, C.)	0	0	739	58	38	79	179	460
(BOL, M.)	0	9	222	22	11	41	205	110
(LISTER, A.)	0	0	92	14	5	20	16	102
(THOMPSON, S.)	0	1	19	8	6	5	3	31
(HANSEN, B.)	7	27	77	69	27	28	3	173
(SMITH, L.)	0	1	256	33	21	44	7	104
(LANE, J.)	0	0	66	17	2	14	1	37
(COPA, T.)	0	0	36	3	2	8	6	48
(McCANN, B.)	0	1	30	6	6	7	4	30

1991–92 REGULAR-SEASON STATISTICAL RESULTS
NBA PLAYERS ORDERED BY POINTS PER GAME

NAME	POS	TEAM	GMs	MINs	MINs per GM	PTs	PTs per MIN	PTs per GM	FG PCT
1. JORDAN, M.	g	CHI	80	3102	38.8	2404	0.775	30.1	0.519
2. WILKINS, D.	f	ATL	42	1601	38.1	1179	0.736	28.1	0.464
3. MALONE, K.	f	UT	81	3054	37.7	2272	0.744	28.0	0.526
4. MULLIN, C.	f	GS	81	3346	41.3	2074	0.620	25.6	0.524
5. DREXLER, C.	g	POR	76	2751	36.2	1903	0.692	25.0	0.470
6. EWING, P.	c	NY	82	3150	38.4	1970	0.625	24.0	0.522
7. HARDAWAY, T.	g	GS	81	3332	41.1	1893	0.568	23.4	0.461
8. ROBINSON, D.	c	SA	68	2564	37.7	1578	0.615	23.2	0.551
9. BARKLEY, C.	f	PHI	75	2881	38.4	1730	0.601	23.1	0.552
10. RICHMOND, M.	g	SAC	80	3095	38.7	1803	0.583	22.5	0.468
11. RICE, G.	f	MIA	79	3007	38.1	1765	0.587	22.3	0.469
12. PIERCE, R.	g	SEA	78	2658	34.1	1690	0.636	21.7	0.475
13. OLAJUWON, H.	c	HOU	70	2636	37.7	1510	0.573	21.6	0.502
14. DAUGHERTY, B.	c	CLE	73	2643	36.2	1566	0.593	21.5	0.570
15. PIPPEN, S.	f	CHI	82	3164	38.6	1720	0.544	21.0	0.506
16. LEWIS, Re.	g	BOS	82	3070	37.4	1703	0.555	20.8	0.503
17. MILLER, R.	g	IND	82	3120	38.0	1695	0.543	20.7	0.501
18. PETROVIC, D.	g	NJ	82	3027	36.9	1691	0.559	20.6	0.508
19. GILL, K.	g/f	CHA	79	2906	36.8	1622	0.558	20.5	0.467
20. MALONE, J.	g	UT	81	2922	36.1	1639	0.561	20.2	0.511
21. BIRD, L.	f	BOS	45	1662	36.9	908	0.546	20.2	0.466
22. HORNACEK, J.	g	PHX	81	3078	38.0	1632	0.530	20.1	0.512
23. ELLISON, P.	c	WAS	66	2511	38.0	1322	0.527	20.0	0.539
24. SCOTT, D.	f	ORL	18	608	33.8	359	0.591	19.9	0.402
25. DUMARS, J.	g	DET	82	3192	38.9	1635	0.512	19.9	0.448
26. ANDERSON, N	g/f	ORL	60	2203	36.7	1196	0.543	19.9	0.463
27. WORTHY, J.	f	LAL	54	2108	39.0	1075	0.510	19.9	0.447
28. COLEMAN, D.	f	NJ	65	2207	34.0	1289	0.584	19.8	0.504
29. JOHNSON, K.	g	PHX	78	2899	37.2	1536	0.530	19.7	0.479
30. MANNING, D.	f	LAC	82	2904	35.4	1579	0.544	19.3	0.542
31. JOHNSON, L.	f	CHA	82	3047	37.2	1576	0.517	19.2	0.490
32. HAWKINS, H.	g	PHI	81	3013	37.2	1536	0.510	19.0	0.462
33. MARCIULIONIS, S.	g	GS	72	2117	29.4	1361	0.643	18.9	0.538
34. THOMAS, I.	g	DET	78	2918	37.4	1445	0.495	18.5	0.446
35. PERSON, C.	f	IND	81	2923	36.1	1497	0.512	18.5	0.480
36. BLACKMAN, R.	g	DAL	75	2527	33.7	1374	0.544	18.3	0.461
37. WILLIS, K.	f/c	ATL	81	2962	36.6	1480	0.500	18.3	0.483
38. HARPER, R.	g	LAC	82	3144	38.3	1495	0.476	18.2	0.440
39. WILLIAMS, R.	f	DEN	81	2623	32.4	1474	0.562	18.2	0.471
40. PORTER, T.	g	POR	82	2784	34.0	1485	0.533	18.1	0.462
41. ADAMS, M.	g	WAS	78	2795	35.8	1408	0.504	18.1	0.393
42. GRANT, Ha.	f	WAS	64	2388	37.3	1155	0.484	18.0	0.479
43. HARPER, D.	g	DAL	65	2252	34.6	1152	0.512	17.7	0.443
44. PRICE, M.	g	CLE	72	2138	29.7	1247	0.583	17.3	0.488
45. THORPE, O.	f	HOU	82	3056	37.3	1420	0.465	17.3	0.592
46. MAJERLE, D.	g/f	PHX	82	2853	34.8	1418	0.497	17.3	0.478
47. CUMMINGS, T.	f	SA	70	2149	30.7	1210	0.563	17.3	0.488
48. SCHREMPF, D.	f	IND	80	2605	32.6	1380	0.530	17.2	0.536
49. MAXWELL, V.	g	HOU	80	2700	33.7	1372	0.508	17.1	0.413
50. SIMMONS, L.	f	SAC	78	2895	37.1	1336	0.462	17.1	0.454
51. JOHNSON, E.	f	SEA	81	2366	29.2	1386	0.586	17.1	0.459
52. NANCE, L.	f	CLE	81	2880	35.6	1375	0.477	17.0	0.539
53. GILLIAM, A.	f/c	PHI	81	2771	34.2	1367	0.493	16.9	0.512
54. CAMPBELL, T.	f/g	MIN	78	2441	31.3	1307	0.535	16.8	0.464
55. TISDALE, W.	f	SAC	72	2521	35.0	1195	0.474	16.6	0.501
56. MUTOMBO, D.	c	DEN	71	2716	38.3	1177	0.433	16.6	0.493

(NAME)	FT PCT	3-PT SHOTS MADE	3-PT SHOTS TRIED	REBs	ASTs	STLs	TURN-OVERS	BLKs
(JORDAN, M.)	0.832	27	100	511	489	182	200	75
(WILKINS, D.)	0.835	37	128	295	158	52	122	24
(MALONE, K.)	0.778	3	17	909	241	108	248	51
(MULLIN, C.)	0.833	64	175	450	286	173	202	62
(DREXLER, C.)	0.794	114	338	500	512	138	240	70
(EWING, P.)	0.738	1	6	921	156	88	209	245
(HARDAWAY, T.)	0.766	127	376	310	807	164	267	13
(ROBINSON, D.)	0.701	1	8	829	181	158	182	305
(BARKLEY, C.)	0.695	32	137	830	308	136	235	44
(RICHMOND, M.)	0.813	103	268	319	411	92	247	34
(RICE, G.)	0.837	155	396	394	184	90	145	35
(PIERCE, R.)	0.917	33	123	233	241	86	189	20
(OLAJUWON, H.)	0.766	0	1	845	157	127	187	304
(DAUGHERTY, B.)	0.777	0	2	760	262	65	185	78
(PIPPEN, S.)	0.760	16	80	630	572	155	253	93
(LEWIS, Re.)	0.851	5	21	394	185	125	136	105
(MILLER, R.)	0.858	129	341	318	314	105	157	26
(PETROVIC, D.)	0.808	123	277	258	252	105	215	11
(GILL, K.)	0.745	6	25	402	329	154	180	46
(MALONE, J.)	0.898	1	12	233	180	56	140	5
(BIRD, L.)	0.926	52	128	434	306	42	125	33
(HORNACEK, J.)	0.886	83	189	407	411	158	170	31
(ELLISON, P.)	0.728	1	3	740	190	62	196	177
(SCOTT, D.)	0.901	29	89	66	35	20	31	9
(DUMARS, J.)	0.867	49	120	188	375	71	193	12
(ANDERSON, N)	0.667	30	85	384	163	97	125	33
(WORTHY, J.)	0.814	9	43	305	252	76	127	23
(COLEMAN, D.)	0.763	23	76	618	205	54	248	98
(JOHNSON, K.)	0.807	10	46	292	836	116	272	23
(MANNING, D.)	0.725	0	5	564	285	135	210	122
(JOHNSON, L.)	0.829	5	22	899	292	81	160	51
(HAWKINS, H.)	0.874	91	229	271	248	157	189	43
(MARCIULIONIS, S.)	0.788	3	10	208	243	116	193	10
(THOMAS, I.)	0.773	25	86	247	560	118	252	15
(PERSON, C.)	0.675	132	354	426	382	68	216	18
(BLACKMAN, R.)	0.899	65	169	239	204	50	153	22
(WILLIS, K.)	0.804	6	37	1258	173	72	197	54
(HARPER, R.)	0.736	64	211	447	417	152	252	72
(WILLIAMS, R.)	0.803	56	156	405	235	148	173	68
(PORTER, T.)	0.856	128	324	255	477	127	188	12
(ADAMS, M.)	0.869	125	386	310	594	145	212	9
(GRANT, Ha.)	0.800	1	8	432	170	74	109	27
(HARPER, D.)	0.759	58	186	170	373	101	154	17
(PRICE, M.)	0.947	101	261	173	535	94	159	12
(THORPE, O.)	0.657	0	7	862	250	52	237	37
(MAJERLE, D.)	0.756	87	228	483	274	131	101	43
(CUMMINGS, T.)	0.711	5	13	631	102	58	115	34
(SCHREMPF, D.)	0.828	23	71	770	312	62	191	37
(MAXWELL, V.)	0.772	162	473	243	326	104	178	28
(SIMMONS, L.)	0.770	1	5	634	337	135	218	132
(JOHNSON, E.)	0.861	27	107	292	161	55	130	11
(NANCE, L.)	0.822	0	6	670	232	80	87	243
(GILLIAM, A.)	0.807	0	2	660	118	51	166	85
(CAMPBELL, T.)	0.803	13	37	286	229	84	165	31
(TISDALE, W.)	0.763	0	2	469	106	55	124	79
(MUTOMBO, D.)	0.642	0	0	870	156	43	252	210

1991–92 REGULAR-SEASON STATISTICAL RESULTS
NBA PLAYERS ORDERED BY POINTS PER GAME

	NAME	POS	TEAM	GMs	MINs	MINs per GM	PTs	PTs per MIN	PTs per GM	FG PCT
57.	PERKINS, S.	f/c	LAL	63	2332	37.0	1041	0.446	16.5	0.450
58.	RICHARDSON, P.	g	MIN	82	2922	35.6	1350	0.462	16.5	0.466
59.	SEIKALY, R.	c	MIA	79	2800	35.4	1296	0.463	16.4	0.489
60.	CHAMBERS, T.	f	PHX	69	1948	28.2	1128	0.579	16.3	0.431
61.	ELLIOTT, S.	f	SA	82	3120	38.0	1338	0.429	16.3	0.494
62.	WEBB, S.	g	SAC	77	2724	35.4	1231	0.452	16.0	0.445
63.	STOCKTON, J.	g	UT	82	3002	36.6	1297	0.432	15.8	0.482
64.	ELLIS, D.	f	MIL	81	2191	27.0	1272	0.581	15.7	0.469
65.	CURRY, D.	g	CHA	77	2020	26.2	1209	0.599	15.7	0.486
66.	MALONE, M.	c	MIL	82	2511	30.6	1279	0.509	15.6	0.474
67.	KEMP, S.	f/c	SEA	64	1808	28.2	994	0.550	15.5	0.504
68.	NEWMAN, J.	f/g	CHA	55	1651	30.0	839	0.508	15.3	0.477
69.	THREATT, S.	g	LAL	82	3070	37.4	1240	0.404	15.1	0.489
70.	WILLIAMS, M.	g	IND	79	2750	34.8	1188	0.432	15.0	0.490
71.	BOWIE, S.	c	NJ	71	2179	30.7	1062	0.487	15.0	0.445
72.	McKEY, D.	f	SEA	52	1757	33.8	777	0.442	14.9	0.472
73.	SCOTT, B.	g	LAL	82	2679	32.7	1218	0.455	14.9	0.458
74.	CATLEDGE, T.	f	ORL	78	2430	31.2	1154	0.475	14.8	0.496
75.	LONG, G.	f	MIA	82	3063	37.4	1212	0.396	14.8	0.494
76.	BOWIE, A.	g/f	ORL	52	1721	33.1	758	0.440	14.6	0.493
77.	SMITH, C.	f/c	LAC	49	1310	26.7	714	0.545	14.6	0.466
78.	OWENS, B.	g/f	GS	80	2510	31.4	1141	0.455	14.3	0.525
79.	GRANT, Ho.	f	CHI	81	2859	35.3	1149	0.402	14.2	0.579
80.	PARISH, R.	c	BOS	79	2285	28.9	1115	0.488	14.1	0.536
81.	SKILES, S.	g	ORL	75	2377	31.7	1057	0.445	14.1	0.414
82.	SMITH, K.	g	HOU	81	2735	33.8	1137	0.416	14.0	0.475
83.	WOOLRIDGE, O.	f	DET	82	2113	25.8	1146	0.542	14.0	0.498
84.	HUMPHRIES, J.	g	MIL	71	2261	31.8	991	0.438	14.0	0.470
85.	BENJAMIN, B.	c	SEA	63	1941	30.8	879	0.453	14.0	0.478
86.	WEST, D.	g	MIN	80	2540	31.7	1116	0.439	14.0	0.518
87.	McHALE, K.	f/c	BOS	56	1398	25.0	780	0.558	13.9	0.510
88.	STARKS, J.	g	NY	82	2118	25.8	1139	0.538	13.9	0.449
89.	SMITS, R.	c	IND	74	1772	23.9	1024	0.578	13.8	0.510
90.	BLAYLOCK, M.	g	NJ	72	2548	35.4	996	0.391	13.8	0.432
91.	STRICKLAND, R.	g	SA	57	2053	36.0	787	0.383	13.8	0.455
92.	McDANIEL, X.	f	NY	82	2344	28.6	1125	0.480	13.7	0.478
93.	ANDERSON, Ro.	f	PHI	82	2432	29.7	1123	0.462	13.7	0.465
94.	GREEN, A.C.	f	LAL	82	2902	35.4	1116	0.385	13.6	0.476
95.	GAMBLE, K.	g/f	BOS	82	2496	30.4	1108	0.444	13.5	0.529
96.	AUGMON, S.	g/f	ATL	82	2505	30.5	1094	0.437	13.3	0.489
97.	EACKLES, L.	f	WAS	65	1463	22.5	856	0.585	13.2	0.468
98.	ANDERSON, W.	g/f	SA	57	1889	33.1	744	0.394	13.1	0.456
99.	ROBINSON, R.	g	ATL	81	2220	27.4	1055	0.475	13.0	0.456
100.	FERRELL, D.	f	ATL	66	1598	24.2	839	0.525	12.7	0.524
101.	GATTISON, K.	f/c	CHA	82	2223	27.1	1042	0.469	12.7	0.529
102.	KERSEY, J.	f	POR	77	2553	33.2	971	0.380	12.6	0.467
103.	EDWARDS, T.	g/f	UT	81	2283	28.2	1018	0.446	12.6	0.522
104.	ROBINSON, C.	f	POR	82	2124	25.9	1016	0.478	12.4	0.466
105.	WILKINS, G.	g	NY	82	2344	28.6	1016	0.433	12.4	0.447
106.	EHLO, C.	g/f	CLE	63	2016	32.0	776	0.385	12.3	0.453
107.	ROBERTSON, A.	g	MIL	82	2463	30.0	1010	0.410	12.3	0.430
108.	PERRY, T.	f	PHX	80	2483	31.0	982	0.396	12.3	0.523
109.	CHAPMAN, R.	g	WAS	22	567	25.8	270	0.476	12.3	0.448
110.	REYNOLDS, J.	g/f	ORL	46	1159	25.2	555	0.479	12.1	0.380
111.	NORMAN, K.	f	LAC	77	2009	26.1	929	0.462	12.1	0.490
112.	DAWKINS, J.	g	PHI	82	2815	34.3	988	0.351	12.0	0.437

(NAME)	FT PCT	3-PT SHOTS MADE	3-PT SHOTS TRIED	REBs	ASTs	STLs	TURN-OVERS	BLKs
(PERKINS, S.)	0.817	15	69	556	141	64	83	62
(RICHARDSON, P.)	0.691	53	155	301	685	119	204	25
(SEIKALY, R.)	0.733	0	3	934	109	40	216	121
(CHAMBERS, T.)	0.830	18	49	401	142	57	103	37
(ELLIOTT, S.)	0.861	25	82	439	214	84	152	29
(WEBB, S.)	0.859	73	199	223	547	125	229	24
(STOCKTON, J.)	0.842	83	204	270	1126	244	286	22
(ELLIS, D.)	0.774	138	329	253	104	57	119	18
(CURRY, D.)	0.836	74	183	259	177	93	134	20
(MALONE, M.)	0.786	3	8	744	93	74	150	64
(KEMP, S.)	0.748	0	3	665	86	70	156	124
(NEWMAN, J.)	0.766	13	46	179	146	70	129	14
(THREATT, S.)	0.831	20	62	253	593	168	182	16
(WILLIAMS, M.)	0.871	8	33	282	647	233	240	22
(BOWIE, S.)	0.757	8	25	578	186	41	150	120
(McKEY, D.)	0.847	19	50	268	120	61	114	47
(SCOTT, B.)	0.839	54	157	310	226	105	119	28
(CATLEDGE, T.)	0.694	0	4	549	109	58	138	16
(LONG, G.)	0.807	6	22	691	225	139	185	40
(BOWIE, A.)	0.860	17	44	245	163	55	107	38
(SMITH, C.)	0.785	0	6	301	56	41	69	98
(OWENS, B.)	0.654	1	9	639	188	90	179	65
(GRANT, Ho.)	0.741	0	2	807	217	100	98	131
(PARISH, R.)	0.772	0	0	705	70	68	131	97
(SKILES, S.)	0.895	91	250	202	544	74	233	5
(SMITH, K.)	0.866	54	137	177	562	104	227	7
(WOOLRIDGE, O.)	0.683	1	9	260	88	41	133	33
(HUMPHRIES, J.)	0.783	42	144	184	466	119	148	13
(BENJAMIN, B.)	0.687	0	2	513	76	39	175	118
(WEST, D.)	0.805	4	23	257	281	66	120	26
(McHALE, K.)	0.822	0	13	330	82	11	82	59
(STARKS, J.)	0.778	94	270	191	276	103	150	18
(SMITS, R.)	0.788	0	2	417	116	29	130	100
(BLAYLOCK, M.)	0.712	12	54	269	492	170	152	40
(STRICKLAND, R.)	0.687	5	15	265	491	118	160	17
(McDANIEL, X.)	0.714	12	39	460	149	57	147	24
(ANDERSON, Ro.)	0.877	42	127	278	135	86	109	11
(GREEN, A.C.)	0.744	12	56	762	117	91	111	36
(GAMBLE, K.)	0.885	9	31	286	219	75	97	37
(AUGMON, S.)	0.666	1	6	420	201	124	181	27
(EACKLES, L.)	0.743	7	35	178	125	47	75	7
(ANDERSON, W.)	0.775	13	56	300	302	54	140	51
(ROBINSON, R.)	0.636	34	104	219	446	105	206	24
(FERRELL, D.)	0.762	11	33	210	92	49	99	17
(GATTISON, K.)	0.688	0	2	580	131	59	140	69
(KERSEY, J.)	0.664	1	8	633	243	114	151	71
(EDWARDS, T.)	0.774	39	103	298	137	81	122	46
(ROBINSON, C.)	0.664	1	11	416	137	85	154	107
(WILKINS, G.)	0.730	38	108	206	219	76	113	17
(EHLO, C.)	0.707	69	167	307	238	78	104	22
(ROBERTSON, A.)	0.763	67	210	350	360	210	223	32
(PERRY, T.)	0.712	3	8	551	134	44	141	116
(CHAPMAN, R.)	0.679	8	29	58	89	15	45	8
(REYNOLDS, J.)	0.836	3	24	149	151	63	96	17
(NORMAN, K.)	0.535	4	28	448	125	53	100	66
(DAWKINS, J.)	0.882	36	101	227	567	89	183	5

1991–92 REGULAR-SEASON STATISTICAL RESULTS
NBA PLAYERS ORDERED BY POINTS PER GAME

	NAME	POS	TEAM	GMs	MINs	MINs per GM	PTs	PTs per MIN	PTs per GM	FG PCT
113.	SMITH, S.	g	MIA	61	1806	29.6	729	0.404	12.0	0.454
114.	WILLIAMS, J.	f/c	CLE	80	2432	30.4	952	0.391	11.9	0.503
115.	HAMMONDS, T.	f	CHA	37	984	26.6	440	0.447	11.9	0.488
116.	BROWN, D.	g	BOS	31	883	28.5	363	0.411	11.7	0.426
117.	ANDERSON, G.	f	DEN	82	2793	34.1	945	0.338	11.5	0.456
118.	GLASS, G.	g	MIN	75	1822	24.3	859	0.472	11.5	0.440
119.	WILLIAMS, H.	f/c	DAL	75	2040	27.2	859	0.421	11.5	0.431
120.	MORRIS, C.	f	NJ	77	2394	31.1	879	0.367	11.4	0.477
121.	BRICKOWSKI, F.	f	MIL	65	1556	23.9	740	0.476	11.4	0.524
122.	AGUIRRE, M.	f	DET	75	1582	21.1	851	0.538	11.3	0.431
123.	BAILEY, T.	f	MIN	84	2104	25.0	951	0.452	11.3	0.440
124.	JACKSON, M.	g	NY	81	2461	30.4	916	0.372	11.3	0.491
125.	WILLIAMS, Bu.	f	POR	80	2519	31.5	901	0.358	11.3	0.604
126.	DIVAC, V.	c	LAL	36	979	27.2	405	0.414	11.2	0.495
127.	BURTON, W.	g/f	MIA	68	1585	23.3	762	0.481	11.2	0.450
128.	LEVER, F.	g	DAL	31	884	28.5	347	0.393	11.2	0.387
129.	REID, J.R.	c/f	CHA	51	1257	24.6	560	0.446	11.0	0.490
130.	ENGLISH, A.J.	g	WAS	81	1665	20.6	886	0.532	10.9	0.433
131.	CARR, A.	f/c	SA	81	1867	23.0	881	0.472	10.9	0.490
132.	RIVERS, Do.	g	LAC	59	1657	28.1	641	0.387	10.9	0.424
133.	GARLAND, W.	g	DEN	78	2209	28.3	846	0.383	10.8	0.444
134.	DUCKWORTH, K.	c	POR	82	2222	27.1	880	0.396	10.7	0.461
135.	TEAGLE, T.	f	LAL	82	1602	19.5	880	0.549	10.7	0.452
136.	MACON, M.	g	DEN	76	2304	30.3	805	0.349	10.6	0.375
137.	VINCENT, S.	g	ORL	39	885	22.7	411	0.464	10.5	0.430
138.	HOPSON, D.	g/f	SAC	71	1314	18.5	743	0.565	10.5	0.465
139.	STEWART, L.	f	WAS	76	2229	29.3	794	0.356	10.4	0.514
140.	ROBERTS, S.	c	ORL	55	1118	20.3	573	0.513	10.4	0.529
141.	JACKSON, C.	g	DEN	81	1538	19.0	837	0.544	10.3	0.421
142.	BATTLE, J.	g	CLE	76	1637	21.5	779	0.476	10.2	0.480
143.	HIGGINS, R.	f	GS	25	535	21.4	255	0.477	10.2	0.412
144.	DAVIS, T.	f/c	DAL	68	2149	31.6	693	0.323	10.2	0.482
145.	GRAHAM, P.	g	ATL	78	1718	22.0	791	0.460	10.1	0.447
146.	EDWARDS, K.	g	MIA	81	1840	22.7	819	0.445	10.1	0.454
147.	COLES, B.	g	MIA	81	1976	24.4	816	0.413	10.1	0.455
148.	MITCHELL, S.	f	MIN	82	2151	26.2	825	0.384	10.1	0.423
149.	DAVIS, W.	g	DEN	46	741	16.1	457	0.617	9.9	0.459
150.	ARMSTRONG, B.J.	g	CHI	82	1875	22.9	809	0.432	9.9	0.481
151.	RODMAN, D.	f	DET	82	3301	40.3	800	0.242	9.8	0.539
152.	CORBIN, T.	f	UT	80	2207	27.6	780	0.353	9.8	0.481
153.	EDWARDS, Ja.	c	LAC	72	1437	20.0	698	0.486	9.7	0.465
154.	AINGE, D.	g	POR	81	1595	19.7	784	0.492	9.7	0.442
155.	LAIMBEER, B.	c	DET	81	2234	27.6	783	0.351	9.7	0.470
156.	ROBERTS, F.	f	MIL	80	1746	21.8	769	0.440	9.6	0.482
157.	SALLEY, J.	f/c	DET	72	1774	24.6	684	0.386	9.5	0.512
158.	PAYTON, G.	g	SEA	81	2549	31.5	764	0.300	9.4	0.451
159.	BONNER, A.	f	SAC	79	2287	28.9	740	0.324	9.4	0.447
160.	IUZZOLINO, M.	g	DAL	52	1280	24.6	486	0.380	9.4	0.451
161.	LIBERTY, M.	f/g	DEN	75	1527	20.4	698	0.457	9.3	0.443
162.	WILLIAMS, Br.	f	ORL	48	905	18.9	437	0.483	9.1	0.528
163.	FLOYD, S.	g	HOU	82	1662	20.3	744	0.448	9.1	0.406
164.	MILLS, T.	f	NJ	82	1714	20.9	742	0.433	9.1	0.463
165.	KRYSTKOWIAK, L.	f	MIL	79	1848	23.4	714	0.386	9.0	0.444
166.	McCRAY, R.	f	DAL	75	2106	28.1	677	0.322	9.0	0.436
167.	GRAYER, J.	g	MIL	82	1659	20.2	739	0.445	9.0	0.449
168.	RASMUSSEN, B.	c	ATL	81	1968	24.3	729	0.370	9.0	0.478

(NAME)	FT PCT	3-PT SHOTS MADE	3-PT SHOTS TRIED	REBs	ASTs	STLs	TURN-OVERS	BLKs
(SMITH, S.)	0.748	40	125	188	278	59	152	19
(WILLIAMS, J.)	0.752	0	4	607	196	60	83	182
(HAMMONDS, T.)	0.610	0	1	185	36	22	58	13
(BROWN, D.)	0.769	5	22	79	164	33	59	7
(ANDERSON, G.)	0.623	0	4	941	78	88	201	65
(GLASS, G.)	0.616	16	54	260	175	66	103	30
(WILLIAMS, H.)	0.725	1	6	454	94	35	114	98
(MORRIS, C.)	0.714	22	110	494	197	129	171	81
(BRICKOWSKI, F.)	0.767	3	6	344	122	60	112	23
(AGUIRRE, M.)	0.687	15	71	236	126	51	105	11
(BAILEY, T.)	0.796	0	2	485	78	35	108	117
(JACKSON, M.)	0.770	11	43	305	694	112	211	13
(WILLIAMS, Bu.)	0.754	0	1	704	108	62	130	41
(DIVAC, V.)	0.768	5	19	247	60	55	88	35
(BURTON, W.)	0.800	6	15	244	123	46	119	37
(LEVER, F.)	0.750	17	52	161	107	46	36	12
(REID, J.R.)	0.705	0	3	317	81	49	84	23
(ENGLISH, A.J.)	0.841	6	34	168	143	32	89	9
(CARR, A.)	0.764	1	5	346	63	32	114	96
(RIVERS, Do.)	0.832	26	92	147	233	111	92	19
(GARLAND, W.)	0.859	9	28	190	411	98	175	22
(DUCKWORTH, K.)	0.690	0	3	497	99	38	143	37
(TEAGLE, T.)	0.767	1	4	183	113	66	114	9
(MACON, M.)	0.730	4	30	220	168	154	155	14
(VINCENT, S.)	0.846	1	13	101	148	35	72	4
(HOPSON, D.)	0.708	12	47	206	102	67	100	39
(STEWART, L.)	0.807	0	3	449	120	51	112	44
(ROBERTS, S.)	0.515	0	1	336	39	22	78	83
(JACKSON, C.)	0.870	31	94	114	192	44	117	4
(BATTLE, J.)	0.848	2	17	112	159	36	91	5
(HIGGINS, R.)	0.814	33	95	85	22	15	15	13
(DAVIS, T.)	0.635	0	5	672	57	26	117	29
(GRAHAM, P.)	0.741	55	141	231	175	96	91	21
(EDWARDS, K.)	0.848	7	32	211	170	99	120	20
(COLES, B.)	0.824	10	52	189	366	73	167	13
(MITCHELL, S.)	0.786	2	11	473	94	53	97	39
(DAVIS, W.)	0.872	5	16	70	68	29	45	1
(ARMSTRONG, B.J.)	0.806	35	87	145	266	46	94	5
(RODMAN, D.)	0.600	32	101	1530	191	68	140	70
(CORBIN, T.)	0.866	0	4	472	140	82	97	20
(EDWARDS, Ja.)	0.731	0	1	202	53	24	72	33
(AINGE, D.)	0.824	78	230	148	202	73	70	13
(LAIMBEER, B.)	0.893	32	85	451	160	51	102	54
(ROBERTS, F.)	0.749	19	37	257	122	52	122	40
(SALLEY, J.)	0.715	0	3	296	116	49	102	110
(PAYTON, G.)	0.669	3	23	295	506	147	174	21
(BONNER, A.)	0.627	1	4	485	125	94	133	26
(IUZZOLINO, M.)	0.836	59	136	98	194	33	92	1
(LIBERTY, M.)	0.728	17	50	308	58	66	90	29
(WILLIAMS, Br.)	0.669	0	0	272	33	41	86	53
(FLOYD, S.)	0.794	37	123	150	239	57	128	21
(MILLS, T.)	0.750	8	23	453	84	48	82	41
(KRYSTKOWIAK, L.)	0.757	0	5	429	114	54	115	12
(McCRAY, R.)	0.719	25	85	468	219	48	115	30
(GRAYER, J.)	0.667	19	66	257	150	64	105	13
(RASMUSSEN, B.)	0.750	5	23	393	107	35	51	48

	NAME	POS	TEAM	GMs	MINs	MINs per GM	PTs	PTs per MIN	PTs per GM	FG PCT
169.	BOGUES, M.	g	CHA	82	2790	34.0	730	0.262	8.9	0.472
170.	FLEMING, V.	g	IND	82	1737	21.2	726	0.418	8.9	0.482
171.	SMITH, Do.	f	DAL	76	1707	22.5	671	0.393	8.8	0.415
172.	CAGE, M.	f	SEA	82	2461	30.0	720	0.293	8.8	0.566
173.	VOLKOV, A.	f	ATL	77	1516	19.7	662	0.437	8.6	0.441
174.	JOHNSON, B.	f	HOU	80	2202	27.5	685	0.311	8.6	0.458
175.	MAYS, T.	g	ATL	2	32	16.0	17	0.531	8.5	0.429
176.	MOORE, T.	f	DAL	42	782	18.6	355	0.454	8.5	0.400
177.	HODGE, D.	c/f	DAL	51	1058	20.7	426	0.403	8.4	0.497
178.	BARROS, D.	g	SEA	75	1331	17.7	619	0.465	8.3	0.483
179.	HILL, T.	c/f	GS	82	1886	23.0	671	0.356	8.2	0.522
180.	POLYNICE, O.	c	LAC	76	1834	24.1	613	0.334	8.1	0.519
181.	CARTWRIGHT, B.	c	CHI	64	1471	23.0	512	0.348	8.0	0.467
182.	JOHNSON, V.	g	SA	60	1350	22.5	478	0.354	8.0	0.405
183.	FOX, R.	g/f	BOS	81	1535	19.0	644	0.420	8.0	0.459
184.	CAUSWELL, D.	c	SAC	80	2291	28.6	636	0.278	8.0	0.550
185.	WINGATE, D.	g	WAS	81	2127	26.3	638	0.300	7.9	0.465
186.	SHAW, B.	g	MIA	63	1423	22.6	495	0.348	7.9	0.407
187.	ELIE, M.	g/f	GS	79	1677	21.2	620	0.370	7.9	0.521
188.	GRANT, Ga.	g	LAC	78	2049	26.3	609	0.297	7.8	0.462
189.	BROWN, M.	c/f	UT	82	1783	21.7	632	0.355	7.7	0.453
190.	LANG, A.	c	PHX	81	1965	24.3	622	0.317	7.7	0.522
191.	HIGGINS, S.	f	ORL	38	616	16.2	291	0.472	7.7	0.459
192.	VAUGHT, L.	f	LAC	79	1687	21.4	601	0.356	7.6	0.492
193.	PINCKNEY, E.	f	BOS	81	1917	23.7	613	0.320	7.6	0.537
194.	BRANDON, T.	g	CLE	82	1605	19.6	605	0.377	7.4	0.419
195.	ALEXANDER, V.	c	GS	80	1350	16.9	589	0.436	7.4	0.529
196.	DOUGLAS, S.	g	BOS	42	752	17.9	308	0.410	7.3	0.463
197.	CEBALLOS, C.	f	PHX	64	725	11.3	462	0.637	7.2	0.482
198.	BAGLEY, J.	g	BOS	73	1742	23.9	524	0.301	7.2	0.441
199.	CAMPBELL, E.	c	LAL	81	1876	23.2	578	0.308	7.1	0.448
200.	SANDERS, M.	f	CLE	31	633	20.4	221	0.349	7.1	0.571
201.	TURNER, J.	f	ORL	75	1591	21.2	530	0.333	7.1	0.451
202.	ANDERSON, K.	g	NJ	64	1086	17.0	450	0.414	7.0	0.390
203.	PAXSON, J.	g	CHI	79	1946	24.6	555	0.285	7.0	0.528
204.	MASON, A.	f	NY	82	2198	26.8	573	0.261	7.0	0.509
205.	KING, S.	f/c	CHI	79	1268	16.1	551	0.435	7.0	0.506
206.	VANDEWEGHE, K.	f	NY	67	956	14.3	467	0.489	7.0	0.491
207.	KERR, S.	g	CLE	48	847	17.6	319	0.377	6.7	0.511
208.	SPENCER, F.	c	MIN	61	1481	24.3	405	0.274	6.6	0.426
209.	McCLOUD, G.	g	IND	51	892	17.5	338	0.379	6.6	0.409
210.	SHACKLEFORD, C.	c	PHI	72	1399	19.4	473	0.338	6.6	0.486
211.	LICHTI, T.	g	DEN	68	1176	17.3	446	0.379	6.6	0.460
212.	TUCKER, T.	g	SA	24	415	17.3	155	0.374	6.5	0.465
213.	JAMES, H.	f	CLE	65	866	13.3	418	0.483	6.4	0.407
214.	WHITE, R.	f	DAL	65	1021	15.7	418	0.409	6.4	0.380
215.	BULLARD, M.	f	HOU	80	1278	16.0	512	0.401	6.4	0.459
216.	ASKEW, V.	g	GS	80	1496	18.7	498	0.333	6.2	0.509
217.	DAVIS, D.	f	IND	64	1301	20.3	395	0.304	6.2	0.552
218.	OAKLEY, C.	f	NY	82	2309	28.2	506	0.219	6.2	0.522
219.	WEST, M.	c	PHX	82	1436	17.5	501	0.349	6.1	0.632
220.	ABDELNABY, A.	f/c	POR	71	934	13.2	432	0.463	6.1	0.493
221.	McMILLAN, N.	g/f	SEA	72	1652	22.9	435	0.263	6.0	0.437
222.	BURTT, S.	g	PHX	31	356	11.5	187	0.525	6.0	0.463
223.	GEORGE, T.	g	NJ	70	1037	14.8	418	0.403	6.0	0.428
224.	FREDERICK, A.	f	CHA	66	852	12.9	389	0.457	5.9	0.435

(NAME)	FT PCT	3-PT SHOTS MADE	3-PT SHOTS TRIED	REBs	ASTs	STLs	TURN-OVERS	BLKs
(BOGUES, M.)	0.783	2	27	235	743	170	156	6
(FLEMING, V.)	0.737	6	27	209	266	56	140	7
(SMITH, Do.)	0.736	0	11	391	129	62	97	34
(CAGE, M.)	0.620	0	5	728	92	99	78	55
(VOLKOV, A.)	0.631	35	110	265	250	66	102	30
(JOHNSON, B.)	0.727	1	9	312	158	72	104	49
(MAYS, T.)	1.000	3	6	2	1	0	3	0
(MOORE, T.)	0.833	30	84	82	48	32	44	4
(HODGE, D.)	0.667	0	0	275	39	25	75	23
(BARROS, D.)	0.760	83	186	81	125	51	56	4
(HILL, T.)	0.694	0	1	593	47	73	106	43
(POLYNICE, O.)	0.622	0	1	536	46	45	83	20
(CARTWRIGHT, B.)	0.604	0	0	324	87	22	75	14
(JOHNSON, V.)	0.647	19	60	182	145	41	74	14
(FOX, R.)	0.755	23	70	220	126	78	123	30
(CAUSWELL, D.)	0.613	0	1	580	59	47	124	215
(WINGATE, D.)	0.719	1	18	269	247	123	124	21
(SHAW, B.)	0.791	5	23	204	250	57	99	22
(ELIE, M.)	0.852	23	70	227	174	68	83	15
(GRANT, Ga.)	0.815	15	51	184	538	138	187	14
(BROWN, M.)	0.667	0	1	476	81	42	105	34
(LANG, A.)	0.768	0	1	546	43	48	87	201
(HIGGINS, S.)	0.861	6	25	102	41	16	41	6
(VAUGHT, L.)	0.797	4	5	512	71	37	66	31
(PINCKNEY, E.)	0.812	0	1	564	62	70	73	56
(BRANDON, T.)	0.807	1	23	162	316	81	136	22
(ALEXANDER, V.)	0.691	0	1	336	32	45	91	62
(DOUGLAS, S.)	0.682	1	10	63	172	25	68	9
(CEBALLOS, C.)	0.737	1	6	152	50	16	71	11
(BAGLEY, J.)	0.716	10	42	161	480	57	148	4
(CAMPBELL, E.)	0.619	0	2	423	59	53	73	159
(SANDERS, M.)	0.766	1	3	96	53	24	22	10
(TURNER, J.)	0.693	1	8	246	92	24	106	16
(ANDERSON, K.)	0.745	3	13	127	203	67	97	9
(PAXSON, J.)	0.784	12	44	96	241	49	44	9
(MASON, A.)	0.642	0	0	573	106	46	101	20
(KING, S.)	0.753	2	5	205	77	21	76	25
(VANDEWEGHE, K.)	0.803	26	66	88	57	15	27	8
(KERR, S.)	0.833	32	74	78	110	27	31	10
(SPENCER, F.)	0.691	0	0	435	53	27	70	79
(McCLOUD, G.)	0.781	32	94	132	116	26	62	11
(SHACKLEFORD, C.)	0.663	0	1	415	46	38	62	51
(LICHTI, T.)	0.839	1	9	118	74	43	72	12
(TUCKER, T.)	0.800	19	48	37	27	21	14	3
(JAMES, H.)	0.803	29	90	112	25	16	43	11
(WHITE, R.)	0.765	4	27	236	31	31	68	22
(BULLARD, M.)	0.760	64	166	223	75	26	56	21
(ASKEW, V.)	0.694	1	10	233	188	47	4	23
(DAVIS, D.)	0.572	0	1	410	30	27	49	74
(OAKLEY, C.)	0.735	0	3	700	133	67	123	15
(WEST, M.)	0.637	0	0	372	22	14	82	81
(ABDELNABY, A.)	0.753	0	0	260	30	25	66	16
(McMILLAN, N.)	0.643	27	98	252	359	129	112	29
(BURTT, S.)	0.704	1	6	34	59	16	33	4
(GEORGE, T.)	0.821	1	6	105	162	41	82	3
(FREDERICK, A.)	0.685	4	17	144	71	40	58	26

1991–92 REGULAR-SEASON STATISTICAL RESULTS
NBA PLAYERS ORDERED BY POINTS PER GAME

	NAME	POS	TEAM	GMs	MINs	MINs per GM	PTs	PTs per MIN	PTs per GM	FG PCT
225.	ADDISON, R.	g	NJ	76	1175	15.5	444	0.378	5.8	0.433
226.	LOHAUS, B.	f/c	MIL	70	1081	15.4	408	0.377	5.8	0.450
227.	KNIGHT, N.	g	PHX	42	631	15.0	243	0.385	5.8	0.475
228.	GMINSKI, M.	c	CHA	35	499	14.3	202	0.405	5.8	0.452
229.	GATLING, C.	c	GS	54	612	11.3	306	0.500	5.7	0.568
230.	BENOIT, D.	f	UT	77	1161	15.1	434	0.374	5.6	0.467
231.	SMITH, O.	g	ORL	55	877	15.9	310	0.354	5.6	0.365
232.	DUDLEY, C.	c	NJ	82	1902	23.2	460	0.242	5.6	0.403
233.	JOHNSON, A.	g	HOU	69	1235	17.9	386	0.313	5.6	0.479
234.	SCHAYES, D.	c	MIL	43	726	16.9	240	0.331	5.6	0.417
235.	ANTHONY, G.	g	NY	82	1510	18.4	447	0.296	5.5	0.370
236.	BREUER, R.	c	MIN	67	1176	17.6	363	0.309	5.4	0.468
237.	KESSLER, A.	c	MIA	77	1197	15.5	410	0.343	5.3	0.413
238.	WALKER, D.	g	DET	74	1541	20.8	387	0.251	5.2	0.423
239.	SMITH, La.	g	WAS	48	708	14.7	247	0.349	5.2	0.407
240.	FERRY, D.	f	CLE	68	937	13.8	346	0.369	5.1	0.409
241.	BROOKS, S.	g	MIN	82	1082	13.2	417	0.385	5.1	0.447
242.	CORCHIANI, C.	g	ORL	51	741	14.5	255	0.344	5.0	0.399
243.	THOMPSON, L.	f/c	IND	80	1299	16.2	394	0.303	4.9	0.468
244.	DONALDSON, J.	c	NY	58	1075	18.5	285	0.265	4.9	0.457
245.	HOWARD, B.	f	DAL	27	318	11.8	131	0.412	4.9	0.519
246.	BROWN, T.	f	SEA	57	655	11.5	271	0.414	4.8	0.410
247.	KLEINE, J.	c	BOS	70	991	14.2	326	0.329	4.7	0.492
248.	CHEEKS, M.	g	ATL	56	1086	19.4	259	0.239	4.6	0.462
249.	PACK, R.	g	POR	72	894	12.4	332	0.371	4.6	0.423
250.	FRANK, T.	f	MIN	10	140	14.0	46	0.329	4.6	0.546
251.	GREEN, S.	f	SA	80	1127	14.1	367	0.326	4.6	0.427
252.	PERDUE, W.	c	CHI	77	1007	13.1	350	0.348	4.6	0.547
253.	YOUNG, D.	g	LAC	62	1023	16.5	280	0.274	4.5	0.392
254.	MUSTAF, J.	f	PHX	52	545	10.5	233	0.428	4.5	0.477
255.	HERRERA, C.	f	HOU	43	566	13.2	191	0.338	4.4	0.516
256.	SMITH, To.	g	LAL	63	820	13.0	275	0.335	4.4	0.399
257.	FOSTER, G.	f	WAS	49	548	11.2	213	0.389	4.4	0.461
258.	WIGGINS, M.	g	PHI	49	569	11.6	211	0.371	4.3	0.384
259.	LONGLEY, L.	c	MIN	66	991	15.0	281	0.284	4.3	0.458
260.	HODGES, C.	g	CHI	56	555	9.9	238	0.429	4.3	0.384
261.	MORTON, J.	g	MIA	25	270	10.8	106	0.393	4.2	0.387
262.	ROYAL, D.	f	SA	60	718	12.0	252	0.351	4.2	0.449
263.	WILLIAMS, K.	f	IND	60	565	9.4	252	0.446	4.2	0.518
264.	PRITCHARD, K.	g	BOS	11	136	12.4	46	0.338	4.2	0.471
265.	MAYES, Th.	g	LAC	24	255	10.6	99	0.388	4.1	0.303
266.	WILLIAMS, Ja.	f/c	PHI	50	646	12.9	206	0.319	4.1	0.364
267.	BRYANT, M.	c	POR	56	800	14.3	230	0.288	4.1	0.480
268.	GREEN, R.	g	BOS	26	367	14.1	106	0.289	4.1	0.447
269.	LYNCH, K.	g	CHA	55	819	14.9	224	0.274	4.1	0.417
270.	MURDOCK, E.	g	UT	50	478	9.6	203	0.425	4.1	0.415
271.	TURNER, A.	g	WAS	70	871	12.4	284	0.326	4.1	0.425
272.	GREEN, Se.	g	IND	35	256	7.3	141	0.551	4.0	0.392
273.	JAMERSON, D.	f	HOU	48	378	7.9	191	0.505	4.0	0.414
274.	LEVINGSTON, C.	f	CHI	79	1020	12.9	311	0.305	3.9	0.498
275.	LISTER, A.	c	GS	26	293	11.3	102	0.348	3.9	0.557
276.	RULAND, J.	c	PHI	13	209	16.1	51	0.244	3.9	0.526
277.	SANDERS, J.	f	ATL	12	117	9.8	47	0.402	3.9	0.444
278.	WILEY, M.	g	ATL	53	870	16.4	204	0.235	3.9	0.430
279.	WOLF, J.	f	DEN	67	1160	17.3	254	0.219	3.8	0.361
280.	LES, J.	g	SAC	62	712	11.5	231	0.324	3.7	0.385

(NAME)	FT PCT	3-PT SHOTS MADE	3-PT SHOTS TRIED	REBs	ASTs	STLs	TURN-OVERS	BLKs
(ADDISON, R.)	0.737	14	49	165	68	28	46	28
(LOHAUS, B.)	0.659	57	144	249	74	40	46	71
(KNIGHT, N.)	0.688	4	13	46	112	24	58	3
(GMINSKI, M.)	0.750	1	3	118	31	11	20	16
(GATLING, C.)	0.661	0	4	182	16	31	44	36
(BENOIT, D.)	0.810	3	14	296	34	19	71	44
(SMITH, O.)	0.769	8	21	116	57	36	62	13
(DUDLEY, C.)	0.468	0	0	739	58	38	79	179
(JOHNSON, A.)	0.654	4	15	80	266	61	110	9
(SCHAYES, D.)	0.771	0	0	168	34	19	41	19
(ANTHONY, G.)	0.741	8	55	136	314	59	98	9
(BREUER, R.)	0.533	0	1	281	89	27	41	99
(KESSLER, A.)	0.817	0	0	314	34	17	58	32
(WALKER, D.)	0.619	0	10	238	205	63	79	18
(SMITH, La.)	0.804	2	21	81	99	44	63	1
(FERRY, D.)	0.836	17	48	213	75	22	46	15
(BROOKS, S.)	0.810	32	90	99	205	66	51	7
(CORCHIANI, C.)	0.875	10	37	78	141	45	74	2
(THOMPSON, L.)	0.817	0	2	381	102	52	98	34
(DONALDSON, J.)	0.709	0	0	289	33	8	48	49
(HOWARD, B.)	0.710	1	2	51	14	11	15	8
(BROWN, T.)	0.727	19	63	84	48	30	35	5
(KLEINE, J.)	0.708	4	8	296	32	23	27	14
(CHEEKS, M.)	0.605	3	6	95	185	83	36	0
(PACK, R.)	0.803	0	10	97	140	40	92	4
(FRANK, T.)	0.667	0	0	26	8	5	5	4
(GREEN, S.)	0.820	0	0	342	36	29	62	11
(PERDUE, W.)	0.495	1	2	312	80	16	72	43
(YOUNG, D.)	0.851	23	70	75	172	46	47	4
(MUSTAF, J.)	0.690	0	0	145	45	21	51	16
(HERRERA, C.)	0.568	0	1	99	27	16	37	25
(SMITH, To.)	0.653	0	11	76	109	39	50	8
(FOSTER, G.)	0.714	0	1	145	35	6	36	12
(WIGGINS, M.)	0.686	0	1	94	22	20	25	1
(LONGLEY, L.)	0.663	0	0	257	53	35	83	64
(HODGES, C.)	0.941	36	96	24	54	14	22	1
(MORTON, J.)	0.842	2	16	26	32	13	28	1
(ROYAL, D.)	0.692	0	0	124	34	25	39	7
(WILLIAMS, K.)	0.605	0	4	129	40	20	22	41
(PRITCHARD, K.)	0.778	0	3	11	30	3	11	4
(MAYES, Th.)	0.667	15	41	16	35	16	31	2
(WILLIAMS, Ja.)	0.636	0	0	145	12	20	44	20
(BRYANT, M.)	0.667	0	3	201	41	26	30	8
(GREEN, R.)	0.722	1	4	24	68	17	18	1
(LYNCH, K.)	0.761	3	8	85	83	37	44	9
(MURDOCK, E.)	0.754	5	26	54	92	30	50	7
(TURNER, A.)	0.792	1	16	90	177	57	84	2
(GREEN, Se.)	0.536	2	10	42	22	13	27	6
(JAMERSON, D.)	0.926	8	28	43	33	17	24	0
(LEVINGSTON, C.)	0.625	1	6	227	66	27	42	45
(LISTER, A.)	0.424	0	0	92	14	5	20	16
(RULAND, J.)	0.688	0	0	47	5	7	20	4
(SANDERS, J.)	0.778	0	0	26	9	5	5	3
(WILEY, M.)	0.686	14	42	81	180	47	60	3
(WOLF, J.)	0.803	1	11	240	61	32	60	14
(LES, J.)	0.809	45	131	63	143	31	42	3

1991–92 REGULAR-SEASON STATISTICAL RESULTS
NBA PLAYERS ORDERED BY POINTS PER GAME

	NAME	POS	TEAM	GMs	MINs	MINs per GM	PTs	PTs per MIN	PTs per GM	FG PCT
281.	ASKINS, K.	g/f	MIA	59	843	14.3	219	0.260	3.7	0.410
282.	SUTTON, G.	g	SA	67	601	9.0	246	0.409	3.7	0.388
283.	CHILCUTT, P.	f/c	SAC	69	817	11.8	251	0.307	3.6	0.452
284.	BENNETT, W.	f	MIA	54	833	15.4	195	0.234	3.6	0.379
285.	BROWN, C.	f	LAL	42	431	10.3	150	0.348	3.6	0.469
286.	BEDFORD, W.	f/c	DET	32	363	11.3	114	0.314	3.6	0.413
287.	OLIVER, J.	g/f	CLE	27	252	9.3	96	0.381	3.6	0.398
288.	CONNER, L.	g	MIL	81	1420	17.5	287	0.202	3.5	0.431
289.	MONROE, R.	g	ATL	38	313	8.2	131	0.419	3.5	0.368
290.	BROWN, R.	g	SAC	56	535	9.6	192	0.359	3.4	0.456
291.	GARRICK, T.	g	DAL	40	549	13.7	137	0.250	3.4	0.413
292.	WILLIAMS, S.	f	CHI	63	690	11.0	214	0.310	3.4	0.483
293.	SCHINTZIUS, D.	c	SAC	33	400	12.1	110	0.275	3.3	0.427
294.	LECKNER, E.	c	CHA	59	716	12.1	196	0.274	3.3	0.513
295.	GRANT, Gr.	g	PHI	68	891	13.1	225	0.253	3.3	0.440
296.	KIMBLE, B.	f	LAC	34	277	8.2	112	0.404	3.3	0.396
297.	EATON, M.	c	UT	81	2023	25.0	266	0.132	3.3	0.446
298.	RAMBIS, K.	f	PHX	28	381	13.6	90	0.236	3.2	0.463
299.	KITE, G.	c	ORL	72	1479	20.5	228	0.154	3.2	0.437
300.	RANDALL, M.	f	MIN	54	441	8.2	171	0.388	3.2	0.456
301.	KONCAK, J.	c	ATL	77	1489	19.3	241	0.162	3.1	0.391
302.	PHILLS, B.	g	CLE	10	65	6.5	31	0.477	3.1	0.429
303.	NEALY, E.	f	PHX	52	505	9.7	160	0.317	3.1	0.512
304.	ACRES, M.	c	ORL	68	926	13.6	208	0.225	3.1	0.517
305.	HENSON, S.	g	MIL	50	386	7.7	150	0.389	3.0	0.361
306.	WHATLEY, E.	g	POR	23	209	9.1	69	0.330	3.0	0.412
307.	RUDD, D.	g	UT	65	538	8.3	193	0.359	3.0	0.399
308.	QUINNETT, B.	f	DAL	39	326	8.4	115	0.353	3.0	0.347
309.	PAYNE, K.	f	PHI	49	353	7.2	144	0.408	2.9	0.448
310.	BROOKS, K.	f	DEN	37	270	7.3	105	0.389	2.8	0.443
311.	DAILEY, Q.	f	SEA	11	98	8.9	31	0.316	2.8	0.243
312.	DAVIS, B.	f	DAL	33	429	13.0	92	0.215	2.8	0.442
313.	TURNER, Jo.	f	HOU	42	345	8.2	117	0.339	2.8	0.439
314.	SPARROW, R.	g	LAL	46	489	10.6	127	0.260	2.8	0.384
315.	PRESSEY, P.	g	SA	56	759	13.6	151	0.199	2.7	0.373
316.	CONLON, M.	c	SEA	45	381	8.5	120	0.315	2.7	0.475
317.	LANE, J.	f	MIL	14	177	12.6	37	0.209	2.6	0.304
318.	LEE, D.	g	NJ	46	307	6.7	120	0.391	2.6	0.431
319.	TOLBERT, T.	f	GS	35	310	8.9	90	0.290	2.6	0.384
320.	HANSEN, B.	g	CHI	68	809	11.9	173	0.214	2.5	0.444
321.	PERRY, E.	g	CHA	50	437	8.7	126	0.288	2.5	0.380
322.	OGG, A.	c	MIA	43	367	8.5	108	0.294	2.5	0.548
323.	BUECHLER, J.	f	GS	28	290	10.4	70	0.241	2.5	0.409
324.	FEITL, D.	c	NJ	34	175	5.2	82	0.469	2.4	0.429
325.	OLIVER, B.	g	PHI	34	279	8.2	81	0.290	2.4	0.330
326.	SELLERS, B.	f/c	DET	43	226	5.3	102	0.451	2.4	0.466
327.	SMITH, L.	f/c	HOU	45	800	17.8	104	0.130	2.3	0.544
328.	HENDERSON, G.	g	DET	16	96	6.0	36	0.375	2.3	0.375
329.	CROWDER, C.	g/f	UT	51	328	6.4	114	0.348	2.2	0.384
330.	COOPER, W.	f	POR	35	344	9.8	77	0.224	2.2	0.427
331.	KING, R.	c	SEA	40	213	5.3	88	0.413	2.2	0.380
332.	SAMPSON, R.	c	WAS	10	108	10.8	22	0.204	2.2	0.310
333.	ANSLEY, M.	f	CHA	10	45	4.5	21	0.467	2.1	0.444
334.	MURPHY, T.	f	MIN	47	429	9.1	98	0.228	2.1	0.488
335.	BATTLE, K.	f	GS	16	92	5.8	32	0.348	2.0	0.647
336.	RIVERS, Da.	g	LAC	15	122	8.1	30	0.246	2.0	0.333

(NAME)	FT PCT	3-PT SHOTS MADE	3-PT SHOTS TRIED	REBs	ASTs	STLs	TURN-OVERS	BLKs
(ASKINS, K.)	0.703	25	73	142	38	40	47	15
(SUTTON, G.)	0.756	26	89	47	91	26	70	9
(CHILCUTT, P.)	0.821	2	2	187	38	32	41	17
(BENNETT, W.)	0.700	0	1	162	38	19	33	9
(BROWN, C.)	0.612	0	3	82	26	12	29	7
(BEDFORD, W.)	0.636	0	1	63	12	6	15	18
(OLIVER, J.)	0.773	1	9	27	20	9	9	2
(CONNER, L.)	0.704	0	7	184	294	97	79	10
(MONROE, R.)	0.826	6	27	33	27	12	23	2
(BROWN, R.)	0.655	0	6	69	59	35	42	12
(GARRICK, T.)	0.692	1	4	56	98	36	44	4
(WILLIAMS, S.)	0.649	0	3	247	50	13	35	36
(SCHINTZIUS, D.)	0.833	0	4	118	20	6	19	28
(LECKNER, E.)	0.745	0	1	206	31	9	39	18
(GRANT, Gr.)	0.833	7	18	69	217	45	46	2
(KIMBLE, B.)	0.645	4	13	32	17	10	15	6
(EATON, M.)	0.598	0	0	491	40	36	60	205
(RAMBIS, K.)	0.778	0	0	106	37	12	25	14
(KITE, G.)	0.588	0	1	402	44	30	61	57
(RANDALL, M.)	0.744	3	16	71	33	12	25	3
(KONCAK, J.)	0.655	0	12	261	132	50	54	67
(PHILLS, B.)	0.636	0	2	8	4	3	8	1
(NEALY, E.)	0.667	20	50	111	37	16	17	2
(ACRES, M.)	0.761	1	3	252	22	25	33	15
(HENSON, S.)	0.793	23	48	41	82	15	40	1
(WHATLEY, E.)	0.871	0	4	21	34	14	14	3
(RUDD, D.)	0.762	11	47	54	109	15	49	1
(QUINNETT, B.)	0.615	13	41	51	12	16	16	8
(PAYNE, K.)	0.692	5	12	54	17	16	19	8
(BROOKS, K.)	0.810	2	11	39	11	8	18	2
(DAILEY, Q.)	0.813	0	1	12	4	5	10	1
(DAVIS, B.)	0.733	5	18	33	66	11	27	3
(TURNER, Jo.)	0.525	0	0	78	12	6	32	4
(SPARROW, R.)	0.615	3	15	28	83	12	33	5
(PRESSEY, P.)	0.683	3	21	95	142	29	64	19
(CONLON, M.)	0.750	0	0	69	12	9	27	7
(LANE, J.)	0.333	0	0	66	17	2	14	1
(LEE, D.)	0.526	10	37	35	22	11	12	1
(TOLBERT, T.)	0.550	2	8	55	21	10	20	6
(HANSEN, B.)	0.364	7	27	77	69	27	28	3
(PERRY, E.)	0.659	1	7	39	78	34	50	3
(OGG, A.)	0.533	0	0	74	7	5	19	28
(BUECHLER, J.)	0.571	0	1	52	23	19	13	7
(FEITL, D.)	0.842	0	0	61	6	2	19	3
(OLIVER, B.)	0.682	0	4	30	20	10	24	2
(SELLERS, B.)	0.769	0	1	42	14	1	15	10
(SMITH, L.)	0.364	0	1	256	33	21	44	7
(HENDERSON, G.)	0.818	3	8	8	10	3	8	0
(CROWDER, C.)	0.833	13	30	41	17	7	13	2
(COOPER, W.)	0.636	0	0	101	21	4	15	27
(KING, R.)	0.756	0	1	49	12	4	18	5
(SAMPSON, R.)	0.667	0	2	30	4	3	10	8
(ANSLEY, M.)	0.833	0	0	6	2	0	3	0
(MURPHY, T.)	0.559	1	2	110	11	9	18	8
(BATTLE, K.)	0.833	0	1	16	4	2	4	2
(RIVERS, Da.)	0.909	0	1	19	21	7	17	1

1991–92 REGULAR-SEASON STATISTICAL RESULTS
NBA PLAYERS ORDERED BY POINTS PER GAME

	NAME	POS	TEAM	GMs	MINs	MINs per GM	PTs	PTs per MIN	PTs per GM	FG PCT
337.	ROLLINS, T.	f/c	HOU	59	697	11.8	118	0.169	2.0	0.535
338.	AUSTIN, I.	c	UT	31	112	3.6	61	0.545	2.0	0.457
339.	DREILING, G.	c	IND	60	509	8.5	117	0.230	2.0	0.494
340.	VRANKOVIC, S.	c	BOS	19	110	5.8	37	0.336	2.0	0.469
341.	McCORMICK, T.	c	NY	22	108	4.9	42	0.389	1.9	0.424
342.	SCHEFFLER, S.	f	DEN	11	61	5.6	21	0.344	1.9	0.667
343.	WINCHESTER, K.	f	NY	19	81	4.3	35	0.432	1.8	0.433
344.	THOMPSON, S.	g	SAC	19	91	4.8	31	0.341	1.6	0.378
345.	PETERSEN, J.	c	GS	27	169	6.3	43	0.254	1.6	0.450
346.	HALEY, J.	f/c	LAL	49	394	8.0	76	0.193	1.6	0.369
347.	BOL, M.	c	PHI	71	1267	17.8	110	0.087	1.6	0.383
348.	COOK, A.	f	DEN	22	115	5.2	34	0.296	1.6	0.600
349.	KOFOED, B.	g	SEA	44	239	5.4	66	0.276	1.5	0.472
350.	BLANKS, L.	g	DET	43	189	4.4	64	0.339	1.5	0.455
351.	ELLIS, L.	f	LAC	29	103	3.6	43	0.418	1.5	0.340
352.	COPA, T.	f/c	SA	33	132	4.0	48	0.364	1.5	0.550
353.	HASTINGS, S.	f	DEN	40	421	10.5	58	0.138	1.5	0.340
354.	OWENS, K.	f	LAL	20	80	4.0	26	0.325	1.3	0.281
355.	THOMAS, C.	g	DET	37	156	4.2	48	0.308	1.3	0.353
356.	McCANN, B.	f	DET	26	129	5.0	30	0.233	1.2	0.394
357.	JONES, Ch.	c/f	WAS	75	1365	18.2	86	0.063	1.2	0.367
358.	JEPSEN, L.	c	SAC	31	87	2.8	25	0.287	0.8	0.375
359.	WITTMAN, R.	g	IND	24	115	4.8	17	0.148	0.7	0.421

(NAME)	FT PCT	3-PT SHOTS MADE	3-PT SHOTS TRIED	REBs	ASTs	STLs	TURN-OVERS	BLKs
(ROLLINS, T.)	0.867	0	0	171	15	14	18	62
(AUSTIN, I.)	0.633	0	0	35	5	2	8	2
(DREILING, G.)	0.750	1	1	96	25	10	31	16
(VRANKOVIC, S.)	0.583	0	0	28	5	0	10	17
(McCORMICK, T.)	0.667	0	0	34	9	2	8	0
(SCHEFFLER, S.)	0.750	0	0	14	0	3	1	1
(WINCHESTER, K.)	0.800	1	2	15	8	2	2	2
(THOMPSON, S.)	0.375	0	1	19	8	6	5	3
(PETERSEN, J.)	0.700	0	2	45	9	5	5	6
(HALEY, J.)	0.483	0	0	95	7	7	25	8
(BOL, M.)	0.462	0	9	222	22	11	41	205
(COOK, A.)	0.667	0	0	34	2	5	3	4
(KOFOED, B.)	0.577	1	7	26	51	2	20	2
(BLANKS, L.)	0.727	6	16	22	19	14	14	1
(ELLIS, L.)	0.474	0	0	24	1	6	11	9
(COPA, T.)	0.308	0	0	36	3	2	8	6
(HASTINGS, S.)	0.857	0	9	98	26	10	22	15
(OWENS, K.)	0.800	0	0	15	3	5	2	4
(THOMAS, C.)	0.667	2	17	22	22	4	17	1
(McCANN, B.)	0.308	0	1	30	6	6	7	4
(JONES, Ch.)	0.500	0	0	317	62	43	39	92
(JEPSEN, L.)	0.636	0	1	30	1	1	3	5
(WITTMAN, R.)	0.500	0	0	9	11	2	3	0

1991–1992 REGULAR-SEASON STATISTICAL RESULTS
NBA PLAYERS ORDERED BY REBOUNDS PER GAME

	NAME	POS	TEAM	GMs	MINs	MINs per GM	OFF REBs	REBs	REBs per MIN	REBs per GM	FG PCT
1.	RODMAN, D.	f	DET	82	3301	40.3	523	1530	0.464	18.7	0.539
2.	WILLIS, K.	f/c	ATL	81	2962	36.6	418	1258	0.425	15.5	0.483
3.	MUTOMBO, D.	c	DEN	71	2716	38.3	316	870	0.320	12.3	0.493
4.	ROBINSON, D.	c	SA	68	2564	37.7	261	829	0.323	12.2	0.551
5.	OLAJUWON, H.	c	HOU	70	2636	37.7	246	845	0.321	12.1	0.502
6.	SEIKALY, R.	c	MIA	79	2800	35.4	307	934	0.334	11.8	0.489
7.	ANDERSON, G.	f	DEN	82	2793	34.1	337	941	0.337	11.5	0.456
8.	EWING, P.	c	NY	82	3150	38.4	228	921	0.292	11.2	0.522
9.	MALONE, K.	f	UT	81	3054	37.7	225	909	0.298	11.2	0.526
10.	ELLISON, P.	c	WAS	66	2511	38.0	217	740	0.295	11.2	0.539
11.	BARKLEY, C.	f	PHI	75	2881	38.4	271	830	0.288	11.1	0.552
12.	JOHNSON, L.	f	CHA	82	3047	37.2	323	899	0.295	11.0	0.490
13.	THORPE, O.	f	HOU	82	3056	37.3	285	862	0.282	10.5	0.592
14.	DAUGHERTY, B.	c	CLE	73	2643	36.2	191	760	0.288	10.4	0.570
15.	KEMP, S.	f/c	SEA	64	1808	28.2	264	665	0.368	10.4	0.504
16.	GRANT, Ho.	f	CHI	81	2859	35.3	344	807	0.282	10.0	0.579
17.	DAVIS, T.	f/c	DAL	68	2149	31.6	228	672	0.313	9.9	0.482
18.	BIRD, L.	f	BOS	45	1662	36.9	46	434	0.261	9.6	0.466
19.	SCHREMPF, D.	f	IND	80	2605	32.6	202	770	0.296	9.6	0.536
20.	COLEMAN, D.	f	NJ	65	2207	34.0	203	618	0.280	9.5	0.504
21.	GREEN, A.C.	f	LAL	82	2902	35.4	306	762	0.263	9.3	0.476
22.	MALONE, M.	c	MIL	82	2511	30.6	320	744	0.296	9.1	0.474
23.	CUMMINGS, T.	f	SA	70	2149	30.7	247	631	0.294	9.0	0.488
24.	DUDLEY, C.	c	NJ	82	1902	23.2	343	739	0.389	9.0	0.403
25.	PARISH, R.	c	BOS	79	2285	28.9	219	705	0.309	8.9	0.536
26.	CAGE, M.	f	SEA	82	2461	30.0	266	728	0.296	8.9	0.566
27.	PERKINS, S.	f/c	LAL	63	2332	37.0	192	556	0.238	8.8	0.450
28.	WILLIAMS, Bu.	f	POR	80	2519	31.5	260	704	0.280	8.8	0.604
29.	OAKLEY, C.	f	NY	82	2309	28.2	256	700	0.303	8.5	0.522
30.	LONG, G.	f	MIA	82	3063	37.4	259	691	0.226	8.4	0.494
31.	NANCE, L.	f	CLE	81	2880	35.6	213	670	0.233	8.3	0.539
32.	KERSEY, J.	f	POR	77	2553	33.2	241	633	0.248	8.2	0.467
33.	GILLIAM, A.	f/c	PHI	81	2771	34.2	234	660	0.238	8.2	0.512
34.	BENJAMIN, B.	c	SEA	63	1941	30.8	130	513	0.264	8.1	0.478
35.	BOWIE, S.	c	NJ	71	2179	30.7	203	578	0.265	8.1	0.445
36.	SIMMONS, L.	f	SAC	78	2895	37.1	149	634	0.219	8.1	0.454
37.	OWENS, B.	g/f	GS	80	2510	31.4	243	639	0.255	8.0	0.525
38.	PIPPEN, S.	f	CHI	82	3164	38.6	185	630	0.199	7.7	0.506
39.	WILLIAMS, J.	f/c	CLE	80	2432	30.4	228	607	0.250	7.6	0.503
40.	CAUSWELL, D.	c	SAC	80	2291	28.6	196	580	0.253	7.3	0.550
41.	HILL, T.	c/f	GS	82	1886	23.0	182	593	0.314	7.2	0.522
42.	SPENCER, F.	c	MIN	61	1481	24.3	167	435	0.294	7.1	0.426
43.	GATTISON, K.	f/c	CHA	82	2223	27.1	177	580	0.261	7.1	0.529
44.	POLYNICE, O.	c	LAC	76	1834	24.1	195	536	0.292	7.1	0.519
45.	CATLEDGE, T.	f	ORL	78	2430	31.2	257	549	0.226	7.0	0.496
46.	WILKINS, D.	f	ATL	42	1601	38.1	103	295	0.184	7.0	0.464
47.	MASON, A.	f	NY	82	2198	26.8	216	573	0.261	7.0	0.509
48.	PINCKNEY, E.	f	BOS	81	1917	23.7	252	564	0.294	7.0	0.537
49.	PERRY, T.	f	PHX	80	2483	31.0	204	551	0.222	6.9	0.523
50.	MANNING, D.	f	LAC	82	2904	35.4	229	564	0.194	6.9	0.542
51.	DIVAC, V.	c	LAL	36	979	27.2	87	247	0.252	6.9	0.495
52.	GRANT, Ha.	f	WAS	64	2388	37.3	157	432	0.181	6.8	0.479
53.	LANG, A.	c	PHX	81	1965	24.3	170	546	0.278	6.7	0.522
54.	DREXLER, C.	g	POR	76	2751	36.2	166	500	0.182	6.6	0.470
55.	TISDALE, W.	f	SAC	72	2521	35.0	135	469	0.186	6.5	0.501
56.	VAUGHT, L.	f	LAC	79	1687	21.4	160	512	0.304	6.5	0.492

(NAME)	FT PCT	3-PT SHOTS MADE	3-PT SHOTS TRIED	ASTs	STLs	TURN-OVERS	BLKs	PTs
(RODMAN, D.)	0.600	32	101	191	68	140	70	800
(WILLIS, K.)	0.804	6	37	173	72	197	54	1480
(MUTOMBO, D.)	0.642	0	0	156	43	252	210	1177
(ROBINSON, D.)	0.701	1	8	181	158	182	305	1578
(OLAJUWON, H.)	0.766	0	1	157	127	187	304	1510
(SEIKALY, R.)	0.733	0	3	109	40	216	121	1296
(ANDERSON, G.)	0.623	0	4	78	88	201	65	945
(EWING, P.)	0.738	1	6	156	88	209	245	1970
(MALONE, K.)	0.778	3	17	241	108	248	51	2272
(ELLISON, P.)	0.728	1	3	190	62	196	177	1322
(BARKLEY, C.)	0.695	32	137	308	136	235	44	1730
(JOHNSON, L.)	0.829	5	22	292	81	160	51	1576
(THORPE, O.)	0.657	0	7	250	52	237	37	1420
(DAUGHERTY, B.)	0.777	0	2	262	65	185	78	1566
(KEMP, S.)	0.748	0	3	86	70	156	124	994
(GRANT, Ho.)	0.741	0	2	217	100	98	131	1149
(DAVIS, T.)	0.635	0	5	57	26	117	29	693
(BIRD, L.)	0.926	52	128	306	42	125	33	908
(SCHREMPF, D.)	0.828	23	71	312	62	191	37	1380
(COLEMAN, D.)	0.763	23	76	205	54	248	98	1289
(GREEN, A.C.)	0.744	12	56	117	91	111	36	1116
(MALONE, M.)	0.786	3	8	93	74	150	64	1279
(CUMMINGS, T.)	0.711	5	13	102	58	115	34	1210
(DUDLEY, C.)	0.468	0	0	58	38	79	179	460
(PARISH, R.)	0.772	0	0	70	68	131	97	1115
(CAGE, M.)	0.620	0	5	92	99	78	55	720
(PERKINS, S.)	0.817	15	69	141	64	83	62	1041
(WILLIAMS, Bu.)	0.754	0	1	108	62	130	41	901
(OAKLEY, C.)	0.735	0	3	133	67	123	15	506
(LONG, G.)	0.807	6	22	225	139	185	40	1212
(NANCE, L.)	0.822	0	6	232	80	87	243	1375
(KERSEY, J.)	0.664	1	8	243	114	151	71	971
(GILLIAM, A.)	0.807	0	2	118	51	166	85	1367
(BENJAMIN, B.)	0.687	0	2	76	39	175	118	879
(BOWIE, S.)	0.757	8	25	186	41	150	120	1062
(SIMMONS, L.)	0.770	1	5	337	135	218	132	1336
(OWENS, B.)	0.654	1	9	188	90	179	65	1141
(PIPPEN, S.)	0.760	16	80	572	155	253	93	1720
(WILLIAMS, J.)	0.752	0	4	196	60	83	182	952
(CAUSWELL, D.)	0.613	0	1	59	47	124	215	636
(HILL, T.)	0.694	0	1	47	73	106	43	671
(SPENCER, F.)	0.691	0	0	53	27	70	79	405
(GATTISON, K.)	0.688	0	2	131	59	140	69	1042
(POLYNICE, O.)	0.622	0	1	46	45	83	20	613
(CATLEDGE, T.)	0.694	0	4	109	58	138	16	1154
(WILKINS, D.)	0.835	37	128	158	52	122	24	1179
(MASON, A.)	0.642	0	0	106	46	101	20	573
(PINCKNEY, E.)	0.812	0	1	62	70	73	56	613
(PERRY, T.)	0.712	3	8	134	44	141	116	982
(MANNING, D.)	0.725	0	5	285	135	210	122	1579
(DIVAC, V.)	0.768	5	19	60	55	88	35	405
(GRANT, Ha.)	0.800	1	8	170	74	109	27	1155
(LANG, A.)	0.768	0	1	43	48	87	201	622
(DREXLER, C.)	0.794	114	338	512	138	240	70	1903
(TISDALE, W.)	0.763	0	2	106	55	124	79	1195
(VAUGHT, L.)	0.797	4	5	71	37	66	31	601

1991–1992 REGULAR-SEASON STATISTICAL RESULTS
NBA PLAYERS ORDERED BY REBOUNDS PER GAME

NAME	POS	TEAM	GMs	MINs	MINs per GM	OFF REBs	REBs	REBs per MIN	REBs per GM	FG PCT
57. MORRIS, C.	f	NJ	77	2394	31.1	199	494	0.206	6.4	0.477
58. DAVIS, D.	f	IND	64	1301	20.3	158	410	0.315	6.4	0.552
59. ANDERSON, N.	g/f	ORL	60	2203	36.7	98	384	0.174	6.4	0.463
60. JORDAN, M.	g	CHI	80	3102	38.8	91	511	0.165	6.4	0.519
61. McCRAY, R.	f	DAL	75	2106	28.1	149	468	0.222	6.2	0.436
62. REID, J.R.	c/f	CHA	51	1257	24.6	96	317	0.252	6.2	0.490
63. SMITH, C.	f/c	LAC	49	1310	26.7	95	301	0.230	6.1	0.466
64. BONNER, A.	f	SAC	79	2287	28.9	192	485	0.212	6.1	0.447
65. ROBERTS, S.	c	ORL	55	1118	20.3	113	336	0.301	6.1	0.529
66. EATON, M.	c	UT	81	2023	25.0	150	491	0.243	6.1	0.446
67. DUCKWORTH, K.	c	POR	82	2222	27.1	151	497	0.224	6.1	0.461
68. WILLIAMS, H.	f/c	DAL	75	2040	27.2	106	454	0.223	6.1	0.431
69. STEWART, L.	f	WAS	76	2229	29.3	186	449	0.201	5.9	0.514
70. CORBIN, T.	f	UT	80	2207	27.6	163	472	0.214	5.9	0.481
71. McHALE, K.	f/c	BOS	56	1398	25.0	119	330	0.236	5.9	0.510
72. MAJERLE, D.	g/f	PHX	82	2853	34.8	148	483	0.169	5.9	0.478
73. NORMAN, K.	f	LAC	77	2009	26.1	158	448	0.223	5.8	0.490
74. CHAMBERS, T.	f	PHX	69	1948	28.2	86	401	0.206	5.8	0.431
75. BROWN, M.	c/f	UT	82	1783	21.7	187	476	0.267	5.8	0.453
76. BAILEY, T.	f	MIN	84	2104	25.0	122	485	0.231	5.8	0.440
77. MITCHELL, S.	f	MIN	82	2151	26.2	158	473	0.220	5.8	0.423
78. SHACKLEFORD, C.	c	PHI	72	1399	19.4	145	415	0.297	5.8	0.486
79. SMITH, L.	f/c	HOU	45	800	17.8	107	256	0.320	5.7	0.544
80. WILLIAMS, Br.	f	ORL	48	905	18.9	115	272	0.301	5.7	0.528
81. WORTHY, J.	f	LAL	54	2108	39.0	98	305	0.145	5.7	0.447
82. SMITS, R.	c	IND	74	1772	23.9	124	417	0.235	5.6	0.510
83. McDANIEL, X.	f	NY	82	2344	28.6	176	460	0.196	5.6	0.478
84. KITE, G.	c	ORL	72	1479	20.5	156	402	0.272	5.6	0.437
85. LAIMBEER, B.	c	DET	81	2234	27.6	104	451	0.202	5.6	0.470
86. MULLIN, C.	f	GS	81	3346	41.3	127	450	0.135	5.6	0.524
87. MILLS, T.	f	NJ	82	1714	20.9	187	453	0.264	5.5	0.463
88. HARPER, R.	g	LAC	82	3144	38.3	120	447	0.142	5.5	0.440
89. KRYSTKOWIAK, L.	f	MIL	79	1848	23.4	131	429	0.232	5.4	0.444
90. HODGE, D.	c/f	DAL	51	1058	20.7	118	275	0.260	5.4	0.497
91. ELLIOTT, S.	f	SA	82	3120	38.0	143	439	0.141	5.4	0.494
92. BRICKOWSKI, F.	f	MIL	65	1556	23.9	97	344	0.221	5.3	0.524
93. ANDERSON, W.	g/f	SA	57	1889	33.1	62	300	0.159	5.3	0.456
94. PERSON, C.	f	IND	81	2923	36.1	114	426	0.146	5.3	0.480
95. CAMPBELL, E.	c	LAL	81	1876	23.2	155	423	0.226	5.2	0.448
96. LEVER, F.	g	DAL	31	884	28.5	56	161	0.182	5.2	0.387
97. McKEY, D.	f	SEA	52	1757	33.8	95	268	0.153	5.2	0.472
98. SMITH, Do.	f	DAL	76	1707	22.5	129	391	0.229	5.1	0.415
99. AUGMON, S.	g/f	ATL	82	2505	30.5	191	420	0.168	5.1	0.489
100. GILL, K.	g/f	CHA	79	2906	36.8	165	402	0.138	5.1	0.467
101. ROBINSON, C.	f	POR	82	2124	25.9	140	416	0.196	5.1	0.466
102. CARTWRIGHT, B.	c	CHI	64	1471	23.0	93	324	0.220	5.1	0.467
103. HORNACEK, J.	g	PHX	81	3078	38.0	106	407	0.132	5.0	0.512
104. HAMMONDS, T.	f	CHA	37	984	26.6	49	185	0.188	5.0	0.488
105. WILLIAMS, R.	f	DEN	81	2623	32.4	145	405	0.154	5.0	0.471
106. RICE, G.	f	MIA	79	3007	38.1	84	394	0.131	5.0	0.469
107. DONALDSON, J.	c	NY	58	1075	18.5	99	289	0.269	5.0	0.457
108. EHLO, C.	g/f	CLE	63	2016	32.0	94	307	0.152	4.9	0.453
109. RASMUSSEN, B.	c	ATL	81	1968	24.3	94	393	0.200	4.9	0.478
110. LEWIS, Re.	g	BOS	82	3070	37.4	117	394	0.128	4.8	0.503
111. THOMPSON, L.	f/c	IND	80	1299	16.2	98	381	0.293	4.8	0.468
112. LANE, J.	f	MIL	14	177	12.6	32	66	0.373	4.7	0.304

(NAME)	FT PCT	3-PT SHOTS MADE	3-PT SHOTS TRIED	ASTs	STLs	TURN-OVERS	BLKs	PTs
(MORRIS, C.)	0.714	22	110	197	129	171	81	879
(DAVIS, D.)	0.572	0	1	30	27	49	74	395
(ANDERSON, N.)	0.667	30	85	163	97	125	33	1196
(JORDAN, M.)	0.832	27	100	489	182	200	75	2404
(McCRAY, R.)	0.719	25	85	219	48	115	30	677
(REID, J.R.)	0.705	0	3	81	49	84	23	560
(SMITH, C.)	0.785	0	6	56	41	69	98	714
(BONNER, A.)	0.627	1	4	125	94	133	26	740
(ROBERTS, S.)	0.515	0	1	39	22	78	83	573
(EATON, M.)	0.598	0	0	40	36	60	205	266
(DUCKWORTH, K.)	0.690	0	3	99	38	143	37	880
(WILLIAMS, H.)	0.725	1	6	94	35	114	98	859
(STEWART, L.)	0.807	0	3	120	51	112	44	794
(CORBIN, T.)	0.866	0	4	140	82	97	20	780
(McHALE, K.)	0.822	0	13	82	11	82	59	780
(MAJERLE, D.)	0.756	87	228	274	131	101	43	1418
(NORMAN, K.)	0.535	4	28	125	53	100	66	929
(CHAMBERS, T.)	0.830	18	49	142	57	103	37	1128
(BROWN, M.)	0.667	0	1	81	42	105	34	632
(BAILEY, T.)	0.796	0	2	78	35	108	117	951
(MITCHELL, S.)	0.786	2	11	94	53	97	39	825
(SHACKLEFORD, C.)	0.663	0	1	46	38	62	51	473
(SMITH, L.)	0.364	0	1	33	21	44	7	104
(WILLIAMS, Br.)	0.669	0	0	33	41	86	53	437
(WORTHY, J.)	0.814	9	43	252	76	127	23	1075
(SMITS, R.)	0.788	0	2	116	29	130	100	1024
(McDANIEL, X.)	0.714	12	39	149	57	147	24	1125
(KITE, G.)	0.588	0	1	44	30	61	57	228
(LAIMBEER, B.)	0.893	32	85	160	51	102	54	783
(MULLIN, C.)	0.833	64	175	286	173	202	62	2074
(MILLS, T.)	0.750	8	23	84	48	82	41	742
(HARPER, R.)	0.736	64	211	417	152	252	72	1495
(KRYSTKOWIAK, L.)	0.757	0	5	114	54	115	12	714
(HODGE, D.)	0.667	0	0	39	25	75	23	426
(ELLIOTT, S.)	0.861	25	82	214	84	152	29	1338
(BRICKOWSKI, F.)	0.767	3	6	122	60	112	23	740
(ANDERSON, W.)	0.775	13	56	302	54	140	51	744
(PERSON, C.)	0.675	132	354	382	68	216	18	1497
(CAMPBELL, E.)	0.619	0	2	59	53	73	159	578
(LEVER, F.)	0.750	17	52	107	46	36	12	347
(McKEY, D.)	0.847	19	50	120	61	114	47	777
(SMITH, Do.)	0.736	0	11	129	62	97	34	671
(AUGMON, S.)	0.666	1	6	201	124	181	27	1094
(GILL, K.)	0.745	6	25	329	154	180	46	1622
(ROBINSON, C.)	0.664	1	11	137	85	154	107	1016
(CARTWRIGHT, B.)	0.604	0	0	87	22	75	14	512
(HORNACEK, J.)	0.886	83	189	411	158	170	31	1632
(HAMMONDS, T.)	0.610	0	1	36	22	58	13	440
(WILLIAMS, R.)	0.803	56	156	235	148	173	68	1474
(RICE, G.)	0.837	155	396	184	90	145	35	1765
(DONALDSON, J.)	0.709	0	0	33	8	48	49	285
(EHLO, C.)	0.707	69	167	238	78	104	22	776
(RASMUSSEN, B.)	0.750	5	23	107	35	51	48	729
(LEWIS, Re.)	0.851	5	21	185	125	136	105	1703
(THOMPSON, L.)	0.817	0	2	102	52	98	34	394
(LANE, J.)	0.333	0	0	17	2	14	1	37

1991–1992 REGULAR-SEASON STATISTICAL RESULTS
NBA PLAYERS ORDERED BY REBOUNDS PER GAME

	NAME	POS	TEAM	GMs	MINs	MINs per GM	OFF REBs	REBs	REBs per MIN	REBs per GM	FG PCT
113.	BOWIE, A.	g/f	ORL	52	1721	33.1	70	245	0.142	4.7	0.493
114.	STRICKLAND, R.	g	SA	57	2053	36.0	92	265	0.129	4.7	0.455
115.	WEST, M.	c	PHX	82	1436	17.5	134	372	0.259	4.5	0.632
116.	GREEN, S.	f	SA	80	1127	14.1	92	342	0.304	4.3	0.427
117.	CARR, A.	f/c	SA	81	1867	23.0	128	346	0.185	4.3	0.490
118.	ROBERTSON, A.	g	MIL	82	2463	30.0	175	350	0.142	4.3	0.430
119.	KLEINE, J.	c	BOS	70	991	14.2	94	296	0.299	4.2	0.492
120.	JONES, Ch.	c/f	WAS	75	1365	18.2	105	317	0.232	4.2	0.367
121.	ALEXANDER, V.	c	GS	80	1350	16.9	106	336	0.249	4.2	0.529
122.	BREUER, R.	c	MIN	67	1176	17.6	98	281	0.239	4.2	0.468
123.	SALLEY, J.	f/c	DET	72	1774	24.6	106	296	0.167	4.1	0.512
124.	LIBERTY, M.	f/g	DEN	75	1527	20.4	144	308	0.202	4.1	0.443
125.	KESSLER, A.	c	MIA	77	1197	15.5	114	314	0.262	4.1	0.413
126.	PERDUE, W.	c	CHI	77	1007	13.1	108	312	0.310	4.1	0.547
127.	RICHMOND, M.	g	SAC	80	3095	38.7	62	319	0.103	4.0	0.468
128.	ADAMS, M.	g	WAS	78	2795	35.8	58	310	0.111	4.0	0.393
129.	WILLIAMS, S.	f	CHI	63	690	11.0	90	247	0.358	3.9	0.483
130.	SCHAYES, D.	c	MIL	43	726	16.9	58	168	0.231	3.9	0.417
131.	JOHNSON, B.	f	HOU	80	2202	27.5	95	312	0.142	3.9	0.458
132.	LONGLEY, L.	c	MIN	66	991	15.0	67	257	0.259	3.9	0.458
133.	MILLER, R.	g	IND	82	3120	38.0	82	318	0.102	3.9	0.501
134.	BENOIT, D.	f	UT	77	1161	15.1	105	296	0.255	3.8	0.467
135.	HARDAWAY, T.	g	GS	81	3332	41.1	81	310	0.093	3.8	0.461
136.	RAMBIS, K.	f	PHX	28	381	13.6	23	106	0.278	3.8	0.463
137.	SCOTT, B.	g	LAL	82	2679	32.7	74	310	0.116	3.8	0.458
138.	JACKSON, M.	g	NY	81	2461	30.4	95	305	0.124	3.8	0.491
139.	JOHNSON, K.	g	PHX	78	2899	37.2	61	292	0.101	3.7	0.479
140.	BLAYLOCK, M.	g	NJ	72	2548	35.4	101	269	0.106	3.7	0.432
141.	ACRES, M.	c	ORL	68	926	13.6	97	252	0.272	3.7	0.517
142.	EDWARDS, T.	g/f	UT	81	2283	28.2	86	298	0.131	3.7	0.522
143.	RICHARDSON, P.	g	MIN	82	2922	35.6	91	301	0.103	3.7	0.466
144.	CAMPBELL, T.	f/g	MIN	78	2441	31.3	141	286	0.117	3.7	0.464
145.	SCOTT, D.	f	ORL	18	608	33.8	14	66	0.109	3.7	0.402
146.	ABDELNABY, A.	f/c	POR	71	934	13.2	81	260	0.278	3.7	0.493
147.	PAYTON, G.	g	SEA	81	2549	31.5	123	295	0.116	3.6	0.451
148.	WHITE, R.	f	DAL	65	1021	15.7	96	236	0.231	3.6	0.380
149.	RULAND, J.	c	PHI	13	209	16.1	16	47	0.225	3.6	0.526
150.	JOHNSON, E.	f	SEA	81	2366	29.2	118	292	0.123	3.6	0.459
151.	BRYANT, M.	c	POR	56	800	14.3	87	201	0.251	3.6	0.480
152.	BURTON, W.	g/f	MIA	68	1585	23.3	76	244	0.154	3.6	0.450
153.	WOLF, J.	f	DEN	67	1160	17.3	97	240	0.207	3.6	0.361
154.	SCHINTZIUS, D.	c	SAC	33	400	12.1	43	118	0.295	3.6	0.427
155.	WILLIAMS, M.	g	IND	79	2750	34.8	73	282	0.103	3.6	0.490
156.	LOHAUS, B.	f/c	MIL	70	1081	15.4	65	249	0.230	3.6	0.450
157.	LISTER, A.	c	GS	26	293	11.3	21	92	0.314	3.5	0.557
158.	McMILLAN, N.	g/f	SEA	72	1652	22.9	92	252	0.153	3.5	0.437
159.	LECKNER, E.	c	CHA	59	716	12.1	49	206	0.288	3.5	0.513
160.	GAMBLE, K.	g/f	BOS	82	2496	30.4	80	286	0.115	3.5	0.529
161.	GLASS, G.	g	MIN	75	1822	24.3	107	260	0.143	3.5	0.440
162.	VOLKOV, A.	f	ATL	77	1516	19.7	103	265	0.175	3.4	0.441
163.	HIGGINS, R.	f	GS	25	535	21.4	30	85	0.159	3.4	0.412
164.	ANDERSON, Ro.	f	PHI	82	2432	29.7	96	278	0.114	3.4	0.465
165.	KONCAK, J.	c	ATL	77	1489	19.3	62	261	0.175	3.4	0.391
166.	GMINSKI, M.	c	CHA	35	499	14.3	37	118	0.237	3.4	0.452
167.	GATLING, C.	c	GS	54	612	11.3	75	182	0.297	3.4	0.568
168.	CURRY, D.	g	CHA	77	2020	26.2	57	259	0.128	3.4	0.486

(NAME)	FT PCT	3-PT SHOTS MADE	3-PT SHOTS TRIED	ASTs	STLs	TURN-OVERS	BLKs	PTs
(BOWIE, A.)	0.860	17	44	163	55	107	38	758
(STRICKLAND, R.)	0.687	5	15	491	118	160	17	787
(WEST, M.)	0.637	0	0	22	14	82	81	501
(GREEN, S.)	0.820	0	0	36	29	62	11	367
(CARR, A.)	0.764	1	5	63	32	114	96	881
(ROBERTSON, A.)	0.763	67	210	360	210	223	32	1010
(KLEINE, J.)	0.708	4	8	32	23	27	14	326
(JONES, Ch.)	0.500	0	0	62	43	39	92	86
(ALEXANDER, V.)	0.691	0	1	32	45	91	62	589
(BREUER, R.)	0.533	0	1	89	27	41	99	363
(SALLEY, J.)	0.715	0	3	116	49	102	110	684
(LIBERTY, M.)	0.728	17	50	58	66	90	29	698
(KESSLER, A.)	0.817	0	0	34	17	58	32	410
(PERDUE, W.)	0.495	1	2	80	16	72	43	350
(RICHMOND, M.)	0.813	103	268	411	92	247	34	1803
(ADAMS, M.)	0.869	125	386	594	145	212	9	1408
(WILLIAMS, S.)	0.649	0	3	50	13	35	36	214
(SCHAYES, D.)	0.771	0	0	34	19	41	19	240
(JOHNSON, B.)	0.727	1	9	158	72	104	49	685
(LONGLEY, L.)	0.663	0	0	53	35	83	64	281
(MILLER, R.)	0.858	129	341	314	105	157	26	1695
(BENOIT, D.)	0.810	3	14	34	19	71	44	434
(HARDAWAY, T.)	0.766	127	376	807	164	267	13	1893
(RAMBIS, K.)	0.778	0	0	37	12	25	14	90
(SCOTT, B.)	0.839	54	157	226	105	119	28	1218
(JACKSON, M.)	0.770	11	43	694	112	211	13	916
(JOHNSON, K.)	0.807	10	46	836	116	272	23	1536
(BLAYLOCK, M.)	0.712	12	54	492	170	152	40	996
(ACRES, M.)	0.761	1	3	22	25	33	15	208
(EDWARDS, T.)	0.774	39	103	137	81	122	46	1018
(RICHARDSON, P.)	0.691	53	155	685	119	204	25	1350
(CAMPBELL, T.)	0.803	13	37	229	84	165	31	1307
(SCOTT, D.)	0.901	29	89	35	20	31	9	359
(ABDELNABY, A.)	0.753	0	0	30	25	66	16	432
(PAYTON, G.)	0.669	3	23	506	147	174	21	764
(WHITE, R.)	0.765	4	27	31	31	68	22	418
(RULAND, J.)	0.688	0	0	5	7	20	4	51
(JOHNSON, E.)	0.861	27	107	161	55	130	11	1386
(BRYANT, M.)	0.667	0	3	41	26	30	8	230
(BURTON, W.)	0.800	6	15	123	46	119	37	762
(WOLF, J.)	0.803	1	11	61	32	60	14	254
(SCHINTZIUS, D.)	0.833	0	4	20	6	19	28	110
(WILLIAMS, M.)	0.871	8	33	647	233	240	22	1188
(LOHAUS, B.)	0.659	57	144	74	40	46	71	408
(LISTER, A.)	0.424	0	0	14	5	20	16	102
(McMILLAN, N.)	0.643	27	98	359	129	112	29	435
(LECKNER, E.)	0.745	0	1	31	9	39	18	196
(GAMBLE, K.)	0.885	9	31	219	75	97	37	1108
(GLASS, G.)	0.616	16	54	175	66	103	30	859
(VOLKOV, A.)	0.631	35	110	250	66	102	30	662
(HIGGINS, R.)	0.814	33	95	22	15	15	13	255
(ANDERSON, Ro.)	0.877	42	127	135	86	109	11	1123
(KONCAK, J.)	0.655	0	12	132	50	54	67	241
(GMINSKI, M.)	0.750	1	3	31	11	20	16	202
(GATLING, C.)	0.661	0	4	16	31	44	36	306
(CURRY, D.)	0.836	74	183	177	93	134	20	1209

1991–1992 REGULAR-SEASON STATISTICAL RESULTS
NBA PLAYERS ORDERED BY REBOUNDS PER GAME

	NAME	POS	TEAM	GMs	MINs	MINs per GM	OFF REBs	REBs	REBs per MIN	REBs per GM	FG PCT
169.	HAWKINS, H.	g	PHI	81	3013	37.2	53	271	0.090	3.4	0.462
170.	WINGATE, D.	g	WAS	81	2127	26.3	80	269	0.127	3.3	0.465
171.	STOCKTON, J.	g	UT	82	3002	36.6	68	270	0.090	3.3	0.482
172.	TURNER, J.	f	ORL	75	1591	21.2	62	246	0.155	3.3	0.451
173.	NEWMAN, J.	f/g	CHA	55	1651	30.0	71	179	0.108	3.3	0.477
174.	REYNOLDS, J.	g/f	ORL	46	1159	25.2	47	149	0.129	3.2	0.380
175.	SHAW, B.	g	MIA	63	1423	22.6	50	204	0.143	3.2	0.407
176.	WALKER, D.	g	DET	74	1541	20.8	85	238	0.154	3.2	0.423
177.	ROBERTS, F.	f	MIL	80	1746	21.8	103	257	0.147	3.2	0.482
178.	WEST, D.	g	MIN	80	2540	31.7	107	257	0.101	3.2	0.518
179.	BLACKMAN, R.	g	DAL	75	2527	33.7	78	239	0.095	3.2	0.461
180.	FERRELL, D.	f	ATL	66	1598	24.2	105	210	0.131	3.2	0.524
181.	WOOLRIDGE, O.	f	DET	82	2113	25.8	109	260	0.123	3.2	0.498
182.	THOMAS, I.	g	DET	78	2918	37.4	68	247	0.085	3.2	0.446
183.	AGUIRRE, M.	f	DET	75	1582	21.1	67	236	0.149	3.2	0.431
184.	PETROVIC, D.	g	NJ	82	3027	36.9	97	258	0.085	3.2	0.508
185.	GRAYER, J.	g	MIL	82	1659	20.2	129	257	0.155	3.1	0.449
186.	FERRY, D.	f	CLE	68	937	13.8	53	213	0.227	3.1	0.409
187.	BOL, M.	c	PHI	71	1267	17.8	54	222	0.175	3.1	0.383
188.	ELLIS, D.	f	MIL	81	2191	27.0	92	253	0.116	3.1	0.469
189.	PORTER, T.	g	POR	82	2784	34.0	51	255	0.092	3.1	0.462
190.	SANDERS, M.	f	CLE	31	633	20.4	27	96	0.152	3.1	0.571
191.	THREATT, S.	g	LAL	82	3070	37.4	43	253	0.082	3.1	0.489
192.	SMITH, S.	g	MIA	61	1806	29.6	81	188	0.104	3.1	0.454
193.	MAXWELL, V.	g	HOU	80	2700	33.7	37	243	0.090	3.0	0.413
194.	JOHNSON, V.	g	SA	60	1350	22.5	67	182	0.135	3.0	0.405
195.	BENNETT, W.	f	MIA	54	833	15.4	63	162	0.195	3.0	0.379
196.	SAMPSON, R.	c	WAS	10	108	10.8	11	30	0.278	3.0	0.310
197.	PIERCE, R.	g	SEA	78	2658	34.1	93	233	0.088	3.0	0.475
198.	GRAHAM, P.	g	ATL	78	1718	22.0	72	231	0.135	3.0	0.447
199.	FOSTER, G.	f	WAS	49	548	11.2	43	145	0.265	3.0	0.461
200.	ASKEW, V.	g	GS	80	1496	18.7	89	233	0.156	2.9	0.509
201.	HOPSON, D.	g/f	SAC	71	1314	18.5	105	206	0.157	2.9	0.465
202.	WILLIAMS, Ja.	f/c	PHI	50	646	12.9	62	145	0.225	2.9	0.364
203.	ROLLINS, T.	f/c	HOU	59	697	11.8	61	171	0.245	2.9	0.535
204.	WEBB, S.	g	SAC	77	2724	35.4	30	223	0.082	2.9	0.445
205.	MACON, M.	g	DEN	76	2304	30.3	80	220	0.096	2.9	0.375
206.	MARCIULIONIS, S.	g	GS	72	2117	29.4	68	208	0.098	2.9	0.538
207.	COOPER, W.	f	POR	35	344	9.8	38	101	0.294	2.9	0.427
208.	MALONE, J.	g	UT	81	2922	36.1	49	233	0.080	2.9	0.511
209.	ELIE, M.	g/f	GS	79	1677	21.2	69	227	0.135	2.9	0.521
210.	LEVINGSTON, C.	f	CHI	79	1020	12.9	109	227	0.223	2.9	0.498
211.	BOGUES, M.	g	CHA	82	2790	34.0	58	235	0.084	2.9	0.472
212.	EDWARDS, Ja.	c	LAC	72	1437	20.0	55	202	0.141	2.8	0.465
213.	MUSTAF, J.	f	PHX	52	545	10.5	45	145	0.266	2.8	0.477
214.	BULLARD, M.	f	HOU	80	1278	16.0	73	223	0.175	2.8	0.459
215.	DAWKINS, J.	g	PHI	82	2815	34.3	42	227	0.081	2.8	0.437
216.	EACKLES, L.	f	WAS	65	1463	22.5	39	178	0.122	2.7	0.468
217.	FOX, R.	g/f	BOS	81	1535	19.0	73	220	0.143	2.7	0.459
218.	CHILCUTT, P.	f/c	SAC	69	817	11.8	78	187	0.229	2.7	0.452
219.	ROBINSON, R.	g	ATL	81	2220	27.4	64	219	0.099	2.7	0.456
220.	SKILES, S.	g	ORL	75	2377	31.7	36	202	0.085	2.7	0.414
221.	HIGGINS, S.	f	ORL	38	616	16.2	29	102	0.166	2.7	0.459
222.	CHAPMAN, R.	g	WAS	22	567	25.8	10	58	0.102	2.6	0.448
223.	HARPER, D.	g	DAL	65	2252	34.6	49	170	0.076	2.6	0.443
224.	EDWARDS, K.	g	MIA	81	1840	22.7	56	211	0.115	2.6	0.454

(NAME)	FT PCT	3-PT SHOTS MADE	3-PT SHOTS TRIED	ASTs	STLs	TURN-OVERS	BLKs	PTs
(HAWKINS, H.)	0.874	91	229	248	157	189	43	1536
(WINGATE, D.)	0.719	1	18	247	123	124	21	638
(STOCKTON, J.)	0.842	83	204	1126	244	286	22	1297
(TURNER, J.)	0.693	1	8	92	24	106	16	530
(NEWMAN, J.)	0.766	13	46	146	70	129	14	839
(REYNOLDS, J.)	0.836	3	24	151	63	96	17	555
(SHAW, B.)	0.791	5	23	250	57	99	22	495
(WALKER, D.)	0.619	0	10	205	63	79	18	387
(ROBERTS, F.)	0.749	19	37	122	52	122	40	769
(WEST, D.)	0.805	4	23	281	66	120	26	1116
(BLACKMAN, R.)	0.899	65	169	204	50	153	22	1374
(FERRELL, D.)	0.762	11	33	92	49	99	17	839
(WOOLRIDGE, O.)	0.683	1	9	88	41	133	33	1146
(THOMAS, I.)	0.773	25	86	560	118	252	15	1445
(AGUIRRE, M.)	0.687	15	71	126	51	105	11	851
(PETROVIC, D.)	0.808	123	277	252	105	215	11	1691
(GRAYER, J.)	0.667	19	66	150	64	105	13	739
(FERRY, D.)	0.836	17	48	75	22	46	15	346
(BOL, M.)	0.462	0	9	22	11	41	205	110
(ELLIS, D.)	0.774	138	329	104	57	119	18	1272
(PORTER, T.)	0.856	128	324	477	127	188	12	1485
(SANDERS, M.)	0.766	1	3	53	24	22	10	221
(THREATT, S.)	0.831	20	62	593	168	182	16	1240
(SMITH, S.)	0.748	40	125	278	59	152	19	729
(MAXWELL, V.)	0.772	162	473	326	104	178	28	1372
(JOHNSON, V.)	0.647	19	60	145	41	74	14	478
(BENNETT, W.)	0.700	0	1	38	19	33	9	195
(SAMPSON, R.)	0.667	0	2	4	3	10	8	22
(PIERCE, R.)	0.917	33	123	241	86	189	20	1690
(GRAHAM, P.)	0.741	55	141	175	96	91	21	791
(FOSTER, G.)	0.714	0	1	35	6	36	12	213
(ASKEW, V.)	0.694	1	10	188	47	84	23	498
(HOPSON, D.)	0.708	12	47	102	67	100	39	743
(WILLIAMS, Ja.)	0.636	0	0	12	20	44	20	206
(ROLLINS, T.)	0.867	0	0	15	14	18	62	118
(WEBB, S.)	0.859	73	199	547	125	229	24	1231
(MACON, M.)	0.730	4	30	168	154	155	14	805
(MARCIULIONIS, S.)	0.788	3	10	243	116	193	10	1361
(COOPER, W.)	0.636	0	0	21	4	15	27	77
(MALONE, J.)	0.898	1	12	180	56	140	5	1639
(ELIE, M.)	0.852	23	70	174	68	83	15	620
(LEVINGSTON, C.)	0.625	1	6	66	27	42	45	311
(BOGUES, M.)	0.783	2	27	743	170	156	6	730
(EDWARDS, Ja.)	0.731	0	1	53	24	72	33	698
(MUSTAF, J.)	0.690	0	0	45	21	51	16	233
(BULLARD, M.)	0.760	64	166	75	26	56	21	512
(DAWKINS, J.)	0.882	36	101	567	89	183	5	988
(EACKLES, L.)	0.743	7	35	125	47	75	7	856
(FOX, R.)	0.755	23	70	126	78	123	30	644
(CHILCUTT, P.)	0.821	2	2	38	32	41	17	251
(ROBINSON, R.)	0.636	34	104	446	105	206	24	1055
(SKILES, S.)	0.895	91	250	544	74	233	5	1057
(HIGGINS, S.)	0.861	6	25	41	16	41	6	291
(CHAPMAN, R.)	0.679	8	29	89	15	45	8	270
(HARPER, D.)	0.759	58	186	373	101	154	17	1152
(EDWARDS, K.)	0.848	7	32	170	99	120	20	819

1991-1992 REGULAR-SEASON STATISTICAL RESULTS
NBA PLAYERS ORDERED BY REBOUNDS PER GAME

NAME	POS	TEAM	GMs	MINs	MINs per GM	OFF REBs	REBs	REBs per MIN	REBs per GM	FG PCT
225. FRANK, T.	f	MIN	10	140	14.0	8	26	0.186	2.6	0.546
226. KING, S.	f/c	CHI	79	1268	16.1	87	205	0.162	2.6	0.506
227. HUMPHRIES, J.	g	MIL	71	2261	31.8	44	184	0.081	2.6	0.470
228. VINCENT, S.	g	ORL	39	885	22.7	19	101	0.114	2.6	0.430
229. McCLOUD, G.	g	IND	51	892	17.5	45	132	0.148	2.6	0.409
230. FLEMING, V.	g	IND	82	1737	21.2	69	209	0.120	2.6	0.482
231. BROWN, D.	g	BOS	31	883	28.5	15	79	0.090	2.6	0.426
232. WILKINS, G.	g	NY	82	2344	28.6	74	206	0.088	2.5	0.447
233. RIVERS, Do.	g	LAC	59	1657	28.1	23	147	0.089	2.5	0.424
234. HASTINGS, S.	f	DEN	40	421	10.5	30	98	0.233	2.5	0.340
235. GARLAND, W.	g	DEN	78	2209	28.3	67	190	0.086	2.4	0.444
236. ASKINS, K.	g/f	MIA	59	843	14.3	65	142	0.168	2.4	0.410
237. PRICE, M.	g	CLE	72	2138	29.7	38	173	0.081	2.4	0.488
238. CEBALLOS, C.	f	PHX	64	725	11.3	60	152	0.210	2.4	0.482
239. GRANT, Ga.	g	LAC	78	2049	26.3	34	184	0.090	2.4	0.462
240. MURPHY, T.	f	MIN	47	429	9.1	36	110	0.256	2.3	0.488
241. COLES, B.	g	MIA	81	1976	24.4	69	189	0.096	2.3	0.455
242. STARKS, J.	g	NY	82	2118	25.8	45	191	0.090	2.3	0.449
243. HERRERA, C.	f	HOU	43	566	13.2	33	99	0.175	2.3	0.516
244. DUMARS, J.	g	DET	82	3192	38.9	82	188	0.059	2.3	0.448
245. CONNER, L.	g	MIL	81	1420	17.5	63	184	0.130	2.3	0.431
246. TEAGLE, T.	f	LAL	82	1602	19.5	91	183	0.114	2.2	0.452
247. BAGLEY, J.	g	BOS	73	1742	23.9	38	161	0.092	2.2	0.441
248. SMITH, K.	g	HOU	81	2735	33.8	34	177	0.065	2.2	0.475
249. FREDERICK, A.	f	CHA	66	852	12.9	75	144	0.169	2.2	0.435
250. ADDISON, R.	g	NJ	76	1175	15.5	65	165	0.140	2.2	0.433
251. SANDERS, J.	f	ATL	12	117	9.8	9	26	0.222	2.2	0.444
252. WILLIAMS, K.	f	IND	60	565	9.4	64	129	0.228	2.2	0.518
253. NEALY, E.	f	PHX	52	505	9.7	25	111	0.220	2.1	0.512
254. SMITH, O.	g	ORL	55	877	15.9	40	116	0.132	2.1	0.365
255. ENGLISH, A.J.	g	WAS	81	1665	20.6	74	168	0.101	2.1	0.433
256. ROYAL, D.	f	SA	60	718	12.0	65	124	0.173	2.1	0.449
257. ANDERSON, K.	g	NJ	64	1086	17.0	38	127	0.117	2.0	0.390
258. BRANDON, T.	g	CLE	82	1605	19.6	49	162	0.101	2.0	0.419
259. BEDFORD, W.	f/c	DET	32	363	11.3	24	63	0.174	2.0	0.413
260. BROWN, C.	f	LAL	42	431	10.3	31	82	0.190	2.0	0.469
261. MOORE, T.	f	DAL	42	782	18.6	31	82	0.105	2.0	0.400
262. HALEY, J.	f/c	LAL	49	394	8.0	31	95	0.241	1.9	0.369
263. WIGGINS, M.	g	PHI	49	569	11.6	43	94	0.165	1.9	0.384
264. HOWARD, B.	f	DAL	27	318	11.8	17	51	0.160	1.9	0.519
265. IUZZOLINO, M.	g	DAL	52	1280	24.6	27	98	0.077	1.9	0.451
266. BUECHLER, J.	f	GS	28	290	10.4	18	52	0.179	1.9	0.409
267. TURNER, Jo.	f	HOU	42	345	8.2	38	78	0.226	1.9	0.439
268. FLOYD, S.	g	HOU	82	1662	20.3	34	150	0.090	1.8	0.406
269. AINGE, D.	g	POR	81	1595	19.7	40	148	0.093	1.8	0.442
270. FEITL, D.	c	NJ	34	175	5.2	21	61	0.349	1.8	0.429
271. ARMSTRONG, B.J.	g	CHI	82	1875	22.9	19	145	0.077	1.8	0.481
272. LICHTI, T.	g	DEN	68	1176	17.3	36	118	0.100	1.7	0.460
273. JAMES, H.	f	CLE	65	866	13.3	35	112	0.129	1.7	0.407
274. OGG, A.	c	MIA	43	367	8.5	30	74	0.202	1.7	0.548
275. CHEEKS, M.	g	ATL	56	1086	19.4	29	95	0.088	1.7	0.462
276. PRESSEY, P.	g	SA	56	759	13.6	22	95	0.125	1.7	0.373
277. SMITH, La.	g	WAS	48	708	14.7	30	81	0.114	1.7	0.407
278. PETERSEN, J.	c	GS	27	169	6.3	12	45	0.266	1.7	0.450
279. ANTHONY, G.	g	NY	82	1510	18.4	33	136	0.090	1.7	0.370
280. KERR, S.	g	CLE	48	847	17.6	14	78	0.092	1.6	0.511

(NAME)	FT PCT	3-PT SHOTS MADE	3-PT SHOTS TRIED	ASTs	STLs	TURN-OVERS	BLKs	PTs
(FRANK, T.)	0.667	0	0	8	5	5	4	46
(KING, S.)	0.753	2	5	77	21	76	25	551
(HUMPHRIES, J.)	0.783	42	144	466	119	148	13	991
(VINCENT, S.)	0.846	1	13	148	35	72	4	411
(McCLOUD, G.)	0.781	32	94	116	26	62	11	338
(FLEMING, V.)	0.737	6	27	266	56	140	7	726
(BROWN, D.)	0.769	5	22	164	33	59	7	363
(WILKINS, G.)	0.730	38	8	219	76	113	17	1016
(RIVERS, Do.)	0.832	26	92	233	111	92	19	641
(HASTINGS, S.)	0.857	0	9	26	10	22	15	58
(GARLAND, W.)	0.859	9	28	411	98	175	22	846
(ASKINS, K.)	0.703	25	73	38	40	47	15	219
(PRICE, M.)	0.947	101	261	535	94	159	12	1247
(CEBALLOS, C.)	0.737	1	6	50	16	71	11	462
(GRANT, Ga.)	0.815	15	51	538	138	187	14	609
(MURPHY, T.)	0.559	1	2	11	9	18	8	98
(COLES, B.)	0.824	10	52	366	73	167	13	816
(STARKS, J.)	0.778	94	270	276	103	150	18	1139
(HERRERA, C.)	0.568	0	1	27	16	37	25	191
(DUMARS, J.)	0.867	49	120	375	71	193	12	1635
(CONNER, L.)	0.704	0	7	294	97	79	10	287
(TEAGLE, T.)	0.767	1	4	113	66	114	9	880
(BAGLEY, J.)	0.716	10	42	480	57	148	4	524
(SMITH, K.)	0.866	54	137	562	104	227	7	1137
(FREDERICK, A.)	0.685	4	17	71	40	58	26	389
(ADDISON, R.)	0.737	14	49	68	28	46	28	444
(SANDERS, J.)	0.778	0	0	9	5	5	3	47
(WILLIAMS, K.)	0.605	0	4	40	20	22	41	252
(NEALY, E.)	0.667	20	50	37	16	17	2	160
(SMITH, O.)	0.769	8	21	57	36	62	13	310
(ENGLISH, A.J.)	0.841	6	34	143	32	89	9	886
(ROYAL, D.)	0.692	0	0	34	25	39	7	252
(ANDERSON, K.)	0.745	3	13	203	67	97	9	450
(BRANDON, T.)	0.807	1	23	316	81	136	22	605
(BEDFORD, W.)	0.636	0	1	12	6	15	18	114
(BROWN, C.)	0.612	0	3	26	12	29	7	150
(MOORE, T.)	0.833	30	84	48	32	44	4	355
(HALEY, J.)	0.483	0	0	7	7	25	8	76
(WIGGINS, M.)	0.686	0	1	22	20	25	1	211
(HOWARD, B.)	0.710	1	2	14	11	15	8	131
(IUZZOLINO, M.)	0.836	59	136	194	33	92	1	486
(BUECHLER, J.)	0.571	0	1	23	19	13	7	70
(TURNER, Jo.)	0.525	0	0	12	6	32	4	117
(FLOYD, S.)	0.794	37	123	239	57	128	21	744
(AINGE, D.)	0.824	78	230	202	73	70	13	784
(FEITL, D.)	0.842	0	0	6	2	19	3	82
(ARMSTRONG, B.J.)	0.806	35	87	266	46	94	5	809
(LICHTI, T.)	0.839	1	9	74	43	72	12	446
(JAMES, H.)	0.803	29	90	25	16	43	11	418
(OGG, A.)	0.533	0	0	7	5	19	28	108
(CHEEKS, M.)	0.605	3	6	185	83	36	0	259
(PRESSEY, P.)	0.683	3	21	142	29	64	19	151
(SMITH, La.)	0.804	2	21	99	44	63	1	247
(PETERSEN, J.)	0.700	0	2	9	5	5	6	43
(ANTHONY, G.)	0.741	8	55	314	59	98	9	447
(KERR, S.)	0.833	32	74	110	27	31	10	319

1991-1992 REGULAR-SEASON STATISTICAL RESULTS
NBA PLAYERS ORDERED BY REBOUNDS PER GAME

	NAME	POS	TEAM	GMs	MINs	MINs per GM	OFF REBs	REBs	REBs per MIN	REBs per GM	FG PCT
281.	DREILING, G.	c	IND	60	509	8.5	22	96	0.189	1.6	0.494
282.	TOLBERT, T.	f	GS	35	310	8.9	14	55	0.177	1.6	0.384
283.	COOK, A.	f	DEN	22	115	5.2	13	34	0.296	1.6	0.600
284.	LYNCH, K.	g	CHA	55	819	14.9	30	85	0.104	1.6	0.417
285.	McCORMICK, T.	c	NY	22	108	4.9	14	34	0.315	1.6	0.424
286.	TUCKER, T.	g	SA	24	415	17.3	8	37	0.089	1.5	0.465
287.	CONLON, M.	c	SEA	45	381	8.5	33	69	0.181	1.5	0.475
288.	CORCHIANI, C.	g	ORL	51	741	14.5	18	78	0.105	1.5	0.399
289.	WILEY, M.	g	ATL	53	870	16.4	24	81	0.093	1.5	0.430
290.	DAVIS, W.	g	DEN	46	741	16.1	20	70	0.095	1.5	0.459
291.	DOUGLAS, S.	g	BOS	42	752	17.9	13	63	0.084	1.5	0.463
292.	GEORGE, T.	g	NJ	70	1037	14.8	36	105	0.101	1.5	0.428
293.	BATTLE, J.	g	CLE	76	1637	21.5	19	112	0.068	1.5	0.480
294.	BROWN, T.	f	SEA	57	655	11.5	32	84	0.128	1.5	0.410
295.	VRANKOVIC, S.	c	BOS	19	110	5.8	8	28	0.255	1.5	0.469
296.	JACKSON, C.	g	DEN	81	1538	19.0	22	114	0.074	1.4	0.421
297.	GARRICK, T.	g	DAL	40	549	13.7	12	56	0.102	1.4	0.413
298.	PACK, R.	g	POR	72	894	12.4	32	97	0.109	1.4	0.423
299.	RANDALL, M.	f	MIN	54	441	8.2	39	71	0.161	1.3	0.456
300.	VANDEWEGHE, K.	f	NY	67	956	14.3	31	88	0.092	1.3	0.491
301.	QUINNETT, B.	f	DAL	39	326	8.4	16	51	0.156	1.3	0.347
302.	TURNER, A.	g	WAS	70	871	12.4	17	90	0.103	1.3	0.425
303.	SCHEFFLER, S.	f	DEN	11	61	5.6	10	14	0.230	1.3	0.667
304.	RIVERS, Da.	g	LAC	15	122	8.1	10	19	0.156	1.3	0.333
305.	BROWN, R.	g	SAC	56	535	9.6	26	69	0.129	1.2	0.456
306.	KING, R.	c	SEA	40	213	5.3	20	49	0.230	1.2	0.380
307.	PAXSON, J.	g	CHI	79	1946	24.6	21	96	0.049	1.2	0.528
308.	YOUNG, D.	g	LAC	62	1023	16.5	16	75	0.073	1.2	0.392
309.	BROOKS, S.	g	MIN	82	1082	13.2	27	99	0.092	1.2	0.447
310.	SMITH, To.	g	LAL	63	820	13.0	31	76	0.093	1.2	0.399
311.	GREEN, Se.	g	IND	35	256	7.3	22	42	0.164	1.2	0.392
312.	JOHNSON, A.	g	HOU	69	1235	17.9	13	80	0.065	1.2	0.479
313.	McCANN, B.	f	DET	26	129	5.0	12	30	0.233	1.2	0.394
314.	HANSEN, B.	g	CHI	68	809	11.9	17	77	0.095	1.1	0.444
315.	AUSTIN, I.	c	UT	31	112	3.6	11	35	0.313	1.1	0.457
316.	PAYNE, K.	f	PHI	49	353	7.2	13	54	0.153	1.1	0.448
317.	BURTT, S.	g	PHX	31	356	11.5	10	34	0.096	1.1	0.463
318.	KNIGHT, N.	g	PHX	42	631	15.0	16	46	0.073	1.1	0.475
319.	COPA, T.	f/c	SA	33	132	4.0	14	36	0.273	1.1	0.550
320.	DAILEY, Q.	f	SEA	11	98	8.9	2	12	0.122	1.1	0.243
321.	BARROS, D.	g	SEA	75	1331	17.7	17	81	0.061	1.1	0.483
322.	MURDOCK, E.	g	UT	50	478	9.6	21	54	0.113	1.1	0.415
323.	BROOKS, K.	f	DEN	37	270	7.3	13	39	0.144	1.1	0.443
324.	MORTON, J.	g	MIA	25	270	10.8	6	26	0.096	1.0	0.387
325.	LES, J.	g	SAC	62	712	11.5	11	63	0.089	1.0	0.385
326.	GRANT, Gr.	g	PHI	68	891	13.1	14	69	0.077	1.0	0.440
327.	BATTLE, K.	f	GS	16	92	5.8	4	16	0.174	1.0	0.647
328.	DAVIS, B.	f	DAL	33	429	13.0	4	33	0.077	1.0	0.442
329.	MAYS, T.	g	ATL	2	32	16.0	1	2	0.063	1.0	0.429
330.	OLIVER, J.	g/f	CLE	27	252	9.3	9	27	0.107	1.0	0.398
331.	PRITCHARD, K.	g	BOS	11	136	12.4	1	11	0.081	1.0	0.471
332.	THOMPSON, S.	g	SAC	19	91	4.8	11	19	0.209	1.0	0.378
333.	SELLERS, B.	f/c	DET	43	226	5.3	15	42	0.186	1.0	0.466
334.	JEPSEN, L.	c	SAC	31	87	2.8	12	30	0.345	1.0	0.375
335.	KIMBLE, B.	f	LAC	34	277	8.2	13	32	0.116	0.9	0.396
336.	GREEN, R.	g	BOS	26	367	14.1	3	24	0.065	0.9	0.447

(NAME)	FT PCT	3-PT SHOTS MADE	3-PT SHOTS TRIED	ASTs	STLs	TURN- OVERS	BLKs	PTs
(DREILING, G.)	0.750	1	1	25	10	31	16	117
(TOLBERT, T.)	0.550	2	8	21	10	20	6	90
(COOK, A.)	0.667	0	0	2	5	3	4	34
(LYNCH, K.)	0.761	3	8	83	37	44	9	224
(McCORMICK, T.)	0.667	0	0	9	2	8	0	42
(TUCKER, T.)	0.800	19	48	27	21	14	3	155
(CONLON, M.)	0.750	0	0	12	9	27	7	120
(CORCHIANI, C.)	0.875	10	37	141	45	74	2	255
(WILEY, M.)	0.686	14	42	180	47	60	3	204
(DAVIS, W.)	0.872	5	16	68	29	45	1	457
(DOUGLAS, S.)	0.682	1	10	172	25	68	9	308
(GEORGE, T.)	0.821	1	6	162	41	82	3	418
(BATTLE, J.)	0.848	2	17	159	36	91	5	779
(BROWN, T.)	0.727	19	63	48	30	35	5	271
(VRANKOVIC, S.)	0.583	0	0	5	0	10	17	37
(JACKSON, C.)	0.870	31	94	192	44	117	4	837
(GARRICK, T.)	0.692	1	4	98	36	44	4	137
(PACK, R.)	0.803	0	10	140	40	92	4	332
(RANDALL, M.)	0.744	3	16	33	12	25	3	171
(VANDEWEGHE, K.)	0.803	26	66	57	15	27	8	467
(QUINNETT, B.)	0.615	13	41	12	16	16	8	115
(TURNER, A.)	0.792	1	16	177	57	84	2	284
(SCHEFFLER, S.)	0.750	0	0	0	3	1	1	21
(RIVERS, Da.)	0.909	0	1	21	7	17	1	30
(BROWN, R.)	0.655	0	6	59	35	42	12	192
(KING, R.)	0.756	0	1	12	4	18	5	88
(PAXSON, J.)	0.784	12	44	241	49	44	9	555
(YOUNG, D.)	0.851	23	70	172	46	47	4	280
(BROOKS, S.)	0.810	32	90	205	66	51	7	417
(SMITH, To.)	0.653	0	11	109	39	50	8	275
(GREEN, Se.)	0.536	2	10	22	13	27	6	141
(JOHNSON, A.)	0.654	4	15	266	61	110	9	386
(McCANN, B.)	0.308	0	1	6	6	7	4	30
(HANSEN, B.)	0.364	7	27	69	27	28	3	173
(AUSTIN, I.)	0.633	0	0	5	2	8	2	61
(PAYNE, K.)	0.692	5	12	17	16	19	8	144
(BURTT, S.)	0.704	1	6	59	16	33	4	187
(KNIGHT, N.)	0.688	4	13	112	24	58	3	243
(COPA, T.)	0.308	0	0	3	2	8	6	48
(DAILEY, Q.)	0.813	0	1	4	5	10	1	31
(BARROS, D.)	0.760	83	186	125	51	56	4	619
(MURDOCK, E.)	0.754	5	26	92	30	50	7	203
(BROOKS, K.)	0.810	2	11	11	8	18	2	105
(MORTON, J.)	0.842	2	16	32	13	28	1	106
(LES, J.)	0.809	45	131	143	31	42	3	231
(GRANT, Gr.)	0.833	7	18	217	45	46	2	225
(BATTLE, K.)	0.833	0	1	4	2	4	2	32
(DAVIS, B.)	0.733	5	18	66	11	27	3	92
(MAYS, T.)	1.000	3	6	1	0	3	0	17
(OLIVER, J.)	0.773	1	9	20	9	9	2	96
(PRITCHARD, K.)	0.778	0	3	30	3	11	4	46
(THOMPSON, S.)	0.375	0	1	8	6	5	3	31
(SELLERS, B.)	0.769	0	1	14	1	15	10	102
(JEPSEN, L.)	0.636	0	1	1	1	3	5	25
(KIMBLE, B.)	0.645	4	13	17	10	15	6	112
(GREEN, R.)	0.722	1	4	68	17	18	1	106

1991–1992 REGULAR-SEASON STATISTICAL RESULTS
NBA PLAYERS ORDERED BY REBOUNDS PER GAME

	NAME	POS	TEAM	GMs	MINs	MINs per GM	OFF REBs	REBs	REBs per MIN	REBs per GM	FG PCT
337.	WHATLEY, E.	g	POR	23	209	9.1	6	21	0.101	0.9	0.412
338.	JAMERSON, D.	f	HOU	48	378	7.9	22	43	0.114	0.9	0.414
339.	OLIVER, B.	g	PHI	34	279	8.2	10	30	0.108	0.9	0.330
340.	MONROE, R.	g	ATL	38	313	8.2	12	33	0.105	0.9	0.368
341.	RUDD, D.	g	UT	65	538	8.3	15	54	0.100	0.8	0.399
342.	ELLIS, L.	f	LAC	29	103	3.6	12	24	0.233	0.8	0.340
343.	HENSON, S.	g	MIL	50	386	7.7	17	41	0.106	0.8	0.361
344.	CROWDER, C.	g/f	UT	51	328	6.4	16	41	0.125	0.8	0.384
345.	PHILLS, B.	g	CLE	10	65	6.5	4	8	0.123	0.8	0.429
346.	WINCHESTER, K.	f	NY	19	81	4.3	6	15	0.185	0.8	0.433
347.	PERRY, E.	g	CHA	50	437	8.7	14	39	0.089	0.8	0.380
348.	LEE, D.	g	NJ	46	307	6.7	17	35	0.114	0.8	0.431
349.	OWENS, K.	f	LAL	20	80	4.0	8	15	0.188	0.8	0.281
350.	SUTTON, G.	g	SA	67	601	9.0	6	47	0.078	0.7	0.388
351.	MAYES, Th.	g	LAC	24	255	10.6	3	16	0.063	0.7	0.303
352.	SPARROW, R.	g	LAL	46	489	10.6	3	28	0.057	0.6	0.384
353.	ANSLEY, M.	f	CHA	10	45	4.5	2	6	0.133	0.6	0.444
354.	THOMAS, C.	g	DET	37	156	4.2	6	22	0.141	0.6	0.353
355.	KOFOED, B.	g	SEA	44	239	5.4	6	26	0.109	0.6	0.472
356.	BLANKS, L.	g	DET	43	189	4.4	9	22	0.116	0.5	0.455
357.	HENDERSON, G.	g	DET	16	96	6.0	1	8	0.083	0.5	0.375
358.	HODGES, C.	g	CHI	56	555	9.9	7	24	0.043	0.4	0.384
359.	WITTMAN, R.	g	IND	24	115	4.8	1	9	0.078	0.4	0.421

(NAME)	FT PCT	3-PT SHOTS MADE	3-PT SHOTS TRIED	ASTs	STLs	TURN-OVERS	BLKs	PTs
(WHATLEY, E.)	0.871	0	4	34	14	14	3	69
(JAMERSON, D.)	0.926	8	28	33	17	24	0	191
(OLIVER, B.)	0.682	0	4	20	10	24	2	81
(MONROE, R.)	0.826	6	27	27	12	23	2	131
(RUDD, D.)	0.762	11	47	109	15	49	1	193
(ELLIS, L.)	0.474	0	0	1	6	11	9	43
(HENSON, S.)	0.793	23	48	82	15	40	1	150
(CROWDER, C.)	0.833	13	30	17	7	13	2	114
(PHILLS, B.)	0.636	0	2	4	3	8	1	31
(WINCHESTER, K.)	0.800	1	2	8	2	2	2	35
(PERRY, E.)	0.659	1	7	78	34	50	3	126
(LEE, D.)	0.526	10	37	22	11	12	1	120
(OWENS, K.)	0.800	0	0	3	5	2	4	26
(SUTTON, G.)	0.756	26	89	91	26	70	9	246
(MAYES, Th.)	0.667	15	41	35	16	31	2	99
(SPARROW, R.)	0.615	3	15	83	12	33	5	127
(ANSLEY, M.)	0.833	0	0	2	0	3	0	21
(THOMAS, C.)	0.667	2	17	22	4	17	1	48
(KOFOED, B.)	0.577	1	7	51	2	20	2	66
(BLANKS, L.)	0.727	6	16	19	14	14	1	64
(HENDERSON, G.)	0.818	3	8	10	3	8	0	36
(HODGES, C.)	0.941	36	96	54	14	22	1	238
(WITTMAN, R.)	0.500	0	0	11	2	3	0	17

1991-92 REGULAR-SEASON STATISTICAL RESULTS
NBA PLAYERS ORDERED BY STEALS PER GAME

	NAME	POS	TEAM	GMs	MINs	MINs per GM	STLs	STLs per MIN	STLs per GM	FG PCT
1.	STOCKTON, J.	g	UT	82	3002	36.6	244	0.081	2.98	0.482
2.	WILLIAMS, M.	g	IND	79	2750	34.8	233	0.085	2.95	0.490
3.	ROBERTSON, A.	g	MIL	82	2463	30.0	210	0.085	2.56	0.430
4.	BLAYLOCK, M.	g	NJ	72	2548	35.4	170	0.067	2.36	0.432
5.	ROBINSON, D.	c	SA	68	2564	37.7	158	0.062	2.32	0.551
6.	JORDAN, M.	g	CHI	80	3102	38.8	182	0.059	2.28	0.519
7.	MULLIN, C.	f	GS	81	3346	41.3	173	0.052	2.14	0.524
8.	BOGUES, M.	g	CHA	82	2790	34.0	170	0.061	2.07	0.472
9.	STRICKLAND, R.	g	SA	57	2053	36.0	118	0.058	2.07	0.455
10.	THREATT, S	g	LAL	82	3070	37.4	168	0.055	2.05	0.489
11.	MACON, M.	g	DEN	76	2304	30.3	154	0.067	2.03	0.375
12.	HARDAWAY, T.	g	GS	81	3332	41.1	164	0.049	2.02	0.461
13.	GILL, K.	g/f	CHA	79	2906	36.8	154	0.053	1.95	0.467
14.	HORNACEK, J.	g	PHX	81	3078	38.0	158	0.051	1.95	0.512
15.	HAWKINS, H.	g	PHI	81	3013	37.2	157	0.052	1.94	0.462
16.	PIPPEN, S.	f	CHI	82	3164	38.6	155	0.049	1.89	0.506
17.	RIVERS, Do.	g	LAC	59	1657	28.1	111	0.067	1.88	0.424
18.	ADAMS, M.	g	WAS	78	2795	35.8	145	0.052	1.86	0.393
19.	HARPER, R.	g	LAC	82	3144	38.3	152	0.048	1.85	0.440
20.	WILLIAMS, R.	f	DEN	81	2623	32.4	148	0.056	1.83	0.471
21.	DREXLER, C.	g	POR	76	2751	36.2	138	0.050	1.82	0.470
22.	BARKLEY, C.	f	PHI	75	2881	38.4	136	0.047	1.81	0.552
23.	OLAJUWON, H.	c	HOU	70	2636	37.7	127	0.048	1.81	0.502
24.	PAYTON, G.	g	SEA	81	2549	31.5	147	0.058	1.81	0.451
25.	McMILLAN, N.	g/f	SEA	72	1652	22.9	129	0.078	1.79	0.437
26.	GRANT, Ga.	g	LAC	78	2049	26.3	138	0.067	1.77	0.462
27.	SIMMONS, L.	f	SAC	78	2895	37.1	135	0.047	1.73	0.454
28.	LONG, G.	f	MIA	82	3063	37.4	139	0.045	1.70	0.494
29.	HUMPHRIES, J.	g	MIL	71	2261	31.8	119	0.053	1.68	0.470
30.	MORRIS, C.	f	NJ	77	2394	31.1	129	0.054	1.68	0.477
31.	MANNING, D.	f	LAC	82	2904	35.4	135	0.047	1.65	0.542
32.	ANDERSON, N.	g/f	ORL	60	2203	36.7	97	0.044	1.62	0.463
33.	WEBB, S.	g	SAC	77	2724	35.4	125	0.046	1.62	0.445
34.	MARCIULIONIS, S.	g	GS	72	2117	29.4	116	0.055	1.61	0.538
35.	MAJERLE, D.	g/f	PHX	82	2853	34.8	131	0.046	1.60	0.478
36.	HARPER, D.	g	DAL	65	2252	34.6	101	0.045	1.55	0.443
37.	PORTER, T.	g	POR	82	2784	34.0	127	0.046	1.55	0.462
38.	DIVAC, V.	c	LAL	36	979	27.2	55	0.056	1.53	0.495
39.	LEWIS, R.	g	BOS	82	3070	37.4	125	0.041	1.52	0.503
40.	WINGATE, D.	g	WAS	81	2127	26.3	123	0.058	1.52	0.465
41.	AUGMON, S.	g/f	ATL	82	2505	30.5	124	0.050	1.51	0.489
42.	THOMAS, I.	g	DET	78	2918	37.4	118	0.040	1.51	0.446
43.	JOHNSON, K.	g	PHX	78	2899	37.2	116	0.040	1.49	0.479
44.	CHEEKS, M.	g	ATL	56	1086	19.4	83	0.076	1.48	0.462
45.	KERSEY, J.	f	POR	77	2553	33.2	114	0.045	1.48	0.467
46.	LEVER, F.	g	DAL	31	884	28.5	46	0.052	1.48	0.387
47.	RICHARDSON, P.	g	MIN	82	2922	35.6	119	0.041	1.45	0.466
48.	WORTHY, J.	f	LAL	54	2108	39.0	76	0.036	1.41	0.447
49.	JACKSON, M.	g	NY	81	2461	30.4	112	0.046	1.38	0.491
50.	REYNOLDS, J.	g/f	ORL	46	1159	25.2	63	0.054	1.37	0.380
51.	MALONE, K.	f	UT	81	3054	37.7	108	0.035	1.33	0.526
52.	PRICE, M.	g	CLE	72	2138	29.7	94	0.044	1.31	0.488
53.	MAXWELL, V.	g	HOU	80	2700	33.7	104	0.039	1.30	0.413
54.	ROBINSON, R.	g	ATL	81	2220	27.4	105	0.047	1.30	0.456
55.	MILLER, R.	g	IND	82	3120	38.0	105	0.034	1.28	0.501
56.	PETROVIC, D.	g	NJ	82	3027	36.9	105	0.035	1.28	0.508

(NAME)	FT PCT	3-PT SHOTS MADE	3-PT SHOTS TRIED	REBs	ASTs	TURN-OVERS	BLKs	PTs
(STOCKTON, J.)	0.842	83	204	270	1126	286	22	1297
(WILLIAMS, M.)	0.871	8	33	282	647	240	22	1188
(ROBERTSON, A.)	0.763	67	210	350	360	223	32	1010
(BLAYLOCK, M.)	0.712	12	54	269	492	152	40	996
(ROBINSON, D.)	0.701	1	8	829	181	182	305	157
(JORDAN, M.)	0.832	27	100	511	489	200	75	2404
(MULLIN, C.)	0.833	64	175	450	286	202	62	2074
(BOGUES, M.)	0.783	2	27	235	743	156	6	730
(STRICKLAND, R.)	0.687	5	15	265	491	160	17	787
(THREATT, S)	0.831	20	62	253	593	182	16	1240
(MACON, M.)	0.730	4	30	220	168	155	14	805
(HARDAWAY, T.)	0.766	127	376	310	807	267	13	1893
(GILL, K.)	0.745	6	25	402	329	180	46	1622
(HORNACEK, J.)	0.886	83	189	407	411	170	31	1632
(HAWKINS, H.)	0.874	91	229	271	248	189	43	1536
(PIPPEN, S.)	0.760	16	80	630	572	253	93	1720
(RIVERS, Do.)	0.832	26	92	147	233	92	19	641
(ADAMS, M.)	0.869	125	386	310	594	212	9	1408
(HARPER, R.)	0.736	64	211	447	417	252	72	1495
(WILLIAMS, R.)	0.803	56	156	405	235	173	68	1474
(DREXLER, C.)	0.794	114	338	500	512	240	70	1903
(BARKLEY, C.)	0.695	32	137	830	308	235	44	1730
(OLAJUWON, H.)	0.766	0	1	845	157	187	304	1510
(PAYTON, G.)	0.669	3	23	295	506	174	21	764
(McMILLAN, N.)	0.643	27	98	252	359	112	29	435
(GRANT, Ga.)	0.815	15	51	184	538	187	14	609
(SIMMONS, L.)	0.770	1	5	634	337	218	132	1336
(LONG, G.)	0.807	6	22	91	225	185	40	1212
(HUMPHRIES, J.)	0.783	42	144	184	466	148	13	991
(MORRIS, C.)	0.714	22	110	494	197	171	81	879
(MANNING, D.)	0.725	0	5	564	285	210	122	1579
(ANDERSON, N.)	0.667	30	85	384	163	125	33	1196
(WEBB, S.)	0.859	73	199	223	547	229	24	1231
(MARCIULIONIS, S.)	0.788	3	10	208	243	193	10	1361
(MAJERLE, D.)	0.756	87	228	483	274	101	43	1418
(HARPER, D.)	0.759	58	186	170	373	154	17	1152
(PORTER, T.)	0.856	128	324	255	477	188	12	1485
(DIVAC, V.)	0.768	5	19	247	60	88	35	405
(LEWIS, R.)	0.851	5	21	394	185	136	105	1703
(WINGATE, D.)	0.719	1	18	269	247	124	21	638
(AUGMON, S.)	0.666	1	6	420	201	181	27	1094
(THOMAS, I.)	0.773	25	86	247	560	252	15	1445
(JOHNSON, K.)	0.807	10	46	292	836	272	23	1536
(CHEEKS, M.)	0.605	3	6	95	185	36	0	259
(KERSEY, J.)	0.664	1	8	633	243	151	71	971
(LEVER, F.)	0.750	17	52	161	107	36	12	347
(RICHARDSON, P.)	0.691	53	155	301	685	204	25	1350
(WORTHY, J.)	0.814	9	43	305	252	127	23	1075
(JACKSON, M.)	0.770	11	43	305	694	211	13	916
(REYNOLDS, J.)	0.836	3	24	149	151	96	17	555
(MALONE, K.)	0.778	3	17	909	241	248	51	2272
(PRICE, M.)	0.947	101	261	173	535	159	12	1247
(MAXWELL, V.)	0.772	162	473	243	326	178	28	1372
(ROBINSON, R.)	0.636	34	104	219	446	206	24	1055
(MILLER, R.)	0.858	129	341	318	314	157	26	1695
(PETROVIC, D.)	0.808	123	277	258	252	215	11	1691

1991–92 REGULAR-SEASON STATISTICAL RESULTS
NBA PLAYERS ORDERED BY STEALS PER GAME

	NAME	POS	TEAM	GMs	MINs	MINs per GM	STLs	STLs per MIN	STLs per GM	FG PCT
57.	SCOTT, B.	g	LAL	82	2679	32.7	105	0.039	1.28	0.458
58.	SMITH, K.	g	HOU	81	2735	33.8	104	0.038	1.28	0.475
59.	NEWMAN, J.	f/g	CHA	55	1651	30.0	70	0.042	1.27	0.477
60.	GARLAND, W.	g	DEN	78	2209	28.3	98	0.044	1.26	0.444
61.	STARKS, J.	g	NY	82	2118	25.8	103	0.049	1.26	0.449
62.	EHLO, C.	g/f	CLE	63	2016	32.0	78	0.039	1.24	0.453
63.	WILKINS, D.	f	ATL	42	1601	38.1	52	0.033	1.24	0.464
64.	GRAHAM, P.	g	ATL	78	1718	22.0	96	0.056	1.23	0.447
65.	GRANT, Ho.	f	CHI	81	2859	35.3	100	0.035	1.23	0.579
66.	EDWARDS, K.	g	MIA	81	1840	22.7	99	0.054	1.22	0.454
67.	CAGE, M.	f	SEA	82	2461	30.0	99	0.040	1.21	0.566
68.	CURRY, D.	g	CHA	77	2020	26.2	93	0.046	1.21	0.486
69.	CONNER, L.	g	MIL	81	1420	17.5	97	0.068	1.20	0.431
70.	BONNER, A.	f	SAC	79	2287	28.9	94	0.041	1.19	0.447
71.	McKEY, D.	f	SEA	52	1757	33.8	61	0.035	1.17	0.472
72.	GRANT, Ha.	f	WAS	64	2388	37.3	74	0.031	1.16	0.479
73.	RICHMOND, M.	g	SAC	80	3095	38.7	92	0.030	1.15	0.468
74.	RICE, G.	f	MIA	79	3007	38.1	90	0.030	1.14	0.469
75.	OWENS, B.	g/f	GS	80	2510	31.4	90	0.036	1.13	0.525
76.	GREEN, A.C.	f	LAL	82	2902	35.4	91	0.031	1.11	0.476
77.	SCOTT, D.	f	ORL	18	608	33.8	20	0.033	1.11	0.402
78.	PIERCE, R.	g	SEA	78	2658	34.1	86	0.032	1.10	0.475
79.	DAWKINS, J.	g	PHI	82	2815	34.3	89	0.032	1.09	0.437
80.	KEMP, S.	f/c	SEA	64	1808	28.2	70	0.039	1.09	0.504
81.	CAMPBELL, T.	f/g	MIN	78	2441	31.3	84	0.034	1.08	0.464
82.	ANDERSON, G.	f	DEN	82	2793	34.1	88	0.032	1.07	0.456
83.	EWING, P.	c	NY	82	3150	38.4	88	0.028	1.07	0.522
84.	BOWIE, A.	g/f	ORL	52	1721	33.1	55	0.032	1.06	0.493
85.	BROWN, D.	g	BOS	31	883	28.5	33	0.037	1.06	0.426
86.	ANDERSON, K.	g	NJ	64	1086	17.0	67	0.062	1.05	0.390
87.	ANDERSON, Ro.	f	PHI	82	2432	29.7	86	0.035	1.05	0.465
88.	ROBINSON, C.	f	POR	82	2124	25.9	85	0.040	1.04	0.466
89.	CORBIN, T.	f	UT	80	2207	27.6	82	0.037	1.02	0.481
90.	ELLIOTT, S.	f	SA	82	3120	38.0	84	0.027	1.02	0.494
91.	PERKINS, S.	f/c	LAL	63	2332	37.0	64	0.027	1.02	0.450
92.	EDWARDS, T.	g/f	UT	81	2283	28.2	81	0.036	1.00	0.522
93.	BRANDON, T.	g	CLE	82	1605	19.6	81	0.051	0.99	0.419
94.	JOHNSON, L.	f	CHA	82	3047	37.2	81	0.027	0.99	0.490
95.	NANCE, L.	f	CLE	81	2880	35.6	80	0.028	0.99	0.539
96.	SKILES, S.	g	ORL	75	2377	31.7	74	0.031	0.99	0.414
97.	SMITH, S.	g	MIA	61	1806	29.6	59	0.033	0.97	0.454
98.	FOX, R.	g/f	BOS	81	1535	19.0	78	0.051	0.96	0.459
99.	REID, J.R.	c/f	CHA	51	1257	24.6	49	0.039	0.96	0.490
100.	ANDERSON, W.	g/f	SA	57	1889	33.1	54	0.029	0.95	0.456
101.	ELLISON, P.	c	WAS	66	2511	38.0	62	0.025	0.94	0.539
102.	HOPSON, D.	g/f	SAC	71	1314	18.5	67	0.051	0.94	0.465
103.	BIRD, L.	f	BOS	45	1662	36.9	42	0.025	0.93	0.466
104.	WILKINS, G.	g	NY	82	2344	28.6	76	0.032	0.93	0.447
105.	BRICKOWSKI, F.	f	MIL	65	1556	23.9	60	0.039	0.92	0.524
106.	SMITH, La.	g	WAS	48	708	14.7	44	0.062	0.92	0.407
107.	GAMBLE, K.	g/f	BOS	82	2496	30.4	75	0.030	0.91	0.529
108.	AINGE, D.	g	POR	81	1595	19.7	73	0.046	0.90	0.442
109.	COLES, B.	g	MIA	81	1976	24.4	73	0.037	0.90	0.455
110.	GARRICK, T.	g	DAL	40	549	13.7	36	0.066	0.90	0.413
111.	JOHNSON, B.	f	HOU	80	2202	27.5	72	0.033	0.90	0.458
112.	MALONE, M.	c	MIL	82	2511	30.6	74	0.030	0.90	0.474

(NAME)	FT PCT	3-PT SHOTS MADE	3-PT SHOTS TRIED	REBs	ASTs	TURN-OVERS	BLKs	PTs
(SCOTT, B.)	0.839	54	157	310	226	119	28	1218
(SMITH, K.)	0.866	54	137	177	562	227	7	1137
(NEWMAN, J.)	0.766	13	46	179	146	129	14	839
(GARLAND, W.)	0.859	9	28	190	411	175	22	846
(STARKS, J.)	0.778	94	270	191	276	150	18	1139
(EHLO, C.)	0.707	69	167	307	238	104	22	776
(WILKINS, D.)	0.835	37	128	295	158	122	24	1179
(GRAHAM, P.)	0.741	55	141	231	175	91	21	791
(GRANT, Ho.)	0.741	0	2	807	217	98	131	1149
(EDWARDS, K.)	0.848	7	32	211	170	120	20	819
(CAGE, M.)	0.620	0	5	728	92	78	55	720
(CURRY, D.)	0.836	74	183	259	177	134	20	1209
(CONNER, L.)	0.704	0	7	184	294	79	10	287
(BONNER, A.)	0.627	1	4	485	125	133	26	740
(McKEY, D.)	0.847	19	50	268	120	114	47	777
(GRANT, Ha.)	0.800	1	8	432	170	109	27	1155
(RICHMOND, M.)	0.813	103	268	319	411	247	34	1803
(RICE, G.)	0.837	155	396	394	184	145	35	1765
(OWENS, B.)	0.654	1	9	639	188	179	65	1141
(GREEN, A.C.)	0.744	12	56	762	117	111	36	1116
(SCOTT, D.)	0.901	29	89	66	35	31	9	359
(PIERCE, R.)	0.917	33	123	233	241	189	20	1690
(DAWKINS, J.)	0.882	36	101	227	567	183	5	988
(KEMP, S.)	0.748	0	3	665	86	156	124	994
(CAMPBELL, T.)	0.803	13	37	286	229	165	31	1307
(ANDERSON, G.)	0.623	0	4	941	78	201	65	945
(EWING, P.)	0.738	1	6	921	156	209	245	1970
(BOWIE, A.)	0.860	17	44	245	163	107	38	758
(BROWN, D.)	0.769	5	22	79	164	59	7	363
(ANDERSON, K.)	0.745	3	13	127	203	97	9	450
(ANDERSON, Ro.)	0.877	42	127	278	135	109	11	1123
(ROBINSON, C.)	0.664	1	11	416	137	154	107	1016
(CORBIN, T.)	0.866	0	4	472	140	97	20	780
(ELLIOTT, S.)	0.861	25	82	439	214	152	29	1338
(PERKINS, S.)	0.817	15	69	556	141	83	62	1041
(EDWARDS, T.)	0.774	39	103	298	137	122	46	1018
(BRANDON, T.)	0.807	1	23	162	316	136	22	605
(JOHNSON, L.)	0.829	5	22	899	292	160	51	1576
(NANCE, L.)	0.822	0	6	670	232	87	243	1375
(SKILES, S.)	0.895	91	250	202	544	233	5	1057
(SMITH, S.)	0.748	40	125	188	278	152	19	729
(FOX, R.)	0.755	23	70	220	126	123	30	644
(REID, J.R.)	0.705	0	3	317	81	84	23	560
(ANDERSON, W.)	0.775	13	56	300	302	40	51	744
(ELLISON, P.)	0.728	1	3	740	190	196	177	1322
(HOPSON, D.)	0.708	12	47	206	102	100	39	743
(BIRD, L.)	0.926	52	128	434	306	125	33	908
(WILKINS, G.)	0.730	38	108	206	219	113	17	1016
(BRICKOWSKI, F.)	0.767	3	6	344	122	112	23	740
(SMITH, La.)	0.804	2	21	81	99	63	1	247
(GAMBLE, K.)	0.885	9	31	286	219	97	37	1108
(AINGE, D.)	0.824	78	230	148	202	70	13	784
(COLES, B.)	0.824	10	52	189	366	167	13	816
(GARRICK, T.)	0.692	1	4	56	98	44	4	137
(JOHNSON, B.)	0.727	1	9	312	158	104	49	685
(MALONE, M.)	0.786	3	8	744	93	150	64	1279

1991–92 REGULAR-SEASON STATISTICAL RESULTS
NBA PLAYERS ORDERED BY STEALS PER GAME

	NAME	POS	TEAM	GMs	MINs	MINs per GM	STLs	STLs per MIN	STLs per GM	FG PCT
113.	SHAW, B.	g	MIA	63	1423	22.6	57	0.040	0.90	0.407
114.	VINCENT, S.	g	ORL	39	885	22.7	35	0.040	0.90	0.430
115.	DAUGHERTY, B.	c	CLE	73	2643	36.2	65	0.025	0.89	0.570
116.	HILL, T.	c/f	GS	82	1886	23.0	73	0.039	0.89	0.522
117.	WILEY, M.	g	ATL	53	870	16.4	47	0.054	0.89	0.430
118.	WILLIS, K.	f/c	ATL	81	2962	36.6	72	0.024	0.89	0.483
119.	CORCHIANI, C.	g	ORL	51	741	14.5	45	0.061	0.88	0.399
120.	GLASS, G.	g	MIN	75	1822	24.3	66	0.036	0.88	0.440
121.	JOHNSON, A.	g	HOU	69	1235	17.6	61	0.049	0.88	0.479
122.	LIBERTY, M.	f/g	DEN	75	1527	20.4	66	0.043	0.88	0.443
123.	TUCKER, T.	g	SA	24	415	17.3	21	0.051	0.88	0.465
124.	DUMARS, J.	g	DET	82	3192	38.9	71	0.022	0.87	0.448
125.	ELIE, M.	g/f	GS	79	1677	21.2	68	0.041	0.86	0.521
126.	PARISH, R.	c	BOS	79	2285	28.9	68	0.030	0.86	0.536
127.	PINCKNEY, E.	f	BOS	81	1917	23.7	70	0.037	0.86	0.537
128.	VOLKOV, A.	f	ATL	77	1516	19.7	66	0.044	0.86	0.441
129.	WALKER, D.	g	DET	74	1541	20.8	63	0.041	0.85	0.423
130.	WILLIAMS, Br.	f	ORL	48	905	18.9	41	0.045	0.85	0.528
131.	PERSON, C.	f	IND	81	2923	36.1	68	0.023	0.84	0.480
132.	SMITH, C.	f/c	LAC	49	1310	26.7	41	0.031	0.84	0.466
133.	CHAMBERS, T.	f	PHX	69	1948	28.2	57	0.029	0.83	0.431
134.	COLEMAN, D.	f	NJ	65	2207	34.0	54	0.025	0.83	0.504
135.	CUMMINGS, T.	f	SA	70	2149	30.7	58	0.027	0.83	0.488
136.	RODMAN, D.	f	DET	82	3301	40.3	68	0.021	0.83	0.539
137.	WEST, D.	g	MIN	80	2540	31.7	66	0.026	0.83	0.518
138.	OAKLEY, C.	f	NY	82	2309	28.2	67	0.029	0.82	0.522
139.	SMITH, Do.	f	DAL	76	1707	22.5	62	0.036	0.82	0.415
140.	TURNER, A.	g	WAS	70	871	12.4	57	0.065	0.81	0.425
141.	BROOKS, S.	g	MIN	82	1082	13.2	66	0.061	0.80	0.447
142.	TEAGLE, T.	f	LAL	82	1602	19.5	66	0.041	0.80	0.452
143.	BAGLEY, J.	g	BOS	73	1742	23.9	57	0.033	0.78	0.441
144.	GRAYER, J.	g	MIL	82	1659	20.2	64	0.039	0.78	0.449
145.	SCHREMPF, D.	f	IND	80	2605	32.6	62	0.024	0.78	0.536
146.	WILLIAMS, Bu.	f	POR	80	2519	31.5	62	0.025	0.78	0.604
147.	SANDERS, M.	f	CLE	31	633	20.4	24	0.038	0.77	0.571
148.	MOORE, T.	f	DAL	42	782	18.6	32	0.041	0.76	0.400
149.	TISDALE, W.	f	SAC	72	2521	35.0	55	0.022	0.76	0.501
150.	WILLIAMS, Jo.	f/c	CLE	80	2432	30.4	60	0.025	0.75	0.503
151.	CATLEDGE, T.	f	ORL	78	2430	31.2	58	0.024	0.74	0.496
152.	FERRELL, D.	f	ATL	66	1598	24.2	49	0.031	0.74	0.524
153.	YOUNG, D.	g	LAC	62	1023	16.5	46	0.045	0.74	0.392
154.	ANTHONY, G.	g	NY	82	1510	18.4	59	0.039	0.72	0.370
155.	EACKLES, L.	f	WAS	65	1463	22.5	47	0.032	0.72	0.468
156.	GATTISON, K.	f/c	CHA	82	2223	27.1	59	0.027	0.72	0.529
157.	ELLIS, D.	f	MIL	81	2191	27.0	57	0.026	0.70	0.469
158.	FLOYD, S.	g	HOU	82	1662	20.3	57	0.034	0.70	0.406
159.	McDANIEL, X.	f	NY	82	2344	28.6	57	0.024	0.70	0.478
160.	MALONE, J.	g	UT	81	2922	36.1	56	0.019	0.69	0.511
161.	NORMAN, K.	f	LAC	77	2009	26.1	53	0.026	0.69	0.490
162.	AGUIRRE, M.	f	DET	75	1582	21.1	51	0.032	0.68	0.431
163.	ASKINS, K.	g/f	MIA	59	843	14.3	40	0.048	0.68	0.410
164.	BARROS, D.	g	SEA	75	1331	17.7	51	0.038	0.68	0.483
165.	BUECHLER, J.	f	GS	28	290	10.4	19	0.066	0.68	0.409
166.	BURTON, W.	g/f	MIA	68	1585	23.3	46	0.029	0.68	0.450
167.	CHAPMAN, R.	g	WAS	22	567	25.8	15	0.027	0.68	0.448
168.	FLEMING, V.	g	IND	82	1737	21.2	56	0.032	0.68	0.482

(NAME)	FT PCT	3-PT SHOTS MADE	3-PT SHOTS TRIED	REBs	ASTs	TURN-OVERS	BLKs	PTs
(SHAW, B.)	0.791	5	23	204	250	99	22	495
(VINCENT, S.)	0.846	1	13	101	148	72	4	411
(DAUGHERTY, B.)	0.777	0	2	760	262	185	78	1566
(HILL, T.)	0.694	0	1	593	47	106	43	671
(WILEY, M.)	0.686	14	42	81	180	60	3	204
(WILLIS, K.)	0.804	6	37	1258	173	197	54	1480
(CORCHIANI, C.)	0.875	10	37	78	141	74	2	255
(GLASS, G.)	0.616	16	54	260	175	103	30	859
(JOHNSON, A.)	0.654	4	15	80	266	110	9	386
(LIBERTY, M.)	0.728	17	50	308	58	90	29	698
(TUCKER, T.)	0.800	19	48	37	27	14	3	155
(DUMARS, J.)	0.867	49	120	188	375	193	12	1635
(ELIE, M.)	0.852	23	70	227	174	83	15	620
(PARISH, R.)	0.772	0	0	705	70	131	97	1115
(PINCKNEY, E.)	0.812	0	1	564	62	73	56	613
(VOLKOV, A.)	0.631	35	110	265	250	102	30	662
(WALKER, D.)	0.619	0	10	238	205	79	18	387
(WILLIAMS, Br.)	0.669	0	0	272	33	86	53	437
(PERSON, C.)	0.675	132	354	426	382	216	18	1497
(SMITH, C.)	0.785	0	6	301	56	69	98	714
(CHAMBERS, T.)	0.830	18	49	401	142	103	37	1128
(COLEMAN, D.)	0.763	23	76	618	205	248	98	1289
(CUMMINGS, T.)	0.711	5	13	631	102	115	34	1210
(RODMAN, D.)	0.600	32	101	1530	191	140	70	800
(WEST, D.)	0.805	4	23	257	281	120	26	1116
(OAKLEY, C.)	0.735	0	3	700	133	123	15	506
(SMITH, Do.)	0.736	0	11	391	129	97	34	671
(TURNER, A.)	0.792	1	16	90	177	84	2	284
(BROOKS, S.)	0.810	32	90	99	205	51	7	417
(TEAGLE, T.)	0.767	1	4	183	113	114	9	880
(BAGLEY, J.)	0.716	10	42	161	480	148	4	524
(GRAYER, J.)	0.667	19	66	257	150	105	13	739
(SCHREMPF, D.)	0.828	23	71	770	312	191	37	1380
(WILLIAMS, Bu.)	0.754	0	1	704	108	130	41	901
(SANDERS, M.)	0.766	1	3	96	53	22	10	221
(MOORE, T.)	0.833	30	84	82	48	44	4	355
(TISDALE, W.)	0.763	0	2	469	106	124	79	1195
(WILLIAMS, Jo.)	0.752	0	4	607	196	83	182	952
(CATLEDGE, T.)	0.694	0	4	549	109	138	16	1154
(FERRELL, D.)	0.762	11	33	210	92	99	17	839
(YOUNG, D.)	0.851	23	70	75	172	47	4	280
(ANTHONY, G.)	0.741	8	55	136	314	98	9	447
(EACKLES, L.)	0.743	7	35	178	125	75	7	856
(GATTISON, K.)	0.688	0	2	580	131	140	69	1042
(ELLIS, D.)	0.774	138	329	253	104	119	18	1272
(FLOYD, S.)	0.794	37	123	150	239	128	21	744
(McDANIEL, X.)	0.714	12	39	460	149	147	24	1125
(MALONE, J.)	0.898	1	12	233	180	140	5	1639
(NORMAN, K.)	0.535	4	28	448	125	100	66	929
(AGUIRRE, M.)	0.687	15	71	236	126	105	11	851
(ASKINS, K.)	0.703	25	73	142	38	47	15	219
(BARROS, D.)	0.760	83	186	81	125	56	4	619
(BUECHLER, J.)	0.571	0	1	52	23	13	7	70
(BURTON, W.)	0.800	6	15	244	123	119	37	762
(CHAPMAN, R.)	0.679	8	29	58	89	45	8	270
(FLEMING, V.)	0.737	6	27	209	266	140	7	726

1991-92 REGULAR-SEASON STATISTICAL RESULTS
NBA PLAYERS ORDERED BY STEALS PER GAME

	NAME	POS	TEAM	GMs	MINs	MINs per GM	STLs	STLs per MIN	STLs per GM	FG PCT
169.	JOHNSON, E.	f	SEA	81	2366	29.2	55	0.023	0.68	0.459
170.	JOHNSON, V.	g	SA	60	1350	22.5	41	0.030	0.68	0.405
171.	KRYSTKOWIAK, L.	f	MIL	79	1848	23.4	54	0.029	0.68	0.444
172.	PERRY, E.	g	CHA	50	437	8.7	34	0.078	0.68	0.380
173.	SALLEY, J.	f/c	DET	72	1774	24.6	49	0.028	0.68	0.512
174.	BLACKMAN, R.	g	DAL	75	2527	33.7	50	0.020	0.67	0.461
175.	LYNCH, K.	g	CHA	55	819	14.9	37	0.045	0.67	0.417
176.	MAYES, Th.	g	LAC	24	255	10.6	16	0.063	0.67	0.303
177.	STEWART, L.	f	WAS	76	2229	29.3	51	0.023	0.67	0.514
178.	GRANT, Gr.	g	PHI	68	891	13.1	45	0.051	0.66	0.440
179.	CAMPBELL, E.	c	LAL	81	1876	23.2	53	0.028	0.65	0.448
180.	GREEN, R.	g	BOS	26	367	14.1	17	0.046	0.65	0.447
181.	KONCAK, J.	c	ATL	77	1489	19.3	50	0.034	0.65	0.391
182.	MITCHELL, S.	f	MIN	82	2151	26.2	53	0.025	0.65	0.423
183.	ROBERTS, F.	f	MIL	80	1746	21.8	52	0.030	0.65	0.482
184.	SMITH, O.	g	ORL	55	877	15.9	36	0.041	0.65	0.365
185.	THOMPSON, L.	f/c	IND	80	1299	16.2	52	0.040	0.65	0.468
186.	McCRAY, R.	f	DAL	75	2106	28.1	48	0.023	0.64	0.436
187.	BROWN, R.	g	SAC	56	535	9.6	35	0.065	0.63	0.456
188.	DAVIS, W.	g	DEN	46	741	16.1	29	0.039	0.63	0.459
189.	GILLIAM, A.	f/c	PHI	81	2771	34.2	51	0.018	0.63	0.512
190.	IUZZOLINO, M.	g	DAL	52	1280	24.6	33	0.026	0.63	0.451
191.	LAIMBEER, B.	c	DET	81	2234	27.6	51	0.023	0.63	0.470
192.	LICHTI, T.	g	DEN	68	1176	17.3	43	0.037	0.63	0.460
193.	THORPE, O.	f	HOU	82	3056	37.3	52	0.017	0.63	0.592
194.	BENJAMIN, B.	c	SEA	63	1941	30.8	39	0.020	0.62	0.478
195.	PAXSON, J.	g	CHI	79	1946	24.6	49	0.025	0.62	0.528
196.	SMITH, To.	g	LAL	63	820	13.0	39	0.048	0.62	0.399
197.	FREDERICK, A.	f	CHA	66	852	12.9	40	0.047	0.61	0.435
198.	MUTOMBO, D.	c	DEN	71	2716	38.3	43	0.016	0.61	0.493
199.	WHATLEY, E.	g	POR	23	209	9.1	14	0.067	0.61	0.412
200.	DOUGLAS, S.	g	BOS	42	752	17.9	25	0.033	0.60	0.463
201.	HIGGINS, R.	f	GS	25	535	21.4	15	0.028	0.60	0.412
202.	MURDOCK, E.	g	UT	50	478	9.6	30	0.063	0.60	0.415
203.	ASKEW, V.	g	GS	80	1496	18.7	47	0.031	0.59	0.509
204.	CAUSWELL, D.	c	SAC	80	2291	28.6	47	0.021	0.59	0.550
205.	GEORGE, T.	g	NJ	70	1037	14.8	41	0.040	0.59	0.428
206.	HAMMONDS, T.	f	CHA	37	984	26.6	22	0.022	0.59	0.488
207.	LANG, A.	c	PHX	81	1965	24.3	48	0.024	0.59	0.522
208.	MILLS, T.	f	NJ	82	1714	20.9	48	0.028	0.59	0.463
209.	POLYNICE, O.	c	LAC	76	1834	24.1	45	0.025	0.59	0.519
210.	BOWIE, S.	c	NJ	71	2179	30.7	41	0.019	0.58	0.445
211.	GATLING, C.	c	GS	54	612	11.3	31	0.051	0.57	0.568
212.	JONES, Ch.	c/f	WAS	75	1365	18.2	43	0.032	0.57	0.367
213.	KNIGHT, N.	g	PHX	42	631	15.0	24	0.038	0.57	0.475
214.	LOHAUS, B.	f/c	MIL	70	1081	15.4	40	0.037	0.57	0.450
215.	ALEXANDER, V.	c	GS	80	1350	16.9	45	0.033	0.56	0.529
216.	ARMSTRONG, B.J.	g	CHI	82	1875	22.9	46	0.025	0.56	0.481
217.	KERR, S.	g	CLE	48	847	17.6	27	0.032	0.56	0.511
218.	MASON, A.	f	NY	82	2198	26.8	46	0.021	0.56	0.509
219.	PACK, R.	g	POR	72	894	12.4	40	0.045	0.56	0.423
220.	PERRY, T.	f	PHX	80	2483	31.0	44	0.018	0.55	0.523
221.	JACKSON, C.	g	DEN	81	1538	19.0	44	0.029	0.54	0.421
222.	RULAND, J.	c	PHI	13	209	16.1	7	0.034	0.54	0.526
223.	BROWN, T.	f	SEA	57	655	11.5	30	0.046	0.53	0.410
224.	LONGLEY, L.	c	MIN	66	991	15.0	35	0.035	0.53	0.458

(NAME)	FT PCT	3-PT SHOTS MADE	3-PT SHOTS TRIED	REBs	ASTs	TURN-OVERS	BLKs	PTs
(JOHNSON, E.)	0.861	27	107	292	161	130	11	1386
(JOHNSON, V.)	0.647	19	60	82	145	74	14	478
(KRYSTKOWIAK, L.)	0.757	0	5	429	114	115	12	714
(PERRY, E.)	0.659	1	7	39	78	50	3	126
(SALLEY, J.)	0.715	0	3	296	116	102	110	684
(BLACKMAN, R.)	0.899	65	169	239	204	153	22	1374
(LYNCH, K.)	0.761	3	8	85	83	44	9	224
(MAYES, Th.)	0.667	15	41	16	35	31	2	99
(STEWART, L.)	0.807	0	3	449	120	112	44	794
(GRANT, Gr.)	0.833	7	18	69	217	46	2	225
(CAMPBELL, E.)	0.619	0	2	423	59	73	159	578
(GREEN, R.)	0.722	1	4	24	68	18	1	106
(KONCAK, J.)	0.655	0	12	261	132	54	67	241
(MITCHELL, S.)	0.786	2	11	473	94	97	39	825
(ROBERTS, F.)	0.749	19	37	257	122	122	40	769
(SMITH, O.)	0.769	8	21	116	57	62	13	310
(THOMPSON, L.)	0.817	0	2	381	102	98	34	394
(McCRAY, R.)	0.719	25	85	468	219	115	30	677
(BROWN, R.)	0.655	0	6	69	59	42	12	192
(DAVIS, W.)	0.872	5	16	70	68	45	1	457
(GILLIAM, A.)	0.807	0	2	660	118	166	85	1367
(IUZZOLINO, M.)	0.836	59	136	98	194	92	1	486
(LAIMBEER, B.)	0.893	32	85	451	160	102	54	783
(LICHTI, T.)	0.839	1	9	118	74	72	12	446
(THORPE, O.)	0.657	0	7	862	250	237	37	1420
(BENJAMIN, B.)	0.687	0	2	513	76	175	118	879
(PAXSON, J.)	0.784	12	44	96	241	44	9	555
(SMITH, To.)	0.653	0	11	76	109	50	8	275
(FREDERICK, A.)	0.685	4	17	144	71	58	26	389
(MUTOMBO, D.)	0.642	0	0	870	156	252	210	1177
(WHATLEY, E.)	0.871	0	4	21	34	14	3	69
(DOUGLAS, S.)	0.682	1	10	63	172	68	9	308
(HIGGINS, R.)	0.814	33	95	5	22	15	13	255
(MURDOCK, E.)	0.754	5	26	54	92	50	7	203
(ASKEW, V.)	0.694	1	10	233	188	84	23	498
(CAUSWELL, D.)	0.613	0	1	580	59	124	215	636
(GEORGE, T.)	0.821	1	6	105	162	82	3	4188
(HAMMONDS, T.)	0.610	0	1	185	36	58	13	440
(LANG, A.)	0.768	0	1	546	43	87	201	622
(MILLS, T.)	0.750	8	23	453	84	82	41	742
(POLYNICE, O.)	0.622	0	1	536	46	83	20	613
(BOWIE, S.)	0.757	8	25	578	186	150	120	1062
(GATLING, C.)	0.661	0	4	182	16	44	36	306
(JONES, Ch.)	0.500	0	0	317	62	39	92	86
(KNIGHT, N.)	0.688	4	13	46	112	58	3	243
(LOHAUS, B.)	0.659	57	144	249	74	46	71	408
(ALEXANDER, V.)	0.691	0	1	336	32	91	62	589
(ARMSTRONG, B.J.)	0.806	35	87	145	266	94	5	809
(KERR, S.)	0.833	32	74	78	110	31	10	319
(MASON, A.)	0.642	0	0	573	106	101	20	573
(PACK, R.)	0.803	0	10	97	140	92	4	332
(PERRY, T.)	0.712	3	8	551	134	141	116	982
(JACKSON, C.)	0.870	31	94	114	192	117	4	837
(RULAND, J.)	0.688	0	0	47	5	20	4	51
(BROWN, T.)	0.727	19	63	84	48	35	5	271
(LONGLEY, L.)	0.663	0	0	257	53	83	64	281

1991–92 REGULAR-SEASON STATISTICAL RESULTS
NBA PLAYERS ORDERED BY STEALS PER GAME

	NAME	POS	TEAM	GMs	MINs	MINs per GM	STLs	STLs per MIN	STLs per GM	FG PCT
225.	SHACKLEFORD, C.	c	PHI	72	1399	19.4	38	0.027	0.53	0.486
226.	BURTT, S.	g	PHX	31	356	11.5	16	0.045	0.52	0.463
227.	MORTON, J.	g	MIA	25	270	10.8	13	0.048	0.52	0.387
228.	PRESSEY, P.	g	SA	56	759	13.6	29	0.038	0.52	0.373
229.	BROWN, M.	c/f	UT	82	1783	21.7	42	0.024	0.51	0.453
230.	McCLOUD, G.	g	IND	51	892	17.5	26	0.029	0.51	0.409
231.	SEIKALY, R.	c	MIA	79	2800	35.4	40	0.014	0.51	0.489
232.	FRANK, T.	f	MIN	10	140	14.0	5	0.036	0.50	0.546
233.	LES, J.	g	SAC	62	712	11.5	31	0.044	0.50	0.385
234.	WOOLRIDGE, O.	f	DET	82	2113	25.8	41	0.019	0.50	0.498
235.	HODGE, D.	c/f	DAL	51	1058	20.7	25	0.024	0.49	0.497
236.	WHITE, R.	f	DAL	65	1021	15.7	31	0.030	0.48	0.380
237.	WOLF, J.	f	DEN	67	1160	17.3	32	0.028	0.48	0.361
238.	BATTLE, J.	g	CLE	76	1637	21.5	36	0.022	0.47	0.480
239.	RIVERS, Da.	g	LAC	15	122	8.1	7	0.057	0.47	0.333
240.	SMITH, L.	f/c	HOU	45	800	17.8	21	0.026	0.47	0.544
241.	VAUGHT, L.	f	LAC	79	1687	21.4	37	0.022	0.47	0.492
242.	WILLIAMS, H.	f/c	DAL	75	2040	27.2	35	0.017	0.47	0.431
243.	BRYANT, M.	c	POR	56	800	14.3	26	0.033	0.46	0.480
244.	CHILCUTT, P.	f/c	SAC	69	817	11.8	32	0.039	0.46	0.452
245.	DUCKWORTH, K.	c	POR	82	2222	27.1	38	0.017	0.46	0.461
246.	DUDLEY, C.	c	NJ	82	1902	23.2	38	0.020	0.46	0.403
247.	DAILEY, Q.	f	SEA	11	98	8.9	5	0.051	0.45	0.243
248.	EATON, M.	c	UT	81	2023	25.0	36	0.018	0.44	0.446
249.	SCHAYES, D.	c	MIL	43	726	16.9	19	0.026	0.44	0.417
250.	SPENCER, F.	c	MIN	61	1481	24.3	27	0.018	0.44	0.426
251.	RAMBIS, K.	f	PHX	28	381	13.6	12	0.032	0.43	0.463
252.	RASMUSSEN, B.	c	ATL	81	1968	24.3	35	0.018	0.43	0.478
253.	BAILEY, T.	f	MIN	84	2104	25.0	35	0.017	0.42	0.440
254.	DAVIS, D.	f	IND	64	1301	20.3	27	0.021	0.42	0.552
255.	HIGGINS, S.	f	ORL	38	616	16.2	16	0.026	0.42	0.459
256.	KITE, G.	c	ORL	72	1479	20.5	30	0.020	0.42	0.437
257.	ROYAL, D.	f	SA	60	718	12.0	25	0.035	0.42	0.449
258.	SANDERS, J.	f	ATL	12	117	9.8	5	0.043	0.42	0.444
259.	HOWARD, B.	f	DAL	27	318	11.8	11	0.035	0.41	0.519
260.	QUINNETT, B.	f	DAL	39	326	8.4	16	0.049	0.41	0.347
261.	WIGGINS, M.	g	PHI	49	569	11.6	20	0.035	0.41	0.384
262.	BREUER, R.	c	MIN	67	1176	17.6	27	0.023	0.40	0.468
263.	CARR, A.	f/c	SA	81	1867	23.0	32	0.017	0.40	0.490
264.	ENGLISH, A.J.	g	WAS	81	1665	20.6	32	0.019	0.40	0.433
265.	HANSEN, B.	g	CHI	68	809	11.9	27	0.033	0.40	0.444
266.	MUSTAF, J.	f	PHX	52	545	10.5	21	0.039	0.40	0.477
267.	ROBERTS, S.	c	ORL	55	1118	20.3	22	0.020	0.40	0.529
268.	WILLIAMS, Ja.	f/c	PHI	50	646	12.9	20	0.031	0.40	0.364
269.	SMITS, R.	c	IND	74	1772	23.9	29	0.016	0.39	0.510
270.	SUTTON, G.	g	SA	67	601	9.0	26	0.043	0.39	0.388
271.	DAVIS, T.	f/c	DAL	68	2149	31.6	26	0.012	0.38	0.482
272.	ACRES, M.	c	ORL	68	926	13.6	25	0.027	0.37	0.517
273.	ADDISON, R.	g	NJ	76	1175	15.5	28	0.024	0.37	0.433
274.	GREEN, Se.	g	IND	35	256	7.3	13	0.051	0.37	0.392
275.	HERRERA, C.	f	HOU	43	566	13.2	16	0.028	0.37	0.516
276.	GREEN, S.	f	SA	80	1127	14.1	29	0.026	0.36	0.427
277.	ABDELNABY, A.	f/c	POR	71	934	13.2	25	0.027	0.35	0.493
278.	BENNETT, W.	f	MIA	54	833	15.4	19	0.023	0.35	0.379
279.	JAMERSON, D.	f	HOU	48	378	7.9	17	0.045	0.35	0.414
280.	CARTWRIGHT, B.	c	CHI	64	1471	23.0	22	0.015	0.34	0.467

(NAME)	FT PCT	3-PT SHOTS MADE	3-PT SHOTS TRIED	REBs	ASTs	TURN-OVERS	BLKs	PTs
(SHACKLEFORD, C.)	0.663	0	1	415	46	62	51	473
(BURTT, S.)	0.704	1	6	34	59	33	4	187
(MORTON, J.)	0.842	2	16	26	32	28	1	106
(PRESSEY, P.)	0.683	3	21	95	142	64	19	151
(BROWN, M.)	0.667	0	1	476	81	105	34	632
(McCLOUD, G.)	0.781	32	94	132	116	62	11	338
(SEIKALY, R.)	0.733	0	3	934	109	216	121	1296
(FRANK, T.)	0.667	0	0	26	8	5	4	46
(LES, J.)	0.809	45	131	63	143	42	3	231
(WOOLRIDGE, O.)	0.683	1	9	260	88	133	33	1146
(HODGE, D.)	0.667	0	0	275	39	75	23	426
(WHITE, R.)	0.765	4	27	236	31	68	22	418
(WOLF, J.)	0.803	1	11	240	61	60	14	254
(BATTLE, J.)	0.848	2	17	112	159	91	5	779
(RIVERS, Da.)	0.909	0	1	19	21	17	1	30
(SMITH, L.)	0.364	0	1	256	33	44	7	104
(VAUGHT, L.)	0.797	4	5	512	71	66	31	601
(WILLIAMS, H.)	0.725	1	6	454	94	114	98	859
(BRYANT, M.)	0.667	0	3	201	41	30	8	230
(CHILCUTT, P.)	0.821	2	2	187	38	41	17	251
(DUCKWORTH, K.)	0.690	0	3	497	99	143	37	880
(DUDLEY, C.)	0.468	0	0	739	58	79	179	460
(DAILEY, Q.)	0.813	0	1	12	4	10	1	31
(EATON, M.)	0.598	0	0	491	40	60	205	266
(SCHAYES, D.)	0.771	0	0	168	34	41	19	240
(SPENCER, F.)	0.691	0	0	435	53	70	79	405
(RAMBIS, K.)	0.778	0	0	106	37	25	14	90
(RASMUSSEN, B.)	0.750	5	23	393	107	51	48	729
(BAILEY, T.)	0.796	0	2	485	78	108	117	951
(DAVIS, D.)	0.572	0	1	410	30	49	74	395
(HIGGINS, S.)	0.861	6	25	102	41	41	6	291
(KITE, G.)	0.588	0	1	402	44	61	57	228
(ROYAL, D.)	0.692	0	0	124	34	39	7	252
(SANDERS, J.)	0.778	0	0	26	9	5	3	47
(HOWARD, B.)	0.710	1	2	51	14	15	8	131
(QUINNETT, B.)	0.615	13	41	51	12	16	8	115
(WIGGINS, M.)	0.686	0	1	94	22	25	1	211
(BREUER, R.)	0.533	0	1	281	89	41	99	363
(CARR, A.)	0.764	1	5	346	63	114	96	881
(ENGLISH, A.J.)	0.841	6	34	168	143	89	9	886
(HANSEN, B.)	0.364	7	27	77	69	28	3	173
(MUSTAF, J.)	0.690	0	0	145	45	51	16	233
(ROBERTS, S.)	0.515	0	1	336	39	78	83	573
(WILLIAMS, Ja.)	0.636	0	0	145	12	44	20	206
(SMITS, R.)	0.788	0	2	417	116	130	100	1024
(SUTTON, G.)	0.756	26	89	47	91	70	9	246
(DAVIS, T.)	0.635	0	5	672	57	117	29	693
(ACRES, M.)	0.761	1	3	252	22	33	15	208
(ADDISON, R.)	0.737	14	49	165	68	46	28	444
(GREEN, Se.)	0.536	2	10	42	22	27	6	141
(HERRERA, C.)	0.568	0	1	99	27	37	25	191
(GREEN, S.)	0.820	0	0	342	36	62	11	367
(ABDELNABY, A.)	0.753	0	0	260	30	66	16	432
(BENNETT, W.)	0.700	0	1	162	38	33	9	195
(JAMERSON, D.)	0.926	8	28	43	33	24	0	191
(CARTWRIGHT, B.)	0.604	0	0	324	87	75	14	512

1991–92 REGULAR-SEASON STATISTICAL RESULTS
NBA PLAYERS ORDERED BY STEALS PER GAME

NAME	POS	TEAM	GMs	MINs	MINs per GM	STLs	STLs per MIN	STLs per GM	FG PCT
281. LEVINGSTON, C.	f	CHI	79	1020	12.9	27	0.027	0.34	0.498
282. BLANKS, L.	g	DET	43	189	4.4	14	0.074	0.33	0.455
283. BULLARD, M.	f	HOU	80	1278	16.0	26	0.020	0.33	0.459
284. DAVIS, B.	f	DAL	33	429	13.0	11	0.026	0.33	0.442
285. EDWARDS, Ja.	c	LAC	72	1437	20.0	24	0.017	0.33	0.465
286. KLEINE, J.	c	BOS	70	991	14.2	23	0.023	0.33	0.492
287. OLIVER, J.	g/f	CLE	27	252	9.3	9	0.036	0.33	0.398
288. PAYNE, K.	f	PHI	49	353	7.2	16	0.045	0.33	0.448
289. WILLIAMS, K.	f	IND	60	565	9.4	20	0.035	0.33	0.518
290. FERRY, D.	f	CLE	68	937	13.8	22	0.024	0.32	0.409
291. MONROE, R.	g	ATL	38	313	8.2	12	0.038	0.32	0.368
292. THOMPSON, S.	g	SAC	19	91	4.8	6	0.066	0.32	0.378
293. TURNER, J.	f	ORL	75	1591	21.2	24	0.015	0.32	0.451
294. GMINSKI, M.	c	CHA	35	499	14.3	11	0.022	0.31	0.452
295. NEALY, E.	f	PHX	52	505	9.7	16	0.032	0.31	0.512
296. HENSON, S.	g	MIL	50	386	7.7	15	0.039	0.30	0.361
297. PHILLS, B.	g	CLE	10	65	6.5	3	0.046	0.30	0.429
298. SAMPSON, R.	c	WAS	10	108	10.8	3	0.028	0.30	0.310
299. BROWN, C.	f	LAL	42	431	10.3	12	0.028	0.29	0.469
300. KIMBLE, B.	f	LAC	34	277	8.2	10	0.036	0.29	0.396
301. OLIVER, B.	g	PHI	34	279	8.2	10	0.036	0.29	0.330
302. TOLBERT, T.	f	GS	35	310	8.9	10	0.032	0.29	0.384
303. KING, S.	f/c	CHI	79	1268	16.1	21	0.017	0.27	0.506
304. PRITCHARD, K.	g	BOS	11	136	12.4	3	0.022	0.27	0.471
305. SCHEFFLER, S.	f	DEN	11	61	5.6	3	0.049	0.27	0.667
306. SPARROW, R.	g	LAL	46	489	10.6	12	0.025	0.26	0.384
307. BENOIT, D.	f	UT	77	1161	15.1	19	0.016	0.25	0.467
308. CEBALLOS, C.	f	PHX	64	725	11.3	16	0.022	0.25	0.482
309. HASTINGS, S.	f	DEN	40	421	10.5	10	0.024	0.25	0.340
310. HODGES, C.	g	CHI	56	555	9.9	14	0.025	0.25	0.384
311. JAMES, H.	f	CLE	65	866	13.3	16	0.019	0.25	0.407
312. OWENS, K.	f	LAL	20	80	4.0	5	0.063	0.25	0.281
313. LEE, D.	g	NJ	46	307	6.7	11	0.036	0.24	0.431
314. ROLLINS, T.	f/c	HOU	59	697	11.8	14	0.020	0.24	0.535
315. COOK, A.	f	DEN	22	115	5.2	5	0.044	0.23	0.600
316. McCANN, B.	f	DET	26	129	5.0	6	0.047	0.23	0.394
317. RUDD, D.	g	UT	65	538	8.3	15	0.028	0.23	0.399
318. BROOKS, K.	f	DEN	37	270	7.3	8	0.030	0.22	0.443
319. KESSLER, A.	c	MIA	77	1197	15.5	17	0.014	0.22	0.413
320. RANDALL, M.	f	MIN	54	441	8.2	12	0.027	0.22	0.456
321. VANDEWEGHE, K.	f	NY	67	956	14.3	15	0.016	0.22	0.491
322. ELLIS, L.	f	LAC	29	103	3.6	6	0.058	0.21	0.340
323. PERDUE, W.	c	CHI	77	1007	13.1	16	0.016	0.21	0.547
324. WILLIAMS, S.	f	CHI	63	690	11.0	13	0.019	0.21	0.483
325. CONLON, M.	c	SEA	45	381	8.5	9	0.024	0.20	0.475
326. McHALE, K.	f/c	BOS	56	1398	25.0	11	0.008	0.20	0.510
327. BEDFORD, W.	f/c	DET	32	363	11.3	6	0.017	0.19	0.413
328. HENDERSON, G.	g	DET	16	96	6.0	3	0.031	0.19	0.375
329. LISTER, A.	c	GS	26	293	11.3	5	0.017	0.19	0.557
330. MURPHY, T	f	MIN	47	429	9.1	9	0.021	0.19	0.488
331. PETERSEN, J.	c	GS	27	169	6.3	5	0.030	0.19	0.450
332. SCHINTZIUS, D.	c	SAC	33	400	12.1	6	0.015	0.18	0.427
333. DREILING, G.	c	IND	60	509	8.5	10	0.020	0.17	0.494
334. WEST, M.	c	PHX	82	1436	17.5	14	0.010	0.17	0.632
335. BOL, M.	c	PHI	71	1267	17.8	11	0.009	0.15	0.383
336. LECKNER, E.	c	CHA	59	716	12.1	9	0.013	0.15	0.513

(NAME)	FT PCT	3-PT SHOTS MADE	3-PT SHOTS TRIED	REBs	ASTs	TURN-OVERS	BLKs	PTs
(LEVINGSTON, C.)	0.625	1	6	227	66	42	45	311
(BLANKS, L.)	0.727	6	16	22	19	14	1	64
(BULLARD, M.)	0.760	64	166	223	75	56	21	512
(DAVIS, B.)	0.733	5	18	33	66	27	3	92
(EDWARDS, Ja.)	0.731	0	1	202	53	72	33	698
(KLEINE, J.)	0.708	4	8	296	32	27	14	326
(OLIVER, J.)	0.773	1	9	27	20	9	2	96
(PAYNE, K.)	0.692	5	12	54	17	19	8	144
(WILLIAMS, K.)	0.605	0	4	129	40	22	41	252
(FERRY, D.)	0.836	17	48	213	75	46	15	346
(MONROE, R.)	0.826	6	27	33	27	23	2	131
(THOMPSON, S.)	0.375	0	1	19	8	5	3	31
(TURNER, J.)	0.693	1	8	246	92	106	16	530
(GMINSKI, M.)	0.750	1	3	118	31	20	16	202
(NEALY, E.)	0.667	20	50	111	37	17	2	160
(HENSON, S.)	0.793	23	48	41	82	40	1	150
(PHILLS, B.)	0.636	0	2	8	4	8	1	31
(SAMPSON, R.)	0.667	0	2	30	4	10	8	22
(BROWN, C.)	0.612	0	3	82	26	29	7	150
(KIMBLE, B.)	0.645	4	13	32	17	15	6	112
(OLIVER, B.)	0.682	0	4	30	20	24	2	81
(TOLBERT, T.)	0.550	2	8	55	21	20	6	90
(KING, S.)	0.753	2	5	205	77	76	25	551
(PRITCHARD, K.)	0.778	0	3	11	30	11	4	46
(SCHEFFLER, S.)	0.750	0	0	14	0	1	1	21
(SPARROW, R.)	0.615	3	15	28	83	33	5	127
(BENOIT, D.)	0.810	3	14	296	34	71	44	434
(CEBALLOS, C.)	0.737	1	6	152	50	71	11	462
(HASTINGS, S.)	0.857	0	9	98	26	22	15	58
(HODGES, C.)	0.941	36	96	24	54	22	1	238
(JAMES, H.)	0.803	29	90	112	25	43	11	418
(OWENS, K.)	0.800	0	0	15	3	2	4	26
(LEE, D.)	0.526	10	37	35	22	12	1	120
(ROLLINS, T.)	0.867	0	0	171	15	18	62	118
(COOK, A.)	0.667	0	0	34	2	3	4	34
(McCANN, B.)	0.308	0	1	30	6	7	4	30
(RUDD, D.)	0.762	11	47	54	109	49	1	193
(BROOKS, K.)	0.810	2	11	39	11	18	2	105
(KESSLER, A.)	0.817	0	0	314	34	58	32	410
(RANDALL, M.)	0.744	3	16	71	33	25	3	171
(VANDEWEGHE, K.)	0.803	26	66	88	57	27	8	467
(ELLIS, L.)	0.474	0	0	24	1	11	9	43
(PERDUE, W.)	0.495	1	2	312	80	72	43	350
(WILLIAMS, S.)	0.649	0	3	247	50	35	36	214
(CONLON, M.)	0.750	0	0	69	12	27	7	120
(McHALE, K.)	0.822	0	13	330	82	82	59	780
(BEDFORD, W.)	0.636	0	1	63	12	15	18	114
(HENDERSON, G.)	0.818	3	8	8	10	8	0	36
(LISTER, A.)	0.424	0	0	92	14	20	16	102
(MURPHY, T)	0.559	1	2	110	11	18	8	98
(PETERSEN, J.)	0.700	0	2	45	9	5	6	43
(SCHINTZIUS, D.)	0.833	0	4	118	20	19	28	110
(DREILING, G.)	0.750	1	1	96	25	31	16	117
(WEST, M.)	0.637	0	0	372	22	82	81	501
(BOL, M.)	0.462	0	9	222	22	41	205	110
(LECKNER, E.)	0.745	0	1	206	31	39	18	196

1991–92 REGULAR-SEASON STATISTICAL RESULTS
NBA PLAYERS ORDERED BY STEALS PER GAME

	NAME	POS	TEAM	GMs	MINs	MINs per GM	STLs	STLs per MIN	STLs per GM	FG PCT
337.	CROWDER, C.	g/f	UT	51	328	6.4	7	0.021	0.14	0.384
338.	DONALDSON, J.	c	NY	58	1075	18.5	8	0.007	0.14	0.457
339.	HALEY, J.	f/c	LAL	49	394	8.0	7	0.018	0.14	0.369
340.	LANE, J.	f	MIL	14	177	12.6	2	0.011	0.14	0.304
341.	TURNER, Jo.	f	HOU	42	345	8.2	6	0.017	0.14	0.439
342.	BATTLE, K.	f	GS	16	92	5.8	2	0.022	0.13	0.647
343.	FOSTER, G.	f	WAS	49	548	11.2	6	0.011	0.12	0.461
344.	OGG, A.	c	MIA	43	367	8.5	5	0.014	0.12	0.548
345.	COOPER, W.	f	POR	35	344	9.8	4	0.012	0.11	0.427
346.	THOMAS, C.	g	DET	37	156	4.2	4	0.026	0.11	0.353
347.	WINCHESTER, K.	f	NY	19	81	4.3	2	0.025	0.11	0.433
348.	KING, R.	c	SEA	40	213	5.3	4	0.019	0.10	0.380
349.	McCORMICK, T.	c	NY	22	108	4.9	2	0.019	0.09	0.424
350.	WITTMAN, R.	g	IND	24	115	4.8	2	0.017	0.08	0.421
351.	AUSTIN, I.	c	UT	31	112	3.6	2	0.018	0.06	0.457
352.	COPA, T.	f/c	SA	33	132	4.0	2	0.015	0.06	0.550
353.	FEITL, D.	c	NJ	34	175	5.2	2	0.011	0.06	0.429
354.	KOFOED, B.	g	SEA	44	239	5.4	2	0.008	0.05	0.472
355.	JEPSEN, L.	c	SAC	31	87	2.8	1	0.012	0.03	0.375
356.	SELLERS, B.	f/c	DET	43	226	5.3	1	0.004	0.02	0.466
357.	ANSLEY, M.	f	CHA	10	45	4.5	0	0.000	0.00	0.444
358.	MAYS, T.	g	ATL	2	32	16.0	0	0.000	0.00	0.429
359.	VRANKOVIC, S.	c	BOS	19	110	5.8	0	0.000	0.00	0.469

(NAME)	FT PCT	3-PT SHOTS MADE	3-PT SHOTS TRIED	REBs	ASTs	TURN-OVERS	BLKs	PTs
(CROWDER, C.)	0.833	13	30	41	17	13	2	114
(DONALDSON, J.)	0.709	0	0	289	33	48	49	285
(HALEY, J.)	0.483	0	0	95	7	25	8	76
(LANE, J.)	0.333	0	0	66	17	14	1	37
(TURNER, Jo.)	0.525	0	0	78	12	32	4	117
(BATTLE, K.)	0.833	0	1	16	4	4	2	32
(FOSTER, G.)	0.714	0	1	145	35	36	12	213
(OGG, A.)	0.533	0	0	74	7	19	28	108
(COOPER, W.)	0.636	0	0	101	21	15	27	77
(THOMAS, C.)	0.667	2	17	22	22	17	1	48
(WINCHESTER, K.)	0.800	1	2	15	8	2	2	35
(KING, R.)	0.756	0	1	49	12	18	5	88
(McCORMICK, T.)	0.667	0	0	34	9	8	0	42
(WITTMAN, R.)	0.500	0	0	9	11	3	0	17
(AUSTIN, I.)	0.633	0	0	35	5	8	2	61
(COPA, T.)	0.308	0	0	36	3	8	6	48
(FEITL, D.)	0.842	0	0	61	6	19	3	82
(KOFOED, B.)	0.577	1	7	26	51	20	2	66
(JEPSEN, L.)	0.636	0	1	30	1	3	5	25
(SELLERS, B.)	0.769	0	1	42	14	15	10	102
(ANSLEY, M.)	0.833	0	0	6	2	3	0	21
(MAYS, T.)	1.000	3	6	2	1	3	0	17
(VRANKOVIC, S.)	0.583	0	0	28	5	10	17	37

1991–92 REGULAR-SEASON STATISTICAL RESULTS
NBA PLAYERS ORDERED BY THREE-POINT SHOTS MADE

	NAME	POS	TEAM	GMs	MINs	MINs per GM	3-PT SHOTS TRIED	3-PT SHOTS MADE	FG PCT	FT PCT
1.	MAXWELL, V.	g	HOU	80	2700	33.7	473	162	0.413	0.772
2.	RICE, G.	f	MIA	79	3007	38.1	396	155	0.469	0.837
3.	ELLIS, D.	f	MIL	81	2191	27.0	329	138	0.469	0.774
4.	PERSON, C.	f	IND	81	2923	36.1	354	132	0.480	0.675
5.	MILLER, R.	g	IND	82	3120	38.0	341	129	0.501	0.858
6.	PORTER, T.	g	POR	82	2784	34.0	324	128	0.462	0.856
7.	HARDAWAY, T.	g	GS	81	3332	41.1	376	127	0.461	0.766
8.	ADAMS, M.	g	WAS	78	2795	35.8	386	125	0.393	0.869
9.	PETROVIC, D.	g	NJ	82	3027	36.9	277	123	0.508	0.808
10.	DREXLER, C.	g	POR	76	2751	36.2	338	114	0.470	0.794
11.	RICHMOND, M.	g	SAC	80	3095	38.7	268	103	0.468	0.813
12.	PRICE, M.	g	CLE	72	2138	29.7	261	101	0.488	0.947
13.	STARKS, J.	g	NY	82	2118	25.8	270	94	0.449	0.778
14.	HAWKINS, H.	g	PHI	81	3013	37.2	229	91	0.462	0.874
15.	SKILES, S.	g	ORL	75	2377	31.7	250	91	0.414	0.895
16.	MAJERLE, D.	g/f	PHX	82	2853	34.8	228	87	0.478	0.756
17.	BARROS, D.	g	SEA	75	1331	17.7	186	83	0.483	0.760
18.	HORNACEK, J.	g	PHX	81	3078	38.0	189	83	0.512	0.886
19.	STOCKTON, J.	g	UT	82	3002	36.6	204	83	0.482	0.842
20.	AINGE, D.	g	POR	81	1595	19.7	230	78	0.442	0.824
21.	CURRY, D.	g	CHA	77	2020	26.2	183	74	0.486	0.836
22.	WEBB, S.	g	SAC	77	2724	35.4	199	73	0.445	0.859
23.	EHLO, C.	g/f	CLE	63	2016	32.0	167	69	0.453	0.707
24.	ROBERTSON, A.	g	MIL	82	2463	30.0	210	67	0.430	0.763
25.	BLACKMAN, R.	g	DAL	75	2527	33.7	169	65	0.461	0.899
26.	BULLARD, M.	f	HOU	80	1278	16.0	166	64	0.459	0.760
27.	HARPER, R.	g	LAC	82	3144	38.3	211	64	0.440	0.736
28.	MULLIN, C.	f	GS	81	3346	41.3	175	64	0.524	0.833
29.	IUZZOLINO, M.	g	DAL	52	1280	24.6	136	59	0.451	0.836
30.	HARPER, D.	g	DAL	65	2252	34.6	186	58	0.443	0.759
31.	LOHAUS, B.	f/c	MIL	70	1081	15.4	144	57	0.450	0.659
32.	WILLIAMS, R.	f	DEN	81	2623	32.4	156	56	0.471	0.803
33.	GRAHAM, P.	g	ATL	78	1718	22.0	141	55	0.447	0.741
34.	SCOTT, B.	g	LAL	82	2679	32.7	157	54	0.458	0.839
35.	SMITH, K.	g	HOU	81	2735	33.8	137	54	0.475	0.866
36.	RICHARDSON, P.	g	MIN	82	2922	35.6	155	53	0.466	0.691
37.	BIRD, L.	f	BOS	45	1662	36.9	128	52	0.466	0.926
38.	DUMARS, J.	g	DET	82	3192	38.9	120	49	0.448	0.867
39.	LES, J.	g	SAC	62	712	11.5	131	45	0.385	0.809
40.	ANDERSON, Ro.	f	PHI	82	2432	29.7	127	42	0.465	0.877
41.	HUMPHRIES, J.	g	MIL	71	2261	31.8	144	42	0.470	0.783
42.	SMITH, S.	g	MIA	61	1806	29.6	125	40	0.454	0.748
43.	EDWARDS, T.	g/f	UT	81	2283	28.2	103	39	0.522	0.774
44.	WILKINS, G.	g	NY	82	2344	28.6	108	38	0.447	0.730
45.	FLOYD, S.	g	HOU	82	1662	20.3	123	37	0.406	0.794
46.	WILKINS, D.	f	ATL	42	1601	38.1	128	37	0.464	0.835
47.	DAWKINS, J.	g	PHI	82	2815	34.3	101	36	0.437	0.882
48.	HODGES, C.	g	CHI	56	555	9.9	96	36	0.384	0.941
49.	ARMSTRONG, B.J.	g	CHI	82	1875	22.9	87	35	0.481	0.806
50.	VOLKOV, A.	f	ATL	77	1516	19.7	110	35	0.441	0.631
51.	ROBINSON, R.	g	ATL	81	2220	27.4	104	34	0.456	0.636
52.	HIGGINS, R.	f	GS	25	535	21.4	95	33	0.412	0.814
53.	PIERCE, R.	g	SEA	78	2658	34.1	123	33	0.475	0.917
54.	BARKLEY, C.	f	PHI	75	2881	38.4	137	32	0.552	0.695
55.	BROOKS, S.	g	MIN	82	1082	13.2	90	32	0.447	0.810
56.	KERR, S.	g	CLE	48	847	17.6	74	32	0.511	0.833

(NAME)	REBs	ASTs	STLs	TURN-OVERS	BLKs	PTs
(MAXWELL, V.)	243	326	104	178	28	1372
(RICE, G.)	394	184	90	145	35	1765
(ELLIS, D.)	253	104	57	119	18	1272
(PERSON, C.)	426	382	68	216	18	1497
(MILLER, R.)	318	314	105	157	26	1695
(PORTER, T.)	255	477	127	188	12	1485
(HARDAWAY, T.)	310	807	164	267	13	1893
(ADAMS, M.)	310	594	145	212	9	1408
(PETROVIC, D.)	258	252	105	215	11	1691
(DREXLER, C.)	500	512	138	240	70	1903
(RICHMOND, M.)	319	411	92	247	34	1803
(PRICE, M.)	173	535	94	159	12	1247
(STARKS, J.)	191	276	103	150	18	1139
(HAWKINS, H.)	271	248	157	189	43	1536
(SKILES, S.)	202	544	74	233	5	1057
(MAJERLE, D.)	483	274	131	101	43	1418
(BARROS, D.)	81	125	51	56	4	619
(HORNACEK, J.)	407	411	158	170	31	1632
(STOCKTON, J.)	270	1126	244	286	22	1297
(AINGE, D.)	148	202	73	70	13	784
(CURRY, D.)	259	177	93	134	20	1209
(WEBB, S.)	223	547	125	229	24	1231
(EHLO, C.)	307	238	78	104	22	776
(ROBERTSON, A.)	350	360	210	223	32	1010
(BLACKMAN, R.)	239	204	50	153	22	1374
(BULLARD, M.)	223	75	26	56	21	512
(HARPER, R.)	447	417	152	252	72	1495
(MULLIN, C.)	450	286	173	202	62	2074
(IUZZOLINO, M.)	98	194	33	92	1	486
(HARPER, D.)	170	373	101	154	17	1152
(LOHAUS, B.)	249	74	40	46	71	408
(WILLIAMS, R.)	405	235	148	173	68	1474
(GRAHAM, P.)	231	175	96	91	21	791
(SCOTT, B.)	310	226	105	119	28	1218
(SMITH, K.)	177	562	104	227	7	1137
(RICHARDSON, P.)	301	685	119	204	25	1350
(BIRD, L.)	434	306	42	125	33	908
(DUMARS, J.)	188	375	71	193	12	1635
(LES, J.)	63	143	31	42	3	231
(ANDERSON, Ro.)	278	135	86	109	11	1123
(HUMPHRIES, J.)	184	466	119	148	13	991
(SMITH, S.)	188	278	59	152	19	729
(EDWARDS, T.)	298	137	81	122	46	1018
(WILKINS, G.)	206	219	76	113	17	1016
(FLOYD, S.)	150	239	57	128	21	744
(WILKINS, D.)	295	158	52	122	24	1179
(DAWKINS, J.)	227	567	89	183	5	988
(HODGES, C.)	24	54	14	22	1	238
(ARMSTRONG, B.J.)	145	266	46	94	5	809
(VOLKOV, A.)	265	250	66	102	30	662
(ROBINSON, R.)	219	446	105	206	24	1055
(HIGGINS, R.)	85	22	15	15	13	255
(PIERCE, R.)	233	241	86	189	20	1690
(BARKLEY, C.)	830	308	136	235	44	1730
(BROOKS, S.)	99	205	66	51	7	417
(KERR, S.)	78	110	27	31	10	319

1991–92 REGULAR-SEASON STATISTICAL RESULTS
NBA PLAYERS ORDERED BY THREE-POINT SHOTS MADE

	NAME	POS	TEAM	GMs	MINs	MINs per GM	3-PT SHOTS TRIED	3-PT SHOTS MADE	FG PCT	FT PCT
57.	LAIMBEER, B.	c	DET	81	2234	27.6	85	32	0.470	0.893
58.	McCLOUD, G.	g	IND	51	892	17.5	94	32	0.409	0.781
59.	RODMAN, D.	f	DET	82	3301	40.3	101	32	0.539	0.600
60.	JACKSON, C.	g	DEN	81	1538	19.0	94	31	0.421	0.870
61.	ANDERSON, N.	g/f	ORL	60	2203	36.7	85	30	0.463	0.667
62.	MOORE, T.	f	DAL	42	782	18.6	84	30	0.400	0.833
63.	JAMES, H.	f	CLE	65	866	13.3	90	29	0.407	0.803
64.	SCOTT, D.	f	ORL	18	608	33.8	89	29	0.402	0.901
65.	JOHNSON, E.	f	SEA	81	2366	29.2	107	27	0.459	0.861
66.	JORDAN, M.	g	CHI	80	3102	38.8	100	27	0.519	0.832
67.	McMILLAN, N.	g/f	SEA	72	1652	22.9	98	27	0.437	0.643
68.	RIVERS, Do.	g	LAC	59	1657	28.1	92	26	0.424	0.832
69.	SUTTON, G.	g	SA	67	601	9.0	89	26	0.388	0.756
70.	VANDEWEGHE, K.	f	NY	67	956	14.3	66	26	0.491	0.803
71.	ASKINS, K.	g/f	MIA	59	843	14.3	73	25	0.410	0.703
72.	ELLIOTT, S.	f	SA	82	3120	38.0	82	25	0.494	0.861
73.	McCRAY, R.	f	DAL	75	2106	28.1	85	25	0.436	0.719
74.	THOMAS, I.	g	DET	78	2918	37.4	86	25	0.446	0.773
75.	COLEMAN, D.	f	NJ	65	2207	34.0	76	23	0.504	0.763
76.	ELIE, M.	g/f	GS	79	1677	21.2	70	23	0.521	0.852
77.	FOX, R.	g/f	BOS	81	1535	19.0	70	23	0.459	0.755
78.	HENSON, S.	g	MIL	50	386	7.7	48	23	0.361	0.793
79.	SCHREMPF, D.	f	IND	80	2605	32.6	71	23	0.536	0.828
80.	YOUNG, D.	g	LAC	62	1023	16.5	70	23	0.392	0.851
81.	MORRIS, C.	f	NJ	77	2394	31.1	110	22	0.477	0.714
82.	NEALY, E.	f	PHX	52	505	9.7	50	20	0.512	0.667
83.	THREATT, S.	g	LAL	82	3070	37.4	62	20	0.489	0.831
84.	BROWN, T.	f	SEA	57	655	11.5	63	19	0.410	0.727
85.	GRAYER, J.	g	MIL	82	1659	20.2	66	19	0.449	0.667
86.	JOHNSON, V.	g	SA	60	1350	22.5	60	19	0.405	0.647
87.	McKEY, D.	f	SEA	52	1757	33.8	50	19	0.472	0.847
88.	ROBERTS, F.	f	MIL	80	1746	21.8	37	19	0.482	0.749
89.	TUCKER, T.	g	SA	24	415	17.3	48	19	0.465	0.800
90.	CHAMBERS, T.	f	PHX	69	1948	28.2	49	18	0.431	0.830
91.	BOWIE, A.	g/f	ORL	52	1721	33.1	44	17	0.493	0.860
92.	FERRY, D.	f	CLE	68	937	13.8	48	17	0.409	0.836
93.	LEVER, F.	g	DAL	31	884	28.5	52	17	0.387	0.750
94.	LIBERTY, M.	f/g	DEN	75	1527	20.4	50	17	0.443	0.728
95.	GLASS, G.	g	MIN	75	1822	24.3	54	16	0.440	0.616
96.	PIPPEN, S.	f	CHI	82	3164	38.6	80	16	0.506	0.760
97.	AGUIRRE, M.	f	DET	75	1582	21.1	71	15	0.431	0.687
98.	GRANT, Ga.	g	LAC	78	2049	26.3	51	15	0.462	0.815
99.	MAYES, Th.	g	LAC	24	255	10.6	41	15	0.303	0.667
100.	PERKINS, S.	f/c	LAL	63	2332	37.0	69	15	0.450	0.817
101.	ADDISON, R.	g	NJ	76	1175	15.5	49	14	0.433	0.737
102.	WILEY, M.	g	ATL	53	870	16.4	42	14	0.430	0.686
103.	ANDERSON, W.	g/f	SA	57	1889	33.1	56	13	0.456	0.775
104.	CAMPBELL, T.	f/g	MIN	78	2441	31.3	37	13	0.464	0.803
105.	CROWDER, C.	g/f	UT	51	328	6.4	30	13	0.384	0.833
106.	NEWMAN, J.	f/g	CHA	55	1651	30.0	46	13	0.477	0.766
107.	QUINNETT, B.	f	DAL	39	326	8.4	41	13	0.347	0.615
108.	BLAYLOCK, M.	g	NJ	72	2548	35.4	54	12	0.432	0.712
109.	GREEN, A.C.	f	LAL	82	2902	35.4	56	12	0.476	0.744
110.	HOPSON, D.	g/f	SAC	71	1314	18.5	47	12	0.465	0.708
111.	McDANIEL, X.	f	NY	82	2344	28.6	39	12	0.478	0.714
112.	PAXSON, J.	g	CHI	79	1946	24.6	44	12	0.528	0.784

(NAME)	REBs	ASTs	STLs	TURN-OVERS	BLKs	PTs
(LAIMBEER, B.)	451	160	51	102	54	783
(McCLOUD, G.)	132	116	26	62	11	338
(RODMAN, D.)	1530	191	68	140	70	800
(JACKSON, C.)	114	192	44	117	4	837
(ANDERSON, N.)	384	163	97	125	33	1196
(MOORE, T.)	82	48	32	44	4	355
(JAMES, H.)	112	25	16	43	11	418
(SCOTT, D.)	66	35	20	31	9	359
(JOHNSON, E.)	292	161	55	130	11	1386
(JORDAN, M.)	511	489	182	200	75	2404
(McMILLAN, N.)	252	359	129	112	29	435
(RIVERS, Do.)	147	233	111	92	19	641
(SUTTON, G.)	47	91	26	70	9	246
(VANDEWEGHE, K.)	88	57	15	27	8	467
(ASKINS, K.)	142	38	40	47	15	219
(ELLIOTT, S.)	439	214	84	152	29	1338
(McCRAY, R.)	468	219	48	115	30	677
(THOMAS, I.)	247	560	118	252	15	1445
(COLEMAN, D.)	618	205	54	248	98	1289
(ELIE, M.)	227	174	68	83	15	620
(FOX, R.)	220	126	78	123	30	644
(HENSON, S.)	41	82	15	40	1	150
(SCHREMPF, D.)	770	312	62	191	37	1380
(YOUNG, D.)	75	172	46	47	4	280
(MORRIS, C.)	494	197	129	171	81	879
(NEALY, E.)	111	37	16	17	2	160
(THREATT, S.)	253	593	168	182	16	1240
(BROWN, T.)	84	48	30	35	5	271
(GRAYER, J.)	257	150	64	105	13	739
(JOHNSON, V.)	182	145	41	74	14	478
(McKEY, D.)	268	120	61	114	47	777
(ROBERTS, F.)	257	122	52	122	40	769
(TUCKER, T.)	37	27	21	14	3	155
(CHAMBERS, T.)	401	142	57	103	37	1128
(BOWIE, A.)	245	163	55	107	38	758
(FERRY, D.)	213	75	22	46	15	346
(LEVER, F.)	161	107	46	36	12	347
(LIBERTY, M.)	308	58	66	90	29	698
(GLASS, G.)	260	175	66	103	30	859
(PIPPEN, S.)	630	572	155	253	93	1720
(AGUIRRE, M.)	236	126	51	105	11	851
(GRANT, Ga.)	184	538	138	187	14	609
(MAYES, Th.)	16	35	16	31	2	99
(PERKINS, S.)	556	141	64	83	62	1041
(ADDISON, R.)	165	68	28	46	28	444
(WILEY, M.)	81	180	47	60	3	204
(ANDERSON, W.)	300	302	54	140	51	744
(CAMPBELL, T.)	286	229	84	165	31	1307
(CROWDER, C.)	41	17	7	13	2	114
(NEWMAN, J.)	179	146	70	129	14	839
(QUINNETT, B.)	51	12	16	16	8	115
(BLAYLOCK, M.)	269	492	170	152	40	996
(GREEN, A.C.)	762	117	91	111	36	1116
(HOPSON, D.)	206	102	67	100	39	743
(McDANIEL, X.)	460	149	57	147	24	1125
(PAXSON, J.)	96	241	49	44	9	555

1991−92 REGULAR-SEASON STATISTICAL RESULTS
NBA PLAYERS ORDERED BY THREE-POINT SHOTS MADE

	NAME	POS	TEAM	GMs	MINs	MINs per GM	3-PT SHOTS TRIED	3-PT SHOTS MADE	FG PCT	FT PCT
113.	FERRELL, D.	f	ATL	66	1598	24.2	33	11	0.524	0.762
114.	JACKSON, M.	g	NY	81	2461	30.4	43	11	0.491	0.770
115.	RUDD, D.	g	UT	65	538	8.3	47	11	0.399	0.762
116.	BAGLEY, J.	g	BOS	73	1742	23.9	42	10	0.441	0.716
117.	COLES, B.	g	MIA	81	1976	24.4	52	10	0.455	0.824
118.	CORCHIANI, C.	g	ORL	51	741	14.5	37	10	0.399	0.875
119.	JOHNSON, K.	g	PHX	78	2899	37.2	46	10	0.479	0.807
120.	LEE, D.	g	NJ	46	307	6.7	37	10	0.431	0.526
121.	GAMBLE, K.	g/f	BOS	82	2496	30.4	31	9	0.529	0.885
122.	GARLAND, W.	g	DEN	78	2209	28.3	28	9	0.444	0.859
123.	WORTHY, J.	f	LAL	54	2108	39.0	43	9	0.447	0.814
124.	ANTHONY, G.	g	NY	82	1510	18.4	55	8	0.370	0.741
125.	BOWIE, S.	c	NJ	71	2179	30.7	25	8	0.445	0.757
126.	CHAPMAN, R.	g	WAS	22	567	25.8	29	8	0.448	0.679
127.	JAMERSON, D.	f	HOU	48	378	7.9	28	8	0.414	0.926
128.	MILLS, T.	f	NJ	82	1714	20.9	23	8	0.463	0.750
129.	SMITH, O.	g	ORL	55	877	15.9	21	8	0.365	0.769
130.	WILLIAMS, M.	g	IND	79	2750	34.8	33	8	0.490	0.871
131.	EACKLES, L.	f	WAS	65	1463	22.5	35	7	0.468	0.743
132.	EDWARDS, K.	g	MIA	81	1840	22.7	32	7	0.454	0.848
133.	GRANT, Gr.	g	PHI	68	891	13.1	18	7	0.440	0.833
134.	HANSEN, B.	g	CHI	68	809	11.9	27	7	0.444	0.364
135.	BLANKS, L.	g	DET	43	189	4.4	16	6	0.455	0.727
136.	BURTON, W.	g/f	MIA	68	1585	23.3	15	6	0.450	0.800
137.	ENGLISH, A.J.	g	WAS	81	1665	20.6	34	6	0.433	0.841
138.	FLEMING, V.	g	IND	82	1737	21.2	27	6	0.482	0.737
139.	GILL, K.	g/f	CHA	79	2906	36.8	25	6	0.467	0.745
140.	HIGGINS, S.	f	ORL	38	616	16.2	25	6	0.459	0.861
141.	LONG, G.	f	MIA	82	3063	37.4	22	6	0.494	0.807
142.	MONROE, R.	g	ATL	38	313	8.2	27	6	0.368	0.826
143.	WILLIS, K.	f/c	ATL	81	2962	36.6	37	6	0.483	0.804
144.	BROWN, D.	g	BOS	31	883	28.5	22	5	0.426	0.769
145.	CUMMINGS, T.	f	SA	70	2149	30.7	13	5	0.488	0.711
146.	DAVIS, B.	f	DAL	33	429	13.0	18	5	0.442	0.733
147.	DAVIS, W.	g	DEN	46	741	16.1	16	5	0.459	0.872
148.	DIVAC, V.	c	LAL	36	979	27.2	19	5	0.495	0.768
149.	JOHNSON, L.	f	CHA	82	3047	37.2	22	5	0.490	0.829
150.	LEWIS, Re.	g	BOS	82	3070	37.4	21	5	0.503	0.851
151.	MURDOCK, E.	g	UT	50	478	9.6	26	5	0.415	0.754
152.	PAYNE, K.	f	PHI	49	353	7.2	12	5	0.448	0.692
153.	RASMUSSEN, B.	c	ATL	81	1968	24.3	23	5	0.478	0.750
154.	SHAW, B.	g	MIA	63	1423	22.6	23	5	0.407	0.791
155.	STRICKLAND, R.	g	SA	57	2053	36.0	15	5	0.455	0.687
156.	FREDERICK, A.	f	CHA	66	852	12.9	17	4	0.435	0.685
157.	JOHNSON, A.	g	HOU	69	1235	17.9	15	4	0.479	0.654
158.	KIMBLE, B.	f	LAC	34	277	8.2	13	4	0.396	0.645
159.	KLEINE, J.	c	BOS	70	991	14.2	8	4	0.492	0.708
160.	KNIGHT, N.	g	PHX	42	631	15.0	13	4	0.475	0.688
161.	MACON, M.	g	DEN	76	2304	30.3	30	4	0.375	0.730
162.	NORMAN, K.	f	LAC	77	2009	26.1	28	4	0.490	0.535
163.	VAUGHT, L.	f	LAC	79	1687	21.4	5	4	0.492	0.797
164.	WEST, D.	g	MIN	80	2540	31.7	23	4	0.518	0.805
165.	WHITE, R.	f	DAL	65	1021	15.7	27	4	0.380	0.765
166.	ANDERSON, K.	g	NJ	64	1086	17.0	13	3	0.390	0.745
167.	BENOIT, D.	f	UT	77	1161	15.1	14	3	0.467	0.810
168.	BRICKOWSKI, F.	f	MIL	65	1556	23.9	6	3	0.524	0.767

(NAME)	REBs	ASTs	STLs	TURN-OVERS	BLKs	PTs
(FERRELL, D.)	210	92	49	99	17	839
(JACKSON, M.)	305	694	112	211	13	916
(RUDD, D.)	54	109	15	49	1	193
(BAGLEY, J.)	161	480	57	148	4	524
(COLES, B.)	189	366	73	167	13	816
(CORCHIANI, C.)	78	141	45	74	2	255
(JOHNSON, K.)	292	836	116	272	23	1536
(LEE, D.)	35	22	11	12	1	120
(GAMBLE, K.)	286	219	75	97	37	1108
(GARLAND, W.)	190	411	98	175	22	846
(WORTHY, J.)	305	252	76	127	23	1075
(ANTHONY, G.)	136	314	59	98	9	447
(BOWIE, S.)	578	186	41	150	120	1062
(CHAPMAN, R.)	58	89	15	45	8	270
(JAMERSON, D.)	43	33	17	24	0	191
(MILLS, T.)	453	84	48	82	41	742
(SMITH, O.)	116	57	36	62	13	310
(WILLIAMS, M.)	282	647	233	240	22	1188
(EACKLES, L.)	178	125	47	75	7	856
(EDWARDS, K.)	211	170	99	120	20	819
(GRANT, Gr.)	69	217	45	46	2	225
(HANSEN, B.)	77	69	27	28	3	173
(BLANKS, L.)	22	19	14	14	1	64
(BURTON, W.)	244	123	46	119	37	762
(ENGLISH, A.J.)	168	143	32	89	9	886
(FLEMING, V.)	209	266	56	140	7	726
(GILL, K.)	402	329	154	180	46	1622
(HIGGINS, S.)	102	41	16	41	6	291
(LONG, G.)	691	225	139	185	40	1212
(MONROE, R.)	33	27	12	23	2	131
(WILLIS, K.)	1258	173	72	197	54	1480
(BROWN, D.)	79	164	33	59	7	363
(CUMMINGS, T.)	631	102	58	115	34	1210
(DAVIS, B.)	33	66	11	27	3	92
(DAVIS, W.)	70	68	29	45	1	457
(DIVAC, V.)	247	60	55	88	35	405
(JOHNSON, L.)	899	292	81	160	51	1576
(LEWIS, Re.)	394	185	125	136	105	1703
(MURDOCK, E.)	54	92	30	50	7	203
(PAYNE, K.)	54	17	16	19	8	144
(RASMUSSEN, B.)	393	107	35	51	48	729
(SHAW, B.)	204	250	57	99	22	495
(STRICKLAND, R.)	265	491	118	160	17	787
(FREDERICK, A.)	144	71	40	58	26	389
(JOHNSON, A.)	80	266	61	110	9	386
(KIMBLE, B.)	32	17	10	15	6	112
(KLEINE, J.)	296	32	23	27	14	326
(KNIGHT, N.)	46	112	24	58	3	243
(MACON, M.)	220	168	154	155	14	805
(NORMAN, K.)	448	125	53	100	66	929
(VAUGHT, L.)	512	71	37	66	31	601
(WEST, D.)	257	281	66	120	26	1116
(WHITE, R.)	236	31	31	68	22	418
(ANDERSON, K.)	127	203	67	97	9	450
(BENOIT, D.)	296	34	19	71	44	434
(BRICKOWSKI, F.)	344	122	60	112	23	740

1991–92 REGULAR-SEASON STATISTICAL RESULTS
NBA PLAYERS ORDERED BY THREE-POINT SHOTS MADE

	NAME	POS	TEAM	GMs	MINs	MINs per GM	3-PT SHOTS TRIED	3-PT SHOTS MADE	FG PCT	FT PCT
169.	CHEEKS, M.	g	ATL	56	1086	19.4	6	3	0.462	0.605
170.	HENDERSON, G.	g	DET	16	96	6.0	8	3	0.375	0.818
171.	LYNCH, K.	g	CHA	55	819	14.9	8	3	0.417	0.761
172.	MALONE, K.	f	UT	81	3054	37.7	17	3	0.526	0.778
173.	MALONE, M.	c	MIL	82	2511	30.6	8	3	0.474	0.786
174.	MARCIULIONIS, S.	g	GS	72	2117	29.4	10	3	0.538	0.788
175.	MAYS, T.	g	ATL	2	32	16.0	6	3	0.429	1.000
176.	PAYTON, G.	g	SEA	81	2549	31.5	23	3	0.451	0.669
177.	PERRY, T.	f	PHX	80	2483	31.0	8	3	0.523	0.712
178.	PRESSEY, P.	g	SA	56	759	13.6	21	3	0.373	0.683
179.	RANDALL, M.	f	MIN	54	441	8.2	16	3	0.456	0.744
180.	REYNOLDS, J.	g/f	ORL	46	1159	25.2	24	3	0.380	0.836
181.	SPARROW, R.	g	LAL	46	489	10.6	15	3	0.384	0.615
182.	BATTLE, J.	g	CLE	76	1637	21.5	17	2	0.480	0.848
183.	BOGUES, M.	g	CHA	82	2790	34.0	27	2	0.472	0.783
184.	BROOKS, K.	f	DEN	37	270	7.3	11	2	0.443	0.810
185.	CHILCUTT, P.	f/c	SAC	69	817	11.8	2	2	0.452	0.821
186.	GREEN, Se.	g	IND	35	256	7.3	10	2	0.392	0.536
187.	KING, S.	f/c	CHI	79	1268	16.1	5	2	0.506	0.753
188.	MITCHELL, S.	f	MIN	82	2151	26.2	11	2	0.423	0.786
189.	MORTON, J.	g	MIA	25	270	10.8	16	2	0.387	0.842
190.	SMITH, La.	g	WAS	48	708	14.7	21	2	0.407	0.804
191.	THOMAS, C.	g	DET	37	156	4.2	17	2	0.353	0.667
192.	TOLBERT, T.	f	GS	35	310	8.9	8	2	0.384	0.550
193.	ACRES, M.	c	ORL	68	926	13.6	3	1	0.517	0.761
194.	ASKEW, V.	g	GS	80	1496	18.7	10	1	0.509	0.694
195.	AUGMON, S.	g/f	ATL	82	2505	30.5	6	1	0.489	0.666
196.	BONNER, A.	f	SAC	79	2287	28.9	4	1	0.447	0.627
197.	BRANDON, T.	g	CLE	82	1605	19.6	23	1	0.419	0.807
198.	BURTT, S.	g	PHX	31	356	11.5	6	1	0.463	0.704
199.	CARR, A.	f/c	SA	81	1867	23.0	5	1	0.490	0.764
200.	CEBALLOS, C.	f	PHX	64	725	11.3	6	1	0.482	0.737
201.	DOUGLAS, S.	g	BOS	42	752	17.9	10	1	0.463	0.682
202.	DREILING, G.	c	IND	60	509	8.5	1	1	0.494	0.750
203.	ELLISON, P.	c	WAS	66	2511	38.0	3	1	0.539	0.728
204.	EWING, P.	c	NY	82	3150	38.4	6	1	0.522	0.738
205.	GARRICK, T.	g	DAL	40	549	13.7	4	1	0.413	0.692
206.	GEORGE, T.	g	NJ	70	1037	14.8	6	1	0.428	0.821
207.	GMINSKI, M.	c	CHA	35	499	14.3	3	1	0.452	0.750
208.	GRANT, Ha.	f	WAS	64	2388	37.3	8	1	0.479	0.800
209.	GREEN, R.	g	BOS	26	367	14.1	4	1	0.447	0.722
210.	HOWARD, B.	f	DAL	27	318	11.8	2	1	0.519	0.710
211.	JOHNSON, B.	f	HOU	80	2202	27.5	9	1	0.458	0.727
212.	KERSEY, J.	f	POR	77	2553	33.2	8	1	0.467	0.664
213.	KOFOED, B.	g	SEA	44	239	5.4	7	1	0.472	0.577
214.	LEVINGSTON, C.	f	CHI	79	1020	12.9	6	1	0.498	0.625
215.	LICHTI, T.	g	DEN	68	1176	17.3	9	1	0.460	0.839
216.	MALONE, J.	g	UT	81	2922	36.1	12	1	0.511	0.898
217.	MURPHY, T.	f	MIN	47	429	9.1	2	1	0.488	0.559
218.	OLIVER, J.	g/f	CLE	27	252	9.3	9	1	0.398	0.773
219.	OWENS, B.	g/f	GS	80	2510	31.4	9	1	0.525	0.654
220.	PERDUE, W.	c	CHI	77	1007	13.1	2	1	0.547	0.495
221.	PERRY, E.	g	CHA	50	437	8.7	7	1	0.380	0.659
222.	ROBINSON, C.	f	POR	82	2124	25.9	11	1	0.466	0.664
223.	ROBINSON, D.	c	SA	68	2564	37.7	8	1	0.551	0.701
224.	SANDERS, M.	f	CLE	31	633	20.4	3	1	0.571	0.766

(NAME)	REBs	ASTs	STLs	TURN-OVERS	BLKs	PTs
(CHEEKS, M.)	95	185	83	36	0	259
(HENDERSON, G.)	8	10	3	8	0	36
(LYNCH, K.)	85	83	37	44	9	224
(MALONE, K.)	909	241	108	248	51	2272
(MALONE, M.)	744	93	74	150	64	1279
(MARCIULIONIS, S.)	208	243	116	193	10	1361
(MAYS, T.)	2	1	0	3	0	17
(PAYTON, G.)	295	506	147	174	21	764
(PERRY, T.)	551	134	44	141	116	982
(PRESSEY, P.)	95	142	29	64	19	151
(RANDALL, M.)	71	33	12	25	3	171
(REYNOLDS, J.)	149	151	63	96	17	555
(SPARROW, R.)	28	83	12	33	5	127
(BATTLE, J.)	112	159	36	91	5	779
(BOGUES, M.)	235	743	170	156	6	730
(BROOKS, K.)	39	11	8	18	2	105
(CHILCUTT, P.)	187	38	32	41	17	251
(GREEN, Se.)	42	22	13	27	6	141
(KING, S.)	205	77	21	76	25	551
(MITCHELL, S.)	473	94	53	97	39	825
(MORTON, J.)	26	32	13	28	1	106
(SMITH, La.)	81	99	44	63	1	247
(THOMAS, C.)	22	22	4	17	1	48
(TOLBERT, T.)	55	21	10	20	6	90
(ACRES, M.)	252	22	25	33	15	208
(ASKEW, V.)	233	188	47	84	23	498
(AUGMON, S.)	420	201	124	181	27	1094
(BONNER, A.)	485	125	94	133	26	740
(BRANDON, T.)	162	316	81	136	22	605
(BURTT, S.)	34	59	16	33	4	187
(CARR, A.)	346	63	32	114	96	881
(CEBALLOS, C.)	152	50	16	71	11	462
(DOUGLAS, S.)	63	172	25	68	9	308
(DREILING, G.)	96	25	10	31	16	117
(ELLISON, P.)	740	190	62	196	177	1322
(EWING, P.)	921	156	88	209	245	1970
(GARRICK, T.)	56	98	36	44	4	137
(GEORGE, T.)	105	162	41	82	3	418
(GMINSKI, M.)	118	31	11	20	16	202
(GRANT, Ha.)	432	170	74	109	27	1155
(GREEN, R.)	24	68	17	18	1	106
(HOWARD, B.)	51	014	11	15	8	131
(JOHNSON, B.)	312	158	72	104	49	685
(KERSEY, J.)	633	243	114	151	71	971
(KOFOED, B.)	26	51	2	20	2	66
(LEVINGSTON, C.)	227	66	27	42	45	311
(LICHTI, T.)	118	74	43	72	12	446
(MALONE, J.)	233	180	56	140	5	1639
(MURPHY, T.)	110	11	9	18	8	98
(OLIVER, J.)	27	20	9	9	2	96
(OWENS, B.)	639	188	90	179	65	1141
(PERDUE, W.)	312	80	16	72	43	350
(PERRY, E.)	39	78	34	50	3	126
(ROBINSON, C.)	416	137	85	154	107	1016
(ROBINSON, D.)	829	181	158	182	305	1578
(SANDERS, M.)	96	53	24	22	10	221

	NAME	POS	TEAM	GMs	MINs	MINs per GM	3-PT SHOTS TRIED	3-PT SHOTS MADE	FG PCT	FT PCT
225.	SIMMONS, L.	f	SAC	78	2895	37.1	5	1	0.454	0.770
226.	TEAGLE, T.	f	LAL	82	1602	19.5	4	1	0.452	0.767
227.	TURNER, A.	g	WAS	70	871	12.4	16	1	0.425	0.792
228.	TURNER, J.	f	ORL	75	1591	21.2	8	1	0.451	0.693
229.	VINCENT, S.	g	ORL	39	885	22.7	13	1	0.430	0.846
230.	WILLIAMS, H.	f/c	DAL	75	2040	27.2	6	1	0.431	0.725
231.	WINCHESTER, K.	f	NY	19	81	4.3	2	1	0.433	0.800
232.	WINGATE, D.	g	WAS	81	2127	26.3	18	1	0.465	0.719
233.	WOLF, J.	f	DEN	67	1160	17.3	11	1	0.361	0.803
234.	WOOLRIDGE, O.	f	DET	82	2113	25.8	9	1	0.498	0.683
235.	ABDELNABY, A.	f/c	POR	71	934	13.2	0	0	0.493	0.753
236.	ALEXANDER, V.	c	GS	80	1350	16.9	1	0	0.529	0.691
237.	ANDERSON, G.	f	DEN	82	2793	34.1	4	0	0.456	0.623
238.	ANSLEY, M.	f	CHA	10	45	4.5	2	0	0.444	0.833
239.	AUSTIN, I.	c	UT	31	112	3.6	0	0	0.457	0.633
240.	BAILEY, T.	f	MIN	84	2104	25.0	2	0	0.440	0.796
241.	BATTLE, K.	f	GS	16	92	5.8	1	0	0.647	0.833
242.	BEDFORD, W.	f/c	DET	32	363	11.3	1	0	0.413	0.636
243.	BENJAMIN, B.	c	SEA	63	1941	30.8	2	0	0.478	0.687
244.	BENNETT, W.	f	MIA	54	833	15.4	1	0	0.379	0.700
245.	BOL, M.	c	PHI	71	1267	17.8	9	0	0.383	0.462
246.	BREUER, R.	c	MIN	67	1176	17.6	1	0	0.468	0.533
247.	BROWN, C.	f	LAL	42	431	10.3	3	0	0.469	0.612
248.	BROWN, M.	c/f	UT	82	1783	21.7	1	0	0.453	0.667
249.	BROWN, R.	g	SAC	56	535	9.6	6	0	0.456	0.655
250.	BRYANT, M.	c	POR	56	800	14.3	3	0	0.480	0.667
251.	BUECHLER, J.	f	GS	28	290	10.4	1	0	0.409	0.571
252.	CAGE, M.	f	SEA	82	2461	30.0	5	0	0.566	0.620
253.	CAMPBELL, E.	c	LAL	81	1876	23.2	2	0	0.448	0.619
254.	CARTWRIGHT, B.	c	CHI	64	1471	23.0	0	0	0.467	0.604
255.	CATLEDGE, T.	f	ORL	78	2430	31.2	4	0	0.496	0.694
256.	CAUSWELL, D.	c	SAC	80	2291	28.6	1	0	0.550	0.613
257.	CONLON, M.	c	SEA	45	381	8.5	0	0	0.475	0.750
258.	CONNER, L.	g	MIL	81	1420	17.5	7	0	0.431	0.704
259.	COOK, A.	f	DEN	22	115	5.2	0	0	0.600	0.667
260.	COOPER, W.	f	POR	35	344	9.8	0	0	0.427	0.636
261.	COPA, T.	f/c	SA	33	132	4.0	0	0	0.550	0.308
262.	CORBIN, T.	f	UT	80	2207	27.6	4	0	0.481	0.866
263.	DAILEY, Q.	f	SEA	11	98	8.9	1	0	0.243	0.813
264.	DAUGHERTY, B.	c	CLE	73	2643	36.2	2	0	0.570	0.777
265.	DAVIS, D.	f	IND	64	1301	20.3	1	0	0.552	0.572
266.	DAVIS, T.	f/c	DAL	68	2149	31.6	5	0	0.482	0.635
267.	DONALDSON, J.	c	NY	58	1075	18.5	0	0	0.457	0.709
268.	DUCKWORTH, K.	c	POR	82	2222	27.1	3	0	0.461	0.690
269.	DUDLEY, C.	c	NJ	82	1902	23.2	0	0	0.403	0.468
270.	EATON, M.	c	UT	81	2023	25.0	0	0	0.446	0.598
271.	EDWARDS, Ja.	c	LAC	72	1437	20.0	1	0	0.465	0.731
272.	ELLIS, L.	f	LAC	29	103	3.6	0	0	0.340	0.474
273.	FEITL, D.	c	NJ	34	175	5.2	0	0	0.429	0.842
274.	FOSTER, G.	f	WAS	49	548	11.2	1	0	0.461	0.714
275.	FRANK, T.	f	MIN	10	140	14.0	0	0	0.546	0.667
276.	GATLING, C.	c	GS	54	612	11.3	4	0	0.568	0.661
277.	GATTISON, K.	f/c	CHA	82	2223	27.1	2	0	0.529	0.688
278.	GILLIAM, A.	f/c	PHI	81	2771	34.2	2	0	0.512	0.807
279.	GRANT, Ho.	f	CHI	81	2859	35.3	2	0	0.579	0.741
280.	GREEN, S.	f	SA	80	1127	14.1	0	0	0.427	0.820

(NAME)	REBs	ASTs	STLs	TURN-OVERS	BLKs	PTs
(SIMMONS, L.)	634	337	135	218	132	1336
(TEAGLE, T.)	183	113	66	114	9	880
(TURNER, A.)	90	177	57	84	2	284
(TURNER, J.)	246	92	24	106	16	530
(VINCENT, S.)	101	148	35	72	4	411
(WILLIAMS, H.)	454	94	35	114	98	859
(WINCHESTER, K.)	15	8	2	2	2	35
(WINGATE, D.)	269	247	123	124	21	638
(WOLF, J.)	240	61	32	60	14	254
(WOOLRIDGE, O.)	260	88	41	133	33	1146
(ABDELNABY, A.)	260	30	25	66	16	432
(ALEXANDER, V.)	336	32	45	91	62	589
(ANDERSON, G.)	941	78	88	201	65	945
(ANSLEY, M.)	6	2	0	3	0	21
(AUSTIN, I.)	35	5	2	8	2	61
(BAILEY, T.)	485	78	35	108	117	951
(BATTLE, K.)	16	4	2	4	2	32
(BEDFORD, W.)	63	12	6	15	18	114
(BENJAMIN, B.)	513	76	39	175	118	879
(BENNETT, W.)	162	38	19	33	9	195
(BOL, M.)	222	22	11	41	205	110
(BREUER, R.)	281	89	27	41	99	363
(BROWN, C.)	82	26	12	29	7	150
(BROWN, M.)	476	81	42	105	34	632
(BROWN, R.)	69	59	35	42	12	192
(BRYANT, M.)	201	41	26	30	8	230
(BUECHLER, J.)	52	23	19	13	7	70
(CAGE, M.)	728	92	99	78	55	720
(CAMPBELL, E.)	423	59	53	73	159	578
(CARTWRIGHT, B.)	324	87	22	75	14	512
(CATLEDGE, T.)	549	109	58	138	16	1154
(CAUSWELL, D.)	580	59	47	124	215	636
(CONLON, M.)	69	12	9	27	7	120
(CONNER, L.)	184	294	97	79	10	287
(COOK, A.)	34	2	5	3	4	34
(COOPER, W.)	101	21	4	15	27	77
(COPA, T.)	36	3	2	8	6	48
(CORBIN, T.)	472	140	82	97	20	780
(DAILEY, Q.)	12	4	5	10	1	31
(DAUGHERTY, B.)	760	262	65	185	78	1566
(DAVIS, D.)	410	30	27	49	74	395
(DAVIS, T.)	672	57	26	117	29	693
(DONALDSON, J.)	289	33	8	48	49	285
(DUCKWORTH, K.)	497	99	38	143	37	880
(DUDLEY, C.)	739	58	38	79	179	460
(EATON, M.)	491	40	36	60	205	266
(EDWARDS, Ja.)	202	53	24	72	33	698
(ELLIS, L.)	24	1	6	11	9	43
(FEITL, D.)	61	6	2	19	3	82
(FOSTER, G.)	145	35	6	36	12	213
(FRANK, T.)	26	8	5	5	4	46
(GATLING, C.)	182	16	31	44	36	306
(GATTISON, K.)	580	131	59	140	69	1042
(GILLIAM, A.)	660	118	51	166	85	1367
(GRANT, Ho.)	807	217	100	98	131	1149
(GREEN, S.)	342	36	29	62	11	367

1991–92 REGULAR-SEASON STATISTICAL RESULTS
NBA PLAYERS ORDERED BY THREE-POINT SHOTS MADE

	NAME	POS	TEAM	GMs	MINs	MINs per GM	3-PT SHOTS TRIED	3-PT SHOTS MADE	FG PCT	FT PCT
281.	HALEY, J.	f/c	LAL	49	394	8.0	0	0	0.369	0.483
282.	HAMMONDS, T.	f	CHA	37	984	26.6	1	0	0.488	0.610
283.	HASTINGS, S.	f	DEN	40	421	10.5	9	0	0.340	0.857
284.	HERRERA, C.	f	HOU	43	566	13.2	1	0	0.516	0.568
285.	HILL, T.	c/f	GS	82	1886	23.0	1	0	0.522	0.694
286.	HODGE, D.	c/f	DAL	51	1058	20.7	0	0	0.497	0.667
287.	JEPSEN, L.	c	SAC	31	87	2.8	1	0	0.375	0.636
288.	JONES, Ch.	c/f	WAS	75	1365	18.2	0	0	0.367	0.500
289.	KEMP, S.	f/c	SEA	64	1808	28.2	3	0	0.504	0.748
290.	KESSLER, A.	c	MIA	77	1197	15.5	0	0	0.413	0.817
291.	KING, R.	c	SEA	40	213	5.3	1	0	0.380	0.756
292.	KITE, G.	c	ORL	72	1479	20.5	1	0	0.437	0.588
293.	KONCAK, J.	c	ATL	77	1489	19.3	12	0	0.391	0.655
294.	KRYSTKOWIAK, L.	f	MIL	79	1848	23.4	5	0	0.444	0.757
295.	LANE, J.	f	MIL	14	177	12.6	0	0	0.304	0.333
296.	LANG, A.	c	PHX	81	1965	24.3	1	0	0.522	0.768
297.	LECKNER, E.	c	CHA	59	716	12.1	1	0	0.513	0.745
298.	LISTER, A.	c	GS	26	293	11.3	0	0	0.557	0.424
299.	LONGLEY, L.	c	MIN	66	991	15.0	0	0	0.458	0.663
300.	MANNING, D.	f	LAC	82	2904	35.4	5	0	0.542	0.725
301.	MASON, A.	f	NY	82	2198	26.8	0	0	0.509	0.642
302.	McCANN, B.	f	DET	26	129	5.0	1	0	0.394	0.308
303.	McCORMICK, T.	c	NY	22	108	4.9	0	0	0.424	0.667
304.	McHALE, K.	f/c	BOS	56	1398	25.0	13	0	0.510	0.822
305.	MUSTAF, J.	f	PHX	52	545	10.5	0	0	0.477	0.690
306.	MUTOMBO, D.	c	DEN	71	2716	38.3	0	0	0.493	0.642
307.	NANCE, L.	f	CLE	81	2880	35.6	6	0	0.539	0.822
308.	OAKLEY, C.	f	NY	82	2309	28.2	3	0	0.522	0.735
309.	OGG, A.	c	MIA	43	367	8.5	0	0	0.548	0.533
310.	OLAJUWON, H.	c	HOU	70	2636	37.7	1	0	0.502	0.766
311.	OLIVER, B.	g	PHI	34	279	8.2	4	0	0.330	0.682
312.	OWENS, K.	f	LAL	20	80	4.0	0	0	0.281	0.800
313.	PACK, R.	g	POR	72	894	12.4	10	0	0.423	0.803
314.	PARISH, R.	c	BOS	79	2285	28.9	0	0	0.536	0.772
315.	PETERSEN, J.	c	GS	27	169	6.3	2	0	0.450	0.700
316.	PHILLS, B.	g	CLE	10	65	6.5	2	0	0.429	0.636
317.	PINCKNEY, E.	f	BOS	81	1917	23.7	1	0	0.537	0.812
318.	POLYNICE, O.	c	LAC	76	1834	24.1	1	0	0.519	0.622
319.	PRITCHARD, K.	g	BOS	11	136	12.4	3	0	0.471	0.778
320.	RAMBIS, K.	f	PHX	28	381	13.6	0	0	0.463	0.778
321.	REID, J.R.	c/f	CHA	51	1257	24.6	3	0	0.490	0.705
322.	RIVERS, Da.	g	LAC	15	122	8.1	1	0	0.333	0.909
323.	ROBERTS, S.	c	ORL	55	1118	20.3	1	0	0.529	0.515
324.	ROLLINS, T.	f/c	HOU	59	697	11.8	0	0	0.535	0.867
325.	ROYAL, D.	f	SA	60	718	12.0	0	0	0.449	0.692
326.	RULAND, J.	c	PHI	13	209	16.1	0	0	0.526	0.688
327.	SALLEY, J.	f/c	DET	72	1774	24.6	3	0	0.512	0.715
328.	SAMPSON, R.	c	WAS	10	108	10.8	2	0	0.310	0.667
329.	SANDERS, J.	f	ATL	12	117	9.8	0	0	0.444	0.778
330.	SCHAYES, D.	c	MIL	43	726	16.9	0	0	0.417	0.771
331.	SCHEFFLER, S.	f	DEN	11	61	5.6	0	0	0.667	0.750
332.	SCHINTZIUS, D.	c	SAC	33	400	12.1	4	0	0.427	0.833
333.	SEIKALY, R.	c	MIA	79	2800	35.4	3	0	0.489	0.733
334.	SELLERS, B.	f/c	DET	43	226	5.3	1	0	0.466	0.769
335.	SHACKLEFORD, C.	c	PHI	72	1399	19.4	1	0	0.486	0.663
336.	SMITH, C.	f/c	LAC	49	1310	26.7	6	0	0.466	0.785

(NAME)	REBs	ASTs	STLs	TURN-OVERS	BLKs	PTs
(HALEY, J.)	95	7	7	25	8	76
(HAMMONDS, T.)	185	36	22	58	13	440
(HASTINGS, S.)	98	26	10	22	15	58
(HERRERA, C.)	99	27	16	37	25	191
(HILL, T.)	593	47	73	106	43	671
(HODGE, D.)	275	39	25	75	23	426
(JEPSEN, L.)	30	1	1	3	5	25
(JONES, Ch.)	317	62	43	39	92	86
(KEMP, S.)	665	86	70	156	124	994
(KESSLER, A.)	314	34	17	58	32	410
(KING, R.)	49	12	4	18	5	88
(KITE, G.)	402	44	30	61	57	228
(KONCAK, J.)	261	132	50	54	67	241
(KRYSTKOWIAK, L.)	429	114	54	115	12	714
(LANE, J.)	66	17	2	14	1	37
(LANG, A.)	546	43	48	87	201	622
(LECKNER, E.)	206	31	9	39	18	196
(LISTER, A.)	92	14	5	20	16	102
(LONGLEY, L.)	257	53	35	83	64	281
(MANNING, D.)	564	285	135	210	122	1579
(MASON, A.)	573	106	46	101	20	573
(McCANN, B.)	30	6	6	7	4	30
(McCORMICK, T.)	34	9	2	8	0	42
(McHALE, K.)	330	82	11	82	59	780
(MUSTAF, J.)	145	45	21	51	16	233
(MUTOMBO, D.)	870	156	43	252	210	1177
(NANCE, L.)	670	232	80	87	243	1375
(OAKLEY, C.)	700	133	67	123	15	506
(OGG, A.)	74	7	5	19	28	108
(OLAJUWON, H.)	845	157	127	187	304	1510
(OLIVER, B.)	30	20	10	24	2	81
(OWENS, K.)	15	3	5	2	4	26
(PACK, R.)	97	140	40	92	4	332
(PARISH, R.)	705	70	68	131	97	1115
(PETERSEN, J.)	45	9	5	5	6	43
(PHILLS, B.)	8	4	3	8	1	31
(PINCKNEY, E.)	564	62	70	73	56	613
(POLYNICE, O.)	536	46	45	83	20	613
(PRITCHARD, K.)	11	30	3	11	4	46
(RAMBIS, K.)	106	37	12	25	14	90
(REID, J.R.)	317	81	49	84	23	560
(RIVERS, Da.)	19	21	7	17	1	30
(ROBERTS, S.)	336	39	22	78	83	573
(ROLLINS, T.)	171	15	14	18	62	118
(ROYAL, D.)	124	34	25	39	7	252
(RULAND, J.)	47	5	7	20	4	51
(SALLEY, J.)	296	116	49	102	110	684
(SAMPSON, R.)	30	4	3	10	8	22
(SANDERS, J.)	26	9	5	5	3	47
(SCHAYES, D.)	168	34	19	41	19	240
(SCHEFFLER, S.)	14	0	3	1	1	21
(SCHINTZIUS, D.)	118	20	6	19	28	110
(SEIKALY, R.)	934	109	40	216	121	1296
(SELLERS, B.)	42	14	1	15	10	102
(SHACKLEFORD, C.)	415	46	38	62	51	473
(SMITH, C.)	301	56	41	69	98	714

1991–92 REGULAR-SEASON STATISTICAL RESULTS
NBA PLAYERS ORDERED BY THREE-POINT SHOTS MADE

	NAME	POS	TEAM	GMs	MINs	MINs per GM	3-PT SHOTS TRIED	3-PT SHOTS MADE	FG PCT	FT PCT
337.	SMITH, Do.	f	DAL	76	1707	22.5	11	0	0.415	0.736
338.	SMITH, L.	f/c	HOU	45	800	17.8	1	0	0.544	0.364
339.	SMITH, To.	g	LAL	63	820	13.0	11	0	0.399	0.653
340.	SMITS, R.	c	IND	74	1772	23.9	2	0	0.510	0.788
341.	SPENCER, F.	c	MIN	61	1481	24.3	0	0	0.426	0.691
342.	STEWART, L.	f	WAS	76	2229	29.3	3	0	0.514	0.807
343.	THOMPSON, L.	f/c	IND	80	1299	16.2	2	0	0.468	0.817
344.	THOMPSON, S.	g	SAC	19	91	4.8	1	0	0.378	0.375
345.	THORPE, O.	f	HOU	82	3056	37.3	7	0	0.592	0.657
346.	TISDALE, W.	f	SAC	72	2521	35.0	2	0	0.501	0.763
347.	TURNER, Jo.	f	HOU	42	345	8.2	0	0	0.439	0.525
348.	VRANKOVIC, S.	c	BOS	19	110	5.8	0	0	0.469	0.583
349.	WALKER, D.	g	DET	74	1541	20.8	10	0	0.423	0.619
350.	WEST, M.	c	PHX	82	1436	17.5	0	0	0.632	0.637
351.	WHATLEY, E.	g	POR	23	209	9.1	4	0	0.412	0.871
352.	WIGGINS, M.	g	PHI	49	569	11.6	1	0	0.384	0.686
353.	WILLIAMS, Br.	F	ORL	48	905	18.9	0	0	0.528	0.669
354.	WILLIAMS, Bu.	f	POR	80	2519	31.5	1	0	0.604	0.754
355.	WILLIAMS, J.	f/c	CLE	80	2432	30.4	4	0	0.503	0.752
356.	WILLIAMS, Ja.	f/c	PHI	50	646	12.9	0	0	0.364	0.636
357.	WILLIAMS, K.	f	IND	60	565	9.4	4	0	0.518	0.605
358.	WILLIAMS, S.	f	CHI	63	690	11.0	3	0	0.483	0.649
359.	WITTMAN, R.	g	IND	24	115	4.8	0	0	0.421	0.500

(NAME)	REBs	ASTs	STLs	TURN-OVERS	BLKs	PTs
(SMITH, Do.)	391	129	62	97	34	671
(SMITH, L.)	256	33	21	44	7	104
(SMITH, To.)	76	109	39	50	8	275
(SMITS, R.)	417	116	29	130	100	1024
(SPENCER, F.)	435	53	27	70	79	405
(STEWART, L.)	449	120	51	112	44	794
(THOMPSON, L.)	381	102	52	98	34	394
(THOMPSON, S.)	19	8	6	5	3	31
(THORPE, O.)	862	250	52	237	37	1420
(TISDALE, W.)	469	106	55	124	79	1195
(TURNER, Jo.)	78	12	6	32	4	117
(VRANKOVIC, S.)	28	5	0	10	17	37
(WALKER, D.)	238	205	63	79	18	387
(WEST, M.)	372	22	14	82	81	501
(WHATLEY, E.)	21	34	14	14	3	69
(WIGGINS, M.)	94	22	20	25	1	211
(WILLIAMS, Br.)	272	33	41	86	53	437
(WILLIAMS, Bu.)	704	108	62	130	41	901
(WILLIAMS, J.)	607	196	60	83	182	952
(WILLIAMS, Ja.)	145	12	20	44	20	206
(WILLIAMS, K.)	129	40	20	22	41	252
(WILLIAMS, S.)	247	50	13	35	36	214
(WITTMAN, R.)	9	11	2	3	0	17

1991–92 REGULAR-SEASON STATISTICAL RESULTS
NBA PLAYERS ORDERED BY TURNOVERS PER GAME

	NAME	POS	TEAM	GMs	MINs	MIN per GM	TURN-OVERS	TOs per MIN	TOs per GM	FG PCT	FT PCT
1.	COLEMAN, D.	f	NJ	65	2207	34.0	248	0.112	3.82	0.504	0.763
2.	MUTOMBO, D.	c	DEN	71	2716	38.3	252	0.093	3.55	0.493	0.642
3.	JOHNSON, K.	g	PHX	78	2899	37.2	272	0.094	3.49	0.479	0.807
4.	STOCKTON, J.	g	UT	82	3002	36.6	286	0.095	3.49	0.482	0.842
5.	HARDAWAY, T.	g	GS	81	3332	41.1	267	0.080	3.30	0.461	0.766
6.	THOMAS, I.	g	DET	78	2918	37.4	252	0.086	3.23	0.446	0.773
7.	DREXLER, C.	g	POR	76	2751	36.2	240	0.087	3.16	0.470	0.794
8.	BARKLEY, C.	f	PHI	75	2881	38.4	235	0.082	3.13	0.552	0.695
9.	SKILES, S.	g	ORL	75	2377	31.7	233	0.098	3.11	0.414	0.895
10.	PIPPEN, S.	f	CHI	82	3164	38.6	253	0.080	3.09	0.506	0.760
11.	RICHMOND, M.	g	SAC	80	3095	38.7	247	0.080	3.09	0.468	0.813
12.	HARPER, R.	g	LAC	82	3144	38.3	252	0.080	3.07	0.440	0.736
13.	MALONE, K.	f	UT	81	3054	37.7	248	0.081	3.06	0.526	0.778
14.	WILLIAMS, M.	g	IND	79	2750	34.8	240	0.087	3.04	0.490	0.871
15.	ELLISON, P.	c	WAS	66	2511	38.0	196	0.078	2.97	0.539	0.728
16.	WEBB, S.	g	SAC	77	2724	35.4	229	0.084	2.97	0.445	0.859
17.	WILKINS, D.	f	ATL	42	1601	38.1	122	0.076	2.90	0.464	0.835
18.	THORPE, O.	f	HOU	82	3056	37.3	237	0.078	2.89	0.592	0.657
19.	STRICKLAND, R.	g	SA	57	2053	36.0	160	0.078	2.81	0.455	0.687
20.	SMITH, K.	g	HOU	81	2735	33.8	227	0.083	2.80	0.475	0.866
21.	SIMMONS, L.	f	SAC	78	2895	37.1	218	0.075	2.79	0.454	0.770
22.	BENJAMIN, B.	c	SEA	63	1941	30.8	175	0.090	2.78	0.478	0.687
23.	BIRD, L.	f	BOS	45	1662	36.9	125	0.075	2.78	0.466	0.926
24.	SEIKALY, R.	c	MIA	79	2800	35.4	216	0.077	2.73	0.489	0.733
25.	ADAMS, M.	g	WAS	78	2795	35.8	212	0.076	2.72	0.393	0.869
26.	ROBERTSON, A.	g	MIL	82	2463	30.0	223	0.091	2.72	0.430	0.763
27.	MARCIULIONIS, S.	g	GS	72	2117	29.4	193	0.091	2.68	0.538	0.788
28.	ROBINSON, D.	c	SA	68	2564	37.7	182	0.071	2.68	0.551	0.701
29.	OLAJUWON, H.	c	HOU	70	2636	37.7	187	0.071	2.67	0.502	0.766
30.	PERSON, C.	f	IND	81	2923	36.1	216	0.074	2.67	0.480	0.675
31.	PETROVIC, D.	g	NJ	82	3027	36.9	215	0.071	2.62	0.508	0.808
32.	JACKSON, M.	g	NY	81	2461	30.4	211	0.086	2.60	0.491	0.770
33.	MANNING, D.	f	LAC	82	2904	35.4	210	0.072	2.56	0.542	0.725
34.	EWING, P.	c	NY	82	3150	38.4	209	0.066	2.55	0.522	0.738
35.	ROBINSON, R.	g	ATL	81	2220	27.4	206	0.093	2.54	0.456	0.636
36.	DAUGHERTY, B.	c	CLE	73	2643	36.2	185	0.070	2.53	0.570	0.777
37.	JORDAN, M.	g	CHI	80	3102	38.8	200	0.065	2.50	0.519	0.832
38.	MULLIN, C.	f	GS	81	3346	41.3	202	0.060	2.49	0.524	0.833
39.	RICHARDSON, P.	g	MIN	82	2922	35.6	204	0.070	2.49	0.466	0.691
40.	SMITH, S.	g	MIA	61	1806	29.6	152	0.084	2.49	0.454	0.748
41.	ANDERSON, W.	g/f	SA	57	1889	33.1	140	0.074	2.46	0.456	0.775
42.	ANDERSON, G.	f	DEN	82	2793	34.1	201	0.072	2.45	0.456	0.623
43.	DIVAC, V.	c	LAL	36	979	27.2	88	0.090	2.44	0.495	0.768
44.	KEMP, S.	f/c	SEA	64	1808	28.2	156	0.086	2.44	0.504	0.748
45.	WILLIS, K.	f/c	ATL	81	2962	36.6	197	0.067	2.43	0.483	0.804
46.	PIERCE, R.	g	SEA	78	2658	34.1	189	0.071	2.42	0.475	0.917
47.	GRANT, Ga.	g	LAC	78	2049	26.3	187	0.091	2.40	0.462	0.815
48.	SCHREMPF, D.	f	IND	80	2605	32.6	191	0.073	2.39	0.536	0.828
49.	HARPER, D.	g	DAL	65	2252	34.6	154	0.068	2.37	0.443	0.759
50.	DUMARS, J.	g	DET	82	3192	38.9	193	0.061	2.35	0.448	0.867
51.	NEWMAN, J.	f/g	CHA	55	1651	30.0	129	0.078	2.35	0.477	0.766
52.	WORTHY, J.	f	LAL	54	2108	39.0	127	0.060	2.35	0.447	0.814
53.	HAWKINS, H.	g	PHI	81	3013	37.2	189	0.063	2.33	0.462	0.874
54.	PORTER, T.	g	POR	82	2784	34.0	188	0.068	2.29	0.462	0.856
55.	GILL, K.	g/f	CHA	79	2906	36.8	180	0.062	2.28	0.467	0.745
56.	LONG, G.	f	MIA	82	3063	37.4	185	0.060	2.26	0.494	0.807

(NAME)	3-PT SHOTS MADE	3-PT SHOTS TRIED	REBs	ASTs	STLs	BLKs	PTs
(COLEMAN, D.)	23	76	618	205	54	98	1289
(MUTOMBO, D.)	0	0	870	156	43	210	1177
(JOHNSON, K.)	10	46	292	836	116	23	1536
(STOCKTON, J.)	83	204	270	1126	244	22	1297
(HARDAWAY, T.)	127	376	310	807	164	13	1893
(THOMAS, I.)	25	86	247	560	118	15	1445
(DREXLER, C.)	114	338	500	512	138	70	1903
(BARKLEY, C.)	32	137	830	308	136	44	1730
(SKILES, S.)	91	250	202	544	74	5	1057
(PIPPEN, S.)	16	80	630	572	155	93	1720
(RICHMOND, M.)	103	268	319	411	92	34	1803
(HARPER, R.)	64	211	447	417	152	72	1495
(MALONE, K.)	3	17	909	241	108	51	2272
(WILLIAMS, M.)	8	33	282	647	233	22	1188
(ELLISON, P.)	1	3	740	190	62	177	1322
(WEBB, S.)	73	199	223	547	125	24	1231
(WILKINS, D.)	37	128	295	158	52	24	1179
(THORPE, O.)	0	7	862	250	52	37	1420
(STRICKLAND, R.)	5	15	265	491	118	17	787
(SMITH, K.)	54	137	177	562	104	7	1137
(SIMMONS, L.)	1	5	634	337	135	132	1336
(BENJAMIN, B.)	0	2	513	76	39	118	879
(BIRD, L.)	52	128	434	306	42	33	908
(SEIKALY, R.)	0	3	934	109	40	121	1296
(ADAMS, M.)	125	386	310	594	145	9	1408
(ROBERTSON, A.)	67	210	350	360	210	32	1010
(MARCIULIONIS, S.)	3	10	208	243	116	10	1361
(ROBINSON, D.)	1	8	829	181	158	305	1578
(OLAJUWON, H.)	0	1	845	157	127	304	1510
(PERSON, C.)	132	354	426	382	68	18	1497
(PETROVIC, D.)	123	277	258	252	105	11	1691
(JACKSON, M.)	11	43	305	694	112	13	916
(MANNING, D.)	0	5	564	285	135	122	1579
(EWING, P.)	1	6	921	156	88	245	1970
(ROBINSON, R.)	34	104	219	446	105	24	1055
(DAUGHERTY, B.)	0	2	760	262	65	78	1566
(JORDAN, M.)	27	100	511	489	182	75	2404
(MULLIN, C.)	64	175	450	286	173	62	2074
(RICHARDSON, P.)	53	155	301	685	119	25	1350
(SMITH, S.)	40	125	188	278	59	19	729
(ANDERSON, W.)	13	56	300	302	54	51	744
(ANDERSON, G.)	0	4	941	78	88	65	945
(DIVAC, V.)	5	19	247	60	55	35	405
(KEMP, S.)	0	3	665	86	70	124	994
(WILLIS, K.)	6	37	1258	173	72	54	1480
(PIERCE, R.)	33	123	233	241	86	20	1690
(GRANT, Ga.)	15	51	184	538	138	14	609
(SCHREMPF, D.)	23	71	770	312	62	37	1380
(HARPER, D.)	58	186	170	373	101	17	1152
(DUMARS, J.)	49	120	188	375	71	12	1635
(NEWMAN, J.)	13	46	179	146	70	14	839
(WORTHY, J.)	9	43	305	252	76	23	1075
(HAWKINS, H.)	91	229	271	248	157	43	1536
(PORTER, T.)	128	324	255	477	127	12	1485
(GILL, K.)	6	25	402	329	154	46	1622
(LONG, G.)	6	22	691	225	139	40	1212

1991–92 REGULAR-SEASON STATISTICAL RESULTS
NBA PLAYERS ORDERED BY TURNOVERS PER GAME

	NAME	POS	TEAM	GMs	MINs	MIN per GM	TURN-OVERS	TOs per MIN	TOs per GM	FG PCT	FT PCT
57.	GARLAND, W.	g	DEN	78	2209	28.3	175	0.079	2.24	0.444	0.859
58.	OWENS, B.	g/f	GS	80	2510	31.4	179	0.071	2.24	0.525	0.654
59.	DAWKINS, J.	g	PHI	82	2815	34.3	183	0.065	2.23	0.437	0.882
60.	MAXWELL, V.	g	HOU	80	2700	33.7	178	0.066	2.23	0.413	0.772
61.	MORRIS, C.	f	NJ	77	2394	31.1	171	0.071	2.22	0.477	0.714
62.	THREATT, S.	g	LAL	82	3070	37.4	182	0.059	2.22	0.489	0.831
63.	AUGMON, S.	g/f	ATL	82	2505	30.5	181	0.072	2.21	0.489	0.666
64.	PRICE, M.	g	CLE	72	2138	29.7	159	0.074	2.21	0.488	0.947
65.	McKEY, D.	f	SEA	52	1757	33.8	114	0.065	2.19	0.472	0.847
66.	PAYTON, G.	g	SEA	81	2549	31.5	174	0.068	2.15	0.451	0.669
67.	WILLIAMS, R.	f	DEN	81	2623	32.4	173	0.066	2.14	0.471	0.803
68.	CAMPBELL, T.	f/g	MIN	78	2441	31.3	165	0.068	2.12	0.464	0.803
69.	BLAYLOCK, M.	g	NJ	72	2548	35.4	152	0.060	2.11	0.432	0.712
70.	BOWIE, S.	c	NJ	71	2179	30.7	150	0.069	2.11	0.445	0.757
71.	HORNACEK, J.	g	PHX	81	3078	38.0	170	0.055	2.10	0.512	0.886
72.	REYNOLDS, J.	g/f	ORL	46	1159	25.2	96	0.083	2.09	0.380	0.836
73.	ANDERSON, N.	g/f	ORL	60	2203	36.7	125	0.057	2.08	0.463	0.667
74.	HUMPHRIES, J.	g	MIL	71	2261	31.8	148	0.066	2.08	0.470	0.783
75.	BOWIE, A.	g/f	ORL	52	1721	33.1	107	0.062	2.06	0.493	0.860
76.	COLES, B.	g	MIA	81	1976	24.4	167	0.085	2.06	0.455	0.824
77.	CHAPMAN, R.	g	WAS	22	567	25.8	45	0.079	2.05	0.448	0.679
78.	GILLIAM, A.	f/c	PHI	81	2771	34.2	166	0.060	2.05	0.512	0.807
79.	BLACKMAN, R.	g	DAL	75	2527	33.7	153	0.061	2.04	0.461	0.899
80.	MACON, M.	g	DEN	76	2304	30.3	155	0.067	2.04	0.375	0.730
81.	BAGLEY, J.	g	BOS	73	1742	23.9	148	0.085	2.03	0.441	0.716
82.	KERSEY, J.	f	POR	77	2553	33.2	151	0.059	1.96	0.467	0.664
83.	JOHNSON, L.	f	CHA	82	3047	37.2	160	0.053	1.95	0.490	0.829
84.	MILLER, R.	g	IND	82	3120	38.0	157	0.050	1.91	0.501	0.858
85.	BOGUES, M.	g	CHA	82	2790	34.0	156	0.056	1.90	0.472	0.783
86.	BROWN, D.	g	BOS	31	883	28.5	59	0.067	1.90	0.426	0.769
87.	ROBINSON, C.	f	POR	82	2124	25.9	154	0.073	1.88	0.466	0.664
88.	ELLIOTT, S.	f	SA	82	3120	38.0	152	0.049	1.85	0.494	0.861
89.	VINCENT, S.	g	ORL	39	885	22.7	72	0.081	1.85	0.430	0.846
90.	RICE, G.	f	MIA	79	3007	38.1	145	0.048	1.84	0.469	0.837
91.	MALONE, M.	c	MIL	82	2511	30.6	150	0.060	1.83	0.474	0.786
92.	STARKS, J.	g	NY	82	2118	25.8	150	0.071	1.83	0.449	0.778
93.	McDANIEL, X.	f	NY	82	2344	28.6	147	0.063	1.79	0.478	0.714
94.	WILLIAMS, Br.	f	ORL	48	905	18.9	86	0.095	1.79	0.528	0.669
95.	CATLEDGE, T.	f	ORL	78	2430	31.2	138	0.057	1.77	0.496	0.694
96.	IUZZOLINO, M.	g	DAL	52	1280	24.6	92	0.072	1.77	0.451	0.836
97.	PERRY, T.	f	PHX	80	2483	31.0	141	0.057	1.76	0.523	0.712
98.	SMITS, R.	c	IND	74	1772	23.9	130	0.073	1.76	0.510	0.788
99.	BURTON, W.	g/f	MIA	68	1585	23.3	119	0.075	1.75	0.450	0.800
100.	CURRY, D.	g	CHA	77	2020	26.2	134	0.066	1.74	0.486	0.836
101.	DUCKWORTH, K.	c	POR	82	2222	27.1	143	0.064	1.74	0.461	0.690
102.	MALONE, J.	g	UT	81	2922	36.1	140	0.048	1.73	0.511	0.898
103.	BRICKOWSKI, F.	f	MIL	65	1556	23.9	112	0.072	1.72	0.524	0.767
104.	DAVIS, T.	f/c	DAL	68	2149	31.6	117	0.054	1.72	0.482	0.635
105.	SCOTT, D.	f	ORL	18	608	33.8	31	0.051	1.72	0.402	0.901
106.	TISDALE, W.	f	SAC	72	2521	35.0	124	0.049	1.72	0.501	0.763
107.	FLEMING, V.	g	IND	82	1737	21.2	140	0.081	1.71	0.482	0.737
108.	GATTISON, K.	f/c	CHA	82	2223	27.1	140	0.063	1.71	0.529	0.688
109.	RODMAN, D.	f	DET	82	3301	40.3	140	0.042	1.71	0.539	0.600
110.	GRANT, Ha.	f	WAS	64	2388	37.3	109	0.046	1.70	0.479	0.800
111.	BONNER, A.	f	SAC	79	2287	28.9	133	0.058	1.68	0.447	0.627
112.	BRANDON, T.	g	CLE	82	1605	19.6	136	0.085	1.66	0.419	0.807

(NAME)	3-PT SHOTS MADE	3-PT SHOTS TRIED	REBs	ASTs	STLs	BLKs	PTs
(GARLAND, W.)	9	28	190	411	98	22	846
(OWENS, B.)	1	9	639	188	90	65	1141
(DAWKINS, J.)	36	101	227	567	89	5	988
(MAXWELL, V.)	162	473	243	326	104	28	1372
(MORRIS, C.)	22	110	494	197	129	81	879
(THREATT, S.)	20	62	253	593	168	16	1240
(AUGMON, S.)	1	6	420	201	124	27	1094
(PRICE, M.)	101	261	173	535	94	12	1247
(McKEY, D.)	19	50	268	120	61	47	777
(PAYTON, G.)	3	23	295	506	147	21	764
(WILLIAMS, R.)	56	156	405	235	148	68	1474
(CAMPBELL, T.)	13	37	286	229	84	31	1307
(BLAYLOCK, M.)	12	54	269	492	170	40	996
(BOWIE, S.)	8	25	578	186	41	120	1062
(HORNACEK, J.)	83	189	407	411	158	31	1632
(REYNOLDS, J.)	3	24	149	151	63	17	555
(ANDERSON, N.)	30	85	384	163	97	33	1196
(HUMPHRIES, J.)	42	144	184	466	119	13	991
(BOWIE, A.)	17	44	245	163	55	38	758
(COLES, B.)	10	52	189	366	73	13	816
(CHAPMAN, R.)	8	29	58	89	15	8	270
(GILLIAM, A.)	0	2	660	118	51	85	1367
(BLACKMAN, R.)	65	169	239	204	50	22	1374
(MACON, M.)	4	30	220	168	154	14	805
(BAGLEY, J.)	10	42	161	480	57	4	524
(KERSEY, J.)	1	8	633	243	114	71	971
(JOHNSON, L.)	5	22	899	292	81	51	1576
(MILLER, R.)	129	341	318	314	105	26	1695
(BOGUES, M.)	2	27	235	743	170	6	730
(BROWN, D.)	5	22	79	164	33	7	363
(ROBINSON, C.)	1	11	416	137	85	107	1016
(ELLIOTT, S.)	25	82	439	214	84	29	1338
(VINCENT, S.)	1	13	101	148	35	4	411
(RICE, G.)	155	396	394	184	90	35	1765
(MALONE, M.)	3	8	744	93	74	64	1279
(STARKS, J.)	94	270	191	276	103	18	1139
(McDANIEL, X.)	12	39	460	149	57	24	1125
(WILLIAMS, Br.)	0	0	272	33	41	53	437
(CATLEDGE, T.)	0	4	549	109	58	16	1154
(IUZZOLINO, M.)	59	136	98	194	33	1	486
(PERRY, T.)	3	8	551	134	44	116	982
(SMITS, R.)	0	2	417	116	29	100	1024
(BURTON, W.)	6	15	244	123	46	37	762
(CURRY, D.)	74	183	259	177	93	20	1209
(DUCKWORTH, K.)	0	3	497	99	38	37	880
(MALONE, J.)	1	12	233	180	56	5	1639
(BRICKOWSKI, F.)	3	6	344	122	60	23	740
(DAVIS, T.)	0	5	672	57	26	29	693
(SCOTT, D.)	29	89	66	35	20	9	359
(TISDALE, W.)	0	2	469	106	55	79	1195
(FLEMING, V.)	6	27	209	266	56	7	726
(GATTISON, K.)	0	2	580	131	59	69	1042
(RODMAN, D.)	32	101	1530	191	68	70	800
(GRANT, Ha.)	1	8	432	170	74	27	1155
(BONNER, A.)	1	4	485	125	94	26	740
(BRANDON, T.)	1	23	162	316	81	22	605

1991–92 REGULAR-SEASON STATISTICAL RESULTS
NBA PLAYERS ORDERED BY TURNOVERS PER GAME

	NAME	POS	TEAM	GMs	MINs	MIN per GM	TURN-OVERS	TOs per MIN	TOs per GM	FG PCT	FT PCT
113.	LEWIS, Re.	g	BOS	82	3070	37.4	136	0.044	1.66	0.503	0.851
114.	PARISH, R.	c	BOS	79	2285	28.9	131	0.057	1.66	0.536	0.772
115.	EHLO, C.	g/f	CLE	63	2016	32.0	104	0.052	1.65	0.453	0.707
116.	REID, J.R.	c/f	CHA	51	1257	24.6	84	0.067	1.65	0.490	0.705
117.	CUMMINGS, T.	f	SA	70	2149	30.7	115	0.054	1.64	0.488	0.711
118.	WILLIAMS, Br.	f	POR	80	2519	31.5	130	0.052	1.63	0.604	0.754
119.	DOUGLAS, S.	g	BOS	42	752	17.9	68	0.090	1.62	0.463	0.682
120.	WOOLRIDGE, O.	f	DET	82	2113	25.8	133	0.063	1.62	0.498	0.683
121.	JOHNSON, E.	f	SEA	81	2366	29.2	130	0.055	1.60	0.459	0.861
122.	JOHNSON, A.	g	HOU	69	1235	17.9	110	0.089	1.59	0.479	0.654
123.	HAMMONDS, T.	f	CHA	37	984	26.6	58	0.059	1.57	0.488	0.610
124.	SHAW, B.	g	MIA	63	1423	22.6	99	0.070	1.57	0.407	0.791
125.	FLOYD, S.	g	HOU	82	1662	20.3	128	0.077	1.56	0.406	0.794
126.	McMILLAN, N.	g/f	SEA	72	1652	22.9	112	0.068	1.56	0.437	0.643
127.	RIVERS, Do.	g	LAC	59	1657	28.1	92	0.056	1.56	0.424	0.832
128.	CAUSWELL, D.	c	SAC	80	2291	28.6	124	0.054	1.55	0.550	0.613
129.	RULAND, J.	c	PHI	13	209	16.1	20	0.096	1.54	0.526	0.688
130.	McCRAY, R.	f	DAL	75	2106	28.1	115	0.055	1.53	0.436	0.719
131.	ROBERTS, F.	f	MIL	80	1746	21.8	122	0.070	1.53	0.482	0.749
132.	WINGATE, D.	g	WAS	81	2127	26.3	124	0.058	1.53	0.465	0.719
133.	ANDERSON, K.	g	NJ	64	1086	17.0	97	0.089	1.52	0.390	0.745
134.	FOX, R.	g/f	BOS	81	1535	19.0	123	0.080	1.52	0.459	0.755
135.	WILLIAMS, H.	f/c	DAL	75	2040	27.2	114	0.056	1.52	0.431	0.725
136.	EDWARDS, T.	g/f	UT	81	2283	28.2	122	0.053	1.51	0.522	0.774
137.	FERRELL, D.	f	ATL	66	1598	24.2	99	0.062	1.50	0.524	0.762
138.	MAYS, T.	g	ATL	2	32	16.0	3	0.094	1.50	0.429	1.000
139.	OAKLEY, C.	f	NY	82	2309	28.2	123	0.053	1.50	0.522	0.735
140.	WEST, D.	g	MIN	80	2540	31.7	120	0.047	1.50	0.518	0.805
141.	CHAMBERS, T.	f	PHX	69	1948	28.2	103	0.053	1.49	0.431	0.830
142.	EDWARDS, K.	g	MIA	81	1840	22.7	120	0.065	1.48	0.454	0.848
143.	ELLIS, D.	f	MIL	81	2191	27.0	119	0.054	1.47	0.469	0.774
144.	HODGE, D.	c/f	DAL	51	1058	20.7	75	0.071	1.47	0.497	0.667
145.	STEWART, L.	f	WAS	76	2229	29.3	112	0.050	1.47	0.514	0.807
146.	KRYSTKOWIAK, L.	f	MIL	79	1848	23.4	115	0.062	1.46	0.444	0.757
147.	McHALE, K.	f/c	BOS	56	1398	25.0	82	0.059	1.46	0.510	0.822
148.	CORCHIANI, C.	g	ORL	51	741	14.5	74	0.100	1.45	0.399	0.875
149.	SCOTT, B.	g	LAL	82	2679	32.7	119	0.044	1.45	0.458	0.839
150.	JACKSON, C.	g	DEN	81	1538	19.0	117	0.076	1.44	0.421	0.870
151.	ROBERTS, S.	c	ORL	55	1118	20.3	78	0.070	1.42	0.529	0.515
152.	SALLEY, J.	f/c	DET	72	1774	24.6	102	0.058	1.42	0.512	0.715
153.	CARR, A.	f/c	SA	81	1867	23.0	114	0.061	1.41	0.490	0.764
154.	HOPSON, D.	g/f	SAC	71	1314	18.5	100	0.076	1.41	0.465	0.708
155.	SMITH, C.	f/c	LAC	49	1310	26.7	69	0.053	1.41	0.466	0.785
156.	TURNER, J.	f	ORL	75	1591	21.2	106	0.067	1.41	0.451	0.693
157.	AGUIRRE, M.	f	DET	75	1582	21.1	105	0.066	1.40	0.431	0.687
158.	TEAGLE, T.	f	LAL	82	1602	19.5	114	0.071	1.39	0.452	0.767
159.	KNIGHT, N.	g	PHX	42	631	15.0	58	0.092	1.38	0.475	0.688
160.	WILKINS, G.	g	NY	82	2344	28.6	113	0.048	1.38	0.447	0.730
161.	GLASS, G.	g	MIN	75	1822	24.3	103	0.057	1.37	0.440	0.616
162.	GREEN, A.C.	f	LAL	82	2902	35.4	111	0.038	1.35	0.476	0.744
163.	ANDERSON, Ro.	f	PHI	82	2432	29.7	109	0.045	1.33	0.465	0.877
164.	PERKINS, S.	f/c	LAL	63	2332	37.0	83	0.036	1.32	0.450	0.817
165.	VOLKOV, A.	f	ATL	77	1516	19.7	102	0.067	1.32	0.441	0.631
166.	SMITH, La.	g	WAS	48	708	14.7	63	0.089	1.31	0.407	0.804
167.	JOHNSON, B.	f	HOU	80	2202	27.5	104	0.047	1.30	0.458	0.727
168.	NORMAN, K.	f	LAC	77	2009	26.1	100	0.050	1.30	0.490	0.535

(NAME)	3-PT SHOTS MADE	3-PT SHOTS TRIED	REBs	ASTs	STLs	BLKs	PTs
(LEWIS, Re.)	5	21	394	185	125	105	1703
(PARISH, R.)	0	0	705	70	68	97	1115
(EHLO, C.)	69	167	307	238	78	22	776
(REID, J.R.)	0	3	317	81	49	23	560
(CUMMINGS, T.)	5	13	631	102	58	34	1210
(WILLIAMS, Br.)	0	1	704	108	62	41	901
(DOUGLAS, S.)	1	10	63	172	25	9	308
(WOOLRIDGE, O.)	1	9	260	88	41	33	1146
(JOHNSON, E.)	27	107	292	161	55	11	1386
(JOHNSON, A.)	4	15	80	266	61	9	386
(HAMMONDS, T.)	0	1	185	36	22	13	440
(SHAW, B.)	5	23	204	250	57	22	495
(FLOYD, S.)	37	123	150	239	57	21	744
(McMILLAN, N.)	27	98	252	359	129	29	435
(RIVERS, Do.)	26	92	147	233	111	19	641
(CAUSWELL, D.)	0	1	580	59	47	215	636
(RULAND, J.)	0	0	47	5	7	4	51
(McCRAY, R.)	25	85	468	219	48	30	677
(ROBERTS, F.)	19	37	257	122	52	40	769
(WINGATE, D.)	1	18	269	247	123	21	638
(ANDERSON, K.)	3	13	127	203	67	9	450
(FOX, R.)	23	70	220	126	78	30	644
(WILLIAMS, H.)	1	6	454	94	35	98	859
(EDWARDS, T.)	39	103	298	137	81	46	1018
(FERRELL, D.)	11	33	210	92	49	17	839
(MAYS, T.)	3	6	2	1	0	0	17
(OAKLEY, C.)	0	3	700	133	67	15	506
(WEST, D.)	4	23	257	281	66	26	1116
(CHAMBERS, T.)	18	49	401	142	57	37	1128
(EDWARDS, K.)	7	32	211	170	99	20	819
(ELLIS, D.)	138	329	253	104	57	18	1272
(HODGE, D.)	0	0	275	39	25	23	426
(STEWART, L.)	0	3	449	120	51	44	794
(KRYSTKOWIAK, L.)	0	5	429	114	54	12	714
(McHALE, K.)	0	13	330	82	11	59	780
(CORCHIANI, C.)	10	37	78	141	45	2	255
(SCOTT, B.)	54	157	310	226	105	28	1218
(JACKSON, C.)	31	94	114	192	44	4	837
(ROBERTS, S.)	0	1	336	39	22	83	573
(SALLEY, J.)	0	3	296	116	49	110	684
(CARR, A.)	1	5	346	63	32	96	881
(HOPSON, D.)	12	47	206	102	67	39	743
(SMITH, C.)	0	6	301	56	41	98	714
(TURNER, J.)	1	8	246	92	24	16	530
(AGUIRRE, M.)	15	71	236	126	51	11	851
(TEAGLE, T.)	1	4	183	113	66	9	880
(KNIGHT, N.)	4	13	46	112	24	3	243
(WILKINS, G.)	38	108	206	219	76	17	1016
(GLASS, G.)	16	54	260	175	66	30	859
(GREEN, A.C.)	12	56	762	117	91	36	1116
(ANDERSON, Ro.)	42	127	278	135	86	11	1123
(PERKINS, S.)	15	69	556	141	64	62	1041
(VOLKOV, A.)	35	110	265	250	66	30	662
(SMITH, La.)	2	21	81	99	44	1	247
(JOHNSON, B.)	1	9	312	158	72	49	685
(NORMAN, K.)	4	28	448	125	53	66	929

1991–92 REGULAR-SEASON STATISTICAL RESULTS
NBA PLAYERS ORDERED BY TURNOVERS PER GAME

	NAME	POS	TEAM	GMs	MINs	MIN per GM	TURN-OVERS	TOs per MIN	TOs per GM	FG PCT	FT PCT
169.	BAILEY, T.	f	MIN	84	2104	25.0	108	0.051	1.29	0.440	0.796
170.	HILL, T.	c/f	GS	82	1886	23.0	106	0.056	1.29	0.522	0.694
171.	MAYES, Th.	g	LAC	24	255	10.6	31	0.122	1.29	0.303	0.667
172.	BROWN, M.	c/f	UT	82	1783	21.7	105	0.059	1.28	0.453	0.667
173.	GRAYER, J.	g	MIL	82	1659	20.2	105	0.063	1.28	0.449	0.667
174.	PACK, R.	g	POR	72	894	12.4	92	0.103	1.28	0.423	0.803
175.	SMITH, Do.	f	DAL	76	1707	22.5	97	0.057	1.28	0.415	0.736
176.	LAIMBEER, B.	c	DET	81	2234	27.6	102	0.046	1.26	0.470	0.893
177.	LONGLEY, L.	c	MIN	66	991	15.0	83	0.084	1.26	0.458	0.663
178.	JOHNSON, V.	g	SA	60	1350	22.5	74	0.055	1.23	0.405	0.647
179.	MAJERLE, D.	g/f	PHX	82	2853	34.8	101	0.035	1.23	0.478	0.756
180.	MASON, A.	f	NY	82	2198	26.8	101	0.046	1.23	0.509	0.642
181.	THOMPSON, L.	f/c	IND	80	1299	16.2	98	0.075	1.23	0.468	0.817
182.	McCLOUD, G.	g	IND	51	892	17.5	62	0.070	1.22	0.409	0.781
183.	CORBIN, T.	f	UT	80	2207	27.6	97	0.044	1.21	0.481	0.866
184.	GRANT, Ho.	f	CHI	81	2859	35.3	98	0.034	1.21	0.579	0.741
185.	ANTHONY, G.	g	NY	82	1510	18.4	98	0.065	1.20	0.370	0.741
186.	BATTLE, J.	g	CLE	76	1637	21.5	91	0.056	1.20	0.480	0.848
187.	LIBERTY, M.	f/g	DEN	75	1527	20.4	90	0.059	1.20	0.443	0.728
188.	TURNER, A.	g	WAS	70	871	12.4	84	0.096	1.20	0.425	0.792
189.	GAMBLE, K.	g/f	BOS	82	2496	30.4	97	0.039	1.18	0.529	0.885
190.	MITCHELL, S.	f	MIN	82	2151	26.2	97	0.045	1.18	0.423	0.786
191.	CARTWRIGHT, B.	c	CHI	64	1471	23.0	75	0.051	1.17	0.467	0.604
192.	GEORGE, T.	g	NJ	70	1037	14.8	82	0.079	1.17	0.428	0.821
193.	GRAHAM, P.	g	ATL	78	1718	22.0	91	0.053	1.17	0.447	0.741
194.	LEVER, F.	g	DAL	31	884	28.5	36	0.041	1.16	0.387	0.750
195.	ARMSTRONG, B.J.	g	CHI	82	1875	22.9	94	0.050	1.15	0.481	0.806
196.	EACKLES, L.	f	WAS	65	1463	22.5	75	0.051	1.15	0.468	0.743
197.	SPENCER, F.	c	MIN	61	1481	24.3	70	0.047	1.15	0.426	0.691
198.	ALEXANDER, V.	c	GS	80	1350	16.9	91	0.067	1.14	0.529	0.691
199.	PRESSEY, P.	g	SA	56	759	13.6	64	0.084	1.14	0.373	0.683
200.	RIVERS, Da.	g	LAC	15	122	8.1	17	0.139	1.13	0.333	0.909
201.	SMITH, O.	g	ORL	55	877	15.9	62	0.071	1.13	0.365	0.769
202.	WILEY, M.	g	ATL	53	870	16.4	60	0.069	1.13	0.430	0.686
203.	MORTON, J.	g	MIA	25	270	10.8	28	0.104	1.12	0.387	0.842
204.	CEBALLOS, C.	f	PHX	64	725	11.3	71	0.098	1.11	0.482	0.737
205.	ENGLISH, A.J.	g	WAS	81	1665	20.6	89	0.054	1.10	0.433	0.841
206.	GARRICK, T.	g	DAL	40	549	13.7	44	0.080	1.10	0.413	0.692
207.	POLYNICE, O.	c	LAC	76	1834	24.1	83	0.045	1.09	0.519	0.622
208.	HIGGINS, S.	f	ORL	38	616	16.2	41	0.067	1.08	0.459	0.861
209.	LANG, A.	c	PHX	81	1965	24.3	87	0.044	1.07	0.522	0.768
210.	NANCE, L.	f	CLE	81	2880	35.6	87	0.030	1.07	0.539	0.822
211.	WALKER, D.	g	DET	74	1541	20.8	79	0.051	1.07	0.423	0.619
212.	BURTT, S.	g	PHX	31	356	11.5	33	0.093	1.06	0.463	0.704
213.	LICHTI, T.	g	DEN	68	1176	17.3	72	0.061	1.06	0.460	0.839
214.	ASKEW, V.	g	GS	80	1496	18.7	84	0.056	1.05	0.509	0.694
215.	ELIE, M.	g/f	GS	79	1677	21.2	83	0.050	1.05	0.521	0.852
216.	MOORE, T.	f	DAL	42	782	18.6	44	0.056	1.05	0.400	0.833
217.	WHITE, R.	f	DAL	65	1021	15.7	68	0.067	1.05	0.380	0.765
218.	SUTTON, G.	g	SA	67	601	9.0	70	0.117	1.04	0.388	0.756
219.	WILLIAMS, J.	f/c	CLE	80	2432	30.4	83	0.034	1.04	0.503	0.752
220.	EDWARDS, Ja.	c	LAC	72	1437	20.0	72	0.050	1.00	0.465	0.731
221.	LANE, J.	f	MIL	14	177	12.6	14	0.079	1.00	0.304	0.333
222.	MILLS, T.	f	NJ	82	1714	20.9	82	0.048	1.00	0.463	0.750
223.	MURDOCK, E.	g	UT	50	478	9.6	50	0.105	1.00	0.415	0.754
224.	PERRY, E.	g	CHA	50	437	8.7	50	0.114	1.00	0.380	0.659

(NAME)	3-PT SHOTS MADE	3-PT SHOTS TRIED	REBs	ASTs	STLs	BLKs	PTs
(BAILEY, T.)	0	2	485	78	35	117	951
(HILL, T.)	0	1	593	47	73	43	671
(MAYES, Th.)	15	41	16	35	16	2	99
(BROWN, M.)	0	1	476	81	42	34	632
(GRAYER, J.)	19	66	257	150	64	13	739
(PACK, R.)	0	10	97	140	40	4	332
(SMITH, Do.)	0	11	391	129	62	34	671
(LAIMBEER, B.)	32	85	451	160	51	54	783
(LONGLEY, L.)	0	0	257	53	35	64	281
(JOHNSON, V.)	19	60	182	145	41	14	478
(MAJERLE, D.)	87	228	483	274	131	43	1418
(MASON, A.)	0	0	573	106	46	20	573
(THOMPSON, L.)	0	2	381	102	52	34	394
(McCLOUD, G.)	32	94	132	116	26	11	338
(CORBIN, T.)	0	4	472	140	82	20	780
(GRANT, Ho.)	0	2	807	217	100	131	1149
(ANTHONY, G.)	8	55	136	314	59	9	447
(BATTLE, J.)	2	17	112	159	36	5	779
(LIBERTY, M.)	17	50	308	58	66	29	698
(TURNER, A.)	1	16	90	177	57	2	284
(GAMBLE, K.)	9	31	286	219	75	37	1108
(MITCHELL, S.)	2	11	473	94	53	39	825
(CARTWRIGHT, B.)	0	0	324	87	22	14	512
(GEORGE, T.)	1	6	105	162	41	3	418
(GRAHAM, P.)	55	141	231	175	96	21	791
(LEVER, F.)	17	52	161	107	46	12	347
(ARMSTRONG, B.J.)	35	87	145	266	46	5	809
(EACKLES, L.)	7	35	178	125	47	7	856
(SPENCER, F.)	0	0	435	53	27	79	405
(ALEXANDER, V.)	0	1	336	32	45	62	589
(PRESSEY, P.)	3	21	95	142	29	19	151
(RIVERS, Da.)	0	1	19	21	7	1	30
(SMITH, O.)	8	21	116	57	36	13	310
(WILEY, M.)	14	42	81	180	47	3	204
(MORTON, J.)	2	16	26	32	13	1	106
(CEBALLOS, C.)	1	6	152	50	16	11	462
(ENGLISH, A.J.)	6	34	168	143	32	9	886
(GARRICK, T.)	1	4	56	98	36	4	137
(POLYNICE, O.)	0	1	536	46	45	20	613
(HIGGINS, S.)	6	25	102	41	16	6	291
(LANG, A.)	0	1	546	43	48	201	622
(NANCE, L.)	0	6	670	232	80	243	1375
(WALKER, D.)	0	10	238	205	63	18	387
(BURTT, S.)	1	6	34	59	16	4	187
(LICHTI, T.)	1	9	118	74	43	12	446
(ASKEW, V.)	1	10	233	188	47	23	498
(ELIE, M.)	23	70	227	174	68	15	620
(MOORE, T.)	30	84	82	48	32	4	355
(WHITE, R.)	4	27	236	31	31	22	418
(SUTTON, G.)	26	89	47	91	26	9	246
(WILLIAMS, J.)	0	4	607	196	60	182	952
(EDWARDS, Ja.)	0	1	202	53	24	33	698
(LANE, J.)	0	0	66	17	2	1	37
(MILLS, T.)	8	23	453	84	48	41	742
(MURDOCK, E.)	5	26	54	92	30	7	203
(PERRY, E.)	1	7	39	78	34	3	126

	NAME	POS	TEAM	GMs	MINs	MIN per GM	TURN-OVERS	TOs per MIN	TOs per GM	FG PCT	FT PCT
225.	PRITCHARD, K.	g	BOS	11	136	12.4	11	0.081	1.00	0.471	0.778
226.	SAMPSON, R.	c	WAS	10	108	10.8	10	0.093	1.00	0.310	0.667
227.	WEST, M.	c	PHX	82	1436	17.5	82	0.057	1.00	0.632	0.637
228.	CONNER, L.	g	MIL	81	1420	17.5	79	0.056	0.98	0.431	0.704
229.	DAVIS, W.	g	DEN	46	741	16.1	45	0.061	0.98	0.459	0.872
230.	MUSTAF, J.	f	PHX	52	545	10.5	51	0.094	0.98	0.477	0.690
231.	SMITH, L.	f/c	HOU	45	800	17.8	44	0.055	0.98	0.544	0.364
232.	DUDLEY, C.	c	NJ	82	1902	23.2	79	0.042	0.96	0.403	0.468
233.	KING, S.	f/c	CHI	79	1268	16.1	76	0.060	0.96	0.506	0.753
234.	CAGE, M.	f	SEA	82	2461	30.0	78	0.032	0.95	0.566	0.620
235.	SCHAYES, D.	c	MIL	43	726	16.9	41	0.057	0.95	0.417	0.771
236.	PERDUE, W.	c	CHI	77	1007	13.1	72	0.072	0.94	0.547	0.495
237.	ABDELNABY, A.	f/c	POR	71	934	13.2	66	0.071	0.93	0.493	0.753
238.	BENOIT, D.	f	UT	77	1161	15.1	71	0.061	0.92	0.467	0.810
239.	DAILEY, Q.	f	SEA	11	98	8.9	10	0.102	0.91	0.243	0.813
240.	CAMPBELL, E.	c	LAL	81	1876	23.2	73	0.039	0.90	0.448	0.619
241.	PINCKNEY, E.	f	BOS	81	1917	23.7	73	0.038	0.90	0.537	0.812
242.	WOLF, J.	f	DEN	67	1160	17.3	60	0.052	0.90	0.361	0.803
243.	RAMBIS, K.	f	PHX	28	381	13.6	25	0.066	0.89	0.463	0.778
244.	FREDERICK, A.	f	CHA	66	852	12.9	58	0.068	0.88	0.435	0.685
245.	WILLIAMS, Ja.	f/c	PHI	50	646	12.9	44	0.068	0.88	0.364	0.636
246.	AINGE, D.	g	POR	81	1595	19.7	70	0.044	0.86	0.442	0.824
247.	HERRERA, C.	f	HOU	43	566	13.2	37	0.065	0.86	0.516	0.568
248.	SHACKLEFORD, C.	c	PHI	72	1399	19.4	62	0.044	0.86	0.486	0.663
249.	KITE, G.	c	ORL	72	1479	20.5	61	0.041	0.85	0.437	0.588
250.	VAUGHT, L.	f	LAC	79	1687	21.4	66	0.039	0.84	0.492	0.797
251.	DONALDSON, J.	c	NY	58	1075	18.5	48	0.045	0.83	0.457	0.709
252.	DAVIS, B.	f	DAL	33	429	13.0	27	0.063	0.82	0.442	0.733
253.	GATLING, C.	c	GS	54	612	11.3	44	0.072	0.81	0.568	0.661
254.	ASKINS, K.	g/f	MIA	59	843	14.3	47	0.056	0.80	0.410	0.703
255.	HENSON, S.	g	MIL	50	386	7.7	40	0.104	0.80	0.361	0.793
256.	LYNCH, K.	g	CHA	55	819	14.9	44	0.054	0.80	0.417	0.761
257.	PHILLS, B.	g	CLE	10	65	6.5	8	0.123	0.80	0.429	0.636
258.	SMITH, To.	g	LAL	63	820	13.0	50	0.061	0.79	0.399	0.653
259.	GREEN, S.	f	SA	80	1127	14.1	62	0.055	0.78	0.427	0.820
260.	DAVIS, D.	f	IND	64	1301	20.3	49	0.038	0.77	0.552	0.572
261.	GREEN, Se.	g	IND	35	256	7.3	27	0.106	0.77	0.392	0.536
262.	LISTER, A.	c	GS	26	293	11.3	20	0.068	0.77	0.557	0.424
263.	TURNER, Jo.	f	HOU	42	345	8.2	32	0.093	0.76	0.439	0.525
264.	YOUNG, D.	g	LAC	62	1023	16.5	47	0.046	0.76	0.392	0.851
265.	BARROS, D.	g	SEA	75	1331	17.7	56	0.042	0.75	0.483	0.760
266.	BROWN, R.	g	SAC	56	535	9.6	42	0.079	0.75	0.456	0.655
267.	KESSLER, A.	c	MIA	77	1197	15.5	58	0.049	0.75	0.413	0.817
268.	RUDD, D.	g	UT	65	538	8.3	49	0.091	0.75	0.399	0.762
269.	EATON, M.	c	UT	81	2023	25.0	60	0.030	0.74	0.446	0.598
270.	FOSTER, G.	f	WAS	49	548	11.2	36	0.066	0.73	0.461	0.714
271.	SPARROW, R.	g	LAL	46	489	10.6	33	0.068	0.72	0.384	0.615
272.	OLIVER, B.	g	PHI	34	279	8.2	24	0.086	0.71	0.330	0.682
273.	SANDERS, M.	f	CLE	31	633	20.4	22	0.035	0.71	0.571	0.766
274.	BULLARD, M.	f	HOU	80	1278	16.0	56	0.044	0.70	0.459	0.760
275.	KONCAK, J.	c	ATL	77	1489	19.3	54	0.036	0.70	0.391	0.655
276.	BROWN, C.	f	LAL	42	431	10.3	29	0.067	0.69	0.469	0.612
277.	GREEN, R.	g	BOS	26	367	14.1	18	0.049	0.69	0.447	0.722
278.	FERRY, D.	f	CLE	68	937	13.8	46	0.049	0.68	0.409	0.836
279.	GRANT, Gr.	g	PHI	68	891	13.1	46	0.052	0.68	0.440	0.833
280.	LES, J.	g	SAC	62	712	11.5	42	0.059	0.68	0.385	0.809

(NAME)	3-PT SHOTS MADE	3-PT SHOTS TRIED	REBs	ASTs	STLs	BLKs	PTs
(PRITCHARD, K.)	0	3	11	30	3	4	46
(SAMPSON, R.)	0	2	30	4	3	8	22
(WEST, M.)	0	0	372	22	14	81	501
(CONNER, L.)	0	7	184	294	97	10	287
(DAVIS, W.)	5	16	70	68	29	1	457
(MUSTAF, J.)	0	0	145	45	21	16	233
(SMITH, L.)	0	1	256	33	21	7	104
(DUDLEY, C.)	0	0	739	58	38	179	460
(KING, S.)	2	5	205	77	21	25	551
(CAGE, M.)	0	5	728	92	99	55	720
(SCHAYES, D.)	0	0	168	34	19	19	240
(PERDUE, W.)	1	2	312	80	16	43	350
(ABDELNABY, A.)	0	0	260	30	25	16	432
(BENOIT, D.)	3	14	296	34	19	44	434
(DAILEY, Q.)	0	1	12	4	5	1	31
(CAMPBELL, E.)	0	2	423	59	53	159	578
(PINCKNEY, E.)	0	1	564	62	70	56	613
(WOLF, J.)	1	11	240	61	32	14	254
(RAMBIS, K.)	0	0	106	37	12	14	90
(FREDERICK, A.)	4	17	144	71	40	26	389
(WILLIAMS, Ja.)	0	0	145	12	20	20	206
(AINGE, D.)	78	230	148	202	73	13	784
(HERRERA, C.)	0	1	99	27	16	25	191
(SHACKLEFORD, C.)	0	1	415	46	38	51	473
(KITE, G.)	0	1	402	44	30	57	228
(VAUGHT, L.)	4	5	512	71	37	31	601
(DONALDSON, J.)	0	0	289	33	8	49	285
(DAVIS, B.)	5	18	33	66	11	3	92
(GATLING, C.)	0	4	182	16	31	36	306
(ASKINS, K.)	25	73	142	38	40	15	219
(HENSON, S.)	23	48	41	82	15	1	150
(LYNCH, K.)	3	8	85	83	37	9	224
(PHILLS, B.)	0	2	8	4	3	1	31
(SMITH, To.)	0	11	76	109	39	8	275
(GREEN, S.)	0	0	342	36	29	11	367
(DAVIS, D.)	0	1	410	30	27	74	395
(GREEN, Se.)	2	10	42	22	13	6	141
(LISTER, A.)	0	0	92	14	5	16	102
(TURNER, Jo.)	0	0	78	12	6	4	117
(YOUNG, D.)	23	70	75	172	46	4	280
(BARROS, D.)	83	186	81	125	51	4	619
(BROWN, R.)	0	6	69	59	35	12	192
(KESSLER, A.)	0	0	314	34	17	32	410
(RUDD, D.)	11	47	54	109	15	1	193
(EATON, M.)	0	0	491	40	36	205	266
(FOSTER, G.)	0	1	145	35	6	12	213
(SPARROW, R.)	3	15	28	83	12	5	127
(OLIVER, B.)	0	4	30	20	10	2	81
(SANDERS, M.)	1	3	96	53	24	10	221
(BULLARD, M.)	64	166	223	75	26	21	512
(KONCAK, J.)	0	12	261	132	50	67	241
(BROWN, C.)	0	3	82	26	12	7	150
(GREEN, R.)	1	4	24	68	17	1	106
(FERRY, D.)	17	48	213	75	22	15	346
(GRANT, Gr.)	7	18	69	217	45	2	225
(LES, J.)	45	131	63	143	31	3	231

1991–92 REGULAR-SEASON STATISTICAL RESULTS
NBA PLAYERS ORDERED BY TURNOVERS PER GAME

	NAME	POS	TEAM	GMs	MINs	MIN per GM	TURN-OVERS	TOs per MIN	TOs per GM	FG PCT	FT PCT
281.	JAMES, H.	f	CLE	65	866	13.3	43	0.050	0.66	0.407	0.803
282.	LECKNER, E.	c	CHA	59	716	12.1	39	0.055	0.66	0.513	0.745
283.	LOHAUS, B.	f/c	MIL	70	1081	15.4	46	0.043	0.66	0.450	0.659
284.	KERR, S.	g	CLE	48	847	17.6	31	0.037	0.65	0.511	0.833
285.	ROYAL, D.	f	SA	60	718	12.0	39	0.054	0.65	0.449	0.692
286.	CHEEKS, M.	g	ATL	56	1086	19.4	36	0.033	0.64	0.462	0.605
287.	RASMUSSEN, B.	c	ATL	81	1968	24.3	51	0.026	0.63	0.478	0.750
288.	BROOKS, S.	g	MIN	82	1082	13.2	51	0.047	0.62	0.447	0.810
289.	ADDISON, R.	g	NJ	76	1175	15.5	46	0.039	0.61	0.433	0.737
290.	BENNETT, W.	f	MIA	54	833	15.4	33	0.040	0.61	0.379	0.700
291.	BREUER, R.	c	MIN	67	1176	17.6	41	0.035	0.61	0.468	0.533
292.	BROWN, T.	f	SEA	57	655	11.5	35	0.053	0.61	0.410	0.727
293.	MONROE, R.	g	ATL	38	313	8.2	23	0.074	0.61	0.368	0.826
294.	WHATLEY, E.	g	POR	23	209	9.1	14	0.067	0.61	0.412	0.871
295.	CONLON, M.	c	SEA	45	381	8.5	27	0.071	0.60	0.475	0.750
296.	HIGGINS, R.	f	GS	25	535	21.4	15	0.028	0.60	0.412	0.814
297.	CHILCUTT, P.	f/c	SAC	69	817	11.8	41	0.050	0.59	0.452	0.821
298.	BOL, M.	c	PHI	71	1267	17.8	41	0.032	0.58	0.383	0.462
299.	SCHINTZIUS, D.	c	SAC	33	400	12.1	19	0.048	0.58	0.427	0.833
300.	TUCKER, T.	g	SA	24	415	17.3	14	0.034	0.58	0.465	0.800
301.	GMINSKI, M.	c	CHA	35	499	14.3	20	0.040	0.57	0.452	0.750
302.	TOLBERT, T.	f	GS	35	310	8.9	20	0.065	0.57	0.384	0.550
303.	FEITL, D.	c	NJ	34	175	5.2	19	0.109	0.56	0.429	0.842
304.	HOWARD, B.	f	DAL	27	318	11.8	15	0.047	0.56	0.519	0.710
305.	PAXSON, J.	g	CHI	79	1946	24.6	44	0.023	0.56	0.528	0.784
306.	WILLIAMS, S.	f	CHI	63	690	11.0	35	0.051	0.56	0.483	0.649
307.	HASTINGS, S.	f	DEN	40	421	10.5	22	0.052	0.55	0.340	0.857
308.	BRYANT, M.	c	POR	56	800	14.3	30	0.038	0.54	0.480	0.667
309.	LEVINGSTON, C.	f	CHI	79	1020	12.9	42	0.041	0.53	0.498	0.625
310.	VRANKOVIC, S.	c	BOS	19	110	5.8	10	0.091	0.53	0.469	0.583
311.	DREILING, G.	c	IND	60	509	8.5	31	0.061	0.52	0.494	0.750
312.	JONES, Ch.	c/f	WAS	75	1365	18.2	39	0.029	0.52	0.367	0.500
313.	HALEY, J.	f/c	LAL	49	394	8.0	25	0.064	0.51	0.369	0.483
314.	WIGGINS, M.	g	PHI	49	569	11.6	25	0.044	0.51	0.384	0.686
315.	FRANK, T.	f	MIN	10	140	14.0	5	0.036	0.50	0.546	0.667
316.	HENDERSON, G.	g	DET	16	96	6.0	8	0.083	0.50	0.375	0.818
317.	JAMERSON, D.	f	HOU	48	378	7.9	24	0.064	0.50	0.414	0.926
318.	ACRES, M.	c	ORL	68	926	13.6	33	0.036	0.49	0.517	0.761
319.	BROOKS, K.	f	DEN	37	270	7.3	18	0.067	0.49	0.443	0.810
320.	BEDFORD, W.	f/c	DET	32	363	11.3	15	0.041	0.47	0.413	0.636
321.	BUECHLER, J.	f	GS	28	290	10.4	13	0.045	0.46	0.409	0.571
322.	RANDALL, M.	f	MIN	54	441	8.2	25	0.057	0.46	0.456	0.744
323.	THOMAS, C.	g	DET	37	156	4.2	17	0.109	0.46	0.353	0.667
324.	KING, R.	c	SEA	40	213	5.3	18	0.085	0.45	0.380	0.756
325.	KOFOED, B.	g	SEA	44	239	5.4	20	0.084	0.45	0.472	0.577
326.	KIMBLE, B.	f	LAC	34	277	8.2	15	0.054	0.44	0.396	0.645
327.	OGG, A.	c	MIA	43	367	8.5	19	0.052	0.44	0.548	0.533
328.	COOPER, W.	f	POR	35	344	9.8	15	0.044	0.43	0.427	0.636
329.	SANDERS, J.	f	ATL	12	117	9.8	5	0.043	0.42	0.444	0.778
330.	HANSEN, B.	g	CHI	68	809	11.9	28	0.035	0.41	0.444	0.364
331.	QUINNETT, B.	f	DAL	39	326	8.4	16	0.049	0.41	0.347	0.615
332.	VANDEWEGHE, K.	f	NY	67	956	14.3	27	0.028	0.40	0.491	0.803
333.	HODGES, C.	g	CHI	56	555	9.9	22	0.040	0.39	0.384	0.941
334.	KLEINE, J.	c	BOS	70	991	14.2	27	0.027	0.39	0.492	0.708
335.	PAYNE, K.	f	PHI	49	353	7.2	19	0.054	0.39	0.448	0.692
336.	ELLIS, L.	f	LAC	29	103	3.6	11	0.107	0.38	0.340	0.474

(NAME)	3-PT SHOTS MADE	3-PT SHOTS TRIED	REBs	ASTs	STLs	BLKs	PTs
(JAMES, H.)	29	90	112	25	16	11	418
(LECKNER, E.)	0	1	206	31	9	18	196
(LOHAUS, B.)	57	144	249	74	40	71	408
(KERR, S.)	32	74	78	110	27	10	319
(ROYAL, D.)	0	0	124	34	25	7	252
(CHEEKS, M.)	3	6	95	185	83	0	259
(RASMUSSEN, B.)	5	23	393	107	35	48	729
(BROOKS, S.)	32	90	99	205	66	7	417
(ADDISON, R.)	14	49	165	68	28	28	444
(BENNETT, W.)	0	1	162	38	19	9	195
(BREUER, R.)	0	1	281	89	27	99	363
(BROWN, T.)	19	63	84	48	30	5	271
(MONROE, R.)	6	27	33	27	12	2	131
(WHATLEY, E.)	0	4	21	34	14	3	69
(CONLON, M.)	0	0	69	12	9	7	120
(HIGGINS, R.)	33	95	85	22	15	13	255
(CHILCUTT, P.)	2	2	187	38	32	17	251
(BOL, M.)	0	9	222	22	11	205	110
(SCHINTZIUS, D.)	0	4	118	20	6	28	110
(TUCKER, T.)	19	48	37	27	21	3	155
(GMINSKI, M.)	1	3	118	31	11	16	202
(TOLBERT, T.)	2	8	55	21	10	6	90
(FEITL, D.)	0	0	61	6	2	3	82
(HOWARD, B.)	1	2	51	14	11	8	131
(PAXSON, J.)	12	44	96	241	49	9	555
(WILLIAMS, S.)	0	3	247	50	13	36	214
(HASTINGS, S.)	0	9	98	26	10	15	58
(BRYANT, M.)	0	3	201	41	26	8	230
(LEVINGSTON, C.)	1	6	227	66	27	45	311
(VRANKOVIC, S.)	0	0	28	5	0	17	37
(DREILING, G.)	1	1	96	25	10	16	117
(JONES, Ch.)	0	0	317	62	43	92	86
(HALEY, J.)	0	0	95	7	7	8	76
(WIGGINS, M.)	0	1	94	22	20	1	211
(FRANK, T.)	0	0	26	8	5	4	46
(HENDERSON, G.)	3	8	8	10	3	0	36
(JAMERSON, D.)	8	28	43	33	17	0	191
(ACRES, M.)	1	3	252	22	25	15	208
(BROOKS, K.)	2	11	39	11	8	2	105
(BEDFORD, W.)	0	1	63	12	6	18	114
(BUECHLER, J.)	0	1	52	23	19	7	70
(RANDALL, M.)	3	16	71	33	12	3	171
(THOMAS, C.)	2	17	22	22	4	1	48
(KING, R.)	0	1	49	12	4	5	88
(KOFOED, B.)	1	7	26	51	2	2	66
(KIMBLE, B.)	4	13	32	17	10	6	112
(OGG, A.)	0	0	74	7	5	28	108
(COOPER, W.)	0	0	101	21	4	27	77
(SANDERS, J.)	0	0	26	9	5	3	47
(HANSEN, B.)	7	27	77	69	27	3	173
(QUINNETT, B.)	13	41	51	12	16	8	115
(VANDEWEGHE, K.)	26	66	88	57	15	8	467
(HODGES, C.)	36	96	24	54	14	1	238
(KLEINE, J.)	4	8	296	32	23	14	326
(PAYNE, K.)	5	12	54	17	16	8	144
(ELLIS, L.)	0	0	24	1	6	9	43

1991–92 REGULAR-SEASON STATISTICAL RESULTS
NBA PLAYERS ORDERED BY TURNOVERS PER GAME

	NAME	POS	TEAM	GMs	MINs	MIN per GM	TURN-OVERS	TOs per MIN	TOs per GM	FG PCT	FT PCT
337.	MURPHY, T.	f	MIN	47	429	9.1	18	0.042	0.38	0.488	0.559
338.	WILLIAMS, K.	f	IND	60	565	9.4	22	0.039	0.37	0.518	0.605
339.	McCORMICK, T.	c	NY	22	108	4.9	8	0.074	0.36	0.424	0.667
340.	SELLERS, B.	f/c	DET	43	226	5.3	15	0.066	0.35	0.466	0.769
341.	BLANKS, L.	g	DET	43	189	4.4	14	0.074	0.33	0.455	0.727
342.	NEALY, E.	f	PHX	52	505	9.7	17	0.034	0.33	0.512	0.667
343.	OLIVER, J.	g/f	CLE	27	252	9.3	9	0.036	0.33	0.398	0.773
344.	ROLLINS, T.	f/c	HOU	59	697	11.8	18	0.026	0.31	0.535	0.867
345.	ANSLEY, M.	f	CHA	10	45	4.5	3	0.067	0.30	0.444	0.833
346.	McCANN, B.	f	DET	26	129	5.0	7	0.054	0.27	0.394	0.308
347.	AUSTIN, I.	c	UT	31	112	3.6	8	0.071	0.26	0.457	0.633
348.	LEE, D.	g	NJ	46	307	6.7	12	0.039	0.26	0.431	0.526
349.	THOMPSON, S.	g	SAC	19	91	4.8	5	0.055	0.26	0.378	0.375
350.	BATTLE, K.	f	GS	16	92	5.8	4	0.044	0.25	0.647	0.833
351.	CROWDER, C.	g/f	UT	51	328	6.4	13	0.040	0.25	0.384	0.833
352.	COPA, T.	f/c	SA	33	132	4.0	8	0.061	0.24	0.550	0.308
353.	PETERSEN, J.	c	GS	27	169	6.3	5	0.030	0.19	0.450	0.700
354.	COOK, A.	f	DEN	22	115	5.2	3	0.026	0.14	0.600	0.667
355.	WITTMAN, R.	g	IND	24	115	4.8	3	0.026	0.13	0.421	0.500
356.	WINCHESTER, K.	f	NY	19	81	4.3	2	0.025	0.11	0.433	0.800
357.	JEPSEN, L.	c	SAC	31	87	2.8	3	0.035	0.10	0.375	0.636
358.	OWENS, K.	f	LAL	20	80	4.0	2	0.025	0.10	0.281	0.800
359.	SCHEFFLER, S.	f	DEN	11	61	5.6	1	0.016	0.09	0.667	0.750

(NAME)	3-PT SHOTS MADE	3-PT SHOTS TRIED	REBs	ASTs	STLs	BLKs	PTs
(MURPHY, T.)	1	2	110	11	9	8	98
(WILLIAMS, K.)	0	4	129	40	20	41	252
(McCORMICK, T.)	0	0	34	9	2	0	42
(SELLERS, B.)	0	1	42	14	1	10	102
(BLANKS, L.)	6	16	22	19	14	1	64
(NEALY, E.)	20	50	111	37	16	2	160
(OLIVER, J.)	1	9	27	20	9	2	96
(ROLLINS, T.)	0	0	171	15	14	62	118
(ANSLEY, M.)	0	0	6	2	0	0	21
(McCANN, B.)	0	1	30	6	6	4	30
(AUSTIN, I.)	0	0	35	5	2	2	61
(LEE, D.)	10	37	35	22	11	1	120
(THOMPSON, S.)	0	1	19	8	6	3	31
(BATTLE, K.)	0	1	16	4	2	2	32
(CROWDER, C.)	13	30	41	17	7	2	114
(COPA, T.)	0	0	36	3	2	6	48
(PETERSEN, J.)	0	2	45	9	5	6	43
(COOK, A.)	0	0	34	2	5	4	34
(WITTMAN, R.)	0	0	9	11	2	0	17
(WINCHESTER, K.)	1	2	15	8	2	2	35
(JEPSEN, L.)	0	1	30	1	1	5	25
(OWENS, K.)	0	0	15	3	5	4	26
(SCHEFFLER, S.)	0	0	14	0	3	1	21

1991–92 REGULAR-SEASON STATISTICAL RESULTS
AVERAGES PER GAME
(Players Listed Alphabetically)

NAME	POS	TEAM	GMs	MINs	FG PCT	FT PCT	3-PT SHOTS MADE	REBs per GM	ASTs per GM	STLs per GM	TOs per GM	BLKs per GM	PTs per GM
1. ABDELNABY, A.	f/c	POR	71	934	0.493	0.753	0	3.7	0.4	0.35	0.93	0.23	6.1
2. ACRES, M.	c	ORL	68	926	0.517	0.761	1	3.7	0.3	0.37	0.49	0.22	3.1
3. ADAMS, M.	g	WAS	78	2795	0.393	0.869	125	4.0	7.6	1.86	2.72	0.12	18.1
4. ADDISON, R.	g	NJ	76	1175	0.433	0.737	14	2.2	0.9	0.37	0.61	0.37	5.8
5. AGUIRRE, M.	f	DET	75	1582	0.431	0.687	15	3.2	1.7	0.68	1.40	0.15	11.3
6. AINGE, D.	g	POR	81	1595	0.442	0.824	78	1.8	2.5	0.90	0.86	0.16	9.7
7. ALEXANDER, V.	c	GS	80	1350	0.529	0.691	0	4.2	0.4	0.56	1.14	0.78	7.4
8. ANDERSON, G.	f	DEN	82	2793	0.456	0.623	0	11.5	1.0	1.07	2.45	0.79	11.5
9. ANDERSON, K.	g	NJ	64	1086	0.390	0.745	3	2.0	3.2	1.05	1.52	0.14	7.0
10. ANDERSON, N.	g/f	ORL	60	2203	0.463	0.667	30	6.4	2.7	1.62	2.08	0.55	19.9
11. ANDERSON, Ro.	f	PHI	82	2432	0.465	0.877	42	3.4	1.7	1.05	1.33	0.13	13.7
12. ANDERSON, W.	g/f	SA	57	1889	0.456	0.775	13	5.3	5.3	0.95	2.46	0.89	13.1
13. ANSLEY, M.	f	CHA	10	45	0.444	0.833	0	0.6	0.2	0.00	0.30	0.00	2.1
14. ANTHONY, G.	g	NY	82	1510	0.370	0.741	8	1.7	3.8	0.72	1.20	0.11	5.5
15. ARMSTRONG, B.J.	g	CHI	82	1875	0.481	0.806	35	1.8	3.2	0.56	1.15	0.06	9.9
16. ASKEW, V.	g	GS	80	1496	0.509	0.694	1	2.9	2.4	0.59	1.05	0.29	6.2
17. ASKINS, K.	g/f	MIA	59	1482	0.410	0.703	25	2.4	0.6	0.68	0.80	0.25	3.7
18. AUGMON, S.	g/f	ATL	82	2505	0.489	0.666	1	5.1	2.5	1.51	2.21	0.33	13.3
19. AUSTIN, I.	c	UT	31	112	0.457	0.633	0	1.1	0.2	0.06	0.26	0.06	2.0
20. BAGLEY, J.	g	BOS	73	1742	0.441	0.716	10	2.2	6.6	0.78	2.03	0.05	7.2
21. BAILEY, T.	f	MIN	84	2104	0.440	0.796	0	5.8	0.9	0.42	1.29	1.39	11.3
22. BARKLEY, C.	f	PHI	75	2881	0.552	0.695	32	11.1	4.1	1.81	3.13	0.59	23.1
23. BARROS, D.	g	SEA	75	1331	0.483	0.760	83	1.1	1.7	0.68	0.75	0.05	8.3
24. BATTLE, J.	g	CLE	76	1637	0.480	0.848	2	1.5	2.1	0.47	1.20	0.07	10.2
25. BATTLE, K.	f	GS	16	92	0.647	0.833	1	1.0	0.3	0.13	0.25	0.13	2.0
26. BEDFORD, W.	f/c	DET	32	363	0.413	0.636	0	2.0	0.4	0.19	0.47	0.56	3.6
27. BENJAMIN, B.	c	SEA	63	1941	0.478	0.687	0	8.1	1.2	0.62	2.78	1.87	14.0
28. BENNETT, W.	f	MIA	54	833	0.379	0.700	0	3.0	0.7	0.35	0.61	0.17	3.6
29. BENOIT, D.	f	UT	77	1161	0.467	0.810	3	3.8	0.4	0.25	0.92	0.57	5.6
30. BIRD, L.	f	BOS	45	1662	0.466	0.926	52	9.6	6.8	0.93	2.78	0.73	20.2
31. BLACKMAN, R.	g	DAL	75	2527	0.461	0.899	65	3.2	2.7	0.67	2.04	0.29	18.3
32. BLANKS, L.	g	DET	43	189	0.455	0.727	6	0.5	0.4	0.33	0.33	0.02	1.5
33. BLAYLOCK, M.	g	NJ	72	2548	0.432	0.712	12	3.7	6.8	2.36	2.11	0.56	13.8
34. BOGUES, M.	g	CHA	82	2790	0.472	0.783	2	2.9	9.1	2.07	1.90	0.07	8.9
35. BOL, M.	c	PHI	71	1267	0.383	0.462	0	3.1	0.3	0.15	0.58	2.89	1.6
36. BONNER, A.	f	SAC	79	2287	0.447	0.627	1	6.1	1.6	1.19	1.68	0.33	9.4
37. BOWIE, A.	g/f	ORL	52	1721	0.493	0.860	17	4.7	3.1	1.06	2.06	0.73	14.6
38. BOWIE, S.	c	NJ	71	2179	0.445	0.757	8	8.1	2.6	0.58	2.11	1.69	15.0
39. BRANDON, T.	g	CLE	82	1605	0.419	0.807	1	2.0	3.9	0.99	1.66	0.27	7.4
40. BREUER, R.	c	MIN	67	1176	0.468	0.533	0	4.2	1.3	0.40	0.61	1.48	5.4
41. BRICKOWSKI, F.	f	MIL	65	1556	0.524	0.767	3	5.3	1.9	0.92	1.72	0.35	11.4
42. BROOKS, K.	f	DEN	37	270	0.443	0.810	2	1.1	0.3	0.22	0.49	0.05	2.8
43. BROOKS, S.	g	MIN	82	1082	0.447	0.810	32	1.2	2.5	0.80	0.62	0.09	5.1
44. BROWN, C.	f	LAL	42	431	0.469	0.612	0	2.0	0.6	0.29	0.69	0.17	3.6
45. BROWN, D.	g	BOS	31	883	0.426	0.769	5	2.6	5.3	1.06	1.90	0.23	11.7
46. BROWN, M.	c/f	UT	82	1783	0.453	0.667	0	5.8	1.0	0.51	1.28	0.41	7.7
47. BROWN, R.	g	SAC	56	535	0.456	0.655	0	1.2	1.1	0.63	0.75	0.21	3.4
48. BROWN, T.	f	SEA	57	655	0.410	0.727	19	1.5	0.8	0.53	0.61	0.09	4.8
49. BRYANT, M.	c	POR	56	800	0.480	0.667	0	3.6	0.7	0.46	0.54	0.14	4.1
50. BUECHLER, J.	f	GS	28	290	0.409	0.571	0	1.9	0.8	0.68	0.46	0.25	2.5
51. BULLARD, M.	f	HOU	80	1278	0.459	0.760	64	3.6	0.9	0.33	0.70	0.26	6.4
52. BURTON, W.	g/f	MIA	68	1585	0.450	0.800	6	3.6	1.8	0.68	1.75	0.54	11.2
53. BURTT, S.	g	PHX	31	356	0.463	0.704	1	1.1	1.9	0.52	1.06	0.13	6.0
54. CAGE, M.	f	SEA	82	2461	0.566	0.620	0	8.9	1.1	1.21	0.95	0.67	8.8

1991–92 REGULAR-SEASON STATISTICAL RESULTS
AVERAGES PER GAME
(Players Listed Alphabetically)

NAME	POS	TEAM	GMs	MINs	FG PCT	FT PCT	3-PT SHOTS MADE	REBs per GM	ASTs per GM	STLs per GM	TOs per GM	BLKs per GM	PTs per GM
55. CAMPBELL, E.	c	LAL	81	1876	0.448	0.619	0	5.2	0.7	0.65	0.90	1.96	7.1
56. CAMPBELL, T.	f/g	MIN	78	2441	0.464	0.803	13	3.7	2.9	1.08	2.12	0.40	16.8
57. CARR, A.	f/c	SA	81	1867	0.490	0.764	1	4.3	0.8	0.40	1.41	1.19	10.9
58. CARTWRIGHT, B.	c	CHI	64	1471	0.467	0.604	0	5.1	1.4	0.34	1.17	0.22	8.0
59. CATLEDGE, T.	f	ORL	78	2430	0.496	0.694	0	7.0	1.4	0.74	1.77	0.21	14.8
60. CAUSWELL, D.	c	SAC	80	2291	0.550	0.613	0	7.3	0.7	0.59	1.55	2.69	8.0
61. CEBALLOS, C.	f	PHX	64	725	0.482	0.737	1	2.4	0.8	0.25	1.11	0.17	7.2
62. CHAMBERS, T.	f	PHX	69	1948	0.431	0.830	18	5.8	2.1	0.83	1.49	0.54	16.3
63. CHAPMAN, R.	g	WAS	22	567	0.448	0.679	8	2.6	4.1	0.68	2.05	0.36	12.3
64. CHEEKS, M.	g	ATL	56	1086	0.462	0.605	3	1.7	3.3	1.48	0.64	0.00	4.6
65. CHILCUTT, P.	f/c	SAC	69	817	0.452	0.821	2	2.7	0.6	0.46	0.59	0.25	3.6
66. COLEMAN, D.	f	NJ	65	2207	0.504	0.763	23	9.5	3.2	0.83	3.82	1.51	19.8
67. COLES, B.	g	MIA	81	1976	0.455	0.824	10	2.3	4.5	0.90	2.06	0.16	10.1
68. CONLON, M.	c	SEA	45	381	0.475	0.750	0	1.5	0.3	0.20	0.60	0.16	2.7
69. CONNER, L.	g	MIL	81	1420	0.431	0.704	0	2.3	3.6	1.20	0.98	0.12	3.5
70. COOK, A.	f	DEN	22	115	0.600	0.667	0	1.6	0.1	0.23	0.14	0.18	1.6
71. COOPER, W.	f	POR	35	344	0.427	0.636	0	2.9	0.6	0.11	0.43	0.77	2.2
72. COPA, T.	f/c	SA	33	132	0.550	0.308	0	1.1	0.1	0.06	0.24	0.18	1.5
73. CORBIN, T.	f	UT	80	2207	0.481	0.866	0	5.9	1.8	1.02	1.21	0.25	9.8
74. CORCHIANI, C.	g	ORL	51	741	0.399	0.875	10	1.5	2.8	0.88	1.45	0.04	5.0
75. CROWDER, C.	g/f	UT	51	328	0.384	0.833	13	0.8	0.3	0.14	0.25	0.04	2.2
76. CUMMINGS, T.	f	SA	70	2149	0.488	0.711	5	9.0	1.5	0.83	1.64	0.49	17.3
77. CURRY, D.	g	CHA	77	2020	0.486	0.836	74	3.4	2.3	1.21	1.74	0.26	15.7
78. DAILEY, Q.	f	SEA	11	98	0.243	0.813	0	1.1	0.4	0.45	0.91	0.09	2.8
79. DAUGHERTY, B.	c	CLE	73	2643	0.570	0.777	0	10.4	3.6	0.89	2.53	1.07	21.5
80. DAVIS, B.	f	DAL	33	429	0.442	0.733	5	1.0	2.0	0.33	0.82	0.09	2.8
81. DAVIS, D.	f	IND	64	1301	0.552	0.572	0	6.4	0.5	0.42	0.77	1.16	6.2
82. DAVIS, T.	f/c	DAL	68	2149	0.482	0.635	0	9.9	0.8	0.38	1.72	0.43	10.2
83. DAVIS, W.	g	DEN	46	741	0.459	0.872	5	1.5	1.5	0.63	0.98	0.02	9.9
84. DAWKINS, J.	g	PHI	82	2815	0.437	0.882	36	2.8	6.9	1.09	2.23	0.06	12.0
85. DIVAC, V.	c	LAL	36	979	0.495	0.768	5	6.9	1.7	1.53	2.44	0.97	11.2
86. DONALDSON, J	c	NY	58	1075	0.457	0.709	0	5.0	0.6	0.14	0.83	0.84	4.9
87. DOUGLAS, S.	g	BOS	42	752	0.463	0.682	1	1.5	4.1	0.60	1.62	0.21	7.3
88. DREILING, G.	c	IND	60	509	0.494	0.750	1	1.6	0.4	0.17	0.52	0.27	2.0
89. DREXLER, C.	g	POR	76	2751	0.470	0.794	114	6.6	6.7	1.82	3.16	0.92	25.0
90. DUCKWORTH, K.	c	POR	82	2222	0.461	0.690	0	6.1	1.2	0.46	1.74	0.45	10.7
91. DUDLEY, C.	c	NJ	82	1902	0.403	0.468	0	9.0	0.7	0.46	0.96	2.18	5.6
92. DUMARS, J.	g	DET	82	3192	0.448	0.867	49	2.3	4.6	0.87	2.35	0.15	19.9
93. EACKLES, L.	f	WAS	65	1463	0.468	0.743	7	2.7	1.9	0.72	1.15	0.11	13.2
94. EATON, M.	c	UT	81	2023	0.446	0.598	0	6.1	0.5	0.44	0.74	2.53	3.3
95. EDWARDS, Ja.	c	LAC	72	1437	0.465	0.731	0	2.8	0.7	0.33	1.00	0.46	9.7
96. EDWARDS, K.	g	MIA	81	1840	0.454	0.848	7	2.6	2.1	1.22	1.48	0.25	10.1
97. EDWARDS, T.	g/f	UT	81	2283	0.522	0.774	39	3.7	1.7	1.00	1.51	0.57	12.6
98. EHLO, C.	g/f	CLE	63	2016	0.453	0.707	69	4.9	3.8	1.24	1.65	0.35	12.3
99. ELIE, M.	g/f	GS	79	1677	0.521	0.852	23	2.9	2.2	0.86	1.05	0.19	7.9
100. ELLIOTT, S.	f	SA	82	3120	0.494	0.861	25	5.4	2.6	1.02	1.85	0.35	16.3
101. ELLIS, D.	f	MIL	81	2191	0.469	0.774	138	3.1	1.3	0.70	1.47	0.22	15.7
102. ELLIS, L.	f	LAC	29	103	0.340	0.474	0	0.8	0.0	0.21	0.38	0.31	1.5
103. ELLISON, P.	c	WAS	66	2511	0.539	0.728	1	11.2	2.9	0.94	2.97	2.68	20.0
104. ENGLISH, A.J.	g	WAS	81	1665	0.433	0.841	6	2.1	1.8	0.40	1.10	0.11	10.9
105. EWING, P.	c	NY	82	3150	0.522	0.738	1	11.2	1.9	1.07	2.55	2.99	24.0
106. FEITL, D.	c	NJ	34	175	0.429	0.842	0	1.8	0.2	0.06	0.56	0.09	2.4
107. FERRELL, D.	f	ATL	66	1598	0.524	0.762	11	3.2	1.4	0.74	1.50	0.26	12.7
108. FERRY, D.	f	CLE	68	937	0.409	0.836	17	3.1	1.1	0.32	0.68	0.22	5.1

1991–92 REGULAR-SEASON STATISTICAL RESULTS
AVERAGES PER GAME
(Players Listed Alphabetically)

NAME	POS	TEAM	GMs	MINs	FG PCT	FT PCT	3-PT SHOTS MADE	REBs per GM	ASTs per GM	STLs per GM	TOs per GM	BLKs per GM	PTs per GM
109. FLEMING, V.	g	IND	82	1737	0.482	0.737	6	2.6	3.2	0.68	1.71	0.09	8.9
110. FLOYD, S.	g	HOU	82	1662	0.406	0.794	37	1.8	2.9	0.70	1.56	0.26	9.1
111. FOSTER, G.	f	WAS	49	548	0.461	0.714	0	3.0	0.7	0.12	0.73	0.24	4.4
112. FOX, R.	g/f	BOS	81	1535	0.459	0.755	23	2.7	1.6	0.96	1.52	0.37	8.0
113. FRANK, T.	f	MIN	10	140	0.546	0.667	0	2.6	0.8	0.50	0.50	0.40	4.6
114. FREDERICK, A.	f	CHA	66	852	0.435	0.685	4	2.2	1.1	0.61	0.88	0.39	5.9
115. GAMBLE, K.	g/f	BOS	82	2496	0.529	0.885	9	3.5	2.7	0.91	1.18	0.45	13.5
116. GARLAND, W.	g	DEN	78	2209	0.444	0.859	9	2.4	5.3	1.26	2.24	0.28	10.8
117. GARRICK, T.	g	DAL	40	549	0.413	0.692	1	1.4	2.5	0.90	1.10	0.10	3.4
118. GATLING, C.	c	GS	54	612	0.568	0.661	0	3.4	0.3	0.57	0.81	0.67	5.7
119. GATTISON, K.	f/c	CHA	82	2223	0.529	0.688	0	7.1	1.6	0.72	1.71	0.84	12.7
120. GEORGE, T.	g	NJ	70	1037	0.428	0.821	1	1.5	2.3	0.59	1.17	0.04	6.0
121. GILL, K.	g/f	CHA	79	2906	0.467	0.745	6	5.1	4.2	1.95	2.28	0.58	20.5
122. GILLIAM, A.	f/c	PHI	81	2771	0.512	0.807	0	8.2	1.5	0.63	2.05	1.05	16.9
123. GLASS, G.	g	MIN	75	1822	0.440	0.616	16	3.5	2.3	0.88	1.37	0.40	11.5
124. GMINSKI, M.	c	CHA	35	499	0.452	0.750	1	3.4	0.9	0.31	0.57	0.46	5.8
125. GRAHAM, P.	g	ATL	78	1718	0.447	0.741	55	3.0	2.2	1.23	1.17	0.27	10.1
126. GRANT, Ga.	g	LAC	78	2049	0.462	0.815	15	2.4	6.9	1.77	2.40	0.18	7.8
127. GRANT, Gr.	g	PHI	68	891	0.440	0.833	7	1.0	3.2	0.66	0.68	0.03	3.3
128. GRANT, Ha.	f	WAS	64	2388	0.479	0.800	1	6.8	2.7	1.16	1.70	0.42	18.0
129. GRANT, Ho.	f	CHI	81	2859	0.579	0.741	0	10.0	2.7	1.23	1.21	1.62	14.2
130. GRAYER, J.	g	MIL	82	1659	0.449	0.667	19	3.1	1.8	0.78	1.28	0.16	9.0
131. GREEN, A.C.	f	LAL	82	2902	0.476	0.744	12	9.3	1.4	1.11	1.35	0.44	13.6
132. GREEN, R.	g	BOS	26	367	0.447	0.722	1	0.9	2.6	0.65	0.69	0.04	4.1
133. GREEN, S.	f	SA	80	1127	0.427	0.820	0	4.3	0.5	0.36	0.78	0.14	4.6
134. GREEN, Se.	g	IND	35	256	0.392	0.536	2	1.2	0.6	0.37	0.77	0.17	4.0
135. HALEY, J.	f/c	LAL	49	394	0.369	0.483	0	1.9	0.1	0.14	0.51	0.16	1.6
136. HAMMONDS, T.	f	CHA	37	984	0.488	0.610	0	5.0	1.0	0.59	1.57	0.35	11.9
137. HANSEN, B.	g	CHI	68	809	0.444	0.364	7	1.1	1.0	0.40	0.41	0.04	2.5
138. HARDAWAY, T.	g	GS	81	3332	0.461	0.766	127	3.8	10.0	2.02	3.30	0.16	23.4
139. HARPER, D.	g	DAL	65	2252	0.443	0.759	58	2.6	5.7	1.55	2.37	0.26	17.7
140. HARPER, R.	g	LAC	82	3144	0.440	0.736	64	5.5	5.1	1.85	3.07	0.88	18.2
141. HASTINGS, S.	f	DEN	40	421	0.340	0.857	0	2.5	0.7	0.25	0.55	0.38	1.5
142. HAWKINS, H.	f	PHI	81	3013	0.462	0.874	91	3.4	3.1	1.94	2.33	0.53	19.0
143. HENDERSON, G.	g	DET	16	96	0.375	0.818	3	0.5	0.6	0.19	0.50	0.00	2.3
144. HENSON, S.	g	MIL	50	386	0.361	0.793	23	0.8	1.6	0.30	0.80	0.02	3.0
145. HERRERA, C.	f	HOU	43	566	0.516	0.568	0	2.3	0.6	0.37	0.86	0.58	4.4
146. HIGGINS, R.	f	GS	25	535	0.412	0.814	33	3.4	0.9	0.60	0.60	0.52	10.2
147. HIGGINS, S.	f	ORL	38	616	0.459	0.861	6	2.7	1.1	0.42	1.08	0.16	7.7
148. HILL, T.	c/f	GS	82	1886	0.522	0.694	0	7.2	0.6	0.89	1.29	0.52	8.2
149. HODGE, D.	c/f	DAL	51	1058	0.497	0.667	0	5.4	0.8	0.49	1.47	0.45	8.4
150. HODGES, C.	g	CHI	56	555	0.384	0.941	36	0.4	1.0	0.25	0.39	0.02	4.3
151. HOPSON, D.	g/f	SAC	71	1314	0.465	0.708	12	2.9	1.4	0.94	1.41	0.55	10.5
152. HORNACEK, J.	g	PHX	81	3078	0.512	0.886	83	5.0	5.1	1.95	2.10	0.38	20.1
153. HOWARD, B.	f	DAL	27	318	0.519	0.710	1	1.9	0.5	0.41	0.56	0.30	4.9
154. HUMPHRIES, J.	g	MIL	71	2261	0.470	0.783	42	2.6	6.6	1.68	2.08	0.18	14.0
155. IUZZOLINO, M.	g	DAL	52	1280	0.451	0.836	59	1.9	3.7	0.63	1.77	0.02	9.4
156. JACKSON, C.	g	DEN	81	1538	0.421	0.870	31	1.4	2.4	0.54	1.44	0.05	10.3
157. JACKSON, M.	g	NY	81	2461	0.491	0.770	11	3.8	8.6	1.38	2.60	0.16	11.3
158. JAMERSON, D.	f	HOU	48	378	0.414	0.926	8	0.9	0.7	0.35	0.50	0.00	4.0
159. JAMES, H.	f	CLE	65	866	0.407	0.803	29	1.7	0.4	0.25	0.66	0.17	6.4
160. JEPSEN, L.	c	SAC	31	87	0.375	0.636	0	1.0	0.0	0.03	0.10	0.16	0.8
161. JOHNSON, A.	g	HOU	69	1235	0.479	0.654	4	1.2	3.9	0.88	1.59	0.13	5.6
162. JOHNSON, B.	f	HOU	80	2202	0.458	0.727	1	3.9	2.0	0.90	1.30	0.61	8.6

NAME	POS	TEAM	GMs	MINs	FG PCT	FT PCT	3-PT SHOTS MADE	REBs per GM	ASTs per GM	STLs per GM	TOs per GM	BLKs per GM	PTs per GM
163. JOHNSON, E.	f	SEA	81	2366	0.459	0.861	27	3.6	2.0	0.68	1.60	0.14	17.1
164. JOHNSON, K.	g	PHX	78	2899	0.479	0.807	10	3.7	10.7	1.49	3.49	0.29	19.7
165. JOHNSON, L.	f	CHA	82	3047	0.490	0.829	5	11.0	3.6	0.99	1.95	0.62	19.2
166. JOHNSON, V.	g	SA	60	1350	0.405	0.647	19	3.0	2.4	0.68	1.23	0.23	8.0
167. JONES, Ch.	c/f	WAS	75	1365	0.367	0.500	0	4.2	0.8	0.57	0.52	1.23	1.2
168. JORDAN, M.	g	CHI	80	3102	0.519	0.832	27	6.4	6.1	2.28	2.50	0.94	30.1
169. KEMP, S.	f/c	SEA	64	1808	0.504	0.748	0	10.4	1.3	1.09	2.44	1.94	15.5
170. KERR, S.	g	CLE	48	847	0.511	0.833	32	1.6	2.3	0.56	0.65	0.21	6.7
171. KERSEY, J.	f	POR	77	2553	0.467	0.664	1	8.2	3.2	1.48	1.96	0.92	12.6
172. KESSLER, A.	c	MIA	77	1197	0.413	0.817	0	4.1	0.4	0.22	0.75	0.42	5.3
173. KIMBLE, B.	f	LAC	34	277	0.396	0.645	4	0.9	0.5	0.29	0.44	0.18	3.3
174. KING, R.	c	SEA	40	213	0.380	0.756	0	1.2	0.3	0.10	0.45	0.13	2.2
175. KING, S.	f/c	CHI	79	1268	0.506	0.753	2	2.6	1.0	0.27	0.96	0.32	7.0
176. KITE, G.	c	ORL	72	1479	0.437	0.588	0	5.6	0.6	0.42	0.85	0.79	3.2
177. KLEINE, J.	c	BOS	70	991	0.492	0.708	4	4.2	0.5	0.33	0.39	0.20	4.7
178. KNIGHT, N.	g	PHX	42	631	0.475	0.688	4	1.1	2.7	0.57	1.38	0.07	5.8
179. KOFOED, B.	g	SEA	44	239	0.472	0.577	1	0.6	1.2	0.05	0.45	0.05	1.5
180. KONCAK, J.	c	ATL	77	1489	0.391	0.655	0	3.4	1.7	0.65	0.70	0.87	3.1
181. KRYSTKOWIAK, L.	f	MIL	79	1848	0.444	0.757	0	5.4	1.4	0.68	1.46	0.15	9.0
182. LAIMBEER, B.	c	DET	81	2234	0.470	0.893	32	5.6	2.0	0.63	1.26	0.67	9.7
183. LANE, J.	f	MIL	14	177	0.304	0.333	0	4.7	1.2	0.14	1.00	0.07	2.6
184. LANG, A.	c	PHX	81	1965	0.522	0.768	0	6.7	0.5	0.59	1.07	2.48	7.7
185. LECKNER, E.	c	CHA	59	716	0.513	0.745	0	3.5	0.5	0.15	0.66	0.31	3.3
186. LEE, D.	g	NJ	46	307	0.431	0.526	10	0.8	0.5	0.24	0.26	0.02	2.6
187. LES, J.	g	SAC	62	712	0.385	0.809	45	1.0	2.3	0.50	0.68	0.05	3.7
188. LEVER, F.	g	DAL	31	898	0.387	0.750	17	5.2	3.5	1.48	1.16	0.39	11.2
189. LEVINGSTON, C.	f	CHI	79	1020	0.498	0.625	1	2.9	0.8	0.34	0.53	0.57	3.9
190. LEWIS, R.	g	BOS	82	3070	0.503	0.851	5	4.8	2.3	1.52	1.66	1.28	20.8
191. LIBERTY, M.	f/g	DEN	75	1527	0.443	0.728	17	4.1	0.8	0.88	1.20	0.39	9.3
192. LICHTI, T.	g	DEN	68	1176	0.460	0.839	1	1.7	1.1	0.63	1.06	0.18	6.6
193. LISTER, A.	c	GS	26	293	0.557	0.424	0	3.5	0.5	0.19	0.77	0.62	3.9
194. LOHAUS, B.	f/c	MIL	70	1081	0.450	0.659	57	3.6	1.1	0.57	0.66	1.01	5.8
195. LONG, G.	f	MIA	82	3063	0.494	0.807	6	8.4	2.7	1.70	2.26	0.49	14.8
196. LONGLEY, L.	c	MIN	66	991	0.458	0.663	0	3.9	0.8	0.53	1.26	0.97	4.3
197. LYNCH, K.	g	CHA	55	819	0.417	0.761	3	1.6	1.5	0.67	0.80	0.16	4.1
198. MACON, M.	g	DEN	76	2304	0.375	0.730	4	2.9	2.2	2.03	2.04	0.18	10.6
199. MAJERLE, D.	g/f	PHX	82	2853	0.478	0.756	87	5.9	3.3	1.60	1.23	0.52	17.3
200. MALONE, J.	g	UT	81	2922	0.511	0.898	1	2.9	2.2	0.69	1.73	0.06	20.2
201. MALONE, K.	f	UT	81	3054	0.526	0.778	3	11.2	3.0	1.33	3.06	0.63	28.0
202. MALONE, M.	c	MIL	82	2511	0.474	0.786	3	9.1	1.1	0.90	1.83	0.78	15.6
203. MANNING, D.	f	LAC	82	2904	0.542	0.725	0	6.9	3.5	1.65	2.56	1.49	19.3
204. MARCIULIONIS, S.	g	GS	72	2117	0.538	0.788	3	2.9	3.4	1.61	2.68	0.14	18.9
205. MASON, A.	f	NY	82	2198	0.509	0.642	0	7.0	1.3	0.56	1.23	0.24	7.0
206. MAXWELL, V.	g	HOU	80	2700	0.413	0.772	162	3.0	4.1	1.30	2.23	0.35	17.1
207. MAYES, Th.	g	LAC	24	255	0.303	0.667	15	0.7	1.5	0.67	1.29	0.08	4.1
208. MAYS, T.	g	ATL	2	32	0.429	1.000	3	1.0	0.5	0.00	1.50	0.00	8.5
209. McCANN, B.	f	DET	26	129	0.394	0.308	0	1.2	0.2	0.23	0.27	0.15	1.2
210. McCLOUD, G.	g	IND	51	892	0.409	0.781	32	2.6	2.3	0.51	1.22	0.22	6.6
211. McCORMICK, T.	c	NY	22	108	0.424	0.667	0	1.6	0.4	0.09	0.36	0.00	1.9
212. McCRAY, R.	f	DAL	75	2106	0.436	0.719	25	6.2	2.9	0.64	1.53	0.40	9.0
213. McDANIEL, X.	f	NY	82	2344	0.478	0.714	12	5.6	1.8	0.70	1.79	0.29	13.7
214. McHALE, K.	f/c	BOS	56	1398	0.510	0.822	0	5.9	1.5	0.20	1.46	1.05	13.9
215. McKEY, D.	f	SEA	52	1757	0.472	0.847	19	5.2	2.3	1.17	2.19	0.90	14.9
216. McMILLAN, N.	g/f	SEA	72	1652	0.437	0.643	27	3.5	5.0	1.79	1.56	0.40	6.0

1991–92 REGULAR-SEASON STATISTICAL RESULTS
AVERAGES PER GAME
(Players Listed Alphabetically)

NAME	POS	TEAM	GMs	MINs	FG PCT	FT PCT	3-PT SHOTS MADE	REBs per GM	ASTs per GM	STLs per GM	TOs per GM	BLKs per GM	PTs per GM
217. MILLER, R.	g	IND	82	3120	0.501	0.858	129	3.9	3.8	1.28	1.91	0.32	20.7
218. MILLS, T.	f	NJ	82	1714	0.463	0.750	8	5.5	1.0	0.59	1.00	0.50	9.1
219. MITCHELL, S.	f	MIN	82	2151	0.423	0.786	2	5.8	1.2	0.65	1.18	0.48	10.1
220. MONROE, R.	g	ATL	38	313	0.368	0.826	6	0.9	0.7	0.32	0.61	0.05	3.5
221. MOORE, T.	f	DAL	42	782	0.400	0.833	30	2.0	1.1	0.76	1.05	0.10	8.5
222. MORRIS, C.	f	NJ	77	2394	0.477	0.714	22	6.4	2.6	1.68	2.22	1.05	11.4
223. MORTON, J.	g	MIA	25	270	0.387	0.842	2	1.0	1.3	0.52	1.12	0.04	4.2
224. MULLIN, C.	f	GS	81	3346	0.524	0.833	64	5.6	3.5	2.14	2.49	0.77	25.6
225. MURDOCK, E.	g	UT	50	478	0.415	0.754	5	1.1	1.8	0.60	1.00	0.14	4.1
226. MURPHY, T.	f	MIN	47	429	0.488	0.559	1	2.3	0.2	0.19	0.38	0.17	2.1
227. MUSTAF, J	f	PHX	52	545	0.477	0.690	0	2.8	0.9	0.40	0.98	0.31	4.5
228. MUTOMBO, D.	c	DEN	71	2716	0.493	0.642	0	12.3	2.2	0.61	3.55	2.96	16.6
229. NANCE, L.	f	CLE	81	2880	0.539	0.822	0	8.3	2.9	0.99	1.07	3.00	17.0
230. NEALY, E.	f	PHX	52	505	0.512	0.667	20	2.1	0.7	0.31	0.33	0.04	3.1
231. NEWMAN, J.	f/g	CHA	55	1651	0.477	0.766	13	3.3	2.7	1.27	2.35	0.25	15.3
232. NORMAN, K.	f	LAC	77	2009	0.490	0.535	4	5.8	1.6	0.69	1.30	0.86	12.1
233. OAKLEY, C.	f	NY	82	2309	0.522	0.735	0	8.5	1.6	0.82	1.50	0.18	6.2
234. OGG, A.	c	MIA	43	367	0.548	0.533	0	1.7	0.2	0.12	0.44	0.65	2.5
235. OLAJUWON, H.	c	HOU	70	2636	0.502	0.766	0	12.1	2.2	1.81	2.67	4.34	21.6
236. OLIVER, B.	g	PHI	34	279	0.330	0.682	0	0.9	0.6	0.29	0.71	0.06	2.4
237. OLIVER, J.	g/f	CLE	27	252	0.398	0.773	1	1.0	0.7	0.33	0.33	0.07	3.6
238. OWENS, B.	g/f	GS	80	2510	0.525	0.654	1	8.0	2.4	1.13	2.24	0.81	14.3
239. OWENS, K.	f	LAL	20	80	0.281	0.800	0	0.8	0.2	0.25	0.10	0.20	1.3
240. PACK, R.	g	POR	72	894	0.423	0.803	0	1.4	1.9	0.56	1.28	0.06	4.6
241. PARISH, R.	c	BOS	79	2285	0.536	0.772	0	8.9	0.9	0.86	1.66	1.23	14.1
242. PAXSON, J.	g	CHI	79	1946	0.528	0.784	12	1.2	3.1	0.62	0.56	0.11	7.0
243. PAYNE, K.	f	PHI	49	353	0.448	0.692	5	1.1	0.4	0.33	0.39	0.16	2.9
244. PAYTON, G.	g	SEA	81	2549	0.451	0.669	3	3.6	6.3	1.81	2.15	0.26	9.4
245. PERDUE, W.	c	CHI	77	1007	0.547	0.495	1	4.1	1.0	0.21	0.94	0.56	4.6
246. PERKINS, S.	f/c	LAL	63	2332	0.450	0.817	15	8.8	2.2	1.02	1.32	0.98	16.5
247. PERRY, E.	g	CHA	50	437	0.380	0.659	1	0.8	1.6	0.68	1.00	0.06	2.5
248. PERRY, T.	f	PHX	80	2483	0.523	0.712	3	6.9	1.7	0.55	1.76	1.45	12.3
249. PERSON, C.	f	IND	81	2923	0.480	0.675	132	5.3	4.7	0.84	2.67	0.22	18.5
250. PETERSEN, J.	c	GS	27	169	0.450	0.700	0	1.7	0.3	0.19	0.19	0.22	1.6
251. PETROVIC, D.	g	NJ	82	3027	0.508	0.808	123	3.2	3.1	1.28	2.62	0.13	20.6
252. PHILLS, B.	g	CLE	10	65	0.429	0.636	0	0.8	0.4	0.30	0.80	0.10	3.1
253. PIERCE, R.	g	SEA	78	2658	0.475	0.917	33	3.0	3.1	1.10	2.42	0.26	21.7
254. PINCKNEY, E.	f	BOS	81	1917	0.537	0.812	0	7.0	0.8	0.86	0.90	0.69	7.6
255. PIPPEN, S.	f	CHI	82	3164	0.506	0.760	16	7.7	7.0	1.89	3.09	1.13	21.0
256. POLYNICE, O.	c	LAC	76	1834	0.519	0.622	0	7.1	0.6	0.59	1.09	0.26	8.1
257. PORTER, T.	g	POR	82	2784	0.462	0.856	128	3.1	5.8	1.55	2.29	0.15	18.1
258. PRESSEY, P.	g	SA	56	759	0.373	0.683	3	1.7	2.5	0.52	1.14	0.34	2.7
259. PRICE, M.	g	CLE	72	2138	0.488	0.947	101	2.4	7.4	1.31	2.21	0.17	17.3
260. PRITCHARD, K.	g	BOS	11	136	0.471	0.778	0	1.0	2.7	0.27	1.00	0.36	4.2
261. QUINNETT, B.	f	DAL	39	326	0.347	0.615	13	1.3	0.3	0.41	0.41	0.21	3.0
262. RAMBIS, K.	f	PHX	28	381	0.463	0.778	0	3.8	1.3	0.43	0.89	0.50	3.2
263. RANDALL, M.	f	MIN	54	441	0.456	0.744	3	1.3	0.6	0.22	0.46	0.06	3.2
264. RASMUSSEN, B.	c	ATL	81	1968	0.478	0.750	5	4.9	1.3	0.43	0.63	0.59	9.0
265. REID, J.R.	c/f	CHA	51	1257	0.490	0.705	0	6.2	1.6	0.96	1.65	0.45	11.0
266. REYNOLDS, J.	g/f	ORL	46	1159	0.380	0.836	3	3.2	3.3	1.37	2.09	0.37	12.1
267. RICE, G.	f	MIA	79	3007	0.469	0.837	155	5.0	2.3	1.14	1.84	0.44	22.3
268. RICHARDSON, P.	g	MIN	82	2922	0.466	0.691	53	3.7	8.4	1.45	2.49	0.30	16.5
269. RICHMOND, M.	g	SAC	80	3095	0.468	0.813	103	4.0	5.1	1.15	3.09	0.43	22.5
270. RIVERS, Da.	g	LAC	15	122	0.333	0.909	0	1.3	1.4	0.47	1.13	0.07	2.0

1991−92 REGULAR-SEASON STATISTICAL RESULTS
AVERAGES PER GAME
(Players Listed Alphabetically)

NAME	POS	TEAM	GMs	MINs	FG PCT	FT PCT	3-PT SHOTS MADE	REBs per GM	ASTs per GM	STLs per GM	TOs per GM	BLKs per GM	PTs per GM
271. RIVERS, Do.	g	LAC	59	1657	0.424	0.832	26	2.5	4.0	1.88	1.56	0.32	10.9
272. ROBERTS, F.	f	MIL	80	1746	0.482	0.749	19	3.2	1.5	0.65	1.53	0.50	9.6
273. ROBERTS, S.	c	ORL	55	1118	0.529	0.515	0	6.1	0.7	0.40	1.42	1.51	10.4
274. ROBERTSON, A.	g	MIL	82	2463	0.430	0.763	67	4.3	4.4	2.56	2.72	0.39	12.3
275. ROBINSON, C.	f	POR	82	2124	0.466	0.664	1	5.1	1.7	1.04	1.88	1.30	12.4
276. ROBINSON, D.	c	SA	68	2564	0.551	0.701	1	12.2	2.7	2.32	2.68	4.49	23.2
277. ROBINSON, R.	g	ATL	81	2220	0.456	0.636	34	2.7	5.5	1.30	2.54	0.30	13.0
278. RODMAN, D.	f	DET	82	3301	0.539	0.600	32	18.7	2.3	0.83	1.71	0.85	9.8
279. ROLLINS, T.	f/c	HOU	59	697	0.535	0.867	0	2.9	0.3	0.24	0.31	1.05	2.0
280. ROYAL, D.	f	SA	60	718	0.449	0.692	0	2.1	0.6	0.42	0.65	0.12	4.2
281. RUDD, D.	g	UT	65	538	0.399	0.762	11	0.8	1.7	0.23	0.75	0.02	3.0
282. RULAND, J.	c	PHI	13	209	0.526	0.688	0	3.6	0.4	0.54	1.54	0.31	3.9
283. SALLEY, J.	f/c	DET	72	1774	0.512	0.715	0	4.1	1.6	0.68	1.42	1.53	9.5
284. SAMPSON, R.	c	WAS	10	108	0.310	0.667	0	3.0	0.4	0.30	1.00	0.80	2.2
285. SANDERS, J.	f	ATL	12	117	0.444	0.778	0	2.2	0.8	0.42	0.42	0.25	3.9
286. SANDERS, M.	f	CLE	31	633	0.571	0.766	1	3.1	1.7	0.77	0.71	0.32	7.1
287. SCHAYES, D.	c	MIL	43	726	0.417	0.771	0	3.9	0.8	0.44	0.95	0.44	5.6
288. SCHEFFLER, S.	f	DEN	11	61	0.667	0.750	0	1.3	0.0	0.27	0.09	0.09	1.9
289. SCHINTZIUS, D.	c	SAC	33	400	0.427	0.833	0	3.6	0.6	0.18	0.58	0.85	3.3
290. SCHREMPF, D.	f	IND	80	2605	0.536	0.828	23	9.6	3.9	0.78	2.39	0.46	17.2
291. SCOTT, B.	g	LAL	82	2679	0.458	0.839	54	3.8	2.8	1.28	1.45	0.34	14.9
292. SCOTT, D.	f	ORL	18	608	0.402	0.901	29	3.7	1.9	1.11	1.72	0.50	19.9
293. SEIKALY, R.	c	MIA	79	2800	0.489	0.733	0	11.8	1.4	0.51	2.73	1.53	16.4
294. SELLERS, B.	f/c	DET	43	226	0.466	0.769	0	1.0	0.3	0.02	0.35	0.23	2.4
295. SHACKLEFORD, C.	c	PHI	72	1399	0.486	0.663	0	5.8	0.6	0.53	0.86	0.71	6.6
296. SHAW, B.	g	MIA	63	1423	0.407	0.791	5	3.2	4.0	0.90	1.57	0.35	7.9
297. SIMMONS, L.	f	SAC	78	2895	0.454	0.770	1	8.1	4.3	1.73	2.79	1.69	17.1
298. SKILES, S.	g	ORL	75	2377	0.414	0.895	91	2.7	7.3	0.99	3.11	0.07	14.1
299. SMITH, C.	f/c	LAC	49	1310	0.466	0.785	0	6.1	1.1	0.84	1.41	2.00	14.6
300. SMITH, Do.	f	DAL	76	1707	0.415	0.736	0	5.1	1.7	0.82	1.28	0.45	8.8
301. SMITH, K.	g	HOU	81	2735	0.475	0.866	54	2.2	6.9	1.28	2.80	0.09	14.0
302. SMITH, L.	f/c	HOU	45	800	0.544	0.364	0	5.7	0.7	0.47	0.98	0.16	2.3
303. SMITH, La.	g	WAS	48	708	0.407	0.804	2	1.7	2.1	0.92	1.31	0.02	5.2
304. SMITH, O.	g	ORL	55	877	0.365	0.769	8	2.1	1.0	0.65	1.13	0.24	5.6
305. SMITH, S.	g	MIA	61	1806	0.454	0.748	40	3.1	4.6	0.97	2.49	0.31	12.0
306. SMITH, T.	g	LAL	63	820	0.399	0.653	0	1.2	1.7	0.62	0.79	0.13	4.4
307. SMITS, R.	c	IND	74	1772	0.510	0.788	0	5.6	1.6	0.39	1.76	1.35	13.8
308. SPARROW, R.	g	LAL	46	489	0.384	0.615	3	0.6	1.8	0.26	0.72	0.11	2.8
309. SPENCER, F.	c	MIN	61	1481	0.426	0.691	0	7.1	0.9	0.44	1.15	1.30	6.6
310. STARKS, J.	g	NY	82	2118	0.449	0.778	94	2.3	3.4	1.26	1.83	0.22	13.9
311. STEWART, L.	f	WAS	76	2229	0.514	0.807	0	5.9	1.6	0.67	1.47	0.58	10.4
312. STOCKTON, J.	g	UT	82	3002	0.482	0.842	83	3.3	13.7	2.98	3.49	0.27	15.8
313. STRICKLAND, R.	g	SA	57	2053	0.455	0.687	5	4.7	8.6	2.07	2.81	0.30	13.8
314. SUTTON, G.	g	SA	67	601	0.388	0.756	26	0.7	1.4	0.39	1.04	0.13	3.7
315. TEAGLE, T.	f	LAL	82	1602	0.452	0.767	1	2.2	1.4	0.80	1.39	0.11	10.7
316. THOMAS, C.	g	DET	37	156	0.353	0.667	2	0.6	0.6	0.11	0.46	0.03	1.3
317. THOMAS, I.	g	DET	78	2918	0.446	0.773	25	3.2	7.2	1.51	3.23	0.19	18.5
318. THOMPSON, L.	f/c	IND	80	1299	0.468	0.817	0	4.8	1.3	0.65	1.23	0.43	4.9
319. THOMPSON, S.	g	SAC	19	91	0.378	0.375	0	1.0	0.4	0.32	0.26	0.16	1.6
320. THORPE, O.	f	HOU	82	3056	0.592	0.657	0	10.5	3.1	0.63	2.89	0.45	17.3
321. THREATT, S.	g	LAL	82	3070	0.489	0.831	20	3.1	7.2	2.05	2.22	0.20	15.1
322. TISDALE, W.	f	SAC	72	2521	0.501	0.763	0	6.5	1.5	0.76	1.72	1.10	16.6
323. TOLBERT, T.	f	GS	35	310	0.384	0.550	2	1.6	0.6	0.29	0.57	0.17	2.6
324. TUCKER, T.	g	SA	24	415	0.465	0.800	19	1.5	1.1	0.88	0.58	0.13	6.5

1991–92 REGULAR-SEASON STATISTICAL RESULTS
AVERAGES PER GAME
(Players Listed Alphabetically)

NAME	POS	TEAM	GMs	MINs	FG PCT	FT PCT	3-PT SHOTS MADE	REBs per GM	ASTs per GM	STLs per GM	TOs per GM	BLKs per GM	PTs per GM
325. TURNER, A.	g	WAS	70	871	0.425	0.792	1	1.3	2.5	0.81	1.20	0.03	4.1
326. TURNER, J.	f	ORL	75	1591	0.451	0.693	1	3.3	1.2	0.32	1.41	0.21	7.1
327. TURNER, Jo.	f	HOU	42	345	0.439	0.525	0	1.9	0.3	0.14	0.76	0.10	2.8
328. VANDEWEGHE, K.	f	NY	67	956	0.491	0.803	26	1.3	0.9	0.22	0.40	0.12	7.0
329. VAUGHT, L.	f	LAC	79	1687	0.492	0.797	4	6.5	0.9	0.47	0.84	0.39	7.6
330. VINCENT, S.	g	ORL	39	885	0.430	0.846	1	2.6	3.8	0.90	1.85	0.10	10.5
331. VOLKOV, A.	f	ATL	77	1516	0.441	0.631	35	3.4	3.3	0.86	1.32	0.39	8.6
332. VRANKOVIC, S.	c	BOS	19	110	0.469	0.583	0	1.5	0.3	0.00	0.53	0.89	2.0
333. WALKER, D.	g	DET	74	1541	0.423	0.619	0	3.2	2.8	0.85	1.07	0.24	5.2
334. WEBB, S.	g	SAC	77	2724	0.445	0.859	73	2.9	7.1	1.62	2.97	0.31	16.0
335. WEST, D.	g	MIN	80	2540	0.518	0.805	4	3.2	3.5	0.83	1.50	0.33	14.0
336. WEST, M.	c	PHX	82	1436	0.632	0.637	0	4.5	0.3	0.17	1.00	0.99	6.1
337. WHATLEY, E.	g	POR	23	209	0.412	0.871	0	0.9	1.5	0.61	0.61	0.13	3.0
338. WHITE, R.	f	DAL	65	1021	0.380	0.765	4	3.6	0.5	0.48	1.05	0.34	6.4
339. WIGGINS, M.	g	PHI	49	569	0.384	0.686	0	1.9	0.5	0.41	0.51	0.02	4.3
340. WILEY, M.	g	ATL	53	870	0.430	0.686	14	1.5	3.4	0.89	1.13	0.06	3.9
341. WILKINS, D.	f	ATL	42	1601	0.464	0.835	37	7.0	3.8	1.24	2.90	0.57	28.1
342. WILKINS, G.	g	NY	82	2344	0.447	0.730	38	2.5	2.7	0.93	1.38	0.21	12.4
343. WILLIAMS, Bu.	f	POR	80	2519	0.604	0.754	0	8.8	1.4	0.78	1.63	0.51	11.3
344. WILLIAMS, Br.	f	ORL	48	905	0.528	0.669	0	5.7	0.7	0.85	1.79	1.10	9.1
345. WILLIAMS, H.	f/c	DAL	75	2040	0.431	0.725	1	6.1	1.3	0.47	1.52	1.31	11.5
346. WILLIAMS, Jo.	f/c	CLE	80	2432	0.503	0.752	0	7.6	2.5	0.75	1.04	2.28	11.9
347. WILLIAMS, Ja.	f/c	PHI	50	646	0.364	0.636	0	2.9	0.2	0.40	0.88	0.40	4.1
348. WILLIAMS, K.	f	IND	60	565	0.518	0.605	0	2.2	0.7	0.33	0.37	0.68	4.2
349. WILLIAMS, M.	g	IND	79	2750	0.490	0.871	8	3.6	8.2	2.95	3.04	0.28	15.0
350. WILLIAMS, R.	f	DEN	81	2623	0.471	0.803	56	5.0	2.9	1.83	2.14	0.84	18.2
351. WILLIAMS, S.	f	CHI	63	690	0.483	0.649	0	3.9	0.8	0.21	0.56	0.57	3.4
352. WILLIS, K.	f/c	ATL	81	2962	0.483	0.804	6	15.5	2.1	0.89	2.43	0.67	18.3
353. WINCHESTER, K.	f	NY	19	81	0.433	0.800	1	0.8	0.4	0.11	0.11	0.11	1.8
354. WINGATE, D.	g	WAS	81	2127	0.465	0.719	1	3.3	3.1	1.52	1.53	0.26	7.9
355. WITTMAN, R.	g	IND	24	115	0.421	0.500	0	0.4	0.5	0.08	0.13	0.00	0.7
356. WOLF, J.	f	DEN	67	1160	0.361	0.803	1	3.6	0.9	0.48	0.90	0.21	3.8
357. WOOLRIDGE, O.	f	DET	82	2113	0.498	0.683	1	3.2	1.1	0.50	1.62	0.40	14.0
358. WORTHY, J.	f	LAL	54	2108	0.447	0.814	9	5.7	4.7	1.41	2.35	0.43	19.9
359. YOUNG, D.	g	LAC	62	1023	0.392	0.851	23	1.2	2.8	0.74	0.76	0.06	4.5

APPENDIX A

TEN KEYS TO WINNING
AT FANTASY BASKETBALL

TEN KEYS TO WINNING
AT FANTASY BASKETBALL

This is our little gift to you for buying our book. It's also a good way for us to point out to all the unsuccessful fantasy owners that we know what they are doing wrong. Also, this is a lot of fun; we feel important when we give advice.

1. Don't Play in Our Fantasy Basketball League.
Okay. This may be carrying ego a little too far.

2. Never Get Attached to a Player.
We don't care if you've had a player on your team for five straight years. People can take advantage of your attachment and bid the player up.

3. Don't Reveal Your True Feelings about a Player.
This, like the preceding piece of advice, is just one of the basics of smart dealing. Why telegraph your moves? Still, you can keep your fellow owners guessing if you appear to slip every once in a while and let your feelings be known.

4. Don't Blow Off Your Taxi Squad.
This could be the most important rule. A good taxi squad can save your team when you suffer from injuries or just poor production. While most people spend all their money on their 12 starters, saving a little bit for your taxi squad will pay off in the long run.

5. Don't Overstock with Information.
You all know the owner who memorizes every magazine and every other source of information that he or she can find before the draft. As this owner is reciting statistics about air-pressure differences among NBA arenas, he or she drafts some bench ornament for 30 units. Don't gather so much information that it gets jumbled up in your head. Keep it simple and plot out your draft strategy beforehand. You will do fine.

6. Don't Spend Too Early or Wait Too Late.
Some people spend all their money in the beginning of the draft and have to wait around until the end to get players for 1 unit—which is all they can afford. As they wait, they painfully watch the bidding on all those other good players. Other people save all of their money until the end. This, too, is a bad strategy; by the end of the draft, there isn't enough talent left to win your league even if you get all the best players left.

7. Don't Pass Up Good Power Forwards for Bad Centers.
Unless you play head-to-head and have to have centers, don't draft centers who won't do much when you can get power forwards who do more. Also, draft only centers who get blocked shots.

8. Only Draft Shooting Guards and Small Forwards Who Do Something besides Score.

Many shooters out there can do other things too. Draft them.

9. Don't Overpay for Rookies.

A rookie rarely lives up to his potential in his rookie season. Don't get sucked in by the hype from scouts and agents. You will only end up regretting it. We aren't saying don't draft rookies, just that the amount you pay should be in line with the production that they are likely to get.

10. Never Draft a Big Ten Center.

Are you ready for this list? Brad Lohaus, Kevin Willis, Jim Rowinski, Steven Scheffler, Mychal Thompson, Herb Williams, Roy Tarpley, Joe Barry Caroll, Tim McCormick, Uwe Blab, Jim Peterson, and Les Jepsen. Okay, Boston sometimes lists Kevin McHale at center, but we aren't going to count him. And that Roy Tarpley guy? Kenny Rogers isn't enough of a gambler to draft him.

APPENDIX B

DRAFT-DAY CHART

THE SUPER-DUPER, ALL-IN-ONE, CAN'T-BE-WITHOUT-IT DRAFT DAY CHART

This is it, the *pièce de résistance,* one of the reasons to choose our book over all the others, the one thing every Fantasy Basketball owner needs: THE SUPER-DUPER, ALL-IN-ONE, CAN'T-BE-WITHOUT-IT DRAFT DAY CHART. This chart will help you tremendously on draft day. When all the others are scratching their heads, wondering whether to pay one more unit, you will know the answer. However, like any good tool, this chart must be used correctly. You can't use this chart to determine a drafting strategy. You can't use this chart to figure out what a player will do this year. For both of those, you will have to read the entire book, and probably a couple of magazines.

But this chart does tell you three very important things. First, it tells you what every player did last year in all the categories. Second, it tells you where each player's total game ranks him with the rest of the league. Third, if you cross off names as you go along, it will tell you which players are left in the draft, and what they can do.

EXAMPLE: Kevin Duckworth is being auctioned off and you need a center. So, you check the chart and realize that Kevin gets almost no blocked shots. You decide to let him slide, and pay the money later for Rony Seikaly, who does get blocked shots.

It is also important that you know how the chart was created. The numbers are all assigned according to rigorous standards created in the laboratories of. . . . Just kidding. We assigned the numbers so that the #1 group in each statistic is always the smallest group, while the #5 group is always the largest.

EXAMPLE: There are only six players in the #1 group for blocked shots. This is because these six players get so many more blocks than anyone else that it would be unfair to assign any more players to that category just to meet a so-called quota.

The last consideration is that the players are ranked according to their stats per game. So, if a player doesn't play all 82 games, his lost statistics aren't reflected in the chart. The only exception to this is three-pointers, in which a player's ranking is based on total three-pointers made, rather than on three-pointers per game. (Larry Bird, for instance, is ranked a 2 even though he made more than one three-pointer per game.) Also, the field-goal and free-throw percentage categories do not reflect the amount of shots taken. For example, Larry Smith's free-throw percentage is only .364, but he'll never shoot enough free throws to affect your team's percentage at all. There is sometimes a big disparity in some of the rankings, especially among the leaders. Conversely, as you move farther down the chart, the difference in performance diminishes. For example, while Rod Strickland and John Stockton are both rated in the #1 group for assists, John had 13.7 assists per game, whereas Rod only had 8.6 assists per game, or about 63% of John's total. Also, while Detlef Schrempf averaged 3.9 assists per game, and was given a ranking of 4, Pooh Richardson averaged 4.0 assists per game, and recieved a ranking of 3. That just happened to be the cutoff point.

THE DRAFT CHART

NAME	POS	TEAM	GMs	MINs	FG PCT	FT PCT	3-PT SHOTS	REBs	ASTs	STLs	TOs	BLKs	PTs
ABDELNABY, A.	f/c	POR	71	934	3	4	5	4	5	5	1	5	4
ACRES, M.	c	ORL	68	926	2	4	5	4	5	5	1	5	5
ADAMS, M.	g	WAS	78	2795	5	2	1	4	2	2	4	5	2
ADDISON, R.	g	NJ	76	1175	5	4	4	5	5	5	1	5	5
AGUIRRE, M.	f	DET	75	1582	5	5	4	4	5	5	2	5	4
AINGE, D.	g	POR	81	1595	4	3	2	5	4	4	1	5	4
ALEXANDER, V.	c	GS	80	1350	2	5	5	4	5	5	1	4	4
ANDERSON, G.	f	DEN	82	2793	4	5	5	1	5	3	3	4	4
ANDERSON, K.	g	NJ	64	1086	5	4	5	5	4	3	2	5	4
ANDERSON, N.	g/f	ORL	60	2203	4	5	3	3	4	2	3	4	2
ANDERSON, Ro.	f	PHI	82	2432	4	2	3	4	5	3	2	5	3
ANDERSON, W.	g/f	SA	57	1889	4	4	4	3	3	4	3	4	3
ANSLEY, M.	f	CHA	10	45	4	3	5	5	5	5	1	5	5
ANTHONY, G.	g	NY	82	1510	5	4	5	5	4	5	1	5	5
ARMSTRONG, B.J.	g	CHI	82	1875	3	3	3	5	4	5	1	5	4
ASKEW, V.	g	GS	80	1496	2	5	5	5	4	5	1	5	4
ASKINS, K.	g/f	MIA	59	843	5	5	4	5	5	5	1	5	5
AUGMON, S.	g/f	ATL	82	2505	3	5	5	3	4	2	3	5	3
AUSTIN, I.	c	UT	31	112	3	5	5	5	5	5	1	5	5
BAGLEY, J.	g	BOS	73	1742	4	5	4	5	2	4	3	5	4
BAILEY, T.	f	MIN	84	2104	4	4	5	3	5	5	1	3	4
BARKLEY, C.	f	PHX	75	2881	1	5	3	1	3	2	5	4	2
BARROS, D.	g	SEA	75	1331	3	4	2	5	5	5	1	5	4
BATTLE, J.	g	CLE	76	1637	3	2	5	5	5	5	1	5	4
BATTLE, K.	f	GS	16	92	1	3	5	5	5	5	1	5	5
BEDFORD, W.	f/c	DET	32	363	5	5	5	5	5	5	1	4	5
BENJAMIN, B.	c	SEA	63	1941	3	5	5	2	5	5	4	2	3
BENNETT, W.	f	MIA	54	833	5	5	5	4	5	5	1	5	5
BENOIT, D.	f	UT	77	1161	4	3	5	4	5	5	1	4	5
BIRD, L.	f	BOS	45	1662	4	1	3	2	2	4	4	4	2
BLACKMAN, R.	g	DAL	75	2527	4	2	2	4	4	5	3	5	2
BLANKS, L.	g	DET	43	189	3	5	5	5	5	5	1	5	5
BLAYLOCK, M.	g	NJ	72	2548	5	5	4	4	2	1	3	4	3
BOGUES, M.	g	CHA	82	2790	4	4	5	5	1	1	2	5	4
BOL, M.	c	PHI	71	1267	5	5	5	4	5	5	1	1	5
BONNER, A.	f	SAC	79	2287	4	5	5	3	5	3	2	5	4
BOWIE, A.	g/f	ORL	52	1721	3	2	4	4	4	3	3	4	3
BOWIE, S.	c	NJ	71	2179	4	4	5	2	4	5	3	2	3
BRANDON, T.	g	CLE	82	1605	5	3	5	5	4	4	2	5	4
BREUER, R.	c	MIN	67	1176	4	5	5	4	5	5	1	3	5
BRICKOWSKI, F.	f	MIL	65	1556	2	4	5	3	5	4	2	5	4
BROOKS, K.	f	DEN	37	270	4	3	5	5	5	5	1	5	5
BROOKS, S.	g	MIN	82	1082	4	3	3	5	4	4	1	5	5
BROWN, C.	f	LAL	42	431	4	5	5	5	5	5	1	5	5
BROWN, D.	g	BOS	31	883	5	4	5	5	3	3	2	5	4
BROWN, M.	c/f	UT	82	1783	4	4	5	3	5	5	1	5	4
BROWN, R.	g	SAC	56	535	4	5	5	5	5	5	1	5	5
BROWN, T.	f	SEA	57	655	5	5	4	5	5	5	1	5	5
BRYANT, M.	c	POR	56	800	3	5	5	4	5	5	1	5	5
BUECHLER, J.	f	GS	28	290	5	5	5	5	5	5	1	5	5
BULLARD, M.	f	HOU	80	1278	4	4	2	5	5	5	1	5	4
BURTON, W.	g/f	MIA	68	1585	4	3	5	4	5	5	2	4	4
BURTT, S.	g	PHX	31	356	4	5	5	5	5	5	1	5	4
CAGE, M.	f	SEA	82	2461	4	4	5	2	5	3	1	4	4
CAMPBELL, E.	c	LAL	81	1876	4	5	5	3	5	5	1	2	4
CAMPBELL, T.	f/g	MIN	78	2441	4	3	4	4	4	3	3	4	3
CARR, A.	f/c	SA	81	1867	3	4	5	4	5	5	2	3	4

NAME	POS	TEAM	GMs	MINs	FG PCT	FT PCT	3-PT SHOTS	REBs	ASTs	STLs	TOs	BLKs	PTs
CARTWRIGHT, B.	c	CHI	64	1471	4	5	5	3	5	5	1	5	4
CATLEDGE, T.	f	ORL	78	2430	3	5	5	2	5	5	2	5	3
CAUSWELL, D.	c	SAC	80	2291	1	5	5	2	5	5	2	2	4
CEBALLOS, C.	f	PHX	64	725	3	4	5	5	5	5	1	5	4
CHAMBERS, T.	f	PHX	69	1948	5	3	4	3	4	4	2	4	3
CHAPMAN, R.	g	WAS	22	567	4	5	5	5	3	5	3	5	3
CHEEKS, M.	g	ATL	56	1086	4	5	5	5	4	3	1	5	5
CHILCUTT, P.	f/c	SAC	69	817	4	3	5	5	5	5	1	5	5
COLEMAN, D.	f	NJ	65	2207	2	4	4	2	4	4	5	3	2
COLES, B.	g	MIA	81	1976	4	3	2	5	3	4	3	5	4
CONLON, M.	c	SEA	45	381	3	4	5	5	5	5	1	5	5
CONNER, L.	g	MIL	81	1420	5	5	5	5	4	3	1	5	5
COOK, A.	f	DEN	22	115	1	5	5	5	5	5	1	5	5
COOPER, W.	f	POR	35	344	5	5	5	4	5	5	1	5	5
COPA, T.	f/c	SA	33	132	1	5	5	5	5	5	1	5	5
CORBIN, T.	f	UT	80	2207	3	2	5	3	5	3	1	5	4
CORCHIANI, C.	g	ORL	51	741	5	2	4	5	4	4	2	5	5
CROWDER, C.	g/f	UT	51	328	5	3	4	5	5	5	1	5	5
CUMMINGS, T.	f	SA	70	2149	3	5	5	2	5	4	2	5	3
CURRY, D.	g	CHA	77	2020	3	3	2	4	4	3	2	5	3
DAILEY, Q.	f	SEA	11	98	5	3	5	5	5	5	1	5	5
DAUGHERTY, B.	c	CLE	73	2643	1	4	5	1	4	4	4	3	2
DAVIS, B.	f	DAL	33	429	4	5	5	5	4	5	1	5	5
DAVIS, D.	f	IND	64	1301	1	5	5	3	5	5	1	3	4
DAVIS, T.	f/c	DAL	68	2149	3	5	5	2	5	5	2	5	4
DAVIS, W.	g	DEN	46	741	4	2	5	5	5	5	1	5	4
DAWKINS, J.	g	PHI	82	2815	5	2	3	5	3	3	3	5	3
DIVAC, V.	c	LAL	36	979	3	4	5	3	5	2	3	4	4
DONALDSON, J.	c	NY	58	1075	4	5	5	3	5	5	1	4	5
DOUGLAS, S.	g	BOS	42	752	3	5	5	5	3	4	2	5	4
DREILING, G.	c	IND	60	509	3	4	5	5	5	5	1	5	5
DREXLER, C.	g	POR	76	2751	4	4	1	3	2	2	5	4	1
DUCKWORTH, K.	c	POR	82	2222	4	5	5	3	5	5	2	5	4
DUDLEY, C.	c	NJ	82	1902	5	5	5	2	5	5	1	2	5
DUMARS, J.	g	DET	82	3192	4	2	3	5	3	4	3	5	2
EACKLES, L.	f	WAS	65	1463	4	4	5	5	5	4	1	5	3
EATON, M.	c	UT	81	2023	4	5	5	3	5	5	1	2	5
EDWARDS, Ja.	c	LAC	72	1437	4	5	5	4	5	5	1	5	4
EDWARDS, K.	g	MIA	81	1840	4	2	5	4	4	3	2	5	4
EDWARDS, T.	g/f	UT	81	2283	2	4	3	4	5	3	2	4	3
EHLO, C.	g/f	CLE	63	2016	4	5	2	4	4	3	2	5	3
ELIE, M.	g/f	GS	79	1677	2	2	4	4	4	4	1	5	4
ELLIOTT, S.	f	SA	82	3120	3	2	4	3	4	3	2	5	3
ELLIS, D.	f	MIL	81	2191	4	4	1	4	5	4	2	5	3
ELLIS, L.	f	LAC	29	103	5	5	5	5	5	5	1	5	5
ELLISON, P.	c	WAS	66	2511	2	5	5	1	4	4	4	2	2
ENGLISH, A.J.	g	WAS	81	1665	5	3	5	4	5	5	1	5	4
EWING, P.	c	NY	82	3150	2	4	5	1	5	3	4	1	2
FEITL, D.	c	NJ	34	175	5	3	5	5	5	5	1	5	5
FERRELL, D.	f	ATL	66	1598	2	4	4	4	5	4	2	5	3
FERRY, D.	f	CLE	68	937	5	3	4	4	5	5	1	5	5
FLEMING, V.	g	IND	82	1737	3	4	5	4	4	4	2	5	4
FLOYD, S.	g	HOU	82	1662	5	4	3	5	4	4	2	5	4
FOSTER, G.	f	WAS	49	548	4	5	5	4	5	5	1	5	5
FOX, R.	g/f	BOS	81	1535	4	4	4	4	5	4	2	5	4
FRANK, T.	f	MIN	10	140	1	5	5	5	5	5	1	5	5
FREDERICK, A.	f	CHA	66	852	5	5	5	5	5	5	1	5	5
GAMBLE, K.	g/f	BOS	82	2496	2	2	5	4	4	4	1	5	3
GARLAND, W.	g	DEN	78	2209	4	2	5	5	3	3	3	5	4

NAME	POS	TEAM	GMs	MINs	FG PCT	FT PCT	3-PT SHOTS	REBs	ASTs	STLs	TOs	BLKs	PTs
GARRICK, T.	g	DAL	40	549	5	5	5	5	4	4	1	5	5
GATLING, C.	c	GS	54	612	1	5	5	4	5	5	1	4	5
GATTISON, K.	f/c	CHA	82	2223	2	5	5	2	5	5	2	4	3
GEORGE, T.	g	NJ	70	1037	5	3	5	5	4	5	1	5	4
GILL, K.	g/f	CHA	79	2906	4	4	5	3	3	4	3	4	2
GILLIAM, A.	f/c	PHI	81	2771	2	3	5	2	5	5	3	3	3
GLASS, G.	g	MIN	75	1822	4	5	4	4	4	4	2	5	4
GMINSKI, M.	c	CHA	35	499	4	4	5	4	5	5	1	5	5
GRAHAM, P.	g	ATL	78	1718	4	4	3	4	4	3	1	5	4
GRANT, Ga.	g	LAC	78	2049	4	3	4	5	2	2	3	5	4
GRANT, Gr.	g	PHI	68	891	4	3	5	5	4	5	1	5	5
GRANT, Ha.	f	WAS	64	2388	3	3	5	3	4	3	2	5	2
GRANT, Ho.	f	CHI	81	2859	1	4	5	1	4	3	1	2	3
GRAYER, J.	g	MIL	82	1659	4	5	4	4	5	4	1	5	4
GREEN, A.C.	f	LAL	82	2902	3	4	4	2	5	3	2	5	3
GREEN, R.	g	BOS	26	367	4	5	5	5	4	5	1	5	5
GREEN, S.	f	SA	80	1127	5	3	5	4	5	5	1	5	5
GREEN, Se.	g	IND	35	256	5	5	5	5	5	5	1	5	5
HALEY, J.	f/c	LAL	49	394	5	5	5	5	5	5	1	5	5
HAMMONDS, T.	f	CHA	37	984	3	5	5	3	5	5	2	5	4
HANSEN, B.	g	CHI	68	809	4	5	5	5	5	5	1	5	5
HARDAWAY, T.	g	GS	81	3332	4	4	1	4	1	1	5	5	2
HARPER, D.	g	DAL	65	2252	4	4	3	5	3	2	3	5	3
HARPER, R.	g	LAC	82	3144	4	4	2	3	3	2	5	4	2
HASTINGS, S.	f	DEN	40	421	5	2	5	5	5	5	1	5	5
HAWKINS, H.	g	PHI	81	3013	4	2	2	4	4	2	3	4	2
HENDERSON, G.	g	DET	16	96	5	3	5	5	5	5	1	5	5
HENSON, S.	g	MIL	50	386	5	4	4	5	5	5	1	5	5
HERRERA, C.	f	HOU	43	566	2	5	5	5	5	5	1	4	5
HIGGINS, R.	f	GS	25	535	5	3	3	4	5	5	1	5	4
HIGGINS, S.	f	ORL	38	616	4	2	5	5	5	5	1	5	4
HILL, T.	c/f	GS	82	1886	2	5	5	2	5	4	1	4	4
HODGE, D.	c/f	DAL	51	1058	3	5	5	3	5	5	2	5	4
HODGES, C.	g	CHI	56	555	5	1	3	5	5	5	1	5	5
HOPSON, D.	g/f	SAC	71	1314	4	5	4	5	5	4	2	4	4
HORNACEK, J.	g	PHX	81	3078	2	2	2	3	3	2	3	5	2
HOWARD, B.	f	DAL	27	318	2	5	5	5	5	5	1	5	5
HUMPHRIES, J.	g	MIL	71	2261	4	4	3	5	3	2	3	5	3
IUZZOLINO, M.	g	DAL	52	1280	4	3	3	5	4	5	2	5	4
JACKSON, C.	g	DEN	81	1538	5	2	3	5	4	5	2	5	4
JACKSON, M.	g	NY	81	2461	3	4	4	4	1	3	4	5	4
JAMERSON, D.	f	HOU	48	378	5	1	5	5	5	5	1	5	5
JAMES, H.	f	CLE	65	866	5	3	2	5	5	5	1	5	4
JEPSEN, L.	c	SAC	31	87	5	5	5	5	5	5	1	5	5
JOHNSON, A.	g	HOU	69	1235	3	5	5	5	4	4	2	5	4
JOHNSON, B.	f	HOU	80	2202	4	5	5	4	4	4	1	4	4
JOHNSON, E.	f	SEA	81	2366	4	2	4	4	4	5	2	5	3
JOHNSON, K.	g	PHX	78	2899	3	3	4	4	1	3	5	5	2
JOHNSON, L.	f	CHA	82	3047	3	3	5	1	4	4	2	4	2
JOHNSON, V.	g	SA	60	1350	5	5	4	4	4	5	1	5	4
JONES, Ch.	c/f	WAS	75	1365	5	5	5	4	5	5	1	3	5
JORDAN, M.	g	CHI	80	3102	2	3	4	3	2	1	4	4	1
KEMP, S.	f/c	SEA	64	1808	2	4	5	1	5	4	3	2	3
KERR, S.	g	CLE	48	847	2	3	3	5	4	5	1	5	4
KERSEY, J.	f	POR	77	2553	4	5	5	2	4	3	2	4	3
KESSLER, A.	c	MIA	77	1197	5	3	5	4	5	5	1	5	5
KIMBLE, B.	f	LAC	34	277	5	5	5	5	5	5	1	5	5
KING, R.	c	SEA	40	213	5	4	5	5	5	5	1	5	5
KING, S.	f/c	CHI	79	1268	2	4	5	5	5	5	1	5	4

NAME	POS	TEAM	GMs	MINs	FG PCT	FT PCT	3-PT SHOTS	REBs	ASTs	STLs	TOs	BLKs	PTs
KITE, G.	c	ORL	72	1479	5	5	5	3	5	5	1	4	5
KLEINE, J.	c	BOS	70	991	4	5	5	4	5	5	1	5	5
KNIGHT, N.	g	PHX	42	631	3	5	5	5	4	5	2	5	5
KOFOED, B.	g	SEA	44	239	4	5	5	5	5	5	1	5	5
KONCAK, J.	c	ATL	77	1489	5	5	5	4	5	5	1	4	5
KRYSTKOWIAK, L.	f	MIL	79	1848	4	4	5	3	5	5	2	5	4
LAIMBEER, B.	c	DET	81	2234	4	2	3	3	4	5	1	4	4
LANE, J.	f	MIL	14	177	5	5	5	4	5	5	1	5	5
LANG, A.	c	PHX	81	1965	2	4	5	3	5	5	1	2	4
LECKNER, E.	c	CHA	59	716	2	4	5	4	5	5	1	5	5
LEE, D.	g	NJ	46	307	5	5	4	5	5	5	1	5	5
LES, J.	g	SAC	62	712	5	3	3	5	4	5	1	5	5
LEVER, F.	g	DAL	31	884	5	4	4	3	4	3	1	5	4
LEVINGSTON, C.	f	CHI	79	1020	3	5	5	5	5	5	1	4	5
LEWIS, R.	g	BOS	82	3070	2	2	5	4	4	2	2	3	2
LIBERTY, M.	f/g	DEN	75	1527	4	5	4	4	5	4	1	5	4
LICHTI, T.	g	DEN	68	1176	4	3	5	5	5	5	1	5	4
LISTER, A.	c	GS	26	293	1	5	5	4	5	5	1	4	5
LOHAUS, B.	f/c	MIL	70	1081	4	5	3	4	5	5	1	3	5
LONG, G.	f	MIA	82	3063	3	3	5	2	4	2	3	5	3
LONGLEY, L.	c	MIN	66	991	4	5	5	4	5	5	1	4	5
LYNCH, K.	g	CHA	55	819	5	4	5	5	5	5	1	5	5
MACON, M.	g	DEN	76	2304	5	5	5	5	4	1	3	5	4
MAJERLE, D.	g/f	PHX	82	2853	3	4	2	3	4	2	1	4	3
MALONE, J.	g	UT	81	2922	2	2	5	5	5	5	2	5	2
MALONE, K.	f	UT	81	3054	2	4	5	1	4	3	5	4	1
MALONE, M.	c	MIL	82	2511	4	4	5	2	5	4	2	4	3
MANNING, D.	f	LAC	82	2904	2	5	5	3	4	2	4	3	2
MARCIULIONIS, S.	g	GS	72	2117	2	4	5	4	4	2	4	5	2
MASON, A.	f	NY	82	2198	2	5	5	2	5	5	1	5	4
MAXWELL, V.	g	HOU	80	2700	5	4	1	4	3	3	3	5	3
MAYES, Th.	g	LAC	24	255	5	5	4	5	5	5	1	5	5
MAYS, T	g	ATL	2	32	5	1	5	5	5	5	2	5	4
McCANN, B.	f	DET	26	129	5	5	5	5	5	5	1	5	5
McCLOUD, G.	g	IND	51	892	5	4	3	5	4	5	1	5	4
McCORMICK, T.	c	NY	22	108	5	5	5	5	5	5	1	5	5
McCRAY, R.	f	DAL	75	2106	5	5	4	3	4	5	2	5	4
McDANIEL, X.	f	NY	82	2344	3	5	4	3	5	5	2	5	3
McHALE, K.	f/c	BOS	56	1398	2	3	5	3	5	5	2	3	3
McKEY, D.	f	SEA	52	1757	4	2	4	3	4	3	3	4	3
McMILLAN, N.	g/f	SEA	72	1652	5	5	4	4	3	2	2	5	4
MILLER, R.	g	IND	82	3120	2	2	1	4	4	3	2	5	2
MILLS, T.	f	NJ	82	1714	4	4	5	3	5	5	1	4	4
MITCHELL, S.	f	MIN	82	2151	5	4	5	3	5	5	1	5	4
MONROE, R.	g	ATL	38	313	5	3	5	5	5	5	1	5	5
MOORE, T.	f	DAL	42	782	5	3	3	5	5	4	1	5	4
MORRIS, C.	f	NJ	77	2394	3	5	4	3	4	2	3	3	4
MORTON, J.	g	MIA	25	270	5	3	5	5	5	5	1	5	5
MULLIN, C.	f	GS	81	3346	2	3	2	3	4	1	3	4	1
MURDOCK, E.	g	UT	50	478	4	5	5	5	5	5	1	5	5
MURPHY, T.	f	MIN	47	429	3	5	5	5	5	5	1	5	5
MUSTAF, J.	f	PHX	52	545	3	5	5	5	5	5	1	5	5
MUTOMBO, D.	c	DEN	71	2716	3	5	5	1	4	5	5	1	3
NANCE, L.	f	CLE	81	2880	2	3	5	2	4	4	1	1	3
NEALY, E.	f	PHX	52	505	2	5	4	5	5	5	1	5	5
NEWMAN, J.	f/g	CHA	55	1651	3	4	4	4	4	3	3	5	3
NORMAN, K.	f	LAC	77	2009	3	5	5	3	5	5	2	4	3
OAKLEY, C.	f	NY	82	2309	2	4	5	2	5	4	2	5	4
OGG, A.	c	MIA	43	367	1	5	5	5	5	5	1	4	5

NAME	POS	TEAM	GMs	MINs	FG PCT	FT PCT	3-PT SHOTS	REBs	ASTs	STLs	TOs	BLKs	PTs
OLAJUWON, H.	c	HOU	70	2636	2	4	5	1	4	2	4	1	2
OLIVER, B.	g	PHI	34	279	5	5	5	5	5	5	1	5	5
OLIVER, J.	g/f	CLE	27	252	5	4	5	5	5	5	1	5	5
OWENS, B.	g/f	GS	80	2510	2	5	5	2	4	3	3	4	3
OWENS, K.	f	LAL	20	80	5	3	5	5	5	5	1	5	5
PACK, R.	g	POR	72	894	5	3	5	5	5	5	1	5	5
PARISH, R.	c	BOS	79	2285	2	4	5	2	5	4	2	3	3
PAXSON, J.	g	CHI	79	1946	2	4	4	5	4	5	1	5	4
PAYNE, K.	f	PHI	49	353	4	5	5	5	5	5	1	5	5
PAYTON, G.	g	SEA	81	2549	4	5	5	4	2	2	3	5	4
PERDUE, W.	c	CHI	77	1007	1	5	5	4	5	5	1	4	5
PERKINS, S.	f/c	LAL	63	2332	4	3	4	2	4	3	2	4	3
PERRY, E.	g	CHA	50	437	5	5	5	5	5	5	1	5	5
PERRY, T.	f	PHX	80	2483	2	5	5	3	5	5	2	2	3
PERSON, C.	f	IND	81	2923	3	5	1	3	3	4	4	5	2
PETERSEN, J.	c	GS	27	169	4	5	5	5	5	5	1	5	5
PETROVIC, D.	g	NJ	82	3027	2	3	1	4	4	3	4	5	2
PHILLS, B.	g	CLE	10	65	5	5	5	5	5	5	1	5	5
PIERCE, R.	g	SEA	78	2658	3	1	3	4	4	3	4	5	2
PINCKNEY, E.	f	BOS	81	1917	2	3	5	2	5	4	1	4	4
PIPPEN, S.	f	CHI	82	3164	2	4	4	2	2	2	5	3	2
POLYNICE, O.	c	LAC	76	1834	2	5	5	2	5	5	1	5	4
PORTER, T.	g	POR	82	2784	4	2	1	4	3	2	3	5	3
PRESSEY, P.	g	SA	56	759	5	5	5	5	4	5	1	5	5
PRICE, M.	g	CLE	72	2138	3	1	1	5	2	3	3	5	3
PRITCHARD, K.	g	BOS	11	136	4	4	5	5	5	5	1	5	5
QUINNETT, B.	f	DAL	39	326	5	5	4	5	5	5	1	5	5
RAMBIS, K.	f	PHX	28	381	4	4	5	4	5	5	1	4	5
RANDALL, M.	f	MIN	54	441	4	4	5	5	5	5	1	5	5
RASMUSSEN, B.	c	ATL	81	1968	3	4	5	4	5	5	1	4	4
REID, J.R.	c/f	CHA	51	1257	3	5	5	3	5	4	2	5	4
REYNOLDS, J.	g/f	ORL	46	1159	5	3	5	4	4	3	3	5	3
RICE, G.	f	MIA	79	3007	4	3	1	3	4	3	2	5	2
RICHARDSON, P.	g	MIN	82	2922	4	5	3	4	1	3	4	5	3
RICHMOND, M.	g	SAC	80	3095	4	3	1	4	3	3	5	5	2
RIVERS, Da.	g	LAC	15	122	5	1	5	5	5	5	1	5	5
RIVERS, Do.	g	LAC	59	1657	5	3	4	5	3	2	2	5	4
ROBERTS, F.	f	MIL	80	1746	3	4	4	4	5	5	2	4	4
ROBERTS, S.	c	ORL	55	1118	2	5	5	3	5	5	2	3	4
ROBERTSON, A.	g	MIL	82	2463	5	4	2	4	3	1	4	5	3
ROBINSON, C.	f	POR	82	2124	4	5	5	3	5	3	2	3	3
ROBINSON, D.	c	SA	68	2564	1	5	5	1	4	1	4	1	2
ROBINSON, R.	g	ATL	81	2220	4	5	3	5	3	3	4	5	3
RODMAN, D.	f	DET	82	3301	2	5	3	1	4	4	2	4	4
ROLLINS, T.	f/c	HOU	59	697	2	2	5	5	5	5	1	3	5
ROYAL, D.	f	SA	60	718	4	5	5	5	5	5	1	5	5
RUDD, D.	g	UT	65	538	5	4	4	5	5	5	1	5	5
RULAND, J.	c	PHI	13	209	2	5	5	4	5	5	2	5	5
SALLEY, J.	f/c	DET	72	1774	2	5	5	4	5	5	2	3	4
SAMPSON, R.	c	WAS	10	108	5	5	5	4	5	5	1	4	5
SANDERS, J.	f	ATL	12	117	4	4	5	5	5	5	1	5	5
SANDERS, M.	f	CLE	31	633	1	4	4	5	4	4	1	5	4
SCHAYES, D.	c	MIL	43	726	5	4	5	5	5	5	1	5	5
SCHEFFLER, S.	f	DEN	11	61	4	5	5	5	5	5	1	5	5
SCHINTZIUS, D.	c	SAC	33	400	5	3	5	4	5	5	1	4	5
SCHREMPF, D.	f	IND	80	2605	2	3	4	1	4	4	3	5	3
SCOTT, B.	g	LAL	82	2679	4	3	3	4	4	3	2	5	3
SCOTT, D.	f	ORL	18	608	5	1	4	4	5	3	2	4	2
SEIKALY, R.	c	MIA	79	2800	3	5	5	1	5	5	4	3	3

NAME	POS	TEAM	GMs	MINs	FG PCT	FT PCT	3-PT SHOTS	REBs	ASTs	STLs	TOs	BLKs	PTs
SELLERS, B.	f/c	DET	43	226	4	4	5	5	5	5	1	5	5
SHACKLEFORD, C.	c	PHI	72	1399	3	5	5	3	5	5	1	4	4
SHAW, B.	g	MIA	63	1423	5	4	5	4	3	4	2	5	4
SIMMONS, L.	f	SAC	78	2895	4	4	5	2	3	2	4	2	3
SKILES, S.	g	ORL	75	2377	5	2	2	5	2	4	1	5	3
SMITH, C.	f/c	LAC	49	1310	4	4	5	3	5	4	2	2	3
SMITH, Do.	f	DAL	76	1707	5	4	5	3	5	4	1	5	4
SMITH, K.	g	HOU	81	2735	3	2	3	5	2	3	4	5	3
SMITH, L.	f/c	HOU	45	800	2	5	5	3	5	5	1	5	5
SMITH, La.	g	WAS	48	708	5	3	5	5	4	4	2	5	5
SMITH, O.	g	ORL	55	877	5	4	5	5	5	5	1	5	5
SMITH, S.	g	MIA	61	1806	4	4	3	4	3	4	3	5	3
SMITH, To.	g	LAL	63	820	5	5	5	5	5	5	1	5	5
SMITS, R.	c	IND	74	1772	2	4	5	3	5	5	2	3	3
SPARROW, R.	g	LAL	46	489	5	5	5	5	5	5	1	5	5
SPENCER, F.	c	MIN	61	1481	5	5	5	2	5	5	1	3	4
STARKS, J.	g	NY	82	2118	4	4	2	5	4	3	2	5	3
STEWART, L.	f	WAS	76	2229	2	3	5	3	5	5	2	4	4
STOCKTON, J.	g	UT	82	3002	3	3	2	4	1	1	5	5	3
STRICKLAND, R.	g	SA	57	2053	4	5	5	4	1	1	4	5	3
SUTTON, G.	g	SA	67	601	5	4	4	5	5	5	1	5	5
TEAGLE, T.	f	LAL	82	1602	4	4	5	5	5	4	2	5	4
THOMAS, C.	g	DET	37	156	5	5	5	5	5	5	1	5	5
THOMAS, I.	g	DET	78	2918	4	4	4	4	2	2	5	5	2
THOMPSON, L.	f/c	IND	80	1299	4	3	5	4	5	5	1	5	5
THOMPSON, S.	g	SAC	19	91	5	5	5	5	5	5	1	5	5
THORPE, O.	f	HOU	82	3056	1	5	5	1	4	5	4	5	3
THREATT, S.	g	LAL	82	3070	3	3	4	4	2	1	3	5	3
TISDALE, W.	f	SAC	72	2521	2	4	5	3	5	4	2	3	3
TOLBERT, T.	f	GS	35	310	5	5	5	5	5	5	1	5	5
TUCKER, T.	g	SA	24	415	4	3	4	5	5	4	1	5	4
TURNER, A.	g	WAS	70	871	5	4	5	5	4	4	2	5	5
TURNER, J.	f	ORL	75	1591	4	5	5	4	5	5	2	5	4
TURNER, Jo.	f	HOU	42	345	5	5	5	5	5	5	1	5	5
VANDEWEGHE, K.	f	NY	67	956	3	3	4	5	5	5	1	5	4
VAUGHT, L.	f	LAC	79	1687	3	4	5	3	5	5	1	5	4
VINCENT, S.	g	ORL	39	885	5	3	5	5	4	4	2	5	4
VOLKOV, A.	f	ATL	77	1516	4	5	3	4	4	4	2	5	4
VRANKOVIC, S.	c	BOS	19	110	4	5	5	5	5	5	1	4	5
WALKER, D.	g	DET	74	1541	5	5	5	4	4	4	1	5	5
WEBB, S.	g	SAC	77	2724	4	2	2	5	2	2	4	5	3
WEST, D.	g	MIN	80	2540	2	3	5	4	4	4	2	5	3
WEST, M.	c	PHX	82	1436	1	5	5	4	5	5	1	4	4
WHATLEY, E.	g	POR	23	209	5	2	5	5	5	5	1	5	5
WHITE, R.	f	DAL	65	1021	5	4	5	4	5	5	1	5	4
WIGGINS, M.	g	PHI	49	569	5	5	5	5	5	5	1	5	5
WILEY, M.	g	ATL	53	870	5	5	2	5	5	4	1	5	5
WILKINS, D.	f	ATL	42	1601	4	3	3	2	4	3	4	4	1
WILKINS, G.	g	NY	82	2344	4	5	3	5	4	3	2	5	3
WILLIAMS, Bu.	f	POR	80	2519	1	4	5	2	5	4	2	4	4
WILLIAMS, Br.	f	ORL	48	905	2	5	5	3	5	4	2	3	4
WILLIAMS, H.	f/c	DAL	75	2040	5	5	5	3	5	5	2	3	4
WILLIAMS, Jo.	f/c	CLE	80	2432	2	4	5	3	4	4	1	2	4
WILLIAMS, Ja.	f/c	PHI	50	646	5	5	5	5	5	5	1	5	5
WILLIAMS, K.	f	IND	60	565	2	5	5	5	5	5	1	4	5
WILLIAMS, M.	g	IND	79	2750	3	2	5	4	1	1	5	5	3
WILLIAMS, R.	f	DEN	81	2623	4	3	3	3	4	2	3	3	2
WILLIAMS, S.	f	CHI	63	690	3	5	5	4	5	5	1	4	5
WILLIS, K.	f/c	ATL	81	2962	3	3	5	1	4	4	2	4	2

NAME	POS	TEAM	GMs	MINs	FG PCT	FT PCT	3-PT SHOTS	REBs	ASTs	STLs	TOs	BLKs	PTs
WINCHESTER, K.	f	NY	19	81	5	3	5	5	5	5	1	5	5
WINGATE, D.	g	WAS	81	2127	4	5	5	4	4	2	2	5	4
WITTMAN, R.	g	IND	24	115	5	5	5	5	5	5	1	5	5
WOLF, J.	f	DEN	67	1160	5	3	5	4	5	5	1	5	5
WOOLRIDGE, O.	f	DET	82	2113	3	5	5	4	5	4	2	5	3
WORTHY, J.	f	LAL	54	2108	4	3	5	3	3	3	3	5	2
YOUNG, D.	g	LAC	62	1023	5	2	4	5	4	5	1	5	5

APPENDIX C

LEAGUE SCHEDULES

LEAGUE SCHEDULES

When looking at these league schedules, remember that once your league plays through a round, the schedule starts over from the beginning. (For example, in the four-team league, the 4th, 7th, 10th, etc. weeks would be the same as the 1st week.) We see no reason to break the teams up into divisions; each team should just play all the other teams the same number of times, and your league will have enough of a barometer to seed the teams for the playoffs.

A note about scheduling a league with an odd number of teams: The boxed games are played against an opponent who has a score either from the previous game, or from the next game to be played. It will be easier to explain by example. In the nine-team league schedule, for instance, the first week has Team 1 playing Team 9, Team 2 playing Team 8, Team 3 playing Team 7, Team 6 playing Team 4, and Team 5 *also* playing Team 4. How can both Team 6 and Team 5 play Team 4? The way it works is that Team 5's Game 1 scores are held, and then compared to Team 4's Game 2 scores to determine a winner. (Example: Team 5, in the Sunday-Monday game, had 61 rebounds, 24 assists, 11 steals, 7 blocks, 2 three-pointers, 16 turnovers, and 134 points. Team 4, in the Wednesday-Thursday game, had 34 rebounds, 34 assists, 14 steals, 6 blocks, 5 three-pointers, 22 turnovers, and 164 points. These two results would be compared, and Team 4 would win the game [its Game 2], while Team 5 would lose [its Game 1].) We found that it works out best if the commissioner does not disclose the starters of the team that plays first until the other team's starters have been reported.

FOUR-TEAM LEAGUE

Game #	1	2	3
Team 1	2	3	4
Team 2	1	4	3
Team 3	4	1	2
Team 4	3	2	1

PLAYOFFS:

In a four-team league you may not need a playoff, but if you want one, take the top two teams and have them play at least a seven-game series.

SIX-TEAM LEAGUE

Game #	1	2	3	4	5
Team 1	2	3	4	5	6
Team 2	1	4	5	6	3
Team 3	5	1	6	4	2
Team 4	6	2	1	3	5
Team 5	3	6	2	1	4
Team 6	4	5	3	2	1

PLAYOFFS: OPTION #1

Take the top two teams and have them play a seven-game series to determine the league champion.

PLAYOFFS: OPTION #2

Take the top three teams and have the second- and third-place teams play a five-game series. The winner advances to play the regular-season champ in a seven-game series. The winner of this second series is the league champion.

EIGHT-TEAM LEAGUE

Game #	1	2	3	4	5	6	7
Team 1	2	3	4	5	6	7	8
Team 2	1	4	8	6	5	3	7
Team 3	4	1	6	8	7	2	5
Team 4	3	2	1	7	8	5	6
Team 5	6	8	7	1	2	4	3
Team 6	5	7	3	2	1	8	4
Team 7	8	6	5	4	3	1	2
Team 8	7	5	2	3	4	6	1

PLAYOFFS: OPTION #1

Seed the top four teams at the end of the regular season. In the first round, have seed #1 play seed #4, and seed #2 play seed #3 (five-game series). The winners then advance to play each other in a seven-game series to determine the league champion. (A consolation series between the two first-round losers is optional.)

PLAYOFFS: OPTION #2

Send the top six teams to the playoffs and seed them according to their regular-season records. The top two finishers get byes in the first round of the playoffs. Of the remaining four teams, have seed #3 play seed #6 and seed #4 play seed #5 (three-game series). The winner of the first series (seeds #3 and #6) advances to play seed #1; while the winner of the second series (seeds #4 and #5) advances to play seed #2 (three-game series). The two winners advance again, meeting in a five-game series to determine the league champion.

NINE-TEAM LEAGUE

Game #	1	2	3	4	5	6	7	8
Team 1	9	7	**8**	6	2	5	3	4
Team 2	8	6	9	5	1	4	**7**	3
Team 3	7	5	8	4	9	**6**	1	2
Team 4	6	**5**	7	3	8	2	9	1
Team 5	**4**	3	6	2	7	1	8	9
Team 6	4	2	5	1	**3**	9	7	8
Team 7	3	1	4	9	5	8	6	**2**
Team 8	2	9	3	**1**	4	7	5	6
Team 9	1	8	2	7	3	6	4	5

PLAYOFFS:

Same as for an eight-team league.

TEN-TEAM LEAGUE

Game #	1	2	3	4	5	6	7	8	9
Team 1	2	3	4	5	6	7	8	9	10
Team 2	1	4	5	6	7	8	9	10	3
Team 3	4	1	6	7	8	9	10	5	2
Team 4	3	2	1	8	9	10	5	6	7
Team 5	7	8	2	1	10	6	4	3	9
Team 6	9	10	3	2	1	5	7	4	8
Team 7	5	9	10	3	2	1	6	8	4
Team 8	10	5	9	4	3	2	1	7	6
Team 9	6	7	8	10	4	3	2	1	5
Team 10	8	6	7	9	5	4	3	2	1

PLAYOFFS:

Same as for an eight-team league, except that the playoffs should be kept to three NBA weeks. Hence, if you use Option #1, play a three-game series in the first round, then a five-game series for the championship. If you use Option #2, all three playoff rounds should be three-game series.

ELEVEN-TEAM LEAGUE

Game #	1	2	3	4	5	6	7	8	9	10
Team 1	11	9	10	8	2	7	3	6	4	5
Team 2	10	8	11	7	1	6	**9**	5	3	4
Team 3	9	7	**10**	6	11	5	1	4	2	**8**
Team 4	8	6	9	5	10	**7**	11	3	1	2
Team 5	7	**6**	8	4	9	3	10	2	11	1
Team 6	**5**	4	7	3	8	2	9	1	10	11
Team 7	5	3	6	2	**4**	1	8	11	9	10
Team 8	4	2	5	1	6	11	7	**10**	**3**	9
Team 9	3	1	4	11	5	10	6	**2**	7	8
Team 10	2	11	3	**1**	4	9	5	8	6	7
Team 11	1	10	2	10	3	8	4	7	5	6

PLAYOFFS:

Same as for an eight-team league, except that the playoffs should be kept to three NBA weeks. Hence, if you use Option #1, play a three-game series in the first round, then a five-game series for the championship. If you use Option #2, all three playoff rounds should be three-game series.

TWELVE-TEAM LEAGUE

Game #	1	2	3	4	5	6	7	8	9	10	11
Team 1	2	3	4	5	6	12	11	7	8	10	9
Team 2	1	4	3	6	7	11	10	8	9	12	5
Team 3	4	1	2	11	9	8	6	12	7	5	10
Team 4	3	2	1	12	10	6	5	9	11	7	8
Team 5	6	7	8	1	11	9	4	10	12	3	2
Team 6	5	8	7	2	1	4	3	11	10	9	12
Team 7	8	5	6	9	2	10	12	1	3	4	11
Team 8	7	6	5	10	12	3	9	2	1	11	4
Team 9	10	11	12	7	3	5	8	4	2	6	1
Team 10	9	12	11	8	4	7	2	5	6	1	3
Team 11	12	9	10	3	5	2	1	6	4	8	7
Team 12	11	10	9	4	8	1	7	3	5	2	6

PLAYOFFS:

Same as for an eight-team league, except that the playoffs should be kept to three NBA weeks. Hence, if you use Option #1, play a three-game series in the first round, then a five-game series for the championship. If you use Option #2, all three playoff rounds should be three-game series.

THIRTEEN-TEAM LEAGUE

Game #	1	2	3	4	5	6	7	8	9	10	11	12
Team 1	13	11	**12**	10	2	9	3	8	4	7	5	6
Team 2	12	10	13	9	1	8	**11**	7	3	6	4	5
Team 3	11	9	12	8	13	7	1	6	2	5	**10**	4
Team 4	10	8	11	7	12	6	13	5	1	**9**	2	3
Team 5	9	7	10	6	11	**8**	12	4	13	3	1	2
Team 6	8	**7**	9	5	10	4	11	3	12	2	13	1
Team 7	**6**	5	8	4	9	3	10	2	11	1	12	13
Team 8	6	4	7	3	**5**	2	9	1	10	13	11	12
Team 9	5	3	6	2	7	1	8	13	**4**	12	10	11
Team 10	4	2	5	1	6	13	7	12	8	11	9	**3**
Team 11	3	1	4	13	5	12	6	**2**	7	10	8	9
Team 12	2	13	3	**1**	4	11	5	10	6	9	7	8
Team 13	1	12	2	11	3	10	4	9	5	8	6	7

PLAYOFFS: OPTION #1

Seed the top four teams at the end of the regular season. In the first round, have seed #1 play seed #4, and seed #2 play seed #3 (three-game series). The winners then play a five-game series to determine the league champion. (A consolation series between the two first-round losers is optional.)

PLAYOFFS: OPTION #2

Send the top six teams to the playoffs and seed them according their regular-season records. The top two finishers get a bye in the first round of the play-offs. Of the remaining four teams, have seed #3 play seed #6, and seed #4 play seed #5 (three-game series). The winner of the first series (seeds #3 and #6) advances to play seed #1; while the winner of the second series (seeds #4 and #5) advances to play seed #2 (three-game series). The two winners advance again, meeting in a three-game series to determine the league champion.

PLAYOFFS: OPTION #3

Seed the top eight teams at the end of the regular season. Have seed #1 play seed #8, seed #2 play seed #7, seed #3 play seed #6, and seed #4 play seed #5 (three-game series). The winner of #1 vs. #8 plays the winner of #4 vs. #5; while the winner of #2 vs. #7 plays the winner of #3 vs. #6 (three-game series). The winners of these two series advance again to play each other in a three-game series for the league championship.

FOURTEEN-TEAM LEAGUE

Game #	1	2	3	4	5	6	7	8	9	10	11	12	13
Team 1	2	3	4	5	6	7	8	9	10	11	12	13	14
Team 2	1	4	5	6	7	8	9	10	11	12	13	14	3
Team 3	4	1	6	7	8	9	10	11	12	13	14	5	2
Team 4	3	2	1	8	9	10	11	12	13	14	6	7	5
Team 5	6	9	2	1	10	11	12	13	14	8	7	3	4
Team 6	5	11	3	2	1	12	13	14	8	9	4	10	7
Team 7	12	13	11	3	2	1	14	8	9	10	5	4	6
Team 8	13	14	12	4	3	2	1	7	6	5	9	11	10
Team 9	10	5	13	14	4	3	2	1	7	6	8	12	11
Team 10	9	12	14	13	5	4	3	2	1	7	11	6	8
Team 11	14	6	7	12	13	5	4	3	2	1	10	8	9
Team 12	7	10	8	11	14	6	5	4	3	2	1	9	13
Team 13	8	7	9	10	11	14	6	5	4	3	2	1	12
Team 14	11	8	10	9	12	13	7	6	5	4	3	2	1

PLAYOFFS:

Same as in a 13-team league.

NOTES

NOTES

NOTES

FANTASY BASKETBALL STUFF

In an effort to provide the Fantasy Basketball owner with everything needed to play and enjoy a good year of Fantasy Basketball, we, the authors at Fantastic Sports Inc., are expanding our services. Not only do we provide the Fantasy Basketball Update, a fan favorite from last year, which will help you catch up with the latest news from NBA camps, but we are also offering the Fantasy Basketball League Organizer, which provides all the forms that a commissioner needs to run a league for a year. Also, if you can't round up enough players to form your own league, let us help with our new FBD Sports Inc. leagues.

But the expansion does not stop there. In the future, we would like to provide you with even more—a scoring service, a computer scoring program for your league, and even fantasy leagues for other sports.

ORDER TODAY!

FANTASY BASKETBALL UPDATE 1992:

Information is power, and many roster moves are made after the NBA raises the salary cap on July 1. Most NBA preview magazines are already set to print by that time, so they may not be able to provide the latest information. Don't get caught with your guard on the wrong team. The update will arrive in two parts. Part One, which will be mailed out in early October, will update all the roster moves to that point and examine their impact on your Fantasy Basketball draft. Part Two will arrive just before the season starts, and will include injury updates, new roster moves, some of the latest scuttlebutt from camp, and our all-important buy/sell list, with players we think have improved or hurt themselves in camp. Both parts of the update can be faxed to all you anxious patrons for a small charge.

FANTASY BASKETBALL LEAGUE ORGANIZER:

Just what every Fantasy Basketball league commissioner needs to run a league smoothly. Among the more important components of the organizer are worksheets for keeping track of rosters, taking down lineups, and scoring for both Head-to-Head and Weekly leagues. It also includes a draft log to help keep track of each franchise's players as well as units spent and units remaining.

FBD SPORTS INC.
FANTASY BASKETBALL LEAGUES:

Test your skills against other players across the country. You may be the king of Fantasy Basketball in your league, but how do you match up against other Fantasy Basketball royalty? Prestige is not all you'll compete for: There's a king's ransom for the victor. Call to receive more information.

ORDER FORM

Please send me the item(s) I have checked below. I have enclosed a check or money order payable to Fantastic Sports, or have included my VISA or MasterCard number.

*Name*_____

*Address*_____

*City*_____*State*_____*Zip*_____

*VISA or MasterCard number and exp.date*_____

Qty:

☐ *Fantasy Basketball Digest 1992*	____	x $11.95	= $_____
☐ Fantasy Basketball League Organizer	____	x $10.00	= $_____
☐ Fantasy Basketball Update 1992	____	x $10.00	= $_____
Any two items, $2.00 off		−2.00	= $_____
Any three items, $5.00 off		−5.00	= $_____
Total			$_____
Wisconsin residents add 5%			$_____

Shipping/Handling Charges:

Up to $30.00	=	$3.00
$30.01 to $40.00	=	$4.00
$40.01 to $50.00	=	$5.00
$50.01 to $75.00	=	$5.50
Over $75.00	=	$6.00	$_____
TOTAL AMOUNT DUE			$_____

Send order and payment to:

Fantastic Sports
P.O. Box 93425
Milwaukee, WI 53203
Or call TOLL-FREE: **1-800-944-7665**